SEAMUS MCCREE

U.P. NORTH

A Compendium of Tales set in Michigan's Upper Peninsula

James M. Jackson

THE SEAMUS MCCREE SERIES
BY JAMES M. JACKSON

NOVELS
Ant Farm
Bad Policy
Cabin Fever
Doubtful Relations
Empty Promises
False Bottom
Granite Oath
Hijacked Legacy

NOVELLAS
Furthermore
Low Tide at Tybee

NONFICTION
BY JIM JACKSON

One Trick at a Time:
How to Start Winning at Bridge

INTRODUCTION

This volume contains reprints of two Seamus McCree novels (*Cabin Fever* and *Empty Promises*), one Seamus McCree short story ("Accidents Happen"), and one bonus short story ("Homework"), all set in Michigan's Upper Peninsula.

ISBN-13 Trade Paperback: 978-1-943166-16-9

Cabin Fever (2014) and *Empty Promises* (2018) are the third and fifth novels of the Seamus McCree series. Those who prefer to read a series in order should put this book down and start with the first novel in the series, *Ant Farm*. But if you enjoy stories set in the wilds of the northwoods, this collection is just up your alley.

The short story "Accidents Happen" also features Seamus McCree. Although it was Seamus's first appearance in print (published in *Fish Tales: The Guppy Anthology*), I had already written drafts of what would eventually become the first two Seamus McCree novels, *Ant Farm* and *Bad Policy*. Chronologically, "Accidents Happen" occurs prior to *Cabin Fever*.

I've added the short story, "Homework" to this collection because it is one of my favorites and set in the same area as the other tales. It first appeared in *A Few Good Words: A Cincinnati Writers Project Anthology*.

Each story stands on its own. I do suggest reading *Cabin Fever* before *Empty Promises* because a few characters who appear in *Empty* Promises are first introduced in *Cabin Fever*.

James M. Jackson
Amasa, Michigan

Printed in the United States of America
109876543

CABIN FEVER

A Seamus McCree Novel (#3)

James M. Jackson

Trade Paperback Edition: April 2017

Cover Design by Karen Phillips

Wolf's Echo Press
PO Box 54
Amasa, MI 49903
www.WolfsEchoPress.com

This is a work of fiction. Any references to real places, real people, real organizations, or historical events are used fictitiously. Other names, characters, organizations, places, or events are the product of the author's imagination.

CABIN FEVER

A Seamus McCree Novel (#3)

ONE

FACING NORTH INTO A BRISK wind, I searched for signs of the aurora borealis but spotted only a front forming in the distance. *It's probably nothing.* The skies above were so clear the Milky Way seemed almost within reach. I never worried about getting lost on nights like this. As long as stars were shining, the reflective snow made it easy to follow my old tracks home.

I checked the northern Michigan sky again. *The stars are bright—stop making excuses, Seamus, and get crackin'.* With my breath crystalizing around me, turning my beard and mustache white, I strapped on snow-shoes and began my trek, the snow squeaking in protest with each step.

I was six miles into an eight-mile loop when I exited the shelter of a cedar swamp. The evergreens had been holding much of the snow in their branches, making travel relatively easy. Deep in thought, I had paid only passing attention as snow-laden clouds from the north brought with them a howling February snowstorm that threatened to erase any trace of my tracks.

That was a stupid mistake for someone living all alone, miles from his nearest neighbor.

To the snare drum rattling of hardwood treetops, I climbed the rise from the frozen swamp to the head of the lake following faint indentations. At first, the trail headed the way I expected, but soon it veered off and I realized the tracks had drifted in. *No problem, I'll cut straight up the hill to the lake.* I pushed through the brush border at the lake's edge and met a fierce blast that tore my breath away. A thousand hypodermic snow needles jabbed my exposed face. I ducked my head into my parka, pulled ski goggles from my knapsack, and fastened them over my mink hat.

I could take the safer approach: go back down the hill and partially retrace my sheltered steps to a road that would eventually lead me home. Or I could move forward and strike directly over the lake toward my property. The wind on the lake would be terrible without cover. The wind also meant there would be less snow, and what there was would be hard-packed, allowing better footing. Walking up the middle of the lake would lop off considerable distance and time. Not wanting to retreat, I rationalized that if conditions worsened, I could cut over to the shoreline and follow it home.

I turned to consult Abigail, remembering in a flush of regret that she'd been gone for a month. To the wind I muttered, "Mad wolves and Irishmen go out in the dark winter storm."

Realizing I needed to stop channeling Noël Coward and get with the program, I strode onto the lake. After ten labored steps, I turned around to block the wind and wipe the snow from my goggles. The shore, a scant twenty-five feet away, was almost invisible. I could picture the headline in the *Iron County Reporter*: "Snowmobiler Finds 'Tourist' Frozen on Shank Lake." I retreated to the shoreline and followed it around toward my place.

An hour later, I located the gaps in the wild cherry bushes marking the start of the path leading past my guest cabin and up to my house. Sections of my dismantled dock stacked next to the path for winter served momentarily as a windbreak while I gathered my strength. I stuffed my mittens between my legs and fished a Petzl headlamp from my knapsack. Flipping the red filter down so I wouldn't lose night vision, I fastened it around my head. Almost home.

Halfway to the cabin, I entered a group of hemlocks blocking the wind. Not paying enough attention as I left the trees' shelter, the wind whipped a maple branch across my nose. Jerking away from the sting, I staggered a step into the unpacked snow and buried my left leg up to my crotch in powder. I threw both arms forward to cushion my fall, bucking as my sleeves filled with snow. It took me two tries to regain my balance. If coyotes were watching, they would howl for hours at my bipedal comedy.

I wiped the snow from my nose with bare fingers, felt a dribble of warmth, and licked away the salty blood.

The guest cabin was rustic: no electricity, no plumbing. I periodically shoveled the stoop to allow access to the bookshelves my son and I had built years ago when it was the only building on the property. I dithered at stopping to get something new to read—I was almost through a Rex Stout collection—or getting to the main house to take care of my nose. The dithering itself was a sign I was overtired and not thinking clearly.

An arc of smoothed snow on the stoop formed a single angel wing. Someone had recently opened the door to the screened porch. Squatting down, I flipped up the headlamp's red filter and spotted prints of bare feet.

Now I knew I was going nuts. Occasionally holding conversations with a disappeared Abigail was one thing, but phantom footprints meant my imagination was reaching a new level of desperation. *Get a grip, Seamus. No one walks around barefoot in this weather.* At the thought, my arms reminded me they were freezing from my nosedive into the snow. My teeth started chattering.

I knelt to inspect the tracks: all faced forward; no departures. Must be guys from one of the nearby camps playing a trick. Peering into the swirling snow, the track of partially filled footprints disappeared down the driveway.

A frisson of disquiet struck me. Although only sixty-five yards away, the house and garage were invisible with their lights off. What if it wasn't a joke? What if someone found this cabin and took refuge? I yanked open the screen door and tromped in, ignoring the scrape of snowshoe claws on the porch floor. I peered in the glass door to the cabin proper. No one had lit the fire preset in the wood stove.

A shiver running from my toes to the top of my head reminded me I needed warmth. A book could wait for morning. Turning from the door, I caught a flash of two bare legs dangling below the chair hammock attached to a porch rafter. I laughed so hard my sides ached and my lungs hurt from the frozen air.

In a place where winter lasts half the year, jokes and jokers get odd. The jerks must have stepped a blow-up doll onto my porch to make the footprints and posed it in the swinging chair. They had concealed their tracks well. In this dark, I couldn't figure out how they did it, but I'd find the evidence in daylight.

Fine. Like pink flamingos mysteriously congregating in front lawns of townies about to return from vacation, this babe was definitely going to show up in someone's sauna in the near future. *Might as well drag it to the house so it'll be close at hand for future revenge.* I grabbed the plastic legs to haul the thing from the chair.

The legs were real.

TWO

HER BREATHING WAS SHALLOW AND slow. Her breath warm and odorless. Her pulse erratic. I moved her to the house using a fireman's carry. It felt about the same as lugging a couple of fifty-pound bags of sunflower seed to the basement so I could feed the birds all winter. After shucking my snowshoes, I deposited her in the tub and ran a tepid bath to defrost her.

First thing I thought of was drugs. Her body was athlete-thin. Her hands and feet were callused. She sported fresh scrapes on the bottom of her left heel, probably from walking barefoot. A chipped fingernail on her right hand added to my impression that her work was physical. A recovering hickey on her neck showed she had recently spent time with someone. Most disconcerting, fresh rope burns on her wrists and ankles had left them raw. I had never been interested in bondage games and these had to have hurt. No needle tracks.

Her cropped hair looked as though she'd run a beard trimmer over her scalp. Or maybe she had shaved her head and let it grow a few weeks. She had three holes in each ear, but no earrings. I found no other punctures, but she had a rose tattooed above her left breast and a Celtic braid on her right ankle. She was not wearing contacts.

I replaced cooled water with hot to return the bath to room temperature. After forty-five minutes her skin tone changed from milky white to mottled pink. I shifted her weight to check her pulse again and her eyes fluttered to consciousness. She jerked away from my hovering hand, cracking her head against the faucet. "Ouch." She closed her eyes and shook her head several times as though trying to shake out cobwebs. "Who . . . the fuck . . . are you?" Her voice rose. "Where the hell . . . am I?"

"I'm Seamus McCree." I slowly and clearly enunciated the "Shay-mus."

Most people haven't heard the name and, if I say it too fast, they usually ask me to repeat it. "And you're . . . ?" I released her shoulders. She slipped into the water, caught herself, and raised her body on extended arms. Her face took on a quizzical expression. She looked at herself in the tub, then at the cathedral ceiling, and finally pinned me to the wall with her glare.

"I . . . don't remember . . . shit. Roofie? Why's this . . . bath so . . . damn cold?" She pointed to my outerwear left strewn on the bathroom floor. "Where are mine?"

She tried and failed to get out of the tub. "Too tired . . . to move. Cold."

"You were frostbitten," I said. "Doesn't look too bad. Only your fingers and toes appear chapped. The rest of you . . ." I realized I was about to say "looks pretty good," which she could easily take the wrong way. "The rest of you was preternaturally white. We can make the bath a little warmer, but not much or it will be really painful—at least that's what I remember from Boy Scouts. You don't remember anything?"

She closed her eyes and furrowed her brow. She was either concentrating intensely or putting on a great act. "No frostbite. I . . . was really . . . hot." In apparent frustration, she slapped the water, spraying me and the floor. "Where . . . am I?"

Hot made sense. People in the last stages of hypothermia sometimes think they're really hot and strip off their clothes. "You're at my camp on Shank Lake." No glimmer of recognition in her eyes. "It's in the northeast corner of Iron County."

Her eyes briefly widened. "Wisconsin?"

"The Upper Peninsula of Michigan."

"You don't sound like a Yooper."

"I wasn't born in the U.P. I found you on the screened porch of my guest cabin. I've been thawing you ever since. You still haven't told me your name."

"Want to . . . call the cops."

"I wish we could," I said, using what I hoped was a nonthreatening voice. "Problem is there's no cell phone coverage. Let me get you some clothes."

"I'm tired." She released a long sigh that appeared to back up her claim. "Need sleep . . . alone."

After lifting her out of the tub and holding her steady while she toweled off, I threw a ratty bathrobe around her. On my six feet two inches, the bathrobe nearly touched the ground; on her slight frame, the robe hung like an Elizabethan gown, fanning out on the floor around her. I led her to the main bedroom, which was next to the bathroom, and pulled back the down comforter. "I can put on fresh sheets if you want." She waved away the offer and crawled into bed still wearing the bathrobe. I tucked the comforter under her chin. From the bureau I pulled a pair of flannel pants with a tie string and a T-shirt advertising the Nature Conservancy's Pine Butte Guest Ranch. "These are way too large, but it's the best I can do."

"Leave them." She pointed to the chair. "My head hurts." She twisted her head back and forth. "Not a hangover. Flu or something. You got pain meds?"

I brought two Advils and a large glass of water. "It would be good if you drink it all. I think you get dehydrated with frostbite."

She downed the tablets and several slugs of water. "Maybe later." She placed the half-emptied glass on the nightstand. Her eyes narrowed. "How is it you're the only person in a thousand miles who uses 'preternaturally' in a sentence, but's too dumb to check my ID to find out who I am?"

I took the hint of humor and the compound sentence as a good sign. "I found you freezing to death on my porch," I said. "No clothes. No purse. Just you. I have no idea where you came from." I heard a testiness entering my voice. Why was that? I consciously lightened my tone. "You're probably suffering from shock. You want a nightlight in the bathroom?" I was talking to a sleeping woman.

I stood at the foot of the bed and watched the comforter rise and fall with her breathing. She looked nothing like Abigail, and yet the memories of standing helplessly next to her hospital bed buckled my knees. Abigail had been shot protecting me, and I almost lost her then. Now I had.

I left the bedroom door ajar, hung the wet towel above the bathtub, and plugged in the nightlight. The house elves were on strike. The fire in the great room stove had burned down to coals. The outside temperature had dropped to minus fifteen, and I needed to keep the fire going to maintain sixty-five indoors. I placed kindling and two logs into the wood stove. Distracted with worry, I cleaned the tub, mopped the melted snow I had tracked in, and returned the coat, snow bib, mittens, and extra socks to their assigned pegs.

Concern for her blurred into concern for myself. Her blurted accusation about roofies and what that implied left me wondering what kind of trouble I would be in if she didn't recover her memory. The cops sure weren't going to believe I found her *au naturel* on the cabin porch. Is that why I had started to lose my temper with her?

I poured a glass of red wine from my favorite box and curled into the chair next to the wood stove, trying to anticipate what tomorrow would bring. Whatever it was, it would wreak havoc on my normal routine. Where had she come from? The closest neighbors were miles away. Was she taking a late snowmobile ride and broke down? Riding by yourself midwinter was dangerous, but so was walking miles away from home, which I did both day and night. Maybe someone would follow whatever tracks the storm hadn't covered and show up here, saving me the trouble of sorting out what happened.

I didn't feel like making up the futon in the guest bedroom, so I laid my sleeping bag on top of the Oriental rug nearest the wood stove. From there, I could easily tend the fire and hear her if she called. Before I crawled into the bag, I tiptoed upstairs and listened at the open bedroom door: her breathing was regular, but raspy.

Stripping off my thermals, I snuggled into the sleeping bag and watched reflections from the wood stove dance on the pitched ceiling. Even if she seemed fully recovered tomorrow, she really should have a doctor examine her, and, depending on what had caused the restraint abrasions, she might need the cops. My next expected visitor was the supply man who came on Tuesdays, five days away. Not exactly timely. *Maybe I should have bought a snowmobile, after all.* Tomorrow I'd have to cross-country ski the eight miles to the permanent residences on Deer Lake and use someone's computer to request help. On that decision I fell asleep.

And awoke to someone shaking me.

Her strong fingers dug into my shoulders with the force of pliers. Sleep vanished. "I'm burning up," she said. Firelight twinkled in the glistening sweat covering her body. "I can't find the Advil."

My mother never gave me anything to reduce fevers. She said fevers are our body's way of burning out what ails us. I wasn't sure if that applied to someone recently frostbitten or, for that matter, why frostbite would cause a fever. Maybe her body was overreacting.

"Let's take your temperature and make sure what we're dealing with," I said. "Turn around and let me get some clothes on."

"I don't give a shit about your body. Just get me the drugs." She plopped down on the couch and braced her head on her hands.

I shucked off the sleeping bag, donned a pair of briefs, and rummaged in the closet containing medical supplies. Found a red thermometer with a pear-shaped tip, a rectal one from when Paddy was a tyke. I was not going to go there if I could avoid it, so kept searching for an oral thermometer, which should have a long, blue tip. Finally, in the medicine cabinet over the sink, I turned up one with numbers on a strip. Not perfect, but preferable.

She didn't open her eyes while I held the thermometer strip on her brow. To my hand she was steaming. I watched the tape's digits start with 94 and rapidly light up the 98.6, 100, 102 and finally settle somewhere between 104 and 105. Paddy, at around three, had a fever that high. Bad for a kid, terrible for an adult. I dressed while she sat up to choke down two more Advil—it had been almost four hours. She slumped onto the couch and coughed a long dry rattle. Pneumonia?

I gathered several self-help medical texts from the nonfiction library in the basement. All agreed I needed to cool her down. If she had viral pneumonia, there was nothing else to do. If bacterial, treat with antibiotics. What did I know about viral versus bacterial pneumonia, or if it was pneumonia at all? A doctor friend, learning Abigail and I were going to spend winter at my isolated camp and would only have someone come in once a week to bring supplies and mail, insisted I fill a prescription for erythromycin. The seal remained unbroken. The girl raised her head and took a dose. Better safe than sorry, as long as she wasn't allergic to the stuff.

"Back in the bathtub, kiddo," I said once she finished the water chaser to the drugs.

She looked at me with glassy eyes. I helped her upstairs and ran another tepid bath, making sure to point her feet at the faucet. She was sufficiently coherent to sit up this time, so I grabbed a washcloth and gave her a sponge bath, without soap and without any rubbing. I was still a little concerned about frostbite, although that didn't seem to be a problem. She had mentioned earlier she had been hot; I wondered if her fever had mitigated the frostbite.

I replaced her soaked sheets with a fresh set. She crawled into bed and quickly fell asleep. The bath had dropped her temperature to a hundred; how long before it spiked again, I didn't know. I added wood to the stove and turned off the two ceiling fans so more heat would stay upstairs. The best place to monitor her was the bedroom, so I scooted the rocking chair away from the bed and wrapped myself in a Hudson Bay blanket.

What am I going to do? I had been either sanguine or fatalistic about my chances living so far from help. Abigail maintained it was necessary for her as a bodyguard to either recognize that life could end at any time or to find another profession. I'm not sure she ever really accepted the philosophy as it pertained to living in the middle of nowhere, but that wasn't why she left me.

This situation, however, didn't affect my mortality. This woman needed medical attention. Unless her fever broke, I didn't think I could leave her for the time it would take to ski the eight miles to Deer Lake and my closest neighbor. If someone was around to snowmobile me back, it was one thing; but if they weren't—and I had to assume the worst—I'd also have to ski back. I could do it, but it would take several hours. I'd given her the Advil at four a.m.; she could have more at eight. By then it would be light enough to see. I closed my eyes.

From the depths of sleep I heard, "Mister, Mister. Snakes are all over the walls." Her forehead was again on fire. She drained the water from the glass I proffered. "No snakes," she said. "Just a bad dream."

Hallucinations, more likely. I gave her a second glass of water. "Drink while I draw a bath."

She latched onto my arms for support as we shuffled from bedroom to bath. She caught sight of herself in the mirror, fingered the hickey, and closed her eyes.

"Does that help you remember anything?" I asked.

Her eyes exhibited a series of flickers, as though she were in REM. She popped them open. Looking straight at me, she mumbled, "No."

The bath again dropped her temperature, and this time I wet her head to help keep her cooler longer. It was too soon to give her more medicine, which left me crossing my fingers. While she toweled off, I put my third and last set of sheets on the bed. Abigail had last washed this set, and the faint scent of the dryer sheets she used remained on them.

The woman placed a fresh glass of water on the end table and slid back into bed. Any thought of leaving her alone while I got help vanished with her renewed fever spikes. I threw the soaked sheets into the washing machine and plunked into the chair next to the wood stove. Gazing into the fire, I prayed for inspiration. Ideas were slow in coming. The most likely possibility was for snowmobilers to pass by. They would travel by road or lake; I needed to mark each route to alert passersby to the emergency and get them to stop.

Another possibility occurred to me. The previous week, a mining company had flown magnetic imagery runs somewhere west of here. I heard them all that day, running a series of parallel courses towing sensors designed to find places where the magnetic direction of the rock layers change, indicating a possible fault into which gold or copper may have flowed. To catch the attention of any planes flying nearby, I wanted to put a distress signal on the ice.

I turned on the radio to NPR. The world still existed, but the bad news/good news ratio was nineteen to one. The weather forecaster predicted an end to the snow by dawn, clearing by afternoon, and winds less than five miles an hour. Predawn slowly arrived. I flicked on an outside light—a whisper breeze juked a few flakes through the bright cone. My guest was sleeping again, so I put on snow gear and retrieved the can I used for ash from the wood stove.

Most people think the Northwoods are dark in winter. They're actually darker in the summer because the maple, birch, and aspen are fully leafed out. At its worst, we do have only eight hours of daylight. But by now in early February, we had around ten; I could easily work outside without a flashlight. The storm had increased our snow depth to more than three feet. Unlike in civilized areas where snow quickly turns dirty, ours would stay luminous white until it melted away in the spring thaw, better known as "mud season."

With snowshoes strapped over boots, I carted the ash bucket up the driveway to the road. The wind had smoothed away any evidence of civilization except for faint traces of one of my cross-country ski trails. A lone coyote had painted the snowy canvas with its characteristic track as it wandered down the middle of the road, occasionally checking something on the edge before returning to the center. For a moment, I forgot why I was standing in the road with an ash bucket in my hand. The air smelled fresh and clean and the silence was so complete that the only sound I heard was the whoosh of blood coursing near my ears. The tickle of a single snowflake reminded me I was outside for a reason.

I stamped HELP in block letters taking up the width of the road. It might work to stop a snowmobiler, but often they traveled forty, fifty, or more miles an hour. At those speeds the tramped area would be a blur. I darkened the letters with ash. Initially, the ash melted the snow with a hiss of steam; soon cooler ash from the can silently covered the bright snow. I stepped away to look at the completed project: it should stop any passing traffic.

Back inside, I checked on the girl—still sleeping—and despite the room smelling of a mixture of Abigail's shampoo and the dryer sheets, this woman was not Abigail, nor would she ever be. No one could be, and I missed her like crazy—maybe the reality was that I was crazy with the missing.

The road was only twelve feet or so across; the lake spanned three-eighths of a mile. Unless I guessed the right spot on the lake, a snowmobile could easily pass by my message, and I had to make it large enough to attract a pilot's attention from a long distance. From the garage I retrieved three blue tarps and cut them into footwide strips.

Light tinted the tips of the evergreens across the lake. Isolated patches of pale blue pockmarked the clouds, providing promise of a clearing sky and warming temperatures. I snowshoed onto the lake and, using the blue tarp swatches, displayed SOS in six-foot letters, finishing with an elongated arrow pointing to my house. The letters and arrow covered as much of the lake between my house and the opposite shore as possible. From the air, the message would be clear; I hoped a snowmobiler would notice at least a flash of blue tarp and slow down to figure out what was going on. I weighted down each letter's corners with packed snow. Without fresh snowfall, they should remain visible. I didn't expect enough sun to cause the tarp to act as a heat trap and melt snow beneath the letters, but, periodically, I'd have to make sure.

I checked on my guest—still sleeping, albeit more fitfully—and I returned outside to unbury my woods truck from the winter's accumulated snow. A serviceable Ford Ranger, I had pulled its battery shortly after Christmas once snow had closed the local roads for the duration of winter. To institute the third component of my plan, I reinstalled it and shattered the silence with three long horn blasts: the universal signal of distress. I figured the sound would travel at least a couple of miles since the leaves were off the trees and the wind had died to a gentle breeze. I planned to repeat the blasts every half hour.

I sent a silent message in all four directions asking someone, anyone, to find me before I had a dead woman on my hands.

THREE

SHORTLY AFTER NINE IN THE morning, Jimmie Heitzmann arrived at Boss's rented cabin accompanied by the roar of a finely tuned snow machine. Attached to his canary-yellow Arctic Cat was a utility sleigh. He circled the camp and parked next to Brett's truck.

Jimmie dismounted and removed his helmet and black balaclava, exposing a clean-shaven face, squashed nose, eyes the color of a Caribbean bay, and a ruffled mess of mud-brown hair. He left the snow machine running and checked to make sure the long gun was still firmly bungee-corded to the sled. He patted the Ruger strapped to his side and followed his breath cloud to the front door.

Inside, his glance took in the nearly empty rum bottle on the table and the inert form under the quilts. He tiptoed to the bed, leaned down, and yelled as loudly as he could, "Wake-up, fuck face!"

Brett groaned and tugged the covers further over his head. Jimmie walked to the sink and started running cold water into a bucket. Took off one glove and tested the water. *Damn near to grabbing ice cubes.* He blew on his hand to warm it, and replaced the glove.

"I'm up, goddamn it. I'm up." Brett threw off the covers and heaved out of bed. "Don't you start with that water shit again. We got time for breakfast?"

"You drank it last night. We need to get tracking. Boss already filled me in. You got three minutes."

"It's freezing in here. What's the hurry? There wasn't hardly any gas in the snow machine she stole. That's why I was in town when she escaped— to get gas, y'know? She's frozen someplace not far. Alls we got to do is follow her tracks. She didn't have long anyway, her fever was way up there."

"Save your excuses for Boss. You did get rid of the guy, right?"

"He's anchored with concrete and feeding fishes." Brett finished dressing and opened the door to the wood stove.

"Leave it," Jimmie commanded. "Pipes won't freeze before we get back. We need to find the girl."

Brett pulled his first beer of the day from the refrigerator—"hair of the dog"— and downed it before they got to Jimmie's sled. Even with the new snowfall and the night's high winds, it took no skill to follow the girl's trail for several miles. Wind had drifted in the runner lines, but the packed center track was still visible. She had followed the main road west, then cut south, skirted a gate, and headed up a camp road.

Brett tapped Jimmie's shoulder and he slowed to a crawl. "This leads into a guy's camp on Long Lake. He wasn't up a few days ago when I got rid of Brandon." Jimmie dipped his head in understanding and sped off, shooting snow rooster tails behind him. They followed her trail to the camp, a two-story log edifice. The yard was a mess of tracks.

Jimmie stopped the machine and both men hopped off. With face masks up and gloves off, they studied the tracks and decided she had backtracked a hundred feet and followed a frozen lead down onto the lake where the track disappeared. "Now what the fuck do we do?" Brett said. "I didn't think there was that much gas in the sled."

"Keep your eyes peeled, asshole. If she ain't in the lake, she musta cut into the woods. We need to find where she came out. If I was her, I'd try the little log cabin across the lake."

They followed the shoreline down to the outlet and started back up the far side. In short order, Jimmie found the state's boat landing, which he remembered led to an old trail. They got off, walked up the bank, and saw recently disturbed dead ferns. *Gotcha, girlie.*

A distant automobile horn honked three times. "Fuck's that?" said Brett.

Jimmie held up his hand for silence. They waited a minute, but heard nothing other than chickadees and a red-breasted ass-up feeding in a gnarled yellow birch. Gunning the snowmobile, Jimmie followed the girl's trail around a bend and saw the stolen sled. She had run it smack under a chain running across the access to the smaller cabin. It must have knocked her ass over teakettle. The snow machine zoomed off without her and buried itself in a snowbank. Written in the snow was her struggle to extract the machine, but it was too stuck and too heavy for a small woman.

"Leave it for now," Jimmie said. "We'll get it on the way back. She can't have gone far in this snow without snowshoes." They remounted Jimmie's snow machine and slowly followed the occasional dimple in the snow that indicated her path. Wherever the woods opened up, everything drifted in and they had to guess which way she went. The problem became more acute once they entered a Plum Creek clear-cut. Whenever their first guess didn't quickly pan out, they strapped on snowshoes and walked arcs until they restruck her trail.

Fifteen minutes into the process, they hit a larger road and again followed the shuffling tracks south. Brett tapped Jimmie's shoulder and pointed to a blue knit hat hanging on a tree limb. Jimmie gave it a good sniff—smelled like the aloe in her shampoo—and pitched it into the sleigh's storage compartment. They soon discovered a glove decorating a bush.

Brett began to bounce up and down on the seat like he was five and about to get Jell-O with canned fruit for dessert. "Can't be much farther," he shouted over the engine. Jimmie ignored him, stared down the road, intent on glimpsing a spot of color or toe sticking up.

Her coat was next. Then her snow bib.

They entered another clear-cut and found her boots perched on a giant white pine stump, tops rising above the four-inch mound of snow, under which they discovered socks, long underwear, bra, and panties neatly folded.

A car honked. Three long blasts: still distant, but closer and in the direction they were heading.

"Fuck *is* that?" Brett asked using the whine that drove Jimmie bonkers. "Ah, man, with all these stumps and piles of snow, she could be lying dead anywhere."

Jimmie left Brett to check the immediate vicinity. He glided down the road searching for tracks. The more he considered those car horn blasts, the more he thought it unlikely they would find a body. At a fork, he followed the wider road to the left. Snow was heavier in this area, and he didn't find either a corpse or her tracks. The road teed at Shank Lake where he struck a well-traveled snowmobile route; nothing had passed by since the storm. Jimmie checked his plat book. There were several camps on this lake and more along the route into town. Taking a left onto Shank Lake Road, he followed it to the head of the lake, where Lukes Road, unmarked by snow machine tracks, came in from the right. He backtracked to the original fork and took the less-used direction. Thought he might have spotted a footprint or two, but never anything he could convince himself was a trail. No body. Hit Shank Lake again and stopped to consider his options.

Three blasts on a car horn. Closer this time. Exactly half an hour since the last three blasts. Jimmie now knew for certain that someone had already found her and that she was alive. He needed to execute Plan B.

He roared back to Brett, motioned for him to hop on, and buzzed their trail to Brett's snow machine that the girl had left stuck in the snowbank. Jimmie parked next to it and told Brett, "Fill 'er up with gas. Let's see if we can blast her out."

Brett hauled one of the gas cans to the trapped sled and poured. Jimmie followed, leaned close, and brought the Ruger an inch away from the hollow in the back of Brett's neck marking the spot where spine entered skull.

IF SOMEONE DIDN'T SHOW UP soon, I was screwed.

With a combination of Advil, erythromycin, and lukewarm sponge baths, I kept the woman's temperature under 102 for most of the day. She wasn't getting better; stabilized was the best I could convince myself about her condition. Before the end of each Advil cycle, her temperature spiked and her skin turned clammy. She spoke little. Each time she tried, a wracking cough doubled her up like a rag doll. She vomited breakfast of toast and jam. I had to hold down my gag reflex while I cleaned up the mess.

She tried to gargle, but it caused her to choke. I gave her a new toothbrush and from then on she smelled like Tom's of Maine's fennel toothpaste. Because she had felt worse the last time she ate, she refused solid food. Throughout the day I needed to coax her into slurping bouillon with its faint taste of chicken overwhelmed by sharp brine. I did get her to drink three glasses of water.

Early in the morning, I thought I heard a snowmobile's buzz, but it never came close. Back inside, I tuned the radio to "Telephone Time" on WIKB in hopes someone would call the talk show to report a missing woman. No luck and nothing on their hourly news report either. A plane flew past shortly after noon, but was probably too far away to spot my signal. I mostly sat outside the bedroom and worried.

I would feel terrible if the woman died on me. It would be one more person I had let down. Besides, I had no doubt the police would suspect me of something— unlawful imprisonment at the least. *Come on, girl. You've got to get better.*

I set an alarm to remind myself to honk the horn every half hour. At the start of the three-thirty routine, she was sleeping soundly. After hitting the truck horn three times, I snowshoed up to the guest cabin to see if I could follow her tracks. The snow and wind had done a fine job of filling in any footprints, although close to the cabin I could pick out what appeared to be a small indentation here and there. Unfortunately, a light breeze was dumping the remaining snow from the trees, producing a minicrater with each plop of snow. I gave up before I got to the end of the driveway. I'd been away no more than ten minutes, but it was enough time for the woman to reprise her Lady Godiva act: walking up the driveway wearing only a hat from the hook by the kitchen door and a pair of work gloves I had left on a nearby counter. I corralled her and asked what she was doing. "Brandon honked for me," she said. "I'm late for school again."

She did remember who I was; she didn't remember how she got here; she didn't remember who she was. She couldn't tell me who Brandon was or whether he was responsible for the hickey or the rope burns. Yet she was not without memory. Propped into a sitting position in the bed by several pillows, an hour before dark she spotted a mature bald eagle cruising the lake, head and tail as pure white as fresh snow. "Size marks her as female," she said. "She's shopping for carrion." She coughed, finally controlled it, took several long glugs of water, and whispered, "If I don't make it, just haul me to the middle of the lake. Everybody out there's a little hungry this time of year."

I protested. She raised her hand to cut me off. "Joke," she whispered. "Just a joke." Minutes later she was asleep.

Her pulse remained strong, but her breathing was increasingly labored and featured a wheeze that sounded like someone sucking air through the wrong end of a reed instrument. I worried that if her fever spiked and I wasn't around, she might hallucinate and walk away, as she had earlier looking for Brandon. Equally treacherous, she might go into convulsions.

With time on my hands and not daring to go out to ski or snowshoe to burn off all the nervous energy, I polished off the Rex Stout. The thought of reading another mystery didn't feel right—I was living a mystery. I pulled a John McPhee from the nonfiction shelf in the basement, thinking that would occupy my brain. Nope.

I reread the letter from Paddy that Owen had delivered earlier in the month along with the weekly supplies. Paddy, a natural networker unlike his dad, packed the letter with news of friends and acquaintances. He filled me in on what his girlfriend, TV investigative reporter Cindy Nelson, was working on. My eyes stuck on his passing mention that while he and Cindy were in a Chicago nightclub they ran across Abigail. *Who was she with? Was it for business or pleasure? Did she at least say hi?* The printed note gave no hint.

I tried journaling about the last few days, but lost focus. Writing about the woman's rope burns got me thinking about the body police had found in my Cincinnati home the previous spring, and how that had touched off a series of events leading to all kinds of things I didn't want to remember.

One lesson from that experience certainly applied here: police were predisposed to focus on the initial suspect long past the point when other evidence—evidence that they didn't find because they weren't looking for it—should have directed them toward the real perpetrator. If she died at my home, how could I prove I had done nothing wrong? With such an improbable story, why would cops spend much time trying to find alternative suspects?

It was Friday, and I had half-convinced myself that one of the locals with a camp on the lake would come out after work to spend the weekend ice fishing and drinking. If so, I'd hear their snowmobile roar down the lake after dark and could risk leaving her for the short time it would take to ski to their camp.

It didn't happen that way.

 FOUR

THE SUN HAD SET AND the wall thermometer read minus four by the time Jimmie finished at Boss's rented camp. He was surprised how good he felt. In the movies, they showed a first-time killer getting wobbly knees and puking his guts out. Bullshit. This was easier than putting down his old hunting dog. He'd loved Bomber; Brett was a pain. Besides, no one paid him for putting down Bomber, whereas Brett was worth decent bucks.

He kept his gloves on except to wash the dishes. He dried those and neatly hung the dishtowel on the rack by the sink. After draining the water lines, he cleaned the wood stove of ash—good thing dumbass Brett had let the fire die—stripped all the linens, and shut off the propane. Brett's gear piled on the sleigh provided cover for the girl's stuff underneath. Camo tarps served as wrappers for foodstuffs, which he also tied down on the sleigh.

Using rubbing alcohol and shop rags from a box, he wiped down every surface where fingerprints could be found. Always liked the smell, maybe because it reminded him of cleaning guns? Although, thinking about it, he concluded gun oil smelled heavier. He let the rags air dry and stuffed them in his parka pocket to toss into his home burn barrel. Using a million-candle torch, he checked the cabin and grounds one last time. Satisfied, he padlocked the cabin and generator shed, pulling on the locks to make sure they were secure even after hearing the satisfying click of the lock engaging. He then used Brett's shotgun to blow off the door hasp, leaving the lock burnished by twenty-gauge shot and buried in the snow.

The shot brought a pair of gray jays from the woods to investigate, their conversation alerting Jimmie of their presence. "Nothing for you camp robbers today," he told them. "Gonna be slim pickings around here for a piece."

Eight long hours after he had dispatched Brett, Jimmie pulled his snow machine and sleigh onto the trailer he'd attached to Brett's truck and left the camp. His stomach protested the lack of food. His only break had been to force down cold pasties, which tasted like shoe leather when they weren't warm. Twenty minutes later, he had cell coverage and called Boss. "She's still missing, but I think I know where. Everything else is cool."

"Meet me tomorrow at eleven," Boss said. "Sooner we solve that problem, the better."

NEITHER THE WOMAN NOR I slept much during the night. Her fever held steady at around a hundred degrees, so maybe the drugs were helping keep it down. The dry wheeze of her cough morphed into a wet rattle. Those episodes occurred more frequently, each one lasting longer. After one particularly long and violent coughing jag she waved me to her. "Am I going to die?"

"Of course not," I said too loudly to fool myself with the false confidence.

"I think someone already has, but I just can't remember. Will you hold me? I need someone to hold me and my mother isn't here." Talking sparked another long coughing spree. "Please?"

I kicked off my shoes and got in the other side of the bed, sliding over to spoon against her muscled back, laying my arm around her warm shoulders. Again, the scent of Abigail surprised me, even though I was the one who had washed her with Abigail's lavender soap.

"Thank you," she whispered into the pillow.

She calmed down and slept. I didn't. Wrapped against her, I measured every shallow breath she took against the previous one, worrying she was getting worse. Despair grew as I held this nameless woman and recognized I had no clue what to do. All my years of education, all my years in business, all my years as a parent, provided no preparation for this moment.

Who was Brandon? What did she mean by someone already died? Did that relate to her rope burns? I wished for so very many reasons that Abigail were still here. If she hadn't left, one of us could have stayed and the other gone for help. This woman would be in a hospital, getting real care.

And I missed Abigail. I'd screwed it up again and lost her for good.

"Do the best you can, and let go of the results," my mother had often told me when I was fussing over something I couldn't control. Had I done my best for the woman today? What did I need to do tomorrow? The dueling calls of barred owls outside interrupted my contemplation. Even if hunting was tough for them with so much snow on the ground, they had it comparatively easy, worrying only about food and sex. Just two days ago, I had stood at the window for the better part of an hour watching a snowshoe hare inspect the clearing around my house. That once-idyllic life now seemed a fantasy.

Lying on my back, I marked the passage of the nearly full moon as it slunk toward its setting an hour before official sunrise. My guest was wasting away. If I didn't get her medical attention, I might justly be accused of letting her die. I had no choice but to act, but what if I made the wrong choice?

* * *

Jimmie figured Boss had already arrived for the meeting: a curl of white smoke drifted into the bluing sky from the single-wide trailer set on top of the hill. He checked for company—no traffic on Rock Crusher Road in either direction—and pulled into the plowed gravel driveway around the single-wide and into the second stall of a pole barn building at the rear of the clearing. In typical Yooper fashion, the pole barn was quadruple the size of the trailer home.

He left his keys in the Chevy Blazer, walked to the edge of the trailer, and listened for traffic. Still nothing, so he slipped around to the front and let himself in. He pulled off his gloves and hat, but left his coat on. The propane furnace was clacking away, but it had some work to do to raise the temperature from fifty—Boss's setting while away—to something comfortable. He grabbed a mug from a tree—they all advertised Hematite National Bank, no surprise there—and poured coffee from the pot left cooking on the hotplate. He liked it plain and black, no mochaccino crap for him. Maxwell House "good to the last drop" was still best in his book. As the boss said, "The closer to diesel fuel, the better." The warmth tumbled down his gullet and into his stomach.

Boss emerged from the bedroom. "Prompt as always, Jimmie. I appreciate that. Set your ass down." Boss waved toward the gawd-awful orange plaid couch in the living room and plunked down in the La-Z-Boy. "Tell me what transpired with Brett."

Typical. Flaunts that college degree using words like "transpired" when "happened" would have done just as well. Well, Jimmie knew all those words too; he just didn't use 'em. He took a couple slurps of the coffee, sagged into the couch feeling it envelop his hips as the springs stretched with pings and pops. Once everything settled, he related the previous day's activities.

"Couldn't you make it look like a hunting accident? Shot himself?"

"Didn't you ever read that book, *The Sweater Letter*? They'd never buy it. I made it look like a drug buy gone bad. Left a stash of blow in a baggie in the tank of his snow machine." He added, in case Boss thought he was asking for more money, "Part of my full-service package." Tried a smile, got nothing back, and plowed on. "Here's the thing. I'm pretty sure someone around Shank Lake found the girl. Every half hour, some guy's nailing his horn three long honks."

"Distress signal, sure as shit."

Boss rustled around in the bookcase and opened an Iron County plat book. "Lukes Road comes in from US 141. That's the only other way in other than up The Grade from Amasa. There are only a few camps on Shank—forty-acre zoning. We hold the mortgages on a couple. Thing I can't get my head around is why they were honking their horn instead of packing her into town."

Jimmie tried out his theory. "What if the girl's alive and somebody staying by theirselves didn't figure he could leave her to get help?"

Boss looked up sharply. "I kinda figured maybe you were gold digging me with your suggestion she was alive, her walking around naked in below zero temps and all. But now I hear you telling it, well, shit, you might be right." Boss tapped the plat book. "Looking at that section, I seem to recall something about a guy name of McCree planning to overwinter, and I see a McCree family trust owns an eighty. Neither of those biologists ever laid eyes on you, right?"

"Even so, if I rode into someone's camp, it might tie me to them. If I found only one guy with the girl, which is what I'm now thinking is the case, I could take care of both of them. But I didn't think of that at the time, and if it was a group up for the weekend, I'd have been totally fucked. Besides, you told me if the girl escaped, I had to take care of Brett . . ."

Boss nodded a few times, which led to a hacking fit. Boss pulled out a handkerchief and coughed something into it Jimmie was clearly not supposed to see or ask about. Supposedly the lung cancer was taken care of, but maybe it was back? Jimmie pretended to concentrate on the plat book, noting it smelled a bit musty.

"Point taken," Boss said. "By now if she were a stiff, she'd be parked in some funeral home and 'Telephone Time' would be chatting away helping the cops figure out who she was—and there wasn't a peep. You've taken care of Brett's stuff?"

"And the girl's. Burned everything except his truck. That's a cube of crushed metal sitting in a recycler's lot in Duluth. He ships the stuff to China. I've never heard of anyone named McCree."

"Tourist, not a local. You've done a good job, Jimmie, but we're not finished by a long shot. You and I need to check the Shank Lake camps. We'll start with McCree. I got an extra sled you can take. You got a choice of weapons." Boss pointed to a gun rack lining one wall of the living room.

"You got your snowmobile duds in the truck, right? Let me get changed while you prepare the sleds. Gas is stored in the pole barn."

Jimmie realized he was jazzed—like before playing a high school football game. How would it go down when their two snow machines drove into McCree's camp? He chugged the last swallow of coffee, cleaned his cup, and hung it on the tree, making sure to wipe off his prints in the process. Never can be too careful.

THE SUN BACKLIT THE EASTERN hill, and I had finally reached the crap-or-get-off-the-pot point regarding how to handle the woman. My style had always been to take in as much data as I could and put off making a decision for as long as possible—but not a moment longer. The good news was that her fever had abated overnight. The bad news was her cough was much, much worse. I needed to get her help, but I needed to minimize the chances she would wander off while I was gone.

My strategy was to tire her out so completely that she would sleep until I returned. I bundled the woman in warm clothes, sleeves and pant legs bunched to the right length with elastic bands. A binder clip cinched in the waist of the old snow pants I had managed to wrestle over pajama bottoms that kept riding up her limp legs. My feet were seven thousand sizes larger than hers, so I stuffed newspaper in the toe boxes and around the heels of the boots.

By the time I finished dressing her, she reminded me of some children in the winter that are clothed in so many layers they can't move—all they can do is stand or fall. I carried her outside and settled her onto my son's old wooden Flexible Flyer, which I towed down to the lake. Across the way, a pair of ravens entertained us with an aerial show and the accompanying soundtrack of raucous croaks before flying away. With the exception of a couple of small snowdrifts I had to dust off, the blue SOS was still okay.

I dragged the sled from the lake to the road and inspected the HELP sign. The dark ashes had absorbed some of yesterday's wan sunlight and caused the message to melt a bit, but it would do for another day.

The house seemed stuffy after our hour-long outing. I cracked open a couple of windows and fixed lunch of split-pea soup laced with chunks of salty bacon. She ate tentatively at first. Once she decided it wouldn't come back up, she wolfed down a bowl and, after a terrible coughing spell, asked for more.

Fortunately, the cold air and warm soup did the trick, and she soon fell asleep. Praying her slumber would last until my return, I attached a note to the back door: "Gone for help. If you get here first, please take the woman to the hospital in Iron River. VERY HIGH fever and possible pneumonia." I strapped on cross-country skis and took off.

At the edge of my property, an old logging road meanders toward a clear-cut. A snowmobile had come down the road and turned around at that intersection. They had been so close; if only they had made it onto my road they would have seen the HELP sign and the woman would be in treatment. My Irish luck was on holiday, probably in a warmer clime.

Birds, normally active feeding in the brief daylight hours, became silent at my approach, no doubt wondering at the intrusion. Only the swish of skis cutting through fresh snow marred the woods' silence. Ice crystals stuck to my mustache and beard and coated the long wool hat that wicked sweat and heat away from my head. After a mile, I was in a zone, having found a strong, easy rhythm that ate up the distance.

The sun was as high in the sky as it was going to get. Even through yellow-tinged goggles, snow sparkled as though laced with diamond chips. Trees lining the road cast blue shadows, giving form to the otherwise smooth landscape. Several camps had access from these roads, but only deer, coyote, and wolf tracks marred the palette of whites.

Skiing through new snow tired me more than I expected, but the thought of the woman waking up with no one around spurred me on. At first, I sensed a ticking clock in my head, but that morphed into an hourglass leaking sand from the realm of the living to the dead. I pressed forward as fast as I could. Trucks had plowed the last two miles of my trip and I didn't have to break trail. I glided around the final corner and spotted both a blue car and red truck parked in a cleared driveway I knew belonged to a couple who lived year-round on Deer Lake. Relief caused a chill to run across my skin with the tingle of a weak electrical current. I'd lucked out; they were home.

I pounded on the door and the woman, dressed in sweats and a heavy wool sweater, informed me her husband had taken off on their snowmobile and was ice fishing with his buddies. She used her satellite internet and tried to find an email address for the Iron County Sheriff's office in Crystal

Falls. No go. She promised to drive the ten miles to Amasa, the nearest town, and call them.

My hourglass was leaking faster. Thoughts of the woman waking up and spacing out drove me to maintain a punishing pace toward home. Reusing tracks I'd made coming to Deer Lake helped speed my return since I didn't have to fight new snow, but my age was starting to tell. I huffed and puffed with the look and sound of an old steam locomotive. For an old fart, I was in outstanding shape, but this exertion proved there was no way I could ever be a professional soccer player again.

Turning onto the A Grade, I discovered snowmobiles had obliterated my path. Their tracks followed mine onto Shank Lake Road, and I gained extra energy from the sense of relief. The cops must have already been in the vicinity when the Deer Lake woman contacted them. By now they were certainly taking care of the woman.

Unless it wasn't them.

I pressed on at top speed. At the head of the lake the snowmobile tracks took Lukes Road instead of staying on my side of the lake. They hadn't made it to my house. My mood crashed and drained my energy.

The steepest hills in the entire eight miles were on my property. By the time I reached them, my legs were whipped; I had to herringbone up them. From the top of the last hill I glided down to my driveway, turned in, and spotted two snowmobiles I didn't recognize parked outside my house.

FIVE

IRON COUNTY SERGEANT LON BARTELLE thought about the story the character sitting on the opposite side of the table had told him. It sounded practiced, bored, too cool, too calm for a guy who had spent the better part of the afternoon and into the evening answering questions from his deputies. "Here's what I don't get," he said, curling his left arm over his head and scratching his gray crew cut. "Instead of relying on some pilot calling us because he sees your SOS on the lake, why didn't you bring her out yourself?"

"Like I told your cohorts," McCree said, "I don't have a snowmobile. I don't have a snow plow. I have an ATV, but that's an All Terrain Vehicle, not an All Snow Vehicle. With three feet of snow my ATV wouldn't make it much past the garage. What did you want me to do, sprout fairy wings and fly?" He puffed out an exclamation of air. "I've been patient and answered the same questions about six times now. I'm tired. I'm hungry. The sun vanished hours ago. I want to go home. Who's my ride?"

"When a sled's free," Bartelle lied with accomplished practice, "we'll take you back. Might be a while, though. Be better if we could do that in the morning. How about we get you a meal and put you up in town?" Bartelle cocked his head, as though he was interested in the response.

"If you're waiting for a search warrant, that's not an issue. I'll grant the county, the state, and/or the DNR full access to my land and buildings and vehicles and anything else you want to look at. Heck, I'll even throw in the Animal Control Officer. Just give me something to sign."

Time to play dumb. Bartelle put on his quizzical expression. "Huh?"

McCree gave him the open-handed "what do you want from me" gesture and said, "I've been cooling my heels for hours since I volunteered," he drew finger quotes around the word volunteered, "to accompany you to town. I told your people everything I know. The questions haven't changed. You think I held her prisoner—I saw the rope burns on her wrists and ankles—and you think I've done who knows what to her over an unknown period of time. Of course I'm a suspect. Problem is I've already told you everything I know."

"Fair enough." Bartelle slapped his hand on the table, stinging his palm. *Dumb.* He heaved up from the chair, walked to the dirty window, and stared out. "Truth: we don't want you alone cleaning the place, and we'd prefer to do the search in daylight. We can arrest you on suspicion and provide a cell for accommodations, or I can treat you to dinner at Mr. T's and put you up at the AmericInn, which will cost the county a whole lot less than the OT. Either way, going home is not one of your options."

MR. T'S FAMILY RESTAURANT WAS nothing fancy: a half-dozen booths and a scattering of Formica tables. Years ago, the place smelled like a burning cigarette pack; now the day's cooking provided the perfume. He judged it had been a big fried onions day. An hour before closing, and without a liquor license, the place was quiet and Bartelle led McCree to a booth. Unasked, the waitress brought Bartelle a diet cola, handed McCree a menu, and said to the Sergeant, "The usual?"

McCree leaned back and locked his fingers behind his head. "So, he's in here so often he has a usual? "

"He claims he's teaching himself how to cook, but I don't see no evidence of it. He's got him a couple different breakfasts, but for dinner—"

"Stop telling all my secrets, Agnes"

A hint of a smile attached itself to McCree's face. "Does he insist on *the usual* for his suspects or will he let me order on my own?"

"You're a suspect?"

He grinned. "The good sergeant seems to think so. I'm not armed, but he still believes I'm dangerous. I'm looking for an independent opinion. Do I look dangerous to you?"

"Only if you're married."

"Divorced for years, but not currently on the market either."

She grinned right back at him. "Well Lon, you put me on the stand, and I'm taking the fifth. Now, sugar, what are we having today?"

"Since you have breakfast all day, I'll take the cheese omelet, breakfast potatoes, and some OJ, please."

"You want that in a four, six, ten, or sixteen-ounce glass?"

"Well, I'm a guest of Iron County, and I don't want my taxes going any higher, so I think I'll stick with the ten ounce. Thank you very much."

The waitress bustled off with the orders.

The interaction between McCree and Agnes, who had to be sixty if she was a day, and not exactly a looker, amazed Bartelle. When had a suspect ever admitted to the first stranger he met that he was one? Never that Bartelle could remember. Was McCree slick or just friendly? He thought it best to ease into the conversation. "Seamus isn't a very common first name," he said. "Family name or just a parental favorite?"

"My father's first name was Seamus, although he went by his middle name. I grew up in an Irish neighborhood so I didn't have to get into too many fights over my name."

"My neighborhood was Italian and everyone wanted to know why we didn't spell Bartelle with an 'i' at the end instead of the final 'e.' Poor penmanship. At Ellis Island the 'i' lost its dot and was kind of loopy. The immigration papers said 'e' and grandpop just wanted in." The pleather seats creaked as Bartelle shifted his weight. "I'd be interested in hearing why you're wintering out in God's country."

McCree seemed to weigh his words carefully. *Too bad, he's not going to be a loquacious bastard who tells me more than he realizes.* Bartelle waited him out.

"Last year, my house in Cincinnati was broken into. My . . ." He paused. *To make sure he used the right word?* "My . . . then girlfriend was nearly killed. A real mess, very traumatic. After she recovered, we spent some time traveling and decided it would be interesting to spend winter at my camp.

"I made arrangements with a guy from Amasa—maybe you know him, Owen Lyndstrom—to bring in supplies once we got snowed in. He comes on Tuesdays. Brings mail, groceries, whatever else I might need as long as I can think of it a week in advance. It's worked pretty well."

"I take it the girlfriend isn't there anymore?"

"Shipped herself out the Tuesday after New Year's. She loved the house, loved the outdoors, loved not having three thousand cable channels. Loved everything except not seeing or talking to people. Snow came early this year, and after three weeks she couldn't hack it. I still had some things to work out, so I stayed." He lifted his hands, which Bartelle interpreted as, "And that's the story."

Bartelle tried waiting him out again while making notes on a pad he kept in his lap. McCree showed no signs of speaking further. The only sound was the scritch of Bartelle's pen. *The problem with McCree is that he doesn't seem to have any problem with silence.* "This girlfriend have a name and address?

"Abigail Hancock." McCree provided an address in Chicago. "But I don't know if she's there. Her work takes her all over. She's a bodyguard."

Bartelle caught himself rubbing his scalp again, left arm crooked over his head like a human Cape Cod. Thought about the gesture for a second and continued to scratch. *I ain't trying to impress anyone, and it feels so good.* He struggled to place this guy's accent. Not from here—didn't use "eh?" to end every third sentence. No way was it Midwestern flat. Reminded him of those presidential candidates from Massachusetts who always got their asses whipped. That was it, like John Kerry or that short guy who looked stupid in the tank, what was his name? This guy dressed like a Yooper, nothing matched, but his clothes were neat without holes or patches. To fill the growing silence, Bartelle asked, "Get laid off, or something? Collecting unemployment?"

The waitress delivered the food, determined neither man needed anything else, and removed the ketchup McCree said he wouldn't need because he didn't spoil his breakfast potatoes with the stuff. She turned to leave, but must have changed her mind because she swung back.

"What does he suspect you of doing?"

"That's a very perceptive question," McCree said. "How about you answer that, Sergeant Bartelle. Two of us are interested."

Mary, Mother of God, how did he turn the tables? "Agnes, you know I can't say anything about an open investigation."

"For Pete's sake why not, Lon? It will be all over town by morning."

McCree laughed. "Just so you know, my name's Seamus McCree." He stuck out his hand. "I'm pleased to meet you, Agnes."

Agnes left with a self-satisfied smile on her face, and McCree picked up his fork and shoveled more food into his mouth. Bartelle decided McCree was using the food to avoid answering his last question. Fine. They would eat in silence, and after McCree put down his fork, he'd ask again.

But McCree surprised him.

"Actually, I retired several years ago."

Bartelle raised his eyebrows to express interest without taking McCree off the hook to continue speaking. He concentrated on chewing the grilled cheese sandwich, letting the sharp taste of the cheddar satisfy him.

"Long ago and far away, I analyzed bank stocks for a Wall Street firm that no longer exists. Quit after someone tried to change one of my reports. Caused a big stink, but that's ancient history."

Bartelle considered the information. McCree couldn't even be a young fifty. Full head of hair, raggedy black beard with a dusting of red highlights. Probably been going native since he left paved-road life and jumped into the woods. Obviously in good shape. No broken blood vessels in his nose, so probably not a drinker. Eyes clear. *In fact, the blue sometimes feels uncomfortably piercing, as though he's looking straight through me.* It reminded Bartelle of a wolf who'd just as soon ignore you and go his own way but, when you pressed, would not back down regardless of the odds— or consequences. "You help make up them Collateralized Mortgage Obligations that got everyone in trouble?"

"Few years ago, no one knew what CMOs were; now everyone's an expert on them and derivatives and a bunch of other fancy financial terms." McCree smiled, like he was remembering something interesting. "I wasn't smart enough to invent new stuff. I told people which bank stocks to buy and which to sell."

"And I suppose you predicted the mess they got themselves in?" Bartelle knew his voice dripped with sarcasm. Didn't want it to; couldn't help it and, underneath the table, he dug his fingernails into his palms to punish himself for the lack of control.

The subject physically tightened after that jab in a way Bartelle couldn't define. McCree used a long sip of water to regain control and replaced a smile on his face. "You caught me," he said. "It's all my fault. That's why I'm in hiding."

Bartelle dug his nails in again to regain concentration. *Shit, I blew that.* Everyone wanted to ring a Wall Streeter's neck after the mess they got us in, but I'm supposed to get this guy to talk. He matched McCree's water drinking trick, put on his own smile, and said, "I'm not buying the *mea culpa*, Mr. McCree. I have a feeling there's a different reason why you quit."

McCree snapped up the bait. "Call me Seamus. My bosses changed a report I wrote that recommended downgrading a now-failed bank's stock because they were early participants in the subprime mortgage market, and I believed their liabilities were understated. The bank was a major client of the firm and making a buck was more important to management than accurate predictions. If they had released the report I wrote, the bank would have taken their business elsewhere. You scratch my back and I'll scratch yours was the corporate style." He tilted his head back and blew a puff of air at the ceiling. "Fact is, I was right, but that was a long time ago. I quit in protest, but it didn't help the world avoid the debacle."

"You get another job, or just take it easy?" Bartelle asked and motioned to Agnes for more diet soda.

"Ever hear of Criminal Investigations Group?"

Bartelle nodded. "I worked with them on a case down in the Mitten before— Mitten's what we call—"

"I know what the Mitten is," McCree interjected, showing Bartelle his left palm. "In lower Michigan they point to their mitten to show where they live. Fact is, we Yoopers refer to people from Lower Michigan as trolls since they live below the Mackinac Bridge."

"I was happy to move somewhere I still had family," Bartelle snapped. He'd intentionally tried a bit of one-upmanship, and McCree had turned it against him, managing to nail his hot button about not being accepted by the locals as a true Yooper. He forced a laugh. "So, yeah, I was a troll before I hired on up here. Anyway, CIG provided computer expertise on that case to help us crack a fencing operation out of one of the big GM plants. Can't remember who we worked with. What do you do with them?"

"About a year after I quit Wall Street, the guy who runs CIG convinced me to set up a group to tackle international financial crimes. Took a couple of years to get all the people in place. It's been successful both here and abroad, and from time to time they ask me to give them a hand. I guess you could say I'm a forensic accountant, or you could think of it as a financial crimes investigator—or at least I will be again once I return to civilization."

Bartelle was pleased. McCree had become animated once he started talking about CIG. "You're an interesting fellow, Seamus. Got any family?"

"A son. Lives and works in Evanston, Illinois." McCree centered the glass on a napkin. "I've been doing all the talking. What brought you to this neck of the woods if you're from the Lower Peninsula?"

Dinner finished with meaningless chit chat, during which Bartelle found himself liking McCree. His mind was so quick, like the way he twisted the Mitten thing back on Bartelle. He was an interesting mixture of big city sophisticate and blue collar regular guy: working in New York City, but son of a Boston cop. Bartelle got no sense that McCree was anything but genuinely interested in Agnes when he was talking with her. He had to remind himself that any really good salesman had that same trick—but if it was a trick, what was McCree selling? Innocence?

When McCree saw him put down a fifteen percent tip, he added a couple of bucks to it. "We're the only ones still in here," McCree said. "And she's living off tips."

While Bartelle checked McCree in at the AmericInn, McCree chatted up the night clerk and discovered the kid was working nights and taking courses at Bay College in Iron Mountain—stuff Bartelle had not known.

"Before you lock me in for the night," McCree said. "Can you ask the hospital how the woman is?"

"That reminds me," Bartelle said, "I've been meaning to ask. Why did you say you'll pay for her medical costs?"

"Because the seventy-ninth time the admitting nurse asked, 'Who's going to pay for this?' I got annoyed. To shut her up I said I would. Okay?" He lowered his voice. "As you can tell, it *still* pisses me off."

Bartelle called the hospital, and the benign feelings he had been developing toward McCree vanished. She had pneumonia, severe dehydration, a fever had spiked to 103 before they could control it. Doctors were clueless as to what she had. He reported all this to McCree, who seemed to take it in stride. One thing Bartelle did not want was a relaxed suspect.

Bartelle checked McCree into his room and left a parting shot, "You better pray she lives."

SIX

AS EXPECTED, I PLAYED HOST to much of the Iron County Sheriff's Department on Sunday. Their search warrant allowed them full access to my land and possessions. They removed ropes from the garage, took dirty bedclothes from the bedroom, and bagged ashes from my burn barrel. They even took the chair hammock I had found the woman in. Two deputies worked outside trying to make sense of the tracks on the property, their task made harder by the three inches of wet overnight snowfall.

From the snatches of conversation I overheard, they were clearly skeptical of my story, but found nothing to contradict it. Their parting words before roaring away on snowmobiles were that I should not leave the area without letting the sheriff's office know. They forgot to say please and thank you. I forgot to tell them that I knew I could go anywhere I damned well pleased until they arrested me.

I went to bed early, too exhausted by the tension of having strangers paw through my belongings to start cleaning up after their search. Returning everything to its proper place took most of Monday. After all the excitement, I appreciated the quiet. Deer returned to the salt lick I had placed between the house and cabin, and the loudest noise I had to put up with was the scolding of a red squirrel when I stuck my head outside.

Tuesday broke sunny and warm. WIKB proclaimed a heat wave: temperatures would reach forty in town, might break freezing around my place and start to reduce the snow pack. Owen Lyndstrom arrived to find me having given up trying to understand the geology in McPhee's book and instead pretending to reread Asimov's *Foundation* series. Still wondering how the girl was doing and fretting about what the police were thinking, I couldn't concentrate on anything for more than fifteen seconds.

Owen was a Northwoods jack-of-all-trades; he had mostly mastered them too. He had cut wood, walked the woods as a timber spotter, worked excavating equipment, graded roads, driven a logging truck, loaded logs onto railcars, plowed snow three seasons of the year, and trapped during the winter of '70–71 when there was no work. He had made more money off an illegal cougar pelt that year than from a whole winter's worth of legal beaver, muskrat, coyote, and snowshoe hare. Although the cougar was the only other witness to the confrontation, I had no reason to doubt Owen when he said he had backtracked it after it jumped him and discovered the cougar had been stalking him for half a day. The DNR didn't fess up to cougars returning to the U.P. until forty years later, so as far as they were concerned, the incident never happened.

He had worked some construction, was handy with hammer and saw, could mix concrete by hand—not the Quickrete stuff either. Liked to keep his feet on the ground, thought any building more than a story high was putting on airs. Hired out as a guide for a year, but couldn't stand having to listen to a bunch of rich folks who "didn't know their dicks from a garter snake." He proudly proclaimed that he'd been no farther from the U.P. than the northern counties of Wisconsin. Never been north to visit "them Canucks," nor as far west as Minnesota.

When it came to talking, Owen was a contradiction. In the woods, Owen could go weeks without uttering a word. Wasn't one of those guys who had to sing or whistle or have the radio blasting so as not to go stir crazy. "Cain't hear what the woods is tellin ya if alls you do is gab."

Yet put a piece of gossip within thirty miles of his elephant ears, and guaranteed before nightfall it was part of the unofficial male grapevine from Copper Harbor to Ironwood to Sault Ste. Marie and all points in between.

Each Tuesday, he'd arrive around noon, we'd unpack the supplies, and then he'd slip in his false teeth. For lunch, I provided soup and he shared some of the sharpest tasting jerky I ever sampled. Between slurps he'd dish the week's news and I'd pump him about his jobs, and the woods, and anything else I could think to ask him. Two weeks ago, I had surprised him with birthday cupcakes to celebrate his eighty-second birthday. Owen was my model for what I wanted to be as an octogenarian—in fact, if I could be half as active and half as interesting as Owen, I would be more than satisfied. I liked the old coot a ton and a half.

For the last two days, I'd listened to WIKB's news and funeral reports and heard squat about my unexpected guest. This week, I was actually looking forward to the gossipy part of Owen's visit.

Owen hardly got his teeth in place before he asked if I'd heard about "that Janie Doe person brought to the hospital."

His face fell when I told him I had.

"I seen from tracks you had all kinds of company. They musta beat me to the story, eh? My Cousin Molly's daughter-in-law—the second one, not the first—she works down there at the hospital. Smarter than a trout, that one. Just this mornin she was tellin me that poor girl is alive, but sicker than a dog chowin down on skunk cabbage. Don't nobody know who she is. Folks sayin some perv kept her tied up somewhere. Had a change in heart when she got sick. Me? I'm leanin toward a sugar daddy. Molly was sayin this guy's payin for her medical expenses. Wish I knew me that feller. Medical expenses are outrageous. You know how much her stay's gonna cost? Geez, I'm thinkin maybe ten grand. She stays in there long enough, could even be twenty. Thank God for the VA, that's all I can say." He cackled at his humor.

If she was uninsured, the stay would cost a lot more than Owen's estimate. Without a competitive market to keep costs in check for the uninsured, hospitals can jack up their prices. They don't have to deal with any insurance companies. It's like allowing a hotel to charge the rates they post on the back of the room's door, which are probably there for some legal reason, but I suspect mostly to make people feel good about how little they paid in comparison.

His rant gave me the idea to talk to an insurance company CEO I knew to see if he could cut me a deal to insure the woman. I'd pay them administrative expenses and reimburse them for all her expenses, but with insurance, the hospital would charge only the insurance company's negotiated rates. It wasn't strictly cricket, but no one would be harmed.

I shoved down anger at an unjust system and used Owen's pause to relate my version of the truth about "Janie Doe." Owen cupped his hands to his ears to make sure he didn't miss a bit. "Nekkid. Well don't that beat all, eh? Say, you hear about the brawl in Gaastra?"

He left quicker than usual, possibly because I was not holding up my end of the conversation, not remembering to ask about his week or about one of his past jobs. Or maybe he left because I gave him the inside scoop on the hottest story of the week.

It would be a week before Owen returned, and I would miss his company, but I had the feeling it would not be a week of solitude. Some say we Irish are superstitious. I say it ain't paranoia if it's true.

Boss first heard Seamus McCree's name mentioned by someone else during the gabbing before a Wednesday morning prayer meeting. Heard the name twice more in the bank before lunch, with more or less the same story attached to it. Jimmie had led the two of them right to the McCree family trust's eighty acres on Shank Lake. Unfortunately, Iron County deputies had beaten them to the scene. Each time Boss heard "McCree," the disappointment of coming to the top of McCree's driveway and seeing the two Iron County snow machines parked at his house reappeared.

For whatever reason, that triggered Boss to hum the opening line from Carole King's "So Far Away." Boss hated songs getting stuck in a loop, replaying over and over until finally the mind's disk jockey replaced it with some other tune. Only thing Boss hated worse right then was the coughing jag the humming triggered, which caused back spasms sharp enough to double over a Greek god.

"You okay, Boss?" the executive secretary called in.

"Fine." *As fine as you can be with stage IV lung cancer and three months left on the year the doc gave me.* Of course, the year had assumed no more cigarettes and no more drinking, and that last part was not going to happen. Boss threw on overclothes and headed outside to think-walk. Wandering up Superior Avenue toward the Iron County Courthouse, Boss picked up the weekly Iron County Reporter. The article on page two took four column-inches to say the unidentified woman had entered the hospital Saturday afternoon, and at press time her condition was still critical. If anyone had information, blah, blah, blah.

Boss checked the rag from stem to stern. Still no news about Brett's murder. The longer it took to find him, the less evidence would remain. At the foot of the courthouse steps, Boss turned around and gazed at the far hills past Crystal Falls, willing a threatening cough to be still. Whispering to stave off the cough, Boss recited the first two verses of the sixth Psalm. "Lord, rebuke me not in thine anger, neither chasten me in thy hot displeasure. Have mercy upon me, O Lord; for I am weak: O Lord, heal me; for my bones are vexed." Boss could still picture the 1875 family Bible all these years after memorizing the complete Book of Psalms in fourth grade from it and winning the Sunday school's Student of the Year Award.

Lost in the reminiscences, but feeling calmer, Boss damn near got bowled over by Sergeant Bartelle. The hairy ape was yapping a mile a minute into his cell phone. He flipped his phone shut, doffed his hat, and pardoned himself up and down, which Boss saw as a natural perk of funding the Democratic ticket in the county; people did tend to bow and scrape.

"What brings you to the courthouse today, Boss?"

Boss glared at the hireling. *Damn his curiosity. We never should have brought him up from the Mitten.* "Care to set me straight on these rumors I hear about that girl down in the hospital, Lon?" Boss vaguely nodded west toward Iron River.

"Open investigation. You know I can't comment, but I will say the rumors are just rumors."

"You saying this McCree guy didn't find her?"

"You know McCree?"

"We had a mortgage on that parcel twenty, thirty years ago, back before it was split up."

Bartelle ignored his cell phone's ringtone version of "God Bless America."

"Well, I've heard a lot of things in the last twenty-four hours and none of them have come from witnesses." Bartelle replaced his hat. "How's the banking business holding up these days? You weren't looking at deeds to foreclose, were you?"

Boss relaxed. Bartelle had provided a perfect excuse for this courthouse visit. "I know deputies hate serving eviction notices. So do I, I'll tell you. Storm's passed, thank goodness. Property's not rising yet, but it's stopped falling. Fortunately, we don't have many foreclosures coming up. Can't say what's happening at the other banks."

Conversation complete, they do-si-doed around each other. Boss decided not to return to the bank, going instead to the single-wide outside of town and toward the passion few living people knew about.

SEVEN

THURSDAY MORNING, A NORTHWEST BREEZE stirred snow devils on Shank Lake, bringing with it a hint of wood smoke: probably someone burning slash from a winter logging operation. The brilliant sun in a clear Paul Newman blue sky hurt my eyes. I decided to combine my normal morning cross-country ski and my evening snowshoe ramble into one long backwoods workout. Skiing is all about rhythm: getting into it and staying in it. You don't feel your legs and arms move. The effortless rhythm is perfect for contemplation; it allows your mind free rein to sort through all the facts, possibilities, impossibilities and perhaps arrive at a "eureka" moment. I had been stirring that pot for well over forty days and forty nights with my twice-daily exercise.

My thinking had come this far: in psychospeak, I had a few issues. My father died when I was young. My mother chose to bury her sorrow in silence; with the exception of five words spoken while under extreme duress, she had not uttered a word for decades. My wife dumped me after I quit Wall Street.

Although I had dated some, I had been skittish about new commitments. I don't blame anyone else; the problems are mine. Abigail told me I was a closed book and took too much responsibility for problems that weren't mine. Every day while we were together, we spent time talking about my issues—our issues. I thought we were making a lot of progress. I really, really wanted us to work out, so I was trying hard—but she left anyway.

Friends I could make—even good women friends. Something was preventing me from staying in a loving relationship. Either I needed to do something differently or admit I was not cut out for "we" life.

On these daily excursions into the woods, I had parsed all of my actions, all of my words and come up with . . . more questions and no answers. I hoped, as I had hoped every other day, that today I would have an epiphany. While concentrating on keeping rhythm and picking lint off the dark blanket of my thoughts, I missed a turn and found myself in new territory. The vegetation began to clog the road, constricting it into a narrow, winding path. The young firs underneath the snow grabbed the poles and jerked me backwards if I strode forward before working them free. My shoulders ached from the repeated evergreen abuse. Skiing became impossible.

Obviously this was not the day for enlightenment-through-skiing. The wrong turn instead offered me the gift of exploring new territory. I shoved the skis into a snowdrift to await the return trip and strapped on snowshoes.

Soon I ran into a second problem, much larger than the first. Literally. A cow moose and her calf blocked the path. They looked at me. I looked at them. Moose can be patient buggers. Five minutes later, they ambled into the tag alder thicket. I took it as a sign that I should turn around. Today was just not my day, period.

By the time I reached the home stretch on Shank Lake Road, I was plumb tuckered out. I concentrated on sliding one sore leg in front of the other without crossing ski tips. It took some time before the distant burr of a snowmobile barreling up the road intruded on my consciousness.

They were either coming to visit me at the house, which was only a quarter mile away, or they would blast on by. Most Yoopers don't expect to see anyone skiing in the middle of "their" road, and I moved to the edge to avoid looking like Wile E. Coyote after a truck ran him over.

The roar diminished and then the woods returned to silence. *Visitors. There might be something to Irish intuition—or paranoia.*

I caught Sergeant Lon Bartelle peering into the house from the screened porch. Another parka-clad figure huddled over a snowmobile in the driveway, removing what looked like fishing tackle boxes. I pulled off my gloves and shook hands with Bartelle. His hands were cold. "Forget something?" I bent down to unclasp my skis.

"Sorry we're here so late in the day. We planned to be here much earlier but something else grabbed us first. Got some more paperwork for you." He handed me a search warrant.

I skimmed it. "Water?"

"We're interested in pathogens, actually, but they'd come from your water. Beautiful day, but I'm freezing . . . Shall we?" He stamped his feet for emphasis.

We shed our gear in the mud room and Bartelle introduced me to the technician, who walked with a hitch in his giddyup. I immediately forgot his name and thought of him as Tex. "Can you give him a tour so he can determine where he needs to take his samples?"

"You guys want to start up or down?"

Tex said, "Basement. That's where the water comes in, eh?"

"My drilled well goes to the pressure tank. It has hard water with some iron, so I installed a prefilter and water softener. Water heater operates off the furnace. Do you care about the heating system?"

"Don't think so," Tex said. "Water at the little cabin where you found the Jane Doe?"

"The little guest cabin? My rustic retreat? No electricity and no running water unless I sprint with a bucket from the lake."

No one cracked a smile at my weak attempt to be funny. After the tour, Tex hauled his tackle cases containing empty sample vials and testing chemicals into the basement.

Bartelle pulled a pocket notebook from his shirt, flipped a few pages, rubbed his head. "While he's working, I got a few follow-up questions—assuming you don't mind? Did the Jane Doe ever take a shower here?"

"Only baths, trying to get her fever down. Why?" I refilled the wood stove and settled him on the chair in the great room that faced the wall of windows.

"This is a great view you've got, McCree. I can see why you love it here."

My stomach growled its discontent with emptiness. "Do I dare offer you my water to drink? Or I've got soda in the cold room downstairs if you want. I assume beer and wine are out? I need to grab something to eat. Want anything?"

"I'll take a rain check. What guns do you keep here?"

"As you know from your search, I don't have any guns. Never owned one."

He rubbed his scalp, leaving his crooked arm resting on the top of his head. "Now that's what confuses me. In the U.P. we've got more guns than people. You're living here all by your lonesome. Some real weirdos out in the woods sometimes and you don't have a gun. Make sense to you?"

I don't answer rhetorical questions.

After another scalp massage he continued, "Here's what else tickles my curiosity: last Sunday, one of the guys found four nine-millimeter jackets in the woods across the road. Care to explain?"

"Abigail set up a little range facing the swamp. Used it to practice with her Sig Sauer. Why the interest in guns?"

"Miss Hancock have any .22s?"

"Sergeant, you have me totally baffled. Tex is sampling my water for pathogens. You're asking about firearms. I assume this has to do with the woman, but I'll be darned if I can understand how."

"Tex?"

I explained my reasons for the name.

"Suits him. By the way, Lieutenant Hastings from the Cincinnati Police said to tell you she's real sorry you and Miss Hancock didn't work out. You're supposed to give her a call when you're back there."

To stall for time while I considered the implications of Hastings' message, I knocked down the damper on the fire, brought water from the kitchen, and filled the Delft porcelain humidifier on top of the wood stove. Obviously, he had researched me, looking for arrests, and found those relating to the killing at my Cincinnati house the previous year. The thought of the dead man lying there caused me to flash back to that scene. I shook it off. Bartelle would also know the prosecutor had dropped all the charges because the guys had broken in, were armed, and had shot Abigail.

He wouldn't know that I still suffered nightmares that caused me to wake up with a racing heart and a deep black knowledge that I had failed to protect Abigail in my house. I switched my thoughts to Lieutenant Hastings, who was the head of Cincinnati's Homicide Unit and a friend. Another not-to-be relationship. I had once been interested in her, but she then hooked up with a Cincinnati Bengal. After the football player dumped her, "for a first-round cheerleader pick"—her words, not mine—she made a move, but by then, Abigail was in the picture. Two ships passing . . .

Taking a cop's perspective, I figured Bartelle probably thought any person who had killed once—like me—was more likely to get into trouble than the average bear. All well and good, but how did any of this relate to the woman?

"How's she doing?" I asked after I finished my domestic duties. "The woman . . ."

"Docs have her stabilized. They're keeping her in the hospital. She still claims not to know who she is, where she came from, how she got to your place or what she did here, or before. Doc says high fevers can wipe all that stuff out, but it's usually temporary. Don't worry, we'll get the real story."

"And in the meantime, here you are, looking at your one and only suspect."

Tex stomped up the basement steps, and I found myself counting each percussive step. From the kitchen he called, "If you filter and soften your water, how come you also use a Brita filter?"

"I liked the taste of my water before conditioning, but it stained every-thing. Hence the softener. With the softener, the water tastes salty, so I filter it."

"You say so. Ever melt snow or anything?"

"Only when I stayed at the cabin and the lake was frozen so deep I couldn't chop a hole through. But that was several years ago, before I built the house."

"Shoulda used an ice auger," Tex laughed. "As a kid we used to ice fish this lake. Got lots of perch and some good northerns too. I'm about done here, just need to pack everything up. Oh hey, is that water you got on the stove?" He walked to the humidifier. "Yes. Look at those crystals." He pumped his fist in celebration. "Sometimes the stove gets so hot the water boils and then the crystals precipitate out. Hot dog!"

He filled two vials with water from the humidifier, then donned fire gloves I kept on the hearth and carried the humidifier to the sink. After dumping the water he scraped samples of the residue clinging to the inside of the vessel. "Perfect," he said. "Let me pack and we'll be out of your hair."

"We'll be back," Bartelle promised.

EIGHT

BOSS STOOD TO ONE SIDE OF the tellers, antennae extended, to gather facts and rumors about the murder up by Long Lake. Everyone agreed some guy snowmobiling from Witch Lake with his son had seen three eagles on the far side of Long Lake. In winter, eagles are primarily carrion eaters, and the kid wanted to see what had died. They discovered an abandoned snowmobile and portions of a frozen corpse, which in the conversations only Boss seemed to know was Brett Aho's carcass. Boss chose not to share that information. Wolves and coyotes had scattered bones over a large area and eagles were picking over the leftovers. The father stayed to keep the eagles away from the evidence, while his son scooted into Amasa to the nearest phone. He was so shaken up by the time he reached the Tall Pines general store and gas station that the clerk had to make the 911 call.

The medical examiner, looking like one of his cadavers, popped in around noon to cash a check. Boss maneuvered across the ME's path on his departure from the teller and cast a line in front of him. "Heard tell the sheriff caught an ugly one."

The ME eased to a stop and extended his head like a turtle reaching for a tasty morsel. "Yep, got ourselves an old-fashioned murder," he rasped through a voice box scarred by a three-pack-a-day habit. "Everybody's been asking if we know who it is."

Boss waited for the ME to continue, but the old man seemed to be enjoying some kind of power game, standing there, bobbing his head at the information he knew but had not yet shared. Boss knew how to play those kinds of games. "And?" Boss stretched the vowel.

"We'll probably have to rely on dental records." The ME eased back on his heels.

"Because?" Boss again drew it out.

"Bartelle would have ordered the state boys to run the prints, 'cept some animal decided they were finger-lickin' good." The ME coughed and grimaced at the pain.

Boss didn't give the ME the satisfaction of groaning at the joke; it would only encourage him. And Boss didn't want to comment on the ME's pained look, which would only lead to a discussion about how the docs had removed one of his lungs and part of the other, but cancer had still spread to his bones. Better to ask another question and avoid any reciprocal health questions. "Bartelle's running the investigation?"

"Caught a real break there. Seems the sergeant was in the area on the Jane Doe matter. Nobody's got more experience than Bartelle at running a grid. He met the lad at Tall Pines a few minutes after the call came in. Settled him down until the rest of the sheriff's boys showed. Everyone followed the kid to the murder scene. They searched for pieces and eventually the state crime scene boys from Marquette arrived."

"They find anything useful?" Boss asked.

He leaned in, bringing with him the hint of death. "I pulled a .22 slug from the deceased's brain pan. Think about it. Everyone knows a .22 is a girl's weapon. Gotta go, probably said too much already." The ME tipped his hat.

"Yeah, woman for sure." Boss said, knowing they were barking up the wrong tree. Watching the ME hobble out the door, Boss thought, "I will not let my cancer do that to me. I'm going out with a bang, not a whimper."

TWO WEEKS AFTER THE GIRL first appeared, Sergeant Lon Bartelle sat at his desk, feet up, arm wrapped around his head, drawing blood from worrying a scab. He stared at the toxicological tests from McCree's house that Tex—thanks to McCree, he couldn't think of him as anything else—had dumped on his desk.

"All negative?" Bartelle felt his face glow with the heat of disappointment. Tex stood mute before him.

Bartelle choked down his anger. No sense shooting the proverbial messenger. "Sheriff know yet?" Bartelle asked.

"Figured you'd be the one to tell him," Tex said. "Anything new on Jane?"

"You figured that, did you?" Bartelle tried a smile to get Tex to relax, but the effort died through lack of practice. "With this, I have exactly nothing I want to tell him. The woman still claims no memory."

"But she's remembering the current stuff."

"Not good enough," Bartelle growled. "Add in the stellar work we've done so far on the murder vic. We got him narrowed down to about one hundred and sixty million possible males. We have no clue who owned the Polaris we found at the murder scene. I wasted four man days of department time looking for spent brass nearby. They turned up a junkyard full of iron, but nothing useful." Bartelle slapped his forehead hard enough to produce a loud thwack. "I know why you're still standing there. You got something useful from your DEA contacts? Please tell me I'm right."

Tex leaned back against the doorframe. "Love to, Sarge, but I wouldn't want to do anything to spoil your mood. They heard nothing about a buy gone bad. All I can tell you is the victim's hair showed no drug use. Don't know about alcohol because his organs were already recycled. You still figure the murder and the Jane Doe are related?"

"Don't you? It's only two miles from the murder site on Long Lake to McCree's camp on Shank Lake where the Jane Doe pops up at approximately the same time. She's a suspect for the murder by proximity alone. Unfortunately, the sheriff and DA want proof, and the distance between me having no doubts and giving them proof looks about as big as the Grand Canyon. McCree has got to be lying—unless he's telling the truth."

"Glad you got that clear," Tex said and gimped through the doorway.

THE SNOWMOBILE'S WHINE ANNOUNCED OWEN'S weekly visit. I threw on a jacket— the temperature was already above freezing—picked up a pair of work gloves and got as far as the back porch before I realized he had a passenger. She placed her helmet on the snowmobile seat and shrugged out of a one-piece snowsuit, which she folded and placed next to the helmet. Her shoulders rose and fell in a huge sigh. Spinning around, she caught me staring at her and flashed a smile. Jane Doe.

I uprooted my feet and helped unload my week's supplies. With three pairs of hands it went quickly, especially since no one chose to break the uncomfortable silence.

Owen disappeared behind the pole barn to pee—he maintained it was a waste of water to use a toilet—and left the woman in the kitchen shifting from foot to foot. I gathered an extra placemat and cloth napkin from the Indiana cupboard. "All recovered?" I asked.

"They've released me." She approached me. "I came to thank you for saving my life."

I slipped around her and grabbed a soup bowl and spoon. "That really wasn't necessary."

"I've got my own questions, but those can wait. The doctors told me that if you hadn't given me the antibiotics and brought my fever down, I would never have made it. Somehow I contracted Legionnaires' disease— don't worry, it's not catching. That's worth at least a thank-you and a hug—saving my life, not the disease."

She wrapped her arms around me and squeezed hard. At least I now knew what Tex was looking for with his pathological sampling. I stood there, arms raised, wondering what to do with them as her body pressed to mine. I could picture her in the bath and it was making me uncomfortable. Owen walked in and barked a short cough. She applied a last bit of pressure and released me. "Soup smells homey," she said. "What kind?"

While I used the bathroom, she served the lentil soup. I returned to hear Owen chuckling. He saw me, choked down the chuckle, and said, "No problem."

Owen had already installed his teeth and between slurps of soup, he jumped to the gossip. "You hear they identified the guy was killed?"

I hadn't, so Owen enthusiastically took the bit. "Lived in Trout Creek or Ewen, 'round there. Went by the name of Brett Aho. Not related to the Ahos in Iron County, I don't think. Had a weekly meet-up with some floozy. Guess it had been two, three years he was seein her for their lay-zon. When he missed and she couldn't contact him, she got to worryin, remembered hearin about the murder, and called the state police.

"Took 'em some time to find his dentist. Geezer was winterin in Arizona. Had enough teeth on the jawbone to match his X-rays. Hear tell there's a sister somewhere. Ain't claimed the body yet. Course there ain't much to claim, neither. More soup?"

I served Owen seconds and motioned to the woman, who shook her head in refusal. I poured a ladleful into my bowl and passed the bread. "What kind of work did he do?" I sucked in a spoonful of soup and burned the inside of my mouth.

"Trucker I heard this from didn't know no more than what I told ya. You all hear the DNR is looking for some jerk who shot hisself a wolf over by Cable Lake?"

The woman dropped her spoon and it clattered into the bowl, splashing drops of soup onto the table. "Where's that?" She dabbed at the spill with her cloth napkin.

Owen waved toward the wall of windows. "Other side of One-Forty-One and a little bit south. Ten, twelve miles maybe. DNR used to think the Cable Lake pack and the one up arounds here was the same ones. I kept tellin them they was separate. Finally, they got radio collars on the alpha pair and proved it was two different packs. Listened to me they could have saved money and used it on somethin useful, like stockin the lakes. The radio signal didn't move no more and the local DNR found the bitch gut shot. I ain't got much good to say about wolves, but shootin 'em like that is lower than snake shit in Death Valley."

The woman flinched when he mentioned the gut shot and looked as though she would be sick.

Owen must have noticed her discomfort as well. "Pardon my French. I ain't used to polite company."

Owen's apology brought a smile to her face and caused me to remember her colorful language when she first came out of her stupor. Whatever had caused her discomfort, it wasn't Owen's swearing.

Owen nattered on about other local happenings, finished his soup, patted his beard and mustache with his napkin, belched to proclaim it had been good, and announced he needed to see a man about a dog—his way of indicating he was going outside to pee again.

Owen had painted the silence with his gossip; now I wondered how to broach the topic of her lost memories. I gave up on clever. "Any luck with your memory?"

"Nothing worthwhile. You're still looking at Jane Doe. I decided on the ride out I was going to adopt a temporary name. I'm feeling like a Niki today. N-I-K-I. What do you think?"

"Isn't it usually with two 'k's?"

"I don't want to be greedy with the consonants. One's all I need."

"Niki's good. Staying with Doe or moving to Smith or Johnson, or something a little more unique?"

"I'll be one of those single-named people. You know, like Madonna or Rihanna."

Outside the snowmobile sputtered to life. "I guess you'd best catch your ride. Miss it and you'll be stranded for a week."

She rose from the table and gathered the dishes. "There's no hurry. I'll wash these."

In the midst of our friendly argument about whether or not she should wash the dishes, the snowmobile engine roared, and through the mudroom window I watched Owen speed up the driveway. "What the . . . ?"

"I guess now would be a good time to fess up," she said from behind me. I spun around and she greeted me with a crooked smile. "Before lunch . . . while you were in the bathroom, I told him you had agreed to let me stay here until I figured out who I was."

NINE

JIMMIE HAD TO PASS BY Boss's place the first time. A logging truck was coming the other way, and he'd agreed that no one should see him here. He pulled as far to the right as he dared and gave the Yooper wave—four fingers raised from the steering wheel while the thumb still steered—as the logging truck rumbled past. "Bastards think they own the damn road," Jimmie grumbled through clenched teeth. He continued moseying down Rock Crusher until he hit the Enstrom Cutoff, where he executed a three-point turn.

Boss's vehicle wasn't in the pole barn. Jimmie parked in the same place he had before, kicked some accumulated snow from around his tires, and entered the unlocked single-wide. He boosted the thermostat to sixty-eight. Figuring Boss would want coffee, maybe even with a drop of brandy being as it was the end of the day, he ran water into a kettle and put it on the hotplate to boil.

Jimmie drummed his fingers on the table, warming them to the rhythm of some Sousa march. The kettle soon whistled. He hunted for the Maxwell House; found it in the same cupboard containing powdered milk and rat poison. Paused to think about that for a moment, then dumped a heaping teaspoon of coffee into the mug. Nothing worse than weak coffee. Jimmie stirred in boiling water, snorting the steam to capture the smell of freshly made instant. He rotated the mug to look at the Hematite National Bank logo and wondered if they shouldn't update their graphic from a miner with a pick to giant earthmovers and three-story dump trucks.

The first mug of coffee warmed Jimmie's insides; the second he carried as a hand warmer while he searched the main room for something to read. Found an ancient *Playboy* stuffed under the couch, checked the centerfold, and read the "Advisor" column before tucking it back where he had found it. He'd never entered the bedroom. Still no sound of Boss, so what the hell.

He set the mug on the table, pulled his sleeves over his fingers, and pushed the door open. Blackout curtains covered the window and he flicked on the overhead light. Except for the bed in the corner, it looked like the reading room of a library: cherry keyhole desk in the middle with a Herman Miller Aeron chair, bookcases on three walls, a locked gun safe in the other corner. Three-by-five cards with Boss's back-slanted printing labeled the sections. He read the cards tacked onto the bookshelves on the left wall: Constitution, Police State, Militia.

The row at eye level contained the last few volumes of "Police State" and ran into the "Militia" section. He perused the spines with titles like *Waste in Waco* and *Your Rights After an Unauthorized Search and Seizure.* Sitting open on the desk was *Life and Hard Times of Mark Koernke: Radio's Voice of Truth.* Huh! He had never heard Boss speak one word about the militia. At the crunch of tires coming up the driveway, he knocked the light switch down with his elbow and, with his sleeve again covering his hand, shut the door.

Boss shucked the parka onto the couch. "Been waiting long? Must have been. Feels decent in here and smells like you made coffee. More water in the pot?"

With a brandy-fortified coffee in hand, Boss asked, "You hungry? I bought some pasties for later, but I can heat one up."

At the mention of food Jimmie realized he was hungry. Breakfast was a long time ago, but he felt a little skittish, and the tour of the bedroom hadn't eased his concern. Boss was one part Chamber of Commerce, one part backroom pol, one part church deacon, and one part certified. "I'm good for now," he said.

"Tell me I was right." Boss settled on the couch.

"As always," Jimmie said, plastering a genuine thousand-watt smile on his face. "I seen that old coot pick her up at the hospital just like you figured. Trailed along until they got to his place in Amasa, then I parked by where the snowmobile trail cuts the highway near Tall Pines and unloaded my snow machine from the trailer. Took off ahead of them, hid my sled in a stand of hemlocks off that back road we seen from the plat book was on McCree's property. Had on my white camo suit. Snuck up on 'em so's they never seen me peeking over the hill spying on 'em."

"Just the two of them?"

"She rode in behind him. While old hairy ears and McCree bring the first bags into the house, she takes the knapsack you give her and stores it inside the woodshed sticking off McCree's pole barn. Then she quick-like grabs some groceries and helps unload the goods."

Jimmie stopped his recital while Boss made another spiked coffee. "Could you hear them?"

"Not then. Later. They was in the house for a good long time. Probably et something. Finally the old coot comes out, steps behind the pole barn, and takes a second leak. Then he cranks up his machine and takes off. Leaves the girl behind."

"You're messing with me, Jimmie."

Jimmie leaned back, held his hands up in the universal I'm-only-telling-the-truth gesture. "I stuck around and a few minutes later the two of them—McCree and the girl—come out the door. She says, 'I put my stuff out here,' and gets her knapsack from the woodshed. He follows her and says—and you can tell he's totally pissed— he says, 'Look Nikki, I'm not going to make you walk to town, but tomorrow first thing . . . ' She kind of shrugs," Jimmie exaggerated a shrug, raising his shoulders almost to his ears, "and walks past him and inside the house. McCree takes off on cross-country skis going lickety-split. We ain't talked about whether you still want her kilt, so I slipped away."

Boss got up and patted Jimmie on the shoulder. "You've done well. You sure you heard McCree call the girl Nikki?"

"Yep." Jimmie had been feeling pretty good about the pats on the shoulder, but now he wasn't so sure.

Boss paced the room two circuits, paused to look out the window, then made a third circuit. Jimmie waited, feeling the vibrations of each step reverberate through the single-wide's floor. Boss faced him. "Good call on leaving the girl alone. Last I heard, she still wasn't remembering anything, and if I'm not mistaken, by now Owen is eating high off the hog on his story about the girl shacking up with McCree." Boss chuckled and Jimmie figured it was good policy to join in. "The cops were wondering about the two of them being in cahoots before. This should frost that cake. She is a cute thing and McCree's been holed up there without any companionship. Too bad we don't have the place wired for video."

Jimmie waited for instructions while Boss slurped down the dregs of the coffee, washed the mugs, and hung them on the tree. Boss tucked the dishtowel over the rack. "I'll keep an ear to the ground in town. You stay away from there until I get back atcha."

THE GIRL'S NAME WAS NOT Nikki. Boss thought back again to the two people selected from more than a hundred who submitted applications to the foundation—a foundation existing only as a downstate Michigan corporation with a postal drop that forwarded mail to another postal drop that was nearer to Boss's home, but not too near. Bethany and Brandon: if those weren't monikers representing white Americans born in the eighties, what were?

Both postdoctoral students, both orphans without close family, both loners, both able to leave everything behind and give their all on a six-month project. Despite assurances to Jimmie that he had done well, Boss worried about Bethany still being alive. A secondary question was whether Seamus McCree also posed an unacceptable risk. If the girl was calling herself Nikki, she obviously didn't know who she was. Nikki wasn't her mother or grandmother or former roommate's name either. Not even close.

If Bethany didn't get her memory of past events back in the five-plus weeks before April Fool's Day, then she could cause no harm to the plans. It seemed, however, too long a time. Since no one knew where the girl came from, if she went missing from the Northwoods without a trace, the cops might decide her disappearance was further proof she had killed Brett Aho—or that McCree had killed them both. Either result was acceptable. So, let Jimmie clean up the loose end once everyone decided McCree and the girl were romantically involved.

Let McCree choose his own fate: either he booted the girl out or he didn't. If he didn't, and Jimmie couldn't catch Bethany alone, McCree would become collateral damage. If Jimmie struck right after Owen Lyndstrom's next Tuesday supply run, it might not be until Owen's visit the following week that someone would discover the bodies.

If McCree ditched the girl, then he could live. If the girl returned to town, it would be harder to kill her, but fortunately Boss had been one of the deacons from the Presbyterian Church who organized the new red knapsack filled with donated clothing to keep her going until she figured out who she was. The fact they had already met might make it easier to lure the girl away when the time was right.

Eschewing more coffee, Boss filled a juice glass with brandy and took it to the office. Moving the Koernke book aside, Boss retrieved an archaic Dell Inspiron 2500 from a cardboard box stored in the office closet. Slower than making toast by solar heat in December, the computer eventually did the trick. Checking email was a four-step process: attach the laptop to the phone line; wait for the dial-up connection to take; download email from NuWrldYooper@gmail.com, an account only a few people knew; delete email. Two messages:

Congratulations on test results. Two out of two healthy students is great! Just think what this will do to old damaged goods.

Cysteine levels remaining sufficiently high and sodium levels now under control. Should be concentrated in three weeks or less.

Boss took a celebratory slug of the brandy and felt the liquor burn a path from throat to stomach. Time to sing a psalm. Interesting when you thought of it: in the Bible, the psalms came immediately after the afflictions of Job. To everything its time and place—Ecclesiastes was two books after the Psalms, leaving room for Proverbs in between.

Boss drained the whiskey and thought of a favorite proverb: "When pride cometh, then cometh shame: but with the lowly is wisdom." Boss put away the laptop and pulled a folder from the drawer and spread its contents on the desk.

TEN

MY CHASE DREAM THAT NIGHT took its typical form: unknown people were after me, and I knew that if they caught me, they'd kill me. I awoke wondering if people who died in their sleep had also suffered chase dreams, and if, in their terminal dream, their demons finally did reach them.

The house was silent except for the metronome ticks from the grandmother clock hanging on the wall. My feet didn't recoil from the cold floor as they usually do. The house was warm. I threw on fresh clothes, tiptoed from the bedroom to the loft and stopped at the sight of Niki downstairs, facing the lakeside wall of windows, performing yoga's Salute to the Sun. Dressed in a tank top, boy shorts, and slouch socks, the glow from the wood stove fire painted her skin a warm orange. She was as supple as I was stiff.

Trying unsuccessfully to ignore her scanty attire, I waited until she had run through the poses before I continued down the stairs.

"I've figured it out," she said at my entry. "I'll stay in your guest cabin. There's plenty of split wood, and I already lit the fire. It'll take all day before it's comfortable for sitting, but it should be fine for sleeping tonight. You've got enough cooking utensils over there for me to take care of my breakfast and lunches, but it would be nice if we could share dinner?" She slipped into blue jeans and a T-shirt with the names of all the Forest Park Trojans football players. "I can only pay you with labor, but you're not exactly domestic. Have you ever washed these windows? Wood heat isn't clean, you know. I can—"

"You hatched this plan this morning, did you?" My voice dripped with skepticism. I had to give her credit. She didn't turn away, didn't look down. She didn't plead or shout. She continued her conversational tone.

"Coyotes yipping and yapping woke me around three. I couldn't get back to sleep, so I borrowed your headlamp and restoked the stove since the fire had burned down. Then I walked on the lake. You missed the northern lights. The borealis showed for maybe twenty minutes. Not exactly bright, just green sheets in the northern sky." She pointed high on the cathedral ceiling on the north side. "While I was walking, I thought about everything you said yesterday. You know, about needing your space and everything. Then I remembered the cabin, so I checked it out."

She grabbed my arm, pulled me to the nearest window, and ran her finger over the window sill. "See this dust? I'd hate to think what it looks like under your refrigerator."

I pulled my arm away. "I appreciate your—"

"I know I'm costing you food, a little extra propane maybe, and wood. I'll replace the wood I use. If I cook and clean, would that compensate for the food?"

I didn't know what to say, so I temporized and poured a glass of water, drank it, and poured another. From the corner of my eye, I watched her follow my movements. "I'm not expressing myself well this morning," I said. "Yesterday's concerns still hold. I appreciate your not wanting to be a financial burden. Believe me, that is the least of it. I need space and . . ." *And what exactly did I need?*

She nodded as though she read my mind. "Here's the thing, Seamus. I don't exactly know who or what I am. I kind of think I'm a loner. The thought of staying at your cabin appeals to me. How about a week's trial? You don't throw me out until Owen returns next Tuesday. What have you got to lose?"

Any hope the cops won't think I'm involved with this person, that's what. With Owen undoubtedly letting the world know she's here, though, I guess that ship has sailed.

She pulled her earlobe a couple of times. "Your house will be clean. I'll leave you alone except we'll eat dinner together? You've got a couple of dead maples on the other side of your cabin. I'll take them down and work them up to replace the wood I use."

"You know how to use a chainsaw?" The inane question leapt from my mouth.

"How hard can it be? Please, Seamus. One week."

Once, in my corporate days, we underwent a Myers–Briggs personality test. I was an INTP. The *P*, which stands for perceiving, came into full play. *P*s like to take in information for as long as possible before they have to make a decision. I didn't have to make a decision this moment. If she had pouted or batted her eyes or tried any other stereotypical female ploy, I think I would have tossed her out. My normal morning routine was to stretch for thirty minutes, then cook oatmeal for breakfast and journal for an hour or so before cross-country skiing the rest of the morning and often into the afternoon. If I decided after journaling to ski to Deer Lake and arrange transportation for Niki, nothing would stand in my way. In the meantime, I might learn something about her.

I moved the footstool to make room for my stretches and started with easy back rocks. "What did the doctors tell you about your memory?" I asked.

"Full recovery," she said with a confident voice. "They're not sure of the timing or whether it will return in bits and pieces or all at once."

I shifted into a one-legged stand and caught her eye as I changed positions.

"Well, that's not exactly right," she answered, the assurance gone. "They're not sure. I could quite possibly never remember whatever happened while I had the high fever, but they gave me, like, a ninety percent chance of remembering all the rest of the stuff."

"What do you know about yourself?" I said in the midst of touching my toes—well, that's what they call the exercise—I was three inches short of the objective.

She paced the great room, careful to avoid interrupting my stretches. A series of emotions played across her face until she regained control of a blank expression. "I have certain . . . competencies. I don't know anything factual about myself. I'm like a scientific puzzle. You know, they find the bones of a new animal and try to determine what it looked like, how it lived, what it ate, who ate it? That's how I feel. I've figured out some things are easy for me and some are hard."

She effortlessly flowed from a standing position to a handstand, legs straight, her shirt falling down past her chest to cover her face, exposing an arched back and the tight body accented by the rose tattoo above her breast I remembered from the sponge baths. She bent her elbows, popped herself to standing, and pulled her shirt into place. "Like that. I knew I could do it, although I haven't tried it. But I don't know if I was a gymnast or I'm just a show-off. I go outside and my spirits lift, but I don't know why."

My next stretch was a shoulder stand. I had never done a hand stand, except with a wall nearby to lean into if I lost balance. I considered skipping that position and then figured, what the heck? I wasn't trying to impress her with my flexibility, I was trying to stretch. "What else," I mumbled with my chin tucked into my chest.

"God," she said. "You are skinny. Don't you eat enough?"

Most people abhor silence and find it necessary in a conversation to fill in the empty space when I leave one. She was no different. Ten seconds and she cracked. "What else? I've got tattoos. Not exactly news to you, is it?" She gave a nervous chuckle. "Unfortunately, they don't tell me shit about anything. Oh, I swear like a sailor, so I'm probably not a fundamentalist anything. I like to read and I seem to have an eclectic taste—as do you, assuming all the books you have around here are yours?"

"All mine." I lay on my back with my arms stretched overhead, feeling my shoulder muscles slowly release their tension. "You know, with your tattoo, I'm surprised you didn't decide to call yourself Rose."

"Really!" She laughed with a Joni Mitchell leap of octaves.

"I haven't always been slim. I put on a lot of extra weight after my divorce. Eating and drinking too much, and exercising too little. My son eventually called me 'Blubber Man,' which forced me to see what I was doing to myself."

"Depression can do that." She stepped over to my stretched frame and pulled my feet out while pushing my rear in. "That's better balance. Yep, depression makes you fat or skinny. Hard to find someone with depression who weighs what they should.”

While I finished stretching, she continued to pace, her socks sounding like two cloth brooms sweeping the wood floor. As I did my final stretch she said, “I gotta tell you, Seamus. I’m not afraid of what I will find, I’m afraid I’ll never find out. Then what do I do?” She stared out the windows toward the snow-covered lake. “You know, you’re tight because of your hamstrings. I can show you some stretches that are really good for that. Some of them need a second person, and while I’m here . . . But you haven’t exactly decided whether to throw me out, have you?”

I banged around in the kitchen. “You want oatmeal?”

“Sure, can I help?”

“No,” I said. “I can boil water all on my own.” Harsh. She didn’t deserve my anger. Anger at what exactly? “I’m sorry. That was rude. You can set the table. Napkins and placemats are in the Indiana cupboard. If you want coffee, filters and stuff are there too.”

“Don’t you drink coffee?”

“Never took it up. Don’t do tea either, but I stock it, in case. So, help yourself.” My mother would approve of my hospitality. Now, why had Niki’s presence caused me to bubble with anger? Yes, she had tricked me into housing her for a night. She should have been honest and asked—but I would have refused. Taking her at her word, she was homeless, penniless, and nameless. I had arguably saved her life, and it surely wasn’t the cost of feeding her I objected to. Was it as simple as I didn’t want the inconvenience of having to worry about someone other than myself? Had I become that self-centered—or depressed, as she had suggested?

“The water’s boiling,” she said so softly the words airbrushed my consciousness.

Once I stirred in brown sugar and added the oatmeal, I turned down the heat and checked the clock to know when six minutes passed. Who in my position didn’t have the right to be a little depressed? My lover was now an ex; my home in Cincinnati was just a repaired building after everything of sentimental value had been burned. I was bored with the recent cases Criminal Investigations Group had assigned me.

Why shouldn’t I enjoy the great outdoors and my freedom to do whatever I wanted, whenever I wanted? My son was well-launched with his anti-computer-hacking startup. Of course I needed new challenges, but those could wait until spring break-up when I returned to civilization. Or so I kept telling myself.

We ate in silence. Every few bites, her chair would squeak as she shifted position to sneak a glance in my direction. She clearly wanted to talk. *Well, let her stew. Nobody asked her here.* On the other hand, I had to admit to myself that breakfast tasted better accompanied by the smells of fresh coffee and slightly burned toast, even though I didn't partake of either.

She poured a second cup of coffee, took a sip, and said, "I've never had oatmeal with brown sugar stirred into the water first. I think I like my brown sugar and raisins on the top. Did you learn that from your parents?"

"Self-taught. I don't like the cardboard taste of plain oatmeal. This solves the problem."

"I add more sugar." Her eyes smiled. "How did the police discover me here?"

"Huh?"

"The doctors told me you saved me and everything. But if the only contact you have is with Owen on Tuesdays, how did the cops pick me up on a Sunday?"

I related how I had unsuccessfully honked the horn to get someone's attention. How I had finally decided to ski for help and how an amateur pilot flying from Marquette to Ironwood had spotted the blue tarp SOS. He called the coordinates in to the airport, who called 911. Iron County Sheriff's officers responded. End of story.

An impish smile played on her face. "Did you hear about the hunter who was lost in the woods and used the three-shot signal like you tried?"

"Nope." I took another spoonful of oatmeal.

"Well, this guy gets all turned around chasing a deer. He knows enough to stop moving and signal his distress with three shots so his buddies, who should be nearby, can find him. He fires his three shots toward the east and waits on a downed log. Nothing. An hour goes by and he fires off three more shots, this time facing south. Still nothing. Later, three more shots to the north. He's getting cold, and it's going to be dark soon. He only has enough for three more shots, but decides to use them, so he faces the setting sun, pulls the last three arrows from his quiver and lets loose."

I burst out laughing, nearly snorting oatmeal out my nose. The laughter surprised me. It was a sound I had not heard since Abigail left.

A smile flickered across her features, but then she became solemn, scratched her head a few times. "Please give it a week, Seamus. Somewhere nearby is the answer to who I am. I know you're taking a risk. I could be faking all this. I could be a cold-blooded killer. The police think maybe I am. Of course, they think maybe you are too." A grin briefly glimmered and retreated. "It's not like I'm exactly hiding or anything. I got the impression over lunch with Owen that he'll be gabbing to the entire world that I'm here.

"I could use your skis if you are snowshoeing or vice versa. And I meant what I said about cleaning this place and . . ." She wiped her eyes with the back of her hands. "I swore I wasn't going to cry."

I dumped the dishes into the sink—a darned good thing they weren't glass—and turned on the hot water. "Alright, a week. I've got extra snowshoes and skis and poles and stuff I bought for Abigail. She's taller than you, so size might be something of a problem."

"Thanks, Seamus. You won't regret it." She threw her arms around me, squeezed hard, and planted a wet kiss on the back of my neck.

I hoped she was right.

Eleven

Two days later, Niki awoke in the middle of the night to the ululations of a wolf pack. Tingles ran up and down her back as she lay in the log cabin's bed listening to the haunting calls. Starlight from the moonless night illuminated the room. She added logs to restore the fire and slipped on every layer of clothes she had.

Standing underneath the sugar maple trees, she gazed at the Milky Way arched overhead, a sparkling promenade for the angels. She followed the path from the cabin to the house to get an unobstructed view of the sky from the yard, startling a deer from the salt lick as she passed. Orion hung above the lake: left shoulder the bright reddish star Betelgeuse that kids in her Girl Scout troop called Beetlejuice; belt—Alnilam, Alnitak, Mintaka— bold as a spit-shined biker's pride; sword—two stars and a nebula—pulsing with 1,500-year-old light from the birth of new stars.

Past Orion's right shoulder shone the Pleiades, the Seven Sisters, except it was so clear Niki could distinguish all nine of the major stars, the first time that had ever happened.

Above her, the sliding door from Seamus's bedroom opened and he stepped onto the small deck dressed in a T-shirt and Jockeys, his head covered by a fur hat. "Get some clothes on, ya dumb fuck" she yelled. "It's five below!" A sympathetic shiver caused her arms and legs to twitch.

He started. "What are *you* doing?"

"Those poor bastards in town never get to see this magnificent sight. I'm heading to the lake to get a better view."

"Hang on. I'll be right down."

For several hours they walked up and down the lake, watched stars wheel across the sky, caught brief glimpses of the northern lights, and eventually witnessed the stars fade away as the sun ascended into the sky. She spent the last hour trying to ignore the cold, but with the last star gone, the cold won. "I'm heading in."

He touched her arm. "Don't leave yet. Watching the sunrise from here is something you need to experience at least once."

She oriented herself to see its first direct light gathering behind the eastern hills.

"The other way." He took her shoulders and pointed her toward the western shore. The sun first gilded the tops of the trees, then as the brilliant orb moved higher into the sky, its light worked down the trees and onto the lake.

It was just a sunrise, but somehow it seemed like magic. Even as a wisp of a breeze brushed her exposed skin and reminded her how cold she was, she remained on the ice feeling . . . what? Excitement? She'd seen sunrises before. Were these the first stirrings of lust? A twinge rocked her at the thought. She fingered her neck where the hickey had once been. Whose lips had branded her? What promises? Dark thoughts returned. What trauma was implied by the rope burns? She closed her eyes and willed the memories to return.

Once inside, she convinced him to let her fix breakfast. She whipped up pancakes only to discover he didn't have maple syrup. Rooting around in the freezer, she discovered frozen cranberries, which she made into a sauce. He devoured the pancakes.

An internal voice said, *the way to a man's heart is through his stomach.* Whose voice, and why think of that now? He was certainly easy to look at.

Lanky with a nicely rounded ass. With a razor and a comb he'd clean up right well. She announced her decision. "I think today is the day."

"Um?" he mumbled through a mouthful of pancakes.

She bit her lip. "You've had two days of solitudenous—is that a word?—forays. Today, I want you to take me to explore where that guy was murdered. Maybe I killed him."

He carefully put down his fork. She gnawed on the inside of her cheek. Maybe being blunt wasn't such a good idea. "Jiminy, maybe you did it! What the hell do I know? I could be a moth drawn to flame, but you know the country around here . . ."

He crossed his arms over his chest. "You know my routine—"

"And I know you won't go into cardiac arrest if you don't follow it for one single day. Take a walk on the wild side, Seamus. Explore with me first, then I'll go to the cabin and you can stretch and journal to your heart's content." That did not come out as she had intended. She brushed a nonexistent tear from the corner of her eye. "Give it a try. Please? Just this once?"

I MENTALLY KICKED MYSELF ALL the way to the murder site. *Where am I going to draw the line? Despite my protests, she insists on cooking breakfast. Then she convinces me to throw my daily routine in the garbage and pretend to be Sherlock Holmes. Next she's going to tell me to trim my beard. Five days.* I counted five snowshoe steps. *And then she's gone for good.*

At the murder site, it was apparent we hadn't been the only voyeurs. Snowmobile tracks crisscrossed the trails around Long Lake. A herd of snowshoed bipeds had trampled the area, packing down the snow. By the expression on Niki's face, I didn't think she recognized the site. We brushed snow from two roadside boulders to serve as seats while we snacked on gorp.

Between mouthfuls she asked, "Do you know they call this stuff 'scroggin' in New Zealand?"

"You've been to New Zealand?"

She closed her eyes in concentration. "Don't know. Maybe it's just a factoid I picked up. Here, you finish the bag. You need to put on weight.

You may have been—what did your son call you?—'Blubber' or whatever once, but you're anorexic now. You need to work through your grief in better ways than eating disorders."

"Grief?"

"Yeah. You know, love's labor lost—the mythical Abigail whose stuff I don't fit into." She sprang to her feet. "Let's head down the lake and see if anything looks familiar."

We found evidence of ice fishing as we skied the length of the lake: circular holes had been drilled into the ice with battery-powered augers and were now refrozen. Near the outlet, we skirted a weird-looking patch of ice: not clear like most of the lake, but opaque with flecks of rotting leaves. We paused to speculate what might have happened and decided someone had broken through the ice with their snowmobile and stirred up the bottom.

On the lake's far shore, we explored a two-story log cabin up a short rise from the ice. I sat down on the porch stoop. Niki walked all around the house, peered into the windows, wandered down the entrance road. "I don't recognize anything," she announced, "but I'd like to determine where that road goes."

"Probably to the A Grade," I said. "It's about a mile away."

She whacked me on the shoulder with a mitten. "That's not what I meant."

At the A Grade, she headed away from Amasa and at the Camp Ten switch picked up the Cut-Across Road. At Camp Ten Creek, we stopped and drank half the water we carried. The day remained crystal clear and the sun had warmed the temperature to the teens. I pulled off my hat to let heat escape. From a snowbank at the edge of the marshy area surrounding the creek, an ermine periscoped his head and chirped. It ran in bursts to a rock outcropping where it dived into the surrounding snow. Periodically, its head reappeared. Sometimes we'd glimpse the entire body; mostly we caught sight of only its black-tipped tail as the weasel punched another hole in the snow to pursue dinner.

"I didn't realize how tired I was until we stopped," Niki said.

We had no sooner started back than we had to hustle out of the road to avoid a canary-yellow snowmobile with flaming red hotrod stripes roaring past us. Its operator returned our waves. Niki stared at its tracks.

"Not too ostentatious, is it?" I said.

"Seamus, I'm not exactly sure . . . but I may have seen it before."

TWELVE

I LAY ON THE COUCH reading a book, partly listening to Niki humming to herself as she stirred the Senate bean soup she was preparing for Owen's Tuesday visit. "You can't put off the decision any longer, Seamus. If you won't let me stay, I need to pack before Owen arrives."

Put-up or shut-up, as my father used to say. The house was clean, but not obsessively so. She had taken over the cooking. She knew how to use spices, so her meals were more varied and better tasting than mine. She was interesting to talk with, but didn't mind quiet. She stayed out of my way when I preferred to be alone. Mostly. We shared a love of the outdoors.

It came down to this: fate threw her on my doorstep, and I felt the responsibility to help. I leaned over the pot and inhaled, the steam clouding my glasses. "Smells great." Stepping back to give her access to the soup I added, "You can stay, I'll—"

She yelped with glee, pulled my head down, and planted her lips on mine. The kiss took me by surprise and into my opened lips she slipped her tongue. Without thinking, I replied in kind, even while my arms remained limply at my sides. She released my head and stepped away.

"Thanks," she said. Her smile preceded a rollicking laugh. My face heated with embarrassment at her laughing at me.

She controlled her laugh sufficiently to sputter, "I forgot I was holding the spoon and splattered your head with soup."

Owen zoomed into the yard while I cleaned up. I towel-dried my hair and helped him bring in the supplies—he had doubled the quantities on my supply list to account for Niki. Before taking in the last load, Owen handed me a small paper bag.

"What's this?" I hefted it to check its weight—light.

He looked down at the ground. "Don't know what kind you like, so I . . ." He motioned at the bag.

Inside was a package of condoms. "It's not like that." My voice rose an octave in protest.

"You don't know nothin about that girl's history. You gotta . . . well, you're old enough to know what you gotta do. You get in there. I need to see a man about a horse." He stomped off around the pole barn.

I tucked the condoms in my pocket. "She's not dangerous," I said to his back. *Is that true?*

Owen reappeared, pulled me by the arm to where his gun was strapped to the snowmobile. In a stage whisper he said, "Don't look at nothin but me. Somebody's spyin on you."

I thought back to the kiss Niki and I had shared and blushed like a teenager caught necking on the couch by his parents.

"I was about to pee when I caught a flash from a scope or somethin. He's dressed in white camo up on the hill between here and the cabin. Don't know how long he's been there. I seen fresh tracks from the road headin in that direction. Shoulda realized they wouldn't be yourn."

To give the impression we were talking about Owen's machine, I projected my voice. "I don't see anything wrong with it either." Under my breath I added, "We might be able to see from the bedroom window."

We removed our boots in the mud room and slipped by Niki, who was putting away the provisions. As Owen passed her, she grabbed his arm and planted a smooch on his cheek. "What lovely produce you brought. From Angeli's?"

Owen's blush made my earlier one pale in comparison. He mumbled a reply and I jumped in. "We'll be back in a minute. I want to show Owen something upstairs."

None of the windows provided a view of the watcher. "We might see from the balcony," I said and dragged Owen into the master bedroom where I stuck the condoms in my sock drawer.

"He could've taken us out while we was bringin in the groceries, so maybe we got ourselves some time. Either way, lettin him know we know ain't a good idea."

"So what do you suggest?"

Owen removed his choppers from his pocket and placed them into his mouth. "It'd be a durnblasted shame to waste the soup."

"So you figure he's interested in Niki?"

"Who's interested in Niki?"

Owen and I spun around to find her standing in the doorway.

"What? You two come in toting a gun and sashay upstairs and what— I'm supposed to be the good little woman slaving away in the kitchen?" She fisted her hands on her hips. "Not likely."

We told her of the spy.

"Let them look," Niki said stomping to the door onto the balcony. "I've got nothing to hide." She pulled her shirt up to her chin. "It's Mardi Gras. He owes me some beads." She let her shirt drop.

"Don't think no voyeur is gonna come out here to look at your tits."

Niki pushed off the doorframe and again placed her hands on her hips, thrusting out her chest.

"I'm not sayin—not that they ain't worth lookin at—not that I'd know. Ah hell, a fellow got killed a couple of miles from here. I think you need to worry about that."

"And you think he's interested in me? Why don't we invite him in for soup and ask his intentions?" Before either Owen or I realized her plan, Niki slid open the door to the bedroom balcony a crack and yelled, "Hey Tom Peeper. Come on in and have lunch with us." To us she said, "Get downstairs and sit before my soup gets cold."

Owen led the way to the table, pulled out his chair and sat. He tucked a napkin into his shirt and looked up expectantly.

"Niki, the guy's in camo," I said. "With a scope."

"He's looking. He's not shooting. Besides, now that he knows we saw him, he's gone." Niki placed a bowl of soup in front of Owen and patted his arm. "I'd give you another kiss for protecting us, but it might cause you or our peeper to faint." She giggled and finished serving the soup. "Where was he, Owen? Sit, Seamus."

Good boy that I am, I sat.

We were almost finished eating when the roar of a snowmobile shooting down the driveway announced a visitor.

Owen grabbed the rifle and quick-walked into the downstairs bedroom where he could cover the rider. "Don't answer the door or go near a window until you know who it is. If he comes to your door, give me a few secs to slip out the side and cover him."

Niki and I ran upstairs to view the visitor from the upstairs window where we could stay low and peek over the sills. The driver eased around the pole barn, momentarily disappearing from our sight, pulled beside Owen's machine, and killed the engine. He stepped off his machine and pulled off his gloves and helmet.

∗ ∗ ∗

SERGEANT BARTELLE DISMOUNTED FROM THE snow machine and before he could even say hello to Seamus McCree or Owen Lyndstrom, the geezer asked, "Is the spy still there?"

Bartelle gave Owen a look that said, "What the hell are you talking about?"

"The tracks comin in from the road, a third of the way from the driveway to the cabin. Didn't you see them? Clear as blaze orange at noon. There was a guy up on the hill spyin on these folks."

"How are you, Owen?" Bartelle drawled, his voice quiet. "That why you're carrying your rifle?" He gave McCree a wink. "He always has it, but the DNR's never caught him doing anything illegal. Now, Seamus, we're going to play act a little. I want you to wave your arms around a lot and tell me to get off your property. I'll take my sled up to where Owen saw the tracks and follow them in. You and Owen go back inside like nothing's happening. Got it?"

In response, McCree turned in an Oscar-winning performance.

"Fine, then," Bartelle yelled in response. "I'll be back with your bleeping warrant." Bartelle slammed his helmet on his head and roared up the driveway. He found the tracks Owen mentioned, but it was clear someone had recently exited in a hurry. Bartelle dismounted and checked the spot the spy had used.

On his return, Bartelle found Jane Doe standing on the stoop. "So, it's true," he said. "You are here." He peeled off his outer layers and she hung them on a hook. They gathered around the wood stove, melting the snow off everyone's boots. The smell of drying wool perfumed the air.

"Well?" Lyndstrom asked Bartelle.

"Rabbited, but probably a good thing I arrived when I did."

McCree shifted from foot to foot and finally said, "No warrants today, Sergeant Bartelle?"

Bartelle felt heat burn on his neck. "You keep telling me you have nothing to hide and I can search anytime for anything. That changed?"

"Boys, boys," Niki's voice came from the kitchen. "I'll get a tape measure if you really want to find out who has the biggest dick. Care for some soup, Sergeant?"

Bartelle waved the idea aside. "Any idea who your visitor was?" To a chorus of "nos" Owen added, "What did you find?"

Time to remind them who was police and who was not. "What did you see, Owen?" Bartelle took a pen and spiral notebook from his flannel shirt pocket and recorded the description of white camo and maybe a scope. Matched what he saw on the hill, except based on the multiple trails in and out, it probably wasn't the first time someone had been there. He discovered the woman watching from the kitchen. "What are you doing here, anyway?"

"Washing dishes. Dishtowel's hanging on the stove if you want to dry."

Bartelle gave her his patented hard stare. It had turned many a knee weak, but had no visible effect on her. He scratched his head, bringing relief that would soon become pain if he kept at it. He forced his arm down to his side. "Owen, how about you git on home so I can chat in private with these two. I don't need to hear a verbatim transcript next time I'm in town."

"I can keep secrets," Lyndstrom looked miffed. "I only started gabbin after Vinnie, my wife, passed. Auto accident. We was married forty-seven years, and I was lonely. Bein with people, and tellin stories come natural to me. Been sixteen years last September." He turned away, but not before Bartelle spotted a tear leaking down his cheek.

"I'm sorry," Bartelle said. "It is official business."

"Before you go," the woman said, "I've got a couple of extra items to add to Seamus's shopping list."

Lyndstrom glanced at the paper she handed him and turned beet red. The woman let loose with a high birdsong laugh and gave him a peck on the cheek. Bartelle tamped down his curiosity and grabbed a dishtowel to start drying. Lyndstrom shrugged into his snowmobile suit and waved goodbye.

"Lyndstrom forgot his gun."

"We're keeping it," McCree said. "You and Niki need privacy?"

Bartelle mentally congratulated himself for not dropping a dish in his excitement. "You remember your name?" He put the plate away, but kept a sharp focus on her reaction.

Her shoulders slumped. "I didn't want to be called Jane Doe any longer."

Disappointment plopped in his stomach. "Sorry to hear that. What did you write on the list that got Lyndstrom to light up like a firecracker?"

She laughed. "Tampons."

Bartelle kept the smile off his face and put on his serious-talk expression.

"I decided to come up here and personally warn each of you. Either one of you could be a killer—unless you're in cahoots and did it together." Pointing at McCree he asked, "You notice anything about her that will help us figure out who she is?"

"Nothing useful," McCree said. "You know anything about someone spying on us? A fellow officer, maybe?"

"I guarantee it's not us. Maybe you should consider coming into town where it's easier to give you protection. Owen's gun won't work if they kill you with the first shot. So, neither of you has anything new to tell me?"

Why did they look at each other first before shaking their heads? Bartelle delayed. He inspected the last bowl, flipping it this way and that before drying and putting it away. "Then I'll move to the second reason I'm here. This is personal. Has nothing to do with any investigation. My research confirms you were a big player for a major New York investment bank. You're good with financial stuff?"

McCree led him to the living room seating. "Some. Why?"

"Know anything about viatical settlements?"

Niki said, "If you two don't need me, I'll head outside." In silence, the men watched her pull outer garments from pegs and leave.

"I know what viatical settlements are," McCree said. "You're not considering investing in them are you? There are all kinds of scams."

"A local company wants to buy my aunt's life insurance policy. She's in a nursing home. She has a few problems, but she's still pretty with it. Anyway, this company is trying to sign up everyone at the nursing home who has life insurance. They're coming by, like, every day or two."

McCree indicated with his hands for him to continue.

"She thinks she's going to live longer than they seem to think. Anything past how to balance a checkbook is beyond me. The truth is I barely even manage that. My antennas are twitching on this deal, and I got to thinking that I was investigating someone who did understand more about finance than how to balance a checking account."

Bartelle pointed at McCree, looked at his finger, and realized how crooked it was. "Can you take a look at this and tell me what you think?" He reached into his jacket and brought out a wrinkled manila envelope, unfolded the flap and shook the contents into his lap.

"I'm not licensed to give financial advice in Michigan."

"I'm just looking for your opinion."

"A viatical assignment is a security. You really should talk to someone who can give you an expert opinion."

"I'm not trying to make a federal crime over it. I'm just trying to help my aunt."

"What has she told you?"

Bartelle hung his left arm over his head and scratched behind his right ear. "They want to pay her $170,000 now if she'll sign over her $200,000 life insurance to them. They claim to have a letter of credit from Hematite Bank to guarantee the check. My aunt says she can earn five percent on her money and, as long as she lives three and a half years, she's ahead of the game. She's healthy as a horse except she's confined to a wheelchair and needs help going to the bathroom, taking showers, that stuff. What do you think?"

"What kind of a policy is it? Whole life? Does it have a cash surrender value or is it term? Is she still paying premiums? How old—"

Bartelle held up both hands. "I give. I don't have a clue what you're asking. I brought all the stuff. She gave it to me to look at, but what do I know, eh? She's seventy-seven, which is pretty darn young these days."

McCree took the file from Bartelle and leafed through it, mumbling about declarations pages and such. Concentration etched his face. "When do you need this?

"They want her to sign by the end of next week. I can come back whenever it's convenient for you. I assume you're not planning any trips to town?"

"Thursday will work. I should warn you, I could end up with more questions than answers. But I'm not writing anything down. It's just a couple of guys talking. Right?"

"I appreciate it. Sure I can't convince you to bring the girl to town?" Bartelle cocked his head and squinted through one eye.

"She would stay where and do what?"

"I don't have a clue what she would do, but we got a female deputy who could give her a room."

"Thanks for the offer. I don't think she wants to be under your microscope, and I can't say I blame her. Thursday, say before noon?"

"I still think you're taking your life in your hands—either with Niki or whoever was hiding on your hill."

* * *

OWEN SHOWED UP AT MY place the next afternoon with a friend whose mouth looked like it came from a nineteenth-century picture: puckered and toothless. "This here's Badger," Owen said. "Got him this snow machine he's hankerin to sell. Runs good so long as you don't mind the color scheme. I got to thinkin you needed to get yourself some snow transportation in case you ever need to get out of here."

I didn't want a snowmobile. They had two big strikes in my book: they were mechanical and noisy. Abigail and I had talked about getting one and had decided we could do without. Besides, this was Yooper ugly. Its right side was blue and the left side Creamsicle orange.

Owen must have read my look. "Think about what you could have done if you had this when that girl showed up, eh? At least give it a try before you say no."

Badger handed me his helmet and said "Try 'er out. She's a real workhorse."

They showed me the throttle, brake, and where to stick my feet. Owen slapped the helmet hard. "Remember to let go of the throttle if you start to tip. Oh, and you ain't got no reverse."

I settled onto the cracked seat, jockeyed around, pinching my butt on a gator-toothed crack, and found a comfortable position for my arms. I arranged my feet and pressed the throttle with my thumb. With a vroom, the sled leapt forward nearly pitching me off the back. The sled and I skidded to a halt after my thumb slipped off the throttle. *Easy does it, Seamus.*

With a lighter touch I engaged the throttle again and crawled up the driveway. Once on the road, I gradually increased the speed. It operated like an ATV, except it was much louder. I began to feel comfortable. Then I made a sharp turn and flipped it. My head rattled around in the too-big helmet, but I didn't see stars. Before extracting myself from the snow, I mentally checked for broken bones and found myself humming the ditty about the ankle bone connected to the leg bone . . .

I righted the machine and it started up without problem. No harm, no foul. On the way back, I inched up the speed and realized it was darned cold creating my own wind. My hands nearly froze solid before I got back. I waited too long to start braking and avoided crashing into Owen's machine by pure luck. "I guess you're right, Owen. I trust your opinion if you think this one will work."

I haggled with Badger over the price, chiefly because Badger expected me to. Owen slapped me on the back once the negotiations concluded. "We'll make you a real Yooper yet, eh? Cain't do nothin about that Tourist accent of yourn though. Open your mouth and everyone knows right off you're an implant."

Transplant. I bit my tongue to avoid correcting him.

"Gonna need you a helmet and some gloves. Dependin on what you got, maybe a bib and jacket too," Owen said. "We'll need a real store." Owen craned his head. "Where's the little woman?"

"Snowshoeing. I'll need to get warmer stuff for her too. Logistics are going to be a real problem. I need to get it registered, notify my insurance company. You willing to be our chauffeur, Owen? I'll pay for the gas and an hourly rate, including getting us from here to your car."

Owen and Badger agreed to return Friday with spare helmets. They'd take us to Owen's place. I'd give Badger the check and get the registration transfer papers, and then Owen would take us into Iron Mountain to get gear and take care of business with the motor vehicle department.

"Almost forgot," Owen said. He handed me a box of shells for the rifle. "Ain't had time to get you a gun, so you keep mine 'til Friday. We can buy you one in town, since we're goin in. Unless'n I scout up a used one afore then."

I made a mental note to recharge my cell phone so I could arrange insurance and give my son a call. The real question was whether I should also call Abigail.

THIRTEEN

BOSS PARKED THE LEXUS HYBRID SUV in a visitor's space, screwed on a smile, and prepared to finalize four sales, bringing the total to eighteen—seven short of the goal. Five more might agree today, and the others were still considering. Onward and upward.

The Crystal Falls brick building had originally housed a hospital. With the expansion of the hospital in Iron River this facility had been vacant for years, and after several false starts was rehabbed into a private senior care center. A local contest named the place the Laughing Loon Senior Care Facility. The logo was a black and white loon floating on water with its head thrown back, beak open and pointed at the moon. Talk about loony.

One really good thing about this place, Boss reflected, it was privately owned and didn't take Medicaid patients. These folks had money, and money meant opportunity. Boss scribbled an illegible signature in the registration book, greeted a couple who passed by, and paused at the elevator to check the green spiral notebook for the first appointment's name and room number.

A blast of heat assaulted Boss as Mrs. Pirhonen opened her door. The rattling of an overworked radiator sounded from inside.

"Hello, Mrs. Pirhonen," Boss said brightly in the too-loud voice one needed to use around here. "I've got the check ready. Just need your signature on a few forms. You all set?"

"K.C., do come in. I've got everything ready right here." She patted a pile of paper on the end table next to her rocking chair. "Pull up a chair and we'll get this done. I can't tell you how much I appreciate your bringing this opportunity to my attention."

Boss pressed down hard on the back of a chair, probably the remains of an ancient dining room set, to make sure it was sturdy enough and brought it to face Mrs. Pirhonen. "Still healthy as a horse?" Boss asked. "Haven't had any setbacks since we last met?"

Mrs. Pirhonen's face cratered with worry and her rocking ground to a halt.

"I only ask because if you have learned some bad news about your health we might have to redo the numbers. We don't want to cheat you. The check I brought assumes you're planning to live for a good long time."

Mrs. Pirhonen smiled and resumed rocking. "Arthritis is still kicking up, but that won't kill me," she said, presenting her twisted hands for Boss to inspect. Then she flipped through the items in her stack. "The birth certificate proves I'm five years older than I tell everyone, but you promised not to let anyone know." She giggled at Boss's nodded agreement to the little lie. "Got the life insurance certificate right here with a note from my agent showing I paid all the premiums. Next one ain't due for a few months."

She shuffled through the papers. "This here's the contract you left and once you hand me the check, I'll sign 'er on the dotted line, eh?"

"As promised, it's certified," Boss said. "Hematite guarantees it in the amount of $65,000."

"And if anyone should know about Hematite's guarantees, it's you." Mrs. Pirhonen inspected the check. "All us girls getting checks today are taking the shuttle to the bank to deposit them this afternoon."

"A very smart idea," Boss said. "Maybe I'll see you there. Now if you'll sign right here," Boss pointed to the contract's signature line, "I'll get out of your hair—speaking of which, I like your new 'do, and is that a new perfume I smell?" Boss made a big deal of inhaling. "Citrus?"

Mrs. Pirhonen glowed. "It's called 'Tangerine Vert.' My granddaughter gave it to me for my birthday. You say 'hi' to your son when you talk to him."

Boss put up with several more minutes of chitchat, returned the chair to its normal position against the far wall, and proceeded to the next crone on the list.

Several hours later, with only Mrs. Ricci left, Boss's mood had picked up. The coterie of women in this place had coalesced around how good the deal was, eventually pressuring the holdouts to sign; even two crotchety guys Boss had previously written off accepted offers.

Boss knocked on the open door. "Mrs. Ricci, is now a good time to talk?"

"Hello, K.C. Didn't we agree I'd get back to you at the end of next week? I still need time to make my decision."

Boss walked in a step and stopped. Mrs. Ricci did not back her wheelchair up or offer a seat. "Is there any additional information I can provide you with?" Boss made sure to use a neutral tone.

"I've given the papers to my nephew. I expect to see him Sunday."

Boss didn't feel comfortable maintaining eye contact with a cripple and so looked over her head. *What the hell did the old prune know anyway? It was a good deal, as anyone with half a brain could see.* Boss mentally counted to three. "Your nephew a financial advisor?"

"I thought you knew. He's the sergeant with the Iron County Sheriff's Department. He told me he would ask an expert." She looked at her watch. "Imagine that, it's gotten so late . . . if you'll excuse me?" She spun around with the squeak of rubber on linoleum and briskly pushed herself into her kitchenette.

Boss turned away from the door, angry enough to punch out the bitch, or at least tip over her damn wheelchair. *So much for the good mood. So Sergeant Bartelle, the damn wop, was sticking his nose into the deal. Well, Bartelle's expert wouldn't find a damn thing wrong because there wasn't a damn thing wrong—at least not with the viatical settlements.*

Boss signed out of the Laughing Loon, held the door for a biddy smelling like day-old piss and bent over her walker making an inchworm look like a roadster. *How can people live like that? Here's a pleasant thought: it's only four weeks to D-day—not Debarkation-day, but Death-day. Well, in fairness, the deaths would come after April 1st, but the mechanism would be in place that day.*

Then we can buy more than enough weapons to take down the high and mighty in Washington who are bankrupting our country.

THURSDAY AFTER LUNCH, I WORKED on the generator: changed the oil and filter, which I had to do every one hundred hours the generator ran. The day showed promise of warming past thirty-two. Despite some unsuccessful attempts in the last two weeks, it would be the first time since mid-November—sixteen weeks ago—that temperatures would be above freezing. Before I left the generator shed, I checked the inverter; the solar panels were charging the batteries at the rate of twelve amps.

Mud season would soon be upon us if it remained this mild. For those three or four weeks of mud each year, activity in the U.P. woods nearly comes to a standstill. The roads change from frozen solid to a goop deep enough and thick enough to swallow a car or truck at least to the floorboards. On unpaved roads, only ATVs work, and both of mine were currently inoperable.

I had brought the ATV batteries inside to avoid draining them in the minus forty temperatures of deep winter. With Niki off snowshoeing across the lake to spot a moose I'd seen browsing in a nearby swamp, I had time to reinstall the batteries and get my two ATVs into working order. Not knowing if we would be faced with more snow or immediate mud, it would be safest to have both the snowmobile and the ATVs tuned and ready to go. With that thought in mind, I left the generator shed and was surprised by a deep rumble coming from the direction of Amasa. I walked into the side yard to get a better fix on the sound. Heavy equipment was moving somewhere nearby. Probably loggers bringing equipment for an early spring cutting, beating the coming restrictions that prohibited anything heavier than a pickup from traveling these roads once thaws started.

Paying the ruckus no more attention, I installed the batteries, gassed the ATVs, and cranked them up. They both started like champs. I left them warming up and figured I might as well put the battery in the skid steer as long as I was in the mood. By the time I left the garage to get its battery, the low rumble had come much closer. The skid steer could wait while I satisfied my curiosity. I donned cross-country ski shoes, hooked the toes into the binding, and hurried toward the noise.

Immediately past the driveway to my cabin I stopped. Had someone taken a video, I suppose they would have caught my jaw bouncing off the snow pack. Lumbering up the hill was a caravan consisting of a Caterpillar D-9 pushing snow to one side, a smaller loader cleaning up after the D-9, and a police car bringing up the rear.

A CLEARED ROAD WAS NOT my idea of an improvement. I kept my trap shut while Bartelle uncharacteristically nattered on. "I got the county probation officer to let these two fine, upstanding citizens, who forgot it isn't legal to drive with blood alcohol levels in excess of point three, work off some of their community service time," he inclined his head in their direction. "Getting double credit since they're using their own equipment." He noticed my less-than-enthusiastic frown. "Don't express your appreciation all at once now."

"Needed to get in to arrest me?"

"Not currently. I'm tired of snowmobiling out here. Actually, I thought it might be a way of saying thanks for looking at the stuff for my aunt." He scratched his head in the arm-curled-over-his-head way I had grown accustomed to seeing. "Doesn't seem like I guessed right. Well, no matter. If you run into some trouble, now you can get out, or at least it will be easier for us to get in. Speaking of which, any more visitors? Where is the Jane—uh, the woman?"

"I am unaware of any visitors," I said. "Niki's searching for a moose. We've seen their sign across the lake, and I saw a cow and yearling nearby."

"She'll be back soon?"

I shrugged and realized the muscles on my neck had tightened up. "You married, Bartelle?"

"Nuh-uh. Why do you ask?"

"Didn't think so. You're married to the job and I'm divorced. I don't think either of us can claim to predict what a woman is going to do next."

"You learn anything more about her?"

"I'm not your spy. You'll have to ask her. Your trip's not wasted, though. I've studied your aunt's issue."

We settled into the chairs near the wood stove, scooching them close to the fire to warm our toes. "I changed my mind and typed my observations so you can give them to your aunt and not rely on memory. I agree with her: the deal seems to be too good—even with the historically low interest rates we have now—assuming your aunt is an average seventy-seven-year-old woman." Bartelle's eyebrows arched at the word average. "Average in a medical sense. This is a great deal. I'd take it, as long as the payment is guaranteed, which appears to be the case."

He sipped a Diet Pepsi and flipped through my calculations and conclusions. "Numbers were never my strong point. You'd take it?"

"I would and I'd wonder if I could get some more life insurance to sell. You should back up a truck and take away as much of this as you can . . . which to me is worrisome. You know the old saw: 'if it looks too good to be true, it probably is'? These aren't the hardest numbers in the world to crunch. If they're buying policies from most of the Laughing Loon residents, you're talking serious money."

"So where's the problem? You mentioned viatical settlement scams?" He clicked his ballpoint a few times while I considered how to answer.

"Most scams involve suckering people who invest in the viaticals," I said. "But this is going the other way. We know your aunt is not the crook, which eliminates a bunch of other malfeasance. So, how can someone cheat your aunt? Number one, she signs over the insurance policy and doesn't get the promised money. Easy to solve: have a third party hold the endorsed policy until the check clears."

"Got it," he said. "What else?"

"They know something about your aunt's health that you don't."

He scratched his head. "How could they?"

"They could be in cahoots with, say, a local doctor. But since they're offering everyone there similar deals, that can't be it. They could plan to change the mortality table."

His face bunched into a question mark. "I'm just a Yooper Trooper. Want to put that into English?"

"Someone hurries their deaths. With enough policies, it wouldn't even have to be by much. A nurse's aide could give too much or too little of a medicine or swap real pills for sugar." A possibility occurred to me that sent a shill up my spine. "In fact, if they make the deaths appear to be from an accident and the policies include accidental death and dismemberment benefits, like your aunt's does, they really make out because they get paid twice the face value."

I popped out of my chair and busied myself with adding a stick of wood to the fire. "Do the residents go on bus outings? Most senior citizen homes have trips to casinos or to something like the Pine Mountain Music Festival in the summer. If they tampered with the brakes on the bus or . . ."

Bartelle had stopped writing and was studying me as though I had grown a second head. Into the silence, broken only by the ticking of my grandmother clock, he finally said, "That would take one sick fuck. Pardon the expression."

"Well, from my experience, if money's involved, there are a lot of sick fucks, and they're not all on Wall Street."

FOURTEEN

FINDING THE ROAD PLOWED WAS the first piss-poor surprise in Jimmie's day. A couple of miles from McCree's place, he met the D-9 and loader returning, widening the cleared road as they went. He quickly slid onto an old skidder road and pulled far enough into the woods so the operators wouldn't have much of a look at him or his sled.

The cleared road ended at McCree's driveway, where he paused to take a peek and received a second shock: an Iron County Sheriff's cruiser sat in the driveway. He was not about to stick around and have some cop wonder why he was in the neighborhood.

Jimmie zipped the sled down the road to its end at the Net River, realized he had trapped himself if anyone was following and worked his way to a deer camp a couple guys he knew maintained about halfway back to McCree's place. There he keyed off the sled, listened to the *dee-dee-dees* of a feeding flock of chickadees working over a stand of white spruce, and considered his options.

Boss wanted him to observe and if the opportunity arose, "put down the girl." Facing Boss and again reporting failure was not something he looked forward to. Unlike boozer Brett, he hadn't screwed up, but Jimmie wasn't sure Boss would see it that way. He remembered the casual shrug Boss had given before ordering Brett's "regrettable termination."

Ah, Christ. He released a long sigh he recognized as resignation. No help for it but to wait out the police and do the girl. If McCree's there, bop him too. He'd tell Boss it was unavoidable. Then cash Boss's bonus and spend mud season in Florida.

Plopping onto a wood plank bench tucked far enough under the eaves to be free of snow, he turned his face to the sun, closed his eyes. Warmth bathed his face and he drifted into a dreamless nap.

JIMMIE AWOKE TO THE SUN perching two fingers above the horizon: thirty minutes to sunset. To the steady *drip, drip, drip* of snow melting from the roof, he firmed up a plan: drive the snowmobile down McCree's driveway, pop whoever came out to greet him, and then pop the other one. If they barricaded themselves in the house, he'd burn them out. No subtlety needed: just two bodies.

At the top of McCree's driveway, he stopped and surveyed the scene. The cop was gone, but two sets of tire tracks now emerged from the driveway. A smile dimpled his cheeks. Maybe McCree had driven into town and left the girl behind? He stuffed the Ruger under his coat and cruised down the driveway, followed it around the pole barn, and parked facing up the driveway, his sled hidden from the house by the outbuilding. He turned off the snowmobile and listened to the tinkling of wind chimes. A solitary red squirrel, a bird wannabe, was gorging on sunflower seeds under one of McCree's many feeders.

He dismounted, removed his gloves and helmet and balanced them on the seat, bent down as though to inspect something on the snowmobile, and waited for the sound of a door opening or the crunch of footsteps on the freshly plowed snow. Nothing. The adrenaline rush was working overtime, and Jimmie knew he wanted to get this done now. Still no movement inside the house.

He swiped at his nose with his hand. Now what? He walked toward the back door. At the corner of the house, invisible from anyone inside, he removed the Ruger from his coat. He rapped on the door with his left hand, stood away from the door's outward swing, and held the revolver behind his back. Nothing.

No footsteps; no call to wait a minute; no whispered conversation from inside. Thirty seconds, a minute. He rapped a second time, using the window instead of the wood to make a sharper sound. Still nothing. He propped open the storm door with his foot and tested the metal door. Unlocked. Had the cop taken them in? Wouldn't it be fucking rich if the cops nailed the girl and McCree for Brett's murder?

Jimmie knocked once more, opened the door, and called, "Hello. Anyone home?" He stepped into the laundry room, gun now leading the way. Boss would want a complete report, so he took his time developing a mental picture of the house. In the laundry room he spotted two empty pegs where their overcoats should be. On the shoe mat was space for two pairs of boots. Should he wait for their return?

Unlike Brett who would have looked for booze, Jimmie concentrated on weapons. No gun safe and no rifle to match a new box of .30–06 shells he discovered under the sink in the upstairs bathroom. Returning to the front room, he appreciated the spectacular winter view from the wall of windows. This place was way nicer than any hunting camp. If he couldn't catch them outside, he'd need to find a good firing position to target the house. After dark, once lights were on inside, he'd have a clear forty-yard backlit shot from the lake edge if someone stepped close to the windows. With the sky clouding over to block the moon, he could get an even closer shot from the woods.

He considered staying. The refrigerator held plenty of food. He could hide the sled and walk in. Problem was, if the cop returned with McCree and the girl, it would get complicated, and he would be the one trapped inside if anything went wrong. Best to head into Amasa, get dinner at the Rusty Saw Blade, and fuel up for some primate hunting tonight.

Decision made, Jimmie hustled from the house, donned his helmet and gloves, and sped toward town. About a mile before the new sawmill, he caught up to an old Ford Ranger. He couldn't see into the cab, but a bumper sticker proclaiming, "AMASA—it's not just a place, it's a state of mind" indicated it was locals. He stuck up a hand in greeting as he blasted past.

Niki pointed to the snowmobile whizzing by Seamus's truck. "You know him? He's waving."

McCree held two hands on the steering wheel. "Looks like the same one we saw up past Long Lake. You want dinner in Amasa or wait until we get to the megalopolis of Marquette? Great pizza at the Rusty Saw Blade. Either way we need to make a quick stop at Owen's and let him know we don't need to borrow his truck."

Niki felt anxious, not hungry. She now knew who she was. She knew she needed to make a phone call without McCree's knowledge. She had regained her memory, except for what happened the last few days before she showed up naked at McCree's cabin. "The excitement of getting to the *big city* has killed my appetite." Well, that sure came out sarcastic. McCree didn't seem to notice. However, with McCree, not seeming to notice and not noticing were two different things. She needed to be careful around him. He was scary smart.

"Okay," he said. "Marquette it is. We'll decide on type of food after your appetite returns. We need to make a list so we don't forget anything. Might be a while before we hit the stores again."

"Which brings me to a question that's been bothering me," Niki said. "I was pretty skeptical at the hospital when they told me some guy was picking up my tab. I mean, who believes in fairy tales where the prince finds the beautiful girl lost in the woods, gives her the kiss of life, and they live happily ever after? Did you know the cops did a rape kit on me? Did they ask you for a DNA sample?"

She raked her fingers through her hair. "I'm rambling all over the place and not getting to the point. The point is, why the fuck are you helping me? You haven't made any moves. You've covered my hospital bill. Now you're taking me to buy clothes to replace the crap the church guild gave me. What do you get out of this? That's the question, Seamus McCree: What do you get out of this?"

Niki evaluated her performance. She had started out being

argumentative, but by the time she asked the last question, it arrived in a whisper.

McCree glanced over and saw her swipe tears from her eyes. "You okay?"

"Of course I'm not okay. Do you realize today is our one-month anniversary?" She blew her nose, looked around for somewhere to store the dirty tissue, and, finding nothing, crammed it into her pocket. "For a month, I haven't known who I am, why I'm here. No one seems to know me. I'm like the twenty-first century version of *Stranger in a Strange Land*—like I got raised on Mars and dropped into the primordial soup of Michigan's Upper Peninsula. Sergeant Bartelle offered to take me off your hands so he could keep me a virtual prisoner until he found out what I know. Did you agree to take me in so you could control me if my memory came back?"

Niki wished she could get a straight answer from McCree. He was layers deep and could do silence like a monk. She stared out the window. After a few minutes she fiddled with the radio dials and settled on a hard rock station. They passed through Covington, then Michigamme, and were approaching Ishpeming before McCree spoke.

"Last year I killed a man. For a while it looked like I was going to have to defend that action in court, so I hired a top-notch criminal lawyer. Guy named Leroy Patterson. I asked him much the same question you're asking me. Why did he do what he did? He told me he was the guy with the white hat who gets the girl in the final reel."

Is he opening up? Niki turned off the radio.

"He clearly had a vision of his role in the judicial system," he continued. "He had earned enough money to be choosy and now only defends people he thinks were wronged by the system. And what, you wonder, does this have to do with you?"

Niki bowed her head and gently waved her hand in a please-proceed-if-you-would-be-so-kind gesture.

"You've heard bits and pieces about my background from my answers to Bartelle's questions. I made a pile of money understanding what made banks tick. I could tell you which bank was overvalued and which was undervalued, and they paid me handsomely. Information is power in Wall Street. To please a humongous client, my bosses changed a negative report I wrote.

"I discovered the chicanery a week before they paid bonuses and quit, giving up a big six-figure payment. After the dust settled, my wife left me. Any successful marriage has to overcome shocks along the way. She was furious that I was no longer the hard-driving winner she had used to cloak her own insecurities. I know it's not PC to say, but many women still determine their own value by their husband's job. In my opinion, most are selling themselves short. She certainly was. That was years ago and if I don't speed this story up, we'll be in Marquette before I get to the present."

Niki reached over and patted his hand, "Take your time." She returned her hand to her lap to join the other one.

"The one good thing remaining from my marriage is my wonderful son, whom I'm going to call while you're shopping. When we're young, we expect to save the world. Unfortunately, it's only a question of time before we discover that saving the entire world is beyond our capabilities. Anyway, footing your hospital bill and buying you a few clothes so you don't have to do laundry three times a week isn't going to cause me any monetary problems. So maybe the answer is I took an opportunity to try on the white hat and see if it still fits."

Niki rocked and wondered if he was also faking it. If so, he deserved an "A."

"And the girl in the final reel?"

"Well," he pulled his lips tightly together, "I guess I didn't think the comparison all the way through. Besides, if my current streak continues, the only way I'll have the girl in the final reel is if I steal all the reels after the one in which the girl and I fall head-over-heels in love. So how about you? No wedding ring, not that that means a whole lot these days, but someone was responsible for the hickey you sported."

She caught herself pulling at the hair around her ears and realized she was trying to block a question she didn't want to answer. She dropped her traitorous hands back into her lap and glanced out the window, all the while deciding how much truth to intersperse with the lies. "Here's what's so freakin' frustrating: I can't remember my name or how I came to pose as the ice queen on your porch hammock. I can't remember anything for at least the last six months and only a few earlier bits and pieces. I can remember everything since I woke up in your bathtub . . ." She tossed him a quizzical look. "Or at least I think I can. Who's to say, I guess? I don't know my name. I don't know who my parents are. I don't know where I grew up.

"But I can tell you the name of my best friend in second grade. I can tell you who the first boy I kissed playing spin the bottle was. He was chewing gum—ick. I know all sorts of stuff like that, but I can't tell you where I went to college, though I'm sure I did. I have no idea what kind of work I do, but I have a feeling it has something to do with the out-of-doors. I have no idea who gave me the hickey."

"I'm sure someday a switch will flip and it will all come back to you."

Well, it wasn't quite a flick of a switch.

"I didn't realize you had memories of the past. With what you remember, I'll bet Paddy could figure out who you are. Will you talk to him and tell him everything you remember?"

"And Paddy is who?"

"My son, the computer whiz, king of databases and, I hope, reformed hacker. He and some friends started a company to help banks keep their IT structure safe from hackers. But to hear him talk, the twenty-first century is all about networking, and I'm sure he can discover who you are."

She quickly faced the window and tugged her short hair hard enough to cause tears to form. *Oh Jesus, what have I done now?*

"Don't you want to know who you are?"

"Of course I do." She slapped her thigh for effect. "But I'm afraid I'll discover I'm wanted, or I abandoned four kids under the age of two or . . ."

Thankfully, he let her hanging question hang. They pulled into the Gander Mountain parking lot at the outskirts of Marquette. She waited until he killed the engine and pulled the parking brake before she faced him, tears streaking both cheeks. "What if I don't like who I am?"

He sat there like a lump, staring at her. Niki turned her gaze toward her hands folded in her lap, but looked up when he cleared his throat.

"If it were me—or is it *if it were I?*—whatever. I'd want to know. And I think you do as well. While you're shopping, I'll call Paddy."

She looked up and damn if he didn't snap her picture with his cell phone. Why hadn't she anticipated that? At least with this butch haircut she didn't look like herself.

"I'll fill him in, and if he agrees to help, you can decide whether to talk with him or not. Fair enough?"

Niki knew she had no choice. She hated that.

FIFTEEN

WATCHING NIKI WALK INTO THE store was like witnessing Atlas shouldering the weight of the world. She would signal me when it was time for me to pay. I dialed Paddy's cell phone and sent a prayer down the line that he would answer.

"Dad," he asked as salutation, "you okay? I didn't expect to hear from you for several more weeks."

My initial shock at his recognizing me before I spoke faded quickly away—his cell phone displayed my name. "A father can't call his son without causing concern? Before we hang up, I have a favor to ask."

We covered his girlfriend (still together), business (going fine) and cats (why didn't I get some?) for several minutes before he said, "You sound distracted, Dad. What's the favor?"

I related Niki's mysterious appearance at the cabin, the Brett Aho murder, the attentions I received from the police and from whoever was spying on me. "Can you help figure out who she is?"

"Should be a piece of cake. Why can't the cops do it?"

"When we were last together, you extolled the virtues of networking. The cops are old fashioned like me. They rely on fingerprints, and hers aren't in any database. They aren't going to spend the time posting information on social websites and sifting through lots of false leads or trolling through information databases to find people who match the bits and pieces of information she remembers about herself. Not unless they decide she killed Brett Aho. Then they'll go all out. So I was thinking, if you set it up as a kind of game—I could post a reward—you could get the whole networked generation helping to solve the problem."

"You thought of this all by yourself?"

I felt my shoulders hunch into my neck as my body tightened to protect me from the expected blow of rejection. "What am I missing?"

"It's a really good idea. Not the game part of it—that's a little hokey—but the idea of getting everyone working on it together. If we get the known facts along with a recent picture out to all the right spots of the blogosphere, I bet we have her name in a couple of days—max."

I smiled at his enthusiasm. He was in charge of sales for his company with good reason. "Your first job is going to be to convince her to do it," I said. "She's not sure she'll like her past and might prefer a fresh start. Shall I have her call you?"

"I can't imagine what it must be like to be cut off from all your friends and family. I know, before you point it out: I'm the extrovert, you're the introvert and often wish you could be done with all of us."

"Well . . ."

"Don't deny it. It's why you stayed in the woods even after Abigail left."

His mention of Abigail brought me back to his cryptic note about seeing her in a club and I missed the next few words he said.

". . .sales meetings tomorrow and the first part of next week. I need part of the weekend to prepare for them, so I won't be able to spend one hundred percent of my time on this. And I want to make sure when we hit with this, it's with a big bang."

He trailed off, mumbling to himself about timing and critical mass. I let him ramble and took the time to reflect on how much I appreciated this adult version of my son. His mother and I divorced while he was in grammar school. Paddy in junior high exhibited all the obnoxiousness of a smart preteen boy combined with a need to act out and garner attention from his parents.

By his sophomore year in high school, he had his act together—or so I thought until I received a visit from the FBI accusing me of hacking into a Defense Department website and posting online the expense reports of top department officials. Paddy's resulting juvenile record has supposedly been expunged, but in today's electronic environment, I'm sure it resides in a computer somewhere like the sword of Damocles hanging by a horse hair over his life.

"So you'll have her call me?" Paddy's voice brought me back to the present.

I couldn't bring myself to ask him about Abigail. We disconnected and I sent him Niki's picture.

The gnawing in my stomach was not hunger.

I checked my phone for messages. Before we had headed into the woods for winter, I told everyone I thought important what our plans were, and so there were only a few messages, several of which were wrong numbers. A part of me knew Abigail wouldn't call because we had agreed she wouldn't. Another part of me hoped she had missed me enough that she had called anyway. That part was disappointed.

With no sign of Niki, I opened the phone's address list and scrolled down to Abigail. I looked again for Niki's appearance to delay my decision to call. Still shopping. I screwed up my courage, pressed the button to connect, and listened to the first ring.

DURING DINNER, I BRIBED NIKI to call Paddy by offering her the first ride on the snowmobile tomorrow after we completed the purchase, registered it, and arranged insurance. Once she understood I intended to accomplish everything the next morning, all reticence she had about finding out who she was seemed to disappear. After dinner and the rest of our shopping, she took my cell phone into her room and returned it an hour later. I checked the logs: she and Paddy had talked for about forty-five minutes; she had made no other calls; she had received no calls.

Nor had I. What I didn't know, and what caused a restless night, was whether Abigail was on assignment and hadn't heard the message I left, or whether she had chosen not to call me back.

At breakfast, as Niki chattered away, I put on my "isn't everything wonderful" smile, but felt like a pumpkin the day after Halloween: a carved smile fixed on my face, hollowed out insides covered with soot from a burned down candle, and a lump of melted wax in the pit of my stomach. I did notice and comment on her perfume— something fresh with a light, fruity touch. She didn't reveal the brand. Fair enough. Everyone has secrets.

I ordered pancakes because they had been tasty the last time I was here. Niki ordered the lumberjack special and polished off the three pancakes, a three-egg omelet, three pieces each of sausage links and rye toast, and a side of hashbrowns. My pancakes tasted like cardboard, but I knew the problem was not the cook. I was in a funk.

Acquiring the snowmobile with its attendant paperwork went off without a hitch. Owen and Badger had the beast ready when we arrived at Owen's. Niki changed into her new snowmobiling outfit. I followed her home in the truck. Actually, she left me in the dust as she roared off.

By the time I arrived home, she was pacing next to the snowmobile. "Get on your snowmobiling clothes," she said with an urgency I had not previously detected. "We're going to try to find where I was imprisoned. I say 'we' to be inclusive. Fact is, I've got the key." She dangled it from her finger. "You can come or not."

I turned away so she couldn't see my smile. The real reason I had agreed to buy a snowmobile was so we could continue our search past the range of skis and snowshoes.

Sitting on the saddle, I snuggled against her back. It felt like I was cuddling the Michelin man given all the insulation and padding. I'd seen the speed at which she took off from Owen's so I wrapped both arms tightly around her waist. She zipped up the driveway, but once we got off my property, she slowed to walking speed. Over her shoulder she shouted, "Look for anything unusual. You see a squirrel squatting to pee, give me a good slap on the shoulder. Understand?"

While giving commands, her voice downshifted into a lower register, the one I found incredibly sexy. I reached in front of her facemask and gave the okay sign. We worked our way toward the spot where Brett Aho had been murdered. A couple of hundred yards before we got there, she stopped and plucked a glove from underneath a bush whose leaf buds had swelled but not yet turned red. Spring was coming.

She returned with her prize and tried it on. Her hands were small and this glove fit. She turned off the engine and yanked off her helmet. I followed suit.

"This is mine. See this small tear?" She held the thumb and first finger apart and revealed a ragged gash in the material. A tuft of insulation stuck out. "Cut it on barbed wire. Meant to slap some duct tape on it. Don't know why I didn't."

The uneasy feeling I'd had that she had somehow been involved with the murdered person began to spread. It was too coincidental. *Lover? Associate? Killer?* I offered up the possibility that it happened while she was sick.

"Could be. Let's see if any of my other stuff is around here."

No luck. Maybe we would find something else after the snow melted more. We briefly stopped at Brett Aho's murder site, but the melting snow had exposed nothing new. I directed Niki across Long Lake to the place where we had previously found numerous snowmobile tracks.

"It's starting to come back to me," she said after we stopped in the yard. "I drove all around that cabin hoping to find someone home. Then I drove onto the lake. Remember when we saw that yellow snowmobile while we skied? Can you get us back to where the places started looking familiar to me?"

Several miles later Niki leaned back against me and shouted, "I think we're almost there. Just around the bend." She gave my leg a good slap.

"What's just around the bend?"

"Don't know, but we'll soon see."

JIMMIE WAS IN A BIND. He had broken into a camp across the lake from McCree's place and had spent the night there. It was cozy enough and with the binoculars he could observe any comings and goings at McCree's. By the time he realized it was the girl who had arrived on the grungy snow machine, McCree returned in the truck he remembered passing the night before on the way to Amasa. He planned to wait for dark before dealing with them; he had plenty of food. But instead of staying put as he expected them to, McCree joined the woman on the snow machine.

He followed their tracks; unless they veered off, they were heading straight to the rented camp where Brett had kept the two human guinea pigs. Like a homing pigeon, the girl was returning to her roost.

According to Boss, "The girl don't know shit about shit."

Had her memory come back? If so, he wasn't in immediate danger since she had never seen him. Problem was, no matter how well he had cleaned the camp, a CSI routine might find a partial fingerprint or two and maybe his DNA somewhere.

He felt the thump of his heartbeat slow to normal. *The girl can't tie me to the camp or to Brett. The camp is the immediate danger. Its forensic evidence might do the implicating without human testimony. Eliminate the camp, eliminate the problem.* He'd take care of Boss's problem with the girl and McCree later.

He parked the snow machine in a cedar grove a half mile from the camp, took the binocs and rifle, and trekked in. Still a quarter mile away, he steadied the binocs on a tree limb and scanned the area around the cabin. They were peering in windows. The girl gesticulated and he heard indistinct but excited words.

She knows.

He thought about shooting them, sticking their bodies in the cabin, and burning it down. Unfortunately, he had never been the best of shots. If he missed . . .

Jimmie watched them circle the cabin to the front door. He had made sure the door was inviting—actually hoped some kids would find it and muck-up the crime scene. McCree reached for the door, but the girl pulled him away. If they had gone in, he might have been able to get close enough to gun them down when they came back out. They circled the cabin again and then inspected the wood shed, carport, and sauna. He thought about his own activities while here. He had never gone into the shed or sauna, but he had been in the carport, which would also have to go. A few minutes later they took off on their machine. Whether they were going to get the cops or heading to Shank Lake didn't much matter, he had work to do before anyone returned.

After the sound of their machine died away, only a gentle breeze stirring the cedars remained. He skirted around the hill and picked up the road, rutted with frozen tracks from Brett's truck. He walked in one track, careful to avoid any soft area, and arrived at the camp without leaving footprints. He found gas containers neatly stacked in the carport and thought about opening the cabin and spreading the gas inside, but figured it would be harder for the cops to get any clues about the arsonist if he did everything from the outside. He scattered enough gasoline around the carport to make sure it would burn completely. He broke all the cabin windows to create a good draft and poured the gas inside. Fumes made him want to puke. With the remnants of the final container, he soaked one end of a cedar stick.

He used a firestarter he found next to the grill to turn the stick into a torch. The carport was handy so he lit it first, and then from as far away as he dared, he tossed the torch inside the cabin and hotfooted it back up the frozen track. He had expected the house would explode, but it didn't. The gasoline caught with a polite little whoosh. Eventually, flames did the work he had intended. He didn't think anyone was nearby, but there was no reason to take chances just to watch a building burn. He wasn't some sick firebug; this was business and his was done here.

Atop the last hill from which he could see the cabin, Jimmie looked backward. Black smoke billowed from the carport—probably chainsaw or motor oil. All the snow on the cabin roof had melted—he hadn't considered the water effect of snow— but yellow flames danced on the near eave. The cabin was history. Now he could take care of McCree and the girl.

He drove a circuitous route of little-used logging trails to the camp he had broken into across the lake from McCree and settled in to await their arrival. A current of warm air shimmered from McCree's chimney, heat from a played-out fire in the woodstove. Their snow machine was not in evidence and he concluded they had not yet returned. This time he was not leaving until McCree and the girl were dead.

Maybe he should walk across the lake and be there to welcome them.

SIXTEEN

SERGEANT BARTELLE WASN'T SURE EXACTLY what he felt. Ever since he received the call from McCree and the Jane Doe—he refused to think of her as Niki—his emotions had been on a rollercoaster. His first reaction to McCree's call from Amasa demanding he and "Tex," the lab technician, get their asses in gear to investigate the camp where she claimed she'd stayed, was relief that the woman had found her memory. Then on the trip out he asked himself why she took McCree there before contacting him. Anger soon blossomed, especially as he considered that they had surely sullied evidence at the scene.

The first acrid smells from the burnt cabin reached him a couple miles away from the site, further fueling his anger. By the time he arrived, it had grown into a boiling rage. High blood pressure ran in his family and he tried to tamp down his feelings so he wouldn't blow a gasket, but all it did was give him a splitting headache.

McCree and Jane Doe swore up and down someone had burned the place after they left. The woman remembered only suspiciously selective information. He didn't put it past them to have torched the place, but then why bring him to the scene?

He ordered Tex and two other Iron County deputies to collect fingerprints and bag whatever evidence they found. They must have sensed his mood because they exchanged only muted conversation as they worked. Bartelle separated the suspects and spoke first with McCree, who cooperated fully, answering his questions no matter how many different ways he asked the same thing. Whenever Bartelle's question required a memory, McCree's eyes shifted to the right, as the Reid Method of Interrogation said they should as a suspect accesses memory. And every time he asked a speculative question, McCree would pause, his eyes shifting upward, marking cognitive thinking. Bartelle would swear McCree wasn't lying— well, almost swear, 'cause what do you really know for sure?

Jane Doe, on the other hand, was not forthcoming. Everything was measured with her. Each question elicited a short silence during which her eyes twitched leftward or upward before she provided an answer. He'd be willing to swear on the proverbial stack of Bibles that she was lying.

"Hey, Sarge," Tex called. "Come lookee here."

The three of them hustled to Tex, who pointed to a fresh set of two-way footprints several hundred yards away from the burned cabin.

"What do you make of them?" Bartelle asked the woman and watched her eyes. Pause. Left flick. "Made today, you can still see the sole pattern. They're a guy's boots, or some honking female Sasquatch. If the three of us make some parallel steps, we can gauge how much he weighed . . . well, assuming he wasn't carrying anything."

Interesting analysis, she clearly knew something about tracking. "Where do these lead?" Bartelle asked as though she should know the answer.

Pause. Right eye flick. "There's a bunch of evergreens on the other side of the hill. I'll bet he parked a sled and walked in."

Bartelle thanked Tex for the find and sent him scouting for any other trails. The three of them followed the boot prints to a cedar grove where they gave way to snow machine tracks.

"All right!" Jane Doe pumped her fist. "Now we're getting somewhere. Let's follow this sucker."

She was glowing; McCree's face showed neutral. If McCree knew about these tracks before, Bartelle figured he should never play poker with the guy. Aloud he said, "The tracks aren't going to disappear. I'll have the boys run them down after they finish collecting samples." He indicated an inclusive circle with his arm. "This spot bring anything else to mind? Jar any memories?"

Left flick. "Not really."

"But you've obviously been here before. When? Why?" Bartelle asked for the thousandth time.

She shrugged and began walking toward the burned cabin.

Bartelle caught McCree's arm. "She tell you anything she hasn't told me?"

"Nope. You figure she's lying, but now you trust me?"

Bartelle was so attuned to eye movement that he felt his own eyes click left while he considered his answer. "She is lying. You—" He waggled his fingers. "My suspicion is we're going to find that the snow machine followed you. Might be safer for all concerned if you bring her into town to stay."

McCree went into his silent mode.

"I've got way more questions than answers," Bartelle said. "Was someone following you to see what you knew and, once you found this place, burned it down? Or were they following you because they didn't know where the place was, and once you led them to it, they burned it down?

"Or was he following you because your 'Niki' told him where you were going? When she used your phone in Marquette to call your son she could have called someone else."

"I checked the logs. No calls other than to my son."

Bartelle made a note to subpoena McCree's phone records as soon as he got to town.

BARTELLE FINALLY RELENTED AND LET Niki and me return home. She again took the driver's seat. Fine by me; I'd rather think than worry about driving. Bartelle clearly suspected Niki of something, and I had to agree: her answers were less than convincing. *Should I use the excuse of the coming mud season to move us into town?*

Once we were out of sight of the cops, she slowed down. "What's up?" I yelled into her ear.

"If I can find where our tail cut off and circled around to the back of that camp, I can follow his tracks."

"Bartelle specifically told us they would do it."

"You scared?"

Was I? I probably should be, but, strangely, that wasn't it. My feelings could be better described as cautious. "I suppose a little," I said. "I'm thinking about the dog that finally caught the car and then wondered what to do with it. I'm not against tracking the guy, but it'll be dark soon and I don't know what we'll find. Besides, we'd screw up the tracks for the cops. They might arrest us for obstruction."

She tilted her head and measured the sun's progress. "Crap. First thing tomorrow then."

She damn near dumped me off the back with her acceleration. I wrapped my arms so tightly around her I could count her ribs through the padded material. By the time we got home, the first stars twinkled in a cloud-free night. It would be a cold one. She zoomed down the driveway and parked behind the garage, close to the path to the cabin.

"I'm going to go change," she said. "Then I'll cook supper. Pasta good?"

"Perfect. I'll work on getting some heat."

I rounded the side of the garage and froze. Lights shone from inside the house, which I hadn't noticed as we passed it because my head was buried into Niki's back to avoid the wind. I was sure we hadn't left any lights on when we drove off the day before. I returned to the snowmobile and grabbed the rifle, then raced up the snowpacked path to the cabin, burst through the door and caught Niki midway through changing.

Backlit by the kerosene lamp hung from a rafter, she turned, surprise painted on her face. "If you were looking for a free show, all you—"

"Someone's in the house. The lights are on."

She stopped mid-motion, arms thrust into a sweater, ready to pull it over her head. "I told you to lock the doors." She pulled the sweater on. "Did you see movement inside?"

"I did lock the doors."

"Sure you did. I'll take the rifle. You take the flashlight. Let's circle around the woods to look in from the front. Don't use the flashlight—we'll let our eyes adjust to the starlight."

It was slow work without snowshoes. With the warmer weather, some snow had melted and packed down, but cooler temperatures had returned and thin ice crusted the snow. Each step I took broke through the crust, chafing my ankles with the rim of ice. With snow past my knee, I had to take baby steps, providing a compacted path Niki easily followed. As the ridge played out, I slipped into a little basin that would soon hold a vernal pond, staying close to its edge. We crawled the rest of the way. After what seemed like ten hours but was probably only a couple of minutes, we lay in position to watch movement through the large windows on that side of the house.

In whispered consultation we agreed lights were on in the kitchen, main room, and upstairs loft. No movement. No sound. The wind had tamped down to dead stillness. The silhouette of a man slid from the kitchen around a corner and down the stairs into the basement, where a light turned on. From our position all we could see was the light spilling onto the snow.

"Anyone familiar?" Niki asked.

"Never got a view of his face," I said. "Seemed pretty tall, but it's hard to tell from this angle."

We waited. I was still in snowmobile attire and didn't feel the cold, but I could hear Niki's teeth rattling.

"Better give me the gun," I said. "You won't be able to hit anything."

"Don't kid yourself," she whispered in a steel tone. "Hopping on one foot, whistling Dixie, I'd still be a better shot than you."

The guy turned off the basement light and I knew he would soon come up the stairs. With quick steps he appeared in the light, giving me full view of his face before he disappeared into the kitchen.

"How the hell did he get here?" I asked.

JIMMIE EXPERIENCED A QUICK FLASH of guilt as he entered the house across the lake from McCree's. He paused to consider what had caused it. Certainly it wasn't breaking into the house. A smile crept onto his face as he looked down at his boots. He was feeling guilty because he had tracked snow into the house. "Take your boots off, Jimmie. This ain't no barn." His mother yelled those words each time he had raced into the house to tell her what he had found in the woods. She would ruffle his hair and make him clean up his mess.

Her number one rule was "Make a mess—clean it up. Your mess—your fix." Worked then; worked now. Jimmie had a plan for cleaning up this mess, but it required waiting for dark.

Two hours later the buzz of a distant snowmobile caught his attention. Through the rifle scope he watched the old geezer, Owen Whateverhisname, drop off someone with a backpack and then zoom away. Not McCree. Not the girl. Who the hell was this guy and what was he doing there? Ah, crap. One more complication.

Anxiety triggered hunger pangs, and he was thirsty. He thought about grabbing a beer from the stocked cold room he had discovered in the basement. He slapped himself upside the head. Drinking beer on an empty stomach was not the best idea. In his excitement he had forgotten to eat.

Across the way, the guy checked all the doors and discovered them locked—Jimmie's fault; he'd unintentionally locked the door when he left. The guy retrieved an extension ladder from behind the garage and scurried up to the balcony off the master bedroom. A few minutes later, the guy exited from the side door and returned the ladder to the garage.

Either he knew the balcony sliding door was unlocked, or he had broken in through that door on the theory no one would notice until it was too late, which was a decent idea Jimmie would keep in mind should the need arise.

A stream of smoke rising from the chimney across the way soon caught Jimmie's attention. Whoever it was had relit the fire. McCree must have told him about the balcony entrance—a fatal mistake. Bullets were cheap.

The day folded to a close. Shadows stretched across the lake toward McCree's place—narrow, reaching fingers first touching the shore and then climbing the trees on the other side as the sun sank lower. Jimmie strained his eyes reading in the deepening darkness. Patience, he counseled himself, patience. It may be too dark to read, but it wasn't dark enough to venture onto the lake.

Anticipation worked in mysterious ways, even if he hadn't eaten or drunk anything. While he was outside watering a tree, he heard a second snowmobile buzz. Peering through the scope he scanned the opposite shore. A snowmobile zipped down the driveway. Two people. Probably McCree and the girl, but in the deepening dusk, he couldn't tell. A cheerleaders' chant from high school football ran through his head: *Victory, victory is our cry. V-I-C-T-O-R-Y.*

A smile creased his face. In an hour the darkness would be complete and he could walk across the lake unseen. The people inside the house, whoever they were, would be backlit like a shooting gallery. *Pop. Pop. Pop.*

SEVENTEEN

JIMMIE MOVED DELIBERATELY CROSSING THE lake, stopping a hundred and fifty feet from McCree's place. He spotted three people by the dining room table. Because McCree had a walk-out basement, the main floor was about nine feet above ground level, and the slope from the lake to the house added another fifteen feet. The large deck hanging off the front blocked his view of the main part of the living space. The dining area was framed on the side by three big windows, and that side had the best cover. Now he had to get into position without being seen.

From hunting, he knew that people look straight ahead to see, but catch movement using peripheral vision. Rather than risk being spotted by moving laterally on the lake, he retreated until he was several hundred yards away from the shore and then shifted ninety degrees and trotted at a half-crouch up the lake, cutting back to land only when he was sure he was out of sight. He came ashore where McCree kept his dock sections stacked neatly on land beyond the cedars lining the shore. One path stayed by the shoreline. Another headed toward the log cabin. He picked the third, which seemed to head toward the house, and was pleasantly surprised to come upon fresh tracks apparently made by McCree and the girl sneaking up on the house.

He inched forward. With no time pressure, the last thing he wanted was to pitch forward into the snow and foul his rifle. He covered the three hundred yards in about fifteen minutes and found the swale he had scouted earlier in the day. A large boulder provided cover and a steady support for the rifle. He was within a hundred feet of McCree's house, which was lit like a black box theater.

The girl and unknown guy sat side-by-side at the dining room table with their backs to him. McCree moved in and out of the frame made by the oversized windows, delivering food to the table. Jimmie wanted all three sitting down before he struck, but McCree was not cooperating. Time to prepare. He screwed in earplugs and replaced the glove on his right hand with a thin latex one. Cold air worked through the plastic, causing his hand to tense. He sent a mental picture of a warm fire to his fingers and focused on the dining room.

Boss wanted the girl stiff, so she was the primary shot. He visualized the action: squeeze the trigger and send one bullet spiraling toward the wo-man's torso. With a tiny rotation to the left he could nail the other guy, whose reaction to the first shot would probably be to rise, not drop. Even if he decided to drop, he was tall and it would take longer for him to get below the window sill than for Jimmie to aim and fire. Leaving McCree. Chances were he would also rise, unless the shock of seeing the other two killed froze him. In any event, Jimmie should have a clear shot. After all three were down, he'd make sure they were dead.

McCree was not cooperating. The girl and the new guy were eating; McCree was still screwing around in the kitchen, off and on bringing something else to the table. Jimmie felt an adrenaline surge about to come on. If his aim was going to be rock solid, he needed to squeeze the trigger before the surge arrived. He altered his plan and focused the scope on the middle of her back, barely putting pressure on the trigger. As soon as McCree returned to the dining room, he would shoot.

The girl laughed, rocking back and forth in her chair. The target he had mentally painted on her back stayed in the bull's eye. From the far end of the dining room, he sensed something that hadn't been there before and added pressure to the trigger. In a rapid, graceful motion he performed the choreography: squeezed the trigger, rotated, squeezed the trigger, rotated; squeezed the trigger. *Pop. Pop. Pop.*

NIKI TURNED TO McCREE WHO was slightly lower than she was in the swale and hissed, "How the hell did who get here?"

"My son's wandering around inside." McCree began to stand up, but she grabbed his arm and yanked him down.

"How did he get here?" she asked. "You're positive it's him?"

"Positive." McCree stared at her. "I certainly didn't expect him. Maybe he's figured out your identity?"

Her fears exactly. In a calm, flat voice she said, "So soon? Let's make sure he's alone."

"You can freeze your ass if you want. I'm going in," McCree said. One by one he pried her fingers off his arm. *Nothing to do but follow the fool.*

McCree opened the unlocked door, stepped into the mud room, and called Paddy's name.

No response.

Niki stood beside him, pointing the gun down at a thirty-degree angle. She whispered, "Why didn't he come to greet us?"

McCree yelled louder, "Hey Paddy. We're here. Where are you?"

Still no response. The hairs at the back of Niki's neck tingled. She tried to restrain McCree but he again broke her grip and walked through the kitchen into the dining area of the great room. She followed, panning the space with the gun barrel.

Heavy steps sounded, coming up from the basement. Niki separated herself from McCree and covered the steps with the rifle.

A twenty-something with the same general build and looks as McCree loped up the steps, bopping to the beat of his iPod. He was halfway up before he saw his father and broke into a wide smile, which vanished when he saw Niki pointing the rifle at him. He stopped and removed the earbuds. Some unidentifiable hip-hop flowed into the room.

"Hey, Dad, welcome home." He faced Niki and said, "You can put the gun down, Agent Pendergast. I come in peace." He raised his right hand in the peace symbol, flashed a toothy smile, and continued up the stairs.

His words struck her like a kidney punch. She wanted to double over and wretch. The faint beat of the music and the off-beat slap of the kid's shoes on the stair treads filled the silence. McCree's mouth moved, but no sound came out. Niki lowered her rifle and watched the young man reach the head of the stairs.

She fixed him with a stare. "What did you call me?"

He reached into his pocket and shut off the iPod, walked to her and stuck out his hand. "Pleased to meet you, Agent Pendergast. I'm Patrick McCree. Dad, you've been harboring Agent Ashley Pendergast, undercover FBI working on a cross-jurisdictional task force with Homeland Security. Niki, by the way, is the name of the pet poodle she had growing up in Missoula, Montana."

Niki shook Patrick's muscular hand, willing her brain to assess the damage. "Who else knows?"

"Only one other person and I've sworn her to secrecy." Patrick paused. "For now, anyway." To his father he added, "Cindy wanted me to give you a kiss from her, but I think I'll just pass on the sentiment. She would have come, but she's in the middle of a probe into the Cook County building inspectors. I brought up a bottle of red wine." He held it up for us to see. "Care to join me in a glass and some conversation?"

Niki rotated her gaze between the two men. Patrick continued to wear an "aw shucks" grin. Seamus glowed with a father's pride. "An excellent suggestion," Seamus said. "We have lots to discuss. Speaking of which, where's your car?"

"After what you'd written about Owen, I wanted to meet the guy and stopped in. He's awesome! Wanted to know all about me. I told him I was coming to check on your guest. He thought that was a *very good* idea. Then he took a look at my tires and suggested that it would be faster and safer if he brought me out on his snow machine. But the roads are fine—I could have made it out easy enough."

Seamus laughed. "He just wanted to see what happened when you surprised me."

"You may be right. He looked at the tracks as we turned into the driveway and said you guys were off somewhere. I just had him drop me off 'cause I was sure I knew where you kept a spare key. I ended up having to drag up a ladder to the balcony."

She watched the two in action. The son struggled with the corkscrew—clearly not an oenophile. The father moved at half-speed gathering glasses from the cabinet and setting them on the table. Niki leaned the rifle against the wall and sat down at the dining room table, back to the windows so she could observe them as they talked.

"You prefer to be called Patrick?" Niki asked.

Patrick extracted the cork with a pop. "I've tried converting my father, but he's too old to change his stripes. Should we call you Agent Pendergast, or Ashley, or are you sticking with Niki? Based on your reaction, you have your memory back. Had you ever lost it?"

"Use Niki," she said. "It's safer. How did you figure this out?"

"I refuse to answer on the grounds it might incriminate me." He poured the wine. "The big clue was the number you dialed from Dad's cell phone. Nice touch wiping the phone's memory for just that one call, but that does not wipe out the record." He faced me. "And yes, Dad, I do have access to your cell phone records. And no, I didn't hack the FBI's computer system. Although I can't answer for some associates who helped me." He distributed the wine glasses.

"Associates? Who knows about me?" Niki asked. Her knee began bouncing underneath the table, trying to burn off excess energy. She willed herself to appear calm.

Seamus putzed around in the kitchen. Patrick took a seat next to Niki. "Okay, here's the scoop. The only people who know the whole story are me, my partner, Cindy, and now Dad. Some other people know your name but have no idea why I wanted the information. They could probably figure out more but don't have any reason to. They aren't the sort of folks who are going to show off what they know, if you get my meaning."

Maybe true, maybe not. Hackers aren't the most reliable group of people. "Who's this Cindy person?"

"We live together. She's an investigative reporter for a Chicago TV station. She's super curious about what's happening here. She and Dad have worked together in the past—in fact I met her through Dad, but that's beside the point. The point regarding Cindy is: she wants the story, but she's not about to endanger whatever you're doing. Dad can vouchsafe her. It's not my intention to screw you up either, which is why I came in person instead of calling or leaving a message or whatever. Also, I wanted to make sure Dad was safe.

"The FBI may be able to protect its undercover agents by getting their fingerprints removed from databases other police have access to, but it doesn't have the best reputation for avoiding collateral damage. Your turn to talk." He flashed his smile and took a sip of wine.

To stall, Niki said, "Let me think about this for a minute."

"I'll fix supper," Seamus said. "Pasta good, Paddy? I can make a meatless sauce."

"Perfect," Paddy said. "You want help?"

"I'm good."

Niki finished her internal debate. "I want to talk with you later about how you uncovered my identity." Patrick stiffened and she quickly continued, "Only to understand the holes in our security. We'll get the lawyers to give you and your . . . associates . . . whatever immunity is necessary." Her leg was bouncing so badly she started to get up, then forced herself back into the chair, and took a sip of wine.

"For now you should continue to call me Niki. The amnesia was real. I picked Niki because it was a name with good feelings. At the time, I didn't remember she was my dog and when I did, I had to laugh at myself since I told your father I was going to be one of those people known only by their first name. The dog, of course, went only by her first name."

She took another sip of wine, barely tasting it, and pressed both hands onto the table, her fingertips turning white.

"My alias is Bethany Palmer. The real Bethany Palmer had qualified for the job here. I took her place and we arranged for her to study the near extinction of wolves in parts of China. I have a field biology degree, experience with rustic living in cold winters, and no family to worry about not hearing from me for months at a time. It was my first—and now probably last—undercover assignment."

Seamus put a plate of cheese and crackers on the table between them. "Something to tide you over until I get dinner ready."

"If it hadn't been for your father, I would have died. The Legionnaires' disease fevers wiped out all my memory. I didn't know who I was, where I was, what I was. Nothing. Your dad is such a mensch. I can't believe how lucky I was to stumble upon him. When they released me from the hospital, I still had no memory. If Seamus hadn't taken me in . . . well, I don't know."

"He tries to show how tough he is," Patrick said. "But everyone knows he's Mr. Softie inside that rough Irish exterior. When did you remember who you really were?"

Niki released her death grip on the table. "Stuff came back in bits and pieces, all scattered. One of the first things I remembered was who Niki really was." She ruffed up both sides of her scalp and smiled at the recollection.

"I won't string this out. Bits of my childhood came back first. Later, I got more recent stuff like what I was doing out in the woods. But I knew that wasn't the full story. A few days ago, everything clicked into place. I tried to figure out a way to get to town to make contact with the Bureau, without success. Sergeant Bartelle—" At the questioning look from Patrick she explained, "Iron County Sheriff's Department. He had the road plowed, and your generous father offered to take me into town to buy new clothes."

She held up a finger to tell Patrick to hold his thought and turned toward Seamus. "My insurance will cover the hospital costs. I'll write you a check for the clothes once I return to being Ashley. I hope the delay won't be too much of a problem."

Seamus waved away her concern with the spoon he was using to stir the sauce, chuckled when he realized what he'd just done, and got a cloth to clean up the Jackson Pollock he'd painted on the stovetop.

"So what are you investigating?" Patrick asked.

"Your father figured out some of it. There's a paramilitary operation in this neck of the U.P., but I'm not allowed to tell you much." She shrugged. "I like you guys, but rules are rules, and the FBI is nothing without rules.

Infiltrating the organization isn't our biggest concern. We need to determine how they're funding it."

"So you already have someone inside?" Patrick asked. "Anyone besides me want another glass of wine?"

Niki shook her head both to refuse the wine and to remind herself the kid was as sharp as the father; she needed to be careful what she did and didn't say.

"We know the master organization has placed a monstrous weapons order to be delivered and paid for this summer. Sources implied the U.P. contingent is not only taking delivery, probably smuggled in from Canada, but are also generating the funds. This wolf research project Bethany was hired for seemed like a possible cover for a drug smuggling operation, which is why the government finagled my switch with her."

"More cheese anyone?" McCree asked. "Dinner's still fifteen minutes away. I'm planning on a garden salad to go with it." With no takers, Seamus began chopping lettuce, carrots, and tomatoes for a simple salad, the whack of the knife punctuating the conversation.

"Listening to your tone of voice," Patrick said, "I have the impression you didn't have much success in unraveling the puzzle."

"Worse. Not only did the yahoo who was our local *guide* not seem to know anything about the militia, there was another researcher, Brandon Newhouse." She began to massage her neck in the spot the hickey had once been. "He got sick before I did. I'm afraid he's dead. The Iron County cops didn't find anything at the camp to indicate he had been there, so I figure they hid his body somewhere. I think we were onto something, though. Our guide, Brett Aho, was murdered not too far from here. Given the timing, I've got to assume it was because I escaped."

"Did you meet anyone other than Aho?" McCree asked.

"Just him. He picked us up at the 'Soo' airport, told us there was a change in plans, and drove us to the camp. Someone else brought in provisions while we were gone. We never saw him or her or them."

Seamus grabbed the empty cheese plate, washed it at the sink, and stood staring at the side yard.

"See something?" Niki asked.

Patrick answered. "Probably deer at the salt lick. There's a real good view from that window." Niki shifted in her seat. "Slowly," Patrick said, "or you'll scare it off."

"Paddy's right, except the deer is staring at something in the swale." Seamus tossed the dishtowel over his shoulder, ducked down and slipped into the dining area and played owl, shifting his head back and forth to try to give shape and substance to whatever it was.

Niki hated having something going on behind her. "What do you see, Seamus?" She slowly rotated her position.

"It's near the big rock at the edge of the vernal pond. Near where we hid. There's a shape—oh, the deer just took off. There's some kind of reflection. Gun!"

Niki ducked and felt a crushing blow strike her back.

EIGHTEEN

JIMMIE REMOVED THE EARPLUGS AND listened for movement in the house. Nothing. No shadows. No one turned off lights, which would be expected if someone was trying to even the odds. His heartbeat sounded a little fast in his ear. Adrenaline at work. He took two deep breaths to regain control.

No one turned on lights anywhere else in the house. He heard no windows or doors open. From this position, he could only see two sides of the house and he briefly considered moving, but decided he was in a good spot for now. He could cover anyone who tried to escape using the laundry room door, the front deck, or the basement door. He couldn't see the screened porch on the other side, but they couldn't get far from there. He'd spot them if they crossed in front of the house toward the lake, and he'd see them if they tried to get to the truck or the snow machine.

Everyone knew that if you met a black bear in the woods you were safe as long as you didn't get between a sow and her cubs—unless it was injured. A wounded bear was unpredictable and dangerous. Jimmie didn't know the condition of the people inside, but it would be pure luck if he had killed all three of them. They had a gun, so there was no reason to rush in. *Time is on my side; yes it is.* He ducked behind the rock and reloaded. Never can be too careful.

If there had only been two people in there, the odds would be much better for sneaking in, maybe through a porch door, and finishing them off. His uncle told him about entering Viet Cong tunnels so narrow in places only one person at a time could squeeze through. Jimmie wasn't sure if he had big enough balls for that. Of course, maybe those guys were juiced up on potent Southeast Asian weed. He gave himself a head slap. *No tunnels. No Cong. No platoon to watch his back. Just him, McCree, the girl, and the new guy. He was the wolf; they were the three little pigs. This time the wolf was winning.*

A vision of roaring flames crossed his mind. Fire had solved one problem today; maybe it would work again. He realized he was warming to the idea and chuckled at the pun. This place had a metal roof, so the thing to do was set the fire low in the house and smoke the vermin out. Any Yooper with gas-sucking toys had to have extra gas cans around—probably in his pole barn.

He backed away from the house and cut around the generator shed to the rear of the garage. The snow machine ignition key glinted in the moonlight. He pocketed the key—should have done that earlier. Did they leave a key in the truck as well? The only doors to the garage were on the house side and putting himself in a box canyon by going in the front wasn't a brilliant move. The extension ladder the new guy had used to climb to the balcony and enter the house hung on a pair of hooks attached to the rear of the garage. Jimmie considered it for about a quarter second. Talk about setting yourself up—halfway up an exposed ladder. The ladder did have another good use, though.

He set it against the garage, climbed three rungs, and smashed the window above the lock with the rifle butt. He unlocked the window and pried it open. In seconds he was standing on a workbench inside the garage. He fastened on his headlamp and explored, pocketing both ATV keys. No key in the truck ignition. He popped the hood and wiggled a cable off the battery and shut the hood. If they escaped the house, at least they would be on foot.

He tossed two five-gallon billycans of diesel, plus a full five-gallon and a partially filled two-gallon can of gasoline, out the garage window onto the snow. As he climbed out, he considered the thousand-gallon propane pig McCree had behind the garage. Would the pig explode with a shot through its innards? With how big an explosion? It worked for 007. Okay, first he'd go with fire; if necessary, he'd try the propane tank.

Another thought occurred to him: maybe he should cut the power to the house. Then if he saw any lights, he would know someone was about with a flashlight. He slipped into the generator shed, found the master switch, and plunged the house into darkness. Walking to the edge of the garage where he could watch the house without showing himself, he waited. No lights. No shadows moving in the moonlight filtering into the house. No sounds except for a pair of distant barred owls trading their hooted, "Who cooks for you? Who cooks for you all?"

One problem with carrying a rifle was it only left one hand for carrying anything else, which meant taking all the diesel and gasoline would require four trips. Jimmie decided the gasoline was sufficient for the task if he made Molotov cocktails and pitched them through a window.

Back inside the garage, he found a recycling bin filled with plastic soda bottles. Those wouldn't do; the bottle needed to break upon contact so the gasoline could spread rapidly. Rooting around in the garage he found another trash can filled with glass and extracted a balsamic vinegar bottle and two of some fancy-Dan extra virgin olive oil. How something became extra virgin he had no clue, but the bottles would do. Once he got a fire started, the dry wood of McCree's house would do the rest. If someone was alive and mobile, they would surely rush to extinguish the fire and become a perfect target. If they ran from the house, he'd have them in the open, which was a fine alternative. If everyone stayed inside—crispy critters.

Jimmie found a funnel near where the gas canisters were stored, tossed the bottles and funnel into the snow. Now he needed something to make a wick. Nothing cloth was on the shelves. He checked McCree's truck and came up with a heavy rag wrapped around a tire iron and realized cloth was not the big issue; the big issue was how to light the rag. McCree might have a lighter inside the house, but that wasn't going to do him any good. He searched the pole barn again and discovered a propane torch and sparker on a shelf, answering his prayers.

The torch lit like a charm. He touched the flame to the rag and it lit, giving off a putrid oily smoke. Dropping the rag on the floor, he ground it into the dirt and extinguished the fire. He stuffed the cloth and clicker in his back pocket and pitched the propane torch out the window. Returning to his post behind the garage he reconnoitered. No lights. No movement. Even the barred owls were quiet.

He stuck the bottles upright in the snow and filled them using the funnel, leaving an inch of room at the top. He tore the rag—had to use his teeth to start the tear— and soaked each wick in gas, then twisted the wicks into the necks so they blocked the openings. From across the lake, a coyote gave a quick bark, which was joined by what sounded like dozens more, although Jimmie knew there were probably fewer than ten in the pack and more likely only five or six.

Back at the edge of the garage for another look-see after the coyotes finished their caterwauling, Jimmie heard, saw, and felt nothing. Could anyone alive keep this quiet for so long? *Not likely.* He considered for the briefest moment sneaking up to look in the windows and make sure those inside were dead. No reason to take a chance; Molotov cocktails were less risky. *Now, which windows do I throw the cocktails through?* All the windows were double-paned, and he didn't want the bottle to break on the outside of the house. If he used an unbroken window, he'd need to shoot it out first, and then get close enough to make sure he pitched the bottle inside.

Best would be to use one of the windows he had already destroyed. Plenty of room under them so he could reach up and toss the gas bombs in. Getting underneath the windows involved either crossing the exposed side yard or working his way around the house using the woods in front. Someone in the basement would see the maneuver, and he'd find himself in the wrong end of a shooting gallery. The porch screens would deflect the bottle. The lakeside windows were too high. Leaving only the windows on the driveway side—if he could get to them safely.

Jimmie scooted around the garage and up the hill behind it to his original observation post where the geezer had spotted him. Seemed a lifetime ago. From there, he could slip below the ridge line and come out opposite the house. Less than one hundred feet away, it would be the best place to start launching the bottles like hand grenades.

He screwed in his earplugs, took aim, and blasted both windows in the downstairs bedroom. He slid down the bank behind the garage, listened at the edge of the garage, and blasted another big window in the dining area. Give 'em something to think about. He calmed himself, removed the earplugs, and listened. A breeze had arisen and maple tree tops softly rattled together like wooden wind chimes. Still no movement or light from inside. Nothing out of place outside. Time to reload, just in case.

He carted the three Molotov cocktails back up the hill and screwed the bottles into the snow so nothing would spill. He placed them enough apart so one wouldn't catch from another. On the second trip he carted the torch and sparker to the attack point.

Wait. Look. Listen.

Houston, all systems are go.

Jimmie leaned the rifle against a tree, opened the valve on the torch, flicked the sparker, and, with a whoosh, the torch burst into life. He brought the torch to a steady flame and screwed it carefully into the snow, well away from the bottles. He slipped on his right-hand glove to give those fingers much-needed extra warmth, and squatted in the snow, just under the ridge line. From that position he practiced the grenade-throwing maneuver. Bulky clothing inhibited smooth motion, so he peeled off his snow jacket. He might be cold for a few minutes, but soon he could warm himself around a very large campfire.

He knelt on the jacket and practiced throwing again. He visualized a perfect arc from his hand straight through the window and brought the first bottle to the torch.

A blue flame danced along the rag. He reached back and launched the bottle.

Time for a cocktail party.

Jimmie watched the bottle with its blue-fire tail arc through the night and explode on the driveway short of the house.

Bummer.

He lit one of the extra virgin olive oil bottles. He'd have to run down the hill to make sure he got the next one into the house. Fortunately, the hill faced the house and had only light snow cover, so it would be easy to run. The flames and smoke from the first cocktail screened him from anyone inside the house. He got up, and started running.

NINETEEN

I REGAINED CONSCIOUSNESS IN STAGES. Colored light appeared at the edge of my vision. I knew I had been unconscious, and blinking my eyes open, I expected to see a circle of teammates staring down at me, saying things like, "You okay, man?" and "How many fingers do I have up?" No faces, no noise.

With eyes closed, I ran a mental check of my body, starting with my toes. Wait. Where were my soccer cleats? I wore . . . socks? Jerking my eyes open, I stared at a ceiling twenty-eight feet above me. *Ah, camp.* Had I taken a spill? My body responded to the inventory with a sharp current of pain in my left thigh. I reached to rub the sore spot and stopped short: a splinter had entered my leg and stuck out eight-inches. Hoping it wasn't in too deeply, I gave it a tug. *Oh, man, don't try that again.*

I carefully patted the other side of my leg: no wood sticking through. Cavalry troops routinely left arrows in their legs until they got to a surgeon. They knew that if they pulled them out, they might bleed to death.

In a burst of recall, I remembered talking with Paddy and Niki, saw a gun barrel glint in the faint moonlight, and slammed into them to knock them to the floor.

I gingerly rolled onto my side. Paddy lay near where I last saw him in an aureole of blood shimmering in light. I rose on one elbow and peered past him. Niki was gone. Whoever had shot us had taken her. I crawled to Paddy and checked his pulse: slow, about forty-eight beats a minute. But steady.

I gently ran my fingers over his body. No compound fractures, so I risked rolling him over. His perfect nose was at an angle; a mixture of snot and blood covered the lower part of his face. Despite looking like something out of a horror movie, he was breathing regularly through his mouth. I ran fingers across his skull to find the source of the blood and discovered a groove in the top of his head, as though someone had lunged at him with a spinning drill bit and created a shallow canal. I gently parted his hair and examined the wound. Through the warm blood I couldn't find any skull or brains peeking through. I exhaled; I had been holding my breath the entire time. He wasn't going to die from anything I had found so far, but he was unconscious and I needed to get him to the hospital in Iron River.

"Paddy," I said, "Can you hear me?"

A low, urgent "shh," came from the other side of the room. Almost as though I dreamed it, I heard a whisper. "The shooter's still out there. Be absolutely quiet."

I spun toward the voice and a galaxy of stars flashed before me. Once the dizziness passed, I saw Niki crawling toward me. Her right arm was bound to her chest in a sling concocted from her shirt. She left a smear of blood in her wake. In her left hand she carried a cleaver from the kitchen. I slid away from the table to meet her partway, making sure to do nothing to snag the wood embedded in my leg.

Niki cupped my ear in her hand and whispered, "Talk this way and he can't hear us."

"How bad?" I whispered into her ear.

"Me? Just a flesh wound, broken clavicle and maybe a cracked rib or two. Nothing major. You accidentally gave Patrick the most vicious head butt I've ever seen. Knocked you both out. His nose may need a surgeon, but the head wound's a scratch. He might need to part his hair differently, is all. Glad you're with it."

"His heartbeat is so slow."

She laughed silently. "Your son is in serious shape. His heartbeat is elevated . . . I bet normal resting it's less than forty bpm."

Took me a moment to convert bpm to beats per minute. Paddy had been the captain of the crew team his last year in college, and after moving to Evanston to work, he'd joined a local Chicago rowing team for exercise.

"That's not our problem," she said. "Our problem is our gun's busted up from a lucky shot. I've heard noises from outside. I hid in the laundry room thinking he might come in that door and I could catch him from behind." She waved the meat cleaver. "With two of us, we've got more options."

"You can stay inside and I can sneak out and try to catch—"

"No can do, hero. He catches you outside, you're dead, and where does that leave me . . . or your son? No, we need him to come to us, but we need to know where and when so we can catch him by surprise. Here's my plan—"

The house plunged into darkness. "Generator shed," I said.

She grabbed my arm and worked her fingers down to my hand. "Take this. Stay below the window line and get behind the laundry room door." She shoved the handle of the meat cleaver into my hand. I went to move, but she held me back. "If he comes in, yell like a banshee and go for his trunk. I'm taking the porch."

I stayed low and again gave wide berth to anything that could snag the splinter in my leg. Without light, my progress was slow, but I reached the laundry room without blundering into anything. As my eyes grew accustomed to the dark, I realized the moon high in the sky provided ample light. What time was it? I peered around the entryway to check the time on the stove clock—which, of course, was dark.

Muffled sounds came from, I thought, the garage. A pair of barred owls called several times from across the lake. I shifted weight from foot to foot only once. Putting extra weight on the injured leg was not a good idea. Half my mind tuned for movement outside, the other half was sending positive energy to Paddy.

Sometime later, it could have been five minutes, it could have been thirty, Niki appeared like a wraith beside me. I bent my head down and she cupped my ear with her hand. "Your son's starting to stir. I don't want to move him, but I'm worried he'll start making noise. I don't know what the hell's going on outside. Obviously cutting off the electricity wasn't in preparation for an immediate attack. I think maybe he's planning to wait us out."

"We can't keep Paddy quiet. If we gag him, he'll struggle." Frustration had me whispering with force. "We can't wait any longer in here for an attack. There's only one of him and two of us. We've got to go after him."

"Just because we haven't been rushed doesn't mean there's only one person out there. Could be three of them, how would we know?"

Good point. "Should we intentionally make noise and entice them to attack?"

I sensed her shrug. "I'll stay here by the door. You get to your son. If he comes to, try to make him lie still and remain quiet. That's our biggest risk right—"

Shots rang and windows shattered in the guest bedroom. The remaining dining room window was next. Niki silently slid away from me. I remained still, willing my senses to bring me information. Finally, I heard a whoosh followed by the sound of breaking glass. Light poured into windows on the driveway side.

I ran past Niki, making no effort to mask my noise. Through the bathroom window I glimpsed a wall of flames. I yanked open the door to the screened porch and, keeping as close to the house as I could, sidestepped to the end of the porch on the driveway side. I peeked around the edge of the screening.

A wall of flame fifteen feet from the house lit up the night. Recognition leapt to mind: Molotov cocktail. I couldn't see through the blaze and, with now-ruined night vision, tried to spot movement on either side of the flames.

A spot of light appeared to the left of the burning and then quickly disappeared behind the hill. I edged toward the door from the porch, hiding my one hundred and seventy pounds behind four-by-four supports. The spot reappeared, and after a moment, began moving down the hill.

I pushed open the screen door, ran down the ramp to the driveway, and realized I would not get to him before he launched his second Molotov cocktail. With all my might I threw the cleaver at the figure slipping and sliding down the snowy embankment.

The man brought the flaming bomb behind him in preparation for his throw. The flame disappeared behind his body and his arm started forward. The cleaver reached the top of its arc, lazily rotating handle over blade. The flame reappeared from behind him moving upward at a rapid pace. The cleaver was on target but would not get there in time.

I screamed at the top of my lungs as the resulting fireball lit the night.

FRIDAY NIGHT AT CAMP, AND Boss was marking time. Jimmie hadn't reported in last night as expected, and the deadline for him to turn up didn't allow time for visiting the neighbors with a six-pack to shoot the breeze.

The viatical settlements had long passed the go/no-go mark. In fact, there were only two left to sign. It would be nice to get a hundred percent of the residents with the right kind of life insurance, but to worry about that now would be greedy. Boss was never greedy. Focused? Yes. Greedy? No. Pa often quoted the Wall Street ditty, "You can make money as a bull. You can make money as a bear. You get slaughtered if you're a hog." Boss decided not to bother contacting the other two holdouts again. They knew the number to call if they wanted to get in on the action; although damn if it wouldn't be nice to include that old bag Mrs. Ricci and flip Sergeant Bartelle the bird after the old coot croaked in a month or two. Of course, she was probably going to die whether or not she signed the agreement.

The second hand on the clock made another full revolution and the deadline passed. Jimmie's failure to report was now officially a threat to

Boss's plans. Time was of the essence. No way was Boss going to have a lung and a half removed, so days were counting down quickly—less than a hundred, if the doc's prediction was right.

This gig was to be Boss's legacy: a gift to allow the nation to get back on track. With the weapons and explosives they would amass, it should be possible to take out at least the majority of the senators and congressmen on the same day. Then America could elect representatives who would work for the people, not the corporations. Wouldn't the local Chamber of Commerce folks be surprised if they knew Boss's thinking?

Time for some outside resources. Boss opened the cooler, extracted a Bud, and held it as a salute. "Bye, Jimmie. It was kicks."

Retrieving a cell phone from a false-bottom drawer in the desk, Boss speed-dialed twenty-six—Michigan was the twenty-sixth state of the union. On the second ring, Boss heard the click of an open connection.

"Got me some varmints," Boss said.

TWENTY

BARTELLE PACED THE HOSPITAL CORRIDORS, his nose twitching at the antiseptic smell. He had waited for hours for the doctors to release someone, anyone, for questioning. He checked his watch for the umpteenth time: nearly midnight. A nurse exited the emergency room door and held it open as Seamus McCree hobbled out on crutches. What an ungodly mess he looked: left pant leg cut off like short shorts, gauze bandage wrapped around his thigh, blackened right eye. Bartelle released a puff of air, put on his neutral face, and approached the pair.

"I wish you could have seen the other guy," McCree said once Bartelle was in range.

Bartelle shook McCree's hand, making sure not to bump the crutches. "You saying he looked worse than you?"

"I meant it literally. Someone with training may have noticed something worthwhile. The only thing I can tell you is he was male and somewhat shorter than I."

Bartelle fixed the nurse with his stare. "You're done with him, eh?"

"No rodeo for a few days, otherwise he's all set. Now Mr. McCree, you make sure to fill the script at the pharmacy. Your leg's going to be real sensitive for a few days. You want to stay ahead of the pain."

McCree indicated he would and thanked the nurse. Said he'd stick around until they finished with the other two.

"I'll bet anything the doctors will keep your son overnight for observation."

"And Niki?" McCree asked.

"Almost done."

McCree shuffled in a half-circle to face the nurse and extended his hand. "I appreciate your help. All of you guys are terrific."

The nurse beamed. Bartelle shepherded McCree to the empty waiting room. This wasn't an ideal interview spot, but it was convenient and the nurse would be able to find McCree to let him know the second she heard anything about his son, which might make it easier for him to concentrate on answering questions.

"Let's work backward, okay?" Bartelle asked. McCree didn't respond. "Last I knew, you didn't get cell service at your place. Who called the incident in?"

"Paddy brought a satellite phone."

Huh, at least someone in the family has sense. "Come to think of it, why didn't you have one?"

"Yeah, it would have been nice when Niki showed up. Put it down to either I'm too cheap, or I wanted to avoid contact with the rest of the world."

Bartelle scratched his head. Felt good. "Why didn't you drive yourself in?"

"Truck didn't start. Wouldn't catch."

"Hmph. Give me your impressions of the guy. I'm recording this, okay? You said he was smaller than you. White?"

"At first I only saw him as an outline through the flames. Really all I saw was a dark blob and the burning wick on his Molotov cocktail."

McCree related the details, starting with when he and Niki left the burned-out camp. McCree, even with half or more of his mind worried about his kid, and maybe the woman, gave a coherent, detailed description of the events up to the point where he'd charged out of the house.

"I don't get it," Bartelle said. "What possessed you to risk your life like that? You bucking to be some kind of hero?"

"It was pretty stupid if you think about it. I mentioned the last case I worked on in Cincinnati? Well, part of the reason I stayed up north this winter was because some asshole damn near burned down my house in Cincinnati, so something inside me snapped when the guy threw the first Molotov cocktail and it landed short. I was damned if I would let anyone burn this house down."

He reached down and, using both hands, tenderly shifted his injured leg. His face scrunched with the pain.

"The tree trunk was already jammed in your leg?"

"Sliver—well, maybe a small piece of kindling." He flashed a half-smile. "I didn't think about anything. Not my leg. Not what I was doing. Not about Paddy being unconscious. Not about Niki being hurt." He lifted and dropped his shoulder, exhaling a long sigh through his nose. "It was not a rational decision, okay? I lost it."

"I get that. I watched a World War II documentary about Medal of Honors winners. Every one of them a real hero. The interviewer asked one guy what he had been thinking at the time. The guy said, 'If I had been thinking, I wouldn't have done it.' So what happened after you left the house?"

"He started running down the hill—it was slow motion because of the snow. Even so, I wasn't going to get there in time to prevent him from heaving the second bomb. I was so pissed. I wanted to split him from stem to stern and I threw the meat cleaver at him. The cleaver had other ideas: it smashed into the bottle midflight and produced a fireball in the air between the guy and me. I think maybe some of the gasoline landed on him because over my yelling—the Irish know how to yell—I heard him scream, too."

McCree hung his head. Bartelle couldn't tell if McCree was dejected or tired. He placed what he hoped would be a comforting hand on McCree's shoulder. Felt the hard muscle and bone. "Then what happened?"

"Dummy that I am, I kept charging him. I was lucky he didn't have a weapon. He took off down the hill at a slant heading away from me toward the side yard. I veered to head him off. At first, I had the advantage. He was in snow and I was on the plowed driveway. Problem was, I was running around in socks."

Bartelle checked McCree's footwear. Boots.

McCree followed the glance. "We were sitting around gabbing away. I was fixing dinner. I had taken my boots off and never thought to put them on again. Another of my less bright decisions. He escaped because I tripped. Drove the splinter right through my thigh. I gimped to the snowmobile with thoughts of running him down, but he had stolen the key. Pretty much as soon as I discovered that, my leg refused to take any more weight."

"Try an experiment for me," Bartelle said. "Close your eyes and go back to the moment when the meat cleaver hit the bottle. Freeze it there and run the movie forward one frame at a time. Let me know if you see anything different."

McCree's eyeballs twitched as he progressed the movie frame by frame. Many people go through the motions but can't do it. McCree was working hard. At one point, he crossed two fingers on the right hand and later crossed two on the left.

"Definitely white. Wasn't wearing a coat. Had on a long-sleeved checked shirt. Carhartt, maybe?" McCree undid one set of crossed fingers. "He must have had a snowmobile at Spruce Point." McCree released his other digital reminder. "Soon after, a snowmobile started up across the lake and headed up their driveway."

"Spruce Point?" Bartelle prompted.

"Camp across the lake from me. Owned by some Chicagoans."

Bartelle made a quick note to check that camp as well. So much for a weekend off. "Think about the Carhartt plaid. The temperatures were what, in the twenties. Why do you think it was a shirt and not a wool jacket, maybe even a quilted jacket?"

McCree squeezed his eyes closed. "Long shirt tails. Coats are squared off, maybe have a flap in the back. Running, his shirttails flared away. Definitely a shirt."

Which led to the obvious question: what had the attacker done with his snowmobile jacket? The emergency room opened and the nurse held the door for the woman calling herself Niki. Bartelle checked his watch, already after one in the morning. She wore a figure-eight sling to immobilize her arm. Her face was pale and drawn, yet, like a feral cat, her eyes took everything in. Every time he saw her, Bartelle's gut told him something was not right, but he was clueless how to convert feeling to fact.

The accompanying nurse addressed McCree, "They will keep your son overnight for observation. The doctors can give you the details, and I'm probably not supposed to be talking, but when did that ever stop me. Right, Lon?"

She didn't wait for Bartelle to respond but chattered without pause. "He's one very lucky guy. The bullet took off a few layers of skin—quarter inch lower . . ." She shook her head. "His two shiners will last a couple of weeks. His nose should heal well, but I see you know something about broken noses." She touched McCree on the bridge of the nose. "Curiosity killed the cat. Your son won't tell us. How did he break it?"

"Head butt," McCree said. "I caught a glint from a gun barrel and dove into Paddy to knock him down. I misjudged and nailed his nose."

"Saved our lives," Niki said. "Seamus's quick action put both Patrick and me on the floor. The bullet clipped me instead of taking out my heart. He's a hero. While I dithered around, he's the one who took charge and drove off the killer."

She kept talking, but Bartelle was more interested in the look McCree had given her as she said she had dithered around: McCree wasn't buying her story, but didn't want to correct her in front of an audience.

The nurse finally broke in. "You two are ready to be discharged. I understand Mr. McCree is on the hook for both of you?" McCree agreed. "Then I'll take you to billing so they can finish their paperwork. I'll get your overcoats and stuff and bring them down there. Questions?"

"Can I see Paddy before we go?"

"He's sleeping." The nurse patted his hand. "Assuming everything is okay, he'll be released between ten and eleven tomorrow morning. You can call in about nine-thirty. We'll know by then."

McCree shot Bartelle a look that said, "That going to be a problem?"

Bartelle had already planned tomorrow, which included getting a subpoena for McCree's phone. "Will this be okay with you, Seamus? Rooms are available at the AmericInn. Stay there. I'll pick you and Niki up in the lobby at five-fifteen? I know it's not much sleep, but we'll get to your place at sunrise. After we go over the scene with you, you can drive back here in plenty of time to pick up your son. Right now, I need to ask Niki some questions while the incident is still fresh."

She laughed at Bartelle. "You mean before I talk with Seamus. No one is fresh this late at night, including you, Sergeant." She walked to Bartelle and slipped her good arm in his and said in a husky voice. "Take me to your interrogation room."

He didn't trust her a lick, but he couldn't help laughing. Yanking his flashlight from his belt, he shone it into her eyes and said in a Dragnet voice, "Where were you on the night of—" Couldn't finish for his giggles and knew he was overly tired. "Take care of the bill, McCree. We'll be here when you're done."

Niki convinced me that with less than three hours before Bartelle picked us up, it was a waste of money to get two rooms at the AmericInn, especially since she had to sleep sitting up because of her arm. The room had a king-sized bed and a sleeper couch. If the county tongue-waggers needed proof we were coupling, they'd have it now. I was too tired to care.

The room was warm, so I gave Niki the blanket and quilt off the bed to make a cocoon; the sheet would be plenty for me. Once we turned the lights off, we acted like two kids on an overnight: instead of trying to sleep, we compared notes from Bartelle's questioning. We agreed Bartelle had no idea who was behind it.

"You need to call in?" I asked.

"You don't have your cell phone, and Bartelle will check the motel phone logs to see if we called out. I'll check in tomorrow after Bartelle finishes with us. Besides . . ."

I waited for her to continue, but the silence lengthened. "Besides what?"

"It can wait for tomorrow."

"It is tomorrow. Besides what?"

From across the room, I heard a long sigh. "I'm sorry. You can't stay in your house. Even if they release it as a crime scene, you've got all those shot-up windows. I'm beating around the bush. Your son was right. I clearly endangered both you and him. I didn't think I would. You have to believe me. There's no way you can be safe there until this whole thing gets resolved. And after tonight I've got to get distance from you guys. I'm too dangerous. Maybe if you don't want to go all the way to Cincinnati you can stay with your son in Chicago?"

She was right. I couldn't stay in the house until I got it fixed up, but I had the cabin. Remembering the broken windows gave me something else to think about: my backup heating system would be trying to heat the entire world to the thermostat setting of forty-five degrees. Fortunately, it would keep the pipes from freezing tonight, but it meant I had to drain the water system tomorrow. It was going to be a busy day.

Earlier in the evening, before all the fireworks, Paddy had implied I was a teddy bear, which I supposed was partly true. But, if someone tells me what I can't do, I tend to get my Irish up—it's not just an expression. Being unable to stay on my property was not an option I was willing to accept. Abigail had wanted me to own guns for my protection. She trained me at a range, and even though I was a good shot, I never agreed to buy any weapons. Owen had lent me a gun, which I didn't want. However, if the price for staying on my property was to have a gun, I was willing to arm myself. I felt a tiny piece of my soul detach and drift into the Michigan night. I couldn't grab it back; but if I didn't stay, I would lose much more.

Deep into my self-talk, I heard Niki offer another "I'm sorry."

"For what?" More heat filled my voice than I intended. "Look, I understand your position, but here's mine: once I can get Paddy to safety, I'm staying at camp. You can decide for yourself where you want to be. We'd have to share the cabin until I get the house habitable. Hopefully, it shouldn't take too long. My mother used to tell me, 'It's better to run away and live to fight another day,' to which my father would append, 'But if it's going to be the same fight, might as well make it today.' "

"Put yourself in my position," she said. "What happens if I agree and it goes wrong and you're killed? What then? What do I say to your son? What if your son says the same to you? 'Fine, Dad. If you're staying, I'm staying.' What will you do then?"

"I'll bluster and shout and order him home, and if he tells me to stuff it, I'll remember I raised him to make his own decisions. I invited you into my home because I wanted to. If someone had told me what would happen because of my invitation, I'd still do it. That's just who I am. Some things I am unwilling to change." I slapped my open palm onto the bed. "That's hard for people to take, which is why I'm divorced and Abigail is who-knows-where. In that unbending way, we're alike, I think. So screw you, Agent Pendergast, and screw your FBI. I won't blow your undercover operation, but I'm not about to have you tell me what to do."

From the chair came rustling noises, but no words of argument, or of agreement. "Let's get some shut-eye," I said. "We're going to need it."

The bed shifted under her weight as she sat down beside me. "I understand. I'd like to stay, but I have to follow orders. They're going to pull me. You say all your tough-guy words. Beneath them, I hear the Seamus who lost his father, and the divorced Seamus who lost his wife, and the current Seamus who lost his lover." Her fingers brushed my cheek. "I hear the Seamus who wonders if he is loveable. If you listened to your son this evening, you should know you are. I know you are."

Lightly caressing my chest with her good hand, she leaned down and kissed my lips. "With this wing, I'll have to be on top. Okay, tough guy?"

TWENTY-ONE

NIKI AND I WERE WAITING for Bartelle in the AmericInn lobby at the appointed time. He arrived carrying two coffees and a bag with cream and sugar. He pointedly looked at my naked bandaged leg and chuckled. "Love the fashion statement. We'll turn the heat up high for the ride."

Once in the car, I handed my cup to Niki—I couldn't remember when I last drank the stuff. Tex drove: he had had more sleep than Bartelle, Niki, and I combined. Bartelle rode shotgun. On US 141, potentially suicidal deer grazed along the edge. Once we hit the gravel roads, the vegetation grew closer in and deer were less visible, but we knew they were there, waiting to spook into our path. With a predawn rose glowing in the east, we crested a hill and Tex slowed down.

"Well looky what we got."

Niki and I nearly bumped heads as we leaned forward to peer between the front seats. A large male wolf, his black coloration flecked with cinnamon-tipped fur, loped down the road. He peered at us, huffed out a breath of warm air, and continued like a Cadillac—owning the middle of the road.

"DNR hasn't gotten to him," Niki said. "No radio collar and no ear tags." Bartelle shot her a quick look and returned his gaze to the wolf, which reached an area where the left snowbank was only four feet high. The wolf gathered itself in two quick steps and, in a graceful bound, jumped the mound. Five seconds later, we had lost it to the woods.

Bartelle spoke the words I had been thinking: "Sights like that are why I love being in the woods."

Several sheriff's deputies had already set up my screened porch as a staging area. Dawn had officially arrived, but the hill behind the house still hid the sun. They had turned on all the house and garage lights, which, combined with the furnace trying to heat the planet, had the generator running at full buzz. We donned blue booties and entered the house. After throwing on sweatpants, my first stop was the basement so I could flip the furnace circuit breaker. Tex followed me as I laboriously picked my way down the stairs.

"Later, we can all help drain the house," he said. "Pipes won't freeze before Bartelle's done with you."

"Thanks," I said, "but I have to winterize every year, so the house is designed for it. Draining the water heater is the longest part. Everything else is easy, although the biggest pain is the toilets. My bigger concern is figuring out what's wrong with my truck. It was working fine before. The guy must have done something to it."

We found Bartelle and Niki examining the southern wall in the dining room. A freshening breeze pushed air through the broken windows. "Once we've got enough light," Bartelle said, "we'll walk the grid. For now, take me through exactly what happened."

He recorded a lot of stuff in his notebook, even though we'd told him all of it before. While they used little flags to mark every exogenous item for photographing and bagging, Niki remained on the porch. I joined her after I completed draining the water from the house. Tex came trotting over.

"You were right. The guy messed with your truck's battery cable. I dusted everything for prints, but I'm not too hopeful. Anyway, I reconnected the battery for you, so you're good to get to your son in town."

"Thank you. This part of the kinder, gentler Iron County Sheriff's Department?" I joked.

He blushed. "More like the sergeant wants you out of here as quick as possible." He included Niki in his gaze. "You too, miss."

I caught Niki raising her eyebrows and sliding me a sideways glance— probably to see how I reacted. I consciously released my tightened shoulders. "Thanks for all your help." I shook his hand. "Let me grab my cell phone, keys, and Paddy's stuff and we'll head out."

Niki waited only long enough for me to steer the truck onto Shank Lake Road before saying, "I'm surprised you didn't take Tex's head off when he told you Bartelle wanted us gone."

"First, he was only the messenger. Second, you had prepared me, so I was ready and could handle it without a kneejerk reaction. Anyway, I do need to check on Paddy, and you," I handed her the cell phone, "need to call your superior. There was no reason to make a stink . . . yet. If Paddy has to remain in town, then I'll stay with him. As soon as I get him to Chicago, I'm back here."

To accommodate an approaching full-size truck towing an enclosed trailer, I pulled so far to the right that I scraped the side of my truck on tag alders. I sucked in my stomach as they approached. The trailer wasn't one of those specialized ones for carrying snowmobiles, but I figured that was what was inside. Every Saturday, town guys drove freshly plowed roads as far as possible and then offloaded their snowmobiles and explored the country. The truck eased to a stop and lowered its window as did I in the rural tradition of never letting an opportunity pass to discover who was out in the woods and why.

A grizzled bear stuck out his head. "You McCree?" I admitted I was. "Owen apologizes he couldn't be here hisself. Had to go down to the VA in Green Bay, but he sent me and my brothers to cover them windows was shot out with OSB?"

I knew he meant the OSB was to cover the windows, but I couldn't help smiling at the image of someone shooting the plywood equivalent through my windows. I didn't offer him a grammar lesson.

"We wasn't sure what you had for tools up to your camp, so we brung all we needed." He tilted his head toward the trailer. "Sorry we're so late. Had to wait for the lumber store to open to get the OSB. Owen said there was four or five big windows shot out. We brought twice as much stuff as we thought we needed, so we should be hunky dory."

I stammered my thanks and wondered once again at both the efficiency of the local grapevine and the willingness of folks to pitch in to help others. Eventually our conversation informed me they were third cousins once removed to Owen. I think. Owen had roused them at six o'clock. Only God, Owen, and his source knew how he found out about the ambush. After we'd chatted long enough that I wouldn't be considered rude, I mentioned we were headed to Iron River to hopefully check Paddy out of the hospital.

"You got plenty of time. Heard tell the doc would discharge him about eleven. They still got big northern in the lake? Back thirty, forty years ago . . ."

Took twenty more minutes before we disengaged to his parting words, "We'll keep an eye out 'til you get back."

Niki craned her neck looking back at the guys. "More examples of not judging a book by its cover. Sweethearts, aren't they? How come you didn't at least offer to reimburse them?"

"Yoopers may not have much money, but they're rightly proud of taking care of people in the community. I'll find out from Owen the best way to handle things so I don't accidentally insult anyone."

AT EXACTLY TEN O'CLOCK, BOSS met Spider and Digger on a quarter-section of land Hematite Bank had recently foreclosed near the Michigamme Reservoir. Boss thought of them as the Mitten Men, given they came from that part of the state. Everyone stood around making small talk, stamping their feet to keep warm in the mid-morning chill, and slurping the coffee Boss had brought in thermoses.

Boss had no trouble guessing which one was Spider. Wearing a T-shirt and a sheepskin vest, his left arm sported the tattoo of a giant web with a black widow ready to pounce from his bicep. He looked like a spider too—drug-addict skinny, all arms, and legs with a little pot belly. Smelled like an ashtray. The look might have worried Boss, except these two came highly recommended. Digger looked like a fire hydrant: short, squat, and his face burned red. "Caught me frying on a beach in Florida," he said by way of explanation. "Looking forward to going back as soon as this is done. Who are the targets?"

Using the cell phone display, Boss brought up several pictures of the still-missing Jimmie, and one of Jane Doe taken in the hospital. "Take as much time as you want to memorize these faces. I don't want any printouts, nothing anyone could use to tie us together. Best for all our sakes."

Boss paid attention to their eyes, which revealed their skepticism. They knew it was one-way protection, but it didn't seem to bother them. Spider took one look at each picture, proclaimed he "got it," and handed the phone to Digger. Digger stared at a picture, closed his eyes, and described the picture in minute detail. Boss was impressed, but the proof would be in the pudding.

"Before my bank acquired this property, I checked it out. There's lots of coyote sign. Let's get acquainted while we do a little tracking and maybe get us some varmints. Tonight, you can start hunting some other varmints."

Digger brayed loudly at the joke. Spider laughed without sound. Boss did not want to be around these two for long. They were scary *hombres*.

It WAS A BIT AFTER noon by the time Niki returned to the hospital waiting room. She found Seamus reading a month-old issue of *The Economist*. "I thought you and your son would be impatiently waiting for me. Sorry I took so long." She plopped on the bench next to Seamus.

"Now you get to wait." He checked his watch. "One last doctor has to sign off on Paddy's release, but I hear he's stitching up a chainsaw accident."

Niki absentmindedly pawed through the magazines scattered on the coffee table: People, Woman's Day, Parents, Field & Stream, Sports Illustrated, North American Whitetail. "Where'd you get that one?"

"Guy was in earlier waiting on his wife. Retired anthropology prof, of all things. Anyway, we got to talking. When his wife came out, he handed it to me—he'd brought it from home. I'm almost done if you want it."

Only Seamus could walk into a podunk hospital, find an anthropologist to talk to, and come out with an Economist *magazine.*

Niki expected Seamus to drill her with questions, but he went back to reading. *This isn't going to get any easier with the waiting.* "Well," she slapped her good hand on her knee, "I just had the best time. I got to talk to my direct supervisor, then he conferenced in the guy he reports to, and finally that guy added in the AIC—Agent in Charge." She checked to make sure he was paying attention. "I'm supposed to provide whatever information I can to Sergeant Bartelle and then disappear. No one, not even Bartelle gets to know my real name. I'm Niki—one name—single 'k.' "

She tried a quick smile, but couldn't make it stick. "You're supposed to talk with the AIC."

"About?"

She dialed the number, pushed the speakerphone button, and handed Seamus the phone. AIC Cooper answered by grunting his name. Seamus introduced himself.

"Listen McCree, this is what you're going to do. First you're going to—" Seamus frowned at the phone and disconnected the call.

"Did you just hang up on him?"

Seamus removed the battery from the phone. "If Agent-in-Charge Cooper conjures a way to contact me and asks politely, I'll consider whatever request he had in mind. Otherwise . . ."

She had sat with her sling next to Seamus. A quick check showed no one was in the area. She danced around him and sat on his other side, leaned in and gave him a good, hard kiss. She closed her eyes and remembered last night. "He is a prick, and you . . . you are something else."

She leaned in for another kiss, but Seamus ducked away. She punched him lightly on the arm.

"One word is obstreperous," Patrick said. "What did Dad do this time? I only heard the last part as they wheeled me down the hall."

Oh, that's why Seamus avoided kissing me. She turned toward the voice. Patrick looked horrible: his swollen face featured a nose even Jimmy Durante would disown. His eyes presented a mixture of black, green, and putrid yellow. White bandages wound around the top of his head. He shifted his weight to get up from the wheelchair but the nurse restrained him with a hand on his shoulder. "Not until you're officially released."

Patrick slumped down, "Can't be too soon. Shall we?" He motioned with a grand sweep of his arm toward the exit. The nurse unlocked the brakes and we followed them out the door. Seamus brought the car around. The nurse reminded Patrick of his instructions about icing everything swollen and making sure he had his prescriptions for pain medication.

No sooner had Patrick shut the passenger door than he inquired about lunch, claiming breakfast was a year ago and he was starved. At the mention of food, Niki felt her stomach grumble.

Patrick grinned and pointed at her. "You're outvoted, Dad. How about Scott's Subs? Leave room for the ice cream. So who did you blow off?"

"FBI. They—"

"Not another word until we know we're alone," Niki said. "People can read lips better than we think. How bad does it hurt, Patrick?"

"Let me put it this way: next time Dad decides to head butt me, I need to remember he used to head a ball half the length of a soccer pitch—and get the hell out of the way." He poked his father in the ribs, causing Seamus to startle. "Were you jealous of my perfect nose and decided I needed to have the new McCree model with a crook?"

Seamus fingered his own crooked nose. "The ladies will love it, right Niki?"

"Oh yes. We swoon at the manly exhibition of broken noses. And if you add a chipped tooth or two . . ."

During lunch, Niki observed the interplay between the two McCrees. The playful banter showed a clear mutual appreciation. Underneath, however, she could feel tension. Seamus was probably contemplating how to convince Patrick to go to Chicago. She guessed Patrick was working on how to protect his old man. Maybe she could broker a deal to keep them all safe and not make either one lose face—to each other or to themselves.

After lunch, Seamus drove to the Wolf Track Trail at the nearby George Young Recreational Complex. The day had warmed to the lower forties with a light southwestern breeze. Most of the snow was gone and, although the trail was slushy, it had the advantage of being deserted.

Patrick asked, "Are you still Niki or Agent Pendergast?"

"Stick with Niki. I'm to inform Sergeant Bartelle about my undercover operation and provide whatever information might help his murder investigation. Then I am to leave, and I quote, 'on the first available flight.' " She added, emphasizing each word, "Oh, by gosh and by golly, can you believe—" She threw up her hands like a fundamentalist Christian. "—that I accidentally left a few things in your Dad's cabin? No? Well, fancy that."

She gave them her most mischievous smile. "I checked the flights." She rotated her attention to Seamus. "Even if I catch Bartelle before he leaves your place, I won't be able to get to either Iron Mountain or Marquette in time. So, you're stuck with me for one more night . . . unless you don't want to be. You heading down to Chicago today, Patrick? We can drop you off at Owen's to pick up your car."

"What makes you think I'm leaving?" Patrick stopped walking and forced Niki and Seamus to turn around. Niki shrugged at Seamus to say she had given it her best try.

Seamus may not have seen the gesture, but Patrick did. "You two in cahoots? I knew something was going on."

Niki didn't dare look at Seamus. She felt a flush reach from the roots of her hair down to her toenails. She hoped it didn't show.

"Like father, like son," she said. "No one's going to tell you what to do.

Patrick, you showed how smart you were to deliver the news about who I am in person. There's nothing else for you to do here. Tell you what: when this is all over, I'll give your investigative reporter girlfriend, Cindy is it? I'll give her a ton of 'anonymous source' background for her story."

"Now I know I'm staying." Patrick glared at her. Seamus looked like he wanted to shoot her.

What a fucking mess she had created.

TWENTY-TWO

WE DROPPED PADDY OFF AT Owen's to get his car. He wanted to grocery shop for fresh fruits and veggies to fill his vegetarian needs. Niki and I kept to ourselves on the drive home. I was lost in thought and not paying much attention to the scenery, but as we crossed the intersection to Long Lake, I realized someone had recently plowed a one-lane path through the drifts. The tracks of a number of vehicles were visible in the melting snow. "In a hurry to get home?" I asked.

At Long Lake, we discovered hordes of uniforms: Iron County deputies, the State Police crime scene unit, and rescue squads from Amasa and Crystal Falls. We joined a group of snowmobilers standing behind yellow tape strung between two trees close enough to the shore to see what was happening on the lake, but sufficiently removed to stay out of the way. Bartelle stood on the ice about fifteen feet away from a watery hole. Niki wandered to the tallest of the snowmobilers and asked what was going on.

"On the police band, they said a snow machine broke through the ice. Got us a camp yonder." He waved toward Michigamme. "Course the problem is they can't get no machines out on the ice, so they had to wait for guys in dry suits. Ain't seen no body yet, but see there?" He pointed toward the near shore. "They snaked a couple hundred feet of towline across the ice and winched out the yellow Arctic Cat with the flaming red stripes. Belongs to Jimmie Heitzmann. Got him a camp around Witch Lake."

Niki and I followed his pointed finger and shared a glance of agreement. We had met that snowmobile the first day we explored this area. Now I was sure that a couple of days ago it had zipped by us on The Grade near Amasa.

"Divers just went in?" Niki asked.

With a *pffft,* the guy ejected a stream of tobacco juice from between his two front teeth. "Only one. Body probably drifted under the ice toward the outlet."

The diver popped up and summoned Bartelle. We were too far away to hear the words, but Bartelle ordered a deputy to slide the towline across the ice again. What else was down there?

The diver hauled the line under the water and popped up a minute later. Bartelle signaled to the guy running the winch, who cranked up the loud gasoline-powered motor. After ten feet of line, Bartelle gave the stop sign. From the water, the diver pushed two concrete blocks onto the ice.

Niki pulled my head toward her so she could whisper into my ear. "I got a bad feeling there's a body attached to those blocks."

I realized what had happened. The spot on Long Lake I had originally thought was a large ice fishing hole wasn't. Someone had chopped through the ice and dumped a body weighted with cement blocks. A shiver ran up my spine as I wondered if the person had been dropped into the lake dead or alive.

The diver ducked under the water and Bartelle reached into the hole and between them they lifted a body onto the ice. From Niki I heard a great intake of air.

"It's Brandon."

Another mystery solved. I had no doubt that if Niki had not escaped, she would have worn her own set of cement blocks.

Two cops laid the body on a tarp and carried it to shore. The police photographer scurried around taking pictures. Other than waterlogged, the body looked in good shape; yet if my supposition was correct, it had been in the lake a month or more.

As if reading my mind, Niki said, "Very cold water slows decomposition. They need to take pictures immediately because once exposed to the air, the corpse will quickly deteriorate. The diver's going back in. Are there more?" She faced the group of guys and asked, "Anyone got a pencil and paper I can use?"

She wrote a short note to Bartelle and handed it to the officer assigned to make sure none of the civilians got too close. After one look at Niki's note, he called another officer over to take it to Bartelle, who read the message and shoved it in his coat pocket. I later caught him frowning at Niki.

After a quarter hour, the diver surfaced. From the reaction of the cops, I surmised he had found something else. The police soon carted a second body to shore. This one was dressed for snowmobiling with helmet, gloves, a heavy wool shirt layered over insulated coveralls, but no coat. He was our fire bomber and justice had been served. He must have been half-frozen driving the snowmobile without a coat. Embarrassed by my pleased reaction, I hoped he'd died of an immediate heart attack when he hit the water rather than the more cruel death by drowning.

The loquacious tobacco expectorator speculated on whether the body was Heitzmann. Too tough to tell with the helmet still on, but he seemed to have the right height and build. The police photographer gave a signal, and one of the cops removed the victim's helmet. With the cops standing around, it took a while before we could catch a decent look at his face.

Next to us, twin jets of brown juice stained the snow. "Hey, I know that guy," he yelled. A smile lit his face. To us, he said, "That *is* Jimmie. Just wait till I tell the missus."

An officer took him aside, notepad in hand, pen at the ready. Bartelle motioned Niki to meet him away from listening ears. I tagged along.

"What's so important that it can't wait?" Bartelle asked.

"Two things. The guy with the concrete weights is Brandon Newhouse." Bartelle put on his steely stare. "What's the second?"

Niki shook her head. "Can't tell you here, but you need to hear it. We're staying at Seamus's cabin. Stop by when you're done."

Bartelle nodded agreement to Niki and jabbed a hard finger into my chest, setting me on my heels. "You're playing with fire, McCree. I hope you have insurance."

BARTELLE SAW THE THREE PAIRS of boots parked outside the sliding door on the screened porch of McCree's cabin. Inside, McCree, his son, and the woman who called herself Niki sat around a table playing cards by the light and hiss of propane lamps. He stamped off the snow—he didn't trust them enough to go shoeless. Warm air rushed out as he opened the door. Quickly getting inside, he shrugged off his jacket.

"Have a seat," McCree said. "Can we get you something to eat? Drink?" He pulled a chair from the wall and added it to the table. "You've had a long day."

Bartelle noticed the clock hung from a nail on the wall. *Jeez-o-Pete, how had it gotten to be nine o'clock already?* He could have sworn it was only about an hour after sunset. What had happened to the time? Had he zoned out? He needed sleep, for sure. While McCree settled the chair into place, he automatically scoped out the cabin: single room, adequate wood stove with a blazing fire. Wet wool scenting the air from a nearby drying rack. Three propane lamps hissed and added to the warmth. A double bed, the table he sat down at, and a chest of drawers furnished the room, which he gauged was a cozy fifteen by twenty-five.

He took the offered chair. "You made sure I came here tonight instead of getting some much-needed rest. Although come to think of it, you've had as little sleep as me."

"Sure you don't want anything?" Patrick asked. "I've got stew ready to warm up." Bartelle looked around and didn't see any pot of stew. "We do the cooking on the porch. All I have to do is light the burner."

"It's tasty, but vegetarian," Seamus said.

Mention of the food triggered his stomach, which growled at its emptiness.

"One vote for stew," Patrick said. Everyone laughed as though it was an inside joke and to Bartelle's surprise, he found himself laughing as well. "Coming right up."

McCree poured him a glass of water from a gallon jug. Bartelle drained it, and McCree poured another. Bartelle tipped the glass toward the woman. "Just start talking. I'll ask questions if something isn't clear. I'm recording it." He pressed the start button on the digital recorder, set it on the table, and announced the date, time, place, and persons present.

McCree interrupted. "It's actually eight-ten. Technically we're in Central Time, but I keep the camp on Eastern Time since we're only a mile south of the Eastern Time Zone."

That at least explained why he thought he'd lost an hour.

"I want to formally introduce myself," the woman said. "I'm an agent for the FBI working undercover, using the name Bethany Palmer. The FBI has not authorized me to provide you with my real name as it may jeopardize national security. I will give you my AIC's name and number and you or the sheriff can hash it out with him."

Bartelle felt a thousand emotions rip through him. He was pretty sure none of them showed on his face. He felt vindicated: he hadn't bought the woman's story. He was ticked off: he hadn't figured her as an undercover agent. He was doubly ticked off: he had forgotten to check on the results of his subpoena of McCree's phone records. He was ticked off squared: a fellow officer had been lying to him all along, preventing him from doing his job.

His anger soon changed to a combination of discouraged and enraged. He was finally making progress on the case—cases—even if he did end the day with two more bodies than he had started with. And now the FBI was going to hijack all the work. He'd be the kid at the candy store pressing his nose against the window.

"Proceed, Agent X." She appeared to ignore his sarcasm, assuming she had even realized it for what it was.

"Brandon Newhouse and Bethany Palmer," she said, "were research biologists hired to study wolves by an outfit we believe has ties to possible domestic terrorist groups. Homeland Security thinks they're funding their operation smuggling stuff in through Canada. I replaced Bethany. You pulled Brandon's body from the lake. He got sick before I did, but I must have been out of it when he died. My AIC can give you Brandon's contact information and pretty much anything else you want to know about him. We researched him thoroughly.

"The project Bethany and Brandon signed up for was supposed to take place near Sault Ste. Marie, which is, of course, a major border crossing with Canada. Brandon and I flew there and Brett Aho picked us up. On the drive to the base camp, he told us plans had changed: they had gotten permits from Michigan DNR to trap and track wolves in the central U.P., so he was taking us there.

"I never saw any contraband: no drugs, no weapons, nothing at Brett's camp— the one someone torched. He's the only person we saw. Someone provisioned the place while we were out tracking wolves. The only thing that really tells me we're onto something is the effort someone made to try to kill me—and they had no idea I was an agent."

"Unless," McCree said, "you said something while you were delirious with fever." Agent X blanched. Patrick came in from the porch, placed a steaming bowl of stew on the table, and handed Bartelle a blue-checked cloth napkin and a soupspoon. Bartelle wafted the stew's aroma like he was some kind of professional taster. He noted a variety of spices he couldn't quite name, so he dug in. Tasted as wonderful as it smelled. Looked like it was simple enough to make. Maybe he should get the recipe.

"There's a little more if you want it," Patrick said. "And be careful of the bay leaf." Bartelle used the cover of eating the excellent stew to formulate his questions. The propane lamp above the table started to lose its full glow, and soon the only light and hiss came from the other two lamps in the room. No one made a move to switch lamps.

"End of story," Agent X said. "Anything from Brandon's body give you a clue about his death?"

"The ME didn't think there was water in his lungs, so he was dead before he was dumped into the lake. Cement was probably to make sure the body didn't float once the ice broke up. Second guy probably drowned. Neither of you recognized him?"

They hadn't, but they told him about recognizing the snowmobile. An uncomfortable silence filled the cabin. Bartelle finished the bowl of stew, pronounced it delicious, and threw the elephant on the table. "FBI bringing in a team tomorrow?"

Agent X gave him a big smile. "Nope. In fact, my orders are to get out of Dodge. We respectfully request that you destroy the recording and notes of this conversation to protect our investigation. It should be easy for your people to 'discover' all this information now you know what to look for." She air-quoted with her fingers. "We expect the mystery of Niki will remain unsolved."

Bartelle could tell that everyone was waiting for his reaction. He slowly drank the remaining water in his glass and leaned back in the chair. He patted his lips with the napkin and carefully folded it along the creased lines. "All well and good for the FBI," Bartelle said. "But, that is one decision that will not be mine."

TWENTY-THREE

SHORTLY AFTER BARTELLE LEFT, I used the outhouse. Upon my exit, I spotted Owen Lyndstrom walking up the drive with two guys dressed head to foot in camo. The camo was summer–fall, shades of greens and browns; the first leaf wouldn't arrive for two months. Owen left the two outside "to stand guard" and lugged three semi-automatic rifles inside. From a canvas bag slung over his shoulder, he produced boxes of ammunition, which he thunked on the table.

"Me and the boys are takin these here woods back startin right now."

"What do you mean?" I said.

"What I mean is these woods are for huntin and fishin and trappin and for breathin free air, and every man's got a right to live out here if he wants to. Me and the boys are puttin on a . . . what's they call it? . . . a 24/7 operation. We ain't allowin anyone to harass you again. Shootin up someone's place. Tryin to burn them out. No sir. That shit's over and done with. Pardon my French, ma'am." Owen doffed his cap in Niki's direction.

"We got two guys stationed at the head of the lake where Lukes Road splits from Shank Lake, and these two," he pointed through the window toward the Camo Boys, "will watch the road where it comes into your property in case someone tries a back way in. We tried walkie-talkies but they aren't workin so good in the woods, so I'll ride the road between 'em. That should do 'er. Oh, I almost forgot: the password for tonight is 'Nessie'—you know, the Loch Ness Monster? Think you can remember?"

I had picked a bad time for a gulp of water. Hearing "Nessie" I snorted, which caused a coughing jag, which I tried to end by slapping my thigh. The instantaneous bolt of pain from my injured leg immediately ended the coughing. They should have that cure in the medical texts. Fortunately, anyone seeing tears in my eyes would assume laughter, not pain was the cause.

I was concerned the boys would be more likely to shoot each other than prevent another attack, so although I was pretty sure arguing with Owen wasn't going to do any good, I needed to try. "Didn't you hear the guy who tried to kill us drowned in Long Lake?"

Niki put her arm around Owen's shoulders. "That's so sweet of you. Wouldn't it be easier if we packed our stuff and stayed in town?"

Owen squirmed away from Niki, stood by the door, hands on his hips—a picture of exasperation. I knew Niki's well-intentioned gambit was about to backfire.

"We don't run from trouble up here. We don't look for it, neither, but if it comes . . . well, we take her on." He turned from Niki and spoke to me. "Jimmie Heitzmann— the drowned guy? Something went wrong with that boy over in Iraq. He was a grunt, not a general. He didn't get no idea himself to kill you. Somebody pointed him, and whoever that asshole is—sorry, ma'am—he's still around and maybe he's already got him another Jimmie Heitzmann. You see what I'm sayin?"

Owen's glare shifted between Niki and me. Paddy looked up from the laptop he had been pecking away on. "What my father forgot to say was 'thank you.' He thinks he can do everything himself, and he's reluctant to ask for help. I hope your trip to the VA wasn't anything serious?"

Owen's countenance smoothed out. "That warn't for me. Guy from the VFW got readmitted last week. He and I both had a little colon cancer a few years ago." He must have seen the concern on our faces. "Me, they just gotta check the exhaust pipe once a year. He ain't been that lucky. Youse folks need anythin else? Otherwise we'll get out of yer hair. You remember the password, right?"

"Nessie," we said simultaneously.

Owen smiled approval. "And load them guns before you get to yackin."

"Speaking of thank-yous," I said. "Who can I pay for the work your cousins did on closing up the house?"

"Them boys don't want nothin. They was happy to do it. It'd be right nice if you could pay them for the supplies. I'll let you know how much it was."

Owen and the Camo Boys drove away. Paddy took one of the guns and loaded ammunition while Niki watched, an approving expression on her face.

"Where did you learn that?" I asked.

"From someone else who doesn't look for trouble but is ready if it comes." At my confused expression he added, "Abigail taught me." He confirmed the safety was on before setting the first gun in a corner and grabbing the second one.

When had that happened? It wasn't while I was around, but since Abigail lived near Paddy maybe . . . The mention of Abigail's name changed the warm stew to a chunk of iron ore in my stomach. The time with Niki had been fine, but she wasn't Abigail. No one else could be. I shook my head, then realized Paddy and Niki were watching me. I'd have to ask about his seeing her when we were alone. "We're going to have to figure some way to get Owen and the other guys to give up this guard duty. I'm afraid one of them will get hurt."

"Let me get this right," Niki said. "You're willing to risk your life—you who would prefer never to touch a gun. You're willing to risk Patrick's life—your only child. But you don't want those guys out there helping protect you and yours because they might get hurt? That about it?"

Paddy laughed. "He may be a math guy, but that doesn't mean he's logical. He is Irish, after all."

BOSS FLICKED ON A LIGHT in the camp to hold back the onset of night. The Mitten Men were off reconnoitering McCree and the girl. They had shown themselves to be excellent trackers and marksmen, each drilling a coyote. Boss planned to give them the pelts as souvenirs from the mission. Late in the afternoon, Boss had wandered through town and gathered the news trickling in from the woods. It was damned ironic: Jimmie killed Brett, and Brett's dropping Brandon through the ice after he died of the Legionnaires' disease had ultimately killed Jimmie when Jimmie drove through the thin ice over Brett's hole. Evened out their karma and saved the Mitten Men the task of tracking down Jimmie and eliminating that loose end. What really cranked Boss's engine tonight was McCree and the girl still staying out in the woods. It would make their removal much easier and that was worth celebrating.

Boss got up, retrieved another beer from the kitchen, and returned to the couch. Sitting down triggered a coughing fit. Two, three, four minutes, Boss kept hacking away. Chest felt like it was in a vice. Thought it was under control and started hacking again. The April Fools' plan was still three long weeks away. According to the doctor's timetable, the lung cancer wouldn't win for another three months. Boss kicked the coffee table. *I will get this done.*

Boss hooked the Inspiron 2500 into the phone line, went through the painfully slow dial-up routine, and downloaded a message from NuWrldYooper@gmail.com.

Short and sweet: "Magic potion concentration working great. Sufficient supplies ready by March 13. Delivery on Sunday the 15th?"

The Ides of March was a week from tomorrow. Boss typed a one-word reply: "Yes."

The excitement kicked off another hacking spree. Maybe they should push up the original timetable. April Fools' had a cachet to it any other date lacked; but really, who would get the joke? Signing up the Loonies at the retirement home had gone better than expected. Maybe an incentive would get Laughing Loon's management to push up the work? Boss imagined the pitch to get management to move the date when they did their annual HVAC maintenance: "We're trying to keep all our people busy and this is a slack time of the year, so if you . . .

Or should I make it an all-of-a-sudden thing? "Another client went bankrupt and so it frees up some time . . ."

A truck crunched into the driveway. Moments later, the Mitten Men were inside. "Looks like five guards," Spider said. "Two got them a checkpoint at the top of the lake. Got two more stationed closer to McCree's place, maybe three-eighths of a mile away. Fifth guy is driving a truck up and down the roads. Going real slow."

"Can you take them?" Boss asked.

Digger grabbed a beer from the fridge without asking, which Boss didn't like, but didn't make a fuss about. Spider answered, "They're sitting ducks, but we'll need one more person. Those trophies on the wall yours or did they come with this place?"

Boss took umbrage but didn't let it show. "What's the plan?"

"We could avoid the guards altogether and get into McCree's place, but killing them will generate a lot of noise. We don't want to have to shoot our way past five alert guys getting out, which means we take care of them first. Supposed to be bad weather tomorrow night, which should help."

"Why not tonight?" Boss asked.

"To get here, we've been up most of the last twenty-four hours. With all those guards we need some planning. We'll do this tomorrow. Relax. A day isn't going to kill you."

Spider waited until Digger downed the beer before continuing.

"When the truck driving between the two checkpoints reaches the head of the lake, we have three of them in the same spot. Your job will be to take care of those three. Problem is, when you hose the three down, the other two guards will be alerted. So I'll take care of the other two at the same time."

"Still leaves the targets," Boss said, seeing the hole in the plan.

"Digger'll wait for them and cut 'em down if they leave the house. If they stay barricaded inside, I'll join him for the turkey shoot. Once you take care of your three, hoof it to our truck, and pick us up."

"Why your truck, not mine?"

"Locals know your truck and our plates aren't traceable."

They spent an hour and a couple of beers discussing contingency plans: what they would do if there were more guys the next night; how they would handle it if anyone got hurt unexpectedly. After planning petered out, the conversation turned to politics, and Boss got into a stump speech. "There is not a lick of difference between the Democrats and the Republicans when it comes to anything that really matters. Big corporations bought them both. Damned regulations nearly killed my bank, but they spend billions to save people who should be in jail. We need to start fresh."

Spider shot Digger a sideways glance; stillbirthed whatever Digger had planned to say. "I mostly agree," Spider said in a neutral voice, "but in our neck of the woods, we all would have been hurting big time if the government hadn't given the automakers a helping hand."

Boss grew red in the face. "Government Motors, you mean? Would have been better off if we let them die. Anybody can't run a profitable business deserves to go bankrupt. This country was founded by individuals for individuals. Nobody told Daniel Boone where and when he could hunt."

Digger stormed outside, which cut Boss's rant short. "What's his problem?"

"Four generations of his family worked for Chrysler. Sometimes that skews his perspective on what government should and shouldn't do. Best we get going."

Boss saw Spider out and popped one last beer to chase down the painkillers before going to bed. It would have been interesting to debate the Mitten Men on the federal government. Didn't matter, though, because in a few months, once the militia eliminated most of the incumbents, they'd see the light. Tomorrow was going to be an interesting day. Boss's last decision before falling asleep was to go ahead and accelerate the schedule at the Laughing Loon.

OWEN'S SOLDIERS HAD CONSTRUCTED A makeshift roadblock using brush and downed trees. I rolled down the window as they opened the path. "We're heading to the Iron Mountain airport. Here's one of the guns. There'll just be the two of us now."

"New password for today," one of the guys said, "Snuffleupagus." Everyone got a good laugh.

At the airport, Niki retrieved a package containing her ID. I assumed the FBI sent it and when I asked, she answered by waggling her eyebrows.

While we waited, she put on a full-court press to convince us to leave the U.P. until this imbroglio played itself out. "You two have nothing to prove to anyone," she summarized.

Paddy crossed his arms. "Except ourselves."

Niki hugged Paddy, gave me a quick peck, and proceeded through the screening. Paddy and I watched from the parking lot as her plane took off, plugging our ears at the jet's blast. As soon as we pulled our fingers from our ears, he said. "We've got a stop to make on the way back."

I gave him my patented sideways look.

"Rita Pirhonen lives at the Laughing Loon Senior Care Center in Crystal Falls. She and Jimmie Heitzmann have been talking on the phone a lot over the last few months. Maybe he told her something that might help."

Myriad thoughts roiled my mind. How had Paddy developed this connection? Having never heard of the Laughing Loon Senior Care Center until I looked at the viatical settlement for Bartelle's aunt who lived there, now it had come up a second time.

"Fill in the blanks," I said.

"You found the guy's gun leaning against a tree with his coat? His cell phone was in the coat pocket and I checked his call logs—only one number. I used the internet to get the owner's name and—"

"We don't have internet."

"When Owen showed up last night, I was working on my laptop, which has satellite internet. The number belongs to Rita Pirhonen, who resides at Laughing Loon."

I could only hope he had obtained all the information legally, but the fact that he didn't discuss this until Niki, also known as Federal Agent Pendergast, was no longer around, left me wondering.

TWENTY-FOUR

IN THE LAUGHING LOON VESTIBULE, we shook the rain off our coats and signed the guest register. After getting lost in the hallways reeking of disinfectant, we eventually arrived at Rita Pirhonen's room. She held out her hand first to Paddy and then to me. The strength in her arthritic hands surprised me.

"You're the fella that took in the lady with amnesia?" she asked after we introduced ourselves. She settled us on a couple of rickety dining room chairs and offered something to wet our whistle, all the while sneaking peeks at Paddy's battered face, his head still wrapped in white. I'd gotten used to it and hadn't considered the effect it would have on others. "How awful that someone tried to shoot you folks. The radio says they found the person drowned?"

"Did you hear who the person was?" I asked.

She scratched her head. "Yes, but I don't remember the name."

"Jimmie Heitzmann?" Paddy offered.

She placed her hand in her lap and looked openly at Paddy. "Could be . . . yes, that does sound right. Why did he do it?"

She gave no indication of recognizing the name. This was not what I'd anticipated. "I know this will sound like a weird question, but please bear with me." I flashed her a smile, which I hoped looked comforting. "Did you happen to loan your cell phone to anyone?"

"Oh, dear no. I used to have one. My daughter made me get it when I still lived at home. She insisted I have it in case I fell down, so that I could call for help. Now we have these gadgets." She retrieved a small electrical device attached to a chain around her neck and held it out for us to see. We leaned in to get a good look. "No matter where I am on the property, all I have to do is press the button and the staff can locate me. Now who was I talking with? It seems so long ago. Was it that nice lady they have here . . . what do they call her? . . . the ombudsman. Yes, I think so. The ombudsman. If I never used the cell phone, she said I should turn it in and cancel the contract."

"When was that?" I asked.

Her hands fluttered in front of her and settled again on her lap. "I'm sorry, I don't remember. You young fellas can't imagine how hard it is when you can't remember everything like you used to. Last year sometime?"

Paddy cleared his throat. "Did you return the phone?"

"It had to go to Iron Mountain where I got it. Of course I have no way to do that. One of the deacons from church took it. They have a collection box for old cell phones and another one for eyeglasses. I don't get bills for it, so I'm sure everything's okay."

I traded glances with Paddy. He had tucked his bottom lip under his teeth, a thinking gesture someone once pointed out he had inherited from me.

"Which church?" I asked. "Those church ladies can be such a comfort, can't they?"

"Oh, my yes, they can," she said. "It's the Presbyterian Church here in town. Young man, I'm sorry to be nosy, but it's a privilege of my age. Does it still hurt?"

Leaving Mrs. Pirhonen and Paddy to chat, I used the facilities, which consisted of a commode, shower stall, and pedestal sink. Grab bars decorated all the walls. This wasn't a hospital, but I still made sure to thoroughly wash my hands with antibacterial soap. While I waited for the hot water to get reasonably warm—it never did get hot—I snooped through her medicine cabinet. TV detectives always find something interesting in people's bathrooms. Maybe they know what to look for; I didn't see anything unusual.

FIFTEEN MINUTES BEFORE SUNSET, PADDY and I reached the roadblock. "Snuffleupagus," I said through the opened truck window. "Owen, who came up with these passwords?"

"Grandkids. Oldest one is into dinosaurs and saw a TV special on the Loch Ness Monster. He wants to check all the lakes around here, see if he can find him his own Nessie. Youngest is into Sesame Street. Loves Snuffy."

"You got any other grandchildren?" I asked.

"Not yet. One in the oven, though. We turned some visitors away. Claimed they come to talk to you. Flashed FBI badges, but wouldn't leave no card. I told them they was on private property and, unless they had a warrant, they wasn't gettin no further. They said they was gonna wait until you returned." Owen indicated with a bob of his head one of the guys who, in response, ejected a stream of tobacco juice through the gap where his front teeth should have been.

The guy towered over Owen, and I realized I'd met him at Long Lake when they pulled out the bodies. "Nice seeing you again," I said.

"You know Bruce?" Owen sounded almost offended that something had happened without his knowing about it. "Bruce started lettin air out of their tire to make sure they stayed. They hightailed it. I'm not sure they were legit. I didn't think them Hoover guys were supposed to swear."

Everyone laughed. I kind of felt bad for whomever Special Agent Whatshisname had ordered up, probably as a response to my hanging up on him. I felt confident I'd see them again.

"Startin tonight," Owen said, penetrating my fog, "we're leaving our trucks down by the Amasa mill and four-wheelin in. Town's already closed their roads to heavy traffic for the duration. The frost is coming up real early with this rain and warm temperatures. Muck'll get so bad on these roads you'll get sucked in up to the runnin boards. Usually gets cold enough for a few days so's the roads freeze at night and you can get out 'fore sunrise. Course, you ain't gonna get in again with anythin bigger than four-wheelers, and not towin no trailer neither. Then, I won't be able to bring in no new supplies. You'll have ta consider headin into town soon."

PADDY PREPARED DINNER WHILE WE still had light on the cabin porch. I restoked the wood stove. My original plans with Abigail had been to stay the winter and leave before mud season. Well, mud season was here with a vengeance, and it was time to "act my age" as my mother would say. My stubborn Irish pride that refused to let me accept help was not a mature response, as evidenced both by Niki's direct arguments and Owen's gentle suggestion.

"Paddy?" I yelled over the knife slapping the cutting board as he chopped carrots for the salad. He jutted out his chin in acknowledgement that he'd heard. "With the roads turning to goop, there's nothing we can do out here. I'm thinking we should head into town. I can arrange for repairs to the house. If we leave early tomorrow while the road's frozen, Owen's guards can follow us out and get back to their lives. We've proved our point."

He deliberately laid the knife on the cutting board. "You trying to get me out of here?"

He'd nailed part of my thinking, but I wasn't going to admit it. "You can stay with me in town if you want, but there's nothing really for you to do."

He picked up the knife and drummed the blade on the table. "Maybe you should hook the trailer to the truck and haul out the ATVs."

"Good idea. Just in case we want to get back in before the roads dry up. Owen will let me store them at his place. He won't even notice they're there with all the junkers decorating his yard."

In the waning light, I donned a headlamp, hooked up the trailer, and discovered Jimmie Heitzmann had stolen the ATV keys the night he tried to kill us.

To avoid breaking the police tape, I used Paddy's method of entering the house and scrambled up the ladder I propped against the railing of the master bedroom deck. The unlocked sliding door yielded to my tug. Besides getting spare keys, I wanted to make sure the repairs were holding with all the rain we'd been having.

The upstairs was unaffected by the attack, but as I walked down the staircase, my legs felt leaden. I crunched broken glass with every step. A broom leaned against the couch next to a small cleared area. One of the workmen had probably started to clean up and the police stopped him. Owen's workers had removed the double-hung windows and stacked them in the kitchen. They cut the OSB to fit into the window frames and, on closer inspection, I realized they had siliconed the heck out of them. They had even filled in the bullet holes on the other side of the house with silicone. Water was not going to get through their repairs.

I grabbed keys from their pegs by the back door and stuck them in my pocket. Sometime later, I found myself slumped in a chair staring at the lake through the wall of windows. Tears streaked my cheeks. I had designed this house, and it was like a child to me. Everything here could be fixed, but its pureness was corrupted. Telling myself it was "only camp" didn't help. I gave into the sobs, realizing the tears were not solely for the losses I had suffered, but for the kindness of strangers. Owen, the old cuss, had gone out of his way to rally his friends to fix my house and now act as guards.

I left the house the way I had come in and replaced the ladder on its hooks behind the garage. After dinner, Paddy worked on his computer. I curled next to the wood stove and read to the sounds of rain pounding on the roof and the hiss of propane lamps. Having made the decision to leave, I felt relaxed. When the book slipped from my hand and clunked to the floor, I called it a day and set the alarm for five a.m.

ALL DAY, BOSS EXPERIENCED AS much anticipation as an elephant in the twenty-second month of pregnancy. It took every scintilla of effort to seem natural on the outside. Whatever the pastor said at church had gone in one ear and out the other. The social hour afterwards had been interminable, with everyone talking about spring breakup coming early this year, maybe winter was over, and wouldn't that be just great, and did Boss know Linda Cather slipped getting out of the bathtub and chipped her elbow, and *blah, blah, blah.*

On the way out the door, Boss learned the cops hadn't let McCree back into his house, which meant they were using the cabin. Digger needed to watch the right structure. Boss begged off lunch, headed straight to camp, and prepared a real Sunday dinner: half a chicken breast, mashed potatoes with gravy, and canned sweet corn. With the meal consumed, dishes washed up and put away, it left plenty of time for a nap that lasted most of the afternoon.

The Mitten Men showed up around ten p.m. and everyone napped again after finalizing the plan with Boss's new information. They scheduled departure for one in the morning so the attack would begin between three-thirty and four, when the guards should be least alert.

The dirt roads were holding up fairly well despite the rain, which had recently morphed to a steady drizzle. At two twenty-five a.m., Spider backed the truck into an old skidder trail a hundred yards past the turn off to Shank Lake. The three warriors, as Boss thought of the group, put on winter camo, donned white packs and, with their assigned weapons, slipped into the woods.

Their GPS allowed them to parallel the road while remaining hidden from it. Twenty-five minutes later, they reached Boss's assigned ambush location. They observed two guards shuffling around behind a makeshift barricade. A whiff of cigarette smoke reached Boss, setting up a desire so strong that the only way to fight it off required clamped teeth, clenched hands, and curled toes. Boss had quit cold turkey, but now wondered why.

Seven minutes later, a four-wheeler *putt-putted* in from the direction of McCree's place. Boss shot Spider a look saying "Where's the truck?"

Spider shrugged. "Swapped the truck for an ATV," he whispered.

The driver made a three-point turn, stopped long enough to steal a cigarette—driving Boss crazy once again—and slowly drove off.

The three synchronized their watches. In whispered consultation they set the assault for as soon after three forty-five as the four-wheeler reappeared. Boss leaned against a tree, taking comfort in its solid feel, and watched the Mitten Men follow their GPS toward McCree's place.

Twenty-Five

PERCUSSIVE BLASTS OF NEARBY GUNFIRE woke me from a comfortable sleep next to the wood stove.

"Paddy," I called across the room to the lump still sleeping on the bed, "Get up! No, stay down! Keep below the windows. We need to get out of here."

Squirming loose of the sleeping bag, I reached for my glasses and knocked them skittering across the floor. Ominously, the shooting stopped. I pulled on a T-shirt and felt the tag sticking into my Adam's apple—backwards—left it, and slipped on a wool shirt. Patting the floor softly in front of me, I crawled around until I found the glasses against the far wall.

Paddy tossed me a coat and slithered on the floor to the back window. "Get rifles, Dad." He raised a window and forced the screen, shattering the quiet with the screech of metal on metal. He tumbled outside. I handed him the two rifles and, favoring my injured leg, climbed through the window headfirst.

"Where to?" he whispered.

I patted my pocket and felt relieved at the hard outlines of the keys I had retrieved from the house. "ATVs are our best bet."

We cut down the hill behind the cabin to a small ravine where we came to the head of an old trail we had created years ago. We followed it along a ridge running between the cabin and the house and came out near the vernal pond, which was now filling with snowmelt.

I didn't see anybody near the house. "You cover me and then I'll cover you. I'll run to the corner of the garage. As soon as I get there, you go. Okay?"

He shot me a thumbs-up, stuck his right glove in his pocket, and released the gun's safety. I mirrored his actions.

Mentally counting to three, I took off across the open yard. Fifty feet had never felt farther. With each step, pain shot from my left thigh down to the sole of my foot and up my back to my neck. To avoid screaming once I stopped at the side of the building, I shoved the glove from my pocket into my mouth and bit down hard. The taste and smell of oil and grease nearly caused me to gag, but had the analgesic effect of making me forget about the pain. Around the material I panted quick breaths and waved Paddy on. He kept low to the ground and covered the distance in a fraction of my time.

In a whispered exchange, I insisted I could handle one of the ATVs— my left leg had nothing to do once we were riding. Riding single, we could go faster and, if something happened to one ATV, we had a spare. He agreed, and since I was more adept with the Honda's manual shift; Paddy took the Polaris with its automatic transmission. We slung the rifles over our shoulders and entered the garage.

I was glad I hadn't had time to drive the ATVs onto the trailer. The moment we cranked the ignitions we would give away our position. Maneuvering the ATVs off the trailer would have taken way too much time. Using my left hand's fingers to count down from five, we both cranked the engines when I curled my last finger. The Honda caught immediately, but the Polaris cranked like it wasn't getting gas. I leaned over and pulled out its choke. It burst to life. "Go. Go. Go!" I yelled and off he went.

Roaring up the driveway, I shifted into second, then third. At the turn onto the road, I heard the close-by triple bark of a rifle. From the corner of my eye, I saw muzzle flashes from the intersection of the road and the cabin driveway. As I roared away, I heard two more bursts, and felt something tug my jacket, nearly knocking me off the ride.

BOSS FELT JAUNTY ON THE walk to the truck, sucking on a cigarette stolen from one of the corpses, celebrating the successful attack. As planned, the first burst caught the guy on the four-wheeler. The second got one of the guards before he figured out what had happened. The third target took off like a rabbit. In the night scope, he showed up fine. The third burst nailed him mid-stride, but wasn't a clean kill. Boss walked to the prostrate form, forgot to change from three-shot burst to single shot for the *coup de grâce*, and blew off the back of his head. He was the one with the cigarettes and clearly couldn't use them in whatever afterlife there was.

Once at the truck, Boss locked down the four-wheel-drive mechanism and, before taking off, mumbled a mantra to remember to keep moving through any mud patches, especially since the Mitten Men's tires didn't have aggressive treads. Stop in the wrong spot and they'd be walking out.

The truck slid sideways before trenching through one soft spot. Otherwise, the road held. The truck's headlights caught Digger approaching on a stolen ATV. Boss didn't dare stop the truck in the low area and kept plowing forward. Digger veered off at the last minute, barely avoiding a collision. Dismounting, he ran hell-bent for leather to Boss's side of the truck, yanked open the door, and yelled something Boss could barely hear.

Digger motioned for Boss to remove the earplugs.

"I said, two of 'em got away on ATVs. Spider took one of these yokel's wheels," he inclined his head toward the bodies sprawled under a hemlock, "and is following them." He waved toward the woods away from the lake. "He says you're to drive to where we hid the truck and block the intersection. Nothing gets by you, hear? Hose down anything that gets there before we do. *Comprendé?*"

"What happened?" Boss asked, keeping the exasperation at bay.

"They snuck out the back while I was watching the front. I winged the one. Spider's on their tail. I'll loop around the top and close the trap. Don't sit there like shit on a stick. Git and be useful." Digger ran to the four-wheeler, spun it in a tight circle spitting mud all over Boss, and took off.

Boss's hands shook. One winged; two untouched. This was not what was supposed to happen. All the way to the intersection, Boss muttered threats at Digger and Spider for not getting their job done and killing all three of the people in the cabin. Boss seethed at the insult of being told what to do, not to mention the indignity of the mud shower from Digger.

Boss lost traction and spun wheels going through the trenched-up area, thought the truck was stuck, then felt first one, then two wheels gain traction and pull the truck out. At the intersection, Boss jockeyed the truck perpendicular to the main road on the Amasa side of the junction with Shank Lake Road. Nothing could get by without stopping, and all roads to Amasa went through the intersection Boss now controlled.

From the east came the first hint of dawn.

I ACCELERATED THE ATV AND tried to catch Paddy. Shank Lake Road came to a dead end at the Net River, and we needed to avoid any traps. In a mile was a cutoff to the other side of the lake. But from there, the only exit not returning us to this side was Lukes Road, which a beaver had flooded last fall. Between the beaver and the current thaw, we had no hope escaping that way. Our only possibility was to outrun them or outfox them by doubling back, because there was no way to successfully cover our tracks. The one advantage I figured I had was a mental map developed over the years of every abandoned road, skidder trail, and path in the vicinity wide enough for an ATV. I caught up to Paddy shortly before an old logging road pushed into the forest. It was our best chance. I motioned for him to take a right.

I had no sooner congratulated myself on picking well when my engine hiccupped. Sounded like a fuel problem. I was sure I had filled both ATV tanks earlier in the week but, leaving nothing to chance, I reached down on the left side and quickly switched the fuel tank to reserve, tapping the bottom gallon of the tank. The engine immediately perked up.

The trail twisted to follow the high ground and, with better suspension on his ATV, Paddy pulled ahead of me. I lost sight of him in the curves and only caught glimpses of him on long straightaways, hunched low to reduce wind resistance. Soon we would come to a T intersection. I sent Paddy a mental image of turning left.

Lowering my head against the wind, I accelerated to catch him and lost ground when I nailed a hole deeper than I anticipated and rooster-tailed through a puddle. Water sprayed the engine and with a hiss, steam bathed both of my legs, warming them well past the point of comfort. Regaining control, I pressed on.

The engine sputtered as though it was running on fumes—much too soon to have depleted the reserve. Was the fuel filter clogged? I used the choke to try to blast out whatever was causing the fuel malfunction and stalled the ATV. It coasted to a stop around a bend. I tried to restart it. And tried again. And again.

No go.

Ahead of me, Paddy roared away.

Behind me, another ATV. Getting closer.

I hopped off my ride and pushed it back into the bend I had just passed. It wasn't much of a plan, but if I could position it at the point where the pursuing ATV would still be going fast, maybe he would run into it or lose control as he swerved to avoid it. Even if he momentarily lost his concentration, I might get the upper hand. I twisted the ATV sideways across the path so it took up more space and looked for a hiding place. In jerking the ATV around, I smelled gas and realized the gas tank had sprung a leak. I cut the lights and removed the gun from the ATV rack. With no night vision, I stumbled around looking for the right place to hide.

This part of the forest consisted mostly of maple, selectively cut maybe twenty years ago, leaving no big trees. No close evergreens to hide in. No big rocks to use as a shield. The best I could do was position myself on the inside of the curve, away from where the pursuer would be looking as he rounded the bend. I closed my eyes to help redevelop night vision and listened to the oncoming ATV.

The simplest thing would be to shoot whoever followed me. The thought of pulling the trigger brought a flashback of the man I had killed when he and an accomplice invaded my Cincinnati house. I did not need more nightmares. I knew I would kill if it was the only way; but maybe I could use the rifle as a club and knock him out before he realized what was happening. If they were riding tandem . . .

Something in the sound of the various ATVs caught my attention. The one chasing me was still coming on. Paddy's was also growing louder as he headed back toward me. I judged the sounds of Paddy's machine and the guy following us—it was going to be close who would get to me first.

Paddy did. He screeched on his brakes and stopped a few feet short of hitting my stalled ATV. "Dad?" he yelled.

"Turn around. I'll hop on," I yelled.

I remained in ambush until he finished maneuvering. The other ATV was almost on us. I grabbed my rifle, limped to Paddy and struggled onto his machine. My left leg now ached with any movement. Before I settled in, Paddy accelerated, slamming my butt onto the ATV and jarring the rifle loose from my grip.

Paddy returned to the intersection where I had hoped he would turn left; his tracks went right. So much for father–son telepathy. I tapped him on the arm and pointed left. This could work to our advantage: if our pursuer wasn't a tracker, he might waste time following the wrong tracks until he discovered Paddy had turned around. At the next intersection, I motioned for Paddy to stop. With his ATV idling, I tried to determine if we were still being followed. No clue; we were too loud. I gave Paddy's shoulder another pat and off we went deeper into the woods.

Wherever we had choices, I pointed Paddy toward the direction I wanted, mentally tracking where we were. I tried for the roughest possible trails while avoiding dead ends. Most of the time, we traveled less than fifteen miles an hour over rock-strewn trails. Although predawn lightened the woods, Paddy continued to steer by the high-beam headlamp.

We finally reached a Y from which we could take the offensive. A mix of pine, hemlock, and balsam grew close to the trail. The evergreens dampened sound, blocked light, and provided a secure hiding place. The two old skidder trails bowed away from each other for three-quarters of a mile before hitting a decent gravel road. From here we could run down one path to the gravel road and cut back on the second trail. We'd ditch the ATV about a quarter mile in and walk through the woods to the first path to set an ambush—assuming he had crashed into my disabled ATV and was far enough behind so we could implement the plan. Once we disabled him, we could make a mad dash down the main road to Amasa and get help.

Time was of the essence. I pointed in the direction I wanted Paddy to take and yelled in his ear, "Goose it!"

Twenty-Six

WE HUDDLED NEXT TO A steep, rocky section of the trail—a place where our pursuer would have to go slowly. Young balsam firs grew densely and hid us from sight. If either Paddy or I had MacGyver's skills, we could have constructed some device to unseat our pursuer as he ATVed by. Without those talents, we ended up in a whispered shouting match, which sounds like an oxymoron, but isn't. We gesticulated, our faces turned red, we said things I later wished we hadn't, and finally I uttered a parent's last resort: *because I said so.* I briefly wondered if those were Custer's last words.

"Fine," Paddy fiercely whispered after I had laid down my parental trump card. "We won't shoot him as he drives by." He yanked the stout branch I had found away from me and ran to the ambush site. I limped behind, each step accompanied by pain sharp enough to take my breath away. When I finally caught up to him he said, "With your leg, you have no prayer of running up and knocking him off his ATV as he goes by. If that's our so-called plan, then I'll do it." He held out his rifle. "If that doesn't work, are you going to be able to pull the trigger?"

Once I caught my breath, I replied. "I already told you. Of course I can . . . and will, if I have to. This isn't like some video game, Paddy. There's no reset button to resurrect the dead."

"I got the point," he said. "Just make sure you hit the right one of us. Here he comes."

The oncoming ATV downshifted at the base of the hill, its engine whining as he maneuvered around and over the rocks in a series of short bursts. Paddy grasped the four-foot-long stave at the end, flexing his fingers like a baseball player waiting for the pitcher to read the signal from the catcher.

Through the trees, I saw a hint of green as the ATV canted toward us while climbing a particularly large rock. Paddy sprang from our hiding place and with a yell modeled on *Braveheart*, swung the limb at the pursuer's exposed neck. A last rock raised the ATV and the blow caught our attacker high on his right shoulder with a muffled thud. Combined with the rider's lean to the left, it was sufficient to knock him off the four-wheeler.

Paddy was right about my leg; it nearly collapsed as I rose to cover them with the rifle. The good news was the guy was unarmed; his rifle was still strapped to the ATV. The bad news was the guy was agile. He came off the ground, and entered a crouch, holding a long blade low, as knife fighters do. So much for being unarmed. I aimed the rifle, but Paddy was moving quickly and I couldn't be sure whom I would hit. I pointed the barrel away from both of them and fired a shot.

Paddy knew I had a gun. He flinched but continued his attack. The shot startled the guy for a fraction of a second—enough for Paddy to start a second swing with the tree limb. The guy leaned away from the blow, but Paddy's actual target was the guy's knife hand. Like a batter tracking a curveball, Paddy adjusted his swing and nailed the hand with a sickening smack. Paddy's follow-through pulled him off balance.

The knife spun into the mud. The guy howled. Instead of grabbing his injured hand he sprang forward and knocked Paddy down, sat on top of him and pounded Paddy's head with his good hand. I grabbed the rifle by the barrel and slammed the stock into his back below his shoulder blades.

Even though his winter coat lessened the impact, the blow reverberated in my arms. As I brought the rifle back for a second try, he turned his head and his mouth formed a perfect "O." If he made any sound, I didn't hear it. I swung again, aiming for the same spot. Paddy heaved to shake off his opponent, and the gunstock slammed into the small of the guy's back, knocking him to the ground.

I brought the rifle above my head to slam it down on the man's knee if he moved, but he didn't. His face showed a frozen scream, his eyes rolled up into his head, his arms shook like he had a seizure.

"You okay, Paddy?" I called over my shoulder.

"Do you think my insurance will cover two broken noses in the same week?"

If he could joke, he was okay. "How's your head?"

"You kidding me? I'll match a McCree hard head to this guy's knuckles any day, but I'm having trouble seeing because of the pain from this nose. Take a look."

Using the ATV's headlights for illumination, I used snow to clear away the blood. His nose was off kilter again and streaming blood. Otherwise, he only had some minor scrapes and bruises. While keeping an eye on our attacker I went through the how-many-fingers routine with Paddy. No concussion. "This is going to hurt," I said. "I'm going to pack your nose with snow to stop the bleeding."

Paddy yowled in anguish during my ministrations. I wasn't cut out to be a doctor: I hated causing Paddy pain, even though I knew what I was doing would lessen future complications. Of course, most doctors don't work on their own kids.

Once his tears stopped he asked, "Now what do we do with this jerk?"

"No way can we take him with us. I'll tie his hands behind him with the elastic thingie from the waist of his jacket. Then we'll take his shoes and socks to make it hard for him to travel."

Paddy paced to ease his pain. "I could whack him on the head with the rifle. That would keep him put for a while." At my glowered disapproval he added, "It was just an idea."

I patted the guy down and found no other weapons or identification. After flipping him face down, I secured his hands behind his back and flipped him back.

From his eyes, I could tell he was in shock. His spasms had stopped but he moaned low, like a cow with indigestion. Paddy sat on his chest while I removed his shoes and socks. Pulling off the last sock, I accidentally scratched him. His foot showed no reaction.

Molten rock filled my stomach.

I pinched the foot. The other foot. Right leg. Left leg. Right arm and he finally flinched.

I spewed last night's dinner like an exploding volcano. Acid burned up my throat and left a vitriolic taste in my mouth.

"What?" Paddy asked.

"Oh my God." I heaved a second time. "I broke his back. He's paralyzed." His running away was not an issue. I rinsed my mouth with snow. Once I stopped shaking, I put his socks and shoes back on as gently as I could. "We need to leave right now." I said to Paddy's back.

Paddy said, "You'll have to drive. I can't see very well. Another ATV's somewhere nearby. I can hear it."

I forced myself to look at the guy on the ground. "We'll bring help as soon as we can."

He stared at the bluing sky and said nothing.

* * *

BOSS SHIFTED FROM FOOT TO foot, needing to pee something fierce. TV cops on stakeout drink endless coffee and never have to go. This wasn't TV and pressure was building. Sure as shoot pull down a zipper and someone would arrive at the intersection.

For a time, when the wind was right, Boss caught a whisper of ATVs, but for the last half an hour had heard nothing more than trees clicking their upper branches together, castanets in the breeze. *Enough already.* Boss turned from the wind to avoid any unpleasantness and was readjusting the zipper when the weak buzz of an engine came from somewhere up the A Grade. Boss rested the gun barrel on the top of a large flat rock, released the safety, and put the gun into full automatic mode. Dawn would arrive in half an hour so visibility was improving, but it wasn't like anyone could really see anything. At least the rain had finally stopped. Boss peered through the scope and listened as the motor grew steadily louder.

Headlights appeared, running fast down the road. Boss treated the light like a sprinting deer, adjusted for its speed and gave a long burst. One headlight shattered and the vehicle jerked right and left before slowing to a stop. The remaining headlight glowed like a Cyclops. *Cripes, I forgot to replace the darn earplugs. I can't hear a thing.*

Boss thought about hosing it down a second time but spotted no movement. From this distance, it looked like one body was crumpled onto the handlebars and a second flung backwards over the back rack. Boss trotted around in a victory dance, sounding like some TV version of Indian warriors.

BARTELLE HAD FORCED HIMSELF TO go to bed by eleven thirty on Monday night and surprised himself by catching five hours of sleep. The case was his for three more hours, until the scheduled conference with the FBI, DEA, ICE—the Immigrations and Customs Enforcement arm of Homeland Security—and God only knew who else would horn in on this mess. Then the power scramble would begin and, with all those initials involved, the chances of the Iron County Sheriff's office retaining control were about zero.

Tex—who had taken a shine to the new nickname—plunked into the chair, pushed a fresh mug of coffee in Bartelle's direction, and tossed a couple packs of blue sweetener across the desk.

"Give me the short version," Bartelle said, "and save the details for the official report." He dumped the chemicals into his coffee, realized Tex had not brought a spoon, and stirred the brew with his finger. "Hot. Hot. Hot." He sucked the finger until the tingling stopped. "Who killed who?"

"Three of Owen's buddies died near the intersection of Shank Lake and Lukes Road. We think it was probably one shooter, based on where we found casings. Ballistics will confirm. Owen's other two friends were killed at a barricade they had set up near the edge of McCree's property. Casings there are from a different caliber weapon. Those match the shells in the gun we found strapped to the ATV in the woods next to the guy with the spider tattoo. He died from a stab wound to the chest.

"I got to give the state crime lab boys in Marquette credit, they are all over this. They just called in a preliminary analysis: the single fingerprint on that rifle belongs to a William Bell—Spiderman."

"So Spiderman killed the two guys and someone else killed the first three?" Bartelle asked.

"We found Spiderman-type shells of the same caliber on the road near the driveway to McCree's little log cabin, so looks like he killed Owen's two guards, fired after the McCrees, and then chased them. Then the McCrees ambushed him in the woods."

Bartelle blew on the coffee and took a slug, felt the warmth slide all the way to his stomach. "Fingerprints on the knife?"

Tex shook his head. "Handle was wiped clean on Spiderman's shirt. There's something else weird: one of the ATVs is missing. Each of Owen's guys brought his own, and we know where all but one of them is."

Bartelle motioned with his hands, asking for more.

"So there has to be three of them—at least. Someone drove away in the missing ATV—someone different from whoever got Spiderman's truck stuck in the mud on Bone Lake Road since there were no ATV tracks in that area. The truck VIN, which sported stolen tags, gave us Bell's name. We pulled his license and the photo matched the stiff. Once we had the name, the lab pulled his prints from the state's records to do the preliminary match. Back to the truck: we can follow its tracks the nine, ten miles from McCree's place. And we only got one set of footprints walking away from the mud wallow."

"Prints in the truck?" Bartelle asked.

"Lots. Gonna take the latent print boys time for those."

"So at least three perps, two of whom got away."

"So far." Tex stretched his arms above his head. "We lost the trail of the truck driver in a swampy area a ways from the truck. We got tracking dogs coming in. Maybe we'll luck out and find the guy has a nearby camp."

"But you don't think so?" Bartelle finished his coffee. Last caffeine this morning or he'd start twitching.

"Anyone with a nearby camp would know not to travel Bone Lake Road after the frost starts coming out. It's a sink hole."

"Think about it," Bartelle said. "These are the same jerks we pull from the lakes each year 'cause they're sure the ice is thick enough to drive their trucks on. It's early spring. He might have thought he could make it."

Tex stood up and paced the room. "We're missing something and I don't think a hundred federales descending on us Northwoods doofuses are going to turn it up. Spiderman was from downstate and had an old record, but he's been clean the last decade. His weapon was top notch, fully automatic. It doesn't look like killing a lot of people caused these guys a lick of concern. It's like the U.P. has become the US–Mexico border."

"Like a drug war? That could explain the DEA's involvement. Sure would be nice if they'd told us something before . . ." Bartelle leaned back in his chair and went into his head-scratching routine. "Are you saying you think McCree is involved somehow? Could he be financing a drug deal?"

"I don't know what I'm saying." Tex flopped back into the chair, which squeaked in protest. "Except we're missing something big. What do you want me to do next? Yesterday, the lab sent the results from the burnt cabin. I can review them or—"

"I don't give a darn about that stuff. I want to nail the missing killers. Work on the weapons. Get all the ballistics right and tell me what kind of gun we're missing. Let me know first thing if the trackers come up with something. Push the state lab on the latents from the truck."

Tex got up to go. "Yes, Sir."

"Wait. I'm about to interview McCree. Has anyone backtracked his movements?"

"It's like he said: they kept the ATV off the main roads and followed a succession of logging roads, skidder trails, and even did some cross-country travel to get around locked gates and such until they hit Tracy Creek Road, which they took to US 141. Couldn't track them once they hit pavement, but it's not too far from there to the gas station in Covington where they made the phone call and waited for us to pick them up."

"Why didn't they go directly to Amasa?" Bartelle asked.

"Claims they heard another ATV heading down the A Grade so they went the other way. I gotta say Sarge, I'll bet the coroner determines McCree did break Spiderman's back, and the guy either didn't want to live a cripple or he didn't want to go back to jail. Who knows? He shoves the knife high into his chest cavity and gets a major artery."

"Why not just slit his throat?'

"You know most suicides don't cut through clothing?" Tex said. "This guy unzipped his jacket, unbuttoned his shirt, and pushed up his undershirt to get to bare skin."

"You sure McCree—the father, that is—doesn't know that fact too?" Bartelle glanced at his watch. "Nothing to say he didn't make it look like a suicide. That Cincinnati homicide lieutenant told us he's killed up close and personal."

"I know you had to arrest him and his kid, just in case, but—"

"Actually, jail is the only place I can be sure McCree is safe, and it allows us to stick a guard outside his kid's hospital room. If they did it, we got 'em locked up. If they didn't, at least they're protected. It'll be the DA's call."

"Sweet. That's why *you're* wearing the stripes. Anyway, I didn't see anything at the various crime scenes to contradict anything McCree said, except he mentioned hearing a burst of gunfire not too long after they had ambushed the Spider guy. We can't match that with anything. At least not yet. I kinda think McCree's on the up and up. He's too nice to have done this."

"Everyone said the same thing about Bernie Madoff."

TWENTY-SEVEN

BEFORE BREAKFAST, A DEPUTY ESCORTED me from my cell in the Iron County jail, where I had spent the night, past the monitoring station and into the interrogation room: drab concrete walls, drab carpeting, four drab chairs arranged around a drab table. This room could depress Little Mary

Sunshine. All that was missing was the one-way mirror, although it was equipped with a camera hanging from the ceiling, and I'm sure it was wired for sound. "Coffee?" he asked.

"I appreciate the offer, but I'm fine, thanks. You know anything about how my son is doing?"

"Sorry." He shut the door behind him. I waited a long time before my first interrogators showed up, my mind wrapped around Paddy's welfare. ICE marched in. They had names. They had badges. They had attitudes. They played good cop/bad cop.

I had innocence—which isn't everything it's cracked up to be—and silence, which is more powerful than most people imagine.

Bad Cop finished his final tirade with, "If you think we can't make you disappear until you talk, you got another thing coming."

I smiled because I would have said I had 'another think coming.' Ain't language grand?

"I'll wipe that grin off your face," Bad Cop snarled and raised his hand as if to strike me. Good Cop hustled him from the room.

"My partner's right. We can keep you under wraps until you tell us what we need to know," Good Cop said. "We really do need your help. Aren't you a patriot?"

Silence.

He patted a four-inch binder. "We know everything there is to know about you . . . and your family. Your father was a decorated police officer. What would he think about your refusal to help us?"

I would have loved to see what was really in that binder, but his sharing was unlikely. "Since it's been more than an hour and you might have early Alzheimer's, I'll repeat what I said when you first introduced yourselves. I'll be happy to help in any way I can after I have conferred with my legal counsel. In case you missed it in English class, the word 'after' means the other event comes first. Legal counsel first, talking with—"

"We told you, that Miranda shit doesn't apply to us. People like you make me sick," Good Cop said as he packed the binder into his briefcase. "Think freedom has no cost, and when they're inconvenienced the tiniest little bit, they go crying to the ACLU."

He slammed the door behind him.

Five minutes later, FBI AIC Cooper walked in. Polished shoes, starched white shirt, rep tie, blue pinstriped suit, Hoover haircut. He enthroned himself in the chair opposite me and leaned into the intervening space poking a finger at my nose.

"I heard you're not talking until you get a lawyer. Fine with me, I'll do the talking. Number one: you hung up on me. Number two: you had a bunch of yahoos prevent us from getting to your house. We're filing obstruction of justice charges against them. Depends on you whether we include you in those charges, starting right now."

"I'll be sure to pass on your expressions of contempt to the families who are mourning the deaths of your so-called yahoos. Were you born an asshole or did you have to work at it?"

"You think you're some kind of hot shit, don't you? Listen up, McCree. If you ever mention our agent's name or anything about our agent's operation to anyone other than an authorized Federal Bureau of Investigation agent, we will charge you and your son with various and sundry felonies. Got it, shithead?"

I did not reply.

After a long bit of silence passed between us, AIC Cooper said, "You should convince your equally stubborn son to tell us how he hacked our computers. If he cooperates, we'll consider reducing the additional charges we're filing against him. And if you don't, we'll add you as a co-conspirator."

So Paddy had sufficiently recovered from the rhinoplasty that the doctors had allowed the cops to talk to him. Was he still in the Iron Mountain hospital where the surgery took place or back in Iron County sharing the jail with me?

AIC Cooper blathered on, but I didn't pay attention. I spent the time trying to understand why ICE and the FBI were so antagonistic. I could have as profitably spent my time wondering when the next meteorite would crash into the earth. My mother, while she still spoke, referred to such questions as "imponderables." After I gave up trying to understand their attitudes, I again obsessed about how Paddy was holding up.

Cooper eventually ran out of steam and left with one last shot: "You're on my list until the day you die."

The two DEA agents were real chums by comparison. They asked me if it was alright to look through a ton of photographs of mostly Hispanic-looking men and women. I gave it an honest effort, but didn't recognize anyone. They left without threats—or thank-yous.

A new sheriff's deputy escorted me to my cell. "Do you know where my son is?" I asked.

"We're not allowed to talk to one inmate about another . . ." He paused for what I took as an internal debate and then continued. "My son? I'd want to know. I'll see what I can do."

BOSS HADN'T FELT THIS SORE since losing a bull-riding dare in college. Everything hurt. Dragging that damned ATV off the road and hiding it deep in the woods with Digger's body was bad. He should have known better than to drive down the road, especially with a bundle attached to the back rack that in poor light looked like a passenger. No way Boss could have walked the twenty-five miles home after getting the truck stuck in the mud on Bone Lake Road. Damned lucky the camp near Four Corners Boss chose to hide out at until darkness had a bonus: parked in the woodshed so flimsy a child could have broken in was a fueled-up ATV with a key sitting in the ignition. Even so, it was midnight by the time Boss got home after burying the clothes and the rifle in a shallow pit carved from the frozen earth on land Hematite National Bank owned.

Fortunately, Boss's first appointment was the noon Tuesday prayer meeting at the church. The only topic of discussion was the horrific attack up in the woods. Two of the congregation's own were among the dead. Boss damn near lost it after a deputy's wife reported the girl hadn't even been at the cabin. No one knew where she was. Boss covered the shock by leading a fervent prayer for all the local families.

After the meeting, the pastor's wife pulled Boss aside. "Where were you last night? I tried to get hold of you to organize the deacons to take care of meals for the two families. You always do a good job."

"Traveling," Boss muttered. "Didn't get home until real late."

"I left you several messages," the witch continued. "I was worried that maybe with your cancer, you'd taken a turn for the worse. How are you feeling? You look worn out."

One more comment about my health, and I'll wear myself out kicking you from here to kingdom come. "Sorry. By the time I heard them, I assumed you had contacted one of the other deacons."

"Well, I was sure you'd get back to me . . ."

Boss glared at her; she faded to quiet with a flutter of helpless hands. Was no one capable of doing anything right? Did Boss have to do everything? Boss sighed, "I'll take care of it this afternoon. Have the funerals been set yet?"

"There was talk about a single combined funeral, but the priest insisted on a mass and our folks don't want that . . ." The pastor's wife gave Boss's arm a tender squeeze. "These are terrible times. Bless you. Bless you, for all your good work." She scurried off.

Boss watched the little ferret disappear. Terrible times indeed. It was hard to understand what Pastor saw in the woman. Maybe she was a tornado in the sack.

Boss grabbed a pad of paper, wrote the two dead guys' names on the top with a vertical line separating them, and scribbled the days of the week down the left with slots for lunch and dinner. Best way to fill in this chart was to appeal directly to the women of the church. Since several of them were related to local law enforcement, a little face-to-face social conversation should draw out whatever the cops knew.

Before starting the rounds, Boss needed to cancel several afternoon meetings at the bank and grab one of those energy drinks so popular with the kids.

Time to do some more good work for God and Country.

NO ONE DISPUTES THE FACT that a few citizens of Crystal Falls stole the court papers from Iron River in 1887. Three years later an election of dubious integrity determined Crystal Falls, and not Iron River, would be the county seat. Given the shaky foundation of justice, I wasn't surprised that the Iron County Courthouse, built of quarried stone, looked directly down the main business street of Crystal Falls and showed Iron River its backside.

An underground tunnel led from the jail to the courthouse, where we took an elevator to the second floor. I entered the courtroom through a set of double wooden doors. With its high ceilings and multitudinous windows, the radiators clacked in their effort to warm the room. The sheriff's deputy steered me to the jury room where I met my new lawyer. Irene Frankle hailed from Traverse City, six plus hours away from Crystal Falls.

"Thanks for coming," I said. "I know it's far for you, but I couldn't think of anyone to call except Leroy Patterson . . . you know, since I had used him in Cincinnati? I thought he could find someone local."

She waited until I settled into my chair before taking her seat. Dressed in a gray checked skirt and jacket, starched white blouse with a colorful scarf, sensible low heels, her most striking feature was the silver dreadlocks. They ran halfway down her back, each one tipped with a string of colored beads that clicked like rosary beads every time she moved. "Leroy and I go back a long, long way. He spoke highly of you, and he knew I'm bored to death in retirement. Now let's discuss what's going to happen this morning."

WE HAD ONLY A FEW minutes before the court clerk called my name. Still shackled, I shuffled past the railing and up two steps. Irene and I took our places at the left-hand table facing the bench. The county prosecutor, a WASP in every sense of the word, sat at the right-hand bench with a pile of folders in front of him and cast a series of side-glances at Irene. I was willing to bet the courtroom had never seen the likes of her, and internally I smiled. The bald judge bent over the papers the prosecutor had given to the clerk, who had passed them to the judge.

The judge informed me of the charges: open murder, various classes of assault, riding an off-road vehicle without a helmet, riding an off-road vehicle on a paved road, operating an off-road vehicle with an unhelmeted passenger. "In Michigan," Irene whispered, "open murder means the jury decides between first and second degree murder."

"How do you plead?"

Irene said, "Not guilty to the open murder and assault charges, Your Honor. Not guilty by reason of insanity to the three ORV charges."

The judge furrowed his brow. "Reason of insanity?"

"Yes, Your Honor. The prosecutor must be insane to bring those charges. It makes a mockery of our judicial system. When the newspapers—"

The judge banged his gavel once and the tittering behind us stopped. "Such antics, Ms. Frankle, may be tolerated elsewhere, but not in this court."

"Yes, Your Honor." Irene said with all the contriteness of a kindergartener caught feeding her brussels sprouts to the family dog under the table. She remained standing, but motioned for me to sit down, which I did.

"Something else?" the judge asked.

"Can you imagine a jury around here convicting my client of the ORV charges?" Irene said. "People were shooting at him. Who in their right mind would take the time to put on a helmet? Would you tell your son, when someone was trying to kill him, that he had to walk because it was illegal to ride double? Puh-lease."

I covered my mouth. The judge's eyes twinkled while he tried to hold a stern face. "I'll look forward to your arguments—at the proper time. Am I clear, Ms. Frankle, or will you be making a donation to the county because of a contempt charge?"

"Crystal clear." She took her time sitting down.

The judge set the preliminary hearing a week hence. The proceedings turned to bail. Not surprisingly, the prosecutor insisted I was a grave flight risk and the court should deny bail. We, of course, thought personal recognizance was sufficient. The judge decided a million dollars would split the difference.

I whispered to Irene, "As long as Paddy's isn't any higher, I won't need a bail bondsman. I can cover it all with mutual funds."

She dipped her head to show she understood. "Excuse me, Your Honor," Irene said after the judge dismissed us. "Could the prosecutor inform us when he plans to hold the arraignment for Mr. McCree's son? Assuming the charges are the same, we are going to have the same issues—other than the issue of insanity—regarding bail. I'd like to start arranging for the release of both my clients."

The judge glared his disapproval of her sneaking in the word insanity, then directed his gaze at the prosecutor. "Is there some reason you are separating these cases?"

"The son may not be released from the hospital early enough to get to court today."

"I don't understand, Your Honor," Irene said. "I was at the hospital two hours ago talking with my client. The doctor told me he could release young Mr. McCree whenever the county provided the necessary forms." She gave the prosecutor her brightest smile.

The prosecutor flushed. "I'll have to check, Your Honor."

The judge leaned forward and peered over his half glasses. "Good idea. I'll expect an answer."

ORANGE WAS NOT MCCREE'S COLOR. "Could you please unshackle him?" Bartelle asked the sheriff's deputy standing outside the interview room.

"We'll be monitoring the room if you need us," the deputy said and shut the door, leaving Bartelle and McCree sitting on opposite sides of the table.

"Where to start?" Bartelle mused.

"The beginning is usually a good place," McCree said.

Bartelle felt a smile crinkle his face. Totally inappropriate, since there was nothing to smile about. "Fair enough. I owe you an apology. If I had trusted you from the beginning, maybe we both wouldn't be in this room." He swept his arm to encompass the room from corner to corner. "Your boss at Criminal Investigations Group, Robert Rand, called today." Bartelle watched McCree and saw a quick widening of his eyes—he hadn't known. "He offered me the complete resources of CIG. If you ever need a character witness, he'd be a good one."

"Let me guess: you're stuck being Mr. Nice Guy to offset Special-Agent-in-Charge Cooper's sparkling personality?"

"Caught me. He does have the personality of a chunk of magnetite. ICE, the FBI, and the DEA are sorting out the power struggle right now. While it's still my case, can we talk, or do you need your lawyer?"

"She's with Paddy, but she told me I could discuss anything prior to the most recent attack. We're as anxious to get to the bottom of this as anyone."

"So why not talk with any of the other agencies?"

"That was before I met with counsel. Besides, they were more interested in telling me how tough they were than understanding what happened."

Bartelle kept a smile off his face. "In response to the request we placed on the radio, we got a call," he flicked open his pocket notebook and rifled through the pages, "from a Mrs. Rita Pirhonen at the Laughing Loon. She happens to be next-door neighbor to my aunt. She said you and your son paid her a visit over the weekend?"

"What have you learned about my son?"

"He's still in a lot of pain, but he's going to be fine."

"Not what I meant," McCree said, his voice filled with exasperation. "What have the Feds told you about his background?"

Bartelle didn't understand the frustration he heard and thought the question odd. After reflection he didn't see any reason not to answer. "Seamus Patrick McCree goes by his middle name. No arrests or warrants prior to yesterday. One of the founding members of a company called LT2P Network Solutions located in Evanston, Illinois. You sit on their board. Earlier this year, it rejected an acquisition offer from IBM, which would have made the founders all rich. He lives in Chicago with some woman whose name I do not remember. Was there something specific you were going for?"

McCree closed his eyes, scrunched his mouth to the left, drummed his fingers on the metal table. "They tell you what LT2P does?" Bartelle shook his head. "They test computer network security, primarily for banks. They make big bucks trying to hack into banks' computers. You can imagine IBM would not want to buy them if they weren't successful."

Bartelle considered the information. "This relates to your conversation with Mrs. Pirhonen?"

McCree raised his eyebrows.

Bartelle considered the hinted implications. He scraped his chair onto its two hind legs, the sound echoing off the harsh white walls, and crooked his arm over his head to scratch his ear. "I think we can work out something your counsel will find satisfactory."

TWENTY-EIGHT

BOSS WATCHED THE ACTIVITY IN the president's office with growing concern. Sergeant Bartelle, holding a piece of paper in his hand, had marched into that office five minutes after the bank's doors opened Wednesday morning. A mop-haired kid from IT soon followed with a fistful of computer paper. Two minutes after that, Bartelle left with the computer paper under his arm and a smile plastered on his face. The kid remained inside.

Checking the president's calendar on Outlook, Boss could see he had canceled a meeting with one of the bank's troubled logging firms in order to make room for Bartelle, which meant it was important. What was Bartelle looking for at the bank? Boss went through every step of the operation. There were no connections between Hematite Bank and the militia. Boss stood and paced the room while listening to "Telephone Time." Some caller was speculating about the week's killings. No news.

In the middle of a step, it hit Boss: the only nexus with the bank was the extra account used to pay the cell phone bill registered in Mrs. Pirhonen's name. Boss willed the kid to leave the office. A minute later, he did. Boss did a fake saunter to the president's office and closed the door with a rattle that shook the walls.

"What the hell did Bartelle want?" Boss demanded.

The president waved to a seat in front of his desk. "Hello, Mother, it's wonderful to see you today. Won't you make yourself comfortable?"

Boss hated her son treating her with orchestrated politeness. She still owned a majority of the shares. She had a right to know. Boss shot him a look only a mother could give. "Well?"

"He had a court order to obtain all the information we had on one account. I can't imagine what for. As near as I can tell, the account was only used to pay a cell phone bill every month. Cash deposits covered the bill. The average balance was only ten bucks. I shudder to think how much money it cost us to maintain that account, especially since the account holder has other accounts with us. I don't know why this one wasn't linked to those. While Sergeant Bartelle was here, we checked the depositor's other accounts: she rarely withdraws cash and never on the same day as the deposits. Very peculiar. I've asked IT to determine which employee opened the account so we can get to the bottom of this."

He spun the papers around and pushed them to her side of the desk.

Of course she knew what she would be looking at, but made a show of flipping through the pages. Each one felt heavy as a stone tablet. She knew they would eventually discover a now-retired employee had opened the account for Mrs. Pirhonen. Once a month, the same retiree recorded a cash deposit for the account. "Mrs. Pirhonen is a resident at the Laughing Loon," Boss said. "She seems to have lucid days and some . . ." She waggled her hand to emphasize the not-so-lucid days. "I've been up at the Loon to talk to her about some investment opportunities. I don't believe I've seen her in the bank in years. You said it pays a phone bill? Maybe one of her family members keeps the account live. You know how things can get screwed up with families and older relatives." Boss shook her head at the sadness of the elderly starting to lose it.

Her son pulled the file back to his side of the desk. "I'll have someone check into this and see if we can't merge it with one of her other accounts." He checked his watch. "We've got those Sunset Hills developers coming in to try to renegotiate their loan, and with this morning's folderol, I'm running behind."

Boss took the hint. It was time to strategize. Bartelle had done a lot of work in a short time if he had come up with the bank account. They obviously discovered the phone number after Jimmie's death—how no longer mattered—and got the information from the phone company. If they subpoenaed the phone company they could also get all the numbers Boss had called or received using Mrs. Pirhonen's phone. It had been good while it lasted. Boss needed to alert her militia contact to destroy his phone, and when she got to camp, she needed to get rid of Mrs. Pirhonen's.

Boss settled into her office chair and turned off the constant chatter of "Telephone Time" to consider the ramifications of this latest news. The firewall she had constructed between various components of the plan was doing its job. Contact with the biochemist had only been through email, and she couldn't see any reason to change the scheduled delivery from Sunday at Da Yooper Tourist Trap in Ishpeming. What she needed were some throwaway phones. A smile twitched her face.

WAUSAU, WISCONSIN WAS THREE HOURS away. No one knew her there, and most people in these parts thought of traveling to Green Bay before they would consider heading to Wausau. On the outskirts of town she spotted a Mom-and-Pop store for one of the phone companies. By way of explanation, she mentioned to the kid tending the counter—hardly looked professional with studs in both nostrils and purple hair—something about purchasing throwaways for each of her six grandkids. At a nearby park, Boss used one to leave a message for her militia contact in the Mitten, telling him to pitch his phone and call her on the second of her six phones. She left the first phone sitting on a picnic table for whomever happened to find it.

With the third phone, she called the facilities manager at the Laughing Loon. She told him a sob story about the plumbing firm they used getting a big job at the "Soo" that had to start exactly on April 1. They would have to refuse it unless they could reschedule the Laughing Loon for an earlier date because, after all, the deal with the Laughing Loon came first.

The manager couldn't be more accommodating, especially after Boss mentioned a 10% discount for his inconvenience. He never asked why she was doing the calling. The manager confirmed the new appointment for eight in the morning, in exactly seven days.

Boss disposed of that phone at a McDonald's in Rhinelander. *Money well spent. Yes siree, Bob.*

I HAD EXPECTED PADDY AND I would be released on bail sometime late Thursday or early Friday since it would take that long to provide the combined two-million-dollar security, so I wasn't surprised when the sheriff's deputy came for me Thursday afternoon. I was surprised, however, when we ended up in the courthouse. Paddy and Irene Frankle were sitting in the first row of courtroom benches, heads together in whispered conversation. Paddy's legs were also free of restraints.

I sat on Frankle's other side. My orange did not clash with her severe charcoal suit, but it rioted with the batik scarf she wore over her dreads. "What's up?" I asked. The guard took the bench behind me.

"All rise," the clerk intoned as the judge stepped from behind the black fabric screen. I peeked at the clock—four forty-one p.m.

The actors in the drama of the State of Michigan against Seamus Anselm McCree and Seamus Patrick McCree took their places on center stage. The assistant prosecutor, a young woman with sloped shoulders and strands of honey-colored hair escaping the clip at the nape of her neck, rose and reported they wished to drop all charges against each of the defendants. In a television show, this would have been a dramatic scene with crowds of reporters rushing to text in their story. Here, the judge looked up from the papers the clerk had placed in front of him and in a monotone said, "Please share with the court the reasons for the prosecutor's sudden reversal of himself."

Without a glance in our direction the assistant prosecutor fell on her sword while trying mightily to justify the original decision. Police had discovered yet another body with the missing ATV. At this time, there was insufficient evidence.

I tuned out the rest of what she said. *Who else had died?*

We traded orange garb for the clothes we were arrested in, and after Irene paid our $12 booking fee and $30-per-day room and board, we were free men. "Let's grab a bite to eat at Generations," she said. "We have a couple of things to discuss."

It felt good to walk without shackles shortening my stride and clinking at every step. The day was unseasonably warm with temperatures in the upper forties. I pointed my face to the sun and soaked in the rays on the two-block walk down Superior Avenue to the restaurant. We settled into a booth, Paddy and I on one side, Irene on the other. Half the patrons wore their Sunday best. It struck me they must have come here from a memorial service. My mouth dried up and tasted like I had eaten ash.

After we ordered a pizza to share, Irene said, "The police have released your house as a crime scene. After we eat, I can run you up there."

"Not going to work," I said. "It's mud season. Nothing but four-wheelers will get in."

"Your ATVs are still evidence, not to mention the issues of riding double and not wearing helmets." Her shoulders gave a little bounce. "I was so looking forward to defending against those ATV charges."

"There's an ATV dealer in Iron Mountain," I said. "Too late to call tonight, but I'd bet for the right price they'll rent us two ATVs, helmets, so we're all nice and legal, and bring them to us tomorrow."

"Sounds like a plan," Irene said. "Then what happens?"

"Then the cops show up," a voice said from behind me, "and spoil the party."

BARTELLE WATCHED ATTORNEY IRENE FRANKLE'S face become granite; her eyes flashed ferocity and she ripped the scarf off her head as though preparing for battle.

"Easy, Counselor," Bartelle said. "We come in peace. We're even willing to break bread together, if you'll have us. Slide over?"

The McCrees moved in and Tex sat beside Patrick. Frankle took her cue from Seamus and made room for Bartelle. He removed his hat and stuck it next to him on the seat. The waitress added two glasses of water and extra silverware. After determining they had ordered pizza, Bartelle ordered another one.

"Not grilled cheese?" McCree asked.

"Different restaurant," Bartelle said, sipped water, felt it cool his mouth and throat, quenching his thirst and calming his nerves. "Okay, I realize right now we're about as welcome as a skunk at a picnic, but let me tell you why we tracked you down. I'm hoping, with you not officially being suspects, we might pick your brains."

McCree pulled the left side of his face into a squint. Bartelle saw Frankle catch his look. She said, "Not officially suspects and not suspects are hardly the same thing. Numerous federal officers have threatened each of the McCrees. Despite that, they have given full and complete statements about what they know. What more do you want, Sergeant Bartelle?"

"I'll be honest," Bartelle said and wanted to kick himself since any time he heard those words from a suspect, he was sure they were about to lie. "As of this second, the FBI is the lead and AIC Cooper isn't much interested in any local input. Tex and I have been impressed with you two and we thought you might have some ideas. So here we are." He pointed to Tex and all eyes focused on him as he drained the glass of water.

"No more DEA?" Seamus asked.

Tex snorted derision. "DEA packed their bags. The only drugs found anywhere were those in the gas tank of Brett Aho's snow machine, which everyone agrees Jimmie Heitzmann probably planted since no self-respecting drug ring would wrap them in a leaky bag. DEA's working this area with a state police taskforce on other stuff. They have no interest in the murders."

"And those fine gentlemen from ICE?" Seamus asked.

Bartelle cleared his throat. "Right now in the background, but still very much interested. Look, Brett Aho and Jimmie Heitzmann were soldiers. Same thing with the two guys who came up from the Mitten to try to take you out. We know they're militia. Everything on them they bought in Iron Mountain in the last week, 'cept the guns. Those were stolen from an armory six years ago. The FBI executed a warrant on all known militia officers and their meeting places in Michigan and came up with squat."

Frankle shook her head and the tinkle of her hair beads caused Bartelle to stop. "Why are you sharing this information with my clients?"

"Because I want them to know I think Seamus stepped into the middle of something really big and really bad when he rescued Jane Doe. Because I think someone evil believes Seamus knows more than he does, and I am concerned said evil person or persons are not going to stop trying to kill him. Because the sheriff's department does not have the resources to protect them. Because I hope to convince both McCrees to leave town tonight. I hope legal counsel will add her esteemed opinion to my own for her clients' wellbeing."

Seamus cleared his throat and got everyone's attention. "Are there any funerals still left?"

Bartelle knew he meant for the five men killed protecting him. "The last one is tomorrow morning."

"I don't exactly have the clothes for a funeral, but I want to attend unless, given the town's mood, you think that would be unwise."

"The surrounding area is naturally in shock," Bartelle said. "But you know, up here we're used to disasters. They lost a lot more than five men in some of the mining accidents a generation or two ago. And just a few years back, we dealt with the tragedy of two cars full of drunk high schoolers playing chicken and meeting head-on. I don't guess anyone will much care what you wear to the church as long as it's not orange."

"And," Paddy said, "since my car and clothes and—I am so screwed if I don't get it soon, my *laptop*—are all up at camp, I'll attend the funerals with Dad."

"It would be a nice gesture," Bartelle said. "The outside media has already left town, and the local paper's not going to bother you. Here come the pizzas. Since you're going to stick around, we'll talk tomorrow after the service. Changing subjects, you guys Cincinnati Reds fans?"

Bartelle's ploy succeeded and conversation turned to the prospects of the Reds, Brewers, Twins, and Tigers in the coming baseball season.

He was glad to learn Frankle was heading downstate in the morning. Since neither McCree had thought to grab a wallet when they were attacked, and the county was no longer responsible for providing a room with barred door and windows, the lawyer would front them for a motel room. Bartelle agreed to arrange for someone to pick them up and take them to the funeral, and he'd arrange transportation to their camp to collect their stuff.

Once Bartelle and Tex were in a squad car, Tex asked, "You didn't really want them to leave, did you?"

Bartelle stopped himself from scratching his head. "Oh, hell no. I'm not a hundred percent convinced they're not involved—not so much the son, but the father. I want him where I can see him."

Twenty-Nine

BOSS WAS DAMNED TIRED OF funerals. This was the last one, but it would be the longest since it involved the Catholic mass for the dead or whatever they called it. Catholic services took forever, and she never knew when she was supposed to kneel or sit or stand. Her knees ached at every change. And she hated the smell of incense—made her want to sneeze. She led her son and daughter-in-law to a pew in the back where she had a good view of the congregation, and not many would notice if she nodded off during the sermon. She was amusing herself flipping pages in the Bible, trying to remember which extra books the Catholics included compared to her Protestant version. The pre-service buzz in the church went up a notch, and she raised her head.

Owen Lyndstrom, dressed in a suit no less, ushered in Seamus McCree and his son. She had heard at breakfast about their release from jail, and she realized it made sense for them to come. Although you would have thought they could have worn some decent clothes. Cops had attended all the funerals, and she was sure they were watching the crowd. She didn't want to stand out as the only one watching father and son. A quick glance around her allayed her fears. Every eye followed Owen as he brought them down and introduced them to the deceased's family before settling into a pew halfway up on the other side of the aisle.

Throughout the service, she snuck glances at the McCrees. The father knew his way around a Catholic service. Had no problem with the ups and downs and mumbled responses. The son, who looked like he'd lost a ten-rounder to Muhammad Ali, was as clueless as she was. Even with the kid's broken nose and swollen face, you could see the family resemblance: same height, same build, even the same walk. Boss had the feeling lots of curious people were going to talk to them after the service, which would allow her to question them without being obvious.

Now if this damned service would just get done.

KNOWING WHAT TO SAY TO a grieving family has never been my strong suit, and this was worse since their deaths rested heavily on my actions. The father of six children, the husband to his wife, the son to his mother, the brother to his siblings, the former altar boy of this church had died protecting me, someone he had never met. What words could I say to justify this loss? I mumbled my way through the condolences, grateful to Owen for making the introductions. No one expressed anger at Paddy or me; each family member thanked us for being there.

As I let the Requiem Mass wash over me, I recalled the shock of my own father's funeral. Our parish church overflowed with uniforms paying respect to one of their own killed in the line of duty. I don't recall a single thing anyone said to me that day and was surprised to discover hot tears now streaming down my cheeks. I wiped them away with the heels of my hands.

Without thought, I responded to the ritual. While I rejected the doctrine, I understood the power of a congregation: voices ranging from deep bass to boy soprano, mouthing words in unison to force my focus from myself toward something larger. I watched the six children sitting in front of me, aged late teenager to toddler—heads in a row of descending height. I could do nothing to replace their father, but I had the resources to at least help all the families financially. During the homily, I came up with the idea of setting up trust funds for the children. I'd need advice about the psychology around how to do that without seeming in any way to imply the families or community couldn't take care of their own.

Immediately following the service, Owen scooted off to attend the burial. My son the extrovert struck up a conversation with the woman who'd sat next to him, which left me alone with my thoughts as we slowly worked our way toward the exit. The entryway was blocked and, in the muddle, the people in front of us stopped to confab. As I waited, a middle-aged man bumped my arm. He apologized, and then recognition dawned on his face.

"You must be Mr. McCree," he said. "What a terrible tragedy. I'm Sam Maki. This is my wife, Jeanne, and my mother, K.C.—stands for Kathryn

Cynthia. No one has called her Kathryn since she socked someone in the eye at age four."

"Sam," the mother said with a look of annoyance, "loves to tell that story. Don't you, Sam?"

I recognized the Maki's names. He was president of the Hematite bank and his mother was Chair of the Board. The previous year the Makis had been interested in selling out and I had performed due diligence on Hematite for one of my clients.

We shook hands all around and I said to Mr. Maki, "You might be able to help me with setting up some kind of memorial fund for the families. I don't know what that exactly means . . ."

"Understood," he said. "And I'm sure done the right way it will be useful and appreciated. It is still early days. When you have a better idea what you have in mind, you should talk to my mother. She's the bank's chair, but she's also the one most experienced with trusts, investments, structured settlements, annuities. That sort of thing. We all call her *the Boss*." He patted his mother's arm. "Right, Mom?"

"Please, call me K.C.—Boss sounds so imposing. I'll be glad to assist however I can. We attend the Presbyterian Church in town and helped that girl you rescued back . . . what . . . five, six weeks ago? We took up a collection of clothes for her. Whatever happened to her? Did she finally regain her memory?"

We had agreed we could not disclose who Agent Pendergast was, but we had not discussed how to describe her departure. To make my temporary confusion worse, I couldn't remember for the life of me what her assumed name was. When in doubt, make a lie sound convincing by mixing the lie with truths people can easily confirm. "Last I heard, she flew to Chicago."

"Did she find out who she was?" K.C asked. The crush in front of us eased and her son and daughter-in-law excused themselves to visit with someone I did not recognize.

Paddy jumped in before I spoke. "Her first name was Bethany. I think she didn't tell us more about herself because she was afraid Dad would change his mind and come after her for all her medical bills. That's not how my father operates, but how would she know? I got the feeling she was visiting friends in Chicago, but I could be mistaken."

"What," K.C. asked, "was she doing in this area? And why was she wandering around in the woods near you?"

Paddy and I shared a look, and I said, "No clue, but she knew the guy they found in Long Lake—not the snowmobiler, the other one. What was his name, Paddy?"

"Brandon, I think."

"They were staying at a camp somewhere nearby."

"I heard they tied some concrete blocks to him," K.C. said. "It's just awful what's happened. I'm surprised the police didn't insist she stay in the area until they clear everything up."

"You know more about it than I do," I said. "Speaking of the police, here comes Sergeant Bartelle now."

K.C. turned from me and offered Bartelle a big smile. "Lon, how nice of you to come to the funerals. We were just talking about that foundling—Bethany is her name? We were hoping she fully recovered her memory and wondered what became of her."

Bartelle pretended to slap her hand. "Now Mrs. Maki, you know I can't talk about active investigations, but I can assure you we're getting closer."

BARTELLE EXTRACTED THEM FROM THE clutches of the senior Mrs. Maki, one of the county's most effective interrogators and worst gossips. Once they were out of earshot, Seamus said, "Thanks for rescuing us. Before Niki left, we never thought to get our story straight about what we could say about her, but I don't think we gave anything away."

Bartelle had them go through the conversation and then burst their bubble. "And how did she get on the plane with no identification?"

The McCrees looked at each other, with "oh, shit" expressions.

Bartelle flicked his key fob and unlocked his personal car. "Don't worry about it. We all should have thought of it earlier. K.C. Maki rivals Owen Lyndstrom for having an ear to the ground. There were so many witnesses when we fished Brandon Newhouse out of Long Lake, I'm sure she heard about Agent Pendergast—er, Niki— or was she back to Bethany?—whoever she was—identifying him. Owen gave me a key to his place. He'll meet us there and make sure you get to your camp." He flashed the key. "I have a proposition."

"Gee," Patrick said, "Dad's been propositioned by cops before, but I never have."

"Get in, Paddy," Seamus said, "And let's listen to what the man has to say."

Despite practicing his speech, Bartelle's words tumbled out. "I told you Robert Rand, your boss at CIG, offered all their resources. I spoke with him again—yesterday—I mean last night. So, the sheriff agreed to sign a contract with CIG—I didn't realize CIG never takes money for its work. Anyway, you, Seamus, can work with me under the auspices of CIG's contract. And Patrick, I have in my briefcase a form Rand faxed to sign you up as a CIG employee—minimum wage, I'm afraid—but it will allow you to also work with me under the CIG contract. Everything's nice and legal."

"It would help," Seamus said, "if you told us what you want us to do."

"Of course," Bartelle smacked the back of his own head, "I was so worried about the legalities, I forgot the main point. I've seen Patrick work magic with computers. We can't do anything illegal—" He glanced in the rearview mirror to gauge Patrick's expression; it was neutral. "Nothing illegal, but we can get court orders if we need them. I'm off track again. We've gotten a mass of electronic data from the court orders on the phones, and we don't have the skills in our office to get through it quickly. I suspect Patrick does."

"Probably," Patrick said, "I'd have to see exactly what you've got in mind. And Dad?"

"We got the records from Hematite Bank. They seem willing to help us understand them, but they could also be leading me by the nose and I'd never know. Your father would. Plus, in trying to track down who owned the property where Niki and Brandon stayed, we've run into a Colorado corporation I can't track down."

"To summarize, then," Seamus said. "You want our brains, not our good looks, which is a good thing in your case, Paddy, because you still look like crap."

"And the horse you rode in on, Dad." To Bartelle he replied, "I'm game, and I know my old man is. Dad's always said the best defense is a great offense, and we need to find whoever tried to kill us."

Seamus emitted a grating sound, and Bartelle's brief feeling of relief faded. "Paddy's observation is spot on," he said. "The only thing jail had going for it was I didn't have to worry about somebody coming to gun us down, which is probably why you had us arrested in the first place, although the county prosecutor didn't get the joke."

Bartelle felt heat rise to his face, but kept his mouth shut until he knew where McCree was going. McCree glanced at his son.

"Have you thought about how you can try to protect us without endangering anyone? So many people have been killed . . ."

"CIG expressed the same concern, Seamus. I think we can best discuss it after we get to Owen's." With a crack of thunder, the skies opened up. Bartelle flicked the wipers on high. "Hope this stays rain and doesn't turn to sleet."

Seamus nodded assent; Patrick looked out the window. Bartelle hoped they would consider the surprise awaiting them at Owen's a good one.

BOSS SAT IN THE CAMP recliner, sipped straight bourbon, and crushed out the half-smoked cigarette. Damn things didn't even taste good, whereas bourbon was like wood smoke—a little sip engaged scent and taste receptors, providing fine memories; too much overwhelmed everything. After all the funerals, shutting down seemed advantageous. The worst part of attending the funerals, she decided, was pantyhose. If she had her brief stint as a women's libber to do over, she'd lobby hard for burning panty hose instead of bras. It's easy to get rid of bras when you're young and everything up top is perky; now she found them comfortable and couldn't imagine hanging loose without one, but pantyhose was something else. With nice-looking pantsuits, not too much required pantyhose these days, but weddings and funerals were still formal affairs.

She found her conversation with Seamus McCree unsatisfactory. The girl's name was Bethany Palmer. She needed a photo ID card to fly. To get one, Bethany needed to prove her identity to the authorities. So Bartelle knew who she was and where she was from.

Boss checked with a friend who worked for the airlines in Iron Mountain and confirmed Bethany Palmer did fly to Chicago. Her friend had found no record of Bethany Palmer flying out of Chicago that day or since; of course, since Bethany hadn't checked any baggage, she could have taken another airline and her source wouldn't know.

After fuming at the dead end while draining the better part of a fifth of bourbon, she came to the upside of the situation: it required her to think about her motives in trying to finish off Bethany Palmer and Seamus

McCree. Tying up loose ends was only a good thing if it didn't unroll another skein of yarn. She had structured all contacts around hiring the wolf biologists and renting the cabin to go through Brett—although he was unaware of it and now it was too late for him to care. Trying to tidy up all the loose ends connecting her to Brett Aho, the scientists, and the cabin was an error on two accounts.

From a practical standpoint, it didn't matter what Bethany Palmer had told Seamus McCree or Sergeant Bartelle or the world because she didn't know anything to tell him. Furthermore, if anyone had seen Boss in the woods after the Mitten Men disaster, the cops would already have visited her. Once she got rid of the remaining cell phones, the only person who could implicate her was the head of the downstate militia and he had already proven, through a stretch of jail time, that he could keep his mouth shut.

The second count against her was she had been vengeful. *Vengeance is mine, saith the Lord. On that, she needed to reflect further.*

She downed the rest of the bourbon in a gulp and waited until the burn settled from her throat to her stomach before retrieving the ancient laptop. On the way back to the recliner, she pulled the first beer of the afternoon from the fridge and downed it while the computer booted up and connected to the internet. One email:

Sunday meeting confirmed.

She whooped at the news, which soon became a coughing jag so bad it rocked the single-wide as she staggered to catch her breath. Amazing she didn't hack her lung onto the floor. She toasted the news with a second beer and then retrieved Mrs. Pirhonen's cell phone and those remaining from her Wisconsin purchase. What was she going to do with them? If it was later in spring, she could stick a canoe into a nearby lake and dump them in, but if anyone saw her on the water now, it would surely raise suspicions. With the effort it took her to get home from the ambush, she didn't feel like she had the strength to bury a cigarette butt in the nearly frozen soil, let alone all those phones. It had been almost impossible to get rid of her clothes that night. Fact was, if she hadn't stolen that ATV, she would never have gotten home. She used two hands to crinkle the beer can and tossed it into the sink, where it rattled around before rimming out and landing on the floor.

The idea arrived in a burst, and she wondered why she hadn't thought of it earlier, especially since she had simply left two phones in Wisconsin. In less than two days, she would pick up the magic potion in Ishpeming. She could throw the phones away somewhere between here and there. If someone found them and used one, so much the better; it would lead the cops on a fine wild goose chase. She put on a pair of dishwashing gloves, took the cell phones apart and carefully cleaned every surface that could contain a fingerprint. She stored the now-cleansed phones in freezer bags.

She plopped into the recliner with the last of the six-pack and returned to reflecting on revenge. It had been un-Christian and flat out wrong. A lesser person might have blamed it on unclear thinking caused by the lung cancer. She would have none of that self-justification. Nope, her sinful thoughts had caused the deaths of Spider and Digger—plus, she supposed, the five locals—of course, their own stupidity did play a major role in their demise.

She didn't have long enough to atone for two deaths, let alone seven, so it didn't much matter. The best she could do was turn the other cheek to McCree and let bygones be bygones.

Unless he got in the way, in which case she'd squash him like a bug. She placed the empty beer can on the floor and tromped it.

THIRTY

I HAD BEEN TO OWEN'S place only a couple of times. Fortunately for the rest of the residents in the Amasa area, he lived at the end of a long driveway, which made a sweeping curve before coming to the house. Following the curve, we arrived at what had once been a clearing but now stored the remains of uncountable cars, trucks, tractors, and logging equipment, all awaiting resurrection in the Second Coming.

Rain drummed on the car's roof. We pulled off the driveway between what I guessed to be the remains of a Model A Ford and a useable trailer with a disemboweled tractor chained to its bed. Bartelle drove his car close to the front of the house to shorten our walk. Unlike the yard, the house was in immaculate condition. We hustled three abreast up the deck stairs.

The door opened and Abigail Hancock, holding a newspaper above her head, walked out.

Bartelle continued up the steps. I stopped, and my quick turn toward Paddy stopped him as well, "Did you know about this?"

He hustled to Abigail and gave her a hug. "Have you come to save my father's ass again?"

"From the looks of it," she said, "you need it more than he does. Get inside before you catch pneumonia. This bodyguard doesn't carry umbrellas."

Her words jarred me into forward movement, but my walk was slow as I tried to understand my feelings. I had last seen her two and a half months ago snowmobiling away, her arms encircling Owen's waist. As the weeks passed, I became more and more convinced she had left me for good. I thought my penance in the wilderness had cauterized the wound. One glimpse of her ripped off the scab and the internal bleeding began again.

Paddy and Bartelle entered the house. I could gauge nothing from Abigail's eyes, which despite the rain were hidden behind mirrored glasses. It may have been my imagination, but I thought the corners of her mouth curled into the slightest hint of a smile. I could not guess its meaning. From my position standing below her, her long legs appeared even longer than I knew they were, and she looked taller than her five feet nine inches. Bulky clothes hid her form, but I still had her shape memorized. She spun around and went inside leaving the door open and me standing in the rain. Once inside, I received a second surprise: Agent Pendergast stood in the far corner of the living room taking in the scene. Abigail was leaning against a wall—as though she had gone to the closest thing to a neutral corner. Bartelle closed the door behind me. "Surprised?" he asked.

Paddy pointed toward Pendergast. "Who are you and what are you doing here?"

"Today, I'm Ashley Pendergast on medical leave of absence from the Federal Bureau of Investigation and temporarily hired by Criminal Investigations Group to assist the Iron County Sheriff's Department in a number of related investigations."

"What's Cooper think?" I asked, still looking at Abigail.

"Cooper thinks I'm sulking at home because he pulled a quick one and had his lap-doctor put me on medical leave. Owen has graciously agreed to allow me to stay here, where it is unlikely AIC Cooper or anyone else will see me. Your Robert Rand arranged for Abigail's reassignment to provide external protection should either of you boys need to leave Owen's lovely establishment." She asked Abigail. "How did I do?"

"Fine as far as it went," Abigail said. "Robert Rand's orders to me were that I was not to let either of, and I quote, 'those ovacaput McCrees with no more sense than a mycoplasma' out of my sight. You know Robert. He won't use a cussword or a contraction but he sure knows how to deliver a highfalutin putdown."

Bartelle still held the door handle. I wasn't sure if it was to prevent my escape or execute an exit himself. Pendergast took the bait Abigail had floated. "For those of us not smart enough to decode Mr. Rand's diss . . .?"

Paddy said, "Ovacaput is concatenated Latin for egg-headed. Mycoplasma are members of the smallest group of bacteria."

"And concatenated?" Bartelle asked.

Paddy continued, "Linking together in a series. Ova for egg. Caput for head. Hence, Robert's Latin concatenation for egghead."

"Enough already," I said. "Let's back up a few steps." I faced Bartelle. "Last I knew, the Feds had grabbed the investigation and pushed you out."

"The FBI, DEA, and ICE couldn't agree on how to proceed. ICE pulled their trump card and grabbed the brass ring. The FBI didn't fold and the pissing match went up to the Director of Homeland Security and the Attorney General.

"About then, your sometime-employer, Criminal Investigations Group in the form of Robert Rand—is there anybody in law enforcement he doesn't know? Anyway, he contacted the director of the state police and found out the state's only role was assisting the Iron County Sheriff's Department and we were currently sidelined. He then contacted the attorney general and gave the AG leverage to use with Homeland Security. The president—you didn't know you were so important, did you?— decided he wanted to slap down the internecine warfare between the two departments and gave the murder investigations back to Iron County. The sheriff, who is a politician first and sheriff second, was smart enough to duck. Yours truly didn't."

"Which," I said, "leaves me wondering what is going on that even the president cares."

"You once asked me," Agent Pendergast said, "if the FBI has people inside the Michigan militias. We do, and they believe the militia is planning a large-scale attack, which they expect to generate large amounts of money. The source hasn't pinned down when or where, but the timing is very soon. The federal agencies are charged with preventing whatever the militia is planning. No president wants another Oklahoma City bombing on his watch."

"And," Bartelle added, "the two guys from downstate were both militia guys. Current thinking is that Agent Pendergast was the target."

"Because?" I asked. "Strike that. Because she's the one that escaped from the camp. Did forensics turn up anything useful at the camp? Who owns the camp? Never mind. Cut to the chase, why are we all here?"

All eyes focused on Bartelle. "Rand wrangled a special deal, which allows Iron County to use the National Security Agency's quick response system for any subpoenas, wire taps, *et cetera*. He convinced everyone that by allowing us to pursue the killers, we might end up providing the rest of them information about their national attack concerns. The NSA's already helping us out."

"Let me guess," Paddy threw in. "Rand specifically required my Dad's involvement since something wonky is going on at Hematite Bank."

Bartelle squirmed a little before answering. "Actually, he said he had given up on your father. He suggested I recruit you for your computer skills, Patrick."

Abigail offered one of her bubbly laughs and it sent a pleasurable shiver down my back. "Don't you believe it," she said. "Robert Rand knows all and sees all. He hasn't given up on Seamus. He's been looking for a way to get your father back in the fold and what better way than to engage his only begotten son. You can trust Rand with your life, but he is a conniving son of a . . . gun."

I smiled as the mere mention of Robert Rand had the effect of cleaning up Abigail's language.

Abigail continued: "Per Robert: Seamus has an innate talent for getting involved with people who want to kill him. I'm supposed to keep him alive as long as he stays up here. Same goes for you, Paddy, so you see, Robert was sure Seamus would stay."

Which left me wondering what her orders or desires were if I left the U.P. "And what about you, Agent Pendergast?" Paddy asked.

"After I got benched, I gave Bartelle a call to let him know how to contact me. Yesterday, he told me his plan and asked if I wanted in. Here I am. Please everyone call me Ashley or Pendergast. The agent part is on medical leave—maybe permanent leave if Cooper discovers I'm here."

"So," I said, "do we have a plan?"

"This rain will soon turn to snow," Bartelle said. "In a few hours, the woods roads will freeze again. Owen will take you to your camp to bring out whatever you need. I've got to get to headquarters and let everyone know CIG and you two are officially on board . . . or am I jumping the gun?"

Paddy and I shared understanding looks. "We're good," I said.

"But I can't do anything until I get my computer," Paddy said.

"Do you have 3G service for your computer?" Bartelle asked. "Verizon's got a tower in Amasa. Or there's a free hotspot here you can pick up with Wi-Fi. Until we get you to your dad's camp, Owen's got a computer he keeps for the grandkids. I'll get you the computerized files relating to the monitored phone calls at the same time I bring Seamus everything we have from Hematite Bank. Should have them to you after dinner sometime. Mr. Maki has agreed to meet us tomorrow early afternoon. It'll be right after the Saturday closing, but he'll make sure his IT guy is there."

"And the security forces?" I asked.

Pendergast answered. "I'm on nightshift since Abigail needs to be available during the day to accompany you guys on the outside. I think we were about to set up security?" She looked at Abigail, who agreed.

Bartelle left to collect the files. Abigail and Pendergast put on rain slickers and took several duffle bags of stuff outside to secure the perimeter. Owen arrived, the rain having curtailed whatever work he was doing.

My mind was a turmoil of competing concerns. Bartelle had not told Paddy and me everything he knew about the case, of that I was sure. It might be a lack of trust—despite Rand vouching for me, there was no way to rule out the possibility I was involved with whatever was really going on. It might be natural police caution to keep things close to his vest. Or it could be some unstated rules Homeland Security or the FBI had insisted upon. Compartmentalized thinking had caused the various intelligence agencies to miss the clues to prevent 9/11. Yet the tsunami of state department material revealed by WikiLeaks demonstrated the downside of allowing too many people access to information. You might as well let everyone know, which was what WikiLeaks had done.

Then there was the awkwardness of staying in the same place with Abigail and Pendergast. They seemed to be working well together, but . . .

There was nothing I could do until Bartelle delivered the files, so when

Paddy gave up trying to use Owen's computer, declaring it an historical artifact, I challenged Paddy and Owen to a game of cribbage. By dinnertime, Paddy had cleaned Owen and me out of a combined two dollars and forty-eight cents. Owen, whom I discovered did not like losing at cribbage, paid his share of the damages in pennies.

OWEN WOKE ME AT TWO a.m. for the trip to camp, and I came up swinging. "Next time," Owen said after avoiding my flailing arms, "I'm usin a stick. No wonder women leave you."

Pendergast sat in front with Owen behind the wheel; Paddy and I crammed into the backseat of Owen's truck. Six inches of untracked snow on the ground gave everyone comfort that no one had preceded us into the woods.

At camp, Pendergast checked the house and cabin to make sure everything was secure. I packed my truck with what I would need until mud season was over. Paddy made several trips to the cabin to collect all his belongings and tossed them into his car. We caravanned out on the return trip. Pendergast again rode shotgun with Owen, who led us out on the theory that if one of us got stuck he could pull us out.

At Owen's, Paddy grabbed my arm and held me back from following the other two into the house.

"I've been thinking," he said.

"Glad the bucks for college did some good," I said.

"Good one, Dad. I'll have to remember it. The Amasa Wi-Fi is insecure, and I'm not sure it's a good idea. Even with my laptop, it's going to be slower than evolution. LT2P has an important sales meeting Monday that I really should lead. Plus, at home, I've got a superfat pipe and—"

"Meaning?"

"Sorry," he said. "Way more bandwidth and I've got the right tools."

"So you're heading out?"

"It's a bit crowded at Owen's. Besides, without me tagging along, it might give you and Abigail some *alone time*. It was a bit frosty around the dinner table."

"Yeah, I was thinking about wearing a parka to breakfast. Speaking of which, when did Abigail take you to the range?"

"Cindy was working on an investigation into some shady characters. After your experience in Cincinnati, I wanted to know how to shoot, so I called her up not too long after she lef—after she returned from here."

"And?"

"And she took me to the range a bunch of times until she thought I was good to go on pistols and rifles. Then she helped me buy a Sig like hers."

My son, a gun owner. It wasn't something we had ever talked about, but I never imagined I would see the day. I understood better than anyone the overwhelming compulsion to protect loved ones, but I still believed guns in a house were more dangerous than valuable. I needed to know his reasoning. Somehow, though, what seemed more pressing was finding out if they had talked about me, but I couldn't ask. I had always made it a point to never talk to Paddy about his mother or our disagreements. He had followed suit and rarely mentioned her. He obviously figured the same philosophy applied to Abigail. Despite my desire for answers, I knew he was right.

"I'll be in Evanston for a late breakfast," Paddy said. "I know I'm supposed to report to Bartelle, but I'll let you know if I find anything."

As his taillights faded, my chest hollowed out. The pressure of the emptiness inside threatened to crack me wide open. For me it's easier being the leaver than being the one left behind, but that hadn't been how things had gone recently. I had even forgotten to tell Paddy "I love you," before he left.

Owen returned to bed and his snores threatened to raise the roof. There was no way I could go back to sleep. To paper over the void caused by Paddy's departure, I spread the bank's records on the dining room table. Pendergast rocked on the porch, a low thump announcing each dip forward.

I called Bartelle as early as I dared. "Is there a reason we can't meet with Hematite as soon as they open up?"

"What did you find?"

"Do you know how long they keep their security tapes?"

"What did you find?"

"Last month, on the twenty-seventh, the same day interest was credited to Mrs. Pirhonen's account, someone deposited thirty-eight bucks well after closing. I know it was after closing because the deposit was recorded *after* the interest credit."

From down the line, I heard a scratching pen. "So what?"

I tamped down my exasperation at his inability to actually answer my question. He was trained to ask questions and not give answers. *I shouldn't hold it against him.* "Bank accounting systems are structured so the interest credit is the last transaction of the day. Traditional banking is all about interest spreads and float. I'm off topic. The point is someone made an entry late at night—someone who has afterhours access to a teller machine and knows how to work it. If the inside video is still around, we can see who it is. Otherwise, we've got some work to do."

"You're suggesting someone at the bank was involved with the killings? Seems hard to fathom."

"Bartelle, you didn't become a sergeant based on easy. Call Maki and tell him we're coming now, and tell him to have that day's security tapes ready if they haven't been overwritten."

"Mr. Maki has a meeting in Marquette in the morning, which is the reason our meeting is in the afternoon. Is that all you've got?"

"So you're saying we're SOL on an earlier meeting. If they don't have that security tape, we're going to need to know who has access to the bank when it's closed and who works late at the end of the month. Make sure Maki knows. Gotta be some IT guys running the month-end programs. Also, who specifically worked that day? Someone could have hidden in a bathroom or something until everyone left."

"Got it. Anything else?" After my silence he added, "Not to put the pressure on you, but NSA is saying militia email and phone traffic has increased substantially."

THIRTY-ONE

BARTELLE HAD NEVER WORKED WITH a bodyguard before. Abigail drove her own armored car and he and McCree sat in the back like tycoons. They arrived at Hematite's main branch five minutes early. Exactly at the appointed time, Sam Maki led them to a conference room. Abigail took an "at ease" position outside the conference room.

"Is she armed?" Maki asked. "We have rules . . ."

Bartelle shut the door behind them. "Did you find the security tape?"

Maki shook his head. "They're on an eight-day cycle. If you can tell me what you're looking for, maybe I can save you some time."

Bartelle motioned for everyone to sit down. He remained standing to remind Maki who was in charge. "Thanks for your offer, Mr. Maki. Here's the issue in a nutshell: we're interested in the account of Mrs. Pirhonen's we discussed the last time I was here. All the deposits were in cash, which is a bit unusual, and if Seamus correctly understood the information you provided, all the transactions were handled by the same teller." With a rustle of paper, he spread the computer printouts in front of Maki and tapped the teller codes circled in red. "Who is this teller?" He took the seat next to Maki.

Maki phoned his head IT guy, who kept him on hold for less than a minute. Maki listened to the answer and said, "Impossible." His voice rose in anger. "She retired at the end of the year." He nodded, obviously agreeing with what he was hearing. "Do that now, please. We'll get back to you with any other questions. No, wait. First change the password and then do a search to determine what other transactions Doris supposedly entered since she retired. Good, let me know."

He set the phone down and spun his chair to face us. "Doris Stanchina retired December thirty-first. Someone signed into the system using her password. You didn't ask, but the codes also show that all the transactions occurred in this building. You heard me tell Kenny to change the password and run a list of any other transactions Doris supposedly entered after the end of the year."

"Did she have a key to the building?" Bartelle asked.

"Of course. She was the head teller. But I know she turned it in because she gave it to me." He opened his desk drawer and extracted a keychain. "A few years ago, we changed our key system to these. They can't be copied."

The answer led directly to the second question on the list Seamus had given Bartelle on their way to the meeting. "Who else has keys?"

"More people than you might think," Maki answered. "All our senior officers, the head teller, some people in IT, our maintenance staff, the outside cleaners. There may be others I'm not coming up with off the top of my head." He made a note on the pad of paper in front of him. "I can find out, and if for some reason I can't, I guess it's time to change the locks. What else?"

"Who of those people know how to use the teller systems?" Bartelle asked. "Logging in, making a deposit, that kind of stuff." Bartelle watched closely for any tells. Maki's eyes clicked right—retrieving information.

"Our head teller, of course. The VP of operations. I'm pretty sure our marketing VP worked summers in high school and college as a teller, so he probably knows."

Bartelle recorded their names.

McCree had been leaning back in his chair, fingers locked behind his head. Now he placed both forearms on the table and asked, "What about your head of IT? Does he know how to use the teller systems? And could he, or anyone in IT, modify the codes after the fact?"

Sam Maki opened his eyes wide. "You don't think . . . ?"

McCree resumed leaning back. "All I have are questions. Does he know how to use the teller systems?"

"Kenny might have picked up enough information helping the tellers solve problems. He does reset the passwords. I guess you already know that, but—"

The telephone interrupted with a long and two shorts, like a D in Morse code. Maki swiveled around and answered it with, "Kenny, what you got? . . . only those? . . . no other tellers? Thanks."

He settled the handset into its cradle and turned around. "The only transactions with Doris Stanchina's code since the beginning of the year are the ones you found. He also checked to see if any other teller who left last year had any transactions for this year, and they didn't. You've got me wondering if I can trust Kenny. Prior to you guys showing up, I would have said, 'unquestionably,' but now . . ."

Bartelle began working on his head under his right ear. With the stress of these murders, he'd rubbed the spot raw and wasn't sure if rubbing felt good or hurt, but it didn't matter because he couldn't stop. He gave McCree a quick eyebrow waggle to indicate he should ask his questions now.

"I'm a director of a firm with expertise in banking computer systems: LT2P. They can sign a confidentiality agreement and run an independent analysis to make sure Kenny is telling you the truth."

"What can they do without his knowing?" Maki asked.

McCree explained how LT2P worked and got Maki to call Patrick McCree while they were there. Bartelle couldn't understand much, listening to only half of the conversation, but before it concluded, an assistant brought Maki a signed nondisclosure agreement faxed from LT2P. He scrawled his name on a contract calling for one dollar in compensation.

Bartelle hid his smile. *Talk about letting the camel's nose under the tent.* Of course, what McCree had just done to the bank wasn't much different than what he'd done to McCree.

BARTELLE HAULED ME TO DORIS Stanchina's home after we grabbed a bite to eat. Abigail remained on the Crystal Falls bungalow's front porch taking in the view of distant hills.

Doris settled us onto chairs in her living room. Everything was neatly in its place and nothing was newer than twenty years old. The smell of fresh apple pie filled the air.

Bartelle again led the questioning. No, she had not been back in the bank since her retirement. She banked using the drive-through, but saw her friends who still worked there at church, the high school football games, around town. Yes, it was possible someone else knew her password; she had taped it to the bottom of her pencil holder. Well no, she wasn't sure whether Kenny from IT knew enough to operate the teller machines; she had never seen him try. Yes, there was one person not on the list of people Sam Maki had given us who had a key and could use the teller system: Sam Maki himself.

When Maki's father died three years ago, his mother temporarily ran the bank until she convinced Sam to return home to take it over. Did we know they had a controlling stock interest? I said I did.

Sam went through a year's training before becoming the president. As head teller, Doris had trained him in teller operations. Afterwards, he had spent two months working in all the branches, getting to know employees and how to interact with the banking public. He was an excellent teller. He also spent time in marketing, human resources, financial services where his mother was the tutor, and she couldn't remember what else. A fine young man. The bank and the city were lucky to have him.

Would we like a piece of her fresh-baked pie; it should be cool enough. Before Bartelle could say anything, I accepted for us. The aroma had been working on me since we walked in the door. Besides, I had a feeling that the new information about Sam Maki meant dinner was going to be late.

She served it with a slice of sharp cheddar. Only the good manners my mother taught me prevented me from begging for a second slice.

ON THE WAY TO BARTELLE'S office, he and I agreed to spend the rest of the afternoon uncovering as much as we could about Sam Maki and Hematite National Bank before we interviewed Maki again. I'd take the Hematite material since in a former life I had been a bank analyst; he'd dig out the skinny on Maki. Paddy was presumably sifting through the bank's computer systems.

"Anything I can do?" Abigail asked as she walked us into the sheriff's office. "We'll give you a call to pick him up," Bartelle tilted his head in my direction. Abigail turned on her heel and left. I had the feeling that if she could have slammed the door, she would have. "She was Secret Service, you know," I said. "She might have been—"

"Not in her contract. Let's get to work."

Several hours later over take-out pizza, we compared notes. My research confirmed my recollections of the work I had performed for All-American Bancorp the previous autumn while they considered acquiring Hematite. The FDIC was not likely to shut down Hematite, but the bank wasn't in great shape either. It had issued a number of bad real estate mortgages and had several unsound business loans. The family controlled 62% of the common stock, with Sam's mother's holding a 51% majority stake. To conserve capital, they had eliminated their dividend, which severely affected the Maki family finances.

After Sam Maki's father died, many thought the family would sell to a larger bank. I was not able to determine if the family found no takers—the bank I was doing work for decided not to place a bid—or the offers they received weren't what they hoped for.

"Sam Maki didn't want to come back," Bartelle said. "His mother made him. What we have is good background, but no smoking gun. He's been clean as an adult, with the exception of one arrest in college for DUI. My federal associates did unlock his juvenile file. His father was commander of the local militia during the nineties. Not a nutcase like the guy who claimed the Oklahoma City bombing was the Japanese retaliating for the subway sarin attack deaths. But active.

"Returning to Sam Maki: the Feds raided the Maki's hunting camp while Sam was in high school. The only thing illegal they found was the kid's stash of weed. They concluded the son was also involved with the militia thing. For example, they found training tapes on which he appeared. Someone local brought those two militia boys up from the Mitten to take you out."

"And you're wondering if he inherited more than the presidency of his father's bank."

Bartelle broke into a grin. "It crossed my mind. The Fed's militia source isn't in a position to know who the U.P. players are. I'm surprised we haven't heard from your son yet."

"He was supposed to call—" I pulled my cell phone from my pocket. "Hard to get me if I don't turn the damn thing on."

For the first time, Bartelle produced a belly laugh loud enough to register on nearby tectonic devices.

Paddy blasted me for my stupidity. "Fine, so we agree," I said. "I'm an idiot when it comes to cell phones. What have you got?"

"If anyone in Hematite's IT department is messing with the files, they're better than us. We found no traces of any electronic changes after the transactions occurred. I checked every teller ID. Absolutely the only squirrelly transactions relate to Mrs. Pirhonen's spurious account. The sole purpose of that account was to pay the phone bill without letting anyone like us determine who controlled the phone. I spent the rest of the time cross-checking that phone's outgoing and incoming phone numbers. I can't find a single instance where one of those numbers contacted another one."

"I could hear the good news faster and leave the dead ends for later," I said.

"Fine. One of the numbers, which was located in Hamtramck, was only used in contact with Mrs. Pirhonen's purloined cell phone until three days ago when it received a phone call from a different number. And here's the interesting part: the different number was newly listed that day—in fact, less than fifteen minutes before the call was made."

"So someone ditched the old phone and bought a new one."

"It gets better," Paddy said. "Whoever bought that new phone bought five others in Wausau, all prepaid throwaways. I checked those numbers as well. One made one other call and one received a call from—get this—another brand new cell phone account in Hamtramck. Dad, it is scary how fast these Homeland Security guys and their NSA friends can get search warrants. They tell me if any of those eight phones is used—"

"Eight?"

"Yeah, Dad. The six bought in Wausau, the new one bought in Hamtramck and a cell phone registered to one M. Mouse, who buys minutes for the phone at WalMart. All I can tell you about the last one is the call came to a Crystal Falls cell tower. Anyway, if anyone uses any of those phones, these guys will know, and know what is said, and probably be able to figure out exactly where the phone is. They promised to give Sergeant Bartelle transcripts for anything related to his investigation." He cleared his throat.

I felt a tingle of concern as my neck tightened.

"You know, Dad. Next time a government guy threatens to take you out of circulation if you don't cooperate, take it as a serious threat."

"Great work, Paddy. Anything else to do on your end?"

"Have you considered leaving? I know Abigail's a great bodyguard . . . forget I said anything."

"Forgotten. Love you, Paddy."

"Love you too, Dad."

Before I shut off the cell phone, I saw I had voicemail. I decided not to discover how many times Paddy had called. I briefed Bartelle and concluded, "Sam Maki has become a person of interest, wouldn't you say? We should determine where he was Wednesday afternoon at the time someone acquired those phones. Of course, even if he has an alibi, someone else could have bought the phones for him."

"True," Bartelle said. "And whoever it is used at least the first of those prepaid phones. What's sticking in my craw is why Maki didn't mention he could get into the teller system. Was he so willing to have us check the computer systems because he knew there was nothing there other than what we had already found? What better way to throw us off track than appear to be helpful? He's a damned fine liar, if he's the one."

"You got enough for search warrants for those throwaway phones?"

"I'd like to hold off until we talk with him again. Thinking out loud: if we interview him on Monday, his administrative assistant will be there and one of us can chat her up while the other talks to Maki. Maybe I'll have a search warrant in hand to check his office for the phones. We can have people simultaneously check his house, his car, his camp and anywhere else we can think of. Frankly, I'm too tired to make a good decision right now. Let's call it a day and get together tomorrow."

I was exhausted too but was a bit miffed at Bartelle putting off what we could do today. I meant to hold my tongue in my back molars to forestall speaking my mind. Instead, I bit it—my tongue, not my mind. I don't know how brains work, but with the sharp pain my thoughts returned to Abigail and me. We needed to talk, and sooner was better than later.

Abigail pulled up and I went to sit in the front seat. "It's safer in the back," Abigail said. "And right now all I'm interested in is your safety."

That effectively ended any consideration I had about talking about us. I got into the back. The air conditioning wasn't on, but it sure felt like it was. I pulled my head into my coat, closed my eyes, and rested against the window.

After a few minutes of silence she asked what we had learned. "Nothing I want to talk about," I said.

In response, the car accelerated.

THIRTY-TWO

PENDERGAST AWOKE TO ABIGAIL STORMING into the bedroom they shared. "Don't ask me," Abigail snarled. "Ask him." She inclined her head toward the living room.

Pendergast exhaled an audible sigh to show her displeasure and left Abigail pounding her pillow. "Time for the nightshift," she said to McCree. "Tell me what happened."

Pendergast thought Seamus was going to reject her request. He looked between her and Owen and finally said, "How about we take a walk. I've been cooped up inside all day."

She took the hint about not saying anything in front of Owen. The downside of everyone staying at Owen's was if anyone said anything interesting, it would be on the county grapevine before the sentence was complete. As she donned her winter gear, she wondered if they could intentionally use Owen to feed something to the masses. From the corner of her eye, she kept Seamus in view. He paced in a short oval as though he were a spinning top.

"Let's walk the perimeter," she said. "I can pretend I'm doing something useful."

"I take it you think you aren't?" Seamus held the door open and they walked outside.

Sweet of him; the world resting on his shoulder, yet he was concerned about her. What a far cry from working with AIC Cooper. She started to take his hand and flashed to Abigail. She wasn't going to get into the middle of whatever was going on there. If she were Abigail, she would have changed the sleeping arrangements and the hell with Owen's sensibilities. Of course, she wasn't Abigail. She needed to find safer ground.

"I'm a *prima donna*," she said. "I prefer center stage. Instead, I'm parked in right field hoping a grounder gets through the infield."

"You play ball?" he asked.

"Softball. Full ride to UCLA. I played second base on three national championship teams. The FBI liked that competitive nature and hired me. I'm not so sure Cooper currently considers it a positive attribute."

"Well, I am in the middle of it and I don't feel like I'm doing anything. At least you have an excuse." He faced her directly. "You know, if Cooper does kill your career, tons of places would hire you in a flash."

"Name one."

"CIG. Why do you think Rand put you on their payroll? Have you remembered anything else from your stay at the camp with Brett Aho and your supposed coworker, Brandon?"

"Nope."

"Speaking of Brandon, I never heard the results of his autopsy."

She had hoped the question wouldn't come up. "You'll have to ask Bartelle. So what did you guys learn today?"

McCree stopped and she walked a couple more steps, hoping to pull him along. He didn't budge, so she retreated. "What?"

"I am so damn tired of being treated as though I can't keep a secret—not that a cause of death should be such a damn big secret. Keep walking your perimeter, Agent Pendergast. I can find my own way back to the house."

She thought she felt the earth tremble as Seamus tromped off.

Anger steamed off him and she couldn't blame him. It wasn't her rule, and it wasn't even Bartelle's. NSA wanted that information locked up, and screwing with them wasn't worth the cost. She completed her circuit and returned to the house, where she plunked down on the rocker.

As near as she could figure, Bartelle was using McCree's banking expertise, while at the same time monitoring his activities. Prudent, but stupid. She had argued they should tell McCree everything they knew, but Bartelle had shut her down. It wasn't her place to slip McCree the information. Maybe she'd argue the issue one more time with Bartelle.

Feeling better about her decision, she popped up from the rocker and went inside. Owen was sharpening chainsaw chains. "Where's Seamus?" she asked.

Owen looked up from his work. "Warn't he with you?"

BOSS WOKE UP EARLY, NEEDING to pee, but feeling as excited as a kid on Christmas morning. Like that kid, she had to wait to get her present. The pastor preached something insipid about how if we weren't true to ourselves, every day was a personal Ides of March. She could see the point, but preferred the fire and brimstone sermons of the Baptist church she had grown up in. She slipped into a reverie about how so much had changed since she was a kid. Nowadays, parents negotiated with their children instead of smacking them if they misbehaved. She could still hear the slap of her father's belt as it welted her butt. She'd never whipped her son, but her hand had buzzed after a few spankings. Kids used to look up to schoolteachers—of course teachers used to wear dresses and ties, didn't come to work in jeans. *We all used to look up to lawyers and politicians too. Hell, doctors made house visits.*

How had it all gone so wrong, with everybody looking out only for number one? That's why she had joined the militia with her husband. That's why, as her dying legacy, she had figured out how to fund it. That's why her son might be blood family, but the militia was her real family.

The congregation rose to sing the last hymn, returning her to the present. Boss spent the requisite time in chitchat, made her excuses for not joining folks for lunch, and headed to Da Yooper Tourist Trap, where everything went smooth as silk. The chemist stored the magic potion in a five-gallon container like Boss had used at camp before she got running water. She placed the container in the well of her passenger seat so it wouldn't spill.

Before leaving, Boss used the restroom and left one of the throwaway phones in the ladies' room towel bin, making sure to hold it with toilet paper so she didn't leave any fingerprints after she had done such a meticulous job of cleaning it. The second phone she left outside the BP station at Koski Korners. The rest she pitched in the woods, one each from the three bridges she crossed between Republic and Amasa. She saved Mrs. Pirhonen's phone for last—why she wasn't sure, maybe because it had treated her so well.

During the rest of the trip home, she went through a mental checklist of all the steps taken and her remaining exposure. All communications with biologists Brandon Newhouse and Bethany Palmer would trace back to Brett Aho. The only person they had seen was Brett, and Brett was dead. Brett had contacted her only through Mrs. Pirhonen's cell phone and the cops had hit a dead end tracking down who paid for the phone. She might possibly come under suspicion, but there would be no proof. Whenever she made the afterhours deposits in Mrs. Pirhonen's account, she'd destroyed the security tapes.

A guy who lived in Colorado owned the camp Brett rented. The guy had a mortgage with Hematite National Bank. Perhaps another tiny circumstantial piece of evidence, but only if the guy happened to remember they had discussed the camp—but everyone talked about their camps.

The cops were convinced Jimmie Heitzmann killed Brett. Jimmie had contacted her only in person at her camp or through the Pirhonen cell phone. No one had ever seen him there, and he wouldn't be telling any tales. If Jimmie had broken the rules and written anything down, the cops would have already been knocking at her door. All dead ends for the cops.

Maybe the chemist at Da Yooper Trap had watched her in a mirror, but what could he tell? Her basic size? She wore camo? Big deal; every third person wore camo. She had covered her hair with a floppy fishing hat. He had arrived after her and left before. They might find him after the deed was done, but then it would be too late.

Only the Hamtramck militia connection remained open. She did need to let him know to lay low and not use his cell phone. If he talked, he'd be a marked man. Once he got to prison, he'd come out in a pine box. Years ago, they had agreed to use each other's local weekly paper as a last-ditch warning system if either one of them became toxic. Unfortunately, the *Hamtramck Citizen* had folded after seventy-five years in business and they hadn't gotten around to another solution. *It's the minor things that trip you up.* She would have to risk making a phone call.

At the trailer she wiped the new container to remove fingerprints and stored it with the gas and diesel containers in the pole barn. Sixty-four hours and then she could put the magic potion to good use.

IN THE MORNING, I RETURNED to the crackle and smell of frying bacon.

"Just in time for breakfast," Owen shouted. He was wearing his funeral outfit, which probably doubled as Sunday church clothes. An apron declaring him the world's best grandpa covered his pressed shirt. The apron suggested a side of Owen I would like to see.

"How you want your eggs?" Owen shouted at me.

"Owen," I shouted. "You forgot to turn on your ears." I tapped both my ears.

He reached beneath the apron into his shirt pocket and found the switch. After a moment's adjustment he spoke in a normal volume. "They're both out lookin for you. You shoulda seen the cat fight when they discovered you was gone. Heard tell you was talkin to Doris Stanchina yesterday. Sweet woman. Did she give you a piece of pie? She makes the finest . . ."

Abigail entered the house and stamped the snow off her shoes. She pulled off a wool watch cap and her brunette tresses tumbled down. I tuned Owen out and tensed for the assault.

"The mighty warrior returns," she said. "Owen, that smells splendid. Could you please fry a couple for me?" She crooked her finger at me. "How about we step outside for a sec."

Although spoken softly, I took it as a command. She waited until we were both outside. "Mind telling me what that was about?"

"I was pissed. I did what I do when I'm pissed and don't want to hurt anyone. I walked away. I'm back. No harm, no foul. Why didn't you ever contact me after you left?"

She jabbed me in the chest. "Because *you* told me not to. *You* needed your space to think about everything. *You* needed your wilderness experience. *You* needed to recover from your self-perceived failure to protect me when I was shot at your home. Because, damn it, *you* pushed *me* away." She teared up. "I can't tell you how many times I wrote letters and tore them up because I didn't want to interfere with your healing. All I could hope was you still wanted me and you'd figure it out."

I retreated a step, dumbfounded. This was not how I remembered her departure at all.

"This time you walked away from the professional me. I trusted you and . . ." Tears trickled from under her shades. "Women want to talk things out, Seamus. Men want to think them through, which is fine up to a point, but then you have to share your thoughts. We had been constant companions for six months, but you could never get to the second stage, could you?

"It's like we were the Blue Nile and the White Nile—together but separate." She demonstrated with her hands. "At your camp, without any outside influences, we became less, not more, just as the Nile starts to evaporate in its run to the sea because there are so few tributaries."

She shoved her shades in a pocket and wiped her eyes with her hands. "And look at you . . . you've evaporated. You're all skin and bones."

She stomped her heel hard enough for the porch floor to shake my legs. "Here we are again: I'm doing all the talking. Damn it. Your turn, Seamus. What's going on? And why don't you start with, why didn't you call me back when I left you messages while I was driving up here?"

"What messages?"

"Where's your cell phone?" She stormed off to retrieve it from the room Owen had assigned me. I stood rooted in place until she returned. "Just once I wish you would recognize cell phones as two-way communication devices. But why would you, since you don't know what two-way communication means? They're not only for you to call someone. Other people call you because they want to talk with you."

She thrust the phone at me. "You have six messages. See how you do this? One is from Robert Rand—remember him? He's your employer. Two are from me, and three are from your son. Oh, Seamus, what am I going to do with you?" She jammed the phone into my hand. "Never mind, you're Pendergast's problem now."

"Meaning?"

"Meaning Rand pulled me."

"But it wasn't your fault."

"You think? Oh, crap, I forgot to let Pendergast know you showed up." She left me shivering on the porch.

I listened to the messages. All six ended with the same request: could I please call as soon as possible?

Talk about feeling like a piece of garbage.

Pendergast returned before I had screwed up my courage to go inside. She mumbled as she went past me, "We need to talk."

Owen left to go to church. Breakfast was silent, after which Abigail went into the women's bedroom and returned with a bag.

Pendergast asked, "How can I get all your electronic ears to you?"

"If Seamus is still alive he can send them back. If not?" She shrugged. "Ball's in your court, Mr. McCree."

"You're really leaving?" I asked.

"I always said you were the intuitive sort," Abigail closed the door behind her.

Thirty-Three

Normally Boss took breakfast in town, but something told her this morning she should hang around camp. Good thing. She met Bartelle and McCree at the door of the single-wide and didn't have to feign shock as they handed her a search warrant. Before she let them in, she slowly read it to give herself time to recover from sweaty palms and a racing heart. They were looking for cell phones: Mrs. Pirhonen's and six with 715 area codes, and the fifty-caliber rifle. Good thing she had dispatched the cell phones the day before. The rifle was buried on Hematite Bank's foreclosed property with the clothes she had worn that awful night.

She ushered them in. "Looks legal to me, but what do I know, other than you're wasting your time? I won't bother asking why you're searching here. I'm sure you won't tell me. Can I get you boys some coffee?" She had expected the cops would look at her, but probably not until after her death. What would they find? The militia material she'd blame on her husband.

They could probably recover emails from the laptop. What would she say if they asked about the new five-gallon container with the magic potion? Nothing. The search warrant didn't cover it. To present a happy face, she visualized deer hunting with her father. Those were such good times.

Bartelle and McCree began in the kitchen and opened every drawer, every cupboard, tapped the floor for false bottoms, pulled out the refrigerator. Next came the living room and bathroom. In the bedroom, they discovered the militia material and the false bottom drawer, but she had already emptied it. Since it didn't fit their search warrant, they couldn't spend too much time with the militia stuff, but she decided to spin it anyway.

From the doorway she said, "Frank's stuff, my late husband. He spent all his free time here, and I haven't wanted to throw out anything of his. I know it's kind of silly. It's been three years, but this is the place where I still feel his presence."

They mumbled understanding while poking under the bed, feeling under the mattress. Boss asked, "Looks like you're almost done in here, you want me to unlock the outbuildings?"

"Give us the keys," Bartelle said. "We'd prefer you to stay inside."

"How about when you're done here, I lock up this place and unlock all the outbuildings? Then you won't need me here, and I can get some work done in town. You'll lock them up when you're finished?"

"We'll have to do your truck next, but it sounds like a plan," Bartelle said.

After they finished inside, she locked the door behind them. McCree crawled underneath the single-wide and she led Bartelle to the old latrine and various sheds and unlocked everything to his satisfaction. "Just snap them shut." she said.

Bartelle searched the truck, which was totally clean, and wished her a great day.

Not today, she thought, but two days from now will be special.

BARTELLE AND I WATCHED MRS. Maki leave. "She seemed nervous," I said. "Especially as we looked at the militia stuff."

"Well, we already knew her husband was a commander in their heyday."

"Any indication she was involved?"

"It was a macho outfit. I'm not even sure women were allowed. I can understand not throwing stuff away, though. My Aunt Angelica still keeps a Hudson Bay wool shirt my uncle wore. She claims to use it on cold nights, but I think she still wants something to remind her of him all these years later."

"So you think she was telling the truth?"

He left my question unanswered and we continued our search. We found no cell phones and no fifty-caliber rifles in any of the structures. Tacked on the back side of a woodshed were two pelts. "Those aren't—"

"Not wolf," Bartelle said, "Coyote. Look at the ears: they're pointed, not rounded. He touched the nose. "And a coyote's muzzle is also more pointed than a wolf's. Don't try to judge by overall size. A young wolf can be smaller than a grown coyote. Huh?" He stepped closer to the pelts. "Look at these holes."

One had two holes; the other had six. Half the holes were round, the other half jagged. "Okay," I said. "They were shot from the right and the bullets exited their left side. What else am I supposed to see?"

"The bullets punched through the coyotes so they were shot with a high-powered gun. Not surprising, but the interesting thing is the pelt with the six holes. Bing, bing, bing. The coyote didn't stand there after getting shot once for the hunter to do it a second and third time."

"A three-shot burst," I said.

"Bingo, just like the ones used to kill those guys at your place."

Bartelle's cell phone rang with a "God Bless America" tune. The state troopers who had searched Sam Maki's home and office found nothing of interest. We spent the rest of the daylight hours scouring Mrs. Maki's forty acres. In the first five minutes, we found the coyote remains, well picked over by scavengers. Otherwise, our search was fruitless. As dark gathered and a light mist began to fall, Bartelle took me to Owen's.

Bartelle pulled up next to Owen's rusted iron menagerie and clunked the car into park before it had completely stopped. "I'm pretty much flat out of ideas. Maybe we'll get lucky and someone will use one of those phones."

"I've been meaning to ask you," I said. "What was it that killed Brandon Newhouse?"

Bartelle looked at me sharply, shifted his gaze to the car roof, and shrugged once. "Pneumonia."

"That kills one theory I was working on. You going to ask Mrs. Maki about the coyotes?"

"It's about all we've got unless someone uses those phones. And Seamus, stay put tonight. Just because you lucked out when you walked into Amasa to the Rusty Sawblade doesn't mean it will happen again. Who knows what might have happened if you hadn't found that guy who poured your foundation and he let you crash on his couch. Walking around alone is crazy right now and I don't want to attend any more funerals."

It felt like a cheap shot. It also felt like I deserved it.

TUESDAY MORNING, THE SMELL OF bacon filled the house as Owen served another artery-clogging breakfast. We sat in our assigned seats, boys on one side, Pendergast on the other next to the empty place where Abigail should have been if I hadn't been so damn stupid. I had tossed and turned all night. Tossing because I was missing something crucial in the investigation. Turning because I had screwed up my personal life. Again.

I knew the best way to come up with missing investigation pieces was to take a break from the problem and let my unconscious work. Unfortunately, my unconscious seemed clueless about my personal life.

"Owen," Pendergast said, "I'm taking Seamus to meet Sergeant Bartelle. I notice you're low on veggies and fruits. Anything in particular you want me to get at the store?"

"What do you mean?" I said. "You can't leave here."

"And you need protection." She resumed eating, as though she had already won the argument. She shrugged, then added: "Besides, lying around all day watching TV isn't my idea of fun. I'd rather be out and about."

I put my fork down. "Rand must not think I do since he ordered Abigail away instead of just chewing me out. There's no reason for you to cross AIC Cooper. It's one thing watching Owen's and my backs while we're sleeping. It's something else if you shove your involvement under his nose."

"Abigail lied to you. Rand didn't order her to protect you. She twisted his arm to let her. That whole line with ovacaput—she made it up. You're an idiot if you don't know she loves you."

"And you know this because?"

"We talked. Something you should try."

I pointed a fork at Owen, who was shoveling in food as though he was eating by himself. "What do you think?"

"Before I got these choppers fixed up, all I could eat was soft stuff." He pulled the dentures from his mouth, studied them like Hamlet contemplating the skull, and then returned them to their proper place. "I got so sick of overripe bananers and pears and mushy vegetables, once they fixed me up I swore off that stuff and, despite what they say on TV, I cain't eat no apples. I can do corn on the cob, but that ain't in season. If you're wantin somethin different, that wouldn't make me no nevermind. I tolerated them soups Seamus made when I'd bring him his supplies. Still got more home fries if you want 'em."

I rubbed my forehead with both hands, trying to make sense of this conversation. "I won't permit you to screw up your life, Agent Pendergast."

"And who made you God?" She kicked me under the table with a socked foot. "This is the twenty-first century, McCree. People get to make their own choices. For better or for worse. Besides . . ." She kicked me again, but this time gently. "You can't drive unless I return your gas cap."

"Gas cap?"

"Yep. One of the things they taught me at Quantico. Within a mile your engine will shut down because without your gas cap the pressure in the engine is all wrong."

"You was in the Marines?" Owen asked.

"You took my gas cap?" I asked.

She smiled at Owen. "The FBI has their training at Quantico." She exaggerated her smile for me. "I wasn't about to have you drive off without me."

Owen cleared his throat. "Don't play checkers with that one. While you're in town, Seamus, you call on them window fellas. Your replacement windows should be in. If we get one last cold spell to freeze the roads, they might get them in before spring. Otherwise, you're lookin at May. How long you fixin to stay?"

"I know we're an inconvenience—"

"That ain't why I'm askin. If I didn't want you here, you'd come back from town and find your stuff on the porch and the door locked. I was wonderin if I should invite the grandkids over for some of their Easter vacation."

"I couldn't possibly impose on you so long," I said. "That's nearly a month away."

"Are you thick in the skull? There's nothin—" Owen slammed his fist on the table, rattling the plates and spilling Pendergast's coffee. His face turned dark purple. "Nothin more important than gettin these people. You can stay here until Christmas as long as you and Bartelle are still lookin at those killins. We lost five fine people, and there ain't nothin I wouldn't do to bring them back. But since I cain't, the next best thing is to string up the polecat that done it."

I mumbled appreciation and forced down scrambled egg, which had now lost its flavor. I wondered if we were making progress.

Pendergast handed me the gas cap after she climbed into the passenger seat.

"I know I can never outlast your quiet," Pendergast said after we reached paved road. "I'm not going to even try. You got both barrels of the shotgun this morning between Owen and me. Not that you didn't deserve it." She gave my thigh a friendly, but not too friendly, pat.

"I'm sorry if our time together got in the way of you and Abigail. She and I talked a lot while you were AWOL. Listen up, Seamus. The woman is crazy in love with you. I'm not saying you two should get hitched, buy a two-story ranch in the suburbs and have two point five kids—well one point five, you've already got Patrick and he's great. You would be a fool if you don't crawl on your knees down to Chicago and make up with her. Besides, you're stupid if you don't realize you love her as much as she loves you."

My jaw ached from clenching my teeth while she talked. I didn't want to be lectured to, but it was justified. Probably.

"I've watched you long enough to know you won't start crawling south until you're done up here. So what did you and Bartelle find with your search warrants? Oh, and in case you were thinking of dumping me, I'm taking permanent possession of your gas cap."

She gave my upper arm a friendly punch and stuck out her hand. "Friends?"

"Either that or I need to drive your side of the car into a tree," I said.

THIRTY-FOUR

PENDERGAST SAT IN THE OFFICE by herself plodding through case files while Bartelle and McCree interviewed Sam Maki. She saw no burning bushes, heard no heralding angels. As soon as the guys returned, she pounced, "Get anything?"

McCree shook his head. "He claimed he was asleep with his wife the night of the killings at my place. Where else would anyone be? He's now hired Paddy's firm to do a complete security analysis of their systems. He sure seemed seriously angry about someone screwing with their software security."

"The man," Bartelle said, "has brass balls. Or isn't our guy. He claims he resigned from the militia as a sophomore in college. Showed me a letter from his father ripping him a new one for deserting the cause. Would you have kept that letter?"

McCree leaned his head back and howled with laughter. "Well, it would be great cover for a moment such as this."

"Yeah right," Bartelle said. "He knew nothing about the coyotes. Only hunts partridge and deer with business colleagues. Never owned a fifty-caliber gun. I verified his alibi for when the phones were purchased down in Wausau.

"Oh, and speaking about those phones, yesterday I got a call from a local Wausau officer who stopped by the store to inquire about the phone sale. The clerk remembered the sale to a late middle-aged white woman. Couldn't remember much else and there's no security tape. The clerk was only twenty and put the buyer's age between forty-five and sixty-five. The girl didn't think it would help to work with a police artist, but thought she might recognize the woman if we had a picture."

Pendergast asked McCree, "What's your *gut* tell you?"

"Sam Maki is either a great actor or we're barking up the wrong tree. Of course, I've been fooled by great actors before. I say the word, 'bodyguard,' what comes to mind? A big strapping hulk of a guy, right? Abigail fights that image all the time because she's not male and, while she's not small, she's also not an Amazon. She often says she's more effective because people don't think she is a bodyguard."

Pendergast witnessed Bartelle crook his arm over his head and start scratching away. She figured he was equally clueless about McCree's point. "And . . ." She gestured to indicate she wanted more.

"It's those coyote pelts. They've kept bothering me and—remember the Feds running over each other trying to figure out how the militia was using the camp that burned down to fund operations? The DEA was convinced they were bringing in drugs from Canada. AFT thought they were smuggling firearms, and Homeland Security suspected they were tied into terrorists. All of them were getting intel from the NSA, but each saw what they wanted to see. What do you think about when someone mentions a militia outfit? A bunch of guys. Assume Sam Maki has been telling the truth all along. Who first ran the bank after his father died?"

"His mother, K.C. Maki," Bartelle said.

"Right, and it's a banking family. I'll lay dollars to donuts she knows how to run the teller machines. Maybe she worked in the bank as a teller when she was young. Where did we find the old militia information? Her camp. Where did we find the coyotes with the three-burst kill pattern? Her camp. There's money involved here somewhere and what does she do for the bank? Personal investments and financial planning. Why couldn't she be the link to everything? Her husband dies and she runs the bank until she can get Sonny up to speed. Maybe she also took over the militia operations from her husband?

"In fact," McCree slapped his forehead so hard it showed white before turning red. "Who guaranteed the viatical settlement payments? Hematite Bank. Who at Hematite is responsible for personal finances? K.C. Maki. Remember what I said about your aunt's policy?"

Bartelle stopped scratching, leaned forward. "You think the militia is going to storm the Laughing Loon and kill all the geezers? That's crazy."

"What," Pendergast asked, "are you two talking about?"

"First things first," Bartelle said. He flipped through his notes and phoned Doris Stanchina. McCree waved Pendergast quiet while Bartelle asked Doris about K.C. Maki.

After listening to the answers, Bartelle pursed his lips and raised his eyebrows. "So Mrs. Maki filled in whenever anyone called in sick?" Bartelle asked. "No reason to apologize for forgetting about her. We didn't think to ask either."

Bartelle replaced the receiver. "You know everyone's nickname for her is 'Boss.' "

"Even her son introduced her to me that way," McCree said.

"How about," Pendergast said "you fax a picture of Mrs. Maki to the phone clerk in Wausau. See if she can identify her. There's a recent picture in the *Iron County Reporter* of her giving me clothes at the hospital. If she's the one, so much for Christian charity!"

Bartelle got the administrative assistant to take care of the details and checked Kathryn Cynthia Maki for a record—all she had accumulated were a few speeding tickets.

"Is there a way to protect the Laughing Loon?" McCree asked after giving Pendergast the viatical details.

Pendergast joined Bartelle in head shaking. "He's got no evidence, Seamus. The best he can do is put a tail on Mrs. Maki. Even if this is her play, it's hard to see her leading the raid. It would come in the middle of the night, just like they tried at your place."

"Crap," spat McCree like a forty-five going off. "Then get her phone records and see if there's a link anywhere."

"We got nothing we can go to a judge with," Bartelle said. "We can't use the militia stuff we found at her camp or the coyote pelts. Even if we could, it's still not near enough."

"Yeah, but the NSA people don't seem to need much of any reason. I'll call Paddy and have him see what they'll say."

BOSS LET HERSELF INTO THE church through the side door off the alley. Taking the darkened stairway to the basement, she ran a gloved hand along the concrete block wall, following its rough edges to the central religious education room. She slipped inside and, using her fingers like spider legs, found the phone hanging on the wall, placed there years ago so the teachers could call nine-one-one without having to leave the room in case a child got hurt. Now, of course, everyone had cell phones.

The number pad lit at her touch, making it easy to dial in the dark. Voicemail answered; she whispered to disguise her voice, "Destroy that phone. No contact at all. The cops are all over this, but after tomorrow morning they'll be too late." Less than ten seconds, she thought. The cops won't be able to trace her call. Only one more link left to destroy, and no time like the present to do it.

At camp she set up the old Inspiron laptop and deleted all the emails from both the inbox and sent folder. Experts could retrieve things from the hard drive unless you used special erasing software, which she didn't have. What she did have was a sledgehammer, and she took great joy in pulverizing the machine. She collected the pieces and put them into a black plastic bag.

A dozen miles away, she threw the bag into a dumpster kept near the Florence Natural and Wild Rivers Interpretative Center picnic grounds. The effort of screeching the lid up pushed her into a coughing jag, which took forever to stop. It was worth the effort, though. The Wisconsin DNR would be more worried about litter than tying this to any investigation across state lines.

Despite the constant pain, she was jubilant. The plan would work. The only thing left to do was apply the five gallons of magic potion the next morning.

PADDY CALLED BACK MUCH QUICKER than even I expected.

"Not yet," he answered to my question regarding access to K.C. Maki's phone records. "Someone just called the Hamtramck cell phone and left a message. The call came from the Presbyterian Church in Crystal Falls two minutes ago. I quote, 'Destroy that phone. No contact at all. The cops are all over this, but after tomorrow morning they'll be too late.' "

"That's it?"

"Yeah, but given the analysis of calls I've done so far, the chances are ninety-nine out of one hundred Mrs. Pirhonen's cell phone was used to order up those two guys from Hamtramck."

"How do you know?"

He cleared his throat. "Remember, NSA's probably monitoring me too. The other thing you should know is that two of the six Wisconsin prepaids have been used. ICE already checked the people out. They appear to be just regular people who found the phones in Marquette County. I'm afraid someone got wise and ditched all the phones. I'll let you know when I have something more."

Bartelle called the Crystal Falls police to have someone run to the church. A minute later the answer came back: it was empty and locked. They would contact the church sexton.

Next, he ordered Tex to meet us at the church. The church sexton greeted us at the main entrance. He had no idea how many people had keys. "Too many, but no one listens to me," he said.

Tex dusted doorknobs, phones in the office, and the phone downstairs. "Too many prints," he kept muttering under his breath.

Outside and away from the sexton's hearing, Bartelle told Tex to start with the prints from the phones. First thing, check them against K.C. Maki." Tex raised one eyebrow, a trick I had never mastered.

"She got prints on file?" Tex asked.

"I'll bet," I said. "She had to be fingerprinted for her NASD exams."

"NA what?" Bartelle asked.

"National Association of Securities Dealers. If she's giving advice or selling annuities, she needs to have passed some of their exams. They require your fingerprints. Broker/dealers need to get the Criminal History Record Information from the FBI." I laughed at myself. "I know, too much information. The point is: her prints are on file somewhere."

"If the sheriff's department took them, they're in Michigan's database," Tex said. "The whole thing is automated. If I'm only trying to match her, we'll know later today."

"Just to be on the safe side," Bartelle said. "Check her son as well. Sam Maki."

With a roar of stressed engine, Tex laid rubber like a teenager on a hot date leaving us breathing burnt rubber.

After tomorrow morning they'll be too late. I had to make Bartelle understand those words from the phone message were a ticking clock and that not acting might seal the fate of those who had signed the viatical settlements.

"Let's make a quick stop at the Laughing Loon," I said. "I don't remember the name of the company buying those policies, and we can ask your aunt who the salesman—or, if my guess is right—saleswoman was."

After a moment's hesitation, Bartelle said, "I'll give her a call."

"It's just around the corner. Pendergast can cool her heels in your office for another ten minutes. I've found talking to someone in person is preferable to the phone." I could see the indecision in his eyes. "Please," I pleaded. "Ten minutes."

Bartelle rubbed his eyes with the heels of his hands. "Ten minutes. Max. Maybe when we get back Tex will have something on the prints."

* * *

BARTELLE SIGNED THEM IN AT the Laughing Loon and led the way to his aunt's room. "Just a second," she called from the back after Bartelle rapped on the door.

She wheeled out in her chair; a huge smile lit her face when she saw Bartelle, who made the introductions. "Seamus McCree, this is my aunt, Mrs. Angelica Ricci."

"Isn't this the man who looked at my viatical settlement?" At Bartelle's nod, she continued. "Everyone who signed the deal had their checks clear, so I decided if some fool wanted to pay more than they should for the investment, I'd be darned if I wouldn't let them. I took the money and laddered a few CDs since interest rates are lousy. That way, if rates go up, I won't be locked in forever."

"Laddered CDs?" Bartelle asked.

"It means," McCree said, "she bought several certificates of deposit with different maturity dates, and she'll roll them over as they come due. Sounds like a good plan to me. I don't recall the name of the company making the viatical settlements."

"Slips my mind too," Mrs. Ricci said. "K.C. Maki made the sale. You know her, don't you, Lon?"

Bartelle and McCree traded sideways looks and Bartelle asked if she still had the papers available. She pulled them from a drawer. Bartelle wrote the name in his notebook: Freedom Settlements of Michigan, LLC.

"What's the big interest all of a sudden?" Mrs. Ricci asked. "You didn't make a math error did you, young man?"

McCree gave her a charming smile. "No, ma'am. How do you like living here? I ask because at some point I'll need to find something similar for my mother."

She chattered on with a little encouragement from McCree, and Bartelle checked his watch, wondering where he was going with his questions, especially when his aunt's biggest complaints were that they kept the rooms too hot and the hot water too cold. He caught on after McCree said, "It's nice they take you on trips. Do you have any in the near future?"

"Oh yes!" she said. "And you know it just came up. Twice a year they try to get as many of us as possible to go to the casino. They make a big deal of it. Serve us a free lunch. Give us five bucks for the slots. We usually have at least two busloads. Normally, it's in April or May and again in October or November, but this year it's pushed up to tomorrow. They must have gotten a better deal."

"Tomorrow?" Alarm filled Bartelle. McCree's supposition just gained traction. "You going?" He heard the anxiety in his voice.

"Of course." She soundlessly laughed and clapped her hands together. "Those old folks play the slots, but I usually do pretty well at blackjack and craps. Do you know the house has the biggest margin on the slots?"

Bartelle stood up. "Sounds like fun," he said. "I'll look forward to hearing all about it. Mr. McCree and I have a few other things to check on the investigation." He leaned down and kissed her cheek. "You take care now and don't bust the casino."

I TAGGED ALONG AS BARTELLE tracked down the Laughing Loon's manager, a thin wisp of a man sporting a comb-over that fooled no one except himself. His voice was whiny, but I was only half paying attention to their conversation. I was plotting how to uncover the ownership of Freedom Settlements of Michigan, LLC and wondering who was behind it.

Bartelle determined the Laughing Loon was using the tour bus company they had always used for the casino trip. They were going to the same casino. The tour bus operator supplied the drivers; Laughing Loon provided the attendants to help the residents on and off the buses. They also used two specialized vans for those with wheelchairs.

"Really, officer, there's nothing unusual about this. We do it twice a year, timed for the HVAC guys doing system maintenance. They need to shut down the furnace and test the air conditioning. Depending on how long it takes, some of the rooms can get cool—not dangerously so—but some older people find it uncomfortable."

"But some people don't go on the trip?" Bartelle said.

"Sure. They're too ill or can't be easily moved. For example, one lady had a recent hip replacement and she's too fragile to go. We bring those left behind to our day room, which we heat with electric heaters for the duration. You haven't told me what this is all about."

Bartelle ignored the implied question and got contact information for the transport company and casino. We left Laughing Loon at a fast walk.

Once safely in Bartelle's car he said, "Are you thinking what I'm thinking?" While talking to the manager, Bartelle had presented a calm exterior with the exception of a nervous tic in his left eye. Now the stress showed all over his face.

"What are you going to do?"

"I'm open to ideas. Should I cancel their trip?"

"Maybe you should let it go forward, but introduce a bunch of safeguards. Sounded like two buses and two vans. Can you add a guard to each, get the vehicles inspected before they leave the company's lot—brakes, fluids, bombs—that sort of thing. Maybe even replace the drivers? If you shut it down, they may change plans and end up mowing everyone down in their beds some night. They've shown they're not averse to killing people. Of course, that may be their plan anyway. Not my call, though, and thank God."

"Point taken. Above a sergeant's pay grade, too."

"Why don't we try to shake up K.C. Maki? Without giving any specifics, let her know we're onto her scheme. Then put on a tail. Maybe she'll call it off or lead us to someone. What have we got to lose? I also want to try to track down who owns Freedom Settlements of Michigan. Maybe we can get a lead that way."

Something niggled at the back of my brain, but I couldn't work it into the light. Bartelle called the sheriff and brought him up to speed. When the conversation concluded, Bartelle motioned to me to follow him. "Let's see if we can rattle Mrs. Maki."

THIRTY-FIVE

BOSS SAW THEM WALK IN the bank's door and head directly toward her office. She picked up the phone and dialed her home number. She conversed with her answering machine, letting Bartelle and McCree hear her give such noncommittal information as "uh-huh" and "I can see how that would work," and "Tell me a little more about that." All the while, she worked to control her bouncing knee. She looked up, gave them the "just a minute" sign and motioned to the chairs in front of her desk.

Once she calmed her leg she signed off the phone call, promising she'd get back to the other party in a day or two. Putting on her brightest smile, she asked, "What can I do for you gentlemen today?"

She expected Bartelle to take the lead and damn near crapped her pants when McCree opened the conversation with, "I hear they call you Boss. Well, Boss, the biggest mistake you made was not killing me. Too late now. I figured out your scheme, and I guarantee this: not one penny from the life insurance proceeds will be paid if those people at the Laughing Loon die in some collective tragedy." He rose partly from his chair as though he was going to vault the desk. "Mark my words, in days or maybe even hours, your life is over. O-V-E-R."

She felt Bartelle's eyes focused on her until McCree started his spelling lesson. Then he reached up and pulled McCree down to his seat, but said nothing.

Boss's mind raced to frame an answer. The threat on her life was nothing. Cancer was going to beat justice. Whatever else, she must protect the plan. She chose righteous anger as her weapon. "Who are you to come into my office and accuse me of . . . of . . . whatever it is you are accusing me of?" She sounded a bit strained to herself, and the words didn't come out as she had intended them. "You may leave right now."

McCree smiled, like he had won some battle.

Bartelle cleared his throat. "We hoped not to have to take you to the jail to talk. We thought it would be easier for you here. Maybe we should close the door?"

Now she got it: bad cop/good cop—even though McCree wasn't one. Bartelle reached behind him and closed the door. The harsh click startled her back to the present.

"We know you stole the phone from Mrs. Pirhonen," McCree said. "And you manipulated the bank's records so it would look like she kept paying the phone bill. Nice setup. And those calls you made right before those two guys from the militia came to the woods and killed five of your neighbors? Wouldn't surprise me if your lawyer doesn't go for a change in venue."

"Now, Seamus," Bartelle said. "We didn't come here to badger her. We wanted to give her a chance to tell us how she got involved in this whole mess. It's probably something her husband sucked her into and she didn't know the details until it was too late. I'm sure we can find some way to smooth this over for one of the county's leading citizens."

McCree's face reddened in anger and Boss thought he might spit at her. Instead he poked his finger at Bartelle. "I'll tell you this," he yelled. "If one more person dies, it is all on her head." He jabbed his finger in her direction and she rocked back in her chair. "I know you can't arrest her yet, but as soon as the clerk verifies she's the one who bought all those phones in Wausau—" He abruptly rose, knocking his chair backwards and leaned over the desk. "You made a big mistake calling Hamtramck again. We're checking prints on the phone you used at the Presbyterian Church."

Boss tamped down fear, surprised anything could still make her afraid. She knew she had a glazed look because she felt as though someone had taken a bat and smacked her on the head. How had they figured out everything? Somehow she managed to say, "If you have specific questions, perhaps I can help you, but I'm really confused by what you're saying."

Bartelle again took charge in his soft, comforting voice, asking once more about Mrs. Pirhonen's phone—she denied having anything to do with it. She thought about having her lawyer present for this questioning, but decided she was better off feigning innocence and stonewalling. She reminded herself: despite what McCree claimed, nothing had really changed. They had nothing solid and could have nothing unless someone talked, and they had yet to mention any names. She relaxed in her chair and, like a wily trout, ignored the lures Bartelle cast in front of her.

Remember, she told herself, get through tomorrow and everything will take care of itself.

OWEN GOT CRUSTY ON ME after I complimented him on the wholesome dinner he had concocted with the fresh ingredients we provided. "Just don't get used to it," he said. "So spill the beans. What's goin on at the Laughin Loon?"

"You tell us," Pendergast said.

"Heard tell there's a big scare about takin the residents to the casino tomorrow. They replaced all the bus drivers with retired cops, and off-duties are ridin shotgun."

"I helped Bartelle with that," Pendergast said. "It's amazing how many police officers or retired cops up here are licensed to drive buses."

Owen snorted. "You usually need two or three jobs around here just to make it. Anyone retirin from a government job keeps workin at somethin else."

"Well," Pendergast said between bites, "Bartelle already got the buses inspected—all clean—and they're under guard. The DNR's going to cover them from the air."

"I hear tell the cops wanted the Loonies to cancel the trip, but I didn't hear nothin about who's supposed to be plannin this ambush. What if it's a roadside bomb type deal?"

"I'm sure they considered all the risks," I said. "While Pendergast was arranging security, I traced who owns the company that bought the insurance policies from folks at the Laughing Loon. I found a spaghetti bowl of interlocking corporations, which ultimately end up being owned by a private foreign corporation."

"Which, I'll bet," Pendergast added, "is located in one of those fine upstanding countries where secrecy is the biggest business."

"Bingo. This is so elaborate it must be set up to launder money."

Owen yanked out his dentures and wiped them with a finger. "Dad-burn seed hurts like a sumbitch root canal." With dentures back in place he asked, "What's all this about dry cleanin money? You know who the baddies are?"

"Sure do, Owen," I said. "But we can't talk about it, so mum's the word."

"You can count on me," he said. " 'Bout time I get to the senior center for bingo." After Owen left, Pendergast asked why I told Owen we had a suspect.

"He'll tell everyone at bingo, they'll tell their families, and by tomorrow morning everyone should know. Maybe then they'll think twice about whatever they planned. The whole idea is to catch them before they do anything, right?"

"I see your point. While Bartelle guards the caravan tomorrow, I thought I'd look through the files one more time. Want to join me?"

"Bartelle say I could look at the files?"

She flashed a smile. "I'm sorry. The tree frogs are so loud tonight, I didn't hear what you asked."

* * *

Boss noticed the tail following her up Rock Crusher Road to camp and wondered when it had started. She pulled into the driveway and parked behind the single-wide, retrieved the five-gallon container of magic potion and placed it in the passenger footwell. Once inside the trailer, she brewed a pot of coffee.

After pouring steaming coffee into a thermos, she grabbed a pint carton of half and half and a nearly full bottle of whiskey and walked down to the road. Sure enough, parked up the road a piece, pointed toward town, was the unmarked Iron County Sheriff's car. Those antennas give them away. She walked up to the driver's window, and the surprised young man lowered it.

"I'd invite you in, but I'm sure you aren't allowed. I don't know how long your shift is, so I brought you coffee." She handed him the thermos. "Half and half?" She held up the whiskey bottle. "Or something a bit stronger? I can get some sugar if you want it sweet."

He tried to return the thermos. "I can't take these, Mrs. Maki."

"Oh, you're going to need them because I'm not going out tonight and don't have to leave until noon tomorrow." The last was a patent lie, but best to set expectations early.

"Please, Mrs. Maki, I can't accept this."

"Well, if you need to use the facilities, come right in. The door won't be locked and I'm a heavy sleeper, so I'll never know. You have a good evening now." She collected her offerings and returned to the single-wide.

Now what the hell was she going to do? If it weren't for the five gallons of stuff, she could slip out the back and walk to town, but she needed the potion and she needed a few plumbing tools. The cop car was pointed toward town. She could escape in her truck going the other way, but there'd be a BOLO on her before she made it to the first turn. She'd planted the seed about her sticking around; she either needed to figure out how to get past him with the car, or rig up some method of carrying the potion and the tools if she walked. That wouldn't be practical—someone would see her.

The rough woods road running from her property onto the adjacent state land was her last chance. If she could make it through without getting stuck and without the cop noticing she was gone, then she had a few hours before they would miss her.

She returned to the cop and he rolled down his window. "Ma'am?"

"I decided to take a little ATV ride. I thought maybe I should tell you so you didn't get worried. I expect to be gone less than an hour. I'll let you know when I get back?"

She wished she could capture a picture of the kid's face. He had no clue what to do and would have to call it in. By then she'd be gone and about the time they had their undies all in a wad, she'd report back.

Good thing she had checked the woods. She had to clear two downed trees from a late-winter storm. She returned from her scouting mission to find the unmarked car had company: an Iron County vehicle towing a trailer with an ATV. She reported in, again offered coffee and/or whiskey, gave them a convincing yawn and a realistic hacking spell. Minutes later, she was asleep.

SHE HAD BEEN A BIT rankled when, for her last birthday, Sam unilaterally replaced her well-used F-150 with a Lexus RX hybrid. Yes, it was fuel efficient. Yes, it was reliable—the point the kids emphasized in their birthday note. Yes, the bank was wooing a Lexus dealership to settle in Crystal Falls. Yes, its ground clearance was acceptable at a touch under seven inches. But what she really appreciated right now was its silent start.

Not until she was several hundred yards away from the single-wide on the two-track to the state land did the gas engine engage. The cop was unlikely to hear it or attribute it to her.

Expecting the buses and vans to leave at nine a.m., she had given them an extra half hour and arrived at the Laughing Loon at nine-thirty a.m. with tools and container in hand. The cops were all gone except for the rent-a-cop manning a makeshift barricade in the driveway.

She lowered her window, smiled at a face she knew, but wasn't coming up with the name. "Problem?" she yelled over his radio blaring "Telephone Time."

"Not hardly, Mrs. Maki. I'm supposed to get everyone to sign in since the receptionist is off to the casino with all the old . . . er, residents." He handed a clipboard through her window. She scrawled an illegible signature on the line and handed it back. "Thanks, ma'am." He waved her on.

What were the chances he would remember her? Well, it would be his word against the cop babysitting her camp, who would swear she never left.

She drove past the facility and took the service road around back. As previously agreed with the manager, the bulkhead doors were unlocked. She pried one up with a squeal of disuse and ducked down the stairs to the furnace room carrying the five-gallon can. The manager had done the initial preparation and turned off the furnace to let it cool. It would only take a few minutes to finish her work.

THIRTY-SIX

PENDERGAST AND I OCCUPIED A pin-drop quiet meeting room in the sheriff's office with the various case files stacked on the table. It was depressing to realize each of the ten red folders reflected a death: Brett Aho—believed to have been killed by Jimmie Heitzmann; Jimmie Heitzmann—drowned when his snowmobile broke through Long Lake's ice cover; Brandon Newhouse—weighted down with cement blocks and pulled out of Long Lake with Jimmie Heitzmann; the first militia guy—a suicide; the second militia guy—finally discovered in the woods with the stolen ATV, either accidently shot or purposefully killed to eliminate a witness; and finally, the five locals—gunned down trying to protect me.

The Laughing Loon trip was scheduled to last all day, leaving shortly after breakfast and returning in time for dinner. Bartelle shadowed the caravan from a DNR plane. The sheriff, ensconced in his office, monitored everyone's position. Ahead of the caravan, police blocked road crossings with the same precision as if the president were touring the U.P. At least that was the plan.

Consequently, we would have an uninterrupted day to scrutinize the files. I had forgotten the amount of mind-numbing detail police investigations involved. Because many of the deaths were related, many pages cross-referenced other files. I was convinced Hematite National Bank and one or more Maki were involved, and so I initially focused on them.

After a couple of hours, I decided bouncing from file to file wasn't getting me anywhere. Pendergast's approach was to read each file from beginning to end. She was the trained investigator, so I modeled her behavior. I picked up Brandon Newhouse's file since his death was first.

Reading his autopsy report, I came across the first piece of critical new information.

"Hey, Pendergast, why didn't you tell me Brandon died of Legionnaires' disease?"

"State secret. Literally. Homeland Security threatened us all. Technically pneumonia killed him, but Legionnaires' was the proximate cause."

I quickly pulled Brett Aho's and Jimmie Heitzmann's autopsy reports. Each had been tested for Legionnaires' disease and each was clean. I sifted through files until I came to the one with the forensic analysis of my home. The chemical analysis of the samples Tex took showed nothing harmful. Penciled in the margin was a note: "no L.D."

Legionnaires' disease? I folded my hands behind my head, closed my eyes, and leaned back in the chair. My heart was pounding blood so strongly I could feel the pressure in my eardrums. I thought I knew, but I couldn't jump to conclusions.

"Where did you and Brandon go that Brett Aho didn't go?"

She looked up from the file she was reading. "He was pretty much with us all the time."

I shook my head. "Can't be. There had to be someplace. Did he avoid a particular part of the cabin?"

"Nope. You saw: the cabin only had three rooms. Everybody went everywhere."

I pulled Tex's notes on his biological search of my house and read them again. He was concentrating on hot water. The camp Brandon and Pendergast had stayed at had running water, but I couldn't remember seeing a hot water heater. "How did you guys stay clean?"

"Sauna."

"Brett ever use the sauna?"

"What are you thinking?" She closed one file and opened another. "Now you mention it, he said he hated saunas—made him feel all woozy on account of asthma or something. He grabbed showers in town someplace."

"You were guinea pigs."

She gave me a what-the-hell-are-you-talking-about look.

"They intentionally infected you and Brandon with Legionnaires' disease in the sauna. Why else would they be so anxious to capture or kill you? The only person you saw was Brett Aho, and they killed him, so they had to be worried about something you could have told someone."

I whacked myself on the forehead. "It all fits. The Laughing Loon casino trip is today because of furnace maintenance. They're infecting the heating system today. Maybe they already have. We've got to evacuate the Laughing Loon and test their system."

"But you get Legionnaires' disease from air conditioning equipment. The FBI was supposed to check every place Brandon and I went."

"And obviously found nothing or you would have heard. The key to Legionnaires' disease is it needs to be transmitted in an aerosol. Hot water can work just as well. The Laughing Loon has steam heat—essentially the same delivery mechanism for Legionnaires' disease as a camp sauna. They're going to infect the old folks with Legionnaires' disease and collect on the life insurance policies Mrs. Maki bought from the residents. They're betting people treat it as a natural tragedy. Probably spur political investigations and lawsuits and whatnot, but the insurance companies will pay off on the life insurance. Whoever controls the secret account at the end of the corporation ownership chain I tried to follow will make a ton of money."

I paused to make sure I had her full attention. "Wanna bet this is how the militia is planning to fund their arms purchase?"

"No Seamus, you're wrong. Boiling water kills the bacteria that cause Legionnaires' disease. Anything over about a hundred and fifty degrees is enough, and you're talking steam heat."

I felt sure she and Brandon had been guinea pigs, but obviously I was wrong about the sauna. "Must be the air conditioning then."

PENDERGAST DECIDED I *COULD* **BE** right. I knew convincing the sheriff was beyond my talents and left Pendergast to the task. I phoned Owen instead. He beat me to the Laughing Loon and I wanted to hug him. He was standing talking to some guy blocking the driveway and making people sign in.

"When you called," Owen pointed toward his truck, "you didn't say nothin about what plumbin tools we'd need, so I brung everythin I had."

I was hardly paying attention to Owen's words. *It can't be air conditioning. Each room has its own unit. Those aren't the type that foster Legionnaires'.* Once out of the guard's hearing, I pointed out the problem to Owen.

"The annex with the dining room has central A/C. Got one of them big-sucker units on the roof."

We were back in business.

The manager and assistant manager were on the casino outing, as were most of the other employees. The guy checking us in didn't know where the maintenance man was and didn't know how to contact him. While I signed my name, I tried to read the names of everyone who had signed before me. I didn't recognize any names and several were such scrawls I figured they must be doctors.

We found the access stairs to the annex roof and I led Owen up. We had climbed several stairs when I held out my arm and stopped Owen. "These stairs are dusty." I said.

"Un-huh."

"And," I continued, "we're leaving footprints but there aren't any on the steps ahead of us. Is there another access to the roof?"

"Blamed if I know," he said.

We pushed open the door to the roof and Owen led the way to the cooling tower. "Sorry, Seamus. No one's been on this here roof. We're leavin tracks and there ain't none around the A/C."

Shit. Shit. Shit. "Maybe they don't know steam kills the bacteria. Let's check the furnace."

Clumping down the stairwell to the basement we sounded like two horses released from Noah's Ark. We found the boiler in a small room lit by a bare forty-watt bulb. On the far wall was a red switch, which I flicked off. "I hope that kills the furnace. You know anything about furnaces and stuff?"

"Never seen one this big, but theys all gotta operate about the same way, eh? Heat water to steam and the steam does the rest. Thermostat somewhere to control the furnace."

Using flashlights, Owen checked the furnace while I inspected the boiler. Dust covered everything. "I don't think anyone's been here," I said.

"They don't need to mess with the heatin elements if alls they gonna do is pump in contaminated water. Just drain off enough so's you can replace it. Let's take us a looksee at the boiler intake and drain." He followed the flashlight's cone and pointed. "Nope, dirtier than a dog that's been dustin himself for fleas."

Damn. Damn. Damn. My head ached from the pressure. I was wrong on all accounts, but my twisted stomach told me I was close to being right. *Think, brain. Damn it. Think.*

I closed my eyes and breathed in deeply through my nose. Owen was talking away, but I ignored it. I released the breath to a count of twenty and inhaled. On the third exhale, I had it.

"Where's the hot water heater, Owen?"

He pointed the light toward another corner. "Lookee there on the floor," he said. "Water ain't fully evaporated. And see here." He shined the light on a copper pipe. "This here's wiped clean and everythin else's dusty. Oh, he's good. Your perp pumped in the contaminated stuff through this intake."

Perp? Owen had been watching too many cop shows on cable. "You sure?"

"How I'd do it. You turn off the water, disconnect this here filter—see, there's some more water on the floor here—drain off whatever you need and then use a cheap little electric pump and, bingo, you sucked water from your container into the hot water holdin tank."

"What kind of container are you talking about?"

He waved the flashlight around and found a five-gallon container against the wall. "Somethin like that."

BOSS FIRST HEARD OF THE ruckus at the Laughing Loon from one of the bank's customers. According to that person, health officials had forced evacuation of the Laughing Loon's residents.

A deep sadness overcame her and she wanted to crawl under her desk and curl into a ball. She tried to tell herself all was not lost. Disposing of the Loonies with an "accidental" spread of Legionnaires' disease was a bust. But, having discovered one plot, the authorities might let down their guard. Then it would be up to someone else to bomb the place or raid it and finish the job.

Come on, K.C. You didn't earn the title "Boss" because you give up easily. She stuck her head into her son's office. "I'm not feeling so hot today. I gotta go home and lie down." Involuntarily she started hacking. "I probably won't be in until Monday. I'll reschedule my appointments."

Her son glanced up from the pile of papers covering his desk. "Maybe you should see your doctor. You've been coughing a lot again."

She waved away the idea that it was her lungs. "Might be coming down with something. I'll be fine."

On the way to her camp she stopped at the Jubilee and loaded up on groceries. The devil wanted her to ask the cop following her to help load the supplies into her SUV, but she refrained.

At camp, hidden from the road by her single-wide, she hitched a five-by-eight trailer to her ATV and packed in the supplies. She added billycans of gasoline, a couple thirty packs of beer, and two bottles of Jack Daniels. Using a duffle bag, she collected a few changes of clothes and threw in her revolver.

At dinnertime, she offered the police officer some freshly warmed pie. He refused the dessert and her offer to join her on an ATV jaunt. She washed the dinner dishes and put everything away before driving away on the ATV, again taking the back trail to the state land. From there, she took back roads to the land Hematite owned near the reservoir, where she dug up the canvas sack with the fifty-caliber automatic and two hundred rounds of ammo. She reburied the clothes. By the time she finished, she was huffing and puffing and coughing like an old-time car on its last legs.

She couldn't go faster than about fifteen miles an hour towing the trailer. She met minimal traffic along her route. No one stopped, and with the heavy clothes she wore against the forty-degree temperatures and the helmet with its dark facemask, no one could recognize her. For the last nine miles, she met only a snowshoe hare, halfway through its camouflage transition from white to brown, and two deer.

She slowed at the intersection where she had accidentally killed Digger—or was it Spider?—it all seemed a blur now—no, it was Digger, the fool. The snow and rain had obliterated most tracks and the police had removed whatever yellow crime scene tape they had put up. More likely they had just barricaded the road for a while.

Reaching the junction of Lukes Road and Shank Lake Road, her thoughts returned to the night she had ambushed the three guys. She had done her job. She had always done her job. If only Digger and Spider had done theirs. No use crying over spilt milk, as dear old Mom used to say. In retrospect, given McCree was the one to figure out the plan, her first instinct to take him out had been right.

It took three hours to get there, but it was the perfect spot. She was pleased to see her sources were correct: the cops had released McCree's house and it was no longer festooned by yellow tape. With mud season going full bore she was sure it would be empty, and who would think to look for her there? After parking the ATV and trailer in the pole barn, she busted a glass pane on the door from the deck, reached in, and undid the dead bolt.

THIRTY-SEVEN

THE NEXT AFTERNOON, PENDERGAST AND I had a command appearance before the collective inquisition of the FBI and ICE. Bartelle waylaid us before we got to the assigned conference room. "Are we heroes or goats?" I asked.

"Tex confirmed a high level of Legionnaires' disease bacteria in the hot water tank and in the bit of water left in the billycan," Bartelle said. "That makes you heroes. Unfortunately, AIC Cooper has been spitting bullets at the sheriff for hiring CIG, knowing CIG had hired Agent Pendergast." Bartelle gave Pendergast's shoulder a squeeze. "We're all skewered goat's meat for that. Sheriff, bless his heart, didn't back down. Thought you should be prepared. Course we're in our own hot water."

I questioned that statement by furrowing my brow.

"Well, we are. We managed to lose the main suspect. When Mrs. Maki didn't leave for work the day after the fireworks, the on-duty officer knocked on her door. No answer. Her car was there, but her ATV and trailer were gone. Apparently, she told the nightshift officer she was planning an after-dinner ride and he never bothered to check."

Inside the room, the sheriff and Bartelle occupied one corner of the table, ICE another, and AIC Cooper a third. Pendergast and I settled into the empty spots.

Cooper fired the first salvo, telling Pendergast she was now on unpaid administrative leave. She showed more restraint than I would have, only turning red at the news. "Where's Owen Lyndstrom?" Cooper snarled. "He was supposed to be with you."

"He's working and needs the money," I said. "He told me to tell you he didn't know anything more than I did, and if you wanted to talk to him, you could come out after dinner and yap all you want. His words, not mine." I gave the moron my best false smile.

Bartelle confirmed they had searched Boss's home, camp, son's home, had talked to everyone they could think of. "We know she had a couple weeks' worth of supplies with her. We have to consider the possibility that she, her ATV, and trailer were all picked up by a larger enclosed trailer and taken someplace far away."

"The FBI has not been sitting still," Cooper said. "We matched the fingerprints on the inside of the billycan cap to a retired biochemist from the Midland area. We found Legionnaires' disease in his home lab and he's under arrest. Not talking . . . yet." He sent a curious look toward the ICE people, but they looked as relaxed as two guys could be. "You guys?"

"With the help of Patrick McCree and the cooperation of several email service providers, we nailed down evidence linking Maki—the mother— and the biochemist." To Cooper he said, "We'll get it to the FBI by the end of the day."

The second ICE agent smiled at me. A crocodile smile—all teeth and no warmth around his eyes.

"I apologize for getting off on the wrong foot with you, Mr. McCree. The federal government wants to thank you for your valuable assistance in this matter. We do have a few remaining questions. Perhaps Agent Pendergast could excuse us?"

Once we were alone, they wanted to know how I came up with the Legionnaires' disease "scenario." I took them through my thinking process, concluding with the final revelation. "While I was in the basement, I finally remembered that when I washed my hands in Mrs. Pirhonen's room, the hot water was not very hot. At the time I didn't think much of it, but in racking my brain for a solution, I realized management wouldn't want residents to accidentally scald themselves, so they wouldn't have the temperature set very high. The residents took showers—there was no bathtub in Mrs. Pirhonen's room—and that could provide the aerosol mechanism."

I didn't expect applause for my brilliance, but I didn't expect a three-hour grilling either. Apparently, someone considered the timing of my "discovery" of the plan a tad too convenient. They figured it was possible I had been in on the plot all along— maybe was even the mastermind—and had "solved" the crime only after it went south to throw off appearances of my collusion.

Only Owen slept well that night.

The next day officially ushered in spring. To celebrate, we had another cold snap with temperatures diving below zero at night. It matched Cooper's treatment of Pendergast. He wanted her gone. The only way the sheriff could appease the FBI without appearing to cave in was to decide he no longer needed CIG assistance on the cases. Without the CIG buffer, Pendergast had no choice but to leave town.

I again put her on a flight from Iron Mountain to Chicago. They called her flight for the Homeland Security inspection and she said in a serious voice, "I wonder if Cooper cut a deal to make sure I get strip-searched."

"He wouldn't—"

"Joke, Seamus. It was a joke. In all seriousness, I doubt we'll run across each other again. You're a great guy, but if I were you, I'd hurry to Chicago and straighten out your love life. Say goodbye to Patrick for me." She leaned in and gave me a dry peck on the cheek.

In the evening, I met a builder Owen recommended who would undertake rehabilitating my house. We agreed on scope and price. All I needed was to give the insurance company pictures of the damage. The agent didn't want to travel into the "dark beyond," so I decided to borrow Owen's ATV and ride up to my camp Sunday afternoon. I had a camera there.

Once I snapped the pictures, I would have no reason to stay. Bartelle let me know he would still be interested in running stuff past me, but I figured it was more *pro forma* than real. Pendergast was right: I needed to see Abigail. I thought she had permanently benched me, but Pendergast insisted I had earned two strikes, so if I was open and honest, Abigail's next pitch might be a batting practice fastball down the center of the plate.

All I could do was try.

I informed Owen of my plan to take pictures at camp and then leave Monday. He thought I should have a bodyguard. "I cain't go," he said. "My oldest grandkid's got a dance recital. I'll get someone to go with ya."

"No, Owen. K.C. Maki is gone. No one else cares a whit about me. I want to do this myself."

The woods roads were in the worst shape I had ever seen them, never having experienced the depth of mud as frost comes out of the ground. The ATV, with its four-wheel drive, got through without a hitch until I took a swale about three-quarters of a mile from my camp too slowly and became mired. Getting off, I sank to my knees in goop. I pushed. I pulled. I pushed again, slipped, and took an unanticipated mud bath. I didn't get my mouth closed and earned the opportunity to taste the mud. Bland, actually, and a bit crunchy.

I had no choice but to walk to camp, grab the come-a-long and chain, and schlep back to extract the ATV. With each step I felt the squish of mud in my boots. Eventually I spit out most of the gunk in my mouth. The socks I could throw away; the boots would clean up once they dried; I'd use lake water and brush my teeth at camp.

This would, of course, provide Owen with gossip fodder. I owed him at least that and, smiling at how he would spin the tale, I started enjoying the walk. Too early for black flies, the earliest spring flowers were luxuriating in the brief period of unobstructed sunlight occurring after the ground thaws and before trees sprout enough leaves to block the sun. An early phoebe repeatedly called its name.

With its characteristic *weep-weep-weep* call, a wood duck exploded from a vernal pond beside the road. From the pond's edge, the first spring peepers tried their voices. If I had been into maple sugaring, this would be the time. I slowed my walk, considering whether I should take it up some spring. It would be a lot of work, but I had plenty of sugar maples.

A hint of wood smoke intruded upon my reverie.

I checked the tops of the trees. No breeze, the fire had to be near, unless one of my neighbors down the lake was burning brush. At the driveway to my cabin I looked up to see if someone had broken in. No smoke from the chimney, which was a major relief.

Thirty yards farther I got the first glimpse of the house roof, from which a curl of smoke drifted. Adrenaline kicked in full force and the concept of flight did not cross my mind. Some asshole had broken in to rob the place and had the audacity to light a fire to keep warm while he took his time leaving nothing unsearched.

BOSS SAT IN THE ARMCHAIR with her feet propped on the ottoman. It had taken better than a day to get the house heated because of the high ceilings and the glass pane she'd broken, but McCree had an adequate supply of kindling and wood stored on the screened porch so it was easy to keep the fire stoked.

Unpacking the trailer had winded her beyond anything she had experienced. She had never done hard manual labor, but thought she had gained a true understanding of the expression, "bone tired." As with most true understandings, this one had come too late for her to put it to much use. The day after she arrived, she couldn't do more than feed the fire and sleep.

Boss wasn't even interested in drinking—the booze had no taste and she no longer liked the warm glow in her stomach. The doctor's calendar said she still had time, yet not wanting to drink convinced her it wouldn't be long. Which, to her surprise, didn't much bother her. She was ready and, with that first realization, came an epiphany of sorts: she was not angry at McCree. She forgave him for doing what he thought was right.

Could he forgive her? She had only been doing what she thought was a moral imperative to wrench the country away from the politicians and return it to the people. Just like if you are planting a crop, you need to till the soil; similarly, the best way to give the country a fresh start was to wipe out much of the current government. Fresh elections would plant new seeds. Everything about this objective required money—a lot of money.

By the second full day, a bit of energy returned, but with it more pain. She had not eaten the day before. She went to light the gas stove and the igniters didn't work. She laughed at herself, the sound echoing in the empty house. Of course they didn't work, the electricity was turned off. She rooted around in the mud room and came up with one of those things you used to light recalcitrant grills—what were they called?

Using a flashlight, she surveyed McCree's library in the basement. It was all nonfiction and much of it liberal bullshit, but she did find an interesting read on the wolves and moose of Isle Royale. Mostly she slept or looked out the windows to the lake. A pair of bald eagles cavorted all day, trading ear-piercing calls. It was time for a new generation.

On the third day she found pads of paper and pens in McCree's study. She decided she needed to write to her son and daughter-in-law. She had expected to have a long sit-down conversation to help them understand her reasons—even if they didn't like them. Now it was best for her to write them down while she still had time.

Sunday, she listened to two church services on the wind-up radio McCree had. To her surprise, she found the message from the Catholic mass more to the point. From the death of winter comes the promise of spring, the priest intoned. Although she had not succeeded, with those words she convinced herself a phoenix would arise from the ashes of her failure.

The fire was burning low; she needed to bring in some more wood. She opened the French door onto the porch, loaded an armful of wood, and was surprised to hear someone yell, "Get the fuck out of my house!"

Thirty-Eight

FRUSTRATION BUILDS ON FRUSTRATION AND, unless we find a way to sublimate, it comes out in anger—or so I think I recall from my minor in psychology so many years ago. Anger at whom or what depends on our personalities. My first thought was to charge inside my house and kick the intruder all the way to Amasa, where I would call the police and press every possible charge.

Anger brought me boiling over the hill at a run. Even as I topped the hill between my cabin and house, two competing thoughts fought for control. First, there might be—indeed, there probably was—more than one person in my house. Second, most Yoopers, especially those committing crimes in the backwoods, were armed. I was not. I had again ignored Owen's advice and come into the woods with only my wits. More accurately, only half of them.

I stopped behind a large maple tree and caught my breath and senses. Anger was not going to make me think more clearly, so I set it aside. My injured leg still throbbed with pain. I did not want to get into a shootout. Much as I loved reading his books, I did not want to become Lee Child's Jack Reacher, for whom violence and killing were justified in a good cause and engendered no internal turmoil. Unless it became a last resort—or to protect Paddy—I needed another way.

I was under no obligation to handle this myself. So said my rational side. I actually took several steps toward the nearest year-round camp on Deer Lake where I could get a ride to Amasa. Then a different part of my brain took control. By the time I made it to Deer Lake, got to Amasa, corralled the police, and returned, hours would have passed and the burglars would be long gone. The police would want a description of the criminals and I'd have nothing.

I hadn't spotted a vehicle in the driveway. Keeping the pole barn between me and the house, I jogged to the rear of the pole barn, and pushed in the OSB covering the broken window. Inside were an unknown ATV and trailer. If they were going for a quick grab, wouldn't they have parked close to the ramp for easy loading?

The trailer would have a license plate. Jimmie Heitzmann had accessed my pole barn through the rear window, and I hadn't heard him until he tried to firebomb us. One other thing Jimmie had done was to steal the keys to my vehicles. My turn.

I levered myself through the window, making a lot more racket than I had intended. If whoever was inside the house heard the noise, I'd be trapped with no quick escape. I waited until I could hear something other than the pounding of my heart, tiptoed to the back of the trailer, and memorized the plate number. I pocketed the key, which, in true Yooper style, was in the ignition. Now at least we had equal transportation. Only one helmet sat on the seat. Looked like the burglar was a solo act. As long as I was in the garage, I might as well get the tools I needed to extract my ATV from the mud. I tossed the come-a-long and a chain out the rear window.

Having the plate number, logic said the thing to do was beat a retreat, free my ATV from the mud and ride for help. Of course if the plate was stolen, just like the plate had been on Spider's truck, the number was worthless. I didn't have binoculars like Jimmie Heitzmann had used to spy on me, but I figured I could at least try to get a description of the guy before leaving.

I stayed hidden on the hill and spent a fruitless thirty minutes waiting to see movement in the house. Limited to peering through the unbroken backside windows, I saw and heard nothing. Normally, I might try to look into the side of the house facing the vernal pond, but OSB covered those windows. The opposite side had the screened porch making it tough to see all the way into the house. The lakeside windows provided a viable option. I could slip around the porch, staying far enough in the woods in case anyone was on it, and find a safe place to observe through the wall of windows.

I was most of the way around the house when someone came out the

French door from the great room onto the screened porch. I dropped to my knees, landing on a rock I hadn't seen. I went through a mental litany of cuss words in every language I knew while crawling backwards to the protection of a too-thin birch. The person groaned as they loaded their arms with split wood for the fire.

As the person walked toward the interior door, I realized it was K.C. Maki. Without thinking I stood and yelled, "Get the fuck out of my house!"

She dropped the wood in a crash and stared at me. "Why Mr. McCree, this is an unexpected surprise. You alone? Of course you are. Why don't you come in and we'll have us some conversation? I brought whiskey and beer, and I noticed you have some nice-looking wines in your basement. I'd recommend the Laughing Stock. Those Canadians sure have a sense of humor, eh? Course I don't know anything about wine, I just like the label."

Her mocking tone had me clenching my teeth. "You can't escape. I've taken your ATV key."

She laughed and waved her upraised hands in mock surrender. "Oh, my goodness, what shall I do? What shall I do? I didn't come here to escape, Seamus. May I call you that? I do wish you would call me K.C." She started another laugh, which changed to a fierce coughing fit. It might have been an opportunity to rush her, except I was too far away from either the deck steps or the porch ramp.

Once she stopped hacking, she leaned against a four-by-four post as though to get support. I had watched many a killdeer feign broken wings to gradually lead me away from their nests. "You can call me K.C." was not going to con me.

"I'm dying of lung cancer. It won't be long. In a true cause, whenever one soldier falls, another rises to take his, or in my case, her, place. You could leave and get your friends. Then, in one grand last stand, I'd feel compelled to defend myself with the rifle and ammunition I brought. But really, what's the point if I kill one or two or three of you and you kill me? Nothing changes."

"So you admit hiring two guys to come here to kill me?"

She gazed toward the porch as though asking for guidance. "I'm not planning on playing twenty questions, Seamus. I would truly love to sit over a drink or two and have a civilized conversation. Here's what I'm going to do: I'm going to put this wood back—seems like I won't need it now.

I'm going to dress more warmly and sit on one of the chairs on the deck with my bottle of whiskey. We'll talk."

She began to cough, which stopped after she slammed her foot down. "If you have a long gun, I'll be an easy target. You got yourself a pistol, you need to be a better shot, 'cause I'm not letting you get close enough to Taser me and take me in. Nor will you get close enough to rush me. I was born free and I'm going to die free. I will not have you or anyone else put me in a cage."

I contemplated my response while she restacked the wood. Before I decided what to say, she had gone inside. Whatever I had expected, this was not it. I had her ATV key, so she was not going anywhere. I could free my ATV from the mud and notify Bartelle. Or take hers. Any scenario involving Bartelle would end in her death—and maybe some others'. If she died, she would cheat all those who needed the catharsis her trial would provide.

I needed to play for time; I needed to keep her alive. Maybe I could get her to drink enough to pass out. Of course, maybe she was going for her rifle to try to gun me down. I used her absence to sneak closer to the house and burrow behind a large hemlock growing on the mound of a nurse tree. I would be safe there, and I had no doubt that even with a gimpy leg I could outrun her if she tried to get to me.

Five minutes later, she came out shivering in bra and panties, carrying an armful of clothes. She pirouetted. "I'm proving I have nothing hidden." She pulled out the pockets on the pants and shirt before pulling them on, following the same routine to show there was nothing up her sleeve or in her socks or under her hat. "This is all I've got." She waved a pistol above her head. "And this." She held aloft what was probably a whiskey bottle. "No ice. No nothing. You show me the same, and I'll let you go into the basement and get whatever wine you want and we can have ourselves a little down-home chat. Otherwise, we'll have to converse from here to there."

"You tried to kill me too many times for me to trust you with a pistol in your hand," I said. Since she brought out whiskey instead of a rifle, getting her inebriated was still my half-baked plan to allow me to eventually rush and subdue her.

She held the whiskey bottle to her lips and tipped it up. She took three large glugs before setting the bottle down. I wondered if she had filled it with water.

"I want you to know that I forgive you," she said.

"Forgive me? For what?"

"For ruining everything I had planned as my sendoff gift to the nation. But I have to say—" She tilted the bottle back and chug-a-lugged another three swallows. "I have to say, once I forgave you, I became much calmer inside. I'm sure that's what Jesus had in mind. Do you forgive me?"

She did not slur her words. Anyone who could belt straight whiskey as she was ostensibly doing would have to consume a fair piece of the bottle before showing its effects. "I haven't given it any thought," I began, but I realized I had actually thought about it and, no, I could not forgive and forget. Maybe it's in the Irish genes to remember longer than we should. I was better at physically turning the other cheek than at forgiving. "If you've done what I believe you've done, then I don't think I can forgive you for the deaths of so many."

"Every righteous war has cost innocent lives. Think of how many families lost fathers and brothers in our Revolutionary War. Look at the hundreds of thousands of lives we lost putting down our Southern Rebellion. Were they justified?"

What could I say to that? While disgusted that she compared her actions to these events, I was curious how she rationalized things. Perhaps she would reveal details of the plot that could help law enforcement. I chose not to interrupt.

"Thomas Jefferson wrote to Jimmie Madison about the necessity of rebellions." She closed her eyes. Was she falling asleep mid-thought? Moments later she stood and, eyes still closed, recited Jefferson's words:

I hold it that a little rebellion now and then is a good thing, and as necessary in the political world as storms in the physical . . . It is a medicine necessary for the sound health of government.

She opened her eyes and put on an expression that seemed to ask if I had a comment. Knowing time was on my side, I chose continued silence.

She sat down. "Deep down, I'm a libertarian—not one of those crazy libertarians who don't think government should even exist. We need a strong government to deal with other countries. We need one for disasters. We even need one to take care of those who can't take care of themselves. Let me ask you this . . ." She downed another healthy glug of liquor.

"In Lincoln's Gettysburg address, he proclaimed that government of the people, by the people, and for the people would not perish. But it has.

Don't you agree that we are now a government of the corporations, by the corporations, and for the corporations?"

"Pretty much," I said.

"And I'll tell you what you'll do about it—not a bloody damn thing. You're the kind who'll vote Democratic or Republican and think you might make a difference. It doesn't matter one bit. They're both owned by the big corporations. The people need to know freedom again."

"And I suppose killing helpless seniors at the Laughing Loon was going to bring back their freedom?"

Another slug of whiskey. "Their families didn't care enough about them to take them into their homes like we used to do. Think of them as superannuated soldiers giving their lives for you." She shrugged, hacked once, and continued. "If that doesn't work, think of them as the flotsam and jetsam of modern society. We need to bring down the entire federal government. All three branches at the same time. That takes money. Don't you think it's poetic justice that insurance companies would have paid for killing them all?"

What were they going to do, buy a cruise missile and take out the president? And Congress, the Joint Chiefs, and the Supreme Court Justices all at the next State of the Union address? "To be honest," I said. "I think it's crazy."

"I felt the same way at your age. Now, it's something—" She tipped the bottle, drank deeply, and then began to cough. She slammed the bottle on the table and doubled over in the coughing.

A film reel of the church service and the six fatherless children played in my head. They needed a villain to juxtapose with their hero father. I scrambled up and ran toward her. Fully expecting her to take a shot at me, I hoped her racking cough would leave her weak enough to spoil her aim. I lasered in on her, forcing my other senses to allow me to avoid trees and boulders. At the bottom of the steps, I lost sight of her, but could still hear her continue to turn herself inside out with coughing. I crested the stairs and launched myself across the deck. That's when she pulled the trigger.

EPILOGUE

MY NAME IS PATRICK MCCREE. If my father brainwashed you, it's all right if you think of me as "Paddy." He can't speak for himself, so I'm taking over the wrap-up report. Of the various law enforcement agencies, in my opinion, the Iron County Sheriff's Department and the Michigan State Police came out looking the best. In the investigations that followed, none of their officers were criticized, and their cooperation was lauded as a model for other agencies to follow.

The FBI has not released their internal investigation, but both Agent Ashley Pendergast—whom I still call Niki as our private joke—and AIC Cooper were put on administrative leave. Cooper quit and took a job with a corporation. Frankly, I couldn't care less what he's doing as long as we never cross paths again. Niki was reinstated but, since bureaucracies aren't usually fond of independent thinkers, they shunted her to some outpost office in Mississippi. Robert Rand heard about that and offered her a job with CIG. I've kept in touch with her, and in her latest email she said she's sticking it out and learning to like grits.

The chemist who cultivated the *Legionella pneumophila* and prepared the mixture that Boss used to try to kill the Laughing Loon residents pleaded guilty and is residing in an unnamed federal secure facility. Niki kept her promise and briefed Cindy Nelson, my investigative reporter girlfriend, about the entire operation. Cindy vowed to protect Niki and not publish anything until she could get independent confirmation, which has so far been impossible because Homeland Security kept a news blackout on the entire affair. Cindy's Freedom of Information Act request produced material so heavily redacted only the prepositions remained. As far as I can tell, there have been no additional arrests.

The Laughing Loon itself is back in operation with a new owner, new facilities operation manager, and a clean bill of health. Mrs. Ricci reports by text message that the residents are delighted to be back in their rooms, and she and Mrs. Pirhonen are now very close friends. None of them knows the true reason for the residents' evacuation or what was wrong with the heating and plumbing systems.

I don't know who spoke with Owen Lyndstrom, but someone convinced him not to talk about his role in this affair, and in fact, he can keep a secret. He's still a U.P. grapevine regular and with the new computer Dad gave him as a thank-you gift for housing all of us, I've shown him how to automatically keep track of his relatives and friends on several social networks. If it's raining, he's on his computer; if it's not, he's outside making ends meet.

WIKB's funeral report took several days before announcing the death of Kathryn Cynthia "K.C." Maki, survived by her son, Samuel, daughter-in-law, Jeanne, and predeceased by her husband of nearly forty years, Frank. Funeral arrangements were private. Owen tells me she was cremated, but not before her brain was donated to science. Sam Maki resigned the presidency of Hematite National Bank and gave his shares and the ones he inherited from his mother to a charity he created to support victims of violence throughout the Upper Peninsula. I understand he and his wife moved downstate, where he is teaching business math at a community college as an adjunct professor.

I followed Dad's wishes and set up trust accounts to assure all six children of the man murdered guarding my father have the financial means to attend college or trade school. It turns out two of the other murdered men had families also in need of financial assistance, and I found ways to accomplish that as well. Since the stock Sam Maki donated to the charity would take some time to liquidate, I contributed $500,000 of Dad's funds for use as the charity's seed money. I managed everything anonymously, although I'm sure Owen has figured it out by now.

The day after K.C. Maki shot herself on Dad's front deck, he showed up at my office. His taxi waited long enough for him to hand me two things. The first document was a notarized power of attorney authorizing me to handle his finances and legal matters until such time as he revoked the powers. The second was a notarized statement about what happened at his camp the day of Maki's death.

After he had finally extracted his ATV from the mud hole—I asked why he hadn't just taken Boss's ATV. He figured he needed to get his ATV sooner or later, so why not then—anyway, he drove out of the woods, phoned Sergeant Lon Bartelle, and informed him of the events. He paid one of Owen's friends to take him to Milwaukee, where he drew up the legal documents and bought a train ticket to Chicago. He taxied from the station to Evanston to see me and then to Abigail Hancock's apartment in the city. They were gone for the better part of a week. Abigail returned alone. They had talked, she said, really communicated, and had an agreement about their relationship. I didn't figure my power of attorney covered relationships, so I left it at that.

She would not tell me where she left my father, or where he was going, or when I might hear from him. A week or so later, I received an invitation to a private message board. I was about to delete it as spam when I saw the subject heading requested an initial password of "Nessie." In the body of the message it said that if I had not accepted the invitation by midnight, the password would change to "Snuffleupagus."

When I signed into the board, he had left a single message, "Heading to New England. Your grandmother wants to talk."

Thank you for reading this story. If you've enjoyed *Cabin Fever*, I would appreciate your writing a short review and posting it at your favorite online retailer.

AUTHOR'S NOTE

This book is a work of fiction. People familiar with the Upper Peninsula of Michigan will recognize many towns, streets, businesses, and geographical references. I have used all of them in a fictional way to serve the needs of the story. I have also taken the liberty of creating new businesses, roads, and geographical features.

While conducting research for this story, I spent several days in the Iron County Courthouse watching the proceedings brought before the Honorable C. Joseph Schwedler, Chief Judge. He and the Court Administrator, Lori Ann Willman, were kind enough to answer my questions between court sessions. Neither one ever hinted even a stone could have figured out the answers to some of my questions. Hal Arenstein of Cincinnati gave me an insider's look at criminal law from a defense attorney's perspective. As any lawyer reading this story will tell you, it is not a legal procedural, as I have taken a number of liberties with court proceedings.

Similarly, this story is not a police procedural. Sgt. Wade Cross of the Iron County Sheriff's Office and D/Sgt. Jay M. Peterson of the Michigan State Police crime lab in Marquette, Michigan took personal time to help me understand the investigation process. Iron County Sheriff Mark Valesano provided me an insider's view of the county jail. The shortcomings of the fictional Sgt. Bartelle should in no way reflect on the officers or conduct of any of Michigan's various police forces, for which I have high regard.

Cathy Sonnenberg and Kaye George of my Guppy chapter of Sisters in Crime critique group provided excellent insight on areas for improvement in an early draft of this work. I also received very helpful suggestions from my beta readers: E.B. Davis, Dottie Caster, Dave and Rita Stull, Marcia Eckstein, and Mary Kellogg.

A special thanks to Barking Rain Press in the person of Sheri Gormley, who again agreed to help bring the story to life. And a ginormous thanks to my editor, Julie Spergel. She not only saved me from howlers such as having people drive automobiles that were not available to them and attending doctor appointments in the middle of a weekend, she sorted through my sometimes idiosyncratic grammar and wording choices to help make the manuscript sing.

As with my earlier publications, Jan Rubens has been my first reader and my last reader; but if there are any errors left, they are all mine. Right, honey?

James M. Jackson
Amasa, Michigan

EMPTY PROMISES

A SEAMUS MCCREE NOVEL (#5)

James M. Jackson

EMPTY PROMISES

A SEAMUS MCCREE NOVEL (#5)

 ONE

EVERYONE AGREES THAT MY DECISION to go into town that day cost one person his life. Attribution for the other deaths wasn't clear-cut, although I thought I also bore that guilt. And it so easily could have been otherwise.

I was pulling my seatbelt over my shoulder when I had second thoughts. Muttering an apology, I left my family cooling their heels in the car and hustled back inside. Elliot was where I had left him, watching a morning financial show in the TV room. "You're sure you're okay being here by yourself? I—"

"Seamus, we discussed this. I'll be fine." He waved me away with both hands. "Have a good time."

"You're positive?"

He leaned back in the chair and looked at the ceiling. "Go, already."

"Okay, okay" My misgivings melted before his certainty. "We'll be back in four hours. Tops."

As it turned out, we both had lied.

I jogged back to the car. Paddy had plugged earbuds into his phone. Megan, my three-and-a-half-year-old granddaughter, was belted into her car seat in the back, "reading" *The Little Engine That Could* to Raff, her stuffed giraffe.

"All aboard for Crystal Falls," I called like a conductor. Paddy shot me a questioning look and Megan ignored me.

Starting the car engine brought up Dylan's "A Hard Rain's a-Gonna Fall" from my MP3 player's random queue—appropriate, given the glowering skies in the southwest. As a teenager struggling to find my way in the world, I had thought of myself as the blue-eyed son being asked by my dead father where I was going. After I became father to Paddy, my own blue-eyed son, the song pivoted to me asking the questions.

I was very contented with the family part of my life. Paddy and his wife were settled and doing well, and they'd given me the most wonderful granddaughter in the world. The business aspects were something of a challenge, but I put thoughts of Elliot behind me and hummed along with Dylan. Life was good.

A couple of miles down Shank Lake Road, right before the switch to the A Grade, a broad-winged hawk flashed through the trees. I followed its flight, taking my focus from the road. Paddy's "Watch out!" startled me back to attention. A blue pickup towing a trailer steamed toward us, punching a dust cloud into the air. We were both taking our half out of the middle. I slammed on the brakes, steered right, and skidded to a stop at the edge of a drainage ditch. He flashed his lights at me and swept past, enveloping me in his dust.

"Asshole," I muttered under my breath so Megan couldn't hear. My heart thumped wildly in my chest, echoed by beating pressure in my ears. After the dust cleared, I drove through the switch and onto the A Grade.

"That's the guy from the mining company," I said. "I've seen him around, towing his ATV. Driving like that, the only pit he'll find is his own grave. Unless he kills someone first. What a—" I cut myself off. No reason to introduce Megan to words she shouldn't repeat. "I went to a big meeting at the library in Iron River a few weeks back to hear about their plans. Half the audience favored anything that might mean a return of the old mining jobs. The other half worried mining will ruin the woods, pollute the water, and destroy everything they value. Feelings ran pretty high."

"What's your take, Dad?"

I puffed a blast of air, feeling my frustration. "I'd force them to post a bond large enough to cover possible environmental damages. Never happen though, so the taxpayers get stuck paying for their empty promises."

"You going to protest it?"

"I'd prefer it somewhere else, but I'm not a NIMBY. We rely on minerals and need to extract them. My issue is I want the full costs to be borne by the mining companies, not the taxpayers. I understand they've been collecting samples, but there's a long road before anything will happen."

The next song was a Judy Collins classic, and I switched to falsetto and sang along. Paddy replaced his earbuds. Megan hadn't stopped reading her story to Raff, which is how we traveled for several miles until Paddy startled and pulled his earbuds out.

"Dad, listen to the radio." He punched the FM button, silencing Grace Slick in full wail, and hit the preset for WIKB, the local station in Iron River. I wondered what treasure he had heard about on *Telephone Time*, the local swap show he had been listening to. It had better be good for him to interrupt my duet with Grace, asking if you want somebody to love. Paddy increased the volume.

". . . severe damage. Winds up to eighty miles an hour. This storm is fast moving, traveling at more than forty miles an hour. Take shelter. The national weather service gives this system its highest alert status. To repeat, this is not a tornado. It is a front of direct wind currently located in Bates Township and heading northeast. Accompanying the wind is heavy rainfall. Areas likely to be affected are Amasa, Deer Lake, Witch Lake, Republic, and points between. Reports are coming in of massive forest destruction."

We were right in the path. Two miles from Deer Lake. Seven from Amasa.

My first reaction was to race the eight miles back home and hunker down. But with a better road going in, I'd reach Amasa quicker than I could return home, and I wasn't sure how fast the storm was moving. If we were caught in the woods, one decent-sized maple or popple or evergreen hitting the car, and we were goners. The Amasa Post Office, squat and brick, would protect us from the wind—if I could get there. I jammed down the accelerator, causing us to fishtail.

"Careful," Paddy said, looking back at Megan. "The road's a giant washboard. Don't lose control."

Behind us, the dust cloud thickened. We hit a dip and went airborne. Megan squealed in delight. "Do it again, Grampa Seamus!"

My mouth was dry with the taste of fear, but at least one of us was having a good time. I eased off the accelerator a titch.

Using *Telephone Time's* frenetic outpouring of information about damage, I tracked the storm's path. It would be close whether I'd get us to Amasa in time. Through a break in the forest, I glimpsed a southwestern sky that reminded me of boiling black clouds over Tolkien's Mordor.

Two miles from safety, the first drops of rain smacked the windshield with fat plops. The treetops were barely moving. Picturing the stretch of straight road ahead of me, I accelerated to sixty-five and forgot the little rise caused by a new culvert under the road. The Subaru became airborne again. My stomach tightened and I squeezed the steering wheel to control the wheels as we slammed to the ground.

Megan clapped. Even while I fought to keep the car on the road, a piece of me smiled in recollection of encouraging my father to take hills fast enough so we could feel our stomachs rise and fall. The lumber mill came into view, and in my relief that we were almost out of the trees, I forgot how bad the stretch immediately before the first blacktop could be and nailed a pothole. The car juked left and skidded right, nearly going off the road on both sides. The ABS prevented the brakes from locking, which probably avoided an uncontrolled skid into the trees. I white-knuckled the steering wheel and we rattled through until finally the tires gripped the hardtop in front of the mill.

Skidding with too much speed through the turn onto Corral Road, Paddy and I had our first unrestricted look at the storm front. Coal-black clouds boiled directly in front of us. Pale blue showed at the edges. In seconds we would meet the southern edge. I blurted the words as the realization came to me, "The post office is too far."

I slammed on the brakes and skidded into a wide arc, barely missing a pile of logs waiting to be loaded onto railcars. Rain changed into a steady downpour. Even with the wipers on high, I could barely see well enough to weave past the piles of logs to an open area next to the mill. The heavens unloaded a torrent of water, turning day into night. I stopped and keyed off the engine.

"Grampa Seamus?" Megan often spoke my name with a question mark. "Raff's scared."

"We're perfectly safe in the car, pumpkin. This will be over soon."

Megan held her stuffed giraffe close to her and told him not to be afraid.

The winds hit with a howl; the rushing air pulsed from around the piled logs, rocking us from side to side. Megan cried in fear. Paddy unbuckled and reached back, caressing her hand. A sixty-foot spruce succumbed to the wind, falling directly across the road we had just taken, its impact so heavy we felt the reverberation.

"Ho-ly mack-er-el," Paddy intoned under his breath.

Lights outside the mill flickered once and went black. The disk jockey of my mind offered the first verse of Dylan's "Shelter from the Storm," with its references to darkness, mud roads, and coming in from the wilderness. At least we were safe, but if these winds struck camp, it would suffer major damage. My earlier glimpse of blue edges to the storm suggested the band was not wide. But how broad was it, and exactly what direction was it taking? Would my house be okay? It had a metal roof— plenty strong to repel a flying branch or two. But it wouldn't survive if the large trees surrounding the house crashed onto it. My guest cabin didn't even have the protection of a metal roof.

Would Elliot, the guy I was supposed to be protecting, know what to do in a wind storm? His accent sounded Midwestern. Maybe he understood tornadoes and was smart enough to take Atty with him to the safety of the basement. What if he'd gone to the cabin where he liked to read? Had I told him he could access the four-foot cement crawl space from the screened porch? I didn't think so.

Twin rivers ran down the street. Any direction I looked, the woods provided rain-blurred images of downed trees. Time crawled until eventually a shaft of sunshine split dove-gray clouds and illuminated a massive pine tree still standing tall. Although it felt like a decade, the meteorologist timed the path through Amasa at under five minutes. The rains petered out. The sun returned in full glory. The rivers on the road narrowed to streams.

I drove to the downed spruce blocking our way to camp. It had taken two maples with it. Beyond that, a mess of broken popple trees splayed across the road. *No way we can get back to camp anytime soon.* I wanted to kick myself. "I should have given Elliot a burner phone in case of emergencies."

"Didn't you tell me that Abigail specifically ordered you not to allow Elliot anywhere near a phone to protect him from himself?"

"Right. Boss's orders. Nothing we can do until the loggers clear a path."

I gave Megan's foot a tug. "That's enough excitement for one day. Right, pumpkin?"

"Right!" Megan parroted.

Except it wasn't. Not even close.

 Two

Jason Graham's whole body relaxed once Seamus and his family left. Not that he didn't appreciate what they were doing for him, and he'd surely go stir crazy if he were out in the woods all by himself. Despite how much he had loved his wife, they had gotten along best when they were both working. Wasn't there one of those humorous country and western songs, something like "How Can I Miss You If You Won't Go Away?"

He clicked the TV volume ten levels higher to hear it wherever he was in the house. How to enjoy this time? He'd promised to be circumspect and make sure no one had any opportunity to even sense his presence, let alone actually see him. He wanted to return a book to the cabin. Maybe he could extend that jaunt to the cabin to include a hike around McCree's property. Where was the danger? He'd be able to hear a truck or ATV from a mile away and have time to hide. It's not like anyone could sneak up on you in this forsaken wilderness.

Atty came into the room, circled a spot on the rug twice, and settled down with a big sigh. Jason gave her a couple of pats, stroking the long, soft fur. Golden retrievers were such satisfactory dogs.

At a commercial break, Jason trotted upstairs to use the bathroom he considered his. While he took a dump, Atty started barking and he heard tires crunching gravel in the driveway. The engine rumble marked it as a diesel. The dog's deep woofs might scare the intruders away unless they saw her. Then they'd discover her tail wagging, as friendly as could be.

He wiped his butt and silently lowered the lid, not daring to flush. Even though no one could see in through the bathroom's frosted bottom window, his shadow might give him away. He lay on the floor and wriggled pants over his hips, zipped up, and fastened the button.

On the first floor, Atty charged from the TV room to the kitchen. Soon, knocking came from the back door by the kitchen. Even with the dog's barking, they could no doubt hear the TV blaring and know someone was here. Would they go away if no one answered? The doors were unlocked; they could walk right in and he'd be trapped.

Loud knocking resumed from the kitchen door. To tamp down his fear, Jason worked up some saliva and forced the fluid down his constricted throat. Had to be a neighbor or someone driving by. They could not possibly know he was here. Unless there was a leak—then they could know.

To give himself more options, he snaked his way from the bathroom to the bedroom. He'd heard the thunk of one vehicle door shutting, and the dog would have reacted to someone on the deck. He'd risk it. He climbed onto the bed and stood to see out the eyebrow window facing the driveway and garage.

Atty and her bark returned to the TV room, so the visitor must be leaving the stoop and heading back to the truck or around to the screened porch. Leaning against the wall, Jason rose on tippy-toes to increase his chances of seeing the intruder walking close to the house. No go. He eased down and checked the truck, a blue Dodge Ram with a white decal or logo on the passenger door, towing a trailer with a matching blue ATV. This looked like a local working rig. Jason told himself to calm down and make a mental picture so he could describe the vehicle to Seamus.

The truck had a light coating of dust. Its bed contained two aluminum cargo carriers, like construction guys use for tools, and another much larger container of unknown use. Attached to the trailer sides were digging tools and pointed wood stakes with variously colored flags blowing in the wind. Sure felt like a local stopping by to visit. If Seamus saw the guy later, he could make a proper excuse to explain the weirdness of the TV being on with no one home: kid had forgotten to turn it off when they went to town, or he'd been in the basement working on a project with ear protectors on—whatever Seamus decided.

Atty's barking stopped. Jason caught a glimpse of a baseball cap heading toward the kitchen door again. The dog's toenails clicked through the dining room into the kitchen, but she continued to be quiet. In the relative silence, he heard footsteps: one, two, three up the steps to the landing. Two more to the door. Then nothing but the TV commentators talking about the sell-off in Asia and how it was spreading to Europe. So far US stocks were shaking it off, down only a tenth of a percent.

The screen door creaked open. Jason forced himself to breathe through his nose. He was sure he'd puke if he opened his mouth. He closed his eyes to hear better. If the door opened, Jason's only hope was to get onto the deck outside the bedroom, climb down the six-by-six posts, and slip to the other side of the garage while the person was occupied inside. Using the garage as a shield, he could disappear into the woods. He looked down at his bare feet and realized how unprepared he was.

Why had he been so complacent? McCree had harped at him to keep the TV sound turned down to make sure he could hear anyone on the road and have time to go silent. Like a rebelling teenager, the first thing he'd done after Seamus and family drove away was to crank up the damn volume. The screen door squeaked shut. Footsteps on the porch, down the stairs. He raised himself on tiptoes to try to get a look at the intruder. Ball cap, hair down to the neck of a blue T-shirt, blue jeans, wide leather belt, work boots.

Just a guy working in the woods.

The visitor knelt and removed a stick wedged under his truck's chassis. With stick in hand, he turned and Jason got the first view of the intruder's face.

Jason's knees wobbled and he nearly fell off the bed. He ducked below the window, leaned into the wall for support. His mouth was a desert. His armpits an ocean. His vision grayed and a tinny ringing assaulted his ears. Never had he felt fear like this.

Frank Cabibi. In McCree's driveway. Just the kind of sycophant the big dogs would send.

Three

EVERY STORE WE ENTERED IN Crystal Falls had WIKB on. *Telephone Time* reported massive damage north of Amasa. The storm's path had crossed US-141 north of town—we'd witnessed that—traveled north of Deer Lake before hitting Witch Lake head-on. Since my place was eight miles mostly north and west of Deer Lake, I had hopes the storm had missed me entirely. Sketchy information suggested another front had crossed US-141 south of Covington. That might have struck a direct blow.

Only being there would answer the question, which didn't stop me from constantly worrying about Elliot and my place.

We ate lunch in town. Paddy and Megan chowed down, but I worried my food around my plate, not feeling hungry, and anxious to return to camp. Lunch done, Megan reminded me that I had promised her moose tracks ice cream. We stopped at Tall Pines in Amasa.

I chatted with the proprietors while Paddy made the ice cream purchase. They didn't know how far north the damage extended. They had two rooms available in their motel if we wanted them. A group of loggers had heard the storm warning in time and returned to town before it struck. They were cutting a path up the Grade toward Deer Lake. If I couldn't drive to camp, I'd send Paddy and Megan to Tall Pines and I'd hike in. Not getting back to make sure Elliot was okay was not an option.

While Megan was finishing her ice cream outside the car (I had already made the mistake of thinking my granddaughter would be neater with food in the car than my son had been at her age), I monkeyed with the chainsaw stored in back, making sure it started and was full of fluids. If we caught up to the crew, Paddy and I could at least help clear the way.

Talking to the folks at Tall Pines gave me a little hope, which drained in a flash seeing fifty trees down next to US-141 right before our turnoff onto Corral Road. Evergreens with huge root balls lay on their sides or stretched out at a low angle. Maples had snapped off twenty or thirty feet up. Seventy-five feet past that massive blowdown, the forest appeared unimpacted. The damage hadn't been caused by a wall of wind, but by a series of microbursts along the front. But where the wind hit, the damage was much worse than I had expected.

Dread joined us in the car. Even normally bubbly Megan grew silent.

Loggers had cut a narrow lane through the sixty-foot spruce I had watched come down at the beginning of the Grade, leaving most of the tree in place and towing the cut section to the side. They'd wasted no time on smaller branches littering the road and were opening up a one-lane path. I tiptoed the Outback over the debris and moved through the gap.

At first the downed trees were scattered, although limbs and branches dotted the entire road. But the further north we drove, the worse the damage became until the downed trees were a nearly continuous hazard. Paddy frequently left the car to remove branches with sharp breaks that might puncture a tire. I was regretting we hadn't taken my old beater truck into town with its multi-ply tires. The Outback carried a donut spare, which wouldn't last thirty seconds on the gravel roads. We had yet to see any other cars or people.

By the time we passed the five- and six-mile markers without any letup in the damage, tightened metal bands had taken up permanent residence around my chest. I feared for Elliot. I feared for my property. I worried whether I'd get a flat. Whether there would still be a hotel room if I had to send Paddy and Megan to Tall Pines. Megan, on the other hand, had given up her concerns and was in the back seat, singing along with a CD, a cheerful canary amidst the devastation.

As we continued up the Grade, I made a concentrated effort to channel her lack of concern. Eventually, we reached a recent clear-cut that provided a quarter mile of respite from the carnage. I never thought I would see any positives in a clear-cut, but not having any trees to push onto the road was definitely a good thing today.

"Thank God for the loggers," Paddy said. "What's your guess, will they follow the road toward Deer Lake or take the A Grade up toward camp?"

"If they headed toward Deer Lake, I'll send you and Megan to Tall Pines, and I'll hike in. If we did get hit, Elliot might need help, and even if we didn't, he'd likely panic if we didn't show until tomorrow. He must be wondering where the he—" I remembered Little Miss Big Ears was riding with us. "Where the heck we are. I told him four hours tops, and we're already past five. Even if the road is open, it will take us the better part of another hour. I just hope he doesn't do something stupid."

"Like what?"

I crept through the detritus of a white pine. "He's a city boy and I sense he gets panicky without me around. I can't tell you how much better his mood has been since you and Megan arrived. He'll be depressed when your two weeks are over. I've taken him ATVing a bunch of times. He bristles because I make him use the helmet with the smoky glass to prevent anyone from seeing his face, and I won't tempt fate by leaving the house Friday night or the weekend. Too many people wandering in the woods. We've argued about his going anywhere alone, which I forbid. I hope he remembered everything I told him and didn't do something dumb."

"He seems like a smart person to me."

"Paddy, there's book smart and there's life smart. Elliot is book smart, which I suspect is what got him into trouble in the first place."

"You don't know?"

"Abigail's reasoning is, the less I know, the less I can accidentally give away. Given the way he reacts when I call him Elliot, I'm sure it's not his real name. And I don't know where he's from or exactly why we're protecting him. He's to be a witness in a trial, so I assumed bad people don't want him to testify. Abigail's going to be pissed that I left him alone."

"You talked it through with him. It even sounded like he was looking forward to a little time by himself."

I offered a wry smile. "All true, but I'm telling you, Paddy. She's going to be ticked off even if nothing bad happens. She'll say I should never have left him by himself. I put family ahead of the job."

"Papa, I have to tinkle."

"Sweetheart," Paddy said, "on a scale of one to ten, how bad do you have to go?"

"Papa. I need to go now!"

I suppressed a giggle at their exchange and pulled the car to the side of the road. "I stuck a roll of toilet paper in the side door pocket."

Paddy extracted Megan and scooted into the woods. Megan thought peeing in the woods was a fine thing. She hadn't mastered squatting, so after pulling down her panties, she held onto Paddy's hands, leaned back, and peed.

I'm not sure which she enjoyed more, the novelty of doing it outdoors or kicking dirt to bury her few sheets of used toilet paper. The process fascinated her. Walking the woods, she could get Grampa Seamus to stop five times in an hour to allow her to squeeze out a few drops and bury her toilet paper.

Nothing can take my mind off concerns more quickly than spending time with my granddaughter. I wondered if she would soon have a brother or sister, but I wasn't the kind of father to ask. They'd let me know if they became pregnant again.

Paddy fastened Megan into her car seat and started an audio book. Whispering behind his hand, he said, "She's ready for a nap but doesn't want to admit it. This will do the trick."

Good news: the loggers had worked up the A Grade. Bad news: the devastation continued. With each obstruction we passed, my concern heightened—would it continue all the way to Shank Lake or would we luck out? A mile before we reached our turn, we ran into the road-clearing crew heading our way. I parked at the side and hopped out to get the scoop.

I plugged my fingers into my ears until one of the four guys spotted me. Two guys were using heavy-duty chainsaws, and the other two were lugging debris to the side of the road. A quarter mile behind them, I spotted Dick Tanni, one of my Shank Lake neighbors. Looking like a toothpick in hunter orange sitting on his John Deere tractor, he was using its bucket to push smaller branches to the side of the road. The air smelled of freshly-cut wood infused with chainsaw exhaust.

One of the loggers noticed me and they killed their saws. Three of them were loggers I had used to selectively cut my property several years ago. The fourth guy was Owen Lyndstrom, an ancient coot I had become friends with the year I wintered up here.

Owen, senior to the others by at least forty years, was my model for how active I wanted to be in my eighties. Choppers had replaced his teeth decades ago, but he still had all the rest of his original parts and his back remained as straight and strong as a pine. He'd been handling one of the saws. "Howdy, Seamus. Helluva mess." He waved vaguely at the woods.

Owen's elephantine ears were useful for catching all the gossip for miles around, so it wasn't a surprise that he wanted me to relate our harrowing race against the storm. Owen had been out Lukes Road west of Shank Lake when the storm hit, and the logging crew had been working an area near Ned Lake. Between them, they had cleared more than a mile and a half of Shank Lake Road, leaving me only three-quarters of a mile to home. If need be, we could leave the car and walk in, although transporting the groceries might be problematic.

"Look," Owen said. "Damage by youse is scattered, but youse need to check your woods pronto and see where you need cuttin. Wait too long and the big owners'll tie up all the loggers. Unless you get them trees before rot sets in, you'll lose most of their value."

Good advice, but while hiding Elliot, I didn't want people working close to the house. I'd have to deal with my eighty acres once Elliot was gone. Owen's advice triggered another thought. In a generation-skipping estate tax move, I had given Megan several sections of land that might have been affected. I asked Owen about damage on Lukes Road where those properties were.

The logging crew was resting nearby and saw an opportunity: if I let them know by the end of the weekend, they'd be happy to put me at the top of their list.

Owen said, "I dang near forgot you bought them sections. I got nothin else planned. I'll come by first thing tomorrow and we'll scout that out, eh? Then I'll give these boys an estimate of how many cords of work they got."

"Paddy's actually the trustee." I pointed to my car. "He's here with my granddaughter. You won't believe how much she's grown. Let's lock it down with him."

Owen followed me to my car. We used the opportunity to let Megan run around.

"Growin like a weed, she is," Owen said. "Where'd she get the carrot top from?"

"Mailman," Paddy said. "Actually, most of the gray in Dad's hair used to be red highlights, and her mom's family also has some redheads, though Megan's is the most prominent."

Megan ran circles around us, arms stretched, pretending to be an airplane or fairy or who knows what. Her squealing abruptly ended. "Does it hurt?" She pointed to a dried bloodstain the size of a russet potato at the bottom of the wool shirt Owen wore in the woods regardless of the weather.

Owen tugged his shirt around to see what we were looking at and removed a work glove. "Cut myself changing the chain on the saw." He showed me the still-oozing wound on his hand. "Didn't have no hankie, so I used the shirt. Good I got me a tetanus shot last year. Ain't got no time to go to the clinic."

One of the loggers fired up his chainsaw. Break time was over. We quickly agreed to meet Owen first thing in the morning, meaning around six o'clock central time—or seven o'clock eastern time, which was what I went by at camp. Since they would evaluate Megan's land, I'd send Paddy with Owen, and I'd stay home with Megan and keep Elliot under wraps.

We do-se-doed past the loggers, and I stopped to talk to my lake neighbor. Dick had come up for a long weekend of fishing. After the storm blew through, he cleared his driveway and eventually linked up with Owen.

"It mostly missed me," he said. "Maybe ten trees across the driveway, but nothing near the house. It's real spotty though. I knew you were up and figured I'd motor over to your place to make sure you were okay."

"Are trees down between us?" I asked.

"I figured there were, which is why I used the boat. Anyhoo, your house and cabin are both fine, though you got a bunch of trees down here and there. I've tried to scrape the road pretty good, but drive careful, 'cause I might have kicked up some gravel. You know what them sharp edges can do to a tire. And if you can't get in all the way, go ahead and borrow the boat."

What a relief knowing the house and cabin had survived unscathed. That brief respite was followed by a new fear. Where were Elliot and Atty when Dick Tanni had stopped at the house and cabin?

FOUR

OUR PROGRESS TOWARD HOME STOPPED at a downed tree a half mile from the house. The massive hemlock had uprooted. It would take forever to clear with the little chainsaw I had in the car, and I'd run out of fuel before I succeeded. My anxiety over Elliot was increasing by the second, and I decided our best bet was to turn around and drive to Dick's and take him up on his offer to borrow his boat. Megan would like the ride and, once home, I'd have access to my larger chainsaws and could fire up the Bobcat to help clear the road from the house.

For all the wind we'd had earlier, the lake was dead calm. The trolling motor started on the first pull, and we were glad to leave the cool of the shady shore and feel our skin warm under the full sun. The motor's drone blocked the whine of the mosquitoes accompanying us onto the lake. The first we knew of them was the prick of their sting. Megan's hand-waving to ward off the mosquitoes rocked the boat, leaving Paddy to steady it with hands on both gunwales while I steered with one hand and slapped with the other.

I'm sure we looked like crazy idiots flailing our arms in our war with the mosquitoes. After a couple of minutes, we settled in to enjoy the slow boat ride. Megan dragged her hand in the lake, soaking her arm and half her shirt. Soon enough, I brought us into the dock without incident. After tying up, we left the borrowed life jackets in the boat, and Paddy and I each grabbed two bags of groceries. Megan led us up the path carrying her library books cradled in both hands and Raff's long neck tucked under her chin. Cute, very cute.

"Hey, pumpkin," I said once I could see the cabin wasn't damaged. "Why don't you run ahead and see if Mr. Elliot is in the cabin."

With her arms full, Megan's dash was more like a fast waddle. I wished I could take a video of her, but our hands were full and the moment lost. Elliot wasn't in the cabin, nor did I catch any whiff of his aftershave. The picnic table still covered the trapdoor to the half-basement, so he wasn't there. "My guess," I said, "is he's in front of the TV watching one of his financial shows."

Megan asked if she and Raff could race to the house. Permission granted, they took off, and I tucked her books under my arm and followed. Through the trees we watched Megan open the door and seventy-five pounds of golden retriever bound down the steps and into the wildflowers to relieve her bladder. Atty ran up the path and greeted us with her big grin and wagging tail. She led us to the house, where we found Raff propping open the screen door, letting in the last of the season's mosquitoes. From inside came Megan's call, "Mr. Elliot. Mr. Elliot. Come out, come out."

Elliot wasn't answering Megan's hide-and-seek calls. The dog had desperately needed to pee. The TV was blasting. The only way he was in the house was if he were dead or comatose. Leaving Paddy to put away the groceries, I raced after Megan, confirming Elliot was not on the first or second floor. On the way to check the basement, I turned off the TV, which was indeed tuned to one of the financial channels.

Megan followed me to the basement where we double-checked the nooks and crannies. She lost interest and plopped down on the rug to play with the wood blocks I kept in a box stored underneath the futon.

His leaving the TV on made no sense to me. He understood the need to conserve energy with my solar panel and battery system. I supposed they might have interrupted the show for the storm warnings, and Elliot was worried enough to forget the TV. Or he could have turned the TV up to hear the bulletins while he hid in the basement. But that was hours ago and didn't explain his continued absence.

My growing anxiety produced an image of my charge killed or trapped by a toppled tree. Had Elliot been curious about the storm damage? He'd taken walks with me in the woods, but preferred ATVing. With the trees down, though, he couldn't have gotten far, and again, it didn't explain the TV.

He sometimes read down by the lake, so I checked the likely spots and hollered his name in case he had somehow missed our arrival. Nothing. On my return to the house, I passed the pole-barn garage where I stored all the "toys." The garage doors were open, as we had left them, but inside a bare section of the gravel floor highlighted that the yellow Polaris ATV was missing. Anger replaced anxiety as I realized the fool had disobeyed my instructions and gone off on his own.

I followed the tracks in hopes of determining which way he went. Fifteen feet from the garage, they crossed marks made by a truck, or at least a vehicle with truck-like tires towing a trailer, which had made a three-point turn in front of the garage.

Through it all, the ATV tracks remained visible, meaning they were the most recent. I followed the various tire marks up the driveway. The truck had come in and gone out from the direction of town. The ATV drove the opposite way, heading up Shank Lake Road toward its end at the Net River.

The teeter-totter of my emotions dropped anger and embraced anxiety, combining it with embarrassment about how quickly I had become angry at Elliot. What had caused him to leave the safety of the house so abruptly that he hadn't turned off the TV? Had the visitor's arrival spooked him? Maybe something on the TV caused his panic. I had no clue how to tell the age of tire markings. I ran to the garage, hopped on my other ATV, the red Honda, and zipped up the driveway, following Elliot's trail. Great idea until in less than a quarter mile I encountered a tangled mess of hemlock, maple, and popple pushed down across the road.

I clambered around the blowdown and confirmed the tracks continued on the other side. Whatever Elliot's reason for leaving, he left before the storm blew through. Another blowdown blocked the road a couple hundred yards ahead. I could track Elliot and my ATV by foot, but that might take too long. Using the other ATV, I could find a way through the woods to skirt the roadblocks, but that wouldn't be fast, either.

I slapped my head with my hand. *Think, Seamus, think.* Elliot's gone. Tracking him would take time and effort. With Megan visiting, my priority had to be to open my road so we could get out in case of an emergency. Once we accomplished that, we could return Dick Tanni's boat and retrieve my car. With luck, Elliot would have returned from his jaunt to wherever.

I briefly considered calling Abigail to let her know I had lost the person

I was supposed to be protecting. To what end? It would just upset her, and she couldn't help find him. Once Elliot showed up, I'd learn the whole story and then consult with Abigail.

What a mess.

ATTY WHIMPERED WHEN PADDY, MEGAN, and I left her in the house again. Paddy operated the chainsaw. I kept Megan on my lap and she "helped" me run the Bobcat, pushing debris to the side of the road. We finished clearing our path to town shortly before dinnertime. I hoped we wouldn't need it.

Elliot remained a no-show.

I still had daylight and intended to use it to try and find him.

"I hate you going into the woods with all those widow-makers waiting to fall," Paddy said. "Let's eat dinner and then Megan and I can return the boat and pick up your car. While we're there, I can ask your neighbor to go with you. He seems like a nice enough guy."

"I understand your concern, but I can't let anyone know Elliot's here. I'll take a come-along to extract myself if I get stuck. And a gas can in case he ran out. And the first-aid kit. And I'll have my cell phone and a walkie-talkie. Man, I wish I knew where he was."

I filled two water bottles and grabbed several granola bars to gobble while I loaded the ATV. Dinner. When I went to fill a two-gallon traveling gas can, I made a disconcerting discovery. Elliot had taken the full five-gallon gas can with him, leaving me with only a gallon sloshing in the bottom of the other container. Huh. Sure enough, the funnel had been recently used and smelled of gasoline. A full tank would take him eighty miles or so, well beyond the range of any place I had shown him. Why did he need extra gas?

He hadn't thought to turn off the TV, but he had found time to fill up the Polaris's gas tank and take an extra five gallons. This felt more planned than I originally thought. What else had he taken?

Back inside the house, I checked the mud-room closet. The ATV helmet with the smoky face guard and a pair of work gloves had grown legs. Also missing were his lightweight jacket and my wool one, which would look ridiculous on him. Our chests were roughly the same size, but he was four inches shorter than my six-two, and the sleeves would swallow his arms. Besides, it was too warm to be wearing wool.

That perplexed me until I discovered empty spaces in the bedroom closet: missing were the new clothes Abigail had purchased for him on their way to meet me in Green Bay, as was a large backpack I stored there.

I told Paddy of my discoveries while he washed dishes from their supper.

"He got curious and is lying injured someplace?" Skepticism poured from him. "That's your theory? What if the mysterious truck and trailer had two guys and they snagged him. Their trailer was pulling ATVs. With Elliot they needed a third. Maybe they threw Elliot in the truck and one of the guys stole your ATV. And they had a long way to go, which is why they grabbed the extra gasoline."

"You're suggesting someone found him and kidnapped him? But the ATV went in a different direction from the truck."

"Kidnapped or he didn't want to stay hidden anymore and staged his own rescue. They could have taken the ATV in a different direction to avoid being seen together. They'd meet up later. As long as you're standing around, let me heat up some leftovers for you. Won't take a minute."

I didn't think Elliot left voluntarily and I wasn't hungry. "He's the one who wanted protection. He could have asked me to take him home any time he wanted. He wasn't a prisoner. What else would you take?"

"I'd take my blankie," Megan said.

I leaned down and ruffled her hair. "What else would you take, pumpkin?"

"Raff and Momma and Papa and Suzie. Can Suzie come here?"

Paddy wiped his hands on the dishtowel and gave her a big hug. "Thanks for taking your Momma and me. We'll see your friend Suzie when we get home."

"Megan's blankie got me thinking," I said. "If I were running away, I'd want a sleeping bag and a tent and food."

Megan tugged at Paddy's pant leg. "Can we FaceTime Momma?"

"I need to get her ready for bed or she'll have a meltdown." Squatting to Megan's level, he tousled her hair. "Bath first and then we'll FaceTime Momma, okay?"

Megan solemnly nodded and marched to the bathroom, disrobing along the way. Paddy followed and I soon heard the tub filling with water.

"Dad?" Paddy called down while I was checking the first-floor closets. "He left a turd in the upstairs toilet."

The Elliot I had known had been fastidious. Even using the outhouse by the guest cabin, he threw in lime.

Revised conclusion: he left in a hurry—TV on and unflushed toilet—but not so much of a hurry that he hadn't provisioned his trip. Further sleuthing revealed we were missing a sleeping bag, plus several boxes of various flavors of granola bars, a large bag of gorp Paddy had concocted to take on walks in the woods with Megan, and two water bottles. He'd taken both a flashlight and a headlamp, found a hunting knife, and added a can opener to his provisions. Empty hooks revealed he'd scarped up my hatchet and bolt cutter.

Face it, Seamus, this is not the behavior of someone about to go for a walk. These are the acts of someone so panicked that he left the TV on and didn't flush the toilet, but somehow had enough time to think about and collect supplies. Who or what had arrived with that truck?

Paddy had come downstairs during my internal musing and interrupted my thinking. "Maybe you should talk to Abigail and get her take on the best approach."

"It's clear that Elliot intentionally went on the lam and left before the storm hit. Regardless of why he left, he might have been injured by the storm. I owe it to him to use every second of daylight to rescue him if he's hurt. There's plenty of time to talk to Abigail."

Paddy held up his hands in surrender. "I just thought . . . she is the senior partner and the one who picked him up. She might know something."

"Give Megan a goodnight kiss for me and say hi to your lovely wife. I'll be careful. I promise."

Five

MY RETURN FOUND THE HOUSE dark, the garage light on, and the missing ATV still missing. I backed my ATV into the garage, where mosquitoes attacked with the whine of kamikaze fighters. My sprint to the house left the blood-thirsty critters behind. Bursting into the screened porch, I startled Paddy, who had been reading on a Kindle, and Atty, who had been sleeping.

"No Elliot?" I said.

Paddy shook his head. Atty came over to receive a scratch behind her ears and to be let outside to do her thing.

"Megan FaceTimed Cindy, and after I put the kid to bed I called her back. She thinks someone knows Elliot's here and I should take Megan home—out of danger."

"I can't disagree. I need to tell Abigail and get her advice." Because it might make the conversation go smoother, I added, "You can listen in if you want."

Paddy excused himself, saying he'd check the nightly news. With a good cell signal and privacy, I had no more excuses and called Abigail, punching on the speakerphone so I wouldn't fry my brain holding the phone to my ear.

"Elliot disappeared?" She sounded incredulous. "He left? And you don't know where he is? That makes no sense."

I told her everything, probably repeated myself because I was so nervous. "Do you think I should contact the police and have them search?"

Her "No!" was emphatic. I waited for more, picturing her pacing a room somewhere in Louisiana where she was protecting a crooked cop while he negotiated with prosecutors, trading his testimony on kickbacks within the department for a new identity under the witness protection program.

"I can't believe you left him alone. What were you thinking? You need to fix this yourself, Seamus. We cannot involve any official police agencies. If one word gets out about his location, it could be his death sentence. You need to find him and learn why he rabbited. Then we can decide how best to protect him. Are you sure no one's seen him?"

"No one has seen him. Or I should say, no one has seen his face. At least until today. Cindy wants Paddy to bring Megan home."

"The whole reason I agreed for you to do this on your own, and Elliot agreed to be with you instead of me, was because your place is remote as all hell and he wouldn't have to be cooped up inside some hotel room or safe house and go stir-crazy for a month. Paddy and Megan shouldn't have been there in the first place.

"Elliot enjoyed their company, especially Megan. He was much happier after they arrived."

"That's not the point. Despite their best intentions, they could have accidentally done or said something to jeopardize our client." A deep inhale and long sigh came over the line. "Look, Seamus, my Louisiana client will not trust someone else to take over for me. You are on your own and you need to fix this. Our reputation—my reputation—is on the line. You can't involve the police—they probably wouldn't help anyway. You can't say some guy whose real name you don't know stole your ATV. You need—"

"Got it." Testiness had entered my voice. I didn't think I'd screwed up. Paddy and Megan had not jeopardized anything. They hadn't mentioned Elliot to anyone. My whole reason for suggesting the business partnership with Abigail had been so we could spend more time together, and that hadn't worked out either.

Abigail was still talking and I had tuned her out.

". . . and for all those reasons. That's what I think."

"I wonder if something on the television might have been his trigger. You're not aware of anything current that intersects with whatever Elliot is involved in? Nothing to spook him today?"

"I can't exactly go to the prosecutor and inquire. They'll immediately wonder what's wrong and start asking questions. I'll sniff around, but you wanted this job, Seamus. And now you have a problem I have never experienced. Go solve it."

My face burned from the heat of her words. "Yes, ma'am." I disconnected and immediately regretted it. I did not want to go to bed mad at Abigail. I called her again, but it went to voicemail. "In our business dealings angst, I forgot to tell you that I love you. I do, and I do appreciate any suggestions you may have in the morning concerning ways I might find Elliot. I'm leaving my cell phone on in case he calls." As soon as I heard the words from my mouth, I knew she'd think I had given Elliot a phone. "He doesn't have a phone, but he may get to one. So, feel free to call whenever. I'll start tracking him again tomorrow at first light."

Atty patiently waited to be let in. I opened the door sufficiently to allow her to squeeze in and rubbed my hands down her back to try to brush off all the mosquitoes I could. Between Megan and the dog, a lot more mosquitoes were getting into the house than usual. A small price to pay for the family's visit, but an itchy price nonetheless.

The dog circled her bed three times and settled in with a long sigh. I needed to follow her example—sleeping, not circling the bed three times before settling in. Before I could go horizontal, I needed to return Dick Tanni's boat and bring my car home.

THERE'S NO VISITING DICK TANNI at night without chewing the fat and drinking a beer. I didn't get home for nearly an hour and found Paddy still watching TV.

"Learn anything from the news?" I asked.

"I assume," Paddy said, "you weren't the one recording all the stock market and business shows."

"I told Elliot to feel free to do what he wanted provided it didn't interfere with the few PBS shows I like."

"I've been checking today's recordings for any startling criminal news. Or a picture of him. Nothing. How can anybody watch this stuff for hours without going bonkers?"

He was pulling my chain, knowing I could get sucked into defending myself. I tweaked him back. "The same way *some* people can write code for hours and think it's fun. I take it nothing popped?"

"Hardly. I don't know if we'll need it, Dad, but maybe we should put together a dossier of everything we know or observed or guess about him."

"Under Abigail's orders, he and I never discussed his personal stuff. He was very knowledgeable about markets, and he spent a lot of time watching the real estate shows—investments, not the makeover ones. He'd talk back to those. I wish I had paid more attention. The way he related to Megan, I have a feeling he has kids of his own. I take him for midforties. No wedding band. No tan line where one had been, so probably divorced for a while."

"Or he's one of those guys who never wears a wedding ring. But he definitely grew up someplace like Kansas or Iowa. He throws an 'r' into words like wash, makes them 'warsh.' "

I acknowledged Paddy's observation. "He is or at least was Catholic. He's made comments only a former altar boy would make. You know what else I want to do? Let's capture his fingerprints while we can. Right now, I can't think of how we might use them, but if we ever need to know who he is, that would do it."

Paddy looked surprised. "You think he has a record?"

"Well," I said. "He is hiding out. But I was thinking that with his interest in real estate and finance, he might have been fingerprinted for his job."

"Right, like when you sat for your Series Seven exam at the investment bank. You know how to capture latents?"

I snorted at the idea. "Not a clue. But every night he takes a clean glass to the bathroom. It might have a few clear prints. I'll use a tripod to get a good digital photo of the prints. We'll need some kind of powder."

"I have talcum power in Megan's bag."

"They use black on TV. I have fine charcoal in the pills I keep for an oogie stomach."

It felt good to be doing something. We left the TV running in the background—just in case. Paddy searched the internet to learn the process of raising a latent print. We practiced on a glass and our own prints before working on Elliot's glass. We raised a partial thumb print, full index and pointer prints and smudged ring finger and pinkie prints, all from his right hand.

By the time we finished collecting the fingerprints and watched the last recorded business show, our observations about Elliot had grown substantially.

Elliot (pseudonym) - White male

I printed a copy of a cellphone picture of him reading to Megan that captured his dark eyes and brown hair receding into a widow's peak.

Right-handed.

5' 10" - 180 lbs.

Midforties

Probably divorced.

He knew several Sandra Boynton books by heart and gave animated performances for Megan. He also liked playing hide-and-seek.

Either has children or had younger siblings.

Catholic upbringing

Probably from the Iowa/Nebraska/Kansas area ("warsh")

Well-educated. Uses proper grammar. Large vocabulary.

Eclectic reader. Primarily interested in nonfiction.

Spent most of his time indoors. Hardly any tan, but gets antsy being in one place for long. Did not like boats, did not swim in lake, preferred ATV to walking in woods. Didn't exercise, but used strength equipment in basement. Former Boy Scout, so may have some outdoor skills.

Has no phone. Has no credit cards or identification.

Has ATV, clothes, sleeping bag, tent, compass, headlamp and flashlight, hatchet and bolt cutter. Limited food. Spare gasoline.

"Not a lot," Paddy observed.

"Let's look at a different question," I said. "What would *you* do if you were escaping from here?"

"Get help. I'd go someplace far enough away to feel safe and contact someone to help me. Of course, I know the area, which he doesn't. How far did you take him on your ATV rides?"

I whacked my forehead with the heel of my hand. "I showed him how to use the plat books."

Both the Iron and Baraga County plat books were missing from the drum table in the living room.

"With those," Paddy said, "he might look for a vacant camp and hole up until he can get help. He has no cell phone, so he needs a place with electricity and a phone line."

"At the point I had to give up following him, he was heading west on logging trails. A few more miles and he'd reach camps with utilities." I glanced at the clock. "Dawn arrives in three hours. I'll pack now and go find him. The night's clear. I can easily follow my path as far as I went. I'll take my sleeping bag and sleep out. Come first light, I'll be closer to him and can get an early start tracking. I agree with Cindy. You and Megan should leave."

"Remember, Owen's coming to check on the damage on Megan's tract. We'll meet him and leave from there. Megan will be really disappointed, especially since you won't be around to see her off."

"She'll live. Take some of the food with you. There's no way I can eat it all."

Paddy gave me a searching look. "You giving up on Elliot?"

"Nope. But even if I find him, I doubt we'll return to camp."

Six

An ATV's headlights, even combined with light from the stars, do not have the same illumination as the sun. In typical Seamus fashion, I underestimated how long it would take me at night to cover the same ground I had covered the previous evening. And I had not anticipated how many obstacles I wouldn't see in the dim light. My face and arms stung from my encounters with protruding branches and brambles.

The one and a half hours I left myself to sleep before my phone alarm sounded felt like a minute. My hip felt like I had slept on a jagged rock and my back was as limber as concrete block. *I'm too old for this shit.* I bungee-corded the sleeping bag onto the ATV and settled myself onto its cold seat to continue tracking Elliot's trail. Over the years, I had added to my GPS all the logging roads and skidder trails I had explored, so I had a great map. If I knew where Elliot was going, I could find the easiest route. An hour into the morning's search, I was relieved to find evidence of Elliot going off-trail to get around a tree downed by the storm. The storm hadn't killed him.

At exactly 8:07, while off-road in an area filled with scraggly black spruce, I spotted a flash of yellow at the bottom of a ravine. I couldn't see well through the trees, but it had the feel of my ATV partially submerged in water. The bottom dropped out of my stomach at the thought of Elliot's neck broken from a fall or the ATV carrying him all the way to the water where he drowned.

Not wanting to end up down in the ravine myself, I dismounted and walked the path of pushed-down spruce and broken branches from Elliot's attempt to maneuver around a downed popple.

To return to the main trail, he had to run the ATV sideways on the hill. In his inexperience, he must not have leaned enough to counterbalance the ATV's shifting center of gravity. The machine had flipped several times and landed in the swampy area. I side-stepped down the slope looking for signs of Elliot. No body. No blood. In the soft earth were prints to and from the ATV, which was sunk up to its footboards.

I followed one set of footprints to a pine tree and discovered a trove of neatly piled clothes: a pair of pants, several shirts and pairs of underwear. Next to them were an empty soda bottle, four granola bar wrappers and, tucked inside a muddy pair of pants, a pair of soaked socks. Elliot had changed clothes, dumped what he couldn't or didn't want to carry, and walked away from the accident.

Knowing he had survived the accident lifted a bit of the weight bearing down on me. Being on foot was safer for him, but it meant he was no longer constrained to logging trails. Growing up on Boston's streets hadn't provided me expertise at tracking humans in the woods. Sure, I could follow a path of bent and broken stems across a weedy understory, but most of this forest wasn't like that. I might be able to find a footprint here or there in the moss or wet leaves, but even if I could, it would take me forever.

He was a city boy too, and my only hope was he'd take a path of least resistance and return to the logging roads. On those, I could spot footprints in the mud. And on trails, an ATV would cover ground a lot faster than hoofing it.

The Polaris he'd taken had a better suspension and was more stable than my Honda and had the winch in case I had problems. It sat on the right side of the downed popple—a winner on all counts if I could get it out.

The ATV looked fine, and the extra gas can was still strapped onto its rear rack. Spattered mud on the surrounding trees suggested Elliot had further made a hash of it by spinning the wheels, digging the ATV in. He had left the key in the ignition; the tailpipe was above the mud and clear. I pulled the choke, turned the key, and the ATV fired up.

The chances were slim to none that I could drive it out, but I tried. Shifting into reverse, I discovered Elliot had failed to engage the four-wheel drive. Changing that setting, I tried gently rocking my way onto solid footing. No go. Elliot had found or created a real mud hole. Fortunately, I had brought a come-along.

I attached it to the cable from the ATV's winch and had enough length to convert a pine tree into an anchor. A few minutes later, I had ratcheted the Polaris onto dry land. Except for being covered with mud, the ATV worked fine. I drove it up the hill to the trail on the far side of the downed tree.

I transferred my supplies from the Honda, bungee-corded the items to balance the weight between the front and rear racks. I recorded the GPS coordinates for the Honda and zipped its key safely into my jacket pocket.

In the distance, a group of ravens jawed with each other. I considered the archaic terms for a flock of ravens: a conspiracy or an unkindness. The conspiracy label was easy to understand. Ravens are dark black and sociable. We humans have painted black as bad. In addition to being playful, ravens are smart. So, to a bunch of straight-laced, God-fearing, hard-working Englishmen, a flock of ravens could represent a conspiracy against God's will: talking in a secret language, heads nodding in agreement to some nefarious plan, heads rotating at strange angles to give one another a "beady eye."

Experiencing the northwoods had provided me with a possible reason for the unkindness appellation, and thinking about it brought back some of the despair I felt about this enterprise. In open areas, turkey vultures are often the ones to first discover death. In woods, curious ravens frequently perform the unkindness of finding the dead. If I didn't find Elliot, it probably meant the death knell of my business partnership with Abigail. Don't ask for whom the ravens croak; they croak for thee.

I pulled myself away from such esoteric musings. I wouldn't find the needle of Elliot in the haystack of the U.P.'s woods if I didn't get my ass in gear. Worse, a haystack provided limited geography. Every minute that slipped away in my search enlarged the circle of where Elliot could be. I caught myself humming the "Mission Impossible" theme and shoved the ATV into gear.

WITH AT MOST AN HOUR of sleep, Patrick was not looking forward to driving six hours with a preschooler after however long it would take to troop through the woods looking at damaged trees. What with packing the car, feeding Megan, and peeing Atty, they were a couple minutes late meeting Owen at the head of the lake.

As they followed Owen's truck west on Lukes Road, Patrick examined the woods for damage. A mile and a half in they hit the first spot where the passable road narrowed to no wider than Owen's truck. Overall, the damage seemed limited. They pulled off near an old skidder trail widened the previous winter by a logging company when it clear-cut an area past Megan's first section. With permission, they had hauled the logs over the trail through Megan's property.

Owen leaned on Patrick's car while Patrick extracted Megan from the back seat. "Where's Seamus?"

"Dad had to take care of something else, and it turns out we need to return to Chicago, so here we are. Fresh air and exercise, and with luck she and the dog will both sleep most of the way home."

"Ain't no reason you have ta go with me. I can check 'er out, and let your dad know what I found."

"Well, I promised him I would, and Megan's looking forward to it. Dog, too, for that matter."

Owen scratched his beard and seemed to Patrick almost disappointed that they were joining him. "Dog'll be fine, but make sure your girl doesn't wander. This storm's left a bunch of widder-makers. We'll cut in this way to the clear-cut and walk its edge west. Iffen I recollect correctly, there's an old access road should bring us back to Lukes, eh? She can do a coupla miles?"

Patrick considered the issue. "No problem, but we'll need another plan for her other two sections."

"I don't think we're gonna find much damage farther west. We'll do a drive-by and if needs be, I can do'er myself. Welp, the sun ain't waitin fur us."

Atty had been wandering, nose to the ground sniffing what had been there before her. Once she realized her humans were heading down a path, she was prepared to lead wherever they wanted to go.

Patrick used his cell phone to record notes: Owen's three cords here, four cords there, estimates of damaged wood. They reached the clear-cut. "Somebody's been through kinda recent on an ATV," Owen pointed to tracks cutting diagonally through the clear-cut. At the far edge of the open area they found the old access road Owen had mentioned.

"Lookee here." The old man pointed to vehicle tracks on the ground. "This here be the busiest little piece of nowhere I ever seen."

"Wonder why," Patrick said. "I don't remember this road from when Dad and I walked the property with the broker."

Owen laughed. "City brokers don't know shit about country acreage. They rely on their plat books and can't find their ass from their elbow. Pardon my French around the little one. I've been gettin better at home, but I fergit out here."

Megan tugged on Patrick's hand. "Papa? I'm thirsty."

Patrick knelt and Megan extracted a juice box from his knapsack. He punched the straw into the hole and handed it back to her. Atty saw the process and wagged her way to them as if asking if the knapsack held a snack for her, too. "Hey girl," Patrick said. "Rustle up your own grub." The dog seemed to take the words under advisement and wandered into the woods.

Owen waited until the juice production was complete and picked up his conversational thread. "This road starts past your section line. It only cuts this far edge of your property. Probably someone checkin to see if partridge are in the area. Less'n two months 'for bird season starts."

Patrick spotted a glint, like reflected sun. Catching the glare through the trees a second time, he pointed it out to Owen. Another hundred yards down the road the glint had become a truck backed off the road behind a thick stand of alders.

"I didn't hear him, did you?" Patrick said. "Somebody must have gotten up real early."

"Before sunrise anyway. There's dew on the bonnet."

An electric tingle set up along Patrick's spine. "From yesterday, before the storm? Could someone be hurt in the woods? Or dead?"

"Could may be."

Atty led the group to the blue truck, which was towing a trailer with its back gate down to form a ramp. Owen ran his finger through the dew on the hood. "Cold. If it had run this morning there should be some heat."

Patrick opened the unlocked door and peered inside. A plat book, opened to the section they were in, lay on the passenger seat. The ashtray contained what Patrick was sure were a couple of roaches, and the interior did have a faint marijuana smell. He found a registration in the glove box: Environmentally Friendly Extraction, LLC—the mining company doing exploratory tests in the county.

Now I got it. "Dad and I met this guy on our way into town yesterday. He had a blue ATV on the trailer."

"Frankie Joe Cabibi. Not seein his ATV might be good. Storm hits and he mighta headed back to town on the ATV. He'll come back later to pick up his truck. He's a local Amasa boy. Left years ago, recently come back. Thinkin on it, I don't recollect him passin me and the boys when we was clearin the road yesterday. Not that he woulda been likely to give a helpin hand. Lazy bastard. Mighta taken Lukes Road to the highway, eh? Fewer obstructions? Maybe those tracks was him goin through the clear-cut?" He tilted his head back and bellowed, "Frankie Joe! You 'round?"

From the direction of a towering hemlock a dozen or so ravens joined the cry.

Patrick thought back to his premonition of death. His father had a saying, "Nothing goes on in the woods without the ravens knowing." He pulled his shoulders down, trying to bring his shoulder blades together.

Thinking of the ravens didn't help loosen the tenseness he felt. "Maybe we should check?"

Owen gave Patrick a squint-eyed look. "Hemlock's some past your section corner and there ain't much timber between here and there. We'd have to work our way around this raspberry patch."

The dog bounded toward them, tail wagging, carrying something in her mouth.

"Hey girl," Owen called. "Let me see whatcha got." The dog trotted to Owen and danced around trying to engage him in tug-of-war.

"Atty, sit," Patrick said. "Good girl. Atty, drop it."

The dog laid the bone on the ground in front of her and grinned.

Owen picked up the bone while Patrick praised the dog and scratched behind her ear. "She can have it, can't she?" Patrick asked. "Deer bones aren't like chicken bones, right?"

"Uh-huh, 'ceptin this here's a human leg bone."

Seven

Iron County Sheriff Lon Bartelle sat at his desk working on manpower reports for the next County Supervisors' meeting when the desk phone rang. Using his shoulder to cradle the phone next to his ear, he answered with his name, and leaned back, the chair creaking in protest.

"This is Patrick McCree from up by Shank Lake. My dog just discovered a human bone."

Bartelle slumped in the chair. "One bone? You wouldn't be the first city sl—the first person to confuse a deer or bear bone for human."

"It's a femur," Patrick McCree said. "Owen Lyndstrom identified it, not me. And even we city slickers know that most animal bones are found lying on top of the earth. This one was caked with dirt. Looks like it's been in the ground for a while."

"Ah, crud." He grabbed the antacids from his pocket. "Where are you?"

"Right now? At my father's camp, but that's only to get a decent cell signal, and my daughter needed a nap. Owen's waiting with the bone where we found it in the woods." Patrick gave him directions and GPS coordinates.

"I'll gather a team. I'd like for you and the dog to meet us there with Lyndstrom. It'll take us an hour, maybe hour and a half tops."

"Dad's out, and if he hasn't returned, I'll need to bring my daughter. Could you stop by here or give me a call when you're close? We planned to head home today. Any reason we can't do that?"

Something was not making sense. The younger McCree was in the middle of nowhere with his daughter, his dog, and Owen Lyndstrom. They find a purportedly human bone, and now he needs to be in Chicago? On a Saturday? People didn't usually leave God's country on Saturday.

"Shouldn't be a problem," he said. "But let's see what you have. Hopefully it's a case of the old man needing new glasses, or maybe it's some old Chippewa or voyageur grave."

"Maybe," Patrick said. "But it didn't feel *that* old."

MY DECISION TO FOLLOW THE abandoned logging road bore fruit soon after I had beaten my way through the woods back to it. I found a smudged shoe print on the right margin of the road. Abigail had taken away the clothes Elliot had traveled in, making purchases for him in Green Bay—where we'd made the switch from her to me—brand new attire, including shoes. Even though he was shorter, we weighed the same, and it showed in our feet: his Rockports were shorter and wider than my boot. The smudge made it impossible to tell the shoe's size or to see the pattern on the sole. Had to be Elliot, though. Who else had been here since the storm?

I zipped along on the ATV as quickly as I dared but slowed anywhere I thought I might catch a print. A half mile later, I found one so clear I could read "Rockport." Seeing his print on the right edge of the road reminded me of his propensity to be a creature of habit. I would have walked in the crowned center where it was generally drier and farther away from the branches of bushes and young trees encroaching from the sides. Having found two prints on the right, I concentrated my attention there.

The storm had damaged fewer and fewer trees the farther west I went, and traveling became easier. The path arrived at a recent clear-cut, where I picked my way through broken branches and other slash left behind from the logging operation. At the far edge of the harvested area, I was stumped. I no longer saw any footprints and didn't see roads or paths leading from the area. If Elliot had headed straight into the woods, I was stuck.

I consulted my GPS and its depiction of the nearby trails. It looked like one might reach the southwest corner of the cut-over area and head to Lukes Road. Elliot had dumped some clothes, but he still had the plat books with him. Was he good enough with a compass to know where he was?

I needed to remind myself that my only hope was if he preferred the ease of walking roads. I scanned the distant tree line and spotted what might be one. Crossing my fingers, I worked my way in that direction and discovered it was a road the loggers had widened for bringing logs out of the clear-cut. No footprints, but recent ATV traffic.

The sun had risen high enough to burn off the dew and make me uncomfortably warm. I peeled a layer, bungee-corded it to the ATV, and downed a slug of water before pressing on. Moving slowly, I scanned the ground for any sign of Elliot's prints and almost ran into a parked truck I didn't recognize. I dismounted for a closer look and was startled by Owen Lyndstrom greeting me from behind a tree with, "When's the sheriff deputies gettin here?"

PATRICK LED THE PROCESSION OF cop cars toward where he had left Owen with the bone. Sheriff Bartelle came next and behind him was a second Iron County vehicle, this one towing a trailer with two ATVs. At the point they left Lukes Road for the skidder trail, he motioned for the police to take the lead. He didn't want his car blocked in since he still hoped he'd be able to take Megan home.

The sheriff drove directly in. The deputies stopped and one of them snapped several digital photographs of the intersection of Lukes Road and the entrance road before they followed the sheriff's car.

"Megan, do you want to go with Papa or stay in the car and watch a movie on the tablet?"

Megan's eyes lit up. "Dorothy!"

Six weeks earlier Patrick and Cindy had come home from a date night to discover *The Wizard of Oz* in the DVD player. The next day Megan reported watching it with the babysitter, and "loved" it. She appeared proud she had to cover her eyes only three times. Cindy and Patrick worried Megan had been traumatized, although she was sleeping fine. When Megan lobbied to see it again, Patrick watched it with her, ready to turn it off at the first sign of distress. Megan was pretty much fearless, covering her eyes only during the flying monkey scene, but even there, she peeked between her fingers. Patrick thought she treated the movie as a challenge: how scared could she get before she had to cover her eyes? Problem now was she'd never watched it alone.

"I'm not going to be here with you, sweetheart. How about Anna and Elsa? Besides, you already watched Dorothy this trip." Since Megan loved *Frozen*, Patrick hoped his suggestion would work.

"Dorothy," Megan countered and began to pout and kick her heels into the seat.

Patrick broke his own rule of not allowing any movie more than once a week and queued it up. "I'll be back as soon as I can. I'm taking Atty with me." He opened the hatch and the dog hopped down, tail wagging, ready for a new adventure. Patrick snapped on the thirty-foot lead. "Sorry, girl. We'll see what they have in mind for us."

With Atty pulling at the end of the lead, they continued up the road to the parked truck where he had left Owen with the bone. In the two hours since he was last here, the woods had become hot and silent. Other than humans, the dog was the only thing moving. Even the birds were quiet. Upon reaching the truck, Atty nearly pulled the lead from Patrick's hand trying to reach his father, who to Patrick's surprise was leaning against the truck, talking with Sheriff Bartelle. The two deputies were to the side, photographing the leg bone.

Spotting Patrick didn't change his father's grim expression. He closed his eyes and gave his son a minute headshake before resuming his discussion with the sheriff. Patrick scanned the area. No Owen. No Elliot. He had no idea what was going on. Time to keep his mouth shut and listen very carefully.

EIGHT

BARTELLE WAS SURPRISED TO FIND Seamus McCree leaning against the mining company truck. "I didn't expect you. Where's Owen Lyndstrom?" In the seven minutes since he had spoken those words, he still hadn't ascertained why McCree was there and Owen was not.

McCree's explanations were reasonable. The same generosity of spirit and time that McCree showed whenever Bartelle consulted him for expert assistance with financial aspects of a crime would make McCree the sort to check up on his neighbors' camps. And there was nothing objectionable in McCree stopping by to see how his son and Owen were doing documenting the storm damage on family property. And it made some sense for Owen to agree to take Seamus's ATV and inspect the rest of the McCree property. But it didn't *feel* right, and Bartelle had learned to pay attention to those feelings.

For starters, Owen had a well-deserved reputation as one of the county's biggest gossips, and it wasn't his nature to voluntarily give up an opportunity to get the scoop on the origins of the bone. And Seamus acted nervous. He'd keep that in mind. But with the son and dog walking up the trail, he needed to shift gears and find the rest of the skeleton, if one existed.

Patrick reined the dog in and gaped at his father with what Bartelle judged to be surprise and, what, concern? Bartelle offered his hand. "Appreciate your time, Patrick. You already know Tex. Have you met Sergeant Denis Engberg? He's my bone expert. Came to us after retiring from the DNR. From which direction did your dog bring the bone?" He offered his closed hand for the dog to sniff. "Beautiful dog."

Patrick waved toward his right. "I had to whistle several times. Either she was far away or didn't want to leave her treasure. Do you want her on lead—it can be up to thirty feet—or let her roam and hope she takes us to the bones? Dad, Megan's in the car. Can you stay with her? Atty, heel."

The dog trotted to Patrick, circled behind him, and came to a stop next to Patrick's leg. "Good dog." Patrick patted her head. "Now down." The golden sighed and lay on the ground, her head tilted up toward her master. "She does protest commands she doesn't like."

Bartelle decided he'd rather have her under control and not allow her to further disturb any additional bones. "Her name is Atty?"

"Atalanta, actually. In Greek mythology, she was—"

Bartelle caught Tex's smirk. He did not have time or interest in mythology. "Fascinating as your story may be, let's see if your dog can find us a skeleton."

Patrick gave the dog a small carrot. He showed her the bone, now contained in a plastic evidence bag. "Let's find some more bones, Atty. Show me. Find a bone." To the humans he added, "Who knows what she understands, but I'm pretty sure she knows the word b-o-n-e." Back to the dog, "Free!"

The dog scrambled to her feet and trotted more or less in the direction Patrick had pointed, Bartelle and two deputies spread out and trailed behind. "Good girl," Patrick said in that voice people use with babies and dogs.

Unlike looking for stuff in thick brambles, here in the open woods, they didn't have to walk side-by-side. Not that he was sure what he was supposed to be looking for anyway—surely not a bony hand sticking from the grave. During his time as a member of the sheriff's department, they had had only one unsolved missing person case—three years ago—and this bone had the appearance of being much older. In fairness though, he didn't know what the *Bones* character from TV, or her real-life equivalent in a lab somewhere, could determine from their evidence. He hoped they'd find the skull or a jawbone. With teeth, they'd have a shot of identifying the victim using dental records.

He realized he was assuming that a crime had occurred. But wasn't it more likely someone had died of exposure years ago? The dirt bothered him. If someone had died of exposure, the wolves, coyotes, bears, eagles, ravens, buzzards, and whatever would not have buried the bone.

Walking slowly so they didn't miss anything allowed him to return to thinking about antsy Seamus McCree. He'd grown to like the guy a lot. He'd deputized him on cases from time to time and McCree threw himself into understanding the financial aspects of whatever Bartelle had him looking at. Freaking genius. Rich guy, but not one who always had to let you know how much money he had. He hadn't known Seamus had bought three sections of land until he had asked a deputy to check the land records before they drove up. What the heck did he want with 1,920 acres?

Something didn't feel right. He made a mental note to pull McCree aside and explore that. A sharp pain across his shinbone returned him to the present. He'd been paying no attention and walked into a stiff branch. He shifted his full attention to the task at hand.

The dog gave a throaty woof and pulled at her lead. Probably wanted to chase the red squirrels Bartelle heard chattering.

"Over here," Patrick yelled, the pitch of his voice raised in excitement.

Bartelle jogged through the woods, alert for any more branch ambushes, and arrived to find Patrick feeding the dog another small carrot and exclaiming what a good dog she was.

Patrick pointed toward the partially collapsed shack. "Atty started pulling hard, and I didn't want us screwing up any evidence."

The structure had seen much better days. A rotted support post canted the building to one side. A youthful white pine had grown up in the open doorway. Bartelle guessed the ridge pole was holding strong, but the sway-back roof meant the rafters were nearly shot. A yellow-birch sapling grew from the moss-covered roof. The four walls still retained their windows, but if the roof went, he wouldn't bet much on the walls standing.

Bartelle ordered Patrick and the dog to remain where they were. Using yellow tape, he marked an area around the decrepit cabin and ordered Sgt. Engberg to mark a path to the doorway for anyone approaching the cabin.

"I don't want that thing collapsing on you. For now, no one enters that building, but I need to know if there's a body inside. Don't touch anything if you can avoid it, and if you do need to touch something, I want Tex to photograph it before and after. Let's make sure it's human. I'd hate to call out the state to investigate a pig roast."

I HAD NO RECOLLECTION WHEN the last time I had seen the *Wizard of Oz* was. I don't think we let Paddy watch the movie until he was ten. Megan seemed fine and was impressed that I knew a few songs well enough to sing along. Mostly, though, I rehashed my decision to get Owen involved looking for Elliot.

Yes, I had promised Abigail I would tell no one about Elliot, and that I would do my level best to track him down. Owen had probably forgotten more tracking lore than I had ever known. Running into him made me recognize there were only two ways I would find my charge: be extremely lucky or get help. Relying on luck was a fool's game. I could keep my promise to Abigail and kiss away any hope of helping Elliot, or I could break it and get help finding him.

Owen, a human magnet for information and one of the county's foremost gossips, had proven he could keep something private if he promised. I swore him to secrecy before giving him the scoop on Elliot's running away from my protection and how my tracking had brought me to finding Owen guarding a bone.

I ran down the list Paddy and I had developed, which he summarized as, "So basically, you don't know jack. You got a picture of 'im?"

I scrolled through my phone and pulled up one of Elliot playing with Megan.

"Welp, I ain't accomplishing anythin sittin here with this leg bone. How abouts you and me trades places? You babysit the bone and I'll see if I can find your Elliot. What do I do with him if I find him?"

"Tell him I'll do anything I can to make sure he's safe. He has no money and no ID. I can drive him anyplace he wants to go. I just need to do my job, Owen. He can fire us if he wants, but I need to make sure he's safe and protect him from any danger."

Owen scratched the back of his head with both hands, a gesture meaning he was thinking. I gave him time.

"I'd find me a camp where I could steal money, a gun to protect myself, and find some transport. Or if I had someone I trusted, I'd give 'em a call. Have 'em pick me up. He brung them bolt cutters to break in somewheres, and he threw away a bunch of clothes to make room to keep that and the hatchet."

Such common sense should have occurred to me.

"Just so you know, if he starts taking potshots, I'm skedaddlin. I'm no hero."

"Do you want my GPS? Plat books? I forgot, I don't—"

"Oh, hell no. I've been through this whole area cruisin timber and huntin and fishin. Drop me blindfolded anywheres, and I'd figure out where I was before you could sing the Pledge of Allegiance."

I tried to picture someone singing the Pledge of Allegiance, and for the first time since I discovered Elliot missing, I cracked a smile. But now, I had no idea where either Elliot or Owen was, Bartelle had wrinkled his brow at a couple of my nonanswers, and I didn't know how Abigail would react to my decision. Oh, the roads we choose to travel.

Meanwhile, Dorothy, the Lion, the Scarecrow, and the Tin Man were entering the poppy fields marking the end of the first act of the movie. And my mental discomfort had become physical: my full bladder required attention.

Megan was fine staying in the car, so I followed a recently-used ATV trail curving into the woods. Walking beyond a fallen maple someone had recently taken a chainsaw to and hauled off the trail, I checked to see if Megan could see me. Nope. A large rock, dropped by a glacier thousands of years ago or dug up by a logging crew cutting this road, dominated one side of the path. I watered the bushes on the other side. I paused while zipping up to appreciate the buzzy song of a great crested flycatcher singing in a nearby tree.

Without binocs I was unlikely to spot it, but I crossed the path to get a clearer view of the tree I thought the bird was in. The song stopped, and a bird flew out the far side. I followed it and nearly blinded myself looking into the sun. Stupid. I ducked my head and blinked away the spots, coming to focus on a patch of dark color staining the far side of the glacial erratic, spreading to the nearby ground. Thinking it might be an interesting lichen, I squatted for a closer look.

Not a plant. It looked like a lot of blood that had dried evenly. I sniffed the area, but couldn't catch the metallic smell I associated with blood. Outside the ring of the stain, I spotted a jagged fist-sized rock tipped in red. Two people were missing: Frank Cabibi had abandoned his truck. Elliot had been nearby.

My mind whirled with questions. What happened? Whose blood? Did this involve Elliot? Was he responsible?

BARTELLE HUDDLED WITH HIS DEPUTIES, peering at the camera's LCD. What appeared to be a small-caliber hole penetrated the human skull. Earth partially filled the skull, and they couldn't see the other side without moving it. Bones were scattered all around an area the former DNR officer said was a bear den, probably from the previous winter. The bear had dug through floorboards rotted from a leak around a stove pipe.

"This clothing?" Bartelle pointed to an area of the picture with a slightly different tint from the surrounding earth.

"Blue jeans, maybe," Tex said. "I got pictures of plastic buttons and a belt buckle. And in this close-up of the jaw, you can see amalgam fillings. If this guy was local, we can identify him."

Bartelle blinked to get his eyes to focus more clearly. "He?"

"Just a guess, or a very tall woman."

Tex scrolled ahead several shots. "Look, Chief, see the changes in the dirt color along these two edges?" He flipped between two pictures. "This one the bear excavated. See how it goes from duff to black topsoil to gray sand to lighter sand? This here?" He switched pictures. "It's all mixed up. Both areas are under the flooring. The guy didn't crawl under the cabin and die. He was buried. There's evidence of rotted rugs in there. It's a leap, but I'll bet they hid where someone took up some flooring to bury the body. 'Course the floor coulda been added after."

"Either way," Sgt. Engberg added, "given the roots going through the burial area, it's been a good long time. At least twenty, thirty years."

From outside the taped area, Patrick spoke. "Something's up. Here comes my father."

Bartelle flashed anger at McCree bringing the kid here like they were on a picnic. Megan bounced up and down on McCree's shoulders, one arm wrapped around the top of his head and the second arm cradling a stuffed giraffe. The two of them were singing "Follow the Yellow Brick Road" for crying out loud.

Then Bartelle noticed the distressed look on McCree's face and a quick negative shake of his head. Another unspoken communication between father and son? Maybe death made him suspicious of everyone and everything. Once again, the McCrees were smack dab in the middle of an Iron County murder investigation. At least this time, assuming Sgt. Engberg's timetable was correct, the bones predated McCree's' first appearance in the county. "What?" he demanded.

McCree spun Megan from his shoulder and set her on the ground. "Do you carry a reagent for blood?"

Acid sloshed in Bartelle's stomach, and his mouth filled with saliva to wash away the bitter taste. He patted his shirt pocket for an antacid. He'd already eaten them all and it wasn't even noon.

BARTELLE COLLECTED A SAMPLE BAG from the trunk of his car and what he still thought of as a "benzidine color test" kit, even though they hadn't contained that powerful carcinogen in years. He beckoned Seamus McCree to lead the way and followed him past the parked cars and up a lightly-used trail to a bear-sized boulder and the purported bloodstains. "What did you touch? Why were you even here?"

"Call of nature. I don't think I touched anything."

Bartelle studied the stains and decided he had a problem: all the blood was evidence and disturbing any of it could screw up the crime scene—if that's what it was. Tex photographed the entire area, and then Bartelle chose an isolated drop to process.

He fiddled with the test kit and McCree asked, "Looking for blue-green or is this the pink stuff?"

"You been watching that *CSI* crap on TV?"

"You don't like the show?"

Bartelle added a drop each of two different chemicals to the stain. "It gives people false expectations about what we can do." Bartelle closed his eyes to think and told his stomach to stop protesting. He didn't imagine McCree was involved since he was the one to point out the blood. Except a niggling part of his brain wondered what the guy had been hiding when they had talked earlier. McCree was chess-master smart, often several steps ahead of everyone else. Maybe he decided they would eventually find the blood, and he'd take suspicion off himself by "discovering" it first.

Give suspects enough rope to hang themselves. "So, from your vast experience watching *CSI*, what do you think happened here?"

"I never said I watched the show. I read about the blood tests. But to answer your question, head wounds bleed a lot. I'm guessing someone got smacked on the noggin with that rock, fell against this boulder, and bled. No *corpus delicti*. Either the victim recovered and didn't report the assault, or the body was hauled away. I have to tell you, Lon, I've been wondering ever since I got here where Frank Cabibi and his ATV are. His truck is here, but Owen mentioned he and Patrick had found it covered in dew.

I'm sure you noticed an ATV recently drove through here after someone cleared a tree from the path. And kept going. One way. All the plants are pushed away from us."

Bartelle chewed over McCree's suppositions. "I need to retire to someplace like Detroit. What with the drugs and gangs, all their crimes make sense. You got any antacids? I've got lava burning in my stomach. No? Let me think here."

McCree may have planted the idea, but Bartelle didn't figure this was someone taking an illegal deer. There'd be a gut pile somewhere, attracting attention from the ravens he'd heard nearby. The state guys had the tools to verify human blood. The question was what to do now. The skeleton wasn't going anywhere. Some living human might be injured. Out loud he said, "We've already totally screwed the pooch with any evidence on this trail. I want to strategize with my guys. Oh, and thanks. I forget to say that sometimes."

Bartelle stopped after two steps and McCree nearly ran into him. "Save me some time at the courthouse," he said. "Who did you buy the land from?"

"The estate of a Mrs. Ripone. Lived in Amasa, though I never met her. The broker said she inherited the property from her husband years ago."

The name didn't ring any bells, which meant all the Ripones had been law-abiding folks since he'd moved to the area. Or, he reminded himself, at least hadn't been caught at anything.

I EAVESDROPPED ON BARTELLE CONFERRING with the two deputies. Several years ago, I'd been the one to give Tex his nickname because of his roped muscles and the hitch in his step. The DNR guy was maybe my height—hard to tell because he slouched. His salt-and-pepper hair and deep wrinkles around his eyes suggested he was maybe midfifties. I wouldn't want to wrestle him; his barrel-chest and long, strong arms could crush me.

The upshot was Bartelle called in reinforcements. He asked me to guard the skeleton: make sure no one, human or animal, wandered into the marked area until the state police arrived. Paddy, with Megan and Atty in tow, agreed to hang out on Lukes Road to direct both the extra deputies and the state guys when they arrived. Once state resources arrived, Paddy would drive to my place and wait to give a formal statement before heading to Chicago.

I hated not knowing the former DNR guy's name, so I offered my hand. "I don't think we've met, I'm Seamus McCree."

"Denis Engberg, one N." We shook, his giant mitt swallowing mine. "Actually, we met fifteen years ago. I stopped by your camp during deer season to check on licenses."

"And you remember?"

"Well," he flashed a warm smile under his walrus mustache, "there was that little issue with Boss a while back that brought your name to my attention." He clapped his hands. "Guess I'd better act like the bloodhound the sheriff expects me to be and see if I can find a trail to Frank Cabibi. You guys ready?"

Bartelle and Tex took positions a few yards from the path and Sergeant Engberg positioned himself to follow the trail.

Before they could start, a circa 1990 Dodge Ram truck pulled up next to our group. The tailgate was covered with stickers proclaiming "Stop Sulfide Mining," "Environment First," and "Cyanide, The Gift That Keeps on Giving" next to decals for several radical environmental groups. A skinny kid with a peach-fuzz goatee, black glasses with lenses as thick as mine, and an orange camo ball cap covering white-guy dreads hopped out of the truck.

"Hey dudes, what's going on?"

Bartelle asked who he was and why he was here.

"Greg Shuett. I heard Cabibi was nearby, staking a site for a test. I plan to evaluate the hydrological impact and stop this shit before it gets started."

"Mister Shuett," Bartelle spoke with a cop-neutral voice. "We have an active investigation here, and I need you to leave the area."

Shuett stuck out his chin. "Or what?"

"Look, son, I got nothing against you," Bartelle said. "But I don't have a lot of time for idle conversation. If you don't leave now, I'll put you in one of our cruisers and sort it out later. Your choice, Mister Shuett."

Shuett swung his arm in a motion intended to include Paddy and me. "I have as much right as anyone to be here."

Paddy flashed a smile at the guy. "Sorry, Greg. I'm the trustee for this land. It's posted. You're trespassing." Paddy nodded to Bartelle, who stepped toward the intruder.

"If this is your property, you should be on my side. There won't be anything left of this," he swept his arm to include the forest, "once the mining corporations get done with it. And there won't be any safe water for your daughter or your dog once they pollute the aquifers. Do you know—"

"Can it," Bartelle said. "This is your last warning. Turn your truck around and drive away or I'll arrest you for interfering in an active investigation."

Shuett opened his mouth, then thought better of it. Mumbling under his breath, he climbed into his truck and rolled down the window, pointing a finger at Paddy. "I remember who my friends are and who are the money-grubbing traitors." He reversed out the track.

Bartelle wrote in his pocket notebook. "I wonder how he knew Cabibi was here. Okay, Patrick, while you're waiting for the backups, would you mind blocking this road with your car? Appreciate it. We don't need any more tourists up here. Seamus, you willing to be deputized again? Good. Consider it done. That way there's no question concerning the chain of evidence and all that jazz. Go guard our skeleton. Find yourself a good spot and park your butt."

I lifted Megan up and gave her a hug, stooped with her in my arms and gave Atty a kiss on the snout and received a wet kiss in return. "You take care of my granddog, you hear, pumpkin?" To Paddy I added, "Have you remembered to let your lovely wife know you're delayed?"

"We have a regular text storm going. She says even with three hundred and fifty murders in Chicago so far this year, she's jealous of us. That's the investigative reporter talking!"

"You guys deserve each other," I said with a grin.

"You betcha. Atty, heel."

Paddy and Megan weren't even out of sight before an empty, hollow feeling overtook me. I retraced my steps to the derelict cabin with its skeleton. The deputies had used yellow tape to mark a path into the burial site and a perimeter around it. A stomach growl reminded me I was hungry, and Owen had my supplies. I wondered what Owen had found and worried how Elliot was faring. To do something while I waited, I began walking a circle twenty feet away from the perimeter.

I didn't have binocs to watch the birds. They'd grown quiet while many humans invaded their woods; now they'd become active again. Somewhere nearby was a family of yellow-bellied sapsuckers. The youngsters made a racket that, based on my many hours watching other nests, meant one of their parents was nearby and the kids thought they should be fed. They'd continue this behavior even after they were fledged, but these guys were probably still in the nest.

Watching them would be a pleasant way to spend the time until the next group of police arrived.

I worked my way clockwise around the marked area, checking the popple trees for the sapsucker nest. Halfway between the skeleton shack and the sentinel hemlock that dominated the forest, I crossed another logging trail, this one heading straight for the hemlock. The sapsuckers had grown silent at my approach, while the ravens regained their perches in the giant tree and croaked with conviction.

Oh, what the heck, I'd take a little detour and check the hemlock, half a soccer pitch away. Standing thirty or forty feet taller than anything else, it had obviously been a dominant tree for years, and I wondered what its circumference was at the base. I'd hear if anyone was approaching and could hustle back to make sure no one further molested the bone site.

Heavy equipment had worked this area while the ground was wet. Rocks jutted from the center of the two-track in which tires had compressed the earth eight inches lower on either side. Water had collected in the ruts and left them muddy in places. Foot-high balsam sprouted in the center, releasing the sweet smell of Christmas trees.

I moved quickly—the superego part of my brain telling me this was a bad idea—watching where I was walking so I didn't slip. Every dozen steps or so, I checked behind to make sure I could still see the building I was supposed to be protecting. I glanced at the path to gauge my next step and stopped my foot midair.

The mud contained a fresh skid mark eighteen inches long. One step beyond the skid was a series of perfect impressions of Elliot's Rockports heading toward the monster hemlock. The confirmation of his presence in the area caused me a spot of dizziness. I squatted to regain balance.

The ravens broke into a Greek chorus of commentary I could not understand. As they quieted, the indistinct sound of voices came to me from the direction of the hemlock.

TEN

BARTELLE WALKED A LINE PARALLEL to Engberg, keeping his mouth shut and his eyes peeled. Engberg, who was doing the actual tracking, moved deliberately, careful not to destroy anything that might later become evidence. He maintained a running commentary, marked by long silences when he had nothing to say.

"Besides the ATV going through here, we got some newer tracks. . . Smudges running on top of the ATV's marks. . . Stick a flag here, Tex. Looks like some dried blood. . . And see how this area's flattened? Looks like something lay here for a while. Body maybe, we got more blood. . . Lots of tracks. . . Couple clear ones. Stick a flag in. Someone's wearing a new pair of Rockports. I mean real new. . . Up this rise, the path curves right and it's graveled . . . All I can tell is an ATV's been through here."

Bartelle tried to construct a mental map of where they were relative to the skeleton. Curving in the general direction? At the top of a short rise, he realized this trail headed for the monster hemlock they'd spotted west of the burial site.

Engberg picked up his pace over ground too hard to show any footprints. With weeds and ferns on the side, even Bartelle wouldn't miss any sign of the ATV veering from the path. As the entourage worked closer to the hemlock, the ravens registered their agitation with frequent hops to new perches accompanied by loud vocalizations. Humans a hundred feet away was too much for the flock, which rose together, their raspy croaks filling the air.

Engberg pointed to an area near the base of the hemlock. "These grasses have been trampled, and they're a little singed. A hot ATV can do that. I think the ATV was parked here. You two stay here and let me widen out and see if I can spot any foot traffic."

Bartelle stepped under the shade of the tree. The drop in temperature made him realize the old heater—his father's way of referring to the sun— was starting to become downright uncomfortable. His tongue felt too big for his mouth, and sweat was dripping down his neck, soaking his shirt. He needed to get hydrated if he wanted to stay sharp.

"Sheriff," Engberg said from the other side of the hemlock, maybe fifty feet away. "I see a hand underneath a pile of brush."

Engberg marked his path with tape. He had already mucked up any evidence on that route and they needed to limit the contamination of the site. Once the precaution was complete, Bartelle and Tex followed Engberg behind the hemlock and confirmed his finding.

"We need to uncover enough to make sure it's attached," Bartelle said, "and the victim's not still alive. Not likely, but I'm not catching any hint of death. You?"

"The pile's got a lot of fresh broken balsam branches," Tex said. "Smells like Christmas."

"Ah crap, Tex," Engberg said, "I sure as shit hope you haven't spoiled Christmas with that image."

Cop humor to break the tension we're all feeling, Bartelle thought.

Tex's photography documented Bartelle and Engberg playing a game of pick-up sticks with real sticks. In less than two minutes they had access to the hand and forearm. Bartelle lay on the ground and wiggled himself to where he could feel the hand's temperature and check the wrist for a pulse. The hand was cool, much cooler than his own. The arm exhibited partial rigor mortis. Either death was within the last few hours or, given the summer heat, somewhere between a half day and one and a half days. With no smell and no carrion beetles, he'd bet on the more recent time.

Which meant the fucking killer could be out there watching them right now.

AFTER FINDING ELLIOT'S FOOTPRINTS AND hearing voices approaching the giant hemlock, I kept a low profile and retreated to where I was supposed to be. Many minutes later, Tex came and informed me they'd found a fresh victim. Bartelle wanted me to remain on ossuary guard duty while they dealt with the immediate crime. The state boys were close. Could he get me anything in the meantime?

Not trusting my voice, I gave a negative shake of my head. I slumped down, pressing my back hard into the rough bark of a sugar maple, hoping the pain could sharpen my thinking. How had this all gone so wrong? With the clearness of a vision, I pictured Elliot under that brush and my failure made me nauseated. Whoever had scared him into fleeing had caught and killed him.

"Hey, Tex," I yelled toward his back. "Do you know who it is?"

"We're waiting for the state boys," he yelled over his shoulder.

The nonanswer left me wondering whether they couldn't see Elliot's face and didn't want to further disturb the brush until the state troopers arrived, or they could see the face but couldn't identify Elliot because they had no clue who he was.

Whoa, Nellie. Slow down and evaluate the situation, Seamus. Stop jumping to conclusions. Put on your thinking cap.

Fact: Elliot had taken off after someone stopped by the house. Fact: Paddy and I had seen the mining guy Frank Joe Cabibi driving toward the area before the storm. Fact: Cabibi and his ATV were missing, and his truck had been parked for some time on Megan's property.

Question: Had Cabibi stopped at the house to let me know he was checking Megan's property for a test-bore location? Had he spotted Elliot and Elliot decided he needed to kill the guy?

No, that makes no sense.

Elliot hadn't followed whoever had been at my house; he went in the other direction. Maybe, if Cabibi had shown up at my house, he had left a note telling me where he'd be. Elliot used the plat maps to find another—

No, if Elliot were following directions, he would take Shank Lake Road to Lukes Road to the spot, not wander all over hell and gone in the woods. Elliot's route suggested he was actively avoiding being seen. Through inexperience, he stuck my ATV in a mud hole and had to walk out, and by luck he stumbled into Cabibi. And killed him? Why?

Because Cabibi saw Elliot and questioned what he was doing in the woods? Elliot panicked and clunked Cabibi on the head with a rock. Unfortunately, Cabibi died, so Elliot hid the body and took the ATV. Why not steal the truck? Because Cabibi was on his ATV when they stumbled on one another and Elliot didn't realize the truck was around. The scenario was scarily plausible and made a whole lot more sense than Cabibi killing Elliot. Except Elliot had fled, maybe because Cabibi had shown up at the house.

My head hurt trying to figure this out.

If Elliot was dead, I could tell Bartelle everything and let him investigate whatever made sense. But if Cabibi was under the brush—or anyone other than Elliot—I had a quandary to resolve. And I needed to do it before I made a statement. Lying to the cops—even if the lies were of omission—could have serious consequences. What would Abigail have me do?

I checked my cell phone again to see if magic had provided a signal. No such luck. In my last talk with Abigail, she had been adamant that I not inform the police about Elliot. I was to tell no one and must find him on my own. I'd promised her and had already shredded the promise by sending Owen to find him.

Did that make it more or less incumbent on me to withhold information from the police? And, again assuming someone other than Elliot was under the brush, what would Abigail now have me do? She was a stickler for following procedure. Her Secret Service agent background led her to trust police—generally—but she had forbidden me to contact them regarding Elliot's disappearance.

And if it was Elliot under the bush, would my not saying anything now make me the primary suspect? Twice before, I'd been falsely accused of murder. When that had happened, the police focused on proving their case, not finding the real culprit. Having Paddy and Megan for an alibi wouldn't impress the cops.

Where was Owen? Maybe if I knew what he had found, it would guide my decision.

BY THE TIME A FEMALE sheriff's deputy came to record my statement, my stomach pinched with hunger and I had a dehydration headache. She handed me a bottle of water and a couple of granola bars. "You've been out here a long time. Sheriff says you can leave once I have your statement."

"Have you identified the person under the brush?"

"Frank Cabibi. Current theory is someone bashed his head at the spot you found the blood-stained boulder. The bad guy carts him to the big hemlock. Covers him with leaves and branches to make it hard for scavengers to get at the body until he can return to dispose of it. We're hypothesizing an argument. Bad guy gets pissed and picks up a handy rock and cracks Cabibi's skull."

I answered her questions using a Joe Friday "just the facts" manner, telling her when I had arrived and what I had done. Ringing in my head were Abigail's words, "If one word got out about the location of our client, it could be his death sentence." The officer never asked why, just what, so I had not made any false statements and dodged a bullet.

The dodge was on a technicality and made me squeamish. Bartelle trusted me. He'd deputized me, and I was withholding evidence in a murder investigation. Even if Elliot wasn't the killer, he might have seen something.

Until I could talk with Abigail again, I couldn't risk discovering her statement was not hyperbole. She was guarding a crooked cop in a corruption investigation; maybe Elliot was part of the same thing. Maybe that's why his name couldn't appear in any police report because other cops could get access.

The deputy finished reading her notes and interrupted my thinking with one last question, "Anything else you can think of?"

I shook my head, not wanting to voice the lie of my headshake. I prided myself on my word being my bond, and twice today I had stomped all over my principles. Was I falling into the trap of end justifying means? Was I no better than the mining companies that I had accused of making empty promises? I was too tired, physically and mentally, to sort this out, but the sickening feeling overwhelming me made it clear I would ignore the issue at my peril.

"Do you know if my son is still around?"

"Sheriff sent him home to wait for one of us to take his statement. Was he leaving an ATV for you? If not, we can run you home."

I found my ATV on Lukes Road. Stuck in the ignition was its key, pinning a note from Paddy indicating that Owen needed to talk to me and would wait for me at the house. Not even an oblique reference to Elliot.

I drove to a rise above Shank Lake where I often obtained solid phone signals, connected with Abigail, and told her how I had spent my day, neglecting to mention I'd enlisted Owen Lyndstrom to help look for Elliot. She listened silently to my recitation. "Even if our man Elliot isn't mixed up in the murder," I concluded, "sooner or later the police will realize my story leaks like a sieve. If you expect me to have any chance of getting to him before the police, or someone else for that matter, I need to know everything you know."

"I am struck," she said, "by both your use of the phrase 'your man Elliot' and your tone of voice. It sounds like you're distancing yourself from this disaster rather than taking ownership. You own this problem, Seamus."

I considered for a moment arguing that I had said "*our* man Elliot," but Abigail was on a roll, and I wanted to make sure I didn't miss anything.

"I don't know much about Elliot," she continued. "His full name is Robert Elliot Savard. He's been a financial planner. Working with the public provided his front. His real job was laundering money. For whom I do not know. Nor do I know why he decided to testify against his illegal clients, but it is my understanding he has. He doesn't trust the US Marshals Service. I don't know why. He did provide a mechanism for me to verify his story. He's paying us to hide him until the trial starts, which I have recently learned from the Marshals Service will be the beginning of next month."

"Who's on trial?"

"A mid-level Chicago mobster, according to the news. Elliot doesn't have family. His wife and daughter were killed in a hit-and-run automobile accident more than a year ago. He's an only child. His parents are not in the country. He worried his former employers would try to use them as leverage, but believes they're safe abroad."

"Where's he live? Where did he go to school? Has he ever been in this part of the country? Who would he contact?"

"Kansas City born and bred. Look, Seamus, I know you can keep coming up with questions forever. It's your style, but I've already told you what I know. I trusted my source at the Marshals Service, and I trusted you to keep him hidden, which includes not letting people know about him unless we absolutely must. If evidence shows he was involved in Cabibi's death, then you should provide whatever support you can to the police. But if all he's done is borrow some of your stuff and Cabibi's ATV . . . then until we know what made him run, I think our job is to protect our client."

"You, Abigail Hancock of the don't-ever-interfere-with-a-police-investigation-because-that's-their-job-and-not-ours, you are now telling me that unless it's murder, Elliot skates?"

"You're twisting my words and wasting time."

I pulled the phone away from my ear and looked at it like it was crazy. Rock-solid Abigail, who invented rules just so she could obey them, was breaking them without hesitation. "You're right, I am wasting time. I'll call you if and when I know something."

ELEVEN

AT THE PURR OF HIS father's approaching ATV, Patrick turned up the flame under the lentil soup. The noise became a roar as the ATV flew down the driveway and into the garage. Standing at the mud room window, an open Killian Red in his hand, Patrick watched his father shuffle toward the house. It saddened Patrick to realize his father was losing a step. Despite keeping himself in great shape, his father dragged after a long day, right now looking like it was all he could do to put one foot in front of the other. Of course, at twenty-eight, Patrick could no longer pull the all-nighters he routinely had in college or in the first years as partner in LT2P, the cyber-security firm he had helped found.

A lot had changed, including having a daughter old enough to play cards with Owen while they waited for his dad's return. Footsteps on the back porch brought the dog woofing to the door. "Oh Atty, shush. It's only your grandfather." The dog required an offering of head scratches and kisses before allowing Patrick to hand his father the beer. "You look like you could use this. Owen's here to talk with you. I'll take Megan upstairs and get her ready for bed. She's exhausted."

Megan made it clear she was not moving until she finished her game with Owen. Patrick dished soup for his father who sat next to Megan and whispered advice on "Go Fish" strategy.

Owen proclaimed two against one wasn't fair. Patrick came up with the rejoinder, "Add their ages together, Owen, and they still don't have your experience."

Owen let Megan win, after which Megan led Atty upstairs. Patrick followed, tiptoeing to allow him to eavesdrop.

"For a while," Owen said, "I thought you and me guessed wrong about Elliot heading for Lukes Road. I didn't see no footprints comin outta the woods, and with the rain yesterday there was plenty of places I might coulda found tracks if he left 'em. Then I got ta recollectin other stuff I seen and returned and followed an ATV track that did come outta the woods before that beaver wash. You know the one?"

His father thought he did.

"I figured I'd follow me that ATV. It went to Pete Bjork's place. 'Ceptin

I know he's down ta Green Bay in the VA gettin his stomach looked at, so that don't make no sense. The gate's closed, but the chain holdin the lock was fresh cut."

Following a typical Owen verbal ramble, he summarized: "Everythin points to Elliot takin Frankie Joe's ATV and cuttin the chain to my friend's camp. He might still be hidin there. I figure he's armed and dangerous—especially if he had a hand in Cabibi's death. All this time waitin for you, I've been thinkin on it. I'm sorry, Seamus, but with that cut chain and all? I gotta tell my friend."

"Owen," his father's weary voice matched his looks. "Can you summarize what happened?"

"Well, Pete's got him a bunch of guns he keeps at camp. I warn't gonna go drivin up the road and get shot if that Elliot fella had found them guns. I sneaked myself around through the woods, see. Warn't no one around outside, but an ATV was parked by the cabin. Then I come back here to confabulate with you."

"Do you know Bjork's ATV?"

"Got him one of them side-by-side jobs now. Easier on him after he had to get a new hip some five, six winters ago. 'Sides, he always gets camo and this was blue. See, Seamus, I don't know if your Elliot done broke into Pete's place or not. I told your son that I feels like, for Pete's sake, I gotta tell the police about the cut chain, especially since they's already in the area. But I promised you I wouldn't say nothin about you guardin this Elliot. I wanted to find you and tell you, but your son was actin like Sheriff Bartelle's watchdog and wouldn't let me past."

"I was under strict orders," Patrick yelled down from upstairs.

"I know you was," Owen yelled back. "I was just tellin your pa—"

"I appreciate all you've done today, Owen," his father said, terminating what Patrick figured might have been a long soliloquy. "Especially waiting for hours to talk with me before talking to the police. Would it be too much to ask you to wait until tomorrow morning? It would give Elliot the night to return."

" 'Spect I can do that."

A throat clear from his father signaled a change in direction. Patrick held his breath to hear better. "Cabibi grew up in Amasa, right?"

"A coupla years older than my daughter. He was smart, captain of the football and basketball teams, and pretty much full of himself. Got him a scholarship to Tech, and after graduation never looked back on us hicks.

Then this spring he shows up acting like God's gift to Iron County with his big plans for opening a mine hereabouts."

"I met him at the meeting he ran down in Iron River. He spoke well."

"Silver-tongued even as a kid. Comin back, he wore his money loud. Rentin a million-dollar spread on Chicaugon Lake. Sportin an Amasa bumper sticker on his brandy-new Escalade SUV was kinda rubbin everyone's nose in it, wouldn't you say? I know he tried callin some of the folks he knew, and they wasn't much interested in seein him, 'cept a few of the guys who thought maybe they could hit him up for a job. My daughter, Jenny, and her husband turned down his offer to buy them dinner. You got me talkin, Seamus, and I don't remember what your question was. I didn't get my nap this afternoon, and I'm feelin beat."

"I'm not even sure I had one, and I don't have the excuse of having a piano key for every birthday either. You want to stay here tonight rather than drive to town?"

"Oh, hell no. I woulda kept drinkin if I was gonna do that. I'm off. You give me a call first thing if Elliot shows. Otherwise, I'll give Pete Bjork a holler, let him decide whether to call the sheriff."

"Can I ask one more favor? Can you drop me near where I left my other ATV? I'll walk in the rest of the way and bring it home."

Owen produced a large yawn. "Roger Wilco that."

What, Patrick wondered, did Owen mean using the name of the main character of the Space Quest science-fiction computer games he had discovered twenty years ago at a church rummage sale? A janitor with a quest for "truth, justice and really clean floors" didn't seem to fit at all.

"Thanks, Owen," his father said, "for everything. Let me tell Paddy what I'm doing."

Patrick heard Owen leave, left Megan and Atty sleeping together on the floor, and joined his father downstairs. "Dad, wait until tomorrow. I'll drop you before we leave. You do realize we're staying the night?"

"I'd rather get it done now, Paddy. Soon, someone from the police will follow all the various ATV tracks, and I don't want them stumbling over my Honda."

"At least take my headlamp and a come-along, Dad."

"Headlamp yes. Come-along, no. I'll follow the same route I took this morning. I didn't have any real problems from there on."

From outside came the rumble of Owen's truck starting.

"Dad, what did Owen mean with his crack about Roger Wilco? I remember those Space Quest games."

"Huh?" Then his father bent over laughing and slapped both knees. "Before your Space Quest Roger Wilco was Owen's Roger Wilco—from radio communications. Roger means received and Wilco means will comply. Owen was just saying he understood." Putting his arm around Patrick's shoulders he continued. "I need you to do some research while I'm gone. Elliot's real name is Robert Elliot Savard. Please find out what you can."

"Roger Wilco," Patrick said. "Get home safe."

WHAT I HADN'T TOLD PADDY, because he would object, was that after retrieving my Honda ATV from where I had stashed it in the woods, I planned to check Pete Bjork's camp and determine if Elliot was there. Dusk was pushing hard into night by the time I reached my ATV. My original plan was to take the fastest way to Bjork's camp, which followed the path I'd taken earlier to the murder site, and continuing to Lukes Road. Problem was, the sky in that direction was lighter than it should be. The state crime-scene guys must be working under lights, and I didn't want to try to explain myself if I ran into them.

Even with my GPS maps showing the logging roads and skidder trails, it was damn near to midnight by the time I weaved through the blowdowns and regained Lukes Road. I was already much later than Paddy expected, so whatever panic he was in wouldn't get any worse by me being gone another hour. With luck, he might be fast asleep and not know how late I was.

Now I faced the next hurdle: would the police have someone stationed on Lukes Road? What excuse could I use for being out this late at night riding an ATV—without a helmet, no less? My tired brain couldn't come up with anything more inventive than a case of insomnia and deciding to be a good neighbor to find out if they needed water or anything. Lame.

Heart in mouth, I putt-putted up Lukes toward the area of bright lights, going slowly to keep my ATV's noise softer than their portable generator running the lights. I cruised without challenge past the trail leading to the murder site. Could I now find Bjork's camp road based on Owen's description? I sped up until I came to the beaver washout. Owen had recently gone through here twice on my Polaris, so it should be safe. I still offered a silent prayer to make sure I kept on the sunken road and didn't wander into deep water and stall the engine. Keeping the ATV at walking speed, I cut around the boulders closing the road to cars and trucks and entered the water.

Something splashed from the far end. I didn't want to risk losing traction by stopping and figured whatever animal I had scared would hightail it before I got there. With headlights on bright, I maintained a steady speed and nervously watched the water rise to my running boards.

The right front tire lurched into a hole, halting my progress. I goosed the throttle and jerked out of the obstruction, the sudden acceleration nearly pitching me over the back. Focusing my attention forward, I spotted a moose. His antlers wide as the road. Ears perked up. Eyes looking straight at me.

I killed the engine, flicked off the headlights, and coasted to a halt—the very thing I had not wanted to do. While I had been wandering through the woods, a front had passed through, sweeping away the heavy clouds and leaving behind a translucent shroud. With my headlights off, the sky was awash with the elfin glow of muted starlight. The velvet of the moose's antlers throbbed with energy. His myopic eyes seemed to search for mine. I held my breath. I had nowhere to go if the moose charged.

He lowered his rack—should I dive left or right if it came at me?—and ducked his head into the water, surfacing with a mouthful of vegetation. Drops from its swaying bell pattered on the still water. I wondered why the flap of skin hanging from his throat is called a bell. He audibly ground the plants with his twenty-four massive molars.

I had never experienced such a close look at this enormous woodland creature. I wished I could share it with Paddy and Megan. What a great story I could tell—if the moose walked away—and if I lived through my exploration of Pete Bjork's camp. *Too many ifs.*

The moose eventually moseyed from the water and lumbered up the road. I waited until he was well up the rise from the beaver wash before I keyed on the vehicle and engaged the throttle. The ATV pulled forward without complaint. The moose stopped and looked at the noise. I crept forward until I escaped the water. The moose had stepped off the road. I couldn't hear him over the engine noise, so I flicked the lights onto low beam and slowly climbed the hill and passed where he must have entered the woods. Driving a few yards further with no sign of him, I flicked on the high beams and opened the throttle.

A gate on the south side of the road was slightly ajar. The ATV's headlights showed the chain was still padlocked to the six-by-six post; on the other side, two ends dangled from the gate. A decent chain costs more than a good lock; a more thoughtful person would snap the lock instead of the chain—but Elliot would not have known that. Recent ATV tracks cut through the mustard garlic on both sides of the gate.

Confirming whether Frankie Joe Cabibi's missing ATV was still around and whether the camp had been broken into required sneaking up to the compound. My engine roar would announce my presence to whoever was there, so I parked the ATV in a bed of common tansy at the side of the road just past the gate. I fastened on Paddy's Petzl headlamp. Although I didn't need it in the open under the sky now brilliant with stars, I would under the forest canopy.

Maintaining quiet, I clambered past the boulders guarding the sides of the gate rather than risk a squeak to announce my presence—and thought how ridiculous the precaution was. If someone were awake, they'd heard the ATV shut off. Stupid thinking showed I was as mentally drained as I was physically exhausted. I walked up the center of the two-track driveway, using the crown in the middle to guide my feet and keep me centered. My toe hit a protruding rock, nearly tripping me. I needed to click on the headlamp to see where I was going—the same headlight that would paint a target on my forehead. I could still bail.

The wind was dead calm. I closed my eyes and sniffed for a hint of human and got only the smell of fecund forest after a rain. The forest animals held their collective silence and waited for my decision.

TWELVE

PATRICK CHOSE TO STAY ON the screened porch on what had become a lovely night. While Megan slept quietly, Atty rested her head on Megan's sleeping bag and sawed wood like a drunken lumberjack.

Patrick's first online search attempt provided zero hits using the string "Robert Elliot Savard," including the quotes. He tried adding an extra 't' to Elliot. Still nothing. He removed both the extra 't' and the quotes and clicked through the suggested links; none had anything to do with Elliot. He eliminated the Elliot and tried Robert Savard in quotes. Plenty of hits, but none of the Facebook profiles or image files were the missing guy.

Elliot was not Robert Elliot Savard or Elliot Savard or Robert Savard. Either Abigail had lied to his father, or someone had lied to her. Lies are supposedly easier to remember the closer they are to the truth.

Patrick considered what else he supposedly knew. The guy was from Kansas City and a financial planner. He checked the Financial Planning Association of Greater Kansas City, clicking through the pictures of their various events looking for one with Elliot. He tried various combinations of Robert, Elliot, Savard, Kansas City, Financial Planner. Nothing.

He grew increasingly frustrated as minutes became an hour and still nothing. The search string "missing financial planner" did the trick. The first result was www.HaveYouSeenJasonGraham.com on which Elliot's picture occupied half a simple website page. Jason Graham's parents, Andrea and Arthur, offered a $25,000 reward payable by PayPal or bitcoin for information leading to finding their son, last seen in Des Moines, Iowa at the end of June. He had been depressed about the deaths of his wife and daughter the previous year, they said. At least part of Abigail's story had been true.

Patrick clicked on a tab labeled Contact Us, hoping to find a phone number or address, and was disappointed to discover a fill-in form to provide lead information. Patrick checked the HTML coding for the form and discovered an email address that wasn't particularly useful: info@HaveYouSeenJasonGraham.com. The website was first registered a few weeks ago, but the owner's personal information was blocked.

With Jason's real name known, additional searches soon revealed his basic life story. He had grown up in St. Louis, gone to the University of Chicago, worked as a commodity pit trader. He and three others formed a white-shoe financial-planning business. Six months after the hit-and-run that killed his wife and eight-year-old daughter, he sold his share to his partners and returned to St. Louis. There he bought an insurance agency.

If the money-laundering story was true, had it happened while he was in Chicago, or had he discovered the agency he bought was involved with fabricating claims? Was he a black hat or white hat, and did it matter?

Patrick decided to leave the financial-crimes aspects to his father. He turned his attention to Frank Cabibi, Amasa boy returned for good.

Cabibi's plans to develop mines in the U.P. had made plenty of news, including the community meeting his father had attended in Iron River.

In one lengthy article, the name Seamus McCree popped from the page. According to the article, environmental activist Greg Shuett had been removed from the room for his disruptive behavior, to applause from both sides. His father had become increasingly agitated when Cabibi refused to provide any details on project financing, his company's historical safety record, and what bonding they would purchase to mitigate the costs of any environmental damage. It sounded just like his father to want to understand the financial underpinnings.

If Shuett didn't grow up in the area, what had brought him here? He represented something called the Environmental Protection Authority, a nonprofit whose name was so close to the government's Environmental Protection Agency to make Patrick wonder why. Did working for the "EPA" provide Shuett more access? Based on the behavior reported in the paper, it wasn't providing credence. Did the organization's name help funding? Couldn't tell. Shuett had moved up to the U.P. from northern Wisconsin, where he'd been active the previous two years. Patrick had never heard of the college in Oregon where Shuett's online profiles indicated he'd earned a B.S. in environmental sciences.

Having enough of that rabbit hole, he returned to researching Cabibi. A three-year letterman at Forest Park High School in both football and basketball, Cabibi had been named one of the top ten U.P. athletes of the year in his senior year. He got in a bit of hot water when he and two close buddies, Christopher Saari and Timothy Javoroski, were caught drinking at a summer party before their junior year. They were suspended for two games. The team made it to the state finals, but their suspension had cost the team an undefeated regular season.

Patrick checked the clock again—tomorrow already. Where the hell was his father? Worrying about something outside your ability to change is wasted effort, he reminded himself, although he'd be a lot happier if his old man would show up. Soon.

He found lots of articles detailing Cabibi's business career—all promotional fluff pieces with no hint of trouble. Since he had time, he searched Christopher Saari's name and discovered not much more other than he had married a local girl and still lived in the area.

Switching to Timothy Javoroski provided a huge surprise. The kid had disappeared thirty years ago at the end of his senior year. His father reported that he and Tim had watched a cop show on TV and gone to bed. The father woke the next morning and his son was gone. The kid's car was still parked in the yard. The only things missing from the house were Tim's wallet and the clothes he was wearing: jeans, T-shirt, Forest Park jacket, sneakers. Friends reported Tim had recently been depressed. Volunteers searched the woods and fields surrounding Amasa, but found no trace of him.

Had Atty uncovered the answer to Timothy Javoroski's disappearance? If so, and Tim had been shot in the head and buried in the woods miles north of Amasa, someone must have picked him up and taken him there— or at least taken his body there.

Again, assuming the skeleton was Tim, and with a bajillion acres of woods around Amasa, it was one hell of a coincidence for his teammate and drinking buddy Frank Cabibi to be killed a couple hundred yards away.

From across the lake a coyote barked, and soon it sounded like a pack of twenty or thirty of them were howling. The pack probably contained fewer than ten individuals, but they sure could make a racket. Atty heard them too and rose to bat Patrick's hand with her snout.

"You need to go out?"

The dog trotted to the door.

"Give me a woof when you're ready to come in."

The dog raced up the driveway, barking her fool head off. Patrick stepped outside to try to hush her and realized how spectacular the night sky had become. The Milky Way arched overhead, filling the sky with twinkling stars. Even on the clearest night in Chicago, the light pollution eliminated any possibility of spectacular night skies.

He should catch some shuteye, but this was too special not to share with his daughter. Twenty some odd years ago his father had showed him these same skies. He had repeated the story so many times that he no longer knew if he remembered the actual event or remembered his own telling of the story. No matter, thinking of it always brought him the warm, fuzzy feeling he was experiencing right now. He owed Megan the same experience, even if it meant his going short on sleep.

Atty returned with a wagging tail, a satisfied grin, and one parting woof to all the wild things. Patrick woke Megan sufficiently to put on her socks and shoes and get her to use the bathroom. He layered a warm jacket over her pj's and cinched on her life preserver. The dog lifted a head at the disturbance, gave a long yawn, and went back to sleep.

Megan held the flashlight while Patrick carried her down the path past the cabin to the dock. He hauled a kayak and paddle down to the water. Megan was fully awake and chattering away, talking her way toward understanding what was happening.

"Just wait. I think you'll remember this your whole life."

Patrick maneuvered the kayak partially into the water, leaving enough of it on land to be anchored. He settled in and had Megan climb onto the seat between his legs. Rocking his weight back and forth and using the paddle as a lever, he launched the kayak onto the smooth surface and guided it to the middle of the lake.He did not want to disturb the quiet and paid careful attention to not whack the kayak with the paddle. Once they stopped moving, he released the tension on the seat, allowing them to lean back and soak in the beauty.

"Papa?" Megan whispered.

Patrick whispered back, "Yes, sweetheart?"

"I don't know which star to choose."

One of the wonderful things Patrick had discovered with three-year-olds was you never knew where a conversation would lead. That she chose to whisper gave him reason to believe she, too, experienced the magic of this magnificent sky. "Why do you need to choose a star?"

"To make a wish. You know." In a high register, she sang in perfect pitch. "Star light. Star bright. First star I see tonight. I wish I may. I wish I might. Have the wish I wish, tonight." She twisted in her seat, scanning the sky, rocking the kayak in the dead calm water.

Across the lake a merganser softly quacked at the disturbance.

"I can see your problem," Patrick used a soft, contemplative voice. "The song mentions star bright, maybe you can choose the brightest star? There's one."

He pointed to a star and wished he knew its name. "Or maybe you can choose the North Star. It's part of the Big Dipper." He stopped himself from providing too much information. He didn't want to spoil the moment with a big astronomy lesson.

Megan shook her head. "No Papa, that's cheating." She no longer whispered, using instead a serious tone. She clenched her fists in her lap.

"How about this," Patrick said. "Close your eyes. I'll spin the kayak around. When you're ready, open your eyes and make a wish on the first star you see."

"Okay." She covered her eyes with both hands and tilted her head back into his lap.

Getting the kayak spinning while reclining with Megan on top of him wasn't the easiest thing to do. "Not yet, sweetheart." Holding the paddle above Megan, he used short sweeping strokes on one side and propelled the kayak into a spin. "Now!" he whispered.

She flung her arms upward and pointed with a finger from each hand. "The orange one."

Patrick followed her pointing fingers and spotted a small star—or a distant one, he reminded himself—with a distinctly orange cast. "Good choice. What's your wish?"

"I wish Atty could see all these stars. Do doggies like looking at stars?"

"Good question. I know some dogs howl at a bright moon."

"Why?"

"I don't know."

"Atty doesn't howl at the moon."

"No, she doesn't." Remembering how a couple of nights ago the dog had awoken to a coyote pack calling and tried howling back, he smiled. It had been pathetic. "Ready for more sleep?"

"See the moving star?" Megan pointed toward the southern sky.

It took Patrick a few seconds to find a slowly moving white light. "That's a satellite traveling high above the earth."

"Why?"

"I don't know, I can't read its label from here."

"Why?"

So much for my joke.

Megan's face turned serious. "I think Atty is worried 'cause we left her."

"Maybe we should go back and the two of you can snuggle in bed?"

"Do stars go to bed in the morning?"

"No, sweetheart, they're always there. Our sun is so bright during the day it doesn't let us see the rest of the stars. Sit up, honey, so I can paddle."

Megan rippled the water with her fingers. "Papa, where is Grampa Seamus?"

"Looking for Mr. Elliot."

"Why can't we stay with Grampa Seamus?"

Patrick was a bit surprised she hadn't asked earlier, which didn't mean he was prepared with an answer. He didn't want to leave his father alone, but he had to put being a parent and Megan's safety ahead of being a son. He could blame it on Cindy, but that wouldn't be fair. "Because we can't."

"Why?"

Thirteen

The Happy Reaper awoke to another gray Scottish day. He should have paid more attention to northwest Scotland's average 118 inches of rain each year. However, booking the entire estate for himself meant he could roam wherever he pleased and practice his long-distance sniper skills without interference. His hosts shook their heads in dismay each day he didn't return with a coveted red stag. He wondered what they would think when later in the year hunters returned with red stag racks, each with a single point on the left antler shot off.

He saw no reason to kill these magnificent beasts since all he wanted was to hone his tracking and shooting skills. He'd spent one whole day tracking the estate's wildlife manager without being seen. Rewarding, that.

He planned the whole day in the field after he partook of the full Scottish breakfast. An alert on his computer changed those plans.

Someone had accessed the honey-trap Have You Seen Jason Graham website. He scrolled through the captured information, recording the IP address, which he hoped would tell him where the computer had been when it accessed the website.

His heart beats quickened. Even better, the person had clicked on the contact page and begun to type an email address, pmccree@.

McCree was not exactly a common name. He had not thought of Seamus McCree or his son Patrick in years. Could it be someone other than Patrick?

The IP address belonged to a satellite internet provider. Access was purported from the northern part of Michigan, but location was unreliable for satellite internet. Seamus McCree owned property in the U.P. How many McCrees were there in northern Michigan? Not bloody many. He smiled at his English phrasing.

It had been, what, nearly nine years? His entanglement with McCree had cost him a fortune. McCree had been a financial crimes investigator at the time. His son was a computer geek in college. Kid had to be twenty-eight, twenty-nine by now.

Wafting up the stairs came the hint of bangers frying. He was sorry this was his last breakfast here; he'd taken a liking to the blood pudding. He rescheduled his flight to the States to leave late that afternoon. He'd make his regrets to his hosts at breakfast. They would add it to their accumulating evidence of their American guest's strange behavior. Since he'd paid in full for the fortnight, they'd have no complaints. Before he departed, he'd learn what he could about McCrees and Michigan.

A bell tinkled above his door, summoning him to the repast. He left his room feeling excited to have a hint of a lead on Graham and—what else?—a twinge of regret that he might have to deal with the McCrees? Seamus McCree had earned his respect, but if they met again, at least Seamus had had nine years. And the boy was now a man.

THE DRIVEWAY OPENED INTO A clearing with a one-story cabin, a squat building that I took to be a generator shed, a sauna, and a pole-barn building twice the size of the cabin. Standing between the generator shed and the sauna was a ten-foot-high crossbar for hanging deer. A small fishing boat sat on a trailer on the near side of the outbuilding. Other than the grass needing a good mowing, the yard was tidy, with a cutesy Dutch windmill covering the wellhead. The ATV was not where Owen had described it. There were plenty of places to hide it. I remained in the starlit shadows at the edge of the driveway and watched and listened for movement.

I startled to attention at a shadow speeding across the yard and caught the last of the silent flight of a short-eared owl as it banked and landed in a white pine. I laughed silently at my nervous reaction and took several deep breaths to regain control.

No way I could sneak up to the cabin in this bright starlight. Someone looking out the window would spot me. And shoot the intruder? I had less chance of that if I boldly walked up to the front door. Nothing was to be gained from rushing.

Fifteen minutes of waiting brought no new activity or knowledge. Even the owl stayed hidden. I psyched myself with a long, released breath and moved into the center of the driveway, walking from the shadows like I owned the place.

At the front steps, I stomped my way up to a front door constructed with a solid bottom and three-by-three windowpanes above. Someone had knocked out the pane nearest the doorknob and cleared the rectangle of jagged glass, leaving a safe space to reach in and unlock the door.

I kept my gloves on to prevent leaving fingerprints and tried the handle. Unlocked.

With this new information, I debated whether my wisest move was to continue my bold approach and loudly knock on the door or to change tactics and sneak in. Owen said the owner was in Green Bay. If Elliot was sleeping here and I knocked, he might escape out the back. If someone else was here and I entered quietly, they might shoot first and ask questions later. Maybe I should try goading anyone inside to come out by throwing a rock through a window.

Somewhat belatedly I realized I should check the other side of the house for an exit. And I should check the outbuildings before making my assault on the cabin. Keeping close to the house and ducking under windows, I circumnavigated the building. No sounds. No lights. No parked ATV. The only thing attached to the cabin was a hose, neatly wound onto a reel and connected to an outside spigot.

I covered the ground between the cabin and the sauna at a trot, footsteps crunching on the gravel. That door was locked. As was the one to the generator shed. The pole barn was unlocked. Without hesitation, I opened the door and slipped into the dark. I flicked my headlamp onto low beam and spotted a Kubota tractor in front of me and, behind it, storage shelving and a Snap-On tool chest along the rear wall. Unlike my garage, here everything was neatly stored.

Parked in front of the tractor was an old jeep, probably their woods car. Closer to me was a mud-spattered ATV pulled in at an angle. Its key glinted in the ignition, in sharp contrast to the vehicle's dark blue coloring. Next to a current ORV sticker on the rear panel was a logo of a miner carrying a pickax above the letters EFE: Environmentally Friendly Extraction, the company Cabibi worked for. No doubt I'd found his ATV stolen from the woods. I checked it for warmth. If anything, it felt cooler than the night air. I knew I could still feel my ATVs' heat several hours after use; so, some hours ago, Elliot—or someone—had moved the ATV under cover.

This garage spoke of neatness and an order to everything, yet something bothered me. Tools were all present, filling their pegboard outlines. The jeep and the tractor had been backed in parallel to the walls and left without keys in the ignition, in stark contrast to the hastily stored ATV. Proof, which I didn't need, that someone other than the owner had parked it. It dawned on me: the side-by-side ATV Owen said this guy owned was not in the garage. Yes, he might have taken it to town for repairs or an oil change. My bet was Elliot had swapped Cabibi's ATV for the side-by-side. I could think of two reasons why someone would trade the more versatile ATV for a wider one. Either they needed comfortable room for two passengers or they were afraid someone was looking for the ATV. Either way, Elliot was gone.

Feeling like a spent balloon, I left the garage, climbed the cabin steps, and pounded on the door. "Police. Open up." If questioned, I was still deputized. Maybe.

Hearing nothing, I opened the door and entered a combination kitchen/family room. Dishes were stacked in the drying rack. A few drops of water remained in the sink, more evidence someone had recently been here. Attached to the kitchen cabinet nearest the door was a series of hooks, each labeled with a piece of masking tape and black ink: Sauna, Gen, Gar, UTV, Jeep, Kub. Only the UTV hook was empty—more support for my assumption once I figured out UTV stood for Utility Task Vehicle.

The kitchen shelves gave no evidence of anything Elliot might have taken, so I moved to the bedrooms. One was a bunk room whose closet was filled with fishing gear. The other, a master bedroom, contained a large gun safe—locked. *Thank goodness.* At least Elliot hadn't armed himself at this camp.

The master bedroom closet contained several empty hangers. Had Elliot stolen more clothes? I made a second circuit of the cabin interior to see if anything else caught my attention. I opened cupboards and drawers. I caught myself going through the motions with no purpose in mind. I was tired. I was dejected. I was not making any progress.

Doing my good neighbor thing, I covered the broken window with a piece of cardboard and locked the place up. It would at least keep the wildlife out.

I'd bet a lot of money Elliot had been here. Even if I knew for sure he had, I wasn't any closer to finding him, and time was running out.

Fourteen

BARTELLE'S ALARM WOKE HIM UP a half hour before sunrise. It might be a day of rest for the Lord, but not for anyone in the Iron County Sheriff's Department. He arrived at the office to find Sergeant Engberg and Tex looking at a display of photos on a computer. Bartelle shucked his jacket and poured a cup of coffee that smelled and looked like motor oil gone bad. "Something interesting?"

Engberg hooked a chair for Bartelle, dragging it next to him. "A few things don't add up." He opened the county plat map to the pages displaying the area around where they had found the bodies. He tapped at the crime scene. "You mentioned feeling something was off with Seamus McCree? Got me thinking." He pointed to McCree's camp on Shank Lake. "McCree says he was checking the nearby camps to make sure they were okay. That's reasonable, but then he says he came to check on Owen and his son. Right?"

Bartelle agreed that was what McCree had said. He choked down a swill of coffee. "Are you guys drinking this battery acid or is this an assassination attempt?"

"You're still talking," Tex clapped Engberg on the shoulder. "I told you we needed three doses of arsenic to kill an Eye-tal-yon."

Engberg shrugged off Tex's hand. "You don't like it, don't drink it. More for me. Why wouldn't McCree follow the road from the last camp he visited on the west side of Shank Lake to Lukes and come in that way?" He traced a line from Shank Lake through the woods to the murder site. "Good solid roads. Already cleared of obstructions from the storm. Instead, he ATVs through woods chock full of downed trees from the wind damage."

"Now here's the other thing we were looking at." Tex moused through thumbnails of pictures taken the day before and enlarged a closeup of a shoe print. "A fresh print of a Rockport shoe so new you can read the name on the sole. Obviously not from us and none of the Staties."

Engberg continued the narrative. "Not our murder victim, who was wearing a pair of custom-made boots. We saw four adult civilians at the scene. Owen Lyndstrom's boots were antiques and had worn heels. We got pictures of the younger McCree wearing New Balance. This picture catches one of Seamus McCree's feet, and he's wearing boots. We're guessing Danners, but in any case, not Rockports. The one person no one remembers for sure is that asshole, Greg Shuett, although Tex thinks he was wearing sneakers."

Engberg was a great officer and tracker, and he liked his details. Bartelle cut to the chase. "You're telling me some unknown was there wearing Rockports."

"Correct. Whoever wore the Rockports headed directly toward where Cabibi was hidden in the brush pile. So did these prints." He snapped his finger and Tex pulled up a triptych of shoe prints. "Which fit our recollection of what the senior McCree was wearing. We need to confirm it, but assume I'm correct here. Why were McCree's footprints there? He was supposed to be watching the shack and the bones?"

"Curiosity?" Bartelle muttered. "We weren't exactly quiet after you found Cabibi. What are you suggesting?"

"Nosy, sure—I woulda probably wandered around myself—but why didn't he mention the prints to us?"

Bartelle counted alternatives on his fingers. "One, he's hiding something. Or two, he didn't notice. He's a city dude and doesn't exactly have your woods skills. Or three, he noticed, but didn't think to mention it. We deputized him, but that doesn't exactly make him a cop."

Engberg ducked his brow, conceding the point. "Fair enough. Still, we have a possible witness or bad guy wearing brand-new Rockports, and McCree was at least in the same area as the prints. You don't remember what Shuett wore, do you?"

"I was looking at his eyes," Bartelle said. "Good work. Whoever interviews Shuett needs to check whether he has a pair of Rockports. I'll request anyone who spent time in that area over the last two days to contact us. We'll see if anyone comes in with Rockports. If we mention the shoes, they're likely to end up in a burn barrel somewhere. Before you coordinate with the State team, why don't you interview Seamus McCree? I'll let you guys decide who does it, or maybe you tag-team him. Shake his story hard and see what falls out. Maybe even take a trip around the lake and check if he visited his neighbors like he said. Something doesn't ring true there, and I want to know what it is."

I AWOKE TO MEGAN, IN her sleeping bag, singing to herself. In the predawn, the hummingbirds were already arguing over who owned the sugar-water feeder. The sky lightened behind the hill in the east. Sunrise was in another ten minutes, although because of the hill, light wouldn't strike the house for another half hour. Blinking away my cobwebs, I realized Paddy was in the shower. They'd depart once they got some breakfast down Megan.

"Good morning, Megan." I yawned. Three hours sleep was hardly enough for me. "How long have you been awake?" I slipped on socks and pants.

"Grampa Seamus! Papa says there are more stars than we can count. I tried counting but I lost my place. Do you want to hear me sing my ABCs?" Without any prompting on my part, she sang the entire song, on pitch and even enunciated the L, M, N, O, P section that I had thought for a long time was a single letter.

"Let's surprise your father. The two of us will make breakfast."

"Goodeeeee," she squealed and scrambled from her sleeping bag. "Cheerios."

I followed her into the kitchen. She struggled open the drawer in the Indiana cupboard and set the table with three mats, putting the correct napkin rings at each person's place. She extracted the plastic container with the Cheerios from the corner cabinet. I had to unscrew the top, and I held my breath while she poured them into her bowl. Earlier in the week, she had lost her grip and half the container ended up on the floor. Atty had scarped up much of the spillage before I could corral her.

Where is the dog? I hadn't seen or heard her this morning.

Megan overfilled her bowl, but didn't spill. We negotiated how much to return to the container. I poured milk from a half-gallon jug into the ceramic bear Megan had found at a sidewalk sale in town. The bear's paws covered its stomach in a way I thought looked as if he was feeling ill. Megan loved it anyway. Because she had found it and was the only one to use it, it had become one of her favorite things at Grampa Seamus's camp.

"Two hands now."

I wished I had my camera to capture her face: tip of tongue sneaking past the wall of baby teeth, pale-blue eyes squinted in concentration.

"Perfect job," I said. "Not a drop spilled. What kind of juice do you want?"

"Orange. Me pour."

I drew the line there, but allowed her to tell me when to stop.

Paddy arrived, showered and shaved. "I heard you come in last night, but I didn't open my eyes to check the time." He lit the burner under the kettle.

"Two maybe? Or three. Thanks for setting up my bed on the porch. I was asleep before my head hit the pillow. I see a nap in my future. I assume you're heading home?"

"Yes, but we need to talk." While Megan chased Cheerios around her bowl with a spoon, Paddy showed me a website with Elliot's picture and a message from his parents. I wondered if Abigail knew the truth and was keeping it from me, or whether Elliot had hidden the truth from her, and why. Maybe the Marshal's Service had set up his assumed name? Paddy was still talking, but with anger bubbling up, I had stopped paying attention.

I apologized for not listening and blamed it on surprise and lack of sleep. Working my jaw to relieve the tension, I concentrated on understanding the information he had printed before going to bed. While he was here, I needed to ask questions to avoid searching the same websites and duplicating his work after he was gone.

The kettle's whistle diverted Paddy's attention. He made his single serving of French-press coffee using equipment he had brought from home, poured in a few drops of cream, and stirred.

"No breakfast?" I asked.

"We'll stop in Green Bay to give Megan a break. I'll get something then. Go brush your teeth, sweetheart, and get changed. I laid your clothes on your sleeping bag."

Megan skipped off, something I had first seen her doing on this visit. Watching her go, I realized how proud I was of my son to make such different choices than I had at his age. He was the stay-at-home parent and had more patience with Megan than I had ever had with him. Fact was, I had worked through Paddy's early childhood, rarely getting home before he went to bed. I really became involved in his life only after he came to live with me following the divorce.

"What did you find last night?" Paddy's question broke through my reverie.

I provided chapter and verse. "I'll call Abigail. Maybe knowing Elliot's real name, she can suggest a way to track him down. I am totally over my head here."

"Which is not a feeling the father I know and love is comfortable with. Don't you need to call Owen?"

I had forgotten. "I think I need a brain transplant. I guess I was repressing that because then Owen calls his friend, who calls the police. If I'm lucky, they won't have time to check because they're busy on the murder. More likely, they'll wonder if there is a link and hop right on it since they're already in the area. Then the shit hits the fan and it's fess up time for me."

"Will you contact Jason's parents?"

I pursed my lips and rubbed my face, rough with whiskers. "I'm sure they're worried sick. If you were the one missing, I'd sure want to know. But what could I tell them that wouldn't endanger him or them? Too many questions and not enough answers."

"Papa? Where's Atty?" Megan was dressed, carrying Raff by his long giraffe neck.

"Outside," Paddy said. "I didn't hear you brush your teeth. I'll call the dog while you do that. We'll put your bed away and be ready to go. Okay?"

Megan held the giraffe out in front of her with both hands. "You need to brush your teeth, Raff. Up and down. Up and down." She skipped to the bathroom. I smiled at the scrape of a stool across the floor and the splash of running water, wondering if Raff would return with a wet mouth.

Paddy called the dog from the back door. "At-teeee. Break-fast." Then "Atalanta McCree, where are you?"

I helped Megan click her toothbrush into its holder and stick it and her pj's into her suitcase. "Do we need to check the house to make sure you haven't left anything?"

We held hands and toured the house, looking behind and under chairs and couches. We discovered one sock—who knew whether its mate was also loose in the wild or safely in the suitcase—and prevented a real crisis when we discovered Megan's blanket on a chair pushed in at the table on the porch.

From outside I heard Paddy cry, "Atalanta! What have you done?"

Megan squeezed my hand. "Oh-oh. Atty's going to have a timeout."

Still hand and hand, me toting her blankie and Megan carrying Raff, we walked down the ramp from the porch to the driveway where Paddy was holding the dog by the collar. The problem assaulted my nose: the dog had rolled in a dead fish. I suppose covering your scent with stink works well for wild dogs, but I couldn't imagine being trapped in a car for six hours with that smell.

"Stinky pooh." Megan pinched her nose.

"While you finish packing," I said, "I can take her down to the lake and clean her up."

"I have a better idea. I don't want to stick around and discover what else delays us getting Megan home. Cindy will kill me if we're late. Can we leave the dog with you? Gives Megan and me an excuse to come back up. Even if we do clean her up, she'll smell like wet dog. Plus, there's no way we can get her dry. She'll soak her bed, and—"

"I'm happy to have her. Megan, give your Grampa Seamus a big hug. I had such a great time with you here. I'm going to miss you more than the whole world." Megan jumped, all of four inches off the ground, and I swept her into a big hug and blew a wet raspberry on her neck, which got her giggling. "Give your mom a kiss from me."

Atty whined as her family drove away. Both of us were happy for the diversion of a bath in the lake. Atty loved anything happening in the lake, and it allowed me to be active rather than wallow in the emptiness that always attacked me whenever Paddy and Megan left. The dog would be good therapy. Plus, I looked forward to seeing my granddaughter again soon. Oh, and Paddy, too.

But what would happen to the dog if they threw me in jail? I should have thought of that earlier.

Fifteen

Patrick pulled his car to the edge of the Grade to allow the oncoming Sheriff's vehicles to pass. The lead one stopped and Bartelle got out. He waved the second vehicle on and walked over. Patrick lowered the window. "Back at it I see, Sheriff. Any progress?"

Bartelle squatted next to the car, bringing his head to Patrick's level. "A couple of quick questions. I'm a little confused on the timing. Who left first yesterday, you or your father?"

It sounded friendly enough, but given the discussion at breakfast, Patrick sensed the noose tightening on his father. "Dad. You know how it is with kids." He nodded toward Megan, who was plugged into a movie playing on an iPad strapped to the back of the passenger seat. Patrick cautioned himself to tell the truth, but not necessarily the whole truth.

"And your father's plan was to check the camps around the lake before meeting up with you and Owen?"

Patrick shook his head and looked straight into the sheriff's eyes. "His showing up surprised me big time. I thought he would clear more debris from our road."

Bartelle gave him a head cock, "Oh?"

Careful what you say. "You know Dick Tanni? He's got a place on Shank, near the head of the lake on the other side from us. He was with Owen clearing Lukes Road and the last mile of Shank Lake Road down to the A Grade. That still left the road on our side of the lake. We'd made it passable, but it was still a mess."

"Owen was here Friday? Doing what?"

"Don't know, Sheriff. You'd have to ask him."

Bartelle jotted something in his pocket notepad. "You mentioned Dick Tanni was with Owen. You happen to know if he wears Rockports?"

"Rockports?" Patrick's surprise did not need to be feigned. "I've seen him in sneakers and work boots and water shoes. I don't remember any old-man shoes like Rockports, but . . ." He completed the sentence with a shrug.

Bartelle made another note. "You were surprised when your father showed up?"

Asked and answered. Don't give more stuff away. "Yep. I was."

"And you had agreed to meet Owen Lyndstrom. How did that happen?"

Patrick related how they had met Owen and the logging crew clearing the road of storm debris, and the crew had agreed to cut Megan's land if they could start next week.

"Your father gave the land to your daughter, not you?"

Patrick gave the sheriff a quick smile. "Yep, but he made me the trustee. I get all the headaches and none of the profits." Seeing Bartelle's confused expression he added, "Just kidding. It's an estate tax maneuver that lawyers get rich on, and I don't even pretend to understand, but that's why the land is in a trust Megan owns, which I'm the trustee of until she turns thirty." Patrick breathed in after what he realized was a too-long, run-on sentence. "TMI, sorry." Had his nervous speech given him away?

The sheriff scribbled something else in his notebook. "You know if those three sections came with their mineral rights?"

"Only on a hundred and sixty acres. The title search was fascinating. The rest were segregated at the time of the original land sale from the Northwest Territories. A regular Who's Who of industry has owned them. One of Carnegie's companies for a while. Ford Motor Company for the first half of the twentieth century. Then one or two of the big paper companies, and now some Canadian company—unless they've been sold again."

Patrick figured over-cooperating on an undisputed fact might blind Bartelle to the evasiveness of some of his earlier answers. "You know, I must have slept through the part of American history in high school where they discussed how the federal government sold the surface land and kept the mineral rights and later sold them separately or gave them to the railroads to encourage them to build more lines."

Bartelle looked about to interrupt, so Patrick changed tactics. "I need to get the munchkin on home, but let me give you a card in case you need to talk to me again." Patrick pulled his wallet from the armrest console and extracted a business card, which he handed to the sheriff.

Bartelle examined both sides of the card. "Cybersecurity means what, exactly?"

Patrick produced a chuckle. "Whatever a client wants to pay me money for. I'm a full-time parent and part-time consultant."

Bartelle shoved the card into his shirt pocket. "You still doing work with the NSA?"

"If I were, I wouldn't be allowed to tell you, and if I'm not, they wouldn't want me telling you that either. Anything else? We've got a long drive ahead of us, and she's only entertained by movies for so long."

Bartelle looked into the car. "Where's the dog?"

Patrick related the dead fish story. With them both laughing about the knack dogs and kids have for getting dirty at the worst time, Bartelle returned to his cruiser.

Patrick waited for Bartelle to leave before checking his cell phone for a signal. No man's land. He wanted to warn his father that they had discovered evidence of Elliot's—Jason Graham's—Rockports. He had a strong feeling the sheriff or his deputies would soon show up at his dad's door.

"Papa?" Megan had one ear bud out.

"Yes, sweetheart?"

"Papa. I need to tinkle."

"We'll be in town in a few minutes. Can you hold it?"

Megan put on her serious expression, which made Patrick want to laugh, but he suppressed the urge. "Now, Papa."

ENJOYING HIS NEW DIGS, JASON Graham settled in to a breakfast of fried eggs, hash browns, and beer, all cadged from the well-stocked pantry. He flicked on the widescreen TV to check the financial news and stumbled across a teaser: *Two dead in woods north of Amasa. Stay tuned for details.*

His neck of the woods. *What the hell is going on?*

The commercial ended, and he learned he was watching a repeat of the late Saturday night news report. The screen filled with a picture of Frank Cabibi. Jason was so shocked that Cabibi's death didn't initially sink in; when it did, he let loose a war whoop, drowning out the commentator.

After a celebratory toast to the miscreant, Jason tuned into the story again. The newsman introduced a clip of the Iron County sheriff gravely announcing Cabibi had been killed, probably by a blow to the head. They had no further information about the skeleton exhumed earlier that day in the same general area.

What?

Had someone killed Cabibi because he had failed to find Jason? Were the bones from a previous victim of these people? He lost his taste for food and put his fork down.

The screen switched to an interview the station had aired following the informational meeting Cabibi had in Iron River—the one Seamus had attended. Cabibi stood next to his truck sporting the logo for Environmentally Friendly Extraction—the logo on the ATV Jason had stolen from the woods.

He was in so much shit. His prints were all over the dead man's ATV. If police found where he had dumped it, he'd be *the* prime suspect, and his real name would be all over the news.

Bile burned his throat as he barfed eggs and hash browns into the sink.

WASHING ATTY WAS A BLAST. The dog loved to race down the dock, launch herself into the air, and land with a loud belly flop. After retrieving the cloth Frisbee, she'd want to do it again. After one throw got her good and wet, I lathered her up with pet-friendly soap Paddy kept at camp. She tolerated my soaping her and enthusiastically flipped onto her back at the "belly rub" command. Once I thoroughly worked in the soap, I used Frisbee-fetching to rinse her off.

While we were at the dock, the sun rose and painted the very tops of the trees on the opposite bank. The light worked down branch by branch until, by the time we were done, the entire opposite shore was lit. With the sunrise, a freshening breeze rippled the lake. A mature bald eagle cruised past.

I toweled the dog dry and gave her a good sniff. Peppermint had replaced dead fish. I attached the lead to avoid her rolling in the woods—or worse, finding the dead fish again, which I'd need to dispose of. But first I wanted to get her into the house and catch up on my beauty sleep.

"Atty, heel."

She obeyed and stayed at my side up the path from the dock to the cabin. At the crest of the hill she lunged, nearly pulling my arm from its socket. Her barking was fierce, but her tail was wagging—a mixed message. Had Paddy and Megan forgotten something and returned? I controlled the dog, but allowed her to lead us down the path from the cabin to the house. Nearly there, I saw the reason for the dog's agitation: a parked sheriff's car.

I reeled the dog in and called out a hello.

Tex and Sergeant Engberg appeared from the direction of my garage. "Mr. McCree," Tex said. "I thought you might be around."

I put on a cheery smile and prepared to lie through my teeth.

Sixteen

Normally I would invite them in, but Paddy's printouts of Jason Graham were scattered on the dining room table. "Sorry if you were waiting long. The dog got into a dead fish."

"Beautiful place you got here," Engberg said. "You still have good-sized northerns in the lake?"

Former DNR. He'd know. "So I'm told. Is Sheriff Bartelle extending my temporary deputy duties?"

"Not that I'm aware," Engberg said. "Confusing crime scene—scenes. We're trying to get a handle on who exactly was in the woods when. Now good?"

"You should see the view from the inside," Tex said. "And you can hardly tell the place got shot up."

Sending them away wouldn't work. "Mosquitoes will be waking up soon," I said. "And I want the dog to dry before I take her into the house. She'll roll if I leave her out. Screened porch work?" They might see Jason's drinking glass in a plastic bag and the papers sitting on the dining room table, but they wouldn't be able to read them from the porch. I jiggled Atty's lead and clucked my tongue. She trotted next to me in perfect heel position up the ramp and onto the porch. "Good girl."

I led them to the table and sat with my back to the lake. Hopefully, the view would distract them from the house. Didn't work. Tex led Engberg to the french doors, pointed out which windows had been shot out in the mayhem a few years back, and exclaimed anew over the view through the west wall of windows overlooking the lake. Despite a pounding headache, I arranged my face into a smile. Watching Engberg's facial expressions, I figured something was bothering him.

They settled in and Engberg's questions led me through the day of the storm: what time we had gone in, who we had met, and our return. "And you never saw Greg Shuett, that environmental jerk?"

My phone rang from its perch on a window sill where it usually had enough bars to get calls. I wondered who was calling, but I wouldn't risk having them follow me into the house. "Last time I saw him was when he got thrown out from the community meeting Cabibi held at the library a couple of weeks ago. Tex was there. He knows how obnoxious the guy was, not letting Cabibi answer anyone's questions."

The phone rang again. "You need to take that?" Tex interjected.

"Probably a wrong number and if not, they can leave a message. I have to say, I thought Cabibi handled Shuett well, didn't let him get under his skin."

Engberg clicked his pen twice slowly. "I heard you were a little heated yourself."

I waved the concern away. "Here's the thing: I'm not against mining. I use stuff produced from minerals extracted from the ground. But I am damned tired of mining companies conveniently going bankrupt and sticking the rest of us with their cleanup once they've distributed bonuses to their officers and profits to their shareholders. Cabibi refused to answer any of my questions relating to the finances behind this proposed mining. I'll be honest, that pissed me off. But you didn't come here for the Seamus McCree stump speech."

Tex wasn't showing anything, but Engberg's eyes crinkled and he broke into a grin. "Not exactly. You knew they planned to do tests on your property?"

"My granddaughter's—not mine. First I heard anything about her property was yesterday when Greg Shuett spat it out. Don't even know if it's true. Last I heard, they were looking up toward the Wilson Creek area. I have to admit, for local news, if it isn't on *Telephone Time* or in the *Iron County Reporter*, I haven't heard it."

Engberg scribbled something in his notepad that I couldn't read upside down, a skill I had honed to a fine art during my Wall Street bank stock analyst days. He pursed his lips, and I suspected I needed to be super careful. "Take me through yesterday, starting with your waking up."

The headache pounded harder; if I were to make a clean breast of it, now was the time.

Instead, I told him I'd left before dawn, checked the neighbors' camps, and then figured I'd make my way to Megan's property to catch my family before they headed to Chicago.

"What time would you say you left your house?"

I pursed my lips and offered a shrug and tilt of my head. "I don't know. Oh-dark-hundred with no light in the east."

"Why so early?"

Thank goodness he didn't ask if I'd seen Paddy or what we had discussed. "Some mornings I wake up and know I'm not getting back to sleep. Yesterday was one of those. I went to bed with my neighbors on my mind, so when I woke up, I left."

"All the camps were okay?"

Time to throw a little truth in with the fabrication. "I didn't bother with Dick Tanni's place since I'd already seen him after the storm."

"So, after checking everyone's camp, making sure they were okay, you finished the loop to Lukes Road—skipping Mr. Tanni's place—and found your family with Owen? That about right?"

"Paddy had already left to call you. Owen was babysitting the bone and the mining company truck. Took me so damn long because I stupidly thought I'd help assess the wind damage in the northern portions of the property. The interlinked skidder trails I followed were choked with blowdowns. Slow going." I told him I'd traded places with Owen, who was bored to tears doing nothing, so he could check the rest of the property.

Engberg clicked his pen a few times: a nervous gesture, or one he used to stall for time while he was thinking? "Not like Owen to give up the opportunity to gain grist for his rumor mill. How long would you say you were waiting?"

"I'd guess I was there for an hour before you showed up. I didn't want to miss anyone in case they returned to the mining company's truck, so I stayed put."

"Those shoes all yours?" He pointed to the mat where I left shoes and boots to avoid tracking mud into the house.

"The little water shoes are my granddaughter's, but otherwise all mine. You need to know which ones I was wearing yesterday to eliminate my tracks?" *Why the hell did I just say that?* Because I had Elliot's Rockport prints on my mind. Crap, were there Rockport prints outside, around the house or down by the dock? Engberg was the tracker; he'd notice. Do not volunteer anything he doesn't ask for.

"Remind me what you did after we arrived."

If they'd seen the same Rockport prints I'd spotted, they'd also seen my shoe prints. I fessed up to wandering around while I was babysitting the bones. After my confession, Engberg seemed more relaxed. Maybe I'd passed a test? The pounding in my head didn't change.

"Last question for now. Did you hear or see anybody or anything in the woods that might be helpful?"

I did my pursed-lips routine and offered my two-word lie. "Nothing. Sorry."

Engberg clicked the pen and shoved it into his pocket. "You one of those guys who hates daylight savings time?" My face must have expressed my confusion because he clarified. "That Seth Thomas clock you got up on the wall is an hour too fast, like you didn't set it back."

Actually, I thought, setting back is in the fall, spring forward is where we are now. But had his sharp eyes also registered the material on the dining room table when he noticed the clock abnormality? "Gotcha. Half the camps on Shank Lake run on central and half on eastern, depending on where people's other homes are. I've always lived in the eastern time zone, so that's what I chose. You look at your cell phone and, depending on which tower you're pulling from, its fifty-fifty whether it'll give you eastern or central time. Unless you want to drive yourself crazy, you need to prevent your phone from automatically changing the time."

They pulled out their phones. Tex's was central; Engberg's eastern. That got everyone laughing. I let my guard down and asked if the old bones were Tim Javoroski's. Engberg's look reminded me Paddy had made that connection, not the police. My headache throbbed. I explained that Paddy's curiosity had led him to uncovering Javoroski's disappearance and our connecting the dots.

Relief spread through me when Engberg closed his notebook. I had dug myself out of a hole without divulging the existence of Elliot—Jason, as I should now think of him. These guys would leave, and I could take a nap.

"Mind if I use the facilities?" Tex asked.

Saying no would make them suspicious. "Sure." I got up and Atty stirred. As I opened the door, she lunged to get inside. I used a knee to trap her to the frame. Struggling to haul her back to the porch, I realized she was my salvation. "Use the other door. Walk through the TV room and the john is immediately on your left." *And you won't be able to see the table or anything on it.*

Engberg whistled the dog to him and entertained her while Tex did his thing in the bathroom. Engberg, Atty, and I met Tex exiting the TV room, and I ushered the officers down the ramp to the driveway.

With them gone, I stored the Jason papers in a folder, fed the dog, and popped two Aleves. While the dog inhaled breakfast, I checked to see who had called. Paddy—twice, leaving warnings both times: Bartelle had grilled him about me, and the police were headed in my direction.

One bullet dodged, but I still had another before I could breathe easy. I punched in Owen's number. On the second ring a female answered, "Hello?"

I asked for Owen and Jenny Kauppi introduced herself as Owen's daughter. "I'm not sure when he'll get back. I usually clean his house on Sunday mornin and then he takes me and the kids to a late brunch. He said he needed to talk to the sheriff and wasn't sure we'd have brunch today."

Crap. Crap. Triple crap. I thought Owen would at least wait to talk to me before going to the cops. I guess Elliot–Jason breaking into his friend's camp had weighed heavy on his conscience, and he decided not to wait. I hadn't done anything wrong harboring Elliot. But half the congressmen who had been convicted in the last century were sent away on the cover-up, not the crime. I asked her to have Owen call me.

It was time, maybe past time, to consult Abigail, and I wanted to see her reaction, not just hear it. Her face popped up on my screen when she answered the Skype call. Using Skype over a satellite connection involves a significant latency. We tended to talk over each other or leave long silences. I delayed my hello and her hopeful voice said, "You've found him?"

"I have not found him, but I have found out about him." I provided an uninterrupted stream of Jason Graham details, ending with Owen talking to the police. I concentrated on her facial expressions for clues about her thinking. Her mouth flattened into a hard, grim line. Her eyebrows pulled together. She brought her coffee mug partway to her mouth and returned it, unsipped, to the desk in front of her.

"Tell me the truth, Abigail. Did you know this or did someone lie to you too?"

She rocketed from her seat. Without adjusting the tilt of her laptop screen, the camera now focused on her middle. Her hands squeezed her waist, elbows pointed out. She paced in front of the camera, running shorts providing glimpses of tanned thighs. While pacing she said, "I have never lied to you, Seamus McCree. To protect our client, I did not tell you everything because it did not matter to you and could have harmed him. But I have never lied. Never. This news is a shock. What was the website?"

I opened the folder and read from Paddy's notes. She sat down at the desk, and we both entered the URL on our machines so we were looking at the same page.

"Clearly him," she said. "Have you no idea where he is?"

"Assume I'm right and Elliot—Jason—took the mining guy's ATV, broke into that camp, and swapped ATVs. The police will believe it's linked to the murder, and I haven't told the police anything about Jason. This will crash on us like the proverbial ton of bricks. We need to get in front of it."

She leaned into the laptop and adjusted it; the screen filled with her angry face. "This is a fucking disaster. I should never have let you talk me into this, and it will not happen again. I have no doubt this would not have happened had I been there. I have never lost a client. Not one, but bad as this is, I cannot be there to save his ass or yours. I'll check with my contact at the US Marshal's office and try to learn anything that might help you. But don't count on anything. Do whatever you have to do."

She wiped a strand of hair from her damp forehead and puffed out a long sigh. "I don't know how to find people, Seamus, I only know how to protect them. Our partnership never really worked, did it? I ignored the old saw to never mix my money with my honey and let you persuade me. That's on me. We're done, Seamus. I cannot take this anymore. When I get home, I'll box up your stuff and send it to you."

"Abigail, we can—"

She broke the connection. With a sad little sound, her picture shrank to a pinpoint of light.

SEVENTEEN

THE HAPPY REAPER CHECKED INTO the first-class lounge for his flight from Edinburgh to JFK. Booting his laptop generated alerts of three additional hits to the Jason Graham website. The first occurred an hour ago and was another IP address assigned to the same satellite provider that had triggered the first alert. The second and third had occurred moments earlier. One of those was again an IP address assigned to that satellite provider; the other was a fixed IP address that he determined belonged to a major hotel near the Baton Rouge, Louisiana airport.

Could the second person possibly be Jason Graham?

A month with no hits, and now to have all this activity suggested it was connected. Databases placed Patrick McCree's home in Chicago, so not a Michigan resident unless he had moved so recently that the database was outdated. His wife was still an investigative reporter for one of the major Chicago television stations, so unlikely. Seamus McCree had property in the Upper Peninsula within possible geographies for the IP address. For now, he'd go with his hunch that Patrick was visiting his father. Each Michigan county maintained separate property records. There were fifteen counties, running alphabetically from Alger to Schoolcraft in the U.P., and by the time his flight was called he had eliminated the first two and was working on Chippewa.

Boarding the plane, he caught himself whistling. It had been a while since he had whistled. It felt good to be on a real hunt, which he could continue onboard once they reached cruising altitude and the pilot allowed internet access.

BARTELLE FELT MENTALLY UNSETTLED AND double-checked the camera position and sound quality for the interview room where Owen Lyndstrom sat, peaceful as a nun in the first pew listening to the organ prelude. "He's been like this the whole time?" he asked the deputy monitoring the room.

"Came in agitated, but once we informed him you were driving in, he settled right down, asking for a cup of coffee. Gave him one and took him to the john once."

"Well, let's find out what's so important it can't wait." Bartelle walked to the interview room. "Roll 'em,"

Bartelle entered, thought about offering Owen his hand, but didn't. "I understand you have something to tell me, but first, since I'm not exactly sure what this is all about, let's make sure you understand all your rights."

He Mirandized him and asked a second time, "You sure you don't want a lawyer here with you?"

"Lawyer ain't got nothin to do with what I'm tellin ya. He got me aggravated no end and I warn't thinkin none and I whomped him upside the head. Picked up the nearest rock and hit him. Didn't mean to kill him—leastwise I don't think so—but what's done is done."

Bartelle blinked in astonishment. "You're saying you killed Frank Cabibi?"

"Per-xactly."

Bartelle waited to see if Owen would offer more without prompting. He didn't, and it was up to Bartelle to keep Owen talking. Once a lawyer did become involved, they might not get anything else.

"What did he do to rile you up?"

"I don't rightly remember. He was flappin his lips, goin on and on about how much good his mine would do. He didn't care nothin for how he'd destroy the woods and the streams and the habitat. I dunno. I think he said somethin like there warn't no damn thing I could do to stop it. Next thing I know he's on the ground, and I got a bloody rock in my hand."

"Let's start from the beginning. Why were you there? Were you planning on meeting him?"

"I was scoutin some property for a logger buddy, and then I was goin to meet . . . I was goin fishin. Then the storm come through. Ain't too bad where I was, see. I cut myself out and I'm workin my way down Lukes Road and hear a chainsaw coming from the woods. I thought maybe someone needed help, see. I drove up that road you found Cabibi's truck on. Well, one thing came to another and you know the rest."

"Give me a time frame, Owen. What time did you leave home? When did you see Cabibi? Did anyone see you?"

"I was inta the woods by first light. You'd have to ask folks if they saw me leavin town. Prolly not. I seen some cars on the road, but not enough light to tell you who. Didn't see no one in the woods until I run into Cabibi. I found that fella up by Shank Lake—Tannin, Tannit, Tan something."

"Tanni?"

"Yeah, but that was later. Fish drinks less than him, but he hadn't started for the day. Anyhoo, we started clearin the road together. I've been in the woods all my life, and I ain't never seen no storm like that. Who-whee. I heard tell we had a bad one while I was gone to Korea, but by the time I got discharged—"

"So, Owen. You argued. You struck his head. The one time?"

"Far as I recollect, but like I told ya, I wasn't exactly in my right mind. Maybe I hit him a second time. I don't remember so clearly. I'm still pretty strong for a toothless geezer."

"Was he facing you or did you hit him from behind?"

Owen rubbed his eyes with the heels of his hands. "Behind. He was walkin away. Laughin at me."

"Laughing?"

"That's probably what did it, eh? Told me nothin anyone could do would stop him. Laughed in my face and walked away. I hit him and hid him."

"Why'd you hide him?"

"Well, the thing was I didn't have no shovel or nothin to get rid of the body. See? Figured I'd come back and do the job right. But if I left him lyin there, somebody might find him. Or coyotes scavenge him. Lotta coyote sign on the road. All the trees and limbs down made it easy to cover him good. Sometimes I don't remember things so hot, and I needed to find him again, so I used that big hemlock. Stuck him on the shadow side."

"You're pretty good friends with Seamus McCree, right? Did you know you were on his property?"

"McCree's treated me fair." Owen shrugged. "He's okay for a foreigner 'cept he uses a lotta fancy words."

Bartelle had to smile at the dead-on characterization of McCree. "You didn't answer my question. Did you know you were on McCree's land?"

"Cain't say I give her any thought at the time. 'Course I knew later, see."

"Why return the next day with Patrick McCree? Weren't you afraid he might find Cabibi's body?"

"I planned ta steer him away from the tree. After we was done, I'd take care of things, see. It gave me an excuse for being there. Like God was smilin on me. When that bone turned up, I realized God was laughin up His sleeve at me. Took me 'til last night to figure God chose yesterday to reveal the bones of Timmy Javoroski for a reason. He wanted me to stand up for my sins."

Lyndstrom's answers held together, but where was the emotion? The smell of fear permeated the interview room walls, but all he was getting from Owen was the smell of his aftershave, reminding him vaguely of his own father's Old Spice. He could see Owen getting mad and clunking Cabibi on the head with a rock. Owen had a temper, though he hadn't been in trouble with the law for sixty years. The last, a D&D, was dismissed: Owen had paid for the bar damages, and the owner wouldn't press charges. Sure, the DNR figured him for a poacher, but in seventy years they hadn't come close to catching him at anything.

Owen's calm demeanor bothered Bartelle. A sociopath might present that level of calm, but an ordinary civilian who had killed someone? That kind of traumatic experience should affect their mannerisms, their speech, nervous tics, something. Yet Owen had crossed his legs, looking no different from him chewing the fat with a bunch of the old boys at breakfast. And he was hiding something.

The penny dropped. Javoroski wasn't common knowledge. The McCrees had come up with the name. Maybe they told Owen? Or was this not the first time Owen had killed someone up there? "Owen, how do you figure the bones are Javoroski's?"

"Well, see now, I've been good with names until recent. Last few years my memory is for shit, but only for new stuff. Somethin old like Timmy Javoroski going missing? Hell, I can tell you what I had to eat that morning before I helped search for him." He tapped his head with his pointer finger. "Holds memories as tight as a bear trap. 'Sides, my recollection is Timmy's dad owned that very same property. He and Frankie Joe Cabibi and Chris Saari was thick as thieves, them three. Maybe Frankie Joe had somethin to do with Timmy. Maybe his guilty conscience was callin him back there. He picked the spot, not me."

Bartelle had already recognized that possibility. More bad guys than the public realized were caught because they felt compelled to return to the scene of their crime. It's why police recorded video of the crowd at crime scenes. But this could go both ways. If Owen had learned Cabibi was considering a mine near Javoroski's burial site, maybe he was concerned the mining operations would uncover the earlier murder. Yet, if true, why would Owen admit to one murder while denying the other?

Bartelle reminded himself to keep Owen talking. "You've got an interesting point. What did people think happened at the time?"

"We never found nothin to show where he went." He leaned back, locking his fingers behind his head. "His car and stuff was still at home. He weren't gonna walk, meanin somebody picked him up. Chris is the only one of them three who stayed around. Well, I guess Timmy did after all, didn't he?"

"You said Javoroski owned the property. McCree told me he bought it from a Mrs. Ripone."

" 'Spect he did. See, Mrs. Ripone was the widder of Jon Ripone, who married her three, four years maybe after her first husband, Donny Javoroski, had a heart attack on his snow machine and plowed into a tree. That was a mess, I'll tell ya. The winter of nineteen—"

"Owen," Bartelle said. "You started to say who you were planning on meeting later in the day."

"Wasn't meetin no one, 'cept maybe some perch for dinner. Speakin of, when do they serve grub in this place?" He crossed his arms.

Bartelle figured those crossed arms indicated he'd gotten all he would get for this round, but he wasn't done with Owen Lyndstrom. Not by a long shot.

SOMEPLACE OVER THE ATLANTIC, THE Happy Reaper pinned down the probable locations of Seamus McCree's Michigan property, all tucked into the northern extremities of Iron County. County tax records showed McCree owned a house on eighty acres bordering Shank Lake. And a McCree trust owned another 1,920 acres of commercial forest nearby. The Happy Reaper could see the exact location of the Shank Lake property using the township's online GIS. The more recent purchase was in another township without the Geographic Information System, and he wouldn't be able to pin down the precise location until he could acquire plat maps for the area. Probably didn't matter: the house was the important key.

Of the storage facilities he maintained across the country, the one in Chicago was closest to McCree. He'd intended to use Chicago as a base to implement his plan for eliminating Jason Graham at the Federal courthouse, if it came to that, which meant he already had in place most of the provisions he would need. He booked a flight from JFK to Chicago, reserved an SUV rental, and booked a nearby hotel room.

Nothing suited him better than the juice of being on a manhunt—made him tingle with antici . . . pation. McCree's involvement set the dial one notch higher. He was most assuredly looking forward to getting McCree in his sights.

EIGHTEEN

THE ALARM WOKE ME FROM a chase dream in which I was treed and the dogs were closing in. Sheets were twisted around me and sweat dripped from my fevered forehead—partly the chase dream's fault and partly mine for allowing the heat of the day to invade the house by forgetting to close the windows before napping.

I wanted to go back to sleep, but the hollowness inside me would not heal by sleeping my life away. Only productive work would do, yet determining what would be productive was elusive. I got up and stared at the rumpled bed, my thoughts moving as sluggishly as a dinosaur wading through the La Brea Tar Pits. I slapped my head—enough with the negative imaging. I might be treed, but the dogs hadn't yet arrived. I needed caffeine.

Leaving the bed to take care of itself, I made my way to the kitchen and poured a Diet Dr Pepper. A series of questions flitted through my attention, fizzing and popping like the bubbles from the soda. Had Owen returned my call? Had Abigail found anything? Any word from Bartelle after Owen ratted me out? My phone claimed it had no voice or text messages. Sometimes the signal is so weak the phone doesn't receive messages, so I brought the remainder of my drink to the deck, where the signal was strongest, and dialed voicemail. The sun-heated decking was uncomfortable on my bare feet. I shifted weight from foot to foot to minimize the discomfort and keyed in my password.

You have no messages at this time.

Back inside, I booted up the computer and checked email. Nothing relevant and no help for my situation.

I had a long, positive history with Sheriff Lon Bartelle. Was it strong enough for him to cut me some slack over my initially lying to him? Surely, the best way to tell him of my malfeasance was face-to-face. Like a man mounting the scaffold for his hanging, I forced leaden legs to return me to the deck. My call to Bartelle brought the information that he was in the office but not available to come to the phone.

I put Atty on a lead to do her business and then shut her in the house. "Sorry girl, I need to leave you home for this one. Don't do anything I wouldn't do."

She trotted to the living room and, without a glance back, crawled onto the couch, where she didn't belong. She pawed the throw pillow resting against one arm, knocking it flat, and stretched out, snuggling into the back of the couch and resting her head on the flattened pillow. Her eyes met mine and she grinned, as if to say, "What? I'm just following orders."

BY THE TIME THEY BUZZED me into the sheriff's office, I had already read the various warning notices on the wall, checked the bail bondsmen cards, and used my phone to deal with emails. Bartelle met me outside his office. "Seamus, I was just thinking of you and poof—by magic you're here."

Let him show his cards first. "Oh?"

"There's a major breakthrough in the Cabibi investigation, but you know how hard it is for us to quickly assess the import of financial records. We found a ton of material in Cabibi's rental house. Can I twist your arm and have you look through it for us? Tell me everything is kosher—or not? It's probably a waste of your time because Owen Lyndstrom confessed to killing Cabibi, but still, I'd rather know if something about his finances was fishy."

My mouth gaped. I caught myself blinking in astonishment with the same woozy feeling I had after a concussion: sound becomes tinny and the world shifts away. Normally I consider myself a good listener, concentrating on what people say rather than thinking how I'll respond. Not then. I lost his words while I wondered what that meant for me and my planned confession. I snapped out of it and Bartelle was still talking.

". . . think it must have been a spur-of-the-moment-type thing. Owen would've shot him had he planned it, and we would never have found the body. It'd be lying at the bottom of an abandoned mine somewhere."

I heard myself ask, "Did he say why?"

Bartelle shifted in his seat, generating a squeak of protest from the chair. "You ever see him really angry?"

I briefly considered the question. "Lose control angry? No, but he's got a temper."

"His record includes a couple of D and Ds. Bar fights decades ago. You know he's eighty-eight, right?"

"Going on sixty-eight. He's like an ancient yellow birch tree, tough and gnarly. He'll stand forever until something like cancer rots him out from the inside."

"Exactly. I've never known Owen Lyndstrom to withhold his opinion on anything. Cabibi had stirred up the whole county over bringing in a mine, but Owen wasn't ranting on *Telephone Time*. You recall any letters to the editor?"

I didn't, and Bartelle told me details of Owen's confession. "Owen sure seemed normal when we saw him later that day," I said. "Now I wonder whose blood was on his favorite woods' shirt." I explained about the dried blood, Owen's cut hand, and his failure to wear that shirt the next day.

"That would provide some corroboration. Right now, my gut's telling me something's not right."

"So, is there anything particular you want me to be looking for?"

"I've been around investigations long enough to know that with Owen's confession, our efforts will change from broad investigation to making a case against him. Unless some huge red flag appears, we'll concentrate on finding evidence to support Owen bashing Cabibi. We'll explain away evidence that points anywhere else. Not intentionally, but we'll have blinders on. Like Owen's drunk and disorderlies and his history of getting into fights. They'll be evidence of an anger issue, a temper that can flare up, and we'll ignore that he hasn't been in a lick of trouble for decades. I'd feel guilty wasting your time, except I know you get off on this money stuff. You'll do it?"

I had come to Bartelle intending to confess my sins. Once a person decides to confess, internal pressure builds until the confession releases it. A part of me was looking forward to that release. I kept my mouth shut, though. Jason Graham was my responsibility, and he had not killed Cabibi. Without a driving reason to reveal Jason's presence in the area, I let the focus stay on Owen.

"Seamus?"

"Sorry, I was woolgathering . . . wondering what records you have. I'm happy to help however I can."

"Now," Bartelle said, "what was so urgent you had to drive in to see me on a Sunday?"

Oh shit. "Um . . . the loggers hoped to start working Megan's—my granddaughter—her land. I can start them away from the murder scene, but—"

Bartelle cocked his head and squinted through one eye. "You drove all the way in to ask me that?"

"I was getting some groceries anyway," I lied. "They told me you were here but not available, so I took a chance."

I judged his shrug to mean he bought my story but thought I was weird.

"I'll check with the state's crime team and let you know." Bartelle rose from his desk and extended his hand. "Thanks, Seamus, I know I can count on you. I'll let you know when you can review Cabibi's finances."

The juxtaposition of his words and my actions gave me pause. I rose slowly, pressing down on my knees as though they were giving me trouble, but actually providing me time to reconsider my decision to not tell the sheriff about Jason Graham.

I shook Bartelle's hand and sealed my fate.

PATRICK KICKED OFF HIS SANDALS at the front door and carried a napping Megan to her room. Cindy, barefoot, in exercise gear, followed them up the stairs. Once Patrick tucked Megan and Raff under the sheet and shut the door, Cindy hit him with, "Where's the dog?"

Patrick described Atty's last-minute stink while he grabbed a juice from the refrigerator. They settled onto the bar stools at the kitchen counter. "Can your parents take care of Megan for a few days? I'd like to try to help Dad with his problem."

Cindy breathed an exasperated sigh. "When you convinced me you should be the primary caregiver, you said you were willing to put Megan's needs ahead of your own. And you have. I know you've given up business opportunities you would have loved to pursue." She leaned in and gave him a quick kiss. "And I appreciate your agreeing without argument to bring Megan home. I have to admit I didn't sleep well last night, worrying about your extra night up there."

In Patrick's experience, Cindy beating around the bush meant the answer was no. "You won't ask your parents?"

"It's not about asking my parents. How many times have we agreed your Dad and Abigail would never make their arrangement work? You can't solve that, Patrick. You have to let it go."

"Yeah, but . . . this Jason Graham guy was nice to Megan. Very nice. That's maybe part of it, but the big thing is I'm afraid Dad will sink into a depression again. I know it's been a long time, but I thought maybe I was seeing signs. If he's all alone—"

"FaceTime him. Have Megan FaceTime him. Visit him next weekend when I'm not working and can look after Megan. Pick up Atty and stay a night if you want. You are a parent to your daughter, not to your father. You need to remember your priorities."

She was right. He knew she was.

Cindy leaned over, placed her hand high up on his inner thigh, her fingers making little circular motions. She planted a kiss at the corner of his mouth. "Speaking of priorities, the munchkin is down, and I've missed you." Her fingers slid forward. "Seems like I have your attention, Mr. McCree."

Again, she was right. He slid off the stool and stepped to her. She pulled her shirt over her head and wrapped her legs around him. "The den," she whispered.

NINETEEN

THE FIRST THING I DID after returning from visiting Sheriff Bartelle was walk my shoreline to find the dead fish. A breeze had kicked up from the south, bringing with it warm, humid air and the chance of late afternoon thunderstorms. I figured I'd combine the dead fish hunt with checking my lake path for storm damage. I started searching from the north property line and cleared the path of branches as I went. Twice I had to skirt around downed trees that would require a chainsaw to clean up.

The gentle rainstick sound triggered by a breeze stirring leaves in a small grove of popple tapped a flood of pleasant memories: singing some choral anthem in church to its accompaniment; Paddy taking a rainstick apart in grammar school while the teacher wasn't looking. He'd discovered what was inside, and I'd bought a replacement.

The pungent smell of rotting fish brought me out of my reverie. Something—an otter?—had partially eaten a large northern pike and left it on the bank. I deposited the remains into a black trash bag and carted the carcass to the garage to get a digging tool. The thought of burying anything in the glacial debris we call soil was daunting, but tossing it back into the water would just allow the dog to find it again. Those same glacial deposits were the reason the old bones had been buried in a shallow grave. Without a sandy area, it required a backhoe or dynamite to dig deep. I knew of no sand deposits on my property, but I did have an old compost pit that would allow me to easily excavate a hole deep enough to dump the fish. Piling rocks on top of the burial would prevent Atty or wild canines from digging it up. Nothing would stop a determined bear.

How had Owen planned to dispose of Cabibi's body? People had used weights to bury bodies under water; and with all the lakes and sloughs and swamps in the area, there were plenty of possibilities. You'd need either a boat on a trailer, or a kayak or canoe, to get on the water—none of which Owen had brought the day he met Paddy to check Megan's property. Bartelle mentioned dumping a body down an abandoned mine shaft, which would require transporting it. I closed my eyes and tried to remember what was in the bed of Owen's truck the day he met Paddy. No tarps, and he wouldn't just toss the body into the truck bed and haul it out in broad daylight.

Even if the old coot planned on digging a grave, he would know enough to bring proper tools: a shovel, maybe a pickax or mattock, and a winch or block and tackle to handle rocks too large to move by hand. I hadn't seen any of that stuff in his truck. Even if he had everything he needed, how would he transport it to Cabibi's body by the hemlock? I suppose he could have planned to use Cabibi's ATV. Owen's line that there was a right tool for every job applied here: only a fool tried to shovel snow from a driveway with a teaspoon. Nope, Owen had not brought the tools to bury a body or even cart it away.

Plus, I'd loaned Owen my ATV to find Elliot—Jason Graham. Even if he'd had some hidden plan, once Atty found the human bone, he must have known that the police search of the area would likely discover Cabibi's body. And yet, even when he had my ATV, he hadn't taken the opportunity to move the body farther away.

Why not? Did Owen not care if someone found the body? No—he didn't immediately confess. Because he didn't figure he'd get caught even if they found it? Sure, I could see Owen brazening it out, and later his conscience kicking in. Or was Bartelle's gut right, and the reason Owen didn't do anything with Cabibi's body when he had the chance was because he had no idea Cabibi was dead? Which would make sense only if Owen was protecting someone. He had a large extended family, but was there anyone other than his daughter for whom Owen would take the blame? I didn't know. And why would she have any reason to kill Cabibi? Did Bartelle think I'd find a reason in Cabibi's financial records?

Tomorrow might tell, but today I still had time before dark to devote to finding Jason Graham.

FISH BURIAL COMPLETED, I OWED it to Atty to give her some exercise before cooping her up again. We enjoyed a long run and cooled down by swimming in the lake. After toweling both of us off, I fed us and then invited her to get into her bed, figuring that with a run and full stomach, she would soon conk out for a nap. She circled her dog bed several times and settled in with a contented sigh. Snores soon told me she was asleep.

I figured my best hope of finding Jason was to continue down Lukes Road and look for signs of another camp he broke into. In case he'd returned to Pete Bjork's camp, I'd check there first. I filled the ATV's tank and jotted a note to myself to buy more gasoline. To get to Pete Bjork's place, where Owen had spotted the ATV, I had to pass the cutoff to the murder site. If nosy Sergeant Engberg or Tex spotted me, I'd have to explain my presence. Birdwatching and picture-taking would do the trick, and I needed to be bold and not appear to be slinking past them. I slung my binocs around my neck and under my right arm so they lay down by my side. I strapped a tripod onto the front of the ATV and stored in a backpack my good digital camera with an all-purpose 80–300 mm zoom lens.

Sergeant Engberg waved me over as I approached the murder site. I pointed to the road going in, which was now muddy and rutted. "Lots of traffic. Anything new?"

"We'll be here until sometime tomorrow. Main thing left is to walk a wide grid. We've done close-in grids, but the honchos want us to walk a larger area before it rains come Tuesday."

"You looking for more bodies?"

"Naw, the cadaver dogs didn't give a hint of any more. Checking for anything the killer might have left behind. We've already enlisted the kids from Mississippi State running their predator–prey project, but we can use more people. You free tomorrow morning?"

Bartelle hadn't given me a time to check Cabibi's financials, so that could wait for the afternoon. Engberg told me a time to meet, and I agreed to check if my neighbor Dick Tanni was still around and willing. I continued down the road, throwing a, "See you tomorrow," over my shoulder.

At the entrance to Pete Bjork's camp, I pulled the gate open and drove the ATV up the driveway. Halfway up, I realized how stupid that was. At some point someone would discover the stolen ATV here, and whose ATV's tire tracks would they find? Mine. Sergeant Engberg predicted rain in two days. I could only hope it would wash away the evidence of my presence. Maybe I was paranoid someone would match my tire tracks. Well, I could say I noticed the cut chain and wanted to make sure the camp was okay. That would fit nicely with my cardboard repair of the window.

I had a feeling my tired, tangled mind was weaving a spider's web of lies and half-truths that would later entrap me. Best to hope no one cared about my tracks.

I did a thorough exploration. Everything appeared the way I remembered, and I learned nothing new. Wasted effort. At the end of the driveway, I closed the gate and arranged the chain to give the impression that the gate was locked. The ruse would not stand up to close inspection, but it would fool anyone zipping by. With no new information, I had to go with my assumption that Elliot had dumped the ATV at Pete's and left using Pete's UTV. Elliot had started going west, so I guessed he'd continue in that direction.

I drove to the end of Lukes Road at US-141, finding no breeched gates or cut chains. There were a lot of cottages across the highway on Cable Lake. Had any traffic recently crossed the road? I dismounted from my ATV and examined the road surface and gravel on both sides of the highway. Finding no evidence of any vehicle crossing from Lukes Road to

Cable Lake Road, I concluded Jason must still be on my side of the highway.

Who was I kidding? With two days under his belt, he could be anywhere in the country—hell, in the world—by now. A nearby pileated woodpecker gave his "wuk" call, a series of high, clear, piping sounds that lasted several seconds. It flew from a large maple, and I spun my binocs around and up to follow the undulating flight of the crow-sized bird with its flame-red crest. He landed in a mixed stand and provided another rendition of his song.

The brief encounter reminded me of why I loved it here. If nothing else went right in this whole endeavor, at least nature was still nature. When the next black feelings threatened to consume me, I needed to recall those ten seconds of the pileated. The sights, sounds—I breathed in deeply—the smells of northwoods in the early evening.

If Jason made it past the invisible border of US-141, I wouldn't find him. I had to concentrate on things that might work and that meant assuming he was still someplace I could catch up with him—meaning a camp off Lukes Road. I checked my GPS to remind myself where other camps were.

Camp after camp was locked up tight with no hint of a break-in. The first possibility came by following a road a mile up the East Branch of the Net River. No one had messed with the locked gate, but someone had driven an ATV through shrubs to get around it. Following the trail of broken branches and smooshed flowers, I soon found myself on a two-track and came to a metal sign proclaiming NO TRESPASSING. Underneath was a carved-wood sign proclaiming "Security Provided by Smith and Wesson." I usually respected people's desire for privacy, but I was looking for someone who didn't. To buck up my courage, I told myself that anybody could buy those signs at places like Winks Woods down in Crystal Falls—it didn't really mean anything.

Hearing the puttering of a generator, my nonchalance about my physical danger vanished in a pool of concern. Pulling around a bend into a clearing, I found a single-story cabin, large pole-barn building with a 500-gallon propane pig at its side, generator shed with room to spare, single-hole outhouse, and several woodsheds stuffed with split, seasoned hardwood. I called a loud hello, prepared to tell a story about seeing that someone had bypassed the gate and, hearing rumors of nearby camp break-ins, doing my good neighbor thing and investigating.

I shut off my ATV and dismounted onto the graveled apron in front of the buildings. The generator was well insulated, its muffled putt-putting competing with the riffling of the river. Projecting my voice, I tried again, "Hello?"

I did a three-sixty, looking for any life in the compound. A trail cam attached to one of the woodsheds had recorded my arrival. Nothing to do but act the script I had written. I walked up to the door, a solid wood affair in a board-and-batten style. No lights on inside that I could see. I pounded on the door with the heel of my hand. Stepped back so I wouldn't be in someone's face when they opened the door.

Nothing.

A tingling crawled up my neck. I spun around, sure I would find someone watching me. No one there. No movement. I walked to the pole barn and peered through the windows. Dark, no lights on. No radio playing. Was someone fishing down by the river and not heard me? I crossed the graveled area, noting myriad ATV tracks, some going into the garage, some headed to the mowed lawn, others turning around in the driveway. The place had witnessed lots of recent activity.

The generator running suggested someone was around, though. The path down to the river was well packed. All I found was an osprey cruising the river for a late-evening snack. Coming back, I discovered the reason for the active generator. An array of solar panels facing south peeked above the top of the pole-barn building. They'd been hidden from me before. The owner must have a setup like mine with a large battery bank that periodically needed recharging.

The energy provided by my fight-or-flight adrenaline surge soon petered out. I could have happily curled up on the dock in the last of the sun and rested. Mentally kicking my own rear end, I trudged to the cabin and looked in the windows. Nothing unexpected.

Two other remote camps off Lukes Road to check and then I was finished. Cooked. Toasted. Broiled. Fried. Done.

TWENTY

JASON GRAHAM WATCHED SEAMUS MCCREE retreat down the driveway. Better lucky than good. If he hadn't decided to leave the house for an after-dinner exploration of the woods, McCree might have spotted him. The mossy oak camo suit he'd put on because it had mosquito netting had worked well for camouflage. He remained prone until the ATV's sounds diminished to nothingness.

He stretched muscles tightened by the stress of staying still for so long.

Was there something particular about this camp that made Seamus check it, or was he checking them all? If he checked every camp along the way from Shank Lake, surely he had discovered the cut chain and broken window at the first place Jason had raided. Had Seamus found Cabibi's ATV and figured out the switch? Likely. He should have made sure no one could get his prints off that ATV.

Could Seamus have tracked the side-by-side here? Well, if he had, wouldn't he have stuck around, maybe even hiding himself, to see if Jason would return? Roles reversed, that's what he would do. And if Seamus had discovered the switch, why weren't cops involved in the search? He released a frustrated yell.

His walk to the cabin was accompanied by the swish of pant legs. Using the key he'd found under the doormat, he let himself inside and turned on the local radio station while keeping watch for McCree's return. Country music was good by him, but what he wanted was local news. At the top of the hour he was subjected to generic national-roundup crap, mostly about the coming election. Nothing local. Nothing to help inform his next decision: should he stay or should he go?

If McCree was returning with or without cops, he'd probably do it before dark. Jason decided to keep a sharp lookout until dark settled, then he'd set his alarm for 2:00 a.m. and go to bed. Hopefully, he could still take care of a few burning issues.

* * *

THE FIRST STARS WERE ALREADY twinkling by the time I found Dick Tanni sitting on his dock, five beers into a six-pack. "Plenty more where these came from." He nodded at the lone soldier. "Feel free."

How he stayed skinny drinking so much beer, I'd never understand. I removed the cap and took a slug. "Fish been biting?"

"You know, a few here, a few there. I heard your chainsaw from up the lake. Much damage from the storm?"

I tipped the bottle again. "Not bad. Nothing like down toward Amasa. You hear about the murders?"

He had not. I was his first visitor. He'd spent the weekend clearing debris on his forty acres during the day and stayed in camp working down his beer supply at night.

His isolation gave me the opportunity to tell him about Atty finding the skeleton and how that led to the discovery of Cabibi's murder.

He wiggled a business card out of his front pocket. "Now I understand the 'call us' written on the back of Sergeant Engberg's card. I figured they were checking camps affected by the storm to make sure everyone was okay."

"And they might have wanted to talk to you about Owen." Or me, but I needn't offer that thought up to Dick. I completed the story of Owen's confession and drained the beer. We walked up to his cabin to work on the next six-pack. He veered off and placed the empties in his truck bed next to what must have been another eight or nine six-packs of empties. Dick's level of alcohol consumption exceeded anything I had done even during my serious drinking days. That wasn't the only difference: he was generally a happy drunk—unless something ticked him off, then he'd become belligerent. I'd been morose.

Inside, he pulled a six-pack from the propane refrigerator and replaced it with another from a stack on the floor. Handed me a cold one.

I tossed the bottle cap into the waste basket on the other side of the room. "Swish," I said and remembered to ask if he was willing to help walk the grid the next morning.

He took a long pull on the beer. "Sure." He squinted at the empty bottle in his hand. "I'm getting another. Want one?"

I wasn't done with the one I had, and I did want another. Not good. Thankfully, I had Atty at home, probably crossing her legs. I used her as my excuse to leave.

* * *

Despite forcing himself to stay up late, the Happy Reaper's Monday morning started too damn early. At 4:00 a.m. Chicago time, he wasn't going back to sleep no matter how many sheep he counted. A hot shower and fresh shave made him feel like he could conquer anything, although he knew he'd be mentally slow from the jet lag for a day or two. He ate lightly at the hotel breakfast, choosing orange juice to go with the oatmeal into which he mixed dried cranberries. The coffee smelled excellent, but he didn't want anything to interfere with steady hands.

He played solitaire until the Evanston storage facility opened. Once they stopped allowing passengers to carry weapons on planes, he switched tactics and maintained twelve climate-controlled armories scattered across the country. All were in the general vicinity of major airports, although he would often fly into nearby regional airports, rent a car, and pick up the necessary gear.

Upon entering the storage facility, he checked the camera. The only pictures were of his last departure from the room and his current arrival. He selected one long gun, an automatic handgun, and a ranger-type knife. He packed a tennis duffel with ample ammunition and grabbed the rucksack prepacked with his "do-all" kit: regular and night-vision binoculars, emergency first-aid kit, burglary tools, two wigs and various makeup, and because you never know, a roll of duct tape. He removed the cold-weather gear from the pack and kept the lightweight change in clothes. The clothing he'd used for Scotland would do well in Michigan's woods. He'd stop at one of the big-box sporting-goods stores and buy a camo suit.

The phone app calculated the drive to reach McCree's property at slightly under seven hours. Before he checked out from the hotel, he downloaded Korpiklaani's "Hunting Song" for the ride. Deer would be safe from his hunting, but the lyrics sure were right that only the strong ones will survive.

Dick Tanni and I were on time, but were last of the twenty-five people, including a handful of women from the Mississippi State project, to arrive for the grid sweep. The temperature was already on the north side of seventy degrees and the weather forecaster had suggested highs might reach ninety. Bushwhacking meant everyone was dressed in long pants and long sleeves. A few desultory mosquitoes tried to penetrate the Deet. Several now-dead deer flies had announced their presence with painful bites under the edges of my ball cap.

Conversations centered on Owen Lyndstrom's confession. No one questioned its veracity. While no one justified the killing, several locals didn't seem overly concerned: if Owen thought the guy needed killing, the guy probably did. To my question, "Will Cabibi's death change whether a mine happens in Iron County?" One guy summed it up best. "If there's money in it, sooner or later, someone'll do it."

We stayed close enough to touch hands with the person on either side of us. Should we spot anything nature hadn't placed in the woods, our orders were to summon an officer to take responsibility for tagging and bagging. With so many people tromping through the woods, the animals had all gone to ground or flown away, leaving the woods silent except for the movement and chatter of us humans.

At the midmorning coffee break I assessed what had been pulled from our property: an empty oil can and used filter, several newish plastic bottles, and a treasure trove of ancient beer cans and bottles. One of the guys from Amasa recalled a Forest Park graduating class had staged its unofficial pre-graduation celebration somewhere in this area with a huge bonfire and kegs some conspiring adult had bought. "Different times. Nobody much worried about underage drinking, and DUI laws only got applied if you ended up in an accident."

I asked if he remembered when this was. "I graduated in ninety and it was already legendary. The hemlock is the reason I know this was the spot. These trees are all young, twenty-five, thirty years old tops, except for that single tree."

By the end of the sweep, the single non-alcohol-related item I had kicked up was a cigarette pack from a cheap generic brand I'd never heard of. I decided before heading home to take one more gander at the collected booty the deputies had displayed on a large tarp. My heart stutter-stepped at seeing a hatchet stored in an evidence bag. It had the same shape as mine, the handle was the same black leather, and it hadn't been left in the woods long because the blade showed no rust. The odds of there being two similar hatchets, given Graham had stolen mine, were zero.

Would it have my fingerprints? Does a bear shit in the woods? Mine, yes—would it have Graham's? How long before they could run prints? Sergeant Engberg had occasionally glanced my way. He could have been glancing at everyone, and my guilty conscience made me notice every time he looked in my direction. With the hatchet now evidence, should I take him aside and admit to owning it and let him know how it got here? I'd have to confess to withholding information and blame it on the stupid theory that keeping Graham a secret gave me a better chance of finding him—or at least of the bad guys not finding him.

My neck stiffened at the thought of confession. Relieving the tension of living the lie would feel good, but I couldn't pull the trigger. Abigail, normally so quick to draw the line between legal and sketchy, had not wanted the police to know.

Could I steal the hatchet?

What the hell was I thinking? I would not steal evidence to protect a guy who'd ditched my protection. The only reason to not say something about the hatchet was Abigail's insistence that I should not tell the police about Jason. The vehemence of her words convinced me that if I released Jason's name—even cloaking it by using the name Elliot—I'd kill any hope of saving my business or personal relationship with Abigail.

With the search concluded, I dropped Dick Tanni at his place, refusing his offer of a beer, and rushed home, where I let Atty out to roam at will. I went online and bought round-trip tickets from O'Hare to Atlanta to Baton Rouge, arriving at 10:30 p.m. that evening. If I packed and left in fifteen minutes, I'd have just enough time to return the dog to Paddy before catching the flight. I'd call Abigail after boarding the flight to Baton Rouge to let her know I was coming, but not give her time to talk me out of it.

TWENTY-ONE

JASON HAD GONE TO BED early, but every branch creak, every hoot, every coyote bark, every everything had kept him awake long past exhaustion. The shrill alarm sounded at 2:00, blasting him from bed—heart racing, fingers trembling from an adrenaline overload. The preemptive work had gone well, and returning to his hideout, he had slept soundly until midmorning.

He turned on the WIKB local news at noon and listened for mention of his name, hearing nothing, although the station did run a background piece on Frank Cabibi.

Cabibi had been in the woods on mining-company business—Environmentally Friendly Extractions—an oxymoronic name if there ever was one. He'd grown up in the area and returned six months before Jason's arrival. Nothing mentioned Cabibi's work in Chicago. So, either Cabibi being near Jason's hiding place was nothing more than a piece of bad luck, or someone found out where Jason was hiding and contacted the closest asset to take care of him. Except Cabibi was the one pushing daisies.

If it had been a piece of bad luck, then Cabibi's death meant the risk was over. Jason could dump his most recent ATV acquisition in the woods a couple of miles from Seamus McCree's place and walk in. And what? Tell Seamus he'd known Cabibi and run off scared? His experience with Seamus suggested the guy would dig for all the details, and Jason didn't want his stealing Cabibi's ATV and breaking into camps to affect his deal with the Marshals Service.

Maybe he should show up on McCree's doorstep the day before the trial began. That was still a week away, assuming no postponement. The Marshals Service was to contact Abigail Hancock to inform her of any timing changes, so how would he know? Could he stay hidden for a week?

And if the crooks had discovered him, the bosses wouldn't stop at sending Cabibi. The next person would start at Seamus's camp, making it the last place he should be.

With McCree's passport and Canadian money, he'd had a brief fling with the idea of running to Canada—a stupid idea now he had time to consider it. He had no way to convert McCree's passport into something to get him across the border, and he had less than $200 Canadian. How long could he live on that?

For now, it made sense to sit, wait, and listen to WIKB's local news for facts and *Telephone Time* for gossip. He'd check the TV news channels evening and night.

At the WIKB funeral report, he flicked off the radio. He wasn't in the mood.

* * *

SEATED IN FIRST CLASS WITH a red wine at my elbow, waiting for coach to board, I decided to text Abigail rather than call her. No one could overhear me, and if she forbade me from coming, I could claim I'd had to shut down my phone and didn't see her reply. A sip later, I typed my message.

On plane to Baton Rouge. Arrives 10:30. Where can we meet?

My phone beeped an immediate response.

A: WTF?????? Seamus WHAT HAPPENED??????

Nothing. Need to talk. Where?

A: And you couldn't call?????

I started a text suggesting I wasn't sure she'd pick up. Erased it and sipped more wine while framing a response. She beat me to it.

A: Take the shuttle bus to my hotel. I'll meet you in the lobby bar. Txt me when you arrive.

ok

The flight attendant stopped at my row and asked if I wanted another wine. I looked in amazement at the empty glass in my hand. "I'm good," I lied and handed her the glass. I put the phone on airplane mode to avoid further communication until I landed. Closing my eyes, I released a long, slow breath and hoped-for oblivion. Memories arrived instead.

A month shy of nine years ago, I'd drowned in her black pupils, deep pools set in caramel-colored eyes. We'd met in the Cincinnatian Hotel bar. My employer, Criminal Investigations Group, had assigned Abigail to be my bodyguard after I had been attacked while on a case. I smiled recalling her response when I'd asked her what I needed to know about having a bodyguard. "Only one thing," she'd said. "If I tell you to do something, you do it immediately, without any thought, without any question. You will do it because if you don't, you may not have a chance to do anything else."

And she had saved my life, as I had later saved hers. We'd shared great times and terrible times. She had been an integral part of one-sixth of my life. We had each been shot in the other's presence and each been the person responsible for the other's injury. We had brought down a lot of bad people. We'd been lovers, exclusively for most of those nine years, and yet we had been apart more than we'd been together. My attempts to draw us closer had resulted in my becoming her business partner—a decision I now realized might drive us permanently apart.

There was probably a better way, a much better way, to save our business and personal relationships than this ill-advised spur-of-the-moment trip. Given time, I might have figured it out. But I have never been a quitter, and despite the tension headache and queasy stomach the anticipation was causing me, I was not quitting on Jason Graham. And I wasn't quitting on Abigail. On us.

Saving us would require more than seeing Abigail and batting my baby blues at her. We needed to talk truth, and for that I needed to hear her words, see her eyes.

"Need any help with your luggage, sir?"

I blinked my eyes open to realize this was the attendant's polite way of telling me we were in Baton Rouge, and I must leave the safety of the plane.

PER ABIGAIL'S INSTRUCTIONS, I FOLLOWED the signs to the lobby bar, stopping in the doorway to scope out a good place to sit. My heart responded faster than my brain. Sitting in the far corner of the room, where she could observe everyone and everything, was the person I loved so much that each time I saw her my breath would catch. My heart's racing brought with it a kettle drum pounding in my head.

I lifted my hand in a wave that died in the thundercloud look she shot me. Sensing disaster, every rational part of me said this was a terrible idea. *Walk away*, logical brain yelled. I forced my feet to move across the burgundy carpet.

She sat with arms crossed, a clear, untouched drink in front of her. Since she was working, I'd bet on seltzer water. If it had been me, the glass would be empty of a double vodka. Opposite her, a red wine sat centered on a napkin. She gave the glass a stiff nod. "House cabernet. My best advice? Drink your wine and leave. We'll part as friends. A few months from now, we'll look at our time together with fondness."

Logic brain agreed. "And your worst advice?" Heart asked.

She shot a look at the ceiling. "You can find that on your own, Seamus. You can find that on your own." She closed her eyes, and I realized how difficult this meeting was for her.

I moved the wine glass and napkin to the place on her left and collapsed into the chair. After a healthy sip of the wine—could have been turpentine for all the attention I paid to its taste—I said, "Jason Graham's trail's gone cold. I still plan to do everything in my power to find and protect him. I'm here to learn everything, every single thing, you know about him. How he became a client. Where you picked him up. What the plan was for delivering him. When and to whom. Anything you know or suspect or even fear without any basis. I need it all, Abigail." I gulped the wine. "I will not give up until he's safely delivered wherever he's supposed to be, or I'm dead. . . . Or he's dead."

Several patrons glanced in our direction. I had not been using my inside voice.

She took a neat sip of whatever was in the glass. No bubbles. Gin? She folded her hands on the table and leaned in. "Do you think I've lied to you? That's what I hear in your tone. Have we fallen so far apart that we distrust each other? My reluctance to have you as my partner had nothing to do with trust, Seamus. Mixing love and work concerned me, and I was right. Each has ruined the other. Here we sit next to each other, but we aren't together. My mind is made up, Seamus. I can't take the pressure of working together and it hurts too much to see you. Maybe sometime we can be friends again, but not now, Seamus. Not now."

Each of us wanted control and, intellectually, I understood any successful partnership, business or love, required giving up control. I had tried. It hadn't always gone smoothly. My emotional response required more time to adjust to the change than my intellectual response, but over the last three years I had grown to feel comfortable with releasing total control. Perhaps Abigail would disagree with my self-assessment. In this crisis, she had reverted to her safety position: the firm ground of relying on herself. If I had ever earned her business confidence, I had lost it the moment I told her Jason Graham had disappeared.

I looked into her eyes and saw hard flint masking great pain. Maybe I was projecting.

"I understand our business partnership is in ashes," I said. "Before you said yes, I told you that if you ever thought it was not working, I wouldn't stand in your way if you wanted to go solo again. So, that's not what this discussion is about. This is about me making a commitment to you and to Elliot to keep him safe. You have nothing to lose by telling me everything you can about him."

A sudden idea struck me. "Unless the guy you're guarding is related to—"

"Totally separate. This is all Louisiana politics and bribery."

"Then it can't hurt to tell me everything you know. I take full responsibility for whatever has or will go wrong with the assignment to protect Graham. I'll give a sworn affidavit, whatever you need so this doesn't affect our business—your business. But you owe me this much."

She sipped her drink, keeping her gaze on me. I judged her single nod as agreement.

"Tell me how we, you, got this assignment."

"Elliot—I'll call him Elliot, since that's how I know him—just showed up one morning. He expected to testify in an August trial and feared for his life. The Marshals Service had offered to put him in protective custody, but he believed the people he was testifying against had penetrated all levels of government, including law enforcement. He did not trust anything the government might do for him because his name would show up in a database somewhere, and the government has proved none of its databases are safe."

Paddy would certainly agree.

"At first, he wouldn't even give me his name. I wondered if he was a nut job. And I had an easy out because his timing conflicted with this assignment in Baton Rouge. Then, he mentioned that the other reason he wanted private protection was to avoid being cooped up in some hotel room. He was going to prison after he testified, and he wanted to enjoy sniffing free air while he could. A lightbulb went off. You'd been lobbying for a more active role in our partnership, and it was abundantly clear you would never develop the skills to do personal protection the way I do it. But your camp would be the perfect place to sniff free air, and all you had to do was make sure no one saw him."

"Abundantly clear" was an understatement. Abigail had become so frustrated with me when I couldn't master even the rudimentary techniques she tried to teach me, like how to spot potential dangers in a room. I was continually distracted by an interesting conversation, or I concentrated too long on one person and ignored everything else happening around me. I never picked up the way Abigail could see everything happening in a room. "But you had to vet him somehow."

"Of course. Turns out, he got my name from one of the federal assistant prosecutors working in Chicago, someone I know fairly well. While Elliot was sitting with me, I called her on speaker phone. Elliot insisted we not use his name. My contact confirmed that they wanted Elliot to use the Marshals Service because they agreed some of their targets might want to kill him. But Elliot had balked, at which point she thought of me. She suggested to Elliot that, to minimize contact with the prosecutor's office, Elliot call them shortly before the trial date to make sure there were no delays."

"And you accepted him as a client."

"No, I told him about you and your place. He agreed for me to call you, and you jumped at the chance to do something for the partnership more than keep the books. After you agreed, he told me his name was Robert Elliot Savard. Well, I knew it was made up."

"How did he pay? Does that offer a hint of who he really is?"

"In full through the end of August by PayPal. We'd refund any time not used. In the unlikely event the trial was delayed into September, we'd bill him. The email address was something like 1xuse4Elliot. I picked him up the next day at a mall in Gurney.

"What happened on your trip up to camp?"

"Our agreement was for us to pay his expenses. He wouldn't need to carry ID, which made sense since he was using an assumed name. As a further safeguard, I insisted he not have anything with him that could point to his real identity. While he stayed in the car, I bought him new clothes in Green Bay. I later parceled the old clothes out to various nonprofits around Chicago. On the drive, we mostly talked world politics. What was going on in the Middle East, whether we'd end up in a conflict with Russia. The presidential race. That kind of stuff. I'm sorry, Seamus, but we discussed nothing personal that could help you guess where he might have gone."

I finished the glass of wine and waved away the waitress. Abigail was accustomed to my silences and sipped her drink. She was neither maintaining eye contact with me nor doing her bodyguard thing of hawking the room. Reading her body language was simple: her mouth formed an unyielding line. Her glass became the subject of her focus. With no sense of a positive vibe from her, I yielded to a strong urge to touch her hand.

She shook her head. "Don't make it harder on either of us. I expected my assignment here would end shortly before Elliot's trial began, and I'd pick him up and see he got to court safely."

"Would your prosecutor friend give you more information if you asked directly?"

"Probably not, but until we know what's happened to Elliot, asking would not be appropriate. Look, Seamus, you need to be realistic. Unless Elliot contacts you, there's nothing you can do. You're not a tracker, and even if you were, it's been more than three days. If by some miracle you did find him, how would you know if your presence helped him or gave the people who are after him a second shot at silencing him?"

She laid her hand lightly on my forearm. "With financial stuff, your knowledge and supremely logical mind make you the best. Dealing with people . . . Well, you're naively optimistic. You assume everyone is as inherently good and as logical as you. But even you—when you find yourself challenged—jettison logic and become impetuous. Proof, you're here right now. You become as unreasonable as a wolf caught in a trap. With no thought for the future, you'll chew off your own foot to escape."

"A wolf in a trap?"

She gave my arm a squeeze and removed her hand. "There's a Chinese proverb that loosely translated says, 'He who rides a tiger is afraid to dismount.' And a limerick goes, 'There was a young lady of Niger who smiled as she rode on a tiger; they returned from the ride with the lady inside, and the smile on the face of the tiger.' If you combine those two, Seamus, you arrive at the solution to the tiger problem."

She was staring directly at me. I raised my hands, palms up in supplication. "I have no idea what that means."

"Have the wisdom to not climb onto a tiger. But if you find yourself riding one, you must find a safe way to dismount or you lose yourself— either by paralysis, fearful of what might happen, or by being swallowed whole. That tiger has been us, Seamus." She closed her eyes for a moment. "We're our own tiger. I turned down your marriage proposal even though I loved you because I knew we—I—was too independent to make it work. But, in a moment of weakness, I let your baby blues and your crooked smile and your earnest proposal for us to work together . . . I let them seduce me up onto the tiger's back. And it's ruined everything. Everything."

I brushed away the tears leaking from my eyes. "I'm sorry to have hurt you. There's nothing I can do or say, is there?"

She pushed her chair away from the table and stood. I sat looking up, dreading the words that would kill my last hope. "If I hear anything regarding Elliot," she said, "I promise to contact you. Otherwise, it would be best if we made a clean break of it."

No words escaped the black hole of my emptiness. After what felt like ten minutes, but was probably really measured in seconds, she walked away. Moments later a ding announced the elevator.

The waitress checked if I wanted anything else. I choked out, "What do I owe you?"

"Oh, Miss Hancock has taken care of everything."

"Indeed, she has," I said.

TWENTY-TWO

THE HAPPY REAPER SHIVERED ON the drive from the Iron River, Michigan motel where he'd spent the night. The current forty-three degrees ushered in by an overnight cold front made Scotland balmy in comparison, and he regretted leaving his cold-weather gear in storage. Why couldn't his targets stay in warm places? Maybe in the future he could add a cold-weather bonus clause to his contracts.

He followed the plat map he'd acquired yesterday from a gas station/ convenience store near the hotel and headed east on US-2. He'd left at 2:00 a.m. to give himself three hours to get into position before Seamus McCree got up—at least that was his routine nine years ago when he'd followed McCree in Ohio.

He hit the first patch of fog in a dip on the Bates–Amasa Road. The water was warmer than the air, and cloud tendrils floated over every place water collected. Hard to know if it would help his surveillance or make it difficult to see what was happening. Not knowing the roads, he slowed down. The bars had recently closed, and he hoped no drunk was coming the other way. Wouldn't that be a kicker?

And from nowhere and everywhere came Radiohead singing "Fog" in his head. The song had struck him hard at first hearing—as though it had been written just for him, with its question in the refrain: *Did you go bad?*

He whistled the tune to the end to avoid it becoming an earworm, then considered his plans for the day. With luck, he'd spot Jason Graham.

Otherwise, he might have to have a conversation with one of the McCrees. He hoped it wouldn't come to that, but . . .

My first stop after an uneventful return flight to Chicago was Abigail's place. One kindness I could perform was to remove my stuff so she didn't have to do it. Nervous hand tremors forced me to use my left hand to steady my right to slot the key. I disarmed the alarm and grabbed several plastic bags from the laundry room.

My knees buckled at the bathroom door. The place smelled of Abigail, a pleasant mixture of her shampoo and scented dryer sheets. I opened the vanity cabinet under the sink and grabbed the small leather Dopp kit that held my items. Rooting through the linen closet, I found my multivitamins and baby aspirin and dropped them into one of the plastic bags.

Into another bag, I emptied the bureau drawer set aside for me containing socks, underwear, and T-shirts. I retrieved a pair of jeans and a flannel shirt hanging in the closet. The sight of a suit carrier reminded me to take the blue pinstriped suit with all its paraphernalia including dress shoes, with socks stuffed inside. I laid those on my side of the bed. Well, it wasn't my side any more, was it? *Now's not the time to wallow in self-pity.*

Taking a position in the center of the room, I slowly rotated to spot anything I'd missed. I caught my reflection in the mirror. Frown lines etched my forehead. Dark bags sagged under my eyes. To say I hadn't slept well was putting lipstick on the pig of my distress. I had not needed the alarm to wake me in time for my four-thirty taxi to the airport. "You look like a caricature of a sad sack," I told the reflection.

Even the attempted repartee with my mirrored image sounded flat and hollow.

A picture of Abigail, Megan, and me that Paddy had taken occupied a corner of her bureau. I lifted it and tried to remember the moment. We were on Navy Pier. Perched on my shoulders, Megan held onto my ears while I supported her back with one arm, my other wrapped around Abigail's waist. Paddy had caught us all laughing. Standing there, I couldn't remember what had tickled our fancies.

If she asked, how would I explain to Megan where Abigail was? I'm not sure how long I remained motionless before snapping out of it. I set the picture down and picked up Abigail's Chanel Coco Parfum bottle. I disengaged the stopper and touched it to the inside of my wrist—a foolish thing to do. My body heat reacted to the perfume and Abigail's scent filled my senses. Again, I lost control of my tears.

In the living room, I spotted one of my John McPhee books, left on the end table next to the chair I read in. I dropped it into the plastic bag with stuff from the bathroom. No reason to check the kitchen, and I never went into her spare bedroom. I had everything and no excuse for remaining.

Stealing a sheet of paper from the printer waiting with the monitor for the return of Abigail's laptop, I sat at the kitchen table and wrote:

> *Abigail—Here is your key. I was in town and figured you would appreciate me removing my things to save you the trouble. I hope I didn't miss anything. I wish I were blessed with an Irish poet's great gift of words, but I have none of that talent. I hope you know that I love you and have always wanted nothing but the best for you. I am so sorry to bring you such distress. I don't want to become maudlin, so I'll stop. Thank you for our years together.*
>
> *Love,*
> *Seamus*

Rereading the note made me realize that even in saying goodbye I was self-centered: all but the first and last sentences started with the word "I." So be it. I removed her house key from my key ring, gave the cold metal a kiss, and laid it on top of the note.

BY MIDMORNING THE HAPPY REAPER knew neither McCree nor Jason Graham were at McCree's place. He retreated to his rental and traded binoculars for the day pack with tools he might need to explore McCree's buildings. The cabin wouldn't take much time, so he tackled it first, slipping on surgical gloves. Both the door to the screened porch and to the interior cabin were unlocked. The picnic table on the porch held a five-gallon container partially filled with water and a two-burner propane stove with instant coffee and a single clean coffee mug next to it. Unless McCree had taken up coffee, someone else had been spending time there.

Two plastic chairs surrounded an empty cooler that probably doubled as a table. A load of wood was neatly stacked against the wall of the one-room cabin. The inside air was tinged with a hint of wood smoke. Crumpled newsprint and split cedar kindling had been laid in the small Jotul woodstove, ready to be lit by a box of safety matches kept in a nearby tin.

Bookshelves lined the walls above the numerous windows. All fiction, alphabetical by author. On a round table, someone had left an opened book flipped upside down. From his search of McCree's Cincinnati house all those years ago, he recollected that McCree had used bookmarks. Was he less caring at his camp or was someone else the reader? *Liar's Poker* in paperback was the kind of book McCree might own, but why have one nonfiction book in a sea of fiction? Jason Graham might also like reading about bond trading at Solomon Brothers in the '80s.

From underneath the unused bed, he extracted a baby doll, complete with Velcro diaper and onesie. Having a little kid around was not a complication the Happy Reaper needed. He returned the doll to its hiding place.

The outhouse had been recently used. Interesting, since the house clearly had indoor plumbing. Why would someone choose to take a dump in a privy when they were only a couple hundred feet away from modern conveniences?

While on the path between the cabin and the house, he heard a vehicle approaching on the road. Was McCree returning? He hurried to a spot where he could watch both the house and cabin and remain hidden from the road. In place, he tapped the pistol strapped to his waist, knowing it was there, but even after all these years, checking. He listened to the vehicle approaching in a series of alternating squeaks and thumps, as it found potholes, and engine accelerations in the smoother areas.

Closer.

Approaching the cabin driveway.

Past the cabin driveway.

Passing his position.

Near the house driveway.

Continuing.

He resumed his normal breathing and scrambled down the hill to the generator shed, where he opened the unlocked door and quickly surveyed the building's contents: generator, battery bank, solar inverter, new and used engine oil. Nothing of interest.

Walking past the garage, he confirmed the closed doors were all unlocked. He doubted there'd be anything of interest there; he'd check the house first and, if he came up empty, then he'd search the garage. Unlike everything else on the property, all the house doors were locked. He chose to pick the lock of the door between the screened porch and the living room. Farthest from the driveway and closest to the woods, it provided a safe escape should someone happen to show up. He spread the lock picks on a porch table and started the timer on his cell phone. Three minutes eighteen seconds to open it.

Cool air from the house met his entrance. He closed his eyes and let his senses take in the house. A ticking pendulum clock. No refrigerator motor. No water heater. No A/C. Was the power on? He sniffed the air. The house smelled fresh, no different than the woods. It hadn't been closed for long. Stepping inside, he left the door open to better hear approaching traffic. He flipped a switch and a fan lazily rotated overhead. Experiment successful, he shut off the fan. Letting warm air in might not tip McCree to the presence of visitors, but leaving a fan on surely would.

The place was no more than 1,500 square feet of living space, but with cathedral ceilings and a wall of glass facing the lake, the deck in front and the large screened porch at the side, it felt much larger. He'd quickly walk through the house to make sure he understood its layout before doing a detailed search. Walking past the dining room table, he glanced at an open packet of material. Jason Graham's name caught his attention. He forced himself to continue to breathe naturally as he leafed through the material that included printouts from his trolling website and handwritten notes in two distinctive styles. A flush of self-congratulation ran through him. His hunch had been right: McCree and Graham were linked.

He continued his survey of the house, through the kitchen with its softly burbling propane refrigerator (freezer and refrigerator working) and found the back door had a disengaged deadbolt. He could leave by that door and use the button on the knob to lock the door behind him when he pulled it closed. Much faster than having to leave by the screened-porch door he entered and use picks to lock the door.

Upstairs he discovered an open laptop plugged into a display and printer. On the corner of the desk was a picture of Seamus and a tall brunette, their arms wrapped around each other. Not family, this had to be Abigail Hancock. Two books sitting on the desk both had bookmarks and the small basket holding pens and pencils had several more. In the basement, he found McCree's nonfiction collection, sorted by topic, with a spot for the missing *Liar's Poker.* Someone had been sharing space with Seamus, he was almost sure.

Quick reconnaissance complete, he gave himself a prioritized list: (1) read the papers on the dining room table, (2) crack McCree's computer and check his browser history and recent documents to figure out why McCree was running searches on Jason Graham, (3) check the house from top to bottom for anything related to Graham.

All keeping in mind that McCree could show up at any minute from wherever he was.

TWENTY-THREE

PATRICK WAS THE THIRD TO reach the front door after its bell rang. Atty raced down the stairs, barking all the way to the front door. Megan engaged in hot pursuit, grabbing onto the railing with one hand while descending each step first with one foot and then the other, all the while ineffectually telling the dog to sit. Patrick wove his way through dog and daughter and was shocked to see his father peering in the side window, watching the circus. It had been less than twenty-four hours since his father had dropped Atty home, and Patrick was surprised he was back so soon.

He unlocked the door, let his father in. The dog, seeing who the visitor was, flipped on her back, blocking the stairs, demanding belly rubs before anyone could pass. Patrick scrutinized his father's appearance. People usually focused first on his brilliant blue eyes and then his crooked nose. Now Patrick's attention was drawn to the worry lines creasing his forehead and deep bags beneath his eyes, sucking all the warmth from them. Protruding cheekbones more dominant than the bumps and off-kilter shape of his thrice-broken nose suggested his father had either lost weight or was severely dehydrated.

Entrance fee extracted, Atty headed upstairs. His father lifted a squealing Megan high over his head, threatening to drop her. She shrieked in the way little girls do to pierce adult ear drums. He set her down on two feet and allowed her to hold his finger with one hand while they inched up the stairs. Even with whatever had increased his concerns, he was a patient grandfather. Megan was so lucky to have that relationship.

"Okay, Megan," Patrick said once they had climbed the stairs, "Grampa Seamus and I need to talk. Why don't you finish coloring the page in your fairy book so you can show Grampa what fine work you do?" To his father, "You eaten?"

"Not hungry, thanks."

"Well, you look like something the cat wouldn't bother to drag in. You're eating something anyway. What's up?"

Dealing strictly with facts, his father related his current understanding of the status of the murder investigations, Jason Graham, and the results of his trip to see Abigail. Patrick felt sick for his father. He and Abigail had been so good for each other, although they often couldn't see it themselves. Patrick made soothing sounds he knew meant nothing and stuck sliced cantaloupe in front of his father. What could a child say to a parent about relationships?

His father brushed aside his murmurs. "I figure I need to find Graham. Are you, by any chance, still in touch with Molly Fitzhugh? I need a tracker I can trust."

Not the reason he was here, Patrick thought. He heard himself reply, "She's Molly Burroughs now. She took Jeff's name, remember? I follow them both on Facebook." He grabbed his cell phone, pulled up the app, and the messenger box. "I don't have her phone number, but she checks Facebook."

His father messaged Molly to call his number concerning a tracking assignment. The dog butted his hand. "Not now, girl. Find your spot."

The dog huffed a complaint and looked at Patrick, her hopeful eyes clearly wanting to elicit a better command. "You heard him, Atty," Patrick said. "Go place." He pointed to her bed in the corner of the room. There had to be something else his father wanted. "What else?"

"Remember how you used crowdsourcing to discover Agent Pendergast's identity?"

Patrick nodded warily. "Eat your melon."

He cut into the flesh with his spoon, releasing a ripe melon smell.

"Can we do something similar with Jason Graham? Something so he'll know to contact me if he wants help or to at least let me know he's okay?" He ate a small bite of the melon. "I don't even know exactly what I'm asking."

"Let's talk it through," Patrick said. "We already know who Jason is, so what I did with Pendergast is moot here. What you want is for him to contact you, right?" His father agreed and Patrick continued. "Consider how we found out who he was. We stumbled onto the website his parents put up. Why not tell them it's important for them to let you know if they hear from their son?"

"I'd need a good reason, and I'd have to lie about seeing Jason or knowing where he's been."

Without either of them noticing, Atty had released herself from her spot and now leaned against the elder McCree, laying her head in his lap. His father cracked a small smile and rubbed her head. "Who could say no to such a hound?"

"Come on, Dad," Patrick said. "One hand for the dog, and one for eating. I suppose I could set up a website that would rank high if he searches his own name. That would require some spectacular SEO and getting a lot of other places to link to it."

Patrick had to explain that SEO stood for search engine optimization, but his father forestalled any longer explanation.

"But how do we alert him," his father asked, "without alerting those who don't want him to testify?"

"You'd have to come up with a search term only he would use. But still he'd have to have access to electronics to do the search and think to search on your chosen term."

His father's head dropped and he rubbed his eyes. "I'm grasping at straws."

Megan sang her way in from the kitchen with her coloring book open. "Look, Grampa Seamus." She placed the open book on top of Atty's head, which the dog found acceptable. His father flipped the pages and oohed and aahed. Megan wasn't at the stage where she was coloring within the lines, but she had paid attention to lines being there and Grampa Seamus told her how delighted he was to see her creative color choices for the butterfly.

Yep, Patrick thought, while thumbing through some quick internet searches, *not too many pink and green butterflies around*. "Okay, sweetheart," he said, "why don't you do another one to show Grampa Seamus before he goes."

She sang herself out of the room and Atty trotted behind, maybe hoping food was involved.

"While you were encouraging the next Picasso," Patrick said, "I tried a bunch of searches with Elliot and Jason Graham. Won't work. One of his former partners was an Elliot. Maybe that's why he picked the name. I don't know what to tell you, Dad. I can gather more details of his life from the internet, but I don't think it'll help. It's not like I could pinpoint the person he's most likely to trust, and he's unlikely to post pictures on an Instagram account showing where he's at."

"I'm beginning to think Abigail was right again. There's nothing I can do, unless someone like Molly can follow a many-days-old trail."

"It sucks, I know. Eat." He waited until his father took another bite. "I don't have anything I need to do today other than take care of the munchkin. While you're driving home, I can get two or three hours of serious research in on Jason Graham. Maybe something will pop. Cindy already checked their clippings morgue to see if they had anything on him, but I can ask her to check with their St. Louis affiliate to see what they have in their files."

"Give your beautiful wife a kiss for me and thank her. And thank you for everything you've done. I really am sorry to have screwed up your trip back to camp with Megan."

"We'll be back. You want to take Atty for company? I know dealing with this and with Abigail and . . . Well, Dad, don't be pissed at me because I mean it in the best way, but I'm a little worried about you."

His father gave a shrug. "Whatever. Let me check on our artist in the kitchen and be on my way."

Patrick realized he had not managed to get much food into his father. "Finish the melon. I'll make oatmeal. No? Then promise me you'll eat. I've got stuff in the freezer I can send along with you." Patrick's feeling that he was pushing too hard was confirmed by his father's response.

"Enough, Patrick. I'm not ready for a nursing home."

* * *

Rain found me at Green Bay and pelted me all the way up US-141. The foul weather matched my mood as the reality of my failed relationship with Abigail continued to eat at me. Molly Burroughs, nee Fitzhugh, a tracker I had met years ago on the same assignment that introduced me to Abigail, had called me back. She was pleased to hear from me, but dismissed as "totally a waste of time" my request for her to try to track an ATV on gravel roads since ridden on by multiple vehicles, especially with the inch of rain expected in the next twenty-four hours. If I came up with a more recent sighting, I should give her a call.

I was running out of options, and disappointment rode on my shoulder like a turkey vulture smelling of death. From nowhere, I started singing the lyrics to "Me and Bobby McGee." Sometimes I have no idea what triggers my internal jukebox selection. This time I suspected my internal search engine had picked up on feeling busted flat, Baton Rouge, and singing the blues. Or maybe the line about freedom being just another word for nothing left to lose had called to me. I finished the song, feeling drained and wondering what tune would pop up next.

"Hey Jude" was it, but I had no more than vocalized the title words when a good idea struck me.

Jason had gotten a real kick listening to *Telephone Time*. If he was holed up in the listening area, I'd bet he'd tune in if he could. I pulled off the highway at the marker for the forty-fifth parallel, the spot on US-141 half between the equator and the north pole, and composed an ad. I connected with the business manager and told her what I had in mind. They'd be happy to run it once an hour for the rest of the week, starting at six tonight. All they needed was my credit card number.

On the road again, I tried to short-circuit the depressed disk jockey in my head and tuned the radio to NPR news. I got so riled up listening to the Republican and Democratic candidates not answer reporters' questions about how they planned to handle illegal immigration issues that I yelled at the radio. That didn't solve any immigration issue but did make me temporarily forget my problems.

At the commercial break, Mr. Bleak returned by realizing Owen had been too busy confessing and must have forgotten to inform Sheriff Bartelle of the break-in at his friend Pete Bjork's place. Sitting in jail with nothing to do but think, he'd eventually correct the omission and my shit would hit the fan.

TWENTY-FOUR

ENTERING MY HOUSE, MY SKIN tingled with unease. I aborted kicking off my shoes in the mud room and listened hard. The grandmother clock ticked, and I caught the movement of air caused by the propane refrigerator. Nothing else. And yet something had triggered my reaction.

I pinched my nose shut, held it to a slow count of sixty, and inhaled through it to try to catch a hint of an out-of-place odor. Couldn't get it. I walked through the kitchen and checked the carbon monoxide monitor plugged into the wall by the dining room. Green light. The stove clock showed the correct time and was not blinking, so the power hadn't gone out—a rare event in any case, given I was off grid.

The windows and doors on the main floor were all locked. I galloped down the basement stairs, but the door into the basement was still locked from this side. I opened the door and checked the two windows in the west wall—no broken panes of glass. Nothing out of place in the basement.

I hustled to the second floor. Windows locked. Door onto the deck outside the bedroom Jason had been using was still locked.

The tingling skin disappeared, but something still felt wrong. Grabbing a couple of yogurts from the refrigerator for lunch, I checked the papers on the dining room table—all there. I carted the food upstairs to eat while I checked email. Had Paddy sent me anything from his internet sleuthing? I opened the lid of the laptop, bringing it out of sleep mode. Before the email program had even loaded, the fan kicked on.

The laptop had been hibernating for more than a day. Why did it need to cool down?

No messages from Paddy, but the fan was still running. I stuck my hand next to the exhaust. Hot air. Despite half of me pooh-poohing the idea, the tingly-skin half of me pulled up the browsers and checked them for recent activity. None. But even I knew how to erase evidence of searches and websites visited. I logged into my satellite provider's website and checked usage during the last forty-eight hours. A burst of activity shortly before Atty and I left. Nothing for a day and then earlier today a new burst of activity.

I closed my eyes to think, but couldn't make any sense of the whole thing. The release I felt with my frustrated, "Oh, screw it," produced a possible solution: a system update while I was away might have wakened the computer from its sleep. The icon for the Windows message center showed no new messages, and the version of Windows 10 I was running had last been updated a week earlier. So that wasn't it.

Could a modem update have roused the computer? I didn't think so. Besides, that would consist of a single download, and this activity lasted more than an hour and involved data moving in both directions.

My network wasn't secured on the assumption no one would come all the way to my place to steal internet access. Had someone visited and brought their phone onto the screened porch? If their phone was set to pick up public Wi-Fi, it would automatically glom onto my network and use it rather than their provider's network to run a bunch of app updates.

Dumb thinking. I was missing the most important clue: my computer was hot. Someone stealing network resources couldn't have affected my computer.

I hadn't touched the yogurts and decided to bring them to the screened porch to eat. The door from the living room to the porch was locked but not in the position I normally leave it. Ratcheting up the handle of the french doors inserts a bar into the frame to keep the door tight and square. Whenever I locked the door, I ratcheted the handle. A habit, yes, but had I ever forgotten? Sure. Often? Less frequently than a blue moon. The builder had pounded it into my head, and it became part of my routine. I checked the door from the TV room to the porch. Locked with the bar extended.

Like a bursting firework, the conclusion blasted over me. Someone had been in the house. Absolutely. Positively. Maybe.

Checking the driveway for tracks in the now pouring rain, I spotted only my recent ones. Maybe after the rain stopped and the water drained through the gravel, I might find evidence of other traffic.

The wildlife camera! I had placed the wildlife camera on the road to capture pictures of animals traveling past my place, mostly at night. In past years I had caught deer, moose, coyotes, wolf, raccoon, fox, and a gazillion trucks and cars. Also humans walking, jogging, bicycling, or ATVing past the camera. Currently set to cover the road on the far side of the driveway to the cabin, the camera had mostly captured pictures of deer crossing to get to a salt block I'd placed between the cabin and the house.

Ten minutes later I had the camera in the house, extracted the microSD card, and plopped it into the laptop. Since I had erased the disk and changed the camera location, even excluding the bumper crop of deer pictures, there were several hundred images to go through. Reviewing them documented my frequent jogs. My car and truck triggered three shots each time they passed the camera. Paddy's vehicle arrived. We all departed for town and returned. I paused at the picture of a truck towing a trailer. I zoomed in on the side of the truck and stared at the screen.

No shit. Friday, between the time Paddy, Megan, and I had gone into town and the storm struck, an Environmentally Friendly Extraction, LLC truck towing a trailer had driven up our road. I wrote the exact time on a notepad. Ten minutes later, the same truck and trailer passed by the camera going the other way. *Why didn't I think to check the camera before?*

Had Cabibi's presence somehow triggered Graham's flight? Questions noted on the pad, I pressed on. Next shots: Me out to clear the road of debris. Me returning, the Subaru finally returning. Then, Paddy, me, Paddy, me. Paddy, me. A doe and fawn with long ungainly legs trailing behind. Me leaving for Chicago. A person walking at the side of the road. The person returning the way he'd come. The person coming again, this time with a backpack.

I zoomed in and my blood drained to my toes. The self-proclaimed Happy Reaper walked down my road. Early forties now, but with the same lanky frame, same short brown hair, same good-looking face that made one young witness call him "hot, but not that hot."

I felt the prick of his knife on my neck. I heard the hiss of his words: "If you keep looking for me, I'll still be a Happy Reaper because you won't get me. You'll be dead. Or maybe it's your son, Patrick, who'll be dead. Understand?"

He had broken into my house at the end of the same assignment that had introduced me to both Molly Fitzhugh and Abigail. In my bullheadedness and stupidity, I had tried to learn who he was. But Paddy and I had hit a brick wall and given up. Periodically I'd ask friends in various law enforcement agencies involved with the case for an update in the search for the Happy Reaper. They never had good news.

And here he was. In my woods. And I knew, without doubt, he had again been in my house and had looked at my computer.

Why now?

Jason Graham.

If the Happy Reaper was on his trail, Jason was in big trouble. I had foiled the Happy Reaper nine years ago and earned his respect—or so he'd said. Not that I cared. The person who called himself the Happy Reaper had killed hundreds of people and, from what I understood, was considered tops in the murder-for-hire business.

I looked at my hands, wondering if the shaking appendages belonged to someone else.

The next trail cam pictures were the last, evidence of my return today. What was I to do? Jason Graham had become a much larger problem than I had ever imagined.

I don't know how long I sat at my desk daydreaming. The crunch of tires on my gravel driveway stirred me from the unprofitable musing. *The Happy Reaper returns?* I dropped to the floor and crawled to the loft window and raised my head and looked out.

The rain had stopped and Chief Bartelle was exiting his cruiser.

Twenty-Five

BARTELLE WAS HEADING FOR THE back door when Seamus McCree hurried down the ramp. The guy looked pasty—sweat pouring down his cheeks—and wobbly—a breath of air might knock him over.

"What the hell's wrong with you?" Bartelle took McCree's arm and steered him up the ramp and onto the screened porch. "Sit. You having a heart attack?"

He claimed he didn't need anything, but then blathered, "I received some disturbing news. I assume you're not here for a social visit. Did you want me to come in and look at Cabibi's finances or something?"

McCree's forehead felt hot to Bartelle, but not fevered. McCree was not thinking clearly if he thought Bartelle would drive twenty-five miles instead of making a phone call. "Stay," he told McCree and rushed inside, finding glasses in one of the cupboards and returning with a glass of water. "You sure you're not sick?"

McCree drank and Bartelle pulled out a chair and sat. "We fingerprinted anything found in the search yesterday that looked like it had been left recently. Your prints came up on a hatchet. Tex thought one of the Mississippi State kids had found it. So, I want to understand how your fingerprints got on it."

"Is Owen still insisting he killed Cabibi?"

Bartelle wondered what that had to do with his question, but McCree did have a habit of asking questions instead of answering them. "He's not saying much of anything, but he has taken responsibility."

"And you think he did it?" McCree squeezed the arms of the chair.

What has upset him so? Bartelle put on his narrow-eyes-stern-cop look, and leaning toward McCree, placed both forearms on the table. "You have a reason to think he didn't? You haven't answered about the hatchet."

"The hatchet was mine. I have some stuff inside you need to see."

He led a surprised Bartelle inside, swept a bunch of papers on the dining room table into a pile and set up his laptop. He grabbed a dirty glass stored in a plastic bag over to the sink, filled his own glass with more water. "You want anything to drink?"

"Thanks, no." Bartelle saw the computer screen contained a blurry picture of Cabibi's truck. The time stamp dated it as the morning of the day Cabibi died. "The time stamp accurate?"

"Within a few minutes. The picture's from my road. I was protecting a guy here until he could testify at a trial. Jason Graham is his name, although I didn't know it at the time. He disappeared after I went into town the day of the storm."

For once McCree was talkative, taking Bartelle through the material lying on the table. McCree explained how Jason had stolen his hatchet. He also confessed to seeing the Rockport print near where they found Cabibi's body and recognizing it as Jason's. "Later, I discovered a nearby camp had a snapped chain. I found Cabibi's ATV, but no Jason Graham. I think he's stolen another ATV from that camp. That's it."

Bartelle had suspected McCree was uneasy about something, but never would have guessed this. "I don't even know how many laws you've broken, Seamus. Obstructing justice at a minimum."

"If Owen hadn't confessed, I'd have told you earlier. But he did. I recalibrated, deciding I owed my client protection if his existence wasn't material to your investigation."

Bartelle cocked his head and squinted one eye. "You changed your mind because we found your prints on the hatchet? Why not lie and tell me you accidentally picked it up. I would've believed you. What's your motivation for telling me now? And why does this mean Owen Lyndstrom didn't kill the guy, which he swears he did?"

"Because I just looked at the trail cam this afternoon and because I haven't gotten to the worst of it yet. Earlier today a hired killer who calls himself the Happy Reaper was here. I was coming back from Chicago, so I didn't see him, but the trail cam caught pictures of him walking up the road. Even though I've only seen him from a distance, I know it's him."

McCree brought a series of pictures up on the screen.

Bartelle shifted his glance between McCree and the screen. "Keep talking. Who is this guy and why does this mean Owen is innocent?"

"He refers to himself as the Happy Reaper. Before I knew that, I thought of him as the Celtic Cross Killer because he has an ornate tattoo of the cross in the small of his back. He's a high-powered hitman who leaves a calling card with the same Celtic cross and the words 'Results Guaranteed.' And he's here."

Catching another contradiction, it took an extreme effort for Bartelle not to cuff the guy and throw his ass into the cruiser. "Wait, which was it? You talked to him or you saw him from a distance?"

"Both. I saw him from a distance. The time we spoke, he was behind me holding a knife to my throat."

"A story I'd like to hear later. I take it you think *he* killed Cabibi?"

"With a rock? Hell no, he's not one of those guys who makes his hits look like accidents. He plants his calling card on his victims to claim them. It's much more likely he's here on Jason Graham's trail."

Bartelle was feeling more and more frustrated. This whole thing made no sense at all. He was missing something, or McCree was addled. "Why would he show up here now? Did this Jason Graham of yours—have I ever told you I always suspect people with two first names? Did he do something to draw attention to himself? Or do you think somehow Cabibi's death attracted him? Or finding the bones?"

"Why would the Happy Reaper pay me a visit if it was any of those? Why would he even know I was here? I am almost positive someone was in here—this house—while I was away. That's what made me look at the wildlife camera in the first place. Nine years ago, the Happy Reaper broke into my house in Cincinnati, and the only way I knew he'd been inside was because he left a card on my refrigerator. He's capable of picking locks. Someone has been here using my computer. Leaping to conclusions I can't justify, I suspect someone noticed internet traffic either Paddy or I generated and sicced the Happy Reaper on me."

Bartelle couldn't control the disbelief that painted his face. "That makes no fucking sense at all."

"Look, I feel terrible that I've been lying to you, and I know it sounds like I created a mythical monster to try to make my misdeeds pale in comparison. You can check with Lieutenant Tanya Hastings of the Cincinnati Police Department—you've spoken to her before. Or I can give you some names at the FBI."

"I could, and maybe I will. Assuming I believe all this. Knowing you, you have a plan. Give."

"I arranged for *TT* to broadcast a coded message to Jason. He doesn't know I know his real name. I knew him as Elliot, and I don't believe many people knew he was using that name. Certainly no one up here apart from Owen."

"Wait." Bartelle laid a hand on McCree's arm. "Lyndstrom knows about the guy you were guarding?"

"Remember? That's the reason I was babysitting the leg bone at Cabibi's truck instead of Owen waiting for you. I had him searching for Elliot."

Bartelle shot him a confused look.

"Oh right," McCree said. "I told you Owen was checking for storm damage."

Bartelle massaged the back of his neck. *What a barrel of snakes. None of this proved Lyndstrom didn't kill Cabibi. And if Lyndstrom was looking for this Jason Graham character, it was more likely that he, rather than McCree, found the cut chain at a camp, which meant McCree was still filtering the truth.* "Assuming you're right, and this Happy Reaper character thinks you know something about Jason Graham, are you now the one needing protection? What are you going to do, Seamus?"

The question knocked McCree off his pins. His eyes grew vacant, and he lost what little color he had.

"Seamus, this isn't the time for your silence act."

McCree snapped back. "He could have killed me and he didn't. During the intervening years, he could have easily found and killed me if he had wanted. My gut says he's targeting Jason. It's less than a week before the trial starts. I was supposed to protect Jason until then, and I aim to do exactly that—if he contacts me."

Bartelle flashed back to a similar conversation several years ago. "You're an obstinate Irishman, and I don't need to remind you that a lot of good people died proving we can't protect people against a determined attack deep in the woods. Come into town. It's safer."

McCree held up his hands as if defending himself from Bartelle's assault. "If he wants to kill me, at least I won't endanger anyone else if I stay here — but, I don't think he does. Look, seeing pictures of the Happy Reaper rattled me, and I jumped to that story without following my whole train of thought. What if an outsider killed Cabibi, say, Jason Graham? Here's one scenario. Cabibi stops by my place while I'm gone. I don't know why. I wasn't expecting him. Jason sees him, steals supplies, and runs away because he's scared someone knows he's at my place. Maybe Cabibi saw him, or Jason knew Cabibi from the past. The tracks showed he didn't follow Cabibi. He was going the other way around the lake. But we know from Jason's footprints that he ended up in the same general area as Cabibi. At first, I didn't think the timing worked, but if they did overlap, picture a confrontation that resulted in Jason picking up a rock and clobbering Cabibi. Then he tried to hide the body and stole Cabibi's ATV and took off."

More fantastic speculation. "You forgot the part where the Martians scooped Jason up and spirited him away. Your fairy tale hasn't explained why Lyndstrom would lie—certainly not to protect some guy he'd never met."

McCree let out a poof of air. "No disagreement. My brain's scrambled eggs. I know you need to talk to the prosecutor and see if he wants to charge me, but Jason Graham was linked to financial crimes and I'm becoming convinced Cabibi frightened him off. If a link exists between him and Cabibi, isn't it possible we'd find it by looking through Cabibi's finances? Or maybe that's where we find the link to Owen to seal your case. I'd like to look through Cabibi's papers, but I understand if I'm tainted in your eyes."

"What you are," Bartelle said, "is fucking crazy and making no fucking sense. Get your ass down to the office tomorrow morning, no later than nine, and we'll revisit this whole thing with the prosecutor. I'm taking all this material. It's evidence. Right now, you are going to show me exactly where Cabibi's ATV is hidden."

Twenty-Six

BARTELLE PULLED OFF LUKES ROAD and snapped pictures of the gate with its cut chain and dangling lock, and of the crushed mustard garlic. Few tracks would remain after the hard rainfall, but in case a sheltered spot still harbored a clue, he told McCree to get out and follow him for the walk up the long driveway.

"Oh crap," McCree said at his first view of the clearing around the cabin. He pointed to the charred remains of an ATV. "I swear, it was in the garage."

"Stay right there. I don't want you fucking anything else up. Hear me? The damn thing wouldn't be like that if you had told me everything earlier, would it? Why would someone destroy this ATV? Because it contained evidence, McCree. Evidence now lost to us."

Bartelle sniffed: no hint of the fire. The storm had blown away the stench of melted plastic and burned petrochemicals. He faced McCree. "If you want me to take you home, you'll have to wait until my tech gets here, and we've collected evidence and dusted the place for prints. Or you can hoof it. Either way I want you at my office at nine tomorrow morning."

"I'll jog home. I could use the exercise. And I'll be there tomorrow. Again, I'm sorry, Lon."

Bartelle wanted to smack the guy, but that wouldn't do any good except make himself feel better for three seconds. "That's Chief Bartelle. Nine sharp."

He watched McCree jog down the driveway. McCree could run home, take a shower, and be sipping wine before the evidence tech even got here. Bartelle wasn't sure he believed McCree, but he didn't disbelieve him either. A possible hitman running around meant he would definitely wait for backup to clear buildings.

He walked to his car and called the office, ordering Tex to get his ass up here with his evidence kit. Bartelle sat under the shade of a spruce. With at least an hour's wait, he could either nap or use the downtime to think through the evidence against Owen Lyndstrom. The confession didn't conflict with anything they knew, but it didn't provide any new information either. Owen could have pieced his confession together based on what he'd gleaned with his big ears. He claimed the storm reached him while he was in the woods near Hemlock Lake. He was working his way out and heard a chainsaw off Lukes Road. Figuring someone might be trapped, he went in to help and found Cabibi. Words were said and riled Owen sufficiently that he picked up a handy rock and killed Cabibi with a single blow.

Owen used Cabibi's ATV to drag the body to the hemlock and covered it with branches, "so the coyotes didn't get to it," until he could return and find a permanent home for the corpse. He hadn't been afraid the McCrees would find the body because he'd keep them away from it.

In fact, the McCrees hadn't found the body; they'd found Cabibi's truck. Why hadn't Owen hidden the truck?

But if Owen was lying, why? Either to protect someone or because someone made it worth his while to make a false confession. Here he was at eighty-eight still doing hardscrabble jobs. The old coot seemed healthy, but what if he knew he wouldn't live long? Bartelle could see Owen making a financial deal to set aside some money for his daughter and the grands. Who had that kind of money? McCree certainly did.

But if the ME had the right time of death, and assuming someone remembered seeing the family in town that day, the McCrees had alibis. While Owen may be wily smart enough to hide a body and lead a timber-cruising walk nearby the next day, both McCrees were scary smart. No way they'd let Owen within ten miles of that body if they'd been responsible.

But this Jason Graham didn't have any alibi and had been in the area. From McCree's tale, by the time Graham reached the vicinity of the murder, the storm had long passed. But the ME's time of death was 11:00 a.m. the day of the storm, plus or minus three hours, meaning it could have happened before, during, or after the storm.

Greg Shuett, the environmental crazy, had shown up the next day, acting all bent out of shape. He had money, although no one knew where it came from. People figured he was funded by one of those radical environmental protection groups, but Bartelle sure didn't know. No scrapes with the police, so no reason to look at his background. Maybe now he had a reason.

Hell, if anti-mining sentiment drove this crime, a lot of people around didn't like mining and had more than enough assets to buy Owen's confession. Jeez-o-Pete, he could drive himself crazy coming up with people who could pay Owen off.

Owen had an old-timer's perspective that the senior male had responsibility for the clan, and he was protective of his extended family. He didn't have a lot of years left—and, in addition to his daughter, son-in-law, and grandkids in Amasa, he had a ton of cousins, nieces, and nephews living in the area. Bartelle couldn't for the life of him come up with a specific reason for any of Owen's family to murder Cabibi. Might not hurt to learn more about the local daughter.

This family thing might be his own Italian ancestry talking. He sure as hell hoped Owen Lyndstrom had done in Frank Cabibi. Otherwise, he was back to square one. A churning acid boiled up in his stomach. He felt like finding a rock and taking it to Seamus McCree. Not to kill him, but a few broken fingers and toes would be fitting.

Did Cabibi have silent partners? McCree might be able to find out—if Bartelle decided they could trust him. Silent partner still meant money and someone paying Owen to confess. Maybe he needed to peek at the Lyndstrom bank accounts.

And what should he do about this Jason Graham? The guy had stolen and probably burned one ATV. And according to McCree, they should add a B&E charge plus another stolen ATV. If they caught Graham, they could stuff him safely in jail and protect him from this Happy Reaper asshole.

Tex, where the hell are ya?

ENDORPHINS GENERATED BY MY RUN home gave me an energy boost, and I spent time with my equipment in the basement to work on muscle strength. If nothing else, maybe the exercise would let me sleep well. Showered, I reheated leftovers from Paddy's cooking and, while scarfing down the food, regenerated all the notes Bartelle had confiscated. Paddy would urge me to eat deliberately, to be more in the moment, to savor the smell of the thyme and rosemary, to taste the spices. Probably not a trick this old dog would learn. I was too impatient for mindfulness, which is obviously the problem mindfulness would correct. It's circular. And the internet was running waaaaay too slowly. It often slowed in the evening as more people used the satellite's limited bandwidth, but tonight it was glacial.

I forced myself to stay awake until after Megan's bedtime, and then I called Paddy and Cindy. The lousy internet meant Skype was out. I dispensed with chitchat and informed them of the Happy Reaper's reappearance and his house visit. Cindy objected to my supposition that the Happy Reaper was here because of Graham.

"Why not to finish what you and he started years ago?"

I laughed. "Because I'm alive and talking with you. I appreciate your concern, but if he wanted me dead, I'd be dead. I can't figure how he made the connection to Graham. The only people who knew were you guys and Abigail. And Jason."

"It's the internet," Paddy said. "That website from his parents. I bet it's trolling for information."

I pulled it up . . . slowly pulled it up . . . on my laptop while Paddy explained how it might capture IP addresses. I complained about my browser.

"Uh-oh," Paddy said. "You remember the Happy Reaper put spyware on your computer the last time?"

"Oh shit, shit, shit. That's why it's so slow. He did it again to find out what I know."

"Seamus," Cindy said, "I strongly suggest you leave. Now. You survived the Happy Reaper once because he kinda liked you. You can't count on that. His way of dealing with obstacles is to kill them."

Twenty-Seven

WEDNESDAY: JASON GRAHAM'S PERSONAL HUMP day with five days of hiding behind him and five days before the trial was to begin. No one had approached the camp he was holed up in since McCree had been by Sunday evening.

Yesterday, Cabibi's murder no longer rated any space on the TV news. He tuned the radio to *Telephone Time* to see if anyone brought it up. If nothing else, listening to what people had for sale or wanted to buy provided entertaining background noise while he worked on a 1,000-piece jigsaw puzzle he had found in a closet. While finishing the border, an announcement rifled into his consciousness.

"To repeat," the announcer said, "this message is for Elliot. You've given us a huge scare, but all is forgiven. We promise to make a safe delivery on Monday if you return to camp. You have our number and email. Let us know you're all right. Love, Abigail."

Neither Elliot nor Abigail were common names. The Monday reference and returning to camp all fit. Seamus must have placed the circumspect ad and used Abigail's name to avoid any attention to himself. Very smart. Very Seamus.

The question was, did this change anything?

Because Seamus couldn't know if anyone else who posed a threat to Jason would show up in Cabibi's footsteps, he'd keep the ATV packed and fueled for a quick getaway.

I ARRIVED EARLY FOR THE meeting with Bartelle and the county's prosecutor. They kept me stewing for an hour and a half in a room with no air conditioning, which I did not think was a good sign. Since I hadn't been smart enough to bring a book or electronic reader, I willed myself to catch up on missed sleep. Bartelle woke me with a rough shake of my shoulder.

"Good news, bad news, McCree. Good news is no cuffs today. The prosecutor does not want anything to muddy Owen Lyndstrom's confession. But if Owen recants and this case goes to trial, they'll charge you with obstruction."

And I figured if Jason Graham was involved in Cabibi's murder, I'd be charged as an accessory. "Where's the prosecutor on charging Graham for breaking and entering, stealing the ATV, etcetera, etcetera?"

"We can arrest and charge away to our heart's content. However, and this is more good news for you, our prosecutor knows the federal prosecutor in Chicago, who was not at all surprised Jason Graham was hiding until the trial. Should it turn out Graham had good reason to take off, our guy might go light on charges against him, provided Graham shows up and testifies in Chicago. Did you know Graham laundered money for the mob? No wonder you got along so well with him."

I chose to ignore the question and the implication that I got along well with financial criminals. "Did the federal prosecutor know of Frank Cabibi?"

"Says not. Now as to this Happy Reaper fellow. I checked—"

"Wait. Back to Graham. Are you guys going to look for him? What's your plan?"

"As a precautionary measure, I'm sending a team to check all the camps on Lukes Road to determine if there are any other break-ins. If we're lucky, we kick him up. I expect he's long gone. By the way, you weren't shitting me on this Happy Reaper's notoriety. FBI in Detroit is thinking about sending someone up here to talk to us."

Talk about a pointless conversation. My thoughts drifted to my earlier encounters with the Happy Reaper. Bartelle interrupted my wool-gathering.

"Our prosecutor wants your help exploring Cabibi's financial records. He's looking for a stronger motive and money often provides it."

"Let me get this right. Even though the prosecutor's ready to charge me with obstruction, he wants my help on the case."

"Hey. You're still deputized. When can you start?"

I WALKED DOWNTOWN FROM THE sheriff's office to grab some takeout, anxious to continue analyzing the hodgepodge of Cabibi's financial records that had so far included everything from credit card statements, $28,000 in cash, pay stubs, and a series of spreadsheets whose purpose was unclear—and, therefore, intriguing. Jenny Kauppi, Owen's daughter, found me while I waited for my order. "Sheriff Bartelle told me you went to grab a sandwich. Can I talk to you for a minute? Privately?"

We'd met a few times at Owen's place. Her husband was a long-haul trucker and not around much. She taught at the high school—I couldn't remember what—and she had three children whose names and ages I couldn't recall. Two girls and a boy? A brunette, she wore her hair down to her shoulders in a style they used to call a pageboy, covering the too-large ears she'd inherited from her father.

My order arrived and we walked to a bench in the shade by the courthouse. We each chose an end, facing each other to talk.

"My father confessed because he thinks I killed Frankie Joe." She saw the questioning look on my face and continued. "I didn't, but I'm pretty sure I know why he thinks it. Seamus, I need your help to prove my father innocent."

"As you can imagine, Jenny," I said, stalling to think of what I should say, "I have a lot of questions. I have no idea how I might be able to help you. But first, are you aware that I've been deputized?"

She waved off my concern. "My father won't see me, and if I tell the police, they'll think I'm concoctin a story to cast doubt on my father's confession. I just heard today that they found the gun with the skeleton. It's—" She pointed to a couple walking toward us.

"My car's parked around the corner," I said. "Do you want to talk there? We'd eliminate the interruptions, although I would understand if you didn't want to get into a car with someone you don't know well."

Again, she waved off my concern. "Oh fiddlesticks. You start anythin, I'll just shoot ya." At my startled expression, she tapped her purse. "Concealed-carry permit."

TWENTY-EIGHT

WITH THE WINDOWS DOWN TO let the thin breeze air out my sun-heated car, she continued where she had left off. "The gun is the exact make and model of one stolen from Dad in 1986. The police haven't released the skeleton's name, but I agree with the speculation that it's Tim Javoroski. Thirty years ago, his parents owned land thereabouts. My father thinks I stole his gun, shot and buried Tim, and now I've killed Frankie Joe."

I had wondered if Owen was protecting family, but this I hadn't anticipated. "Forgive me for asking, but does he think you stole his handgun? Otherwise, finding out someone used his handgun to kill Javoroski doesn't necessarily point to you. What am I missing?"

Her face worked through several expressions I could not interpret. Her hands worried each other. I had the feeling she was deciding how much to tell me and wondered again if I needed to remind her that I couldn't withhold certain information from the sheriff.

"I'm sorry, Seamus. I practiced this part, but even thirty years later, it's hard."

"Take as much time as you need." I turned my gaze toward the front window to give her some visual space.

She huffed an explosion of air. "It's like this. I was a sophomore in the spring of eighty-six. Hard to believe it now, but I was trim and attractive, and I hung out with three of the senior boys. Frankie Joe Cabibi, Tim Javoroski, and Chris Saari thought of themselves as the Three Musketeers. Dad was workin second shift at the mill, which made my house a popular hangout. Real popular. Dad kept that gun in a bedside drawer. Loaded. Not somethin I would ever do with my kids, but times were different and that was Dad. He made sure I treated guns with care, and he taught me how to shoot all of the ones we had in the house." A smile creased her face. "Bet you didn't know I took second in a statewide 4-H target-shootin contest."

She rubbed her cheeks as though she were cold, although the day was sunny, in the midseventies. I provided some encouraging noises to keep her talking.

"Anyway, one night that spring, the three boys were over. We were drinkin. Underage drinkin was normal. As long as you didn't weave on your way home, no one bothered you. Well, there were some busybodies who would call the cops if they got a whiff of a party. It's tough on the jocks 'cause they get suspended from the team. Nothin happened to any of the girls or guys *not* on teams. Anyway, that night it was the four of us, and Dad was workin twelve-hour shifts, so he was gone all night.

"One of them slipped me a roofie. You know, the date-rape pill?" Tears trickled down her cheeks. "I was a virgin. Not that I had anythin against sex before marriage or anythin, but I wanted it to be with a guy I loved. I mean really loved."

She reached into her bag and came out with tissues rather than the pistol, which relieved me a little. I was starting to understand why Owen thought she had reason to kill Javoroski and, thirty years later, Cabibi. "Do you have an alibi for the day of the storm?"

"Doubtful. I dropped the kids at a neighbor's to carpool to church day camp and headed up to Little Pickerel Lake, which isn't all that far from where Frankie Joe got killed. I was up early. Thing is, I drove the highway up to Lukes Road and came in from the west, and I left the same way. I was never in the area where Frankie Joe got killed, but my father doesn't know that. He knows I was supposed to be at Little Pickerel because he planned to join me once he finished up by Hemlock, which is the next lake down. The storm wasn't bad there, and if Dad went lookin for me, I was already gone."

"No one saw you?"

"Sure. But they saw me after I'd left the woods. That's not givin me an alibi, is it? Just the opposite. It confirms I was around. Which I admit, is no biggie. But alibi? Not even close unless Frankie Joe was killed later than people are sayin, and I was back in town."

"I diverted you from your story. I'm sorry. What happened after the—thirty years ago?"

"Frankie Joe woke me up at five the next mornin. He said he was surprised I was as out of it as I was. Years later I figured out they slipped me a roofie. Anyway, he told me they each—you know—spent time with me in a closed room. They didn't watch each other or nothin. He says he was last, and I was bleedin and everythin, and he didn't do nothin. He waited in the room long enough to fool the other guys."

"Did you believe him? Did you tell anyone?"

"I swear to God, I felt guilty. You know, I was sixteen. I had fantasized about having sex, what girl that age doesn't? Especially if your friends are . . . active. I thought I had gotten blitzed and they took advantage of me. I made it my fault. I cleaned myself up and washed and dried the sheets. I had to keep it to myself. I didn't want Dad killing them." She blanched at her words.

"Afterwards, I tried to act natural around them, but it didn't work. They were nervous . . . and I never quite trusted them. We drifted apart. Then I missed a period. I told Frankie Joe. He collected money from the other guys, and I got an abortion in Iron Mountain. I had fake ID, so I didn't have to get Dad's permission. He might have killed me along with them if he'd learned about that."

Anger churned inside me as I thought of three guys getting away with rape. It made no difference that it had occurred at a time when men's accepted excuse was "she was asking for it." Wrong was wrong. But one part of her story I didn't buy. Owen Lyndstrom had a gossip network running from Copper Harbor to the Soo and all points in between. Ben Franklin's line that three can keep a secret only if two of them are dead would certainly apply in a situation with four high school kids. Add in the second secret of her pregnancy and abortion, and I considered it unlikely Owen had been unaware of something bad happening to his daughter. And, how did the kids explain the sudden disappearance of the money necessary for the abortion? I'm sure my skepticism showed on my face.

"Not a soul. Not ever."

"Jenny, I'm sure you kept quiet, but I have a lot of trouble thinking three teenage guys didn't tell anyone. And you know your dad is a vacuum for gossip."

"I know, but it woulda come back to me if they had. Besides, Frankie Joe left for college, and hasn't been back but a few times until recently. Tim disappeared before I had the abortion. Only Chris stayed in the area. He got married within a year, and they're still hitched. Born again Christians. Got him a good job with Connor Sports. I can't imagine him tellin anyone. We see each other in town and say hello, but that's it."

"What if Cabibi said something while drinking with his buddies. Your father might have heard, even if you didn't."

"And not said anythin to me? That's not like Dad. Not at all. You're right, he's a gossip and hears everythin. Whenever he learned somethin involvin me in high school, he was in my face. Mom had died and Dad treated me like a guy." She tossed her head and gave a laugh. "Except with the birds and bees talk. He had grandma set me down and tell me the facts—like I didn't already know."

She laid a soft hand on my arm. "Look Seamus, I'm not sayin my father couldn't have killed Frankie Joe if he knew what happened to me. But he would've shot him, cut off his prick and stuffed it in his mouth, then gotten rid of the body where no one would ever find it. Can you seriously believe someone who's spent his whole life in the woods would leave a body where it could be found? The storm wouldn't have stopped my father.

"I'm sure he knows somethin happened thirty years ago that caused us kids to all grow apart. But he's warned me about my quick temper. He probably went lookin for me after the storm, and when he couldn't find me—and Frankie Joe turns up dead, and Tim Javoroski's bones are in the same area with Dad's stolen gun—he put two and two together and figures I killed 'em both."

"What if Cabibi threw the past in your father's face?"

She shook her head in denial. "You know my dad used to poach. The DNR never caught him. Does that sound like a man who cracks someone on the head with a rock and leaves the body to be discovered?"

"I follow your logic."

She flashed a smile. "Dad said you were super smart. He refuses to let me see him in jail, but I think he would talk to you. If you make him believe I didn't do it, he won't need to lie."

I broke eye contact and looked at my uneaten sandwich. "Problem is, if the police learn of your troubles with Cabibi, they'll say that gives your father a motive." I held up a hand to delay her objections. "It would be easier if there were other credible suspects."

She jerked away from me, clunking her head into the passenger window. Her eyes were wide with fright. "Oh God, I've made everything worse." She gripped my arm and whispered. "Do you have to tell them?"

The exact question I was asking myself—the reason I'd said *if* they learn, not *when*. "Let me think for a minute." Believing Jenny's tale—and I did—it seemed likely that Tim Javoroski's and Frank Cabibi's deaths were linked by more than geographical proximity. If I added to the mix finding Owen's gun in Javoroski's grave, it all pointed to the Lyndstroms. But if Owen had killed Javoroski, he'd acted stupidly by burying the gun with the victim since he could have pitched it in any of a hundred lakes, never to be found.

Jenny had no alibi for either murder and had access to Owen's pistol. And she admitted to a hot temper. She had a gun in her bag now. I did not need to see it in action. "Let's do this," I said. "I'll try to talk with your father, tell him you have a rock-solid alibi, and confront him with your belief that he's only confessing to protect you. See what he says. I'm reviewing Cabibi's financial records for the sheriff. Maybe those will provide a reason for the police to look at alternatives."

"But I don't have an alibi . . . and Dad knows it. I told him I didn't see anyone."

"We'll create one. What if someone's trail camera proves you weren't anywhere near where Cabibi died?"

"Dad doesn't trust the date and time on trail cams. He says people forget to set them for the right day or change them for daylight savings."

True enough. "So, how can we build on the truth to create something your father *will* accept."

"The truth is, the storm caught me by surprise and I made it to shore while the winds blew through. It was the edge of the storm, so there wasn't much damage. I didn't see anyone on Lukes Road all the way to the highway. Tall Pines was dark when I passed, so I didn't bother stoppin. No one saw me at home until late afternoon. The truth sucks."

"I've got it. We'll say some guy from Wisconsin heard about Cabibi's murder and contacted the sheriff's office to report they'd seen your vehicle come out from Little Pickerel and head toward the highway. We'll give the guy a name, so it sounds like a fact. You heard about this from a deputy following up on the license plate."

She kneaded her purse with nervous fingers. "Maybe. But if you tell the police what happened . . . thirty years ago, and Dad hears it, he'll get as stubborn as a diesel engine at forty below. He'll never move off his story."

I bit into the sandwich to give myself thinking time. I was through making empty promises I could not keep. Sheriff Bartelle believed I was helping look for motives for Cabibi's murder, and I had kicked up a big one. But I hadn't said I'd run to him immediately with every new thing I learned. Since this information only supported the case against Owen, I could justify waiting to include it in my complete report. Had I found something to dispute Owen's story, I'd need to inform him immediately. "Jenny, I promise I'll hold onto your information until we try everything else first."

She appraised me with narrowed eyes. A part of me wanted to hop a plane to New Zealand and permanently avoid Jenny and her handgun. And avoid the sheriff and the threat of prosecution. And evade the Happy Reaper and whatever he wanted. And leave Owen Lyndstrom and Jenny Kauppi and Jason Graham to their fates.

Problem was, I couldn't get away from myself if I did that. Maybe I would learn to live with it, as I needed to learn to live without Abigail. *Who the hell am I kidding?* The fantasy would last all of fifteen minutes, and I'd start eating myself up. That was not who I was, nor who I wanted to be.

"What would happen," Jenny asked, "if I went in and confessed?"

Like father, like daughter? "Wouldn't fly. They'd ask specific questions. Unless you really did it, you wouldn't know the answers. Your father knows because he was around when we discovered the bones and the body."

She bit her lip and squinched her eyes. "My father has often said you're a straight shooter and he'd trust you with his life. He'd better be right."

TWENTY-NINE

AFTER CHECKING OUT OF THE motel, the Happy Reaper settled in for brunch in a cafe in Florence, Wisconsin, over the border from Iron County,

Michigan. He picked up a copy of a paper whose blaring headline read, "MURDER SUSPECT CONFESSES." Amateur hour, but it could prove entertaining while he waited for his breakfast.

Reading the article, he realized the timing of the murder coincided with the sudden interest shown by McCree in Jason Graham. Were the two related? Nothing in the article gave a hint, but the Happy Reaper had not attained his exalted hitman status by ignoring possibilities. A link might provide insight into where Graham was. Or maybe even permit a well-placed anonymous tip to prompt the police into joining the hunt for Graham.

If ever there was a time to use TOR, "the onion router" initially designed by the Navy but now open sourced, to hide his IP addresses, this was it. He left a simple message on a private bulletin board established specifically for this client.

Is a Frank Cabibi, deceased July 22 in Iron County, MI, in ANY way related to your issue?

He set the paper aside when breakfast arrived. Sunny-side eggs not overdone, rye toast done right, hash-browns nicely browned, and spiced sausage that flared his nostrils with anticipation of the seasoning. He sniffed in the steam from his coffee. Rich, slightly acrid, and in no need of milk or sugar. Perfect.

The text-message answer came as he sopped up the last of his eggs with a slice of toast. *Cabibi a bit player. Likely met Graham several years ago in Chicago.*

Chicago—the trial's location and now this link. It made him wonder which McCree was initially involved with Graham. The notes sitting on McCree's dining room table suggested Patrick McCree, who was Chicago based, had done most of the computer work discovering Graham's real identity. The question was why he had undertaken it; and would knowing the answer help the Happy Reaper execute his assignment before the trial began?

He had nearly given up on the possibility of earning the bonus, doubling his fee if he took care of Graham before the trial started. His backup plan might squeak in before the deadline with a cat's whisker to spare—and after the hits on the fake website he set up, hope for an earlier solution had returned. Not earning that bonus felt like losing. Hell, that's why they had offered it, wasn't it? They knew he was goal-oriented and wanted everyone to agree he was the best.

While absently stabbing hash browns with his fork, he decided it didn't matter how or which McCree was involved with Jason Graham; the single question worth considering was whether he should continue to stumble around like some bumpkin looking for Sasquatch or return to his original plan to take care of business at the Chicago courthouse. His woolgathering ended when his fork came up empty, and he realized he had finished everything without tasting anything other than Tabasco sauce, which had left a tingling burn on his tongue. He raised his coffee cup to ask the waitress for more.

From the radio playing in the background, something grabbed his attention. "*To repeat,*" the *Telephone Time* host said, *"this message is for Elliot. You've given us a huge scare, but all is forgiven. We promise to make a safe delivery on Monday if you return to camp. You have our number and email. Let us know you're all right. Love, Abigail.*"

Abigail, such an old-fashioned name. The internet provided her picture—it matched the one on McCree's desk—and the pieces clicked into place. Abigail Hancock, not any of the McCrees, was the driver. She also lived in Chicago when she wasn't on assignment protecting people. Assume Abigail was protecting Jason Graham until the trial on Monday— the safe delivery referred to in the message. She'd hidden him at McCree's camp.

His mind raced through the bits and pieces of information he had collected. Shortly after Cabibi was murdered in a most bizarre fashion, the McCrees discovered the fake website, but chose not to contact Jason Graham's "parents." They wrote down information about Jason pulled from the internet and added notes about the person they had called Elliot.

Jason Graham is using Elliot as an assumed name.

The list—ATV and extra gas and bolt cutters, etc.—made sense now. Graham steals a bunch of McCree's stuff and takes off for parts unknown. McCrees do their internet search and come up with Jason Graham's real name and stumble into the internet honey trap he had laid.

He found no evidence of any women living at McCree's place, so where was Abigail? Unknown, but the message suggested they thought Graham was still in the area. Any plan to take out Graham at the Chicago courthouse carried a lot more risk than killing the jerk up here in the boonies—if he could just find him.

Sipping the coffee the waitress had delivered, the Happy Reaper opened the plat book to the page with McCree's place, spotted Lukes Road, where the newspaper indicated they had found Cabibi. The two places were close. Very close. The message for Elliot had referred to "we" and "us." Until he spotted Abigail Hancock, he'd need to stick to McCree and see what happened. To do that, he needed a safe way to monitor McCree's place.

Using his cell phone, he placed an online order. *Even if you hate Amazon, you have to love Amazon.* For less than the price of a small car, the Happy Reaper would receive morning delivery of two fully equipped drones able to stream video to a remote pickup more than a mile away.

A SENSE OF UNEASE ACCOMPANIED me as I signed in at the Iron County Jail and was escorted to an interview room. Owen Lyndstrom was already seated at the table, facing the camera. Years ago, I'd occupied the same seat Owen now sat in. Nothing much had changed. The room still had drab concrete walls, drab carpeting, a drab table, all designed—intentionally or not—to be depressing as hell. Place stunk of pine cleaner. In the three days Owen had been jailed, he'd aged twenty years. The fluorescent lighting gave his skin a yellowish cast. Was he becoming a little jaundiced? Dark bags hung under his eyes.

"Thanks for seeing me, Owen" I settled into a chair opposite him.

Owen waited to speak until the guard shut the door behind himself. "The only time I ever been cooped up was when I had my appendix out."

"I know what you're saying, Owen. Anything I can bring you other than a file in a cake?"

He did not respond to my attempted humor. He leaned in toward me and whispered conspiratorially, "Find Elliot?"

"Not a trace. I've told the sheriff, so they're aware of the break-in at your friend's camp."

"Good, good. With this other stuff, I done forgot." He leaned away from the table and pinned me to the chair with his stare. "You didn't come here to tell me that."

"Your daughter's real upset. You really ought to see her."

He scrunched his eyes shut and grimaced.

"She believes you confessed because you think she did it and you're covering for her." I tapped his arm and his now-dull eyes looked at me. "I might do the same thing in your position. Especially now that Paddy's a father. And from what Jenny told me, I can see why you might think she did it. But she's learned she has an airtight alibi. Wisconsin guy saw her leaving Little Pickerel and heading west."

"Now ain't that somethin." Owen leaned back into the chair. "Bring him along next time and we can trade fishin stories. Time we ended this parlay. They serve dinner real early here. I don't want to miss the fine home cookin."

THIRTY

I **WAITED IN AMBUSH BY** Chris Saari's house, a vinyl-sided two-story on the east side of town. A 250-gallon propane tank rested on a concrete slab away from the house. Two tricycles adorned the recently mowed front lawn. A Chevy sedan dating from the last decade was parked on one side of the driveway. On the nearside, a stain suggested a second vehicle, which I presumed was Chris's ride.

I hoped if I caught Chris when he pulled up, I could talk to him without any of his family knowing. Even with the windows down and a slight breeze, the late afternoon sun baked me. Checking the clock every three minutes did not make it run faster. If anything, it slowed it down.

A guy driving a green Toyota Tundra pulled into the driveway. I drove in behind the truck in time to watch the tricycle owners pour from the house yelling, "Grampa, Grampa."

"Chris Saari?" I called to the large man as I opened the car door.

"You got him."

"My name's Seamus McCree. Can I talk with you for a minute in private?"

He lifted a child in the crook of each elbow, gave them a bear hug, and set them on the ground. "Tell Grandma I'll be in shortly." He swatted their rumps in a friendly manner and they careened back up the path and into the house, leaving the front door wide open. Their greeting had given me time to reach him by the front walk.

Chris faced me, legs wide, arms crossed. I guessed him a solid six-six and, even thirty years after his football days, he still looked like he could walk onto the field and handle himself well. "What's this about?"

"Won't keep you long. I'm hoping you can clear up a couple of inconsistencies for me about some ancient history having to do with the class of 1986."

"Who'd you say you worked for?"

We both knew I hadn't. "The sheriff has me looking at some of Mr. Cabibi's papers." True enough. "One of the things I came across was next month's class reunion. To make sense of this, I need to tell you a secret." A flicker of interest showed in his eyes. "Some people don't believe Owen Lyndstrom killed Frank Cabibi, and I'm looking into other possibilities." True, although he might mistakenly get the impression I was considering possibilities for the Iron County Sheriff's Office. "Someone called you guys the Three Musketeers. And now you're the only one alive. You've heard they believe the bones found near where Cabibi was murdered are your buddy Tim's?"

A quick head bob provided assent.

"Who besides Frankie Joe, Tim, you, and Jenny Kauppi—well, Jenny Lyndstrom at the time—know what happened? Did you tell anyone about that night? Did either of the others?"

His face turned pasty. His mouth opened and closed, breath stuck in his throat. His arms fell limp. I worried he might faint and prepared to catch him, although he'd be a lot of dead weight to handle. He closed his eyes and slowly opened them. "I don't know what you are talking about."

"Actually, I'm sure you do." I lowered my voice. "You three all had sex with Jenny one night, and it wasn't consensual." I held both hands up in a gesture to indicate I meant no aggression. "The statute of limitations has long since passed for whatever transpired. I'm not trying to get you in trouble and Jenny isn't either. But I do need to understand what happened with the three of you, and you're the only one who can tell me."

He shoved his hands deep into his jeans pockets. His gaze sought the ground before rising to meet my eyes. "That experience is what brought me to the Lord, and that brought me to Kim." He tilted his head to indicate his wife, now standing in the doorway. "I confessed my sins to the Lord, and He has forgiven them. "

With his wife watching, I kept my voice low. "I have no doubt, but I am more interested in whether any of you told any humans. Guys in the locker room? A minister or priest?"

"I did not, and I would have heard if Frankie Joe talked. This has to be coming from Jenny."

"Frankie Joe took Jenny for the abortion?"

"She told you that too?" Shooting a worried look at his wife, he said in a louder voice, "I'll be in in a minute, dear. You're letting the skeeters in." She closed the door. "Why in God's name is Jenny dredging this up now? My wife knows I was a wild kid before I met her, but she knows nothing of this. Thirty years we've been married. Our kids are grown. We're enjoying the blessing of grandchildren. It was a stupid teenager mistake. That's not who I am now."

With surprising speed, he yanked his hands out of his pockets and jammed me in the chest. "What's *your* purpose in all this?"

A curtain in what was surely the living room stirred. "I'm not digging up the past to cause problems. I'm wondering if what happened then is connected to Frank Cabibi's death—or Tim Javoroski's, assuming the bones are his. How did you guys get the money to pay for Jenny's abortion?"

"I don't have to tell you." His spine lengthened with renewed energy. He crossed his arms to confirm his defiance.

"Between us is the easy way, Mr. Saari. The hard way is for the police to show up at your workplace and talk with you there. Here, you just have to come up with a convincing line for your wife." I paused a beat before pretending to throw up my hands in resignation and turn away.

"Wait."

I faced him, keeping a neutral expression on my face.

"Jenny told Frankie she was pregnant. He thought she was shaking us down for money. Tim and I believed her, but Frankie convinced us to go to her house the next Saturday morning. We made her take one of those home pregnancy tests. That was the longest twenty minutes of my life, but the blue told the story. I haven't been to that house since. My share came from money I saved up to buy a car. I didn't ask the others, and I didn't see them much after that.

"Tim split. Well, that's what we thought. He'd been real depressed. And Frank was Frank. Nothing bothered him much. It bothered me, though. A lot. Jesus found me and I accepted him as my personal Savior. I gave up drinking and smoking, and so I didn't hang with the old crowd anymore."

"Did Cabibi contact you after he returned to the area?" I caught movement of the curtains again.

"He invited us to a party at his place. I told him I didn't party anymore—not like that. He tried to get me to invite him here to the house. To be honest with you, I didn't want him to meet Kim. Look, what I did was wrong. I can't make it up to Jenny. She and I see each other occasionally. We say hello and can make small talk for a few minutes. I don't think Frank grew up much from high school. I heard from other guys that he had tried to talk them into investing in something to do with the mine he was working on." He flicked his hands, mimicking flinging off something unpleasant. "I'm sorry he's dead—"

His eyes widened in understanding. "Oh, you think Old Man Lyndstrom killed Frank because of what happened all those years ago. If Jenny's talking, then it could be, but I never saw him raise his hand in anger. The missus is gonna be getting worried if I don't get in there."

"You said Tim was depressed before he went missing?"

"I thought he ran away from his old man to join the Army. Later, I realized that was stupid because the Army only wants you if you graduate high school, and part of the reason he was feeling low was because he was flunking English and he'd probably have to get a GED. Tim and I talked one time without Frank around. He felt as bad as me. We should never have let Frank talk us into it. If I had known he had slipped her something . . . If I could take it all back, I would."

Kim stuck her head out the door. "Chris, I need you to light the grill. We've got to get a move on so we're not late for services."

"Wednesday prayer service," he said.

A new idea popped into my head. "Were you worried Tim was so depressed he'd killed himself?"

"I didn't think so, but Frank suggested he might have gone into the woods somewhere and taken his own life. I gotta go."

He nearly jumped when I touched his turned shoulder. "Sorry," I said. "Here's my card in case you think of anything else I should know."

For a moment, I thought he wouldn't take the card. He grabbed it in a manner suggesting I had cooties and tucked it into his front pocket before going into the house.

Driving home I considered the information I had gained from Chris Saari. He contradicted Jenny's understanding of Cabibi's role in the events. Since Chris admitted his involvement in the rape, I felt confident his version was much closer to the truth than Cabibi's self-serving story to

Jenny. While Tim Javoroski might have been sufficiently depressed to kill himself, he hadn't been so resourceful he could bury himself afterward.

And Cabibi had been looking for investors. Given his stubborn refusal to talk about the mine's finances at the open meeting, my antennae twitched. Sketchy investments had led to more than one murder.

Thirty-One

OVER THE TELEVISION PUNDITS YAPPING about Brexit as if they actually understood the situation, Jason Graham heard the ATVs puttering up the road to his hideaway. He switched off the electronics, made sure there were no lights on, and shoved the plate with the remains of lunch under the couch. He raced upstairs to the bathroom, taking binoculars he had discovered in the house, and waited in the shadows, looking out the front windows.

He tried to settle his hummingbird heart and racing mind by telling himself that Wednesday afternoon was an unlikely time for the owners to return. He frantically went through steps he had taken: all doors and windows locked on both the house and the garage. He had not moved anything in the house, other than shove the lunch plate under the couch. The stolen ATV was in a darkened part of the garage not visible from the side window. The generator was silent.

Two ATVs came into view, both dark green and sporting brush guards. Not McCree's. The helmeted guys driving them wore jackets—weird for a day in the low eighties. He eased onto the floor to avoid detection. Nervously patting his front pocket, he confirmed the keys were there. If they came into the house, his only chance was to slip out of the bathroom window onto the porch roof and jump from there to the ground. And hope like hell he didn't sprain an ankle. Then either make a break with the packed ATV in the garage, steal one of the arriving ATVs, or slip into the woods.

The visitors were close enough he could hear the crunch of gravel under their tires. The ATVs stopped. No talking though. He pressed fingers to his neck and counted the beats. In the quiet, he could feel and hear the whoosh of each heartbeat, the blood pulsing through his arteries, racing past his ears, giving him a pile-driver headache.

Low voices now. Heavy footsteps on the front porch. A rattle of the doorknob. Pounding on the door frame. "Anybody in there? Sheriff's deputies."

Why were they here? Was this a routine visit that caught this camp on this day? Doubtful. Had they found the first break-in and were checking all camps? Possible, but would they travel in pairs? Or were they hunting specifically for him? Had McCree told the cops about him? It went against their agreement, but so did his running away. Yet, why would McCree be so circumspect with the messages he left on *Telephone Time* if he was going to tell the cops. Had they decided he killed Cabibi?

Another series of loud knocks, followed by the words, "Find anything?"

He did not hear the response and speculated the second guy was checking the other buildings.

More footsteps on the porch, which he gauged was the cop walking to the window to look in. Jason smiled. Wasn't he the smart one to make sure nothing was out of place?

The footsteps crossed the porch and their pitch flattened as the cop walked down the three steps. Attuned to the pitch changes, he listened as the footsteps reached gravel and then became silent. Walking around the house looking in?

Oh shit. He'd left the clicker lying on the footstool, and if they looked carefully, they might see the DirecTV box was on. Did people who owned solar-powered houses turn everything off when they left or were some lazy? Would the glow give him away? Could the cop even see it, and would he wonder why it was on?

Jason closed his eyes and could see little flashes of pure white, three times a second in sync with his heartbeat and head-splitting pain. "Leave," he told them using mental telepathy. "There's nothing here." Despite his rising discomfort, he smiled at his attempt to channel The Force as if he were Obi-Wan Kenobi convincing stormtroopers that the droids weren't the ones they were looking for.

He counted the seconds to give his mind an alternative to panic. At eight hundred and three, an ATV cranked over, followed by a second one. In a flood of relief, he realized he had to take a leak, but he wasn't moving a muscle until he was sure they were gone. Now instead of counting, he concentrated on his bladder pain, which pulsed in time with the pain behind his eyes.

After considerable time, an ATV engine roared to life, but his relief at their imminent departure died as the sound headed down a path that dead-ended a quarter mile into the woods. The second ATV idled in the driveway. Had they spotted something?

Oh man, he really needed to pee.

The ATV soon returned; the second cranked its RPMs, and the two sped down the road.

One thing was for sure: he was not cut out for a life on the lam. He raced to the bathroom and unzipped, barely in time to avoid a mess.

What was the safest way to get himself to Chicago for the trial starting in four and a half days? Now that the cops had checked this place, it felt safer, but as the weekend approached, the owner might return. Some guys probably worked long four-day shifts to have an extended weekend.

One way or the other, the next day had a good chance of being moving day. But where was he moving to and how would he get there?

SEEING SEAMUS MCCREE STANDING IN his office doorway, Bartelle held up a finger and pointed to the visitor chairs. McCree settled into the rightmost one.

Bartelle sent an email, heard the confirming swish sound, and looked up at McCree. The guy looked as bushed as Bartelle felt. "Solve everything?" he said and burst into laughter.

"It's that positive attitude that won over the voters of Iron County and gave you a landslide victory."

"More likely they figured electing me sheriff meant they didn't have to pay me overtime." Bartelle checked his wristwatch, which triggered his stomach to growl in hunger. "Already a quarter to seven. What have you got?"

"Impressions and ideas, nothing firm, but they add up to my presumption Cabibi was at least a little crooked. How do you guarantee making money from a new mining operation?"

Bartelle's chair squeaked as he leaned back, one arm over his head, fingers scratching behind the opposite ear. "Hell, there is no guarantee in mining. Prices fluctuate, other mines come online, you get sued polluting an aquifer."

"All good points, which means you have to make your money up front before the actual mining." McCree motioned his hands in a gimme gesture, which Bartelle figured meant he was supposed to perform like some schoolkid.

He wasn't playing that game. "Just spit it out so I can finish this damned paperwork and get dinner."

McCree looked disappointed. "Mineral rights and infrastructure development, and he was into both of them. . . . I think."

Sometimes Bartelle was willing to sit patiently for the long explanations. Not today. "Seamus, give me the *Reader's Digest* version. If you convince me, then we can go through the Russian novel page by page."

"Doesn't matter if the mine never extracts a single rock, all the infrastructure needs to be in place first. It's ten, twelve miles to the nearest electricity from where Cabibi was doing his sampling. Someone has to run power in. Current roads won't stand up to dump trucks full of rock. Means you either improve them or extend a rail line. You need a processing plant. All that and more must be in place before the mine produces a single buck of return. *Reader's Digest* version: Cabibi was able to steer contracts and line his pockets doing it.

"Second way is if you can buy mineral rights cheap and sell them dear. You can be lucky, of course, or discover valuable minerals and buy up the rights. If you already own the rights, then you need to discover something that makes them more valuable."

Bartelle stopped scratching his head and leaned forward, resting his weight on his forearms. He thought he saw where this was going, but it was best to make sure. "Point?"

"Tons of companies have gone bankrupt trading mineral rights. But if you salt the land, you can sell worthless rights for a lot of money."

A flash of irritation crossed Bartelle's mind. "Sometimes it hurts my brain to follow your reasoning. I thought if you salted the land, you made it worthless."

"Sorry," McCree said and seemed to mean it. "Bad choice of words. In ancient times armies did salt enemy farmlands to make them worthless. To salt a mine, you add something to the mine that appears to make it more valuable. After the *discovery*, worthless land now has great value. In the old days, people did that with gold mines and diamond mines . . . invest in a few nuggets or stones, sprinkle them around in a new digging, sell the mine to outsiders, and leave town."

Bartelle circled his hands like wheels going around in mud and getting no traction.

"So," Seamus said in a marginally faster tempo, "Cabibi was the middle man between the tests—all legal—and the testing lab—also legal. What wasn't legal was substituting test results from a mine already in operation for the results on the holes he drilled here. He modified the stated location and time of the test and produced a new document."

Bartelle rose and paced behind his desk. "But that would only profit the mineral-rights owner."

"Which is Canadian, but whose largest owner is an offshore corporation. Or it provides reason for that corporation to invest in all the required infrastructure. At this point, I don't *know* anything. I'm seeing hints of two deals in the works that smell like that dead fish I buried. I need to find some locals he was talking with to see what he was selling. I think he was looking to have his palm greased for the infrastructure contracts. On the rights, I don't know if they're being ginned to justify the infrastructure or if there's some kind of stock fraud. I need you . . . Sorry, Lon . . . I'd like your permission to talk to people."

Bartelle shooed away a mosquito that had somehow found its way into the office. "You never ask permission. Why now?"

"Because I'm walking a thin line and you're threatening me with some heavy charges."

"There is that. Do you actually have a plan?"

Thirty-Two

I KNEW IT HAD BEEN Owen Lyndstrom's habit to meet with a bunch of old timers for breakfast and trade gossip in a private room at one of the local restaurants. The group was invitation only, so I entered their sanctuary prepared for rejection. Of the seven men, I had passing acquaintance with three. Central casting had dressed them all in work boots, jeans, T-shirts with holes or grease stains to mark them as working men, and ballcaps covering gray hair.

They pointed to Owen's reserved seat. One guy flipped over a mug and the other poured coffee from a communal pot on the table. Looked like liquid coal, smelled like burnt tar, and tasted like battery acid. I hate coffee and drank it down anyway.

My questions precipitated a collective reminiscence of Cabibi's athletic accomplishments and the teams he'd played on. I kicked off a four-against-three brouhaha by shifting the conversation to discussing whether mining would benefit Iron County. Waiting patiently for a break didn't pay off, and I finally broke in, asking where Owen stood on the issue.

"Around here," the one with the Husqvarna cap said, "there's two kinds of men who make their living off the land. They farm or they timber. Only difference between them is where they store their junk. Farmers throw stuff into the woods. Timbermen throw stuff into fields. But neither one of them cottons to anything that destroys their land."

"That's us," a guy wearing a Kubota tractor cap said, and two other guys plus Husqvarna Cap raised their hands.

"Which," Husqvarna Cap said, "leaves these three city slickers." He slapped one on the back. "To them, more jobs means more people and more people means more business. And I can see that."

"These boys are being polite," Kubota Cap said, raising his voice to be heard over one of the city slickers. "If Owen seen someone littering in the woods, he'd want to stick the trash up the guy's ass so far it'd poke out his nose like a booger. He hated the idea of a mine so much we couldn't discuss it. Doesn't surprise me at all that he killed Cabibi. Only thing surprises me is him fessing up."

Six heads nodded agreement.

"You know," Kubota hat said, "Cabibi didn't bother with the mature set." He waved his hand to include all present. "I seen him mostly with guys 'round about his age. Spent a lot of time on the golf course. What I hear."

If there's one thing I hate worse than drinking coffee, it's ruining what could be a pleasant four hours outdoors by chasing a golf ball.

The Happy Reaper accepted delivery of the pair of drones at his hotel in

Iron Mountain. He registered them online using the email and credit card that matched his current ID and printed his registration card. He supposed using a false identity was his first felony of the day. He nicknamed them "Sky Spy" and "To Die For" and marked the one with a large SS and the other TDF. He didn't want to screw up and accidentally send one up with a low battery.

He rated his second felony of the day by practicing with the things near the Iron County airport. His third felony, had they caught him, was not keeping the drones in visual sight. The whole purpose of these babies was to be his eyes at a distance. He hadn't mastered the drones' controls with the hour's practice, but he was sure he could keep them in the air and focus their cameras for a live feed. The things were louder than he'd hoped, but if he kept them far enough away, they might not be noticed.

His drive to the woods around McCree's place was uneventful, and he parked down the road in an area denuded of growth the previous winter. With no trees, takeoffs and landings would be easy if he used the logging road for his runway and avoided the stumps littering the place.

Launching SS for its first business flight, he felt like a kid on Christmas morning. Clearing the trees, he maintained it at a hundred feet altitude and hovered over McCree's compound doing circles. He turned on the radio to keep an ear tuned to the *Telephone Time* chatter in case there were any messages to or from "Elliot."

His excitement drained away as the drone displayed McCree's empty driveway. The guy was gone, and it had become just another stakeout, this one with mosquitoes and deer flies. He bombed the area with Deet and concentrated on the task.

Unless you were military, one problem with drones was the limited flight time on a battery charge. He launched TDF, parked it doing circles above McCree's, and recalled SS. As the drone approached its landing, the *Telephone Time* announcer indicated he had a special message for Elliot from Abigail.

"Heard you needed a lift to the Windy City over the weekend. Would love your company but I lost your number. Call mine to arrange a ride." He gave a knowing chuckle. "And all you guys, don't get any brilliant ideas about calling the *TT* offices to get Abigail's number because we don't have it. So, Elliot, it's up to you, but I'd give her a call if I was you, bud."

The Happy Reaper lost concentration and the drone nearly smacked into a towering pine. After landing it safely, he considered his options. Jason Graham had not yet made himself known to Abigail/Seamus, which was good; it meant following Seamus to find Jason still made sense. Unfortunately, he had no idea where either one was, and he hadn't received any additional feeds from McCree's laptop in more than a day. Either McCree hadn't used it, or he had discovered the software and removed it. For now, the Happy Reaper was flying blind.

He still had forty-eight hours before his self-imposed mid-Saturday deadline to leave for Chicago and still have enough time to set up everything for Graham's expected court appointment on Monday.

A freshening breeze manifested itself in the slight sway of nearby treetops. Cirrus clouds gathered on the western horizon. Rain within the day. Rain wasn't supposed to affect the drones, but high winds could, and judging by the damage he had seen driving around, these woods could experience some exceptionally high winds.

He used TDF to check the other properties on the lake. Only one had any activity, a guy fishing from his dock. Using the opportunity to test his focusing skills, he zoomed in on the guy: rod in one hand, beer in the other, remainder of a six-pack sitting next to a tackle box. The resolution on the video was spectacular.

During the third flight of SS, he was rewarded with a perfect view of McCree's car pulling into the driveway and parking next to the garage. McCree walked into the garage and soon left, scooting up his driveway on an ATV.

The Happy Reaper sent the drone in pursuit, increasing its altitude to obtain a wider view. He was pleased with how easily the drone followed McCree, who headed to his recently purchased acreage. When McCree pulled into the woods, the drone lost him. Without infrared sensors to look through the leaves, he had to anticipate where McCree was headed.

From the limits of the drone's video range, a truck pulled into view and drove to McCree's ATV. The Happy Reaper returned the drone to a hundred feet and captured good shots of the truck driver—not Jason Graham—setting up survey equipment. McCree walked into the picture and talked with the truck driver. Too bad the drones didn't have microphones.

He left SS monitoring the two guys and sent TDF into a much higher orbit to do a loop around the area. He spotted another truck tucked deep in the woods, its windshield sparkling in the afternoon sun. He moved TDF in for a closer look.

No one was near the second truck, and he got the sense of a path from the truck down to a swampy area. Its near edge was delineated by sloppy rows of plants and a fence. Sure looked like someone had an illegal grow operation.

Movement from around McCree's ATV refocused his attention. He used TDF to follow McCree home and left SS monitoring the surveyor's area until it threatened to run out of battery.

Swapping in spare batteries and charging up the old ones, he maintained surveillance of McCree's place and waited to see what would happen next. He had not anticipated how exhausting it was to control the two drones, keep track of battery life, watch the monitor, and keep listening for more radio messages addressed to Elliot. Worse, he was no closer to finding Jason Graham.

Either something happened soon or he'd need to stir the pot.

I TOYED WITH THE IDEA of bracing Chris Saari again to see if I could get names of locals who might do deals with Frank Cabibi. On the way to Crystal, I decided instead to show up at Jenny Kauppi's place and ask who she thought I should look into.

She stepped outside, closing the door behind her. "Dad still won't see me."

I expressed my understanding of how difficult it was for her, but I still had hope for some leads I was working on. "If Frank Cabibi was setting up a crooked deal for constructing roads, or bringing in electric, or maybe even building a processing mill, which local guys might he use?"

Her face shut down. "Why would I know that?"

She looked like she might bolt. "Jenny, I apologize if I came across as accusing you of anything. I was asking because you've lived here your entire life, and I haven't. And your father knew everything happening around here and couldn't help but share the gossip with you. I'm trying to find an alternative motive for killing Cabibi. And if Cabibi was into something shady, he might go to the people he knew from high school."

By the time I finished my *mea culpa* and explanation, her face had relaxed into a smile.

"If you're talkin roads, there's two local outfits, one in Crystal, one in Iron River. I never met the guy in Iron River, but Mouse spent a stretch downstate for a construction scheme. Dad would know the details. Anyway, he was in the class between me and Frankie Joe."

"Mouse?"

"George Otto. Mouse is because he played a mouse in a school play in like second grade or somethin, and he was the biggest kid in the class. Goes like six-eight and is kinda mean."

THIRTY-THREE

I FOLLOWED THE SOUND OF Marine-worthy cursing and found Mouse behind an open shed full of heavy equipment. Holding a pipe wrench in one hand, he was berating a grader decades past its sell-by date. He wore a full beard, no mustache. His pimply face and bulked muscles made me think of steroids. Had my arrival set the stage for a game of Clue: Mouse killed Knucklehead Seamus behind the shed with a wrench?

Despite every rational cell in my brain screaming, "Run!" I walked toward him. I was close enough to see prison tats on his fingers before he acknowledged my presence and asked, in a deep bass voice any choir director would love, how he could help me.

I had planned to mention I was working with the sheriff's office. I revised my approach to, "Owen Lyndstrom's a friend of mine. I don't think he killed Frank Cabibi, so I'm trying to learn more about Cabibi to figure out why someone would kill him."

He stared at me as though I had two heads. Or none. What a terrible opening line. I added, "I understand you hung out with Cabibi and thought maybe you'd've heard if he had anything—"

He straightened to his full height, topping me by a half-foot. Plus, he outweighed me by at least a hundred pounds. He balled one hand into a fist; the other held the pipe wrench. Both hands stayed by his waist, but when he took a step toward me, my knees felt a little wobbly.

"Look," I tried a third time, "I'm making a hash out of this." I extended my hand. "My name is Seamus McCree. I'm hoping you can help Owen Lyndstrom."

He stopped, and looked skyward. "Oh," he said. "I've heard of you." He shifted the wrench to his left hand and we shook hands. "Buddy of mine's sister-in-law's ex-husband was one of the guys killed up by your place, what five, six years ago? I have to say, what you're doing for those kids—sending them to college and trade school and all—that goes a long way in my book. I don't want to know who sent you here. All it would do is piss me off. I made some really bad decisions as a kid. Some folks can't let that go."

The scholarships were supposed to be anonymous, but I supposed nothing really was in a small town.

He walked to the grader before turning around again and flashing me a smile, his teeth so straight they had to be dentures. "Besides, if I were to kill Frankie Joe Cabibi, I would have choked the shit out of the peckerwood."

"Oh?" The juxtaposition of his scruffy apparel and grooming and his precise language—including the proper use of "were" for the hypothetical conditional sentence—added to my confusion.

He waved the wrench at the grader. "You mind getting your hands dirty? I could use a third hand."

I laughed. "I have no problems with dirty hands, but my knowledge of graders stops at the general concept of what they do."

"Hold the hose in place while I tighten the connections. It has a mind of its own."

I did as he requested. The thought flitted through my mind that I had placed my hands in a position that would allow him to smash them with the pipe wrench if that was his intention. I inhaled slowly through my nose and caught the smells of grease and aftershave from him. He fastened the wrench on the recalcitrant nut and twisted.

"Look," he said. "I can't tell you much because I threw the asshole out of here. We'd had a few beers together. Reliving the glory days of the football and basketball teams a couple of times was enough. We didn't have much else in common. He's driving his fancy car, living in a fancy house. I run a small business and worry whether I can save enough to make it through the next recession. Anyway, one day he shows up here and asks if I can keep a secret."

He finished tightening the connection and gave it a tug. "Thanks, that saved me considerable time." He shook his head and scrunched his mouth in distaste. "He's been telling the world he plans to open a mine. No secret there. He tells me he's greased the wheels so the mine will get its permits. He raised his bushy eyebrows at me, like I was supposed to be impressed or something. Hell, spend enough money in Lansing, you can buy anything, especially with the current bunch of crooks running the place. I didn't give him any encouragement."

"But he kept talking."

"Oh yeah," Mouse nodded like he was remembering the conversation. "He casually mentioned he was responsible for all the construction contracts. There is only one reason he would imply he's bribing government people and all contracts go through him while talking to a guy who works with heavy equipment."

Agreed, but he was animated and on a roll, so I assumed what I hoped was a wise expression and kept my trap shut.

"He'd guarantee me a sweetheart deal if I slid him cash under the table. I told him I ran a clean business and to get the fuck off my property. I didn't want to see him here again."

"So, you didn't get details."

"I didn't want to be in a position to lie to the cops if they asked—and just like you're here, if they heard any hint of what he was planning, they'd be up my ass." He sneered. "Otto the Mouse has got a sheet, and he's doing okay for himself. Must be he's still a crook. Well, that is total bullshit. I work my ass off six days a week, sometimes seven. I learned a lot of stuff in prison. I even earned a college degree with honors. English Lit. But the thing I learned best was that I do not want to go back."

I offered him my hand. "Mr. Otto, I appreciate you telling me this. Cabibi didn't hint who else he might have tried to involve?"

He accepted my proffered hand. "Call me Mouse, everyone does. The other thing I learned real well doing time is to live and let live. Frankie Joe thought everything and everybody was his business. Someone disagreed. I don't figure to end up like Frankie Joe. You hear what I'm saying?"

Wise words, but I've struggled to follow that advice.

Thirty-Four

Jason Graham figured his best chance of staying alive was to get to Chicago. Abigail had offered to get him there, so he needed to contact Seamus and find out what their plan was. He had no clue whether it was legal to drive ATVs after dark. They had headlights, but driving north to Covington to find a phone meant he'd have to drive next to US-141. If it was illegal at night, he was asking for trouble. Better to hide in plain sight and travel midday.

If he could safely get to a phone far enough from town so the cops weren't around the corner, he'd be well gone before they could trace the call if they had McCree under surveillance. He'd bring his tools in case he saw a phone line going into a camp along the way. In fact, he'd bring everything. He dressed in camo, strapped on the helmet, put the visor down, and checked himself in the mirror. He couldn't recognize himself with a week-old beard. If he kept the gear on, he should be okay.

It took him until after one o'clock central time to pack the ATV. Covington was in the eastern time zone, so past two there. He had no idea what he would find there, but the lunch crowd should be gone, little kids napping, bigger kids gone swimming. It should be dead.

A grim thought entered his mind: better the town dead than him dead.

He mounted the ATV and turned the key. Damn thing ground like it wasn't getting enough gas. He pulled out the choke and the engine roared to life. Driving, he suffered from second thoughts. What if the police were patrolling Lukes Road looking for him? What if the message on *Telephone Time* was a hoax? He slapped himself on the helmet. No, it had to be real. He locked the garage behind him, replaced the garage key on the hook, locked the door to the cabin, and returned its key under the mat. He looked down at his bare fingers with a mounting wave of anxiety. He'd left fingerprints everywhere.

Traveling a sedate fifteen miles an hour shouldn't attract anyone's attention. Soon after turning north along the highway, he passed a swampy area he remembered Seamus saying often contained moose and was the scene of a moose-truck accident that had killed both moose and driver. The last thing he needed was a moose charging him, although he supposed he could outrun it if he needed to. Driving by, he glanced nervously all around the swamp. No moose, only a beaver lodge sitting in the middle. A breeze ruffled the reeds, but he couldn't hear it over the ATV's engine. Reaching the end of the swamp without any moose sightings, he breathed a sigh of relief and fogged his face mask. A sign announced the eastern time zone, which meant he was in Baraga County. Still no signs of electrical power, so probably no telephones, either.

An eighteen-wheeler sped by no more than a foot away in a place where a guardrail on the right side pinched off most of the shoulder. The backdraft pulled at him, kicking his heart into high gear. Lesson learned, he split his attention between the gravel below him and whatever was coming from behind him. What a nervous Nellie he was.

He passed through a small cut of what he figured was pre-Cambrian shield—much different from the landscape he had seen before. It reminded him of fishing trips into parts of Ontario. Up ahead, he spotted a cell tower. Might there be a phone there? Probably not, but it wouldn't hurt to look. He followed a sign proclaiming Drummond Lake Road, crossed what had probably been the original highway, and found the cell tower on the right behind a gated fence. The gate was closed, not locked. Ignoring the no-trespassing signs and microwave warnings, he opened the gate and walked in. No phone.

On the highway north, he finally passed an electrical pole sprouting next to the road. A rail crossing presaged civilization. A rusted silo on the left and a steeple poking above the trees on the right marked the entrance to the village. A brick post office squatted before the church, flag snapping in the breeze. No exterior phone.

He stopped at Bethany Lutheran, hoping some true Christian inside would allow him to make a phone call. No one responded to his pounding on the door. He backtracked and curved around Elm Street, past the town hall and garages, checking whether any of the parked cars had an obvious cell phone he might borrow. This was much harder than he had expected.

A Marathon station calling itself the North 141 Travel Plaza occupied the southwest corner of the intersection of US-141 and M-28. He circled the building looking for a phone. No luck. Maybe a pay phone inside? It did contain the Hard Wood Cafe.

He parked on the side of the building away from the pumps and walked past plastic-wrapped firewood. What a joke. A billion acres of forest all around and people would pay five bucks for a handful of pine? Too late, he realized wearing a helmet inside was kind of dorky; at least he could flip up the visor.

His eyes adjusted to the relative darkness. The cafe, currently a half-dozen empty tables, was tucked into a corner. Shelves loaded with junk food and motor oil occupied the space between the door he had used and the main entrance where a cashier stood, not paying any attention to him. No phone, but he figured he might as well use the restroom.

What a ridiculous sight he was: too-large helmet, his dick in one hand, standing in front of a stained urinal lower than his knees, wondering what he should do next. *The new me.*

He grabbed two packages of Grandma's cookies—a sucker for the oatmeal raisin—and brought them to the counter. "Take Canadian?" he asked the clerk.

The corners of her mouth curved into a disgusted frown. "We don't take no Loonies." The ess hissing through a gap in her front teeth. "Toonies neither."

Jason pulled a crumpled twenty out of his pocket.

"What did I say? No Canadian. Discount ain't so good these days."

"Sorry, I thought you meant you just didn't take coins. This is all I have. Let's call it the equivalent of ten American. It gives you a nice profit if you take it to the bank."

She crossed her arms over her ample chest. "You know how much time it'll take to cash out the register?"

"We're even." Jason threw the twenty on the counter, grabbed four more cookie packages, and marched toward the door.

"Hey. Hey! Put those cookies back."

Outside, he wolfed down the snack. His stomach rebelled against the glut, but soon the sugar buzz would hit his system. He shook his head at the absurdity of his position. He would give anything to curl up in his own bed, listen to music he wanted to listen to, read a book he wanted to read, and ignore the rest of the world. He wanted to go home, but he had no home. If he made it through this alive, would he enjoy whatever new life the Marshals Service gave him, or would he retain this feeling of wanting to go home again?

He walked the cookie wrappings to a trash barrel. At the ATV, he consulted the Baraga County plat book and found a few nearby streets with isolated houses. Remembering to choke the engine before starting it, he dismounted minutes later in front of a white bungalow at the end of a narrow dead-end road. No car in the driveway, but a ton of tracks showing a car routinely entered and exited. Grass grew in front of the garage, suggesting it was used for storage, not to shelter a vehicle.

He parked at the side of the driveway, left the motor running, and prepared himself to politely ask to borrow the person's phone if someone answered the door. After no response, Jason drove the ATV around to the rear, where it was hidden. The back door was locked and had a dead bolt. Jason hoped this person was like most people and didn't use it. He'd soon find out.

Taking a couple of quick breaths, he psyched himself up, and kicked hard next to the doorknob. The wood splintered but held. With another good kick that reverberated up his leg, the door burst open, and he entered the house. A half-empty cup of coffee sat in the sink along with a plate crusted with the remainders of runny eggs. The landline phone was attached to the kitchen wall next to a two-person table with only one chair.

He lifted the handset, heard a dial tone, and punched in the digits for McCree's cell phone.

One ring. Two rings. Three rings. Voicemail.

You've reached the phone of Seamus McCree. Please leave a message at the beep, and I'll get back to you soon as I can.

"It's Elliot," he said. "I need you to get me to Abigail and have her take me to Chicago in time for . . . in time. Meet me at the cell tower on Drummond Lake Road not far from highway one-forty-one."

He disconnected, grabbed a few tissues, and wiped the handset down, taking care of the fingerprints. He hoped. Live and learn.

The rattle of a truck coming down the road alerted him to company. He'd picked a dead-end road. What had he been thinking? He ran through the broken door and mounted the ATV, pulled out the choke, and keyed the ignition. The damn thing whined, but wouldn't kick on.

You're flooding the engine. He shoved in the choke and tried again. The ignition ground away, nearly caught, died. The next go brought it to life. He jammed it in gear and circled the yard looking for a path into the woods. Nothing. He had no choice but to blast past the truck and hope to outrun it if they decided to follow.

He thumbed the throttle hard. The ATV spewed twin rooster tails of grass and dirt behind him as he roared out of the backyard. The tires gained traction once he reached the driveway. The truck was slowing down and had pulled all the way to the left to turn into the driveway. Without looking at the driver, Jason cut sharply onto the road and accelerated until he was bumping along at forty-five miles an hour.

Where to go? He tried to visualize the plat map, but all he remembered of the immediate vicinity were the few streets comprising Covington proper and a bunch of roads wandering off US-141. Some dead-ended at a river, some in the forest. He skidded onto the highway and peeked over his shoulder. The truck was coming. *Think, Jason, think.*

Can't stay on the highway.

He cut onto the first road to the left, pushed the speed up to fifty-five, and held on so tight his forearms ached.

THIRTY-FIVE

I FOUND BARTELLE IN HIS office hunched over a stack of paperwork. He waved at a chair. "How much would the county have to pay you to permanently leave?"

I gave him my patented furrowed-brow look.

"Ever since you built your place, we've had murders every which way I turn. My overtime budget is shot to hell."

"May I point out I built here years before they hired you? Only after they brought in an experienced homicide detective did the murders start."

A faded grin graced his face. "*Touché.* What have you got?"

Ten minutes of questioning were enough for him to suck out everything I had learned or not learned: I'd found no documents corroborating Mouse's story. "I'd like to talk with Owen again."

"So would I, but he's refusing to talk to anyone. We lucked out on one front. The skeleton is Timothy Javoroski. We found his orthodontia records in Iron Mountain. Here's another—what was that highfalutin word you like?—synchronicity. I went through our case files from around the time Javoroski disappeared to see if anything would pop. Owen

Lyndstrom had reported someone stole a pistol from his bedroom. Same make and model as the pistol buried with Javoroski. What are the chances?"

The wise-ass in me wanted to say, "One hundred percent," since both events had, in fact, occurred. Bartelle did not look in the mood for sophomoric, math-geek humor, so I kept my mouth shut.

He massaged his forehead with the heels of his hands. "Prosecutor needs more to make a charge."

"But I take it you have a working theory?"

Bartelle leaned back, curved his arm over his head and scratched behind his ear. "Theory. Don't know if it's working. For reasons not yet known, Lyndstrom shoots Javoroski with his pistol. To cover himself, he reports the gun missing. Years later, Lyndstrom hears Cabibi is testing for a mine near where he buried the body and realizes the body will be discovered. To prevent that, he lures Cabibi to the area."

"And whacks him with a rock he picked up nearby?"

Bartelle sat up straight, his voice harder. "And, knowing everyone thinks he would shoot somebody, whacks Cabibi with a rock he brought with him."

"Which he leaves at the scene?"

Bartelle shrugged. "The better to convince everyone it wasn't him."

"But," I said, "he confessed. Why go through the effort to make it look like it couldn't be you if you plan to confess? And why, under your theory, would he confess to Cabibi's death and not to Javoroski's?"

Bartelle's shoulders sagged. "That's the not-so-working part of the theory. He got old. He felt guilty. Unlike thirty years ago, he doesn't have a long life ahead of him. Confession's good for the soul."

"So say the priests," I said. "For someone like Owen, being confined in a cell would kill his soul. If he felt the need to confess, why not leave a note and take off? Besides, if valuable ores are around, it's only a matter of time before someone digs them up."

"Sure, but at Owen's age a few years' delay might be all he needs."

"Point taken," I said. "Let's find out if he'll see me, shall we?"

THE DOOR TO THE INTERVIEW room opened and a deputy ushered Owen inside. I was shocked by the sallow color of his skin, the lethargy in his step. I thought I kept an impassive face, but my thoughts must have shown.

"I don't think I'll make it long enough for them to take me to trial," he said. "Save the county some money, anyway."

"Are you ill?"

"Not yet," he said. "But I'm workin on it. I'd rather be dead than cooped up. Heard tell the Natives could will themselves dead. Figured I give 'er a try."

We settled into the chairs. He didn't need anything, or so he said. I'd confer with the jailers in case this was part of Owen's effort to shut down his life. I tried to share recent gossip I'd picked up, but Owen was uncharacteristically disinterested.

Time to shift gears. "I hear the pistol they found with Tim Javoroski was likely the one you reported stolen. I assume you didn't kill him since you didn't admit to it?" His expression did not change. "Any idea how your gun got there?"

Owen was a speak-his-mind kind of guy, so I grew suspicious as he considered his answer.

He let loose a theatrical sigh. "I suppose I should let the sheriff off the hook on that one, too. I didn't reckon people would think unkindly of me for riddin the world of Frankie Joe Cabibi. People liked Timmy Javoroski, though. That's why I didn't say nothin."

It felt wrong to me, but I decided to play along. Something Owen would say might provide insight into this imbroglio. "Why would you kill Tim Javoroski?"

A spark flashed in Owen's eyes and his voice hardened with anger. "You never had a daughter, so you wouldn't understand, would ya? No, you wouldn't. But you got a granddaughter now. What would you do if someone took advantage of yer granddaughter? How would you protect her?"

He knew of the rape? "I'm not understanding you, Owen. Whatever you're hinting at, I'm too thick to get."

"What would you do, Seamus McCree, if three boys you knew from when they was in nappies, and who you trusted, took advantage of your daughter? They screwed her and forced her to get an abortion."

He did know.

"I," he thumped his chest. "I gave Timmy Javoroski the gun to kill himself. I don't feel guilty, but what do they call that? Accessory to murder or somethin? I found him in the woods and I buried him and the gun. That I did. Frankie Joe Cabibi chose to leave town and stay away. He waited thirty years to return. I confronted him in the woods. He got me so goldurn mad that I picked up the rock and kilt him. I was gonna bury him next to Timmy. 'Course I didn't have no tools with me, and then God intervened by lettin your dog find one of Timmy's bones. He was telling me to confess my sins, and I did." He crossed his arms and glared at me with hard eyes and a straight-line mouth.

"You said three boys."

"I did. Timmy told me. That's how I knew. I gave the third one a second chance. I don't cotton much to the born-again crap, but it's done good by him."

"Chris Saari."

He uncrossed his arms, leaned into the table, squinting eyes lasered into mine. "How do *you* know that?"

"Your daughter told me. She believes you're taking the blame for killing Cabibi because you think she did it."

He pursed his lips and shook his head. "No. No. No. You've got that all wrong. I'm the one—"

"I listened to you, now you listen to me. If you had buried Tim Javoroski, you'd know he didn't kill himself. People do not commit suicide by shooting themselves twice in the head. Javoroski was murdered and you think your daughter did it because she had access to the gun. And you think she's justified because if you had known, you would have killed all three of them. No second chance for Frank Cabibi if he went away. That's a crock of shit, Owen Lyndstrom, and you know it. You love your daughter and would rather die in jail than see her tried for those crimes."

He continued to shake his head, but he hadn't gotten up, and he hadn't called the guard to take him to his cell.

"Here's the thing, Owen. I'm convinced your daughter did not kill Cabibi. And if she didn't kill Cabibi, chances are strong she didn't have anything to do with Javoroski's death either. Oh yeah, and I talked to Chris Saari, so I know he never told you. And I know Jenny never told you. You're lying through your teeth to protect your daughter, and she doesn't need protecting. You're killing yourself in here, Owen. Is that how to show your daughter that you love her?"

His head drooped, but his voice had a hard edge. "You just won't leave this alone, will you, Seamus? Unless you was with Jenny the whole time, you cain't know where she was or what she was doin. But if I thought Jenny kilt Timmy, why would I report the gun stolen? You're like a mutt who gets its teeth on a disgustin old boot and won't let go no matter how bad it tastes or how bad it smells up the house. I forgive you. Nothin you can do about it. It's who you are, Seamus. So, go on stinkin up the place with your smelly boot, but I've said all I have to say."

Thirty-Six

THE ATV WAS KICKING UP a fierce cloud of dust, which Jason figured meant would make it easy for the guy to follow him. He had to get far enough ahead so the dust settled before the guy arrived. He was running fast down the road and spotted rail cars through the trees. Should he try to cut through the woods and drive on the ballast? The truck couldn't follow, but he'd have to drive slower, giving the truck time to catch up. If the road and the rails came together . . . He wished he'd spent more time studying local plat maps instead of watching how the markets were doing.

The woods opened and he sped over a paved bridge with a clear view to the rails lined with empty cars for carrying lumber. Soon he was back on dirt, spewing cloaking dust behind him with no sign of the truck. He passed several camp roads marked by red Baraga County fire signs—dead ends to avoid. The road soon narrowed and became a less-used two-track. Still dusty, but less so, and his ATV could go faster on this stuff than any truck could.

Barely keeping control while speeding through a series of protruding rocks, he throttled down: better alive and caught than wrapped around a tree. Glimpses of a lake flashed by on his right, and soon he came to a T intersection. He had no idea where he was, but the place he had told Seamus to meet him was south, so he headed right. Slowing through the turn, he looked past his shoulder, the scared part of him sure the truck was close behind, and the logical part telling him an old truck had crap suspension and couldn't possibly go fast enough to keep up.

He couldn't see through the damn dust, and the noise of his engine drowned out every other sound. Having stopped, his own dust cloud enveloped him, tickling his nose and triggering a sneezing fit. Hitting the throttle, the acceleration nearly jerked him off the ATV. He slowed a titch to regain control and slowed again at a sign pointing to the King Lake State Campground. Then he caught a break. Approaching him was a cloud of dust so thick he could see only the cab of an oncoming logging truck.

He found a wide spot to let the logging truck past. He'd seen McCree do the same thing and wave at the drivers. Graham stuck up his left arm, gave a wave, and was pleased the driver waved back as he rumbled past. The dust Jason had kicked up was nothing compared to the dense cloud produced by the truck's passage. No way anyone could follow him through that.

Once the logging truck cleared, Jason inched the ATV forward into the choking dust. Even with raspberry bushes clawing at his arm, he stayed far to the right. He'd experienced logging trucks traveling in pairs, like girls going to the bathroom, and sure enough, a second logging truck materialized out of the dust and ground past him.

Dust had breached his helmet. It was up his nose, in his mouth, and stinging his eyes, dust fucking everywhere. With the logging trucks running interference, he could hide and learn whether the pickup truck was still on his tail. He passed a driveway on the right—its camp too close to the road—and found a two-track on the left, heading for the lake he had passed. With two shallow curves between him and the road, he judged himself safe from being spotted, but near enough to hear any nearby traffic. He shut down the ATV.

After removing his helmet, he created enough saliva to spit most of the dust from his mouth. From the distance came the grumble of the logging trucks crawling toward the highway. Nearby, waves softly lapped the shore. No pursuing truck, but he'd rest in this warm, sheltered spot to make sure.

He consulted the plat book and traced his path from Murphy Road to King Lake Road. From here, he could get to Tracy Creek Road and out to US-141. Except he couldn't find Drummond Lake Road in the plat book. He spotted Drummond Lake itself. Whatever. Once he hit the highway, he'd be able to find that cell tower. All assuming he'd lost his tail; otherwise he was stuck with running on back roads. But would Seamus be there?

* * *

THE HAPPY REAPER DID NOT like hanging around places where cops congregated, and flying a drone in Crystal Falls was sure to gather someone's attention, so that was out. He'd parked on a side street where he could see McCree's car, pretending to read a paperback—a regular Joe patiently waiting for his wife. He should have attached a GPS tracker to McCree's car. Shoulda, woulda, coulda was wasted time. Maybe he could buy some on Amazon and ship them to his new hotel in Iron Mountain. He'd need a bunch: one for McCree's car, one for his woods truck, one for each ATV. Hell, it'd be easier to stick one up the guy's ass.

He checked his watch again, frowned and looked around, thinking, "Where is that woman," so anyone watching him would see the picture he was trying to paint. He could give his search for Graham only one more day in this God-awful place before he headed to Chicago and set up for Monday. Surely, McCree would have been quicker if he had gone to the sheriff's office or jail to retrieve Jason Graham. Something else, then. What? A silver-haired lady came out onto her stoop, shielded her eyes, and looked directly at his car. Time to vamoose.

He started the engine and checked traffic before pulling away from the curb. His backward glance caught Seamus McCree jogging from the sheriff's office toward his car. Timing is everything. Tailing someone in a two-traffic-light town was not the easiest thing in the world. On the other hand, there weren't a lot of places McCree could go, which meant he could leave plenty of room between the two of them. He waited until McCree headed in a direction suggesting he was going west on US-2. That was the way to McCree's place, but what was his hurry?

He circled the block, reaching US-2 from a different street, made his left, and saw McCree a half-dozen cars ahead of him. At the split of US-2 and US-141, McCree signaled north—again the direction home. Two of the five cars between them made the same turn. The Happy Reaper followed, allowing the distance between predator and prey to grow.

One car in front of him dropped out at the Paint River Landing parking lot. The other left the highway at Swan Lake. McCree was going well over the speed limit, so by the time there were no cars between McCree and him, the Happy Reaper had left enough space that he didn't worry. He accelerated to match McCree's sixty-five miles an hour—the fastest

McCree had gone so far. He fully expected McCree to visit Amasa or head home and was surprised when McCree drove past Corral Road, the last possible road to take him home.

His interest quickened. With no intervening cars, he didn't dare pull any closer and lost sight after McCree crested a hill. He kept a lookout for dust clouds that might indicate McCree had exited the highway. At the top of the hill, he spotted McCree again and breathed a sigh of relief.

Halfway to Covington, McCree signaled a right and kicked up dust heading toward a cell phone tower rising high above the trees. Had Jason Graham contacted McCree at the sheriff's office? The Happy Reaper eased onto a switch a hundred yards before McCree's turnoff. He found the correct page on the plat map and traced his finger down the road McCree had taken. From here, you could work your way down to Lukes Road, but why would you go so far out of the way?

Had Graham been hiding nearby all along? Perhaps. Or maybe they were meeting at the tower, an easy place to describe. Sitting wouldn't tell him. He left the plat map open on the passenger seat and put the car in gear.

THE SUBARU'S CLOCK SHOWED A quarter past five. I punched the code to recall the phone message left by Jason Graham—Elliot, as he called himself—from two hours earlier while I was at the jail with Owen Lyndstrom. The message was clear. I was at the right cell tower; he was not. Had something happened and he didn't make it, or had he given up and left? How would I know?

At least he had picked a spot with good 4G coverage. I used my cell phone to reverse white-pages the number he'd left the message from. My GPS claimed the landline in Covington was eight crow-miles away. If Jason still had his stolen ATV, he should have gotten here way before me. If he was on foot, he should be here soon. If he walked at a more leisurely three-miles-an-hour pace, I had the better part of an hour to wait.

My stomach churned with excess acid caused by nerves and skipping lunch. A car drove slowly by, the driver shot a glance my direction. No passenger. Not the right shape for Jason.

With the car engine ticking down, I had time to call Abigail. She picked up with a wary, "Yes?"

My heart raced like I had pressed on the accelerator but forgotten to take the car out of neutral. *Focus on business, Seamus.* I told her of the phone message and my current situation. "Did you discuss an extraction plan with Jason Graham?"

"If I was available, I'd pick him up the day before the trial date and deliver him to the courtroom the next morning. If I was still tied up on the Louisiana job, you'd make the delivery. I got home last night." Her voice softened. "Thank you for removing your stuff from my place. That was thoughtful. I appreciate it."

"If he shows, I'll take him away from here. But, with everything happening, I'll really need your help to protect him until Monday."

"This doesn't change anything." A hint of anger tinged her voice. "If and when you have your charge in hand, give me a call."

With a click, she was gone. A gnawing emptiness replaced my previous hunger. *One step at a time.*

In the next hour, several cars drove past the tower. My heart quickened at the sound of an ATV, but unlike the automobile and truck drivers who had all glanced my way, the ATV roared past, heading to US-141.

How long should I wait? Sitting in the car was getting old. Should I call the number back? No, if he was still there, he could have called me. My imagination whirled with possibilities—none good. I slipped the cell phone into my pocket, grabbed the pair of old binoculars I kept in the car, and began birding the area around the cell tower. If he came, I'd see him, and getting outside and doing something would burn off some worry. *Jason Graham, where are you?*

THE HAPPY REAPER PEEKED PAST his arm, crooked to hide his face, as he drove past McCree's car. McCree had pulled through an open gate onto the gravel around the base of the tower and was pointed facing the road. From the brief look, he was waiting for something or someone. This had to be a meet with Graham. Had to be.

He continued down the road a piece. Balancing the risk of Graham showing up and leaving with McCree against the risk of his SUV being seen twice by McCree too soon, he waited three minutes before returning past the cell tower. McCree had not moved.

The Happy Reaper chose to park under the shade of planted pine trees on the dirt road running parallel to US-141, probably the original highway. Opening the hatch of the SUV, he dug under the drones and their batteries and removed the long gun and slipped an ammunition clip into his pocket. He jogged through the hardwood forest until he was within a hundred feet of the cell tower. He slowed and deliberately made his way to a spot where he could watch McCree through the scope.

Still by himself. Still in the car.

If he knew where Graham would be coming from, he could ambush him before he got to McCree and McCree could live. To his surprise, he realized he was sentimental about good ol' Seamus, despite McCree costing him a seven-figure payout after their first contretemps. He had liked the way the guy figured stuff out and appreciated his integrity. Fact was, he had promised that if McCree stopped looking for him, the Happy Reaper would not harm him.

McCree had put his cell phone on speaker. He had one of those voices that naturally carried, his baritone clear and precise. The Happy Reaper heard everything McCree said and most of what Abigail Hancock had said.

Now he knew for sure that Graham had tried contacting McCree and McCree was hoping the meet was still on.

He prided himself on his word being his bond. During the recession, hit men were a dime a dozen, all scrounging to make ends meet. His reputation had allowed him to maintain his top-dollar fees. But he couldn't be held to promises made under different circumstances. It was McCree's bad luck if Graham showed up. Maybe an anonymous donation to the foundation McCree had set up to help victims of violence would make reasonable recompense. The irony of that put a smile on his lips and soothed the uneasiness he had about breaking his promise to McCree.

Seconds became minutes became quarter hours. Camo and quiet, the perfect combination. He had been still long enough for woodland birds to resume singing: trills in one spot, soft whistles in another. A red squirrel scurried over his shoes, realized those obstructions belonged to a human, and stood tall, lecturing the Happy Reaper in a loud chattering voice. He enjoyed a silent laugh.

A car slowed down to look at McCree. The Happy Reaper scoped the driver: a woman in a tank top. She could be hiding Graham under a blanket or in the trunk. The car accelerated away.

He settled in for a wait, content in the hunt. *If Jason Graham shows, one bullet will provide a happy customer and a fattened bank account.* McCree rummaged in his car, leaning over the seat, looking for something. Then, he opened the door.

The Happy Reaper kept his eye to the scope and forced a slow exhale. *This could be it.*

Thirty-Seven

I WAS WATCHING A PAIR of eastern phoebes use the tower as a launching platform to gather flying bugs when a state trooper rolled up. I nervously moistened the inside of my cheeks with my tongue and waited.

"Evening sir," he said. "Been here long?"

I settled on a noncommittal answer. "A bit."

"I need to ask you to leave. This is posted private property."

"Didn't realize that. The gate was open when I arrived."

"Gate's supposed to be closed," he said. "Have you by any chance seen a green ATV piled high with gear?"

"One passed, but it didn't have any gear. And it was red, I think. What's up?"

"If you do see it, we'd appreciate it if you could give us a call." He handed me a card with his name and number. "A homeowner up by Covington found some guy tear-assing out of his backyard. He lost the guy's trail and found his house broken into. The same ATV had been spotted earlier in town at several locations including the Marathon station, where he left Canadian money even though the clerk told them they didn't take the stuff. Clerk said he didn't talk like a Canuck. Anyway, you spot him, don't do anything foolish, use your cell phone," he pointed to his card, "and give us a call."

I tamped down my strong desire to ask where the break-in had occurred, suspecting I knew both the answer and that Elliot was driving that ATV.

"Am I in danger?" I thought an uninvolved person might ask the same thing.

"I noticed a parked SUV." He motioned with his head toward the highway. "Thought if it was towing a trailer, maybe our guy was using this as a base. No trailer and the vehicle's a rental. You spot the guy, don't use those binoculars to get a better view. Call us. Clear out. By the way, what are you doing?"

"I enjoy birdwatching. It's a good excuse to get outside."

"The wife's into it. Puts up feeders in the winter. You have a good day, sir. The road's wide enough to safely park and continue your birdwatching. And shut the gate after you." He touched his cap with a finger and drove off.

I parked the car on the side of the road, facing US-141, and returned to close the gate, noticing for the first time the sign proclaiming, "No Trespassing! Authorized Personnel Only." I replayed the officer's words and was suddenly struck by a new worry: if the police checked the phone at the house with the break-in, they'd find it had dialed my number. Oh boy.

THE POSITION OF THE STATE cop and his car made it impossible for the Happy Reaper to hear their conversation. The trooper left and McCree got into his car. The Happy Reaper retreated in a jog to his rental to follow McCree, not worrying about the branch snap that sounded like a pistol shot.

He listened to McCree's progress: the crunch of tires on gravel; the screech of the gate closing. He quickened his pace, bursting into a trot once he got to the road.

And then McCree's engine turned off. Whatever the cop had told McCree, the meet was still on. The Happy Reaper silently slipped into the woods.

JASON GRAHAM WOKE WITH A start from an unintended nap, his heart racing. He held his breath and listened for whatever had woken him. A splash in the lake drew his attention. Two otters feeding. One flipped on his back and proceeded to eat a fish the same way Jason ate corn on the cob, spinning the food in his paws.

The sun was noticeably lower in the sky. He chided himself for falling asleep, then realized the adrenaline surge of the chase had shut off and his body's safety mechanism combined with the warm day had done the trick.

Now he needed to get to Seamus and get to safety. Was Seamus still at the meeting spot? Had he even received the message?

MY MOVEMENT HAD DRIVEN THE birds into the forest, leaving my unengaged mind time to do its own thinking. A younger me would have tried to cram the conversation with Abigail into a logic trunk, slam the lid, wrap the trunk with chains, and drown the whole thing so feelings wouldn't affect me. My mind might be willing, but my body was screaming bullshit. My chest hurt, my back hurt, my neck hurt, my stomach hurt, my head hurt. I caught myself preparing arguments to convince Abigail this was only a bump in our road together, not a dead end. Logical brain identified the internal conversation as early-stage grief: the shock and denial stage. Maybe when this was resolved she'd listen to reason?

I set the binocs on the front bumper and stretched the muscles kinked by my self-induced tension. Ten minutes of stretches and deep breathing reduced the physical pain to a throb. I didn't know any exercises to reduce the heartache.

The air shimmered with late July heat and a light breeze ruffled the top branches, making it difficult to distinguish whether a branch moved because a bird had landed on it or because it had been stirred by the wind. Not ideal for birdwatching, but I was here, so why not discover which birds and mammals were in the vicinity in addition to the phoebe still calling from the tower. I slung the binocs over my neck and shoulder so they hung on my right side and walked up the road.

Novice birders often spend gobs of time moving, looking for where the birds are. More experienced birders find a location attractive to birds and let the birds come to them. Birding is often good at edges of habitats. I walked down the road until I found a marsh bordered by conifers. On the other side of the road was a mix of maple, birch, and popple. Three habitats, one spot. I tucked in next to a white pine to hide my shape and let the woods settle.

A red squirrel ran up a nearby tree and stared at me with its tail curled, protecting its back. I remained still, watching. Following a half-hearted round of chattering, the squirrel disappeared, leaping from tree to tree until I could no longer follow it.

I heard a gray jay before I saw it. Calling softly, it received a response from deeper in the woods. It moved from branch to branch, cocking his head this way and that to try to get a better view of me. These guys often show up at campfires during hunting season, looking for handouts. Soon, the woods filled with chickadee song, the *ank-ank* of red-breasted nuthatches, and the high trill of a kinglet.

As though someone had pulled a plug, they all went silent.

Only my eyes had moved. Something else had disturbed them. I dismissed my first thought of a hawk. The jays would screech their warnings, and the little dicky birds would dive for cover in the conifers. The jays were as silent as monks, and a pair of chickadees sat without fear on an popple branch hanging over the road.

If not a raptor, a mammal? Pine marten? They're curious and I've had them come within reach on more than one occasion. I closed my eyes to let my ears take charge.

A chipmunk high in the evergreens broke the silence with a series of scolding chirps that gave him his name. A distant red squirrel joined with a rattle.

Slowly and smoothly, I brought the binoculars to my eyes and scanned the woods opposite me, stopping at an undefined mass behind the leaves. For a while, nothing moved and I thought I had been wrong. Then the fawn raised its head from browsing. With the movement, its dappled fur became clear, as did a doe behind it. She looked in my direction, her ears folded forward to gather sound.

We watched each other for some minutes before the deer slipped into the underbrush. The birds had resumed their little chips and tweets. Who knows what had caused them to go silent; it wasn't the deer. I rose on stiff legs and focused on the tops of the trees opposite, keeping a mental list of the birds I saw, adding a ruby-crowned kinglet and several species of warblers. A growing sense of failure dragged at my mood. The time was going on seven-thirty, nearly four hours since Jason Graham's phone call. I doubted he would show, but gave him fifteen more minutes because I'd hate to leave and then have him arrive.

Scanning the woods, I caught a reflection, and focused the binocs in its direction. Nothing. Must have been a trick of light. Pulling the binocs away from my eyes, I spotted a shape. I changed the focus and brought the camouflaged man into view.

Sweat popped on my forehead, dampened my armpits. Adrenaline coursed through me. My nostrils widened to smell the danger, but found only the rich scent of the northwoods. Those physical reactions were instinctual. Moments later my cognitive facilities named the danger. I had spotted the Happy Reaper.

Calm overtook me. With the binocs I pretended to watch a bird in flight, scanning away from the Happy Reaper. With a sideways step, I mimed getting a better look at the tree in which this phantom bird had landed. For several seconds, I presented an Oscar-winning performance: the perplexed birdwatcher who couldn't quite figure out which bird had flown off.

I was alive, so the Happy Reaper wasn't here to kill me; he was here for Jason. Thank God Jason had not come. How could I lose the assassin? If I tried to evade him, would I lose my value and he'd shoot me? Call Bartelle? No, the Happy Reaper would hear me on the cell phone. Act naturally. Get to my car. Then call Bartelle.

In what I hoped looked like an unconcerned amble, I headed toward my car.

Nothing fast. Nothing suspicious. Look at a flying bird. Dihedral wings. Turkey vulture. Not for me, please. Not today. Get into your car and leave, leave, leave. He's here because he's following me and if he doesn't shoot me, I need to lead him away from Jason. How had he found me? Check again for a GPS tracker on the car. Could he have cloned my phone? Hacked it and followed its GPS?

Blue of wings flashed by. "Hey, blue jay," I called in a voice that almost sounded natural, "where you going?"

I decided to keep talking to myself. "Bring any of your grosbeak friends? I didn't see any, but someone said they'd seen both rose-breasted and evening." At my car, I removed the binocs from around my head and fished car keys from my pocket with nervous fingers. I badly wanted to turn around and see where the Happy Reaper was. I tamped down the urge and, with the thought of electronic cloning in my mind, used the physical key to unlock the door to prevent the Happy Reaper from capturing my electronic door-opening signal.

Crazy thinking—but fearful people do crazy things, even if they are full of logic.

Car motor on, I zipped down the windows to let out the accumulated heat. Bonus, I might hear him in the woods. Pulling out, I scanned the woods for movement. Nothing. Nothing at all. Was I safe?

THIRTY-EIGHT

DRIVING AWAY FROM THE CELL tower, I tried to act normal so the Happy Reaper wouldn't suspect I'd seen him. He had to be stopped, but how? He was armed, I was not. I needed to get the police involved.

And I needed to stay alive.

Had the Happy Reaper overheard my conversation with Abigail? If so, would he follow me or wait for Jason? Could I lure him into a police trap? I had done that once in Cincinnati, but then I had the full cooperation of the Cincinnati police. Would Bartelle cooperate?

Now that I was driving, I questioned myself: had I actually seen anything?

At US-141, instead of heading south toward Amasa and home or Crystal Falls and Bartelle, I chose north, parking at the side of the road a hundred yards on. I ran down the slope, through the trees to the road paralleling the highway and found the rental SUV the state trooper had mentioned.

Now it was a race between my act and the Happy Reaper returning through the woods to this vehicle. Keeping on the safe side of the SUV, I unscrewed the tire valve and used my car key to let out the air. The hiss of escaping air sounded as loud as a trumpet voluntary played to announce the Queen's arrival. If he heard the sound and found me, I was dead. This was crazy stupid. My knuckles turned white and my fingers ached as I pressed the key on the stem. Pressing harder wouldn't make it lose air faster, but I couldn't help it.

With one tire pancaked, I duck-walked to the front tire and worked on flattening it. If this wasn't the Happy Reaper's ride, someone would be pissed. Well, someone would be pissed in any event, especially if I succeeded in getting the cops here.

Second tire flattened, I kept low and ran up the hill to my car. My hands were shaking so hard, I needed my left to steady my right enough to insert the key in the ignition. I did a U-ey and sped south, eyes shifting between the road and my cell-phone address book. I tapped Bartelle's cell-phone number and initiated a call.

His response to my story was, "That is the stupidest thing you have ever done, McCree. You weren't in my county. All I can do is contact the state police and Baraga county sheriff. You do realize that if you're right and we don't catch this guy, you put a giant target on your back? He knows where the fuck you live. Jesus, Seamus, what were you thinking?"

"I'm thinking if you stop fucking haranguing me and call in the troops, we can capture a seriously bad person." I disconnected. "Asshole," I shouted at my phone.

Okay, Seamus, slow down and try to think like Jason Graham. It had been more than four hours since his phone call and he had neither shown up at the cell tower nor called again. Conclusion: he was running, presumably still on the ATV. Maybe lost, maybe not. We needed a different meeting place, and the only place other than the cell tower that Jason and I knew in common was my home. If he wanted to meet somewhere else, he'd have to contact me. I needed to go home. For a stretch of six or seven miles between Amasa and my place I would not have cell coverage. I called my voicemail and set a new message. "Sorry we couldn't meet. I'm heading home."

Hopefully Jason would call. Hopefully the Happy Reaper would not.

THE UNEASY FEELING THE HAPPY Reaper experienced when McCree started talking to the birds and the squirrels kept growing until he was certain McCree had spotted him. The Happy Reaper had practiced following the guy in Scotland all day without being spotted, and in one momentary lapse, he'd given himself away to McCree. The cat-and-mouse switched roles, and he froze in place until he was sure McCree could no longer see him, and then he carefully followed.

Hearing a car start up triggered him to hurry toward his rental. He stayed away from the woods' edge, which kept him out of sight, but brought him to a marshy area. By the time he worked around the marsh, he knew he had lost McCree.

He squatted with his back against a tree and considered his options. McCree obviously had no way of contacting Jason Graham to warn him off, nor did he know where Graham was. If he were McCree, what would he do? *Secure my own safety first. I couldn't help Graham if I were dead.* Check—McCree had skedaddled. Then I'd try to keep Graham safe. That meant expelling the Happy Reaper from the meeting area before Graham showed up.

Since McCree had driven off, he'd obviously rejected personal confrontation, which meant he'd probably called the cops. The Happy Reaper ran to the rental car. Breaking out of the woods several yards away from the vehicle, he recognized its cant meant two flat tires.

"Strike three," he muttered. "No more Mr. Nice Guy."

The wail of a distant siren spurred him to action.

JASON GRAHAM SPOTTED THE CELL tower poking above the trees. Checking the plat book, he concluded the Tracy Creek Road of the plat book and the Drummond Lake Road of the sign had somewhere become the same road. The chances of Seamus still waiting—assuming he even got the message—were not huge. Should he drive up or park the ATV and walk to the meet through the woods? Walking seemed the better plan, providing more options in case something went wrong.

Once the cell tower appeared to be just around the next bend, he drove off the road through tall grass and parked the ATV behind a large bush. To maintain cover on his approach, he walked through the evergreens on the north side of the road. After a hundred yards, the tower didn't seem a lot closer. He'd underestimated the distance, but the exercise would do him good.

As evergreens edged into deciduous forest, strobing blue and red lights flickered through the trees. *Cops.*

He ducked behind a low balsam. *McCree called the cops?*

The distance was too far to hear anything. Watching provided no clues why the cops were there or what they were doing. Being in a uniform didn't mean you hadn't been bought. No choice but return to the ATV and try something else. He hadn't realized he was feeling hopeful until he now felt despair. He needed a plan B, but first he needed to get out of there.

The trip back through the deciduous woods seemed to take forever, but he made it into the conifers without being seen. Why wasn't he seeing the ATV? Had he overshot?

He cut to the road and started jogging, reached a bend he knew he'd passed while still riding the ATV. Turning around, he jogged back and was flooded with relief when he found and followed the ATV tracks into the tall grass where they ended behind the bush.

The ATV was gone.

SEVERAL MILES DOWN THE ROAD, the Happy Reaper pulled the loaded ATV into the grass driveway of a small camp. He needed to assess what had happened, inventory the material at his disposal, and make a plan.

Pawing through the material strapped to the ATV, he discovered local plat maps—useful—and Seamus McCree's passport—ah crap. Why had he not understood the situation while passing the guy in the woods? Because he'd been in escape mode, not hunt mode, and hadn't recognized Jason Graham with the helmet on. A missed opportunity, but he forgave himself the error and contemplated what this new information meant.

Jason Graham had almost made it to the meeting with McCree, except McCree had left the field of play to the Happy Reaper. The cops would soon track his rental and compromise the ID he had been using. He had others, but currently he was riding around on a stolen ATV with a half-tank of gas. Jason Graham was somewhere nearby and on foot.

Should he return and kill Graham? The cops would swarm at the sound of a rifle shot. Without an escape plan, he'd be caught.

The plat maps allowed him to plot a route on dirt roads to McCree's place. With luck, he'd run into Jason Graham and earn his bonus. If McCree had returned home, he'd deal with him there. At a minimum, he'd steal one of McCree's vehicles and drive to Chicago.

FINALLY REACHING CELL PHONE COVERAGE, my phone dinged to let me know I had missed a call and had a voicemail.

"Good call on that rental," Bartelle's message said. "I heard from the state boys. They ran the plates and got the rental agency to divulge the driver information. It's a fake license."

I hadn't embarrassed myself by disabling some tourist's rental. *Whew.*

Bartelle kept talking. "The rental company gave them permission to open the car. The guy had an arsenal plus some other disturbing stuff. Call me."

Dread returned full force. Nothing had changed for the better: the Happy Reaper knew I did it. They hadn't captured him. He'd kill me if he found me. Life in black and white. Like I'd thrown a switch, I became calm and calculating.

Albert Einstein supposedly said insanity could be defined as doing the same thing repeatedly and expecting different results. More than once, I had put my foot down and insisted no one would scare me out of my home. That had not gone well for those around me—or my homes. The Happy Reaper knew where I lived, and I did not plan to be around when he showed up—as he surely would.

Right now, the smart thing would be to go somewhere far away. Ellesmere Island came to mind. But with a chance Jason Graham was waiting at my house in the woods for me to take him to safety, I couldn't leave him to the Happy Reaper. Plus, if I wanted to leave the country, I needed my passport, which was at camp. With a head start, I had time to check for Jason and pack a few things before leaving.

* * *

THE HAPPY REAPER STOPPED AT a large washout on Lukes Road. One problem with plat maps was they didn't show beaver construction projects like this one. On his side, the road went into the water without obstruction. The far side was blocked with large boulders, and he was not sure whether an ATV could get past. Without immediate pursuit, he could afford to be cautious.

Air temperature had dropped to the high sixties, but testing the water with his hand, he found it much warmer. Before taking each step, he made sure he was balanced on the other foot. He did not want to go swimming.

The first few steps were shallow and had a solid gravel bottom. Soon he was calf-high in water and walking on slick mud. Underneath the mud, the ground continued to feel solid. He reached an area where the water tugged his legs. He shuffled forward with baby steps, wet climbing his thighs.

With the next step, the water was lower and the pressure on his legs less. The bottom remained solid. On the far side, a well-worn path wormed around the boulders. Vehicles apparently went through here all the time.

Taking equal care, he returned to the ATV and eased it through the water and around the rocks.

Not far to McCree's now.

THIRTY-NINE

JASON WATCHED THE COPS FROM the safety of the woods. One car blocked the road at the cell tower. Two others blocked an SUV whose contents they were removing, photographing, and tagging. He couldn't hear the words, but their voices were excited by the find, which had nothing to do with him.

Probably.

Time to risk a little play-acting. He retreated through the woods to the road and walked toward the police convention. When he came in sight of the cop car, he yelled, "Hey! Somebody stole my ATV." He pointed back down the road.

The county deputy stayed behind the car and drew his gun. "Sir! Please keep your arms out and walk forward." The cop spoke into his chest.

Jason raised his arms to the side and looked around.

"Sir! Please walk forward."

Jason focused his attention on the officer and walked at a deliberate pace. "But the guy stole my ATV." Jason was pleased with the whine in his voice.

"We have a situation," the cop said. "I need you to lie on the ground and keep your hands where I can see them."

Jason complied and a second officer patted him down while the first one kept his gun at the ready. Once they determined he was unarmed, they helped him to his feet and asked for ID.

"It's with the ATV," Jason said. Under their questioning, he dished a shaggy dog story: He had gotten off the ATV and run into the woods to follow a grouse he had seen from the road—something he and Seamus had done on one of their excursions around McCree's place. The grouse had exploded from a thicket, nearly scaring the crap out of him. He stopped to let his heart settle and take a leak. He returned to the ATV and found it was gone. He'd been walking to the highway to hitchhike and stumbled into the officers. Were they looking for the person who stole his ride?

They didn't tell him anything; he hadn't expected they would. They sent two cars screaming after the stolen ATV and ducked him into the back of a cruiser, promising that when they were done, they'd take him to Tall Pines, where he could call his "friend" to pick him up.

MY NEIGHBOR DICK TANNI PULLED his silver truck across Lukes Road where it overlooks the head of Shank Lake, forcing me to stop. He walked to my window. "I'm not happy about your drone," he yelled over the clacking of his diesel engine.

"What drone? Dick, I'm kind of in a hurry here."

"You saying you don't own a drone that you've been flying all around the lake? I figured it was you 'cause we're the only ones on the lake this week. Big sucker with cameras and stuff. Totally invading my privacy."

"Not me, I promise. Sorry to be rude, but I'm supposed to Skype with my granddaughter."

He pointed at the bank of dark clouds boiling in the west. "Probably lose your internet in fifteen, twenty minutes. That sucker looked expensive, not one of those cheap things folks get from Walmart. I wonder if the mining guys are using them. I'll keep asking around to see who's the culprit. I'll shoot the sucker down next time—" A deep growl of thunder interrupted him. "Nope. Satellite internet is heading for a rain delay. I've got both kids coming up in a couple of weeks. We'll do us some fishing. Always a competition to see who gets the most fish, the biggest fish, the heaviest. We'll have a good time. Maybe you can come for a fish fry if we get enough perch. Last time—"

"Dick?"

"Right. Let me get out of your way." He moseyed to his truck and pulled to the side to let me pass.

I gave him a honk and a wave and made sure to wait until I was well past to accelerate. It would not be nice to envelop him in dust.

At home, everything was as I had left it. I raced down to the basement to grab a duffel from the storage room and my passport from the fireproof box. Jason had stolen my larger duffel, but the smaller one would do for a few changes of clothing. The passport was not where I expected it to be. The Happy Reaper could arrive any moment, and that pressure was surely causing me to have butter blindness—like standing in front of the refrigerator unable to find the butter even though it's sitting at the front of the middle shelf. Cure: slow down; check again.

A flash of lightning triggered me to count seconds until the thunder. Three. Getting close.

I methodically opened each envelope in the fireproof box. Home and vehicle insurance policies, proofs of purchase for ATVs, kayaks, the canoe, health insurance policy, checkbook for my money market account. Nothing left in the damn box and no damn passport.

Had I left it in a desk drawer?

I grabbed the pile of stuff and tossed it back into the box and ran upstairs to more lightning and closer booms that rattled the windows. The skies had noticeably darkened. I tossed several changes of clothes, running attire and shoes, and my Dopp kit into the duffel. I rifled through the desk drawers, grabbing my checkbook. Still no passport. I tried to laugh away the pressure of not being able to leave the country, but that just made my need to leave quickly even stronger.

Two sharp cracks startled me. Distant gunfire? What the hell was Dick shooting at? Did he spot the drone again and try to shoot it down?

I raced through the house, checking to make sure the doors were all locked. I remembered to flip the kill switch for the hot water heater—no reason to waste propane while I was gone. Passing the peg rack in the hallway, I grabbed a rain jacket. Running through the kitchen to the back door, it occurred to me that the food in the refrigerator would spoil before I returned. I briefly considered filling a cooler and taking it to Dick, but the patter of the first raindrops on the garage's metal roof persuaded me to get a move on. I'd call him later and offer the food. He could use the key I hid outside.

After a last mental check, I locked the door and hauled the duffel to the car.

One final thought occurred to me. What if Jason did come here yet tonight? I wrote a quick note on a page from the pocket notebook I kept in the car to record gas mileage and tucked the note into the gap in the doorframe where it would stay dry.

Elliot. If you get this, I'll wait until 10:00 p.m. at the campground we explored."

~ Seamus

Someone pinched heaven's hose and the first patter of rain abruptly stopped. Even so, driving up the driveway, I flicked on the headlights. Did I have everything I needed? What was my plan if Jason didn't show at the Deer Lake campground by ten? Where the hell should I go? When should I tell Bartelle I had split the arca?

Dust boiled around me as I raced down the road. Visions of meeting the Happy Reaper prompted me to keep my speed a skosh under reckless. It had been a couple of years since the logging companies had last graded the road, and the potholes were growing. Keeping a steady forty-five, I avoided most of the bigger ones from muscle memory, but by the time I got to the end of Shank Lake Road, my car probably needed a front-end alignment.

No Happy Reaper, and no rain. If I drove the usual way to the campground, I'd have three and a half miles to potentially meet the Happy Reaper if he were heading my way. Instead, I chose the long way that added fifteen miles but avoided any risk of confrontation with the killer.

The A Grade was in decent shape and I could keep my speed. The Cut Across Road had not been maintained since logging two years ago, and I bumped through at fifteen to twenty miles an hour, still kicking up a dust storm until, halfway through, the clouds vomited rain so heavy I could barely see forward, even with my wipers on high. I couldn't see anything behind me.

The deluge stayed with me all the way to the Deer Lake campground. I met no one, but twice sensed headlights from a vehicle far behind me. Whatever it was never caught up to me; it might even have been my imagination.

If Jason had gotten to my house, seen the note, and taken the direct route to the campground, he might beat me there. I drove down to the boat launch and slowly around the campsites, looking for any sign of him. My sense of hopelessness grew with each empty campsite. The note had been a last-minute effort to assuage my guilty feelings over running away and leaving Jason to fend for himself, and it didn't look likely to pan out. I wasn't exactly superhero material.

I pulled to the side of the campground entrance and checked my cell phone for messages. None. Killing the engine, I settled in to wait to redeem myself if Jason showed. Or, I realized, wait for an ignoble death if the Happy Reaper read my note before Jason did.

THE HAPPY REAPER HAD NOT paid much attention to the weather, and riding on the ATV, he felt more than heard the first deep rumble from the west. He eased to a stop and waited until the dust following him settled before donning the raincoat Jason had so thoughtfully packed in the duffel.

He wasn't sure of the distance to McCree's, but if he didn't get there before the rain, he wouldn't melt.

Steaming around the next bend in the road, he saw a silver Dodge Ram truck ambling toward him, taking his half out of the middle, diesel causing a racket. The Happy Reaper pulled far to the side to let the truck past, but the damn thing pulled itself across the road. The woods tucked in close to the road, the asshole had him blocked.

The Happy Reaper recognized the guy who exited the truck: he owned a camp on the other side of the lake from McCree and had given the drone the finger.

"Seems like I've seen you around. Black SUV? You know anything about a drone?" The guy was staring hard at him, like he was burning the impression into his brain. "Seems funny that SUV showed up same time as the drone."

The Happy Reaper slid a leg across the body of the ATV and stepped onto the road. "You got it wrong." He used his pleasant voice. "I'd like to get home before this rain hits. Mind moving your ride?"

"You got a camp around here? Where at?" The guy widened his stance, hands now on hips.

The Happy Reaper looked down at the ground and witnessed the first drops of rain explode in the dust, miniature bombs pushing up tiny mushroom dust clouds. He kept his eyes down, to give the impression of meekness, and shuffled to the side of the road. With one hand, he waved vaguely to the right while he mumbled, "Down the road a piece." With the hidden hand, he unsnapped the holster at his hip.

"I don't believe you," the guy said. "Look at me."

The Happy Reaper did. The cell-phone flash surprised him. "Well, shit," he said. With no wasted motion, he drew the pistol and put two bullets into the jerk's center mass. The guy had time for a surprised look and a half-step backward before he dropped like yesterday's garbage.

The Happy Reaper avoided the pooling blood and grabbed the dead man's cell phone. With deliberate speed, the Happy Reaper unloaded the ATV and stored everything in the extended cab area of the truck. He dumped the corpse into a natural depression on one side of the road and drove the ATV into the woods on the other side, parking it behind a shrub.

Between his caution crossing the beaver wash and this delay, he had probably lost any advantage over McCree, even assuming McCree had returned to his camp. Nothing to do but check. If McCree wasn't there, he'd clear out his motel room since he had used the same credit card and ID as he had for the rental. The earlier he returned his key, the more likely a maid would clean the room before the police made the connection. If he was lucky, a guest or two would stay before the police searched the room for his DNA.

He turned the diesel around, and, at the top of the hill heading toward the intersection with Shank Lake Road, caught a glimpse of McCree's red Subaru driving away from the lake. Seconds later the car was obscured in the trailing dust. The Happy Reaper followed the dust trail, speeding up whenever it became thin. McCree was driving crazy fast for the road conditions and the truck's stiff suspension jarred his back at every pothole, but he didn't dare lose the dust trail. At the end of Shank Lake Road, he expected McCree to head toward town, but he turned left. Where to?

At the 12A mile marker the dust curved right. He made the turn too wide and fast and had to stand on the brakes to avoid running into the trees. The road was terrible, rocks sticking up all over the place. He should be getting hazardous duty pay. With a crack of lightning and boom of thunder, the skies opened, raining cats, dogs, and bears. With deepening darkness and no more dust, he didn't dare put his lights on lest he alert McCree to his presence. He plowed forward.

Up ahead a shape. He had McCree in sight.

Forty

Jason Graham sat behind the screen in the cruiser, pondering his fate. He was lucky to be alive, but he wasn't sure the odds were good for him staying that way. Overhearing the cops' conversations, Jason learned Seamus had summoned them. No one had pieced together that the SUV driver had most likely been waiting in ambush to kill Jason.

He might be self-centered and paranoid, but only that kind of thinking would keep him alive. If he survived, he'd request that the Marshals Service relocate him to the high plains or the desert, somewhere without trees so he could see trouble coming from miles away.

Seamus's actions had saved his life. Obviously, Frank Cabibi was not the only one who knew Jason was holed up in this godforsaken place. And the only way anyone could know Jason was heading to the cell tower was through Seamus: either he had loose lips and someone heard, or somebody followed him.

Was one person targeting him or multiple people? Did they have Seamus under surveillance and contacting him might sign Jason's death warrant? Or had there been one individual who had followed Seamus and stolen the ATV to escape the police?

Seamus was dangerous to his health. Yet, what viable alternative did he have other than calling the guy? Tell the cops he was wanted so they would lock him up? Arrests become public information, the Chicago pricks would pick it up, and he'd be dead before he got near the courtroom.

The rain announced itself with window-rattling boomers before letting loose a torrential downpour. For sure, the cops would never catch the guy they were chasing. But the clerk at the gas station *had* taken a good long gander at him. Eventually, the police would link him to that house in Covington, so staying in their company was fraught with risk. He'd have to take his chances on calling Seamus.

The cop dripped his way into the cruiser. "Sorry this is taking so long. The crime-scene boys are on another assignment in Ironwood. Who are you calling? If you're like me, everything is in your cell phone and you hardly know your own number anymore. Maybe I can get the number and call him for you."

"I have a good head for numbers," Jason said. "But thanks. If we can get ahold of him, where and when should he meet me? Tall Pines in Amasa good?"

The officer opened a pocket notepad. "What's your friend's name and number?" The officer wrote down Jason's answers, flipped through his pad, mumbled, "McCree, that's odd," gave Jason a pensive look. "Excuse me for a minute, I'll be right back."

Jason's stomach performed a series of flips worthy of an Olympic champion. Was the guy piecing it together? Or had they gotten to the cops up here, too?

THE HAPPY REAPER LUCKED INTO a fine spot to observe McCree: the cabin next to the state campground on Deer Lake was not occupied. He backed in, killed the engine and lights. Once his eyes adjusted, he looked down on McCree's car.

At exactly 8:17 p.m., with the sun down or soon to be—impossible to tell with the steady drizzle and heavy cloud cover—McCree answered his phone. A minute later, headlights nearly blinded him. McCree was leaving.

The game was afoot. Where to now?

MY THROAT FELT SO CONSTRICTED, I was surprised I didn't pass out from the tension. Someone was following me. All down Deer Lake Road, headlights flickered in my rear-view mirror. Not constant. Here and there. Abigail would say there were two viable explanations. Happenstance: an innocent party going in the same direction and, in the gloom of early evening darkness, I was catching glimmers of headlights in the distance. Possible.

My churning stomach voted for the second explanation: The Happy Reaper was on my tail and waiting for me to lead him to Jason, which was exactly what I would do unless I switched something up. The Happy Reaper must have gone to my camp, read my note to Jason, and figured out which campground I was referring to. He hadn't killed me because he might still use me to find Jason.

I was to meet the state trooper in the Tall Pines parking lot, answer his questions—or evade them if necessary—and hightail it with Jason. I kept driving sedately, bypassing the turnoff for the DNR Road I had planned to take into Amasa, while I considered my options. There were lots of camps along the way, but I wasn't familiar enough with any of them to plan a way to hide where he couldn't find me—or double back and work my way into Amasa.

Besides, what if another car was behind the first one? I had no reason to assume the Happy Reaper was by himself. Doubling back wouldn't necessarily work.

Once I reached the end of Deer Lake Road, I'd be in an area with several options and some quick turns. Unless the vehicle behind me committed itself to close pursuit, which it hadn't so far, I could duck into one of the dead ends, kill my lights, leave the car parked, and run to the intersection to observe who was following. Depending on which way they went, I could find an alternate approach to Tall Pines.

If the car pulled up tight in pursuit, I'd run hard to the waiting patrol car at Tall Pines. Maybe I should do that anyway, but I'd give away that I knew he was there. Allowing the Happy Reaper to think I didn't know he was following had advantages. No running; at least not yet.

At the end of Deer Lake Road, I didn't signal my hard right onto Premo Creek Road. Accelerating through the turn, I drove hard on the decent surface. At Carlson Road, I screeched to a stop and doused my lights. No lights behind me. I reversed up Carlson and parked at the side, killed the interior light. Leaving the car door open for quick getaway, I ran in a crouch down the edge of the road toward the intersection.

The whine of a stressed diesel told me he was coming lickety-split. I kneeled and waited. His brake lights flashed red through the intersection— checking Carlson Road for my taillights? Pickup. Silver? His brakes squealed before crossing the railroad tracks with the double whomp-whomp of tires smacking the rails, and I caught white spilling from the left taillight.

A silver pickup with a hole in the left taillight was Dick Tanni's ride. Why was Dick following me? Did he not believe me about the drone? Was he mixed up in this? He was a Chicago guy, but he was a plumber. He couldn't be mixed up in this. Now wasn't the time to sort it out. I sprinted to my car.

* * *

THE HAPPY REAPER HATED HAVING no idea where his quarry was going and promised himself to add GPS trackers to the kits he kept in storage. Continuing his run of bad luck, the truck he stole didn't have its own GPS device. If he were a regular schmo, he could use his cell phone to pull up a map, but cell phones could be tracked, so he didn't carry one.

Wait! He did have that sumbitch's phone. He thumbed it on and found the damn thing wanted a fingerprint to open. He zipped down his window and pitched it.

He largely matched McCree's pace, speeding up on straightaways with his headlights off until he caught the glow of McCree's red tail lights, then coasting until the taillights disappeared and he could use his lights again. It felt like McCree was heading for Crystal Falls; surely they were already well south of Amasa.

The road wandered this way and that, ending in a T. He instinctively chose right toward the main highway McCree would take into Crystal Falls and accelerated to try to catch sight of the taillights. Nothing. A street entered on the right, he slowed to look down it. No lights. Slamming his foot on the accelerator in frustration, he had to jam on the brakes to keep control rattling across another railroad crossing.

At US-141 he picked left and screamed toward Crystal Falls until he came to a rise with a long-distance view: two trucks far ahead and no Subaru taillights. Fuck. Fuck! FUCK!

He braked his speed to a cop-resistant sixty. He'd cruise past the sheriff's office and jail—McCree had been there before. If no McCree, he needed to retrieve his gear from the Iron Mountain hotel room and skedaddle to Chicago to prepare for Monday.

Fuck.

FORTY-ONE

THE YELLOW CONCRETE WALLS OF the Portage, Wisconsin Best Western weren't particularly attractive, but at two in the morning, I'd take any bug-free bed. I parked in the lot next to Abigail's armored limo.

She met us at the entrance, handing a room key to Jason and told him to keep the connecting door unlocked. At his raised eyebrows, she added, "We're taking you on an obscure route to Chicago. I believe this place is safe, but tomorrow you and I will relocate somewhere even Seamus won't know. If something *does* happen, I want to have quick access to you. I'll fill you in on the plan tomorrow."

With a nod of understanding, Jason took a step away, then turned around and shook my hand. "Thank you for everything, Seamus. I owe you my life. I am truly sorry I caused you so much trouble. I should have trusted you to take care of things after Frank Cabibi showed up at your house, and that's on me. Will I see you tomorrow? Er, later today?"

I shook his hand "Testify well, you hear?"

Abigail answered his question. "We'll be leaving before Seamus gets up. It'll be better that way." She was looking at Jason, but I knew the message was for me. "I need to debrief Seamus. Now scoot." She finger-waved him away and dragged me into the darkened breakfast room off the lobby. We listened to the ding of the elevator door open and the whoosh of its closing before she asked if I had learned anything new on the drive down.

I related how Jason had spotted Frank Cabibi, someone he'd run into during his Chicago days perpetuating his financial fraud. "He panicked. He's sure his parents didn't set up the website Paddy discovered. The Happy Reaper is computer savvy. Probably his work. Jason had never heard of Dick Tanni, my neighbor who's also from Chicago. I asked because I'd swear his truck followed me from the Deer Lake campground. Maybe the Happy Reaper has me feeling paranoid. Dick just doesn't feel right."

"And you're sure you weren't followed down here?"

"I performed every tail-discovery trick you ever taught me, Abigail. Unless they are using multiple cars, I have no tail."

"You look about to collapse. Let's sit." She pointed us to a small round table. "Jason say anything else that might be useful?"

My legs collapsed halfway into sitting down and my butt hit the chair hard, scraping it across the floor. "Sorry. We didn't talk much. Given the trouble I'm in with Sheriff Bartelle and the prosecutor, I'd rather be ignorant of what he did than have to decide whether to lie. To shake Jason loose, I did have to tell the state trooper that I was guarding him. He was suspicious of me calling in the police and Jason showing up a little later at the same spot, wanting to contact me. I'm sorry. One more thing I probably should not have done, but it was the only way I could satisfy the officer."

"Water over the dam."

I wanted nothing more than to wrap Abigail in my arms and hold her. Feel her curves tight against me. Even allowing that thought did not respect her wishes, and I willed myself to become an ice cube. "Anything else I can tell you?"

Seamus, get a grip. If this is the last time you see Abigail, don't let her last impressions be of a beaten dog, shoulders slumped, head down. I raised my head to look directly at her. I brought my shoulders against the seat cushion, opening my chest. Of its own accord, a smile cracked my face.

"What?" she said.

Nothing I could say could do justice to my feelings, so I reverted to form and kept silent. Going on three a.m. in a darkened hotel lobby in the center of Wisconsin, and we had nothing more to say.

She eventually stood. I followed her lead. She gave a little head shake, then said words I had heard years ago in much different circumstances. "Seamus, what the fuck am I going to do with you?"

I didn't have an answer then; I didn't have one now.

She grabbed my hand and pulled me toward the elevators.

THE BEEP OF A TRUCK backing up brought me awake to sunlight streaming in the hotel window. I brushed crusties from the corner of my eyes and put on my glasses. My clothes were still scattered across the floor where they had landed in a flurry of tangled fingers getting in each other's way. I closed my eyes and replayed the scene: Tumbling into bed, we broke apart long enough to play rock, paper, scissors. Her scissors cut my paper, and she pushed me onto my back. We made love with the urgency of our first time. We made love again, savoring each moment. Throughout, we spoke not a word. I had been afraid anything I said would break the magic.

She had slipped away without disturbing me. I wondered if she had slept after our lovemaking, and I wondered where she and Jason were now, and I wondered if I would ever see her again. I looked in vain for a note.

The time showing on the room's clock let me know I had missed the free breakfast—no real loss, but the grumble of my stomach reminded me I had also missed dinner the previous night.

I had not given any thought to where I should go once I delivered Jason.

Perhaps I harbored some hope Abigail would take me with her. With the Happy Reaper hanging around camp, returning there didn't seem like a good idea.

Gazing out the window at a squadron of swallows diving on insects, my first impression was barn swallows because of the dark wings, but I quickly decided on cliff swallows: squared tail, not split like barn swallows, and a band of white between beak and forehead. They must have nests clinging to the concrete. My appreciation for the older hotel increased significantly. I'd look more carefully at them with the binocs stored in my car.

They, at least, had nests. Until I considered it safe to return to camp, I was homeless. Why not visit my mother and Uncle Mike in Boston? Then maybe rent a camper and visit a bunch of national parks. It was a solid plan, but did nothing to fill the hole inside.

Food wouldn't fill that hole either, but I needed it to live. First, I wanted a shower. I was soaped up when my cell phone rang. Thinking—no, *wishing*—it was Abigail, I dripped my way to the phone and swiped it to answer.

"McCree," Sheriff Bartelle said. "Where the hell are you? Be in my office in an hour or I'm putting a BOLO out on you."

"Time out. Time out. What's the matter?"

"You'll find out when you get here. Where are you?"

Jason Graham's fear of police had infected me. Was Bartelle involved? Ridiculous. Still, better to be cautious. "Hours away." I looked at the phone. "I can't get there until two o'clock. What's happened?"

"Two-oh-one, I'm broadcasting the BOLO."

THE HAPPY REAPER DUMPED THE silver truck in O'Hare's long-term parking and used a different agency and a different persona to rent another vehicle, this time a white Toyota Corolla. Couldn't be much more boring and unobtrusive than that. He returned to the silver truck and transferred his remaining cargo into the Corolla, then drove to his storage. He had seventy-two hours to prepare for the courthouse.

Yes, taking care of things up in Michigan would have been preferable, but that was history, and now he focused on his original plan. The thought of executing it brought him a warm glow. He would prove again he was the best and most creative member of his profession. Money wasn't the driver—he was already richer than anyone deserved to be—and he didn't get off on killing like some sick fucks. Recognition drove him. He sat atop the pyramid and he planned to stay there, which meant he would focus on the future, not dwell on the past.

This had already been a costly job. Replacing the lost weaponry and the drones was a minor inconvenience. Allowing cops to collect his fingerprints and DNA from the rental car was a major issue. DNA they had from earlier jobs, but with the fingerprints, they'd soon know who he was. He'd blown one of his better identities. Good ones required time and a lot of money to create. He still had several, even so . . . This was all on McCree's account. The guy had become something of a nemesis. If their paths crossed, he'd take him down, although it wouldn't make him happy.

Ha! Having reminded himself that the past was written, couldn't be changed, and to succeed he must concentrate on the near future, here he was replaying his most recent run-in with McCree. His anger at McCree was wounded pride. A splinter under his fingernail: a minor aggravation, which, if he wasn't careful, could pull his attention away from Jason Graham. Focusing on revenge was the kind of mistake others made. Not him.

He felt a smile coming on. Killing Jason Graham would once again make him the Happy Reaper.

Seventy-two hours to get the chemicals, perfect his aim and delivery, and determine the best location from which to pull it off. Seventy-two hours hidden beneath wigs and hats and dressed in forgettable-tourist clothes. Until Monday. On Monday, he'd wear a suit.

And spit-shined black shoes.

FORTY-TWO

HEADING NORTH FROM THE MOTEL, I tried calling Sheriff Bartelle to clarify the situation. He wasn't available—at least not to me. Not sure when I would next eat, I fortified myself with a full meal. At five minutes before two, I buzzed the intercom button for the sheriff's office. I'd overeaten and felt bloated and tired, wondering what the summons was about.

Tex and Sergeant Engberg came through the door. "We need to pat you down," Engberg said, "before we let you in. Tex has something to read to you."

I acknowledged that I understood my rights under the Miranda warning Tex read. "You arresting me?" I faced the wall and leaned in, hands on the wall, feet spread wide apart.

"That," Engberg said, "depends on what you tell the sheriff."

They ushered me away from Bartelle's office and toward the jail facilities, which meant they planned to record my interrogation. "Before you stick me in the interview room and leave me," I said, "could you take me to the men's room. I had two glasses of water with lunch and . . . you know."

In the interview room, I tried to clear my mind. Into the void popped the name of the downstate lawyer I had used the last time I had been arrested by Bartelle. I remembered my surprise, in this same room, seeing Irene Frankel's beaded hair and meeting her sharp wit. Was she still taking the odd case to keep from being bored in retirement?

Bartelle did not keep me waiting long. No handshake, no preliminaries. He sat down, told me they were recording our conversation "for my protection," and asked me where Jason Graham was.

"I have no idea."

"You do remember those obstruction of justice charges the prosecutor has deferred pressing?"

I treated it as a rhetorical question and waited for him to ask something else or give me information. Bartelle knew I had no need to fill silence, and wasted no time playing silly waiting games.

"Before we start, will you give us permission to search your car?"

I don't think I let my surprise show. What did they think I had? I wriggled the keys out of my front pocket. "Knock yourself out."

Tex limped in, refusing to look me in the eye, and accepted the keys from Bartelle. Once the door was closed, Bartelle said, "Take me through everything that happened after you called me with your Happy Reaper lead."

"I drove home, got a call from the state police, and drove to Amasa to pick up Jason. I delivered him to Abigail Hancock, and I have no idea where they are. That's the truth. Why are we having this conversation?"

"I want to walk through your timetable, not fly over at thirty-thousand feet."

He forced me through the details and pinned down time frames: meeting Dick Tanni and having him accuse me of flying a drone, arriving home, what I packed, the note I left Jason, sitting in the Deer Lake campground, being followed, picking up Jason at Tall Pines and my conversation with the state trooper, ending with taking Jason to meet Abigail. I told him to check my cell phone to confirm the time I received the call from the state trooper.

"Where did you meet her?" he asked.

Abigail and Jason had left the motel at least four hours ago and could be anywhere. Probably not Chicago—Rockford maybe, or down toward Springfield, or even into the northwest corner of Indiana. Bartelle knew of the Chicago trial. If he wanted to have someone call all the hotels and motels in a rather large area to find them, I could do nothing. Plus, I had given them permission to look at my cell phone; I'd had it on the whole way down to Portage, so they could track me using cell-tower history. "I do not see how that is at all relevant to any of your investigations. We stayed at the Best Western in Portage, Wisconsin. She made the reservations. Three rooms."

He pursed his lips and, crooking his arm, scratched behind his ear. He was either thinking or would soon switch gears.

"You told me this Happy Reaper guy always leaves a card to proclaim his kill?"

"Who did he kill?"

He stared at me and I remembered his question. "To the best of my knowledge he has signed all his hits with his Celtic cross business card with 'Results Guaranteed' on the back. Who did he kill? Or who do you think he killed since he obviously did not leave a card?"

"I need to remember how quick you are. Here's where we stand. We've released Owen Lyndstrom. The lab found two blood stains on the rock. The large area was mixed with hair and skin, all consistent with the victim, Mr. Cabibi. A second spot had a small smear of blood. Type O negative. Problem is both Cabibi and Lyndstrom have type A. Our current theory is the person who cracked Cabibi with the rock cut themselves on a sharp edge."

"I'll save you the trouble. I have type A positive."

"We know. We don't know your Happy Reaper's blood type, which is why I wondered if he ever killed without leaving his card. Then shortly before I called you, we discovered your boy Jason Graham is a universal donor, O negative. I need you to contact your pal Abigail and have her bring Graham in for questioning."

He ticked the points on his fingers. "He had a motive. The guy knew who he was. It's why he claimed to have run away, right? Two, he had opportunity. We know he walked through the crime scene within the window of death determined by the autopsy. Three, he has the right kind of blood. Four, he's committed multiple felonies. He stole your ATV and various stuff, stole Cabibi's ATV, broke into that camp and stole another ATV from there. We want to talk with him, Seamus. And not that I need to remind you, but you're looking at obstruction of justice at a minimum and possibly co-conspirator on any of the charges relating to the break-ins. If you don't cooperate. . ."

"Do I need to call a lawyer now?"

"Up to you. Make it easy on yourself, Seamus. Don't make me get a court order to look at the directory on your cell phone. Just make the call."

"I gave Abigail my word I wouldn't contact her. I won't make this into another empty promise. Breaking my promise to her that I'd make sure nothing happened to Elliot got me into this fix, and you know our mothers always told us that two wrongs don't make a right."

Putting up a stink wasn't going to help me, though, so I offered to let them look at my phone. "Even if you get her, she won't give him up. And, I'll bet a ton of money that her phone is in a Faraday bag, anyway, so no one can use her cell phone to track her. It's all a waste of your time. I was the one who told you all along Owen hadn't killed Cabibi. I'm telling you now, Jason didn't either. Cabibi had something corrupt going on with his proposed mine, and I'd lay money his death is related to that."

I got a flash of inspiration and went with it. "I'll make you and your prosecutor an offer. Put a leg monitor on me so you know exactly where I am, but let me continue to look through Cabibi's material. The answer is in there, and I'm your best hope of finding it. Jason Graham's trial starts Monday in Chicago. If you get your warrant, arrest him there. This gives me the weekend to come up with the real killer. What do you have to lose?"

"That's exactly what I told the prosecutor you'd offer us. He's already approved it. Right leg or left? And you can't leave the county."

* * *

I SPENT THE AFTERNOON AND early evening pouring through Cabibi's files and decided the odds were good that he was salting the planned mine. To prove it would take much longer than the weekend. I thought about taking a motel room, but decided to fuck it. I didn't have anything the Happy Reaper wanted. By the time I got home, I was tired, hungry, and dejected.

When had I last exercised? It was often an antidote to frustrated thinking or even depression if I was slipping in that direction. The temperature had dropped into the high sixties, not bad running weather for the end of July—and I still had plenty of light. I snugged an ace bandage around the ankle bracelet so it wouldn't rub my leg and eased into an easy trot.

Once I hit my stride, I knew this was a good idea and decided to enjoy the six-mile loop around the lake. If nothing else, I'd see if any of the other neighbors had come up for the weekend.

I emptied my mind of all thoughts and concentrated on avoiding puddles and rocks in the road. I kept a mental list of calling birds: chickadees led a mixed flock including nuthatches and a downy woodpecker. A great-crested flycatcher sounded its whee-ep call from high in the canopy, and a sapsucker beat a rat-a-tat-tat-tat on a yellow birch. I startled a covey of grouse that exploded in a whirring of wings. Jumping at the sound, I lost concentration on the road and tripped on a frost-heaved rock, nearly tumbling ass over teakettle.

I'd settled into a running zone by the time I reached Lukes Road and headed up the hill, sucking in the pleasant smells of my woods after a summer rain. Rounding a bend, a profusion of ravens flew away from my advance. Having nearly spilled once, I kept my head down and didn't follow their flight. In focusing on the road, I spotted storm-blurred tracks of a truck pulling across the road before turning around. Curious. Twenty feet further, an ATV heading in the opposite direction had made a similar maneuver.

They met in the road and both turned around? That didn't make sense.

Several steps later, ATV tracks cut onto a dead-end skidder trail. No return tracks and no easy route back through the woods. Hairs on my neck tingled.

I about-faced and jogged up the skidder trail. Around a bend I found a blue ATV, one I didn't recognize, carrying a bolt cutter similar to mine bungee-corded onto the front rack and a duffel attached to the rear rack. Rummaging through the duffel, I found Jason's clothes, some Canadian money, and my passport. Holy shit! This was the last ATV Jason Graham had commandeered—the one the Happy Reaper later stole—sitting less than two miles from my house.

A shadow glided past. I glanced up to see the red head of a turkey vulture looking down on me.

Ravens and a vulture. My stomach clenched, reacting before my brain added the carrion birds to the picture of Dick Tanni's truck following me from the Deer Lake campground to the abandoned ATV the Happy Reaper had stolen. I choked down vomit, leaving a burning in my throat, and followed the glide path of the vulture into the woods on the other side of the road. My crashing through the underbrush startled it into the air with deep wingbeats I could hear and feel.

Dick Tanni lay behind a downed tree. Dead.

Forty-Three

THE NEXT MORNING, I BROUGHT the memory card from my trail camera to the sheriff's office and gave it to Tex. "I know this isn't much, but it proves no one drove up to my camp after Jason Graham left the phone message for me."

He looked at it skeptically. "What's it show?"

"You'll see me coming and going. On Thursday, you can see me leaving. I was on my way to talk to Jenny Kauppi and eventually down here to talk with Owen. I left from here to pick up Jason. It shows me returning to leave the message on the door for Jason to meet me at Deer Lake campground. After I leave again, you get a fox walking down the road. Friday, it recorded my return. Next, you see me jogging past, running back after I found Dick Tanni and covered him with the sleeping bag that pissed you guys off so much because I messed with the scene—but I wasn't about to let the vultures and the ravens chew on him any more than they already had—and lastly, me returning on the ATV to wait for you guys. You can use my ankle bracelet to verify that the times recorded for the pictures are accurate."

"Calm down, Seamus. The point being?"

Why was this so tough? "The point being that no one else drove or walked down the road to my place. No one saw my note to Jason."

"They could have gone in from the other side."

"Why would they do that?"

"Because," he looked up at the ceiling like I was a complete idiot, "they knew you had the wildlife cam up and didn't want to be on it."

I held out my hand to retrieve the memory card.

"We'll keep it. You never know. I was about to watch surveillance footage from the drones the state guys confiscated. You interested? Troopers sent us a computer file."

I hadn't known they had found drones in the abandoned rental SUV. Bartelle had mentioned weapons and other interesting things but had never elaborated. Dick Tanni had been steamed seeing a drone. Had he gotten into it with the Happy Reaper, and it resulted in his death? I swallowed hard at the thought. Another innocent victim because of me.

Tex adjusted the monitor so we could both see it and started the video. "The drone transmitted continuously, but the recording was manually controlled. The tape is looped, so we have the last hour's worth of recording. Unlike your trail cam, we don't have a time stamp on any of this."

"That's my house." I sat dumbfounded, watching myself hop on an ATV and drive to meet the guy surveying Megan's property preparatory to logging the storm-damaged trees. The drone flew away from where we were talking and, keeping at a distance, followed me home. Next time, I'd use a drone to determine a storm's impact on the woods.

"That looks strange." I pointed to an area of the screen showing a tamarack swamp. "Looks like someone planted rows of something, doesn't it?"

Tex replayed those frames. "Got me, but it wasn't anything the drone was interested in. Let's look at the last fifteen minutes."

Those fifteen minutes proved to be unenlightening. So was the rest of my day at the sheriff's office. I managed to pinpoint a series of banking transactions for the sheriff to pursue with a court order. I also found ore sample reports confirming my suspicions that Frank Cabibi had been using data from core samples drilled in other, richer ore deposits and labeling them as coming from Iron County. I found nothing to tell whether he was in cahoots with the mining company or whether he was also pulling the wool over their eyes.

Tex walked me to my car and summarized my situation at the end of the day, "You've proved what we already knew. Cabibi was a schemer. But you're no closer to knowing who with or whether it resulted in his death. Now that Owen recanted his confession—"

"He has?" That was news to me.

"And because of that, the prosecutor has you in his cross-hairs for hindering the investigation."

"I can't help that," I said.

"Oh hell, you've given us much more than we had. All I'm saying—as a friend, you understand—is that if there's something you need to do before he locks you up, you'd best get to it tomorrow. Come Monday, all hell will break loose."

ON THE WAY HOME, I stopped in at Owen's to see how he was faring. Jenny's car was parked in front of the house. Owen answered my knock. He looked no better than the last time I saw him in jail. He waved me in. "Beer?"

I crossed the threshold and had a strong impression of electricity and tension filling the air. "Am I interrupting something?"

Owen said, "No." Jenny said, "Yes." And the two of them laughed.

I figured I should leave but wanted to learn why Owen had falsely confessed. Staying won.

Owen pulled me in far enough to close the door. "You're lettin in the damn mosquitoes. We was fixin to crack some beers, and we need a referee."

Jenny did the bartending honors and had me join them at the table. "If I'm refereeing, what are the rules?"

"Shortly before you arrived, I told Dad he was a stupid fool if he thought I had killed either Frankie Joe or Tim. I said we needed to be totally honest with each other. So those are the rules. One hundred percent honesty. Any question is fine. You have to answer. You ready, old man?"

Owen removed his dentures and examined them much as Hamlet had examined the skull. He replaced his choppers. "You sure you want the truth? No takin it back once it's out there. Seamus have to play too?"

"That's the price of admission for drinkin your beer. And Seamus has another thirty-six hours to unravel the murders or he's the one behind bars."

"How do you know that?"

Jenny tilted her bottle toward Owen. "Old man's grapevine's been active."

"I'm in." I opened my mouth wide to release the tension. "How do we decide who asks whom?"

Owen retrieved three ancient dice. "Low asks high the question, and no cheatin."

We rolled. Jenny asked Owen, "Did you kill Frankie Joe?"

"Of course not."

Jenny: "Then why—?"

Owen: "Roll the damn dice."

Me for Jenny: "Did you steal your father's pistol thirty-odd years ago?"

Jenny: "No, and I don't know who did."

Jenny for me: "Have you learned what Frankie Joe was up to?"

I told them what I had pieced together and that I was stymied until Bartelle got court orders. I had no idea if I'd still be participating by the time he did.

Me for Owen: "Why did you falsely confess to killing Cabibi?"

Owen drained his beer and started in on another before answering. "I thought Jenny done it. She was in the area supposedly fishin, 'cept she didn't bring home no fish. She's got a damn temper. Be just like her."

Jenny: "I left after the storm, Dad."

Me: "Don't the rules require the whole truth?"

Jenny nodded. Owen tightened his mouth, opened it long enough to take a slug of beer. He smacked the bottle on the handmade maple table. "Fine. Because she had every reason in the world to kill the bastard. Because one of the three of them boys got her pregnant, and the three of them ganged up on her and made her get rid of the baby."

Jenny sucked in a shocked breath, which I judged meant she now realized her father had indeed known her secrets. What I wondered was when he had learned the truth and exactly how much of it he knew. Not my questions to ask, though.

Jenny, silent tears running down her cheeks: "How did you know, Dad?"

He glared at her, and I expected him to require us to throw dice. "Truth? The truth is I knew you missed your monthly time. Who's the one who burned our trash? You thought you could hide it? Your feminine products? And everything was different between you and them boys, wasn't it? Then you and Frankie Joe both skipped school and suddenly you have bleeding again, except its different. Don't take no genius to figure out." He looked sheepishly at his beer. "Well, that plus a fella I know saw you both in Iron Mountain by the clinic."

Jenny: "And you never said anything?"

Owen: "You didn't. I didn't. Then Timmy confessed and told me the whole thing. Oh, honey." Getting up he scraped the chair away from the table and the two of them held each other. Jenny looked miserable and Owen looked older than old. The slump of his shoulders, his drawn face, all made him look like a shell of the vigorous octogenarian I had known only a week ago.

Owen spoke over Jenny's shoulder. "I didn't know how to handle it or how to talk with you. I coulda used your ma. Then Timmy went missing. Everyone figured he run off. Like I told Seamus. I found him and buried him. I confronted Chris Saari. He was a wreck, that one. Attending his new church. Looking for answers. I told him to stick to it because if I ever heard tell of him involved with you again, he wouldn't live to the end of the day. Frankie Joe said he had nothin to do with gettin you pregnant, but he did admit to helpin you . . . you know . . . in Iron Mountain. I didn't believe him and told him if I ever found out different, he wouldn't see no more sunsets. I guess I put the fear of God in him because for thirty years he only visited long enough to bury his folks."

Jenny: "I'm sorry, Dad. I should have trusted you. But I was young, and scared, and . . ."

I let myself out of the house, convinced Owen hadn't killed Cabibi, but still wondering about his role in Tim Javoroski's death. Those two bullet holes in his head still said murder to me, and Owen had admitted to burying him. If Owen hadn't killed Javoroski, he was covering up for someone who did. Jenny?

I had no clue what was going on and now had less than thirty-five hours to figure it all out.

FORTY-FOUR

ATTY'S BARK ALERTED PATRICK TO his father's arrival. He watched from the top of the ramp from the screened-in porch as his father greeted the dog. One glance at his old man was enough to make Patrick glad he had convinced Cindy to let him take the dog for a quick visit to see how his father was doing. "If you kept your cell phone on," he yelled down to the melee of dog and father, "people could tell you they were coming."

His father pulled his cell phone from his pocket. "Sorry, police powered it down and I never thought to check. Not that I'm not thrilled to see you, but why are you here?"

"I could bullshit you and tell you I drove up to see how the loggers were doing on Megan's land, but the truth is I came to check on you. The last time you and Abigail split, you went into a major funk and Cindy and I are worried. I baked some fresh bread and have soup on the stove. You can bring me up to speed over dinner."

"I had planned to take a run. My last one kinda got screwed up."

"Fine. Soup can wait. Atty and I'll go with you. You can fill me in and then after showers we'll have the nice dinner I made. Sound like a plan?" Patrick searched his father's face and saw resignation. "What, old man? You afraid I'll run your butt off?"

His father cracked a smile at the jab. Once they were on the road, to keep his father's mind off Abigail, Patrick encouraged him to relate everything that had gone on regarding the murders. They slow-jogged the still-wet roads, and he let his father talk, interrupting only to ask clarifying questions or indicate he was listening and wanted to hear more.

Until his father mentioned the drone video.

"Can you find the place," Patrick said, "where you thought stuff had been planted? What you're describing sounds like a grow operation."

His father echoed "grow operation," apparently not understanding.

"Pot, Dad. It's a real problem in national forests. People bring in marijuana plants and grow them in open areas, usually around wetlands."

"I know what it is, it just hadn't occurred to me. A few years back, a state drug task force busted an operation in Iron County on the other side of US-141. Involved a crew of Mexicans who were part of a California drug gang. The crew boss was a honcho in the gang. The workers, illegal immigrants who had been promised jobs in Green Bay, found themselves cultivating weed and sleeping in the woods. You think this is on Megan's property?"

"One way to find out," Patrick said, "but it means cutting this run short."

I WHISTLED ATTY INTO THE truck—the loggers would have muddied up the area, and I wanted the stronger engine and four-wheel drive to make sure we didn't get stuck. I hopped into the driver's seat and watched Paddy retrieve a padded gun case and a box of shotgun shells from his car.

My stomach clenched and my mind brought flashes of people I had seen killed with guns, the latest being Dick Tanni. I thought of objecting to Paddy's literally riding shotgun, but we'd been down that path and had agreed to disagree. He had respected my wishes to not bring the gun into the house. If it was a grow site, maybe we needed the protection.

IT HAD BEEN SEVERAL DAYS since the police had removed their crime-scene tape, and the loggers had been busy. All along Lukes Road, they had created tall stacks of eight-foot-long logs, grouped by tree type, waiting for logging trucks to pick them up. We followed the main road to the far edge of Megan's property, driving past the place where Frank Cabibi had died, and parked next to a skidder not far from where we had found his truck.

Atty romped in elongated loops, periodically checking in with us while Paddy removed the shotgun and loaded the magazine with shells. I pretended to ignore him. We walked past where Tim Javoroski's bones had rested for thirty years. The yellow police tape now festooned nearby tag alder and chokecherry bushes. Bypassing the shack, we headed cross-country toward the tamarack swamp and stumbled across a path wider than a deer trail. Once the dog saw we were going to take it, she nearly took out our knees in her rush to lead.

The path skirted a dry vernal pond and plunged down a hill toward the tamarack swamp, its edges guarded by mature cedar trees. Atty caught sight of a red squirrel and barreled after it, barking in the chase. I watched the squirrel climb and spotted the trail camera ten feet up a forest-straight maple. "Smile," I pointed to the camera focused down the trail we were walking. "We're on *Candid Camera.* I suppose it could be a hunter checking for game."

"Sure, Dad, and next we'll meet the Easter Bunny tending his bed of leaf lettuce."

Paddy was right, but I considered it a good sign to spot the camera. It made it less likely we'd run into armed guards. Paddy brought the shotgun into a ready position.

We spotted one more trail camera before we found the marijuana grow site. Paddy stood guard with his shotgun at the ready, while I shot video of the operation with my cell phone. Trees surrounding the site had been cleared to let sunlight stream onto the field. A solar-powered electric fence guarded the pot farm from animals. Under a camo tarp, I found a small gas generator and a tubing system that drew water from the swamp and tied into a drip irrigation system. Paddy found an extension ladder nearby. I counted one hundred and twenty healthy plants and one more trail camera.

We searched the field's perimeter and found no sign of anyone camping out; someone was making regular visits.

"We should get out of Dodge, Dad. This place gives me the creeps."

"Okay, but first, let's collect those cameras."

"We have their ladder, Dad, but nothing to cut the cables. Besides, won't you get in trouble for messing with evidence, assuming there's something recorded that's worth seeing?"

"With all the murders, you think the sheriff will drop everything and send someone to collect the evidence? Maybe, since it's close enough to where Cabibi died, but more likely he's got to contact some state drug taskforce, and they may have to contact the DEA. Who the hell knows how long it will take. And it could all disappear. But to your point, I'll wear gloves to make sure I don't add any prints. And I want to document everything we do to try to preserve a chain of evidence. Can you use your phone and video the whole process?"

"I think you should call them first, and if they don't respond, then collect the cameras."

"No time, Paddy. I'll ask for forgiveness, but I'm not waiting for permission. If I tell them about the cameras, they'll insist we leave everything alone."

"Probably true," Paddy conceded. "But you still don't have anything to cut the cables."

"My chainsaw's in the truck. I'll take the trees to the ground, cut below the camera, and slip the whole thing off. Or if it's too damn tight, cut above and below. We take the cameras and cut the cables at home."

"I don't want you killing my dog when you don't drop a tree where you wanted." Paddy whistled for the dog. "Come on, Atty. Let's get you locked into the truck while your Grampa Seamus plays lumberjack."

ATTY SNORED BENEATH THE DINING-room table while Patrick and his father ate a late dinner and browsed the trail camera images. Starting with the one at the grow site, the first dozen images were twisted, blurred images the camera had recorded while being set up. The time-date stamp said those pictures were taken on July 13, more than two weeks ago.

The first clear picture showed a three-shot burst of the silhouette of a man walking away. It could have been almost anyone. Within the camera's view were several pot plants, and every time they moved in the wind, the camera shot three images. We clicked through several thousand pictures of nothing before being rewarded with the side view of a man.

Patrick pointed to the time stamp: July 22, 7:15 a.m. "The day Cabibi was killed, right?"

Eighteen frames later, a shot included the guy's face. "I don't know who I expected," his father said, "but it wasn't Greg Shuett. He's not local. How did he find this spot?"

Patrick pointed out the Mexicans had also been outsiders.

They scrolled through the pictures and batted around ideas. On the 4,339th picture, a second identifiable person entered the frame. Time: July 22, 9:22 a.m.

Frank Cabibi.

The next thirty pictures showed the two men standing nose to nose. In picture 4,373, Greg Shuett remained, the middle fingers of both hands raised.

No more pictures of Frank Cabibi; a few more of Greg Shuett, the last being 9:31 a.m. The memory disk filled with a long series of pictures showing pot plants pushed sideways under a strong wind.

They reviewed the other two memory cards, making sure to don gloves every time they touched the cameras or the memory cards. In addition to a good-looking buck and a doe with twin fawns periodically showing up, the cards contained images dated July 22 of Greg Shuett walking down the path shouldering a large backpack; an empty-handed Frank Cabibi coming down the path; Frank Cabibi returning up the path carrying a pot plant; Greg Shuett returning, empty backpack slung over his shoulder. One shot caught his facial expression.

Patrick's assessment, "He looks agitated," was shared by his father.

"I wonder," his father said, "if Greg Shuett has type O negative blood. Can you make copies of these for my computer? Put on gloves. We need to call Bartelle and get these to him."

"I don't think he's going to be happy." Patrick said.

"That reminds me." His father held up a finger, opened a desk drawer, and pulled out a rubber-banded stack of business cards. "I need to give you my lawyer's contact information so you can call her when they lock me up."

FORTY-FIVE

THE WHEELS OF JUSTICE SOMETIMES run on flat tires. It took until Sunday afternoon before Greg Shuett and his lawyer sat in the same Iron County interview room where Sheriff Bartelle had threatened me. This time, I was watching and listening from the control room, sitting next to the prosecutor.

Bartelle spoke the introduction, giving the date, time, and people present, followed by the Miranda warning, after which the lawyer told Shuett to not answer any question until he had permission from the attorney.

Attorney: "Why are we here?"

Bartelle: "What's your blood type?"

Attorney shook his head at Shuett: "I asked, why are we here?"

Bartelle: "Let me lay my cards on the table to help this go a little smoother. Your fingerprints, Mr. Shuett, were on the memory cards of three trail cameras found in the woods. We were lucky the hunter who found and removed them wore gloves. Thumb print and index print. Plus, three fingers of the left hand on the metal box the trail cam was in."

The attorney's expression did not change; Shuett showed a flash of shock before going deadpan. Bartelle was a facile liar and I sure appreciated his withholding Paddy's and my names.

Bartelle paused to give counsel and Shuett an opportunity to speak before continuing. "The prosecutor is chasing down the judge, who's fishing with his grands, to sign a search warrant that covers pretty much everything you own. This is Mr. Shuett's opportunity to explain why he was there, why those cameras were there, and anything else he would like to tell us before we arrest him. Your client should know he will be required to provide a DNA sample once we arrest him for a felony."

Shuett glanced at his attorney, who produced a short head bob.

"Probably a blood sample, too. If you cooperate, it might help the judge look favorably upon you. But, Mr. Shuett, now is the time."

Attorney: "I'd like to talk with my client, please."

Bartelle stood, but kept talking. "You realize, don't you, that, if all we wanted to know about was the grow site, we'd contact the DEA to roll up the whole operation and then talk. While you confab with your client, make sure to discuss his relationship with Frank Cabibi. We're thinking your client may have been involved with murder."

Shuett: "I didn't kill him."

The attorney grabbed Shuett's arm. "Quiet." Looking up at Bartelle he said, "Let us have that conversation now."

"You help us," Bartelle said, "and maybe we forget how to count. Twenty pot plants is four years, twenty grand. Judge might be willing to accept a suspended sentence. Your operation? Seven years and a half-million in fines. All that pales compared with murder, which can get you life. We pretty much think you had an argument with Frank Cabibi down by your vegetable patch. Then you followed him to his ATV where the argument continued, and you picked up a handy rock and clobbered him."

"Wasn't me and I can prove it. I help you, you help me, right?" Shuett's head swiveled to look between his lawyer and Bartelle. Getting no reaction from Bartelle, Shuett sat up straight and shook off his lawyer's hand. "I can handle this. I've got proof, but you'll never get it unless we make a deal.

Yeah, sure, I followed him. That's how I got the proof. Now, I'll take my lawyer's advice and not say anything more until you and him make a deal."

WHILE SHUETT'S ATTORNEY AND THE prosecutor inked their agreement, I cooled my heels in Bartelle's office. After three hours and take-out pizza, we gathered in the prosecutor's conference room. Shuett, looking composed in his orange jail attire, sat with Sergeant Engberg on one side of him and his counsel on the other. The prosecutor and Bartelle sat across from them. I joined Tex at a side table, where he operated a computer whose display was projected onto a portable screen at the front of the room. With so many participants, the room was warm and the air stale. Everyone's body language suggested they were antsy. I was too; depending on what happened here, I might be the next one sporting an orange jumpsuit.

At the prosecutor's command, Tex dimmed the lights and typed in Shuett's username and password for a cloud storage site. Following Shuett's instructions he double-clicked a file with an .M4A extension. Mid-sentence, a strident male voice I did not initially recognize said, ". . . it alone. It's been thirty years. Everybody's moved on. Get over it old—"

"I ain't gettin over nothin." The quality was not great and the voice was low and angry. The missing 'g' suggested Owen Lyndstrom.

"So, you heard she got rid of a baby. Big fucking deal. She wasn't the first and she won't be the last to make that trip."

Now I recognized Frank Cabibi's voice from the mining meeting I had attended at the library. It continued, "Jenny was nothing special. You should have heard her asking for it. She begged—"

"Shut the fuck up."

Definitely Owen.

"Or what. No one's gonna believe a rape charge now. Jenny's never told because she doesn't want anyone to know what a slut she was. Are you gonna—?"

A whump sound was followed by something large and soft, like a fifty-pound sack of sunflower seed dropping onto something solid.

Shuett's rapid breathing dominated the low hiss of the recording. A veery's flute-like call sounded from a distance. I held my breath, leaning forward to hear better. Owen's angry voice startled me. "I told you to shut the fuck up."

The background hiss increased. I couldn't make sense of any of the sounds, and with a click the recording stopped. The conference room filled with the ragged breath of seven people. Bartelle spoke first. "And you never saw the guy?"

Shuett stared across the table. "No way I'd get any closer than I was. Like I told you, I waited until I was sure the other guy was gone. Then I went and checked Cabibi for a pulse." He shook his head. "Obviously, I didn't want anyone messing around there, which is why I moved the body. I didn't want the rock the guy had used to be next to the blood, so I tossed it and cut my finger." He held up his right index finger.

Bartelle was letting Shuett give a short version. Obviously, there had been conversations I had not been privy to, so why was I even there?

Shuett continued: "That storm blowing through was a blessing. I had lots of downed limbs to cover him with. I was finishing up when . . . well, play the video and you'll see."

Tex downloaded a second file from the cloud and hit the play button.

A shaky image filled the screen, causing me temporary vertigo. The picture steadied to show Jason Graham carrying a duffel toward Cabibi's ATV. Tex froze the picture.

"Jason Graham," I said, "but the voice wasn't his. The voice is—"

Bartelle interrupted, "We know. Let's see what happens."

Tex pressed play and we watched Jason walk to the ATV and do a slow spin. I judged he was looking for its owner. He walked a few feet in several directions before he stole the vehicle. The video's final scene was zoomed in to catch Jason, duffel on his lap, disappearing into the distance.

The prosecutor cleared his throat. "Mr. Shuett, how do we know you didn't cut yourself on the stone when you used it to finish the job Owen Lyndstrom started?"

Shuett's voice sounded whiny. "Because I told you the truth. That was our deal."

Tex whispered to me, "The prosecutor's acting cagey. The autopsy showed a single strike."

Keeping my voice low, I asked, "Does Shuett's attorney know that?"

Tex shook his head. "But the prosecutor does."

The prosecutor marked a tick on his paper. "Thank you, Mr. Shuett. As agreed, we will not object to reasonable bail at tomorrow's hearing." He waited until Sergeant Engberg escorted Shuett and his attorney from the room before continuing. "Sheriff, we need to question Owen Lyndstrom. We'll eventually need expert testimony to match the voice, but everyone agrees that was Lyndstrom, right?" No one disagreed. "I should have given more credit to his confession and less to . . ."

He gave me a pointed look, and I was sure he was going to say my name. Instead he continued, "exculpatory evidence. We presume the second voice was Frank Cabibi. We'll need confirmation, which is harder since he's deceased."

"If you're looking for a voice recording," I said, "the Iron County Reporter had one of their people at the open meeting in Iron River. He was using a digital recorder. If he still has it . . ."

"You'll check, Sheriff? Good. And Mr. McCree, if you come back tomorrow morning for the court session, our office will agree to removing your tracking device. You are a very lucky man."

Yeah? Why did I feel like shit? Without my intervention, Owen's confession would have held, and in that parallel universe, Dick Tanni might still be alive. No guarantees for Dick, but I did know my determination to keep digging had muddied the waters.

Regardless of the exact reasons Owen had confessed, he'd experienced the reality of jail and let me stir up doubt and secure his release. What would happen when they tried to re-arrest him?

Forty-Six

GUILT DROVE ME TO FOLLOW the two Iron County Sheriff's cars up to Owen's place. Not that they asked me to, or even wanted me to. It's a public road and they weren't speeding, so I tagged along. On the way, I marveled at how easily Owen had produced his bald-faced lies during the "truth" game, which got me to wondering. Had Jenny known he was lying? Was that Owen's only lie? Had he killed Tim Javoroski?

I waited at Owen's driveway until the police cars drove past the first curve, then followed them up and parked behind a rusted tractor that might not have operated since before I was born. I rolled down windows, letting in two persistent mosquitoes along with the whisper of a breeze. Using the binocs I stored in the car for impromptu birdwatching, I followed the action from a distance. Two of the officers jogged around either side of the house. Tex and Sergeant Engberg waited in front until their communication devices squawked.

Attached to the door with nails, top and bottom, was a piece of notepaper with writing I could not read even with the binocs. Tex pounded on the door. No answer. Sergeant Engberg looked through windows, shook his head, and placed a call with his cell phone. The two officers from the back joined the ones in front and soon all four were sitting in the chairs on the front porch.

My curiosity was in the red zone, but I stayed in my car, away from their business, until Jenny Kauppi drove up with her kids. She left the children in her car, and she and I reached the porch at the same time.

Seeing me, Jenny said, "Oh good. Dad left a note for you, too."

I read the note nailed to the doorframe. "I ain't here. Call my daughter to get in." The note concluded with a phone number.

She unlocked the door. "He left separate envelopes for Sheriff Bartelle and Seamus on the kitchen table."

Tex stayed with Jenny and me on the porch until the rest cleared the house. No Owen. Two envelopes with block printing lay on the kitchen table. The police handled them as evidence. Showing Jenny the material, now housed in large plastic bags, Sergeant Engberg asked, "You know what's in these?"

"More or less. I haven't seen 'em. He's gone, you know. He said he didn't want anyone else to get in trouble for somethin he did, but he wasn't doin jail time. He left a full confession for the sheriff. The note to Seamus is an apology."

Owen had amended his confession to include more details, starting with Tim Javoroski. According to Owen's statement, Tim had tried to commit suicide with the gun Owen had given him for that purpose. But the bullet Tim put into his brain hadn't killed him. Owen had agreed to bury him and instead found Tim still breathing. Owen finished the job with a second bullet. Killing a human, Owen wrote, wasn't the same as a game animal and he had acted like a zombie, burying Tim and the gun under the flooring of the hunting cabin. He killed Cabibi in a fit of rage over the way he was speaking about Jenny and Cabibi's lack of any remorse at what he had done. He returned to his truck to get a tarp to collect the body, intending to dump it. Returning, he spotted the "Environmental Nazi" carting the body away.

His note to me apologized for misleading me, but he'd had to do it to avoid living the rest of his life cooped up in some jail. Could I help Jenny get ownership of his property?

Jenny read the note. "Don't mind him, he thinks you walk on water, Seamus." She teared up. "In the end, his temper got the better of him. I wish I knew how to tell the kids they're never gonna see their grandpa again. I'd better tell them now before they hear somethin from their friends."

I gave her an encouraging hug and asked loud enough for the police to hear, "Do you think he might go after Chris Saari?"

THE HAPPY REAPER LOOKED RATHER spiffy if he did say so himself. His black shoes were polished, his suit draped perfectly on his shoulders, an American flag pin his only jewelry. He surrendered his briefcase and belt to the X-ray machine and stepped through the metal detector, waved on by the bored guard, likely a contract "court security officer."

He told the officer to have a good day and, while scanning the area for Jason Graham or Abigail Hancock, followed the crowd to the elevators. He was betting the prosecutor would want to make sure Jason showed up, which meant having Jason check in at the US Attorney's office on the fifth floor. What he couldn't know was whether Abigail had already handed Jason off to the Marshals Service. Either way, he'd stake out the prosecutor's office, hoping for Jason's arrival or departure. If all else failed, he'd take out the judge, causing a mistrial and giving himself more time.

"Come out, come out, wherever you are," he whispered under his breath. A smile curled his lips. Softly he whistled the dwarfs' "Whistle While You Work" from *Snow White.*

Forty-Seven

Driving into Chicago, Jason Graham had felt as nervous as a turkey the week before Thanksgiving. Now that they were here, he felt surprisingly calm considering he would soon lose his identity, his name, everything he had been. Abigail parked the armored car near the courthouse in the S. Clark Street lot, undid her shoulder rig, and slid it under the front seat. She checked the brunette wig in the vanity mirror, then turned and faced Jason. "You ready?"

"I'll be glad to ditch the wig. It itches something fierce."

"Stop bitching and be glad I didn't make you wear heels."

He guffawed and, listening to the sound, decided maybe he was still nervous.

"And keep your trap shut. We don't want any attention at all. Let me do all the talking."

He mimed zipping his mouth shut, which earned him a faint smile and shake of the head from Abigail. She opened his door. Like flipping a switch, moisture disappeared from his mouth. His stomach burned, and he felt sure the sweat popping on his brow would wash away the makeup she had put on him. He gave his dripping underarms a quick sniff and caught the faint whiff of deodorant.

"Don't forget your bag," she said. "And small steps."

He followed in her wake, dragging the wheeled suitcase with his change of clothes behind him and matched her stride. She herded him into the corner of the elevator, let everyone else leave first and shepherded him up to Jackson and over to Dearborn. "Remember, no eye contact."

The wait to get to security was interminable. The guard did not want to let him in with his oversized bag, which didn't fit the X-ray machine. Abigail said something to the guard that Jason couldn't hear. The guy gave him a speculative look and sent them through the body scanner. A second guard escorted them to a small room where he meticulously emptied the bag. With everything removed, the guy tested the bag for false bottoms or sides.

"Go ahead and repack," he said. "US Attorney's office is on the fifth floor."

"Can I change here?" Jason asked.

" 'Fraid not."

"Besides," Abigail said, "you need facilities to remove your makeup."

Abigail again sheep-dogged him into a corner of the elevator—out of habit, he figured, since they were safe once they passed security. A jerk signaled they were starting up. "Before we go in," he asked, "can I use the men's room to change?"

Several heads swiveled in his direction and Abigail elbowed him in the ribs. "Quiet."

Jeez, Jason thought, *lighten up. That hurt.*

She herded him from the elevator to the attorney's office door. He reached it, grabbed the handle, and said, "After you."

I SAT IN THE IRON County courthouse watching rain sheet down the second-story windows of the courtroom. Shuett's case was third on the Monday morning docket.

The prosecutor made his pitch for why Greg Shuett should be subject to minimal bail. The defendant's attorney concurred. The judge did not agree and remanded Shuett to jail without bail. Bartelle whispered in my ear that the judge's son was middle management at the Cliffs mine in Ispheming and the judge didn't think much of Shuett's protests against mining. Shuett was returned to the jail.

The prosecutor told the judge he no longer needed me tethered to a GPS device. I had offered financial reimbursement for any property stolen or damaged by Jason Graham and for any other expenses incurred, and they were not interested in pressing charges. Which meant they saw little point in prosecuting me for obstructing justice.

Afterward, in the prosecutor's office, I was disappointed to discover he would not ask the judge for search warrants related to Frank Cabibi's activities. "He's dead," he said. "We have limited resources. This is not worth our time."

I understood the logic, but a cynical part of me wondered if someone's relation had been involved with Cabibi. When I met later with Bartelle, he claimed no. He also told me that despite Jenny Kauppi insisting Owen would never harm Chris Saari, deputies had warned him to be cautious until Owen was found.

That might not happen soon. That morning, Owen's car had been discovered abandoned in Minnesota's Boundary Waters region near one of the canoeing entry points. Bartelle wondered if Owen was paddling to Canada. I'd never seen Owen with a paddle in his hand, and wondered to myself if he had paid someone to drop his car in Minnesota while he remained hidden in Iron County.

I headed home to let Paddy know he no longer needed to worry about me being prosecuted. Passing the road toward Owen's place, I wondered where he was. He could be anywhere, and I was surprised to discover I hoped the police never caught the old coot. Owen was probably legally wrong, and certainly morally wrong, to encourage a troubled young man to commit suicide. And even scum like Frank Cabibi, with all his schemes and empty promises to the locals, didn't deserve to be killed. Yet, given his age, Owen having to desert his family and friends seemed a sufficient punishment.

Somehow my relationship with Owen Lyndstrom had affected my moral compass much the way chunks of magnetite in Iron County could throw off true north and make a real compass unreliable. I'd need to do some soul-searching to understand how I had reached such shaky moral ground.

And I needed to address my failed relationship with Abigail, to reflect on our last night together. She could have told me goodbye again, but hadn't. I figured that meant she was amenable to future conversation. Probably best to let a little time pass, but time was something we still had plenty of.

Forty-Eight

THE HAPPY REAPER WOULD HAVE missed them entering the door to the US Attorney's office if the second woman hadn't said, "After you," in a clearly masculine voice. Abigail Hancock was either wearing a wig or had dyed her hair a dark brown and had slumped to make herself appear shorter. But her face matched the picture he had seen on McCree's desk. Holding the door open for her was a feminine version of Jason Graham: woman's clothes, hair, and makeup, but male Adam's apple and voice.

Caught off-guard, the Happy Reaper fumbled in his pocket for the weapon, but by the time he had it out, Abigail had pressed Jason inside.

The first opportunity was lost, but they had to leave for the court.

JASON COUNTED THE SECONDS BETWEEN Abigail announcing themselves to the receptionist and a marshal coming out to greet them. Five hundred eighty-eight, a dozen seconds under ten minutes. The marshal's forehead wrinkled in what Jason guessed was concern. "Quite the outfit, isn't it?" Jason rose. "It's the disguise Abigail insisted on. Is there a place I can get rid of this makeup?" He pointed to the suitcase. "And put on my own clothes."

The marshal introduced himself and said he'd have to accompany Jason to the men's room at the end of the hall.

"Something private would be better." Abigail pointed toward the interior of the building.

"Negative. You saw the security in this building. I'll be with Mr. Graham to make sure no one tries to strangle him or anything. It'll be fine. Thanks for bringing him in."

A clear dismissal, but Abigail appeared skeptical. Jason was tickled to see she followed the agent and him to the men's room. "I don't think they're going to let you in there," he said.

She acknowledged his humor with a crinkle of a smile. "I'll make sure no one goes in until you're done."

He and the marshal traded eye messages and shrugs. At the men's room door, Abigail ordered the agent to make sure the inside was clear while she waited with Jason. The marshal returned and motioned Jason in. "We're good."

Forty-Nine

THE HAPPY REAPER HEARD THE door open with the squeak of a hinge needing a drop of oil. He pulled his feet up so nothing would show if someone looked for legs in the three stalls. Footsteps approached and retreated. Door squeak. "We're good," a voice said.

Next came someone wheeling a bag across the tiled floor, thunkity-thunkity-thunk to the sink. Had to be them: Jason taking care of makeup and a marshal guarding the door.

"I don't think you're gonna have to worry about anyone else coming in," the voice by the sink said. "That bodyguard of yours is a force to be reckoned with."

"I can only imagine."

The Happy Reaper closed his eyes and tried to be a bat and use echolocation to precisely define where the suitcase was being unzipped. Next came the sounds of a bottle being squeezed. Water running meant Jason was into his makeup removal at the sink. He silently slid the latch open and gave the guard time to relax while Jason became fully engaged in his transformation.

In one continuous motion, he opened the stall door and stepped out. The guard squared his position and unsnapped his holster.

The Happy Reaper pointed toward the end sink, indicating his intention. A look of confusion grew on the guard's face and his draw slowed, giving the Happy Reaper enough time to take a small step, setting up a spin and powerful chop with the side of his hand to the guy's carotid artery.

Down the guard went. Maybe dead. Didn't matter.

Jason, his eyes squinched against the soap, turned toward the commotion. The Happy Reaper slammed his foot into Jason's throat, snapping his head against the sink.

Shit, too much noise. He stabbed a plastic dart into Jason's neck, feeling it scrape along the guy's spine. Facing the door, he balanced on the balls of his feet, waiting for act two. Abigail came in fast and low. He knife-chopped her neck, partially catching the collar bone, sending a tingle up his forearm. She tucked to roll, and as she rose with a scream, he timed his kick to crush the hinge of her jaw. At contact, her head snapped onto the tile like a coconut hitting concrete.

He blew out a rush of air. *Stay calm. Stay calm.* Act three. He tucked a "Results Guaranteed" card into Jason Graham's hand. Used the mirror to straighten his tie. Shot his cuffs. Put a worried look on his face in case he needed to play act that a guy was having a seizure in there, and opened the door.

ATTY GREETED MY ARRIVAL HOME with fierce barks and a wagging tail. Paddy stood on the stoop in the drizzle with pinched eyes and tight jaw.

I stopped petting the dog. "What?"

"I got a text from Cindy. She was at the courthouse this morning to cover the trial Jason Graham is to testify at. Two killed. One man. One woman. A US marshal hospitalized. No names."

The world narrowed to a pinprick of light. Somehow my body kept going. My heart beat. My lungs processed oxygen and released carbon dioxide. One foot followed the other without falling or tripping over the dog as Paddy led me inside, where he'd been using his laptop to follow live feeds from the Chicago news stations.

"We don't know anything," Paddy said.

My son is a terrible liar.

FIFTY

PATRICK HAD NEVER, EVER SEEN his father cry. After dialing Abigail's cell phone a thousand times without getting an answer, his father received a phone call from Abigail's brother, confirming her death. His body convulsed with heartbreaking sobs. Atty whimpered at the sound and laid her head in the suffering man's lap.

After the crying, his father simply shut down.

For most of Patrick's life, his grandmother McCree had been institutionalized because she'd stopped speaking after her husband's murder. His father was supremely comfortable with silence, and while

Patrick could see him slipping down the same rabbit hole of mental illness, he knew his father was stronger than that. For now, Patrick wouldn't press it. He helped his father into the rocking chair on the screened porch, tucking a blanket around him so he'd stay warm. The old man looked at the woods with unseeing eyes. Atty lay beside the chair, resting her head on her front paws.

Patrick normally listened to music while working on a computer. To make sure he could hear his father, should he break his silence, Patrick laid the earbuds aside and kept the door to the porch open. He searched the internet for answers to exactly what had happened in Chicago.

Every half hour or so, he tried to engage his father, who had taken his blanket to the front deck, staring toward the lake and the storm clouds darkening in the west. Patrick wondered what his father saw.

Patrick brought out lunch for the two of them. His father did not eat. He would not take a nap; he wouldn't even lie down. Later, Patrick tried peanut butter and crackers, then wine and cheese. Nothing doing. With raindrops pattering onto the leaves and a black sky approaching, Patrick led his father inside. Again waving off Patrick's offer of food or drink, he wrapped himself tightly in the blanket and sat in silence, facing the west wall of windows with its lake view.

Patrick retreated to the loft to watch the storm boil in; it would shortly deprive him of satellite internet. Wind pressed against the trees, bending them to its will. Rain pelted down, stripping maple and birch leaves, throwing them against the windows with distinct taps. The first bolt of lightning branched toward the earth, with the boom of thunder rattling the windows seconds later.

"Hey, Dad," Patrick said. "You remember how we used to go to the third floor of your house in Cincinnati and watch the storms roll up the Ohio valley? I loved that." He didn't get a response from his father. The next lightning flash arced across the sky, followed by a loud crack.

Patrick leaned over the loft railing to call down to his father.

The chair was empty except for the blanket.

Patrick's first thought was "bathroom," but some instinct told him to make sure. The bathroom door was open. "Dad?" he raised his voice against the storm. He checked the kitchen. Nothing. Another flash and boom of thunder lit the sky and shook the house. TV room was empty, but Atty was standing by the windows, tail wagging, watching his father rooting through

Patrick's car. Half in the car, his soaked T-shirt and shorts were plastered to his body. He hadn't bothered to grab a hat or rain jacket or shoes. What the hell was he doing?

Patrick opened the door from the TV room to the screened porch and yelled to his father, who probably couldn't hear with the rolling thunder and rain pelting on the metal roofs of the house and garage. His second yell froze in his throat as his father backed out of the car carrying Patrick's shotgun.

Patrick raced down the ramp. His nose pinched at the pungent smell of ozone. Had the lightning hit something?

His father rose at Patrick's approach. "Where are the shells?"

"You're soaked. Come on inside."

His father slapped away Patrick's hand. "Where, Paddy?"

Patrick couldn't see past his father's rain-streaked glasses to make eye contact. He needed to get through to his father. "What do you need them for, Dad?"

Sharp voice. "Where, Paddy? Where did you put them?"

His father hated guns, didn't use them. Patrick could think of only one reason his father would want shotgun shells. He didn't know if his father had ever been attracted to suicide during his bouts of depression. It wasn't the sort of thing a father, particularly his father, would tell his son. The past didn't matter, he realized, only the present. His father wouldn't find the shells, which he had stored in the cold room in the house, but with axes and knives and chainsaws there were many ways to die if one were so inclined.

Leaving his father to the fruitless search, he sprinted inside to his laptop. No internet service. He pulled the cell phone from his pocket. One bar and 3G service. He fired up FaceTime. "Come on. Be there Cindy."

The screen opened with a bruup to show his wife. "How's your father doing?" she asked before he could say anything.

"Terrible," Patrick said. "I need Megan to talk to her Grampa Seamus."

While Cindy called to Megan, Patrick walked the phone to the screened porch, hoping he didn't lose the signal. The rain had let up, but more grumbling thunder in the distance suggested the storm was not over.

"Hi, Papa."

"Hey, Megan. I need you to tell Grampa Seamus how much you love him and ask him to read you the choo choo story. Can you do that? Please?"

"Why?"

"Please Megan, it's important. Really important."

She spun a circle in front of the screen, and Patrick wanted to reach out and shake his daughter into compliance.

She stopped her spin and clapped her hands. "Um-hm. Where's Grampa Seamus?"

"Just a minute. I've got to walk the phone out to him."

He curled his body over the phone to guard it from the weather and jogged to his father, who was peering beneath the front seats. He pointed the phone so Megan could see his father.

"Grampa Seamus! You're all wet. Read me a story. Choo choo. Read me choo choo."

His father lifted his head and looked at the screen. Gave Patrick a confused look. Looked back at the screen. In a flattened tone he said, "I'm busy right now, pumpkin. Let your father read you a story."

"You, Grampa. I love you. *You* read choo choo."

Patrick held his breath. He was stronger than his father, but if it came to a knock-down drag-out to prevent his old man from hurting himself, luck and desperation might turn the tables. He sent a silent message to Abigail's spirit, *I need your help here. Please!*

His father blinked once. Then again. He continued to stare at the screen.

Patrick didn't dare breathe.

"Choo choo," Grampa Seamus said. "Okay, let's read choo choo together."

Patrick steered his father like he was punch drunk up the ramp and onto the screened porch. He settled him into a chair, and propped the cell phone upright on the table in front of him.

"Megan," he said, "tell Grampa Seamus what you did today while I get the book." Without waiting for a response, he raced into the house, found the book with those stored for Megan's visits, grabbed the blanket, and raced back. He threw the blanket over his father's lap and thrust the book, opened to the first page, into his father's hands.

His father cleared his throat. "Chug, chug, chug," he said. "Puff, puff, puff. Ding-dong, ding-dong, ding dong."

Patrick closed his eyes. *Thank you, Abigail.*

His father read *The Little Engine That Could* from beginning to end three times before he gave Megan a virtual goodnight kiss and promised he would see her soon.

Thank you for reading this story. If you've enjoyed *Empty Promises*, I would appreciate your writing a short review and posting it at your favorite online retailer.

Seamus McCree's adventures in Michigan's Upper Peninsula continue in the seventh novel of the series, *Granite Oath*. Seamus agrees by "pinkie swear" to "work" for his eight-year-old granddaughter to find her best friend's missing mother. He uncovers a tangled web of drugs, prostitution, and dummy corporations.

You can order *Granite Oath* from your favorite physical or online bookstore.

Author's Note

Thank you for Reading *Empty Promises*. I am tremendously grateful for all the information, assistance, and support I received during the creation of this novel. I love the writing community, especially my cohorts at Booklovers Bench (Karla Brandenburg, Maggie Toussaint, Nancy J. Cohen, Terry Odell, and Tina Whittle), and at Writers Who Kill (Carla Damron, Debra H. Goldstein, Debra Sennefleder, E.B. Davis, Gloria Alden, Grace Topping, Julia Tollefson, KM Rockwood, Linda Rodriguez, Margaret S. Hamilton, Paula Gail Benson, Shari Randall, and Warren Bull). During much of the work on this novel, I was president of the Guppy Chapter of Sisters in Crime and appreciate you all. Whenever I'm banging my head against a wall, at least one Guppy is there to make me put on a helmet or better yet, move the wall.

A special shout-out to my two eagle-eyed early readers, Carol J. Baldridge and Dottie Caster. They catch stuff others miss, for which I am very grateful.

I continue to follow my practice of using real places and adding a new road or marsh or business when the story needs them. I also invent all the characters, although it's sometimes hard for me to remember because they keep talking to me. (Which means more stories in the future.)

If you found an error, it's my screw-up. Sometimes I have the opportunity to modify future versions of the manuscript, so I'd like you to drop me an email and tell me what you found. And if you enjoyed this tale, I'd love to hear about that too. My email is jmj@jamesmjackson.com.

James M. Jackson
Amasa, Michigan

SHORT STORIES

SET IN MICHIGAN'S UPPER PENINSULA

James M. Jackson

Cover Design by Jim Jackson

Wolf's Echo Press
PO Box 54
Amasa, MI 49903
www.WolfsEchoPress.com

These are works of fiction. Any references to real places, real people, real organizations, or historical events are used fictitiously. Other names, characters, organizations, places, or events are the product of the author's imagination.

ACCIDENTS HAPPEN

ON MY DRIVE THROUGH THE woods to meet Glen at the mine's security gate I passed two gutted deer hanging in hunters' camps and one more posed rack forward strapped to the top of a car. November 15th—first day of deer season in Michigan's Upper Peninsula—was proving successful for the hunters, less so for the deer. Every camp I passed had a smear of smoke drifting from its chimney and a half dozen trucks parked in the yard. Opening day is almost a national holiday hereabouts and many businesses shut down for the first week of deer season. Not the mine; it ran 24/7. Since I don't hunt, it seemed like a good day for the fool's errand I was on.

Glen and I owned neighboring camps deep in the woods, fifteen miles from the nearest place you can buy anything. Toward the end of his annual Halloween party, his wife, Margie, cornered me and Jon Nyland, Glen's boss. She convinced Jon to bring me onsite to look into the mine's mysterious deaths. "A serial killer is on the loose," she said. "Glen could be next."

I asked myself again what a forensic accountant, city born and raised, was doing investigating mine accidents. Sure, Margie knew that, working for Criminal Investigations Group, I had solved a couple of murders. Fortunately, my financial sleuthing uncovered the killers before they claimed me as their next victim. Once Margie laid her hand on my arm and asked, "Seamus McCree, are you going to help me?" my desire to be useful trumped my common sense.

At the guard's booth, Glen handed me the visitors pass, and I followed him to Jon's office, a closet so small we both had to stand.

Jon cleared his throat. "I relooked at the accident files," he said. "The three electricians worked here a combined eighty-seven years. Before their fatal accidents, the worst thing that happened to any of them was one guy slammed a car door on his pinkie."

"You know this is a waste of everyone's time," Glen said. "Margie's just paranoid."

"Look, Seamus," Jon said. "I know Margie caught us after we'd had a few. I got no budget to pay you, and I don't even know what you can do, but I do have a bad feeling about these accidents."

"I'm not a licensed investigator," I said. "But if you want, I can look around, ask some questions. Best hope is to kick up something to get the cops interested again."

"Can't ask for more," Jon said, "but I can't pay you."

I dismissed his concern with a wave. "After the party I talked to Margie again. She wouldn't take no for an answer. She's so worried she promised to take me to Glen's secret spot for brook trout next spring."

"She did what?" Glen squealed.

"Fair enough." Jon removed a file from a dented cabinet that might have been beige a century ago. "Here's a list of the guys in the Electrical Department. I don't think anyone else could rig these deaths. If there is a killer, he's here. Shift change is in fifteen minutes. I'll get both groups together and let them know what you're doing . . . or is that a bad idea?"

"Might as well address it head on," I said. "I don't know enough about electricity to fake being an inspector."

He circled three names. "It's an old seniority list. These are the fatalities. The top six guys are on vacation. These twelve," he placed a circled "1" in front of their names, "are on the shift that's about to end. Glen and the others are on second shift. We got some replacements who aren't on this list, but since they weren't here you don't need to worry about them. I'll have Glen take you around. If you need to talk to the first shift guys, stick around for shift change again or come back in the morning. They ain't gonna stay here any longer than my speech."

"Do you know who was working when each of the supposed accidents happened?" I asked.

"Not off hand. I'll get the information from personnel. Might not be until tomorrow though."

"They got *us* working twelve-hour shifts," Glen said. "But *they're* long gone."

Jon checked his watch. "Showtime."

SHELVES AND BINS CONTAINING WIRES and electrical equipment lined the walls in the change room. Bunched in the center were lockers and benches. A huge "Safety is Job #1" poster covered the inside of the door. Guys changed in and out of steel-toed shoes, Carhartt bibs and coveralls while Jon introduced me. To my disappointment, no one immediately confessed.

The only question when Jon was finished was from a short, baby-faced guy, "We done here?"

Glen and I hopped into his Silverado. "Learn anything interesting?" Glen asked.

"Safety is Job #1."

"So they say. Let's do them in the order they occurred. Used to be five separate lakes on this property," Glen said as we drove to the first accident site. "Pumped them dry, like we do with the big hole. All we got left is the evaporation pond."

The "pond" turned out to cover over 1,000 acres, larger than most Upper Peninsula lakes. Our arrival startled a flock of mergansers, which skittered across the cerulean water. With a flash of white tail feathers, juncos flitted from the road into tag alders growing near the edge of the pond. Across the road a stand of aspen grew, mute testimony to a self-seeded clear-cut from years ago.

"This one was labeled a hunting accident?" I asked. "Isn't the mining property posted?"

"No legal hunting, which is why Arnold was here. The deer love this grove. Lots of browse, close to water, coyotes but no wolves, and no hunting . . . except Arnold. Everyone knew he hunted this area. Hell, even management knew. They figured it was better that Arnold thinned the population and gave the meat to charity than to let the deer starve. Arnold got a processor in Marquette to make steaks and sausage from his kills and gave them to a food bank. All under the table, eh? See the road past the gate?"

In the distance, I made out a fence and gate. "He parked there and walked in?"

"Yeah, that's a public road. Cops figure he tripped, discharged his twenty-gauge into his left shoulder—not fatal—and fell into the pond. Hit his head and drowned in six inches of water."

"Tough way to go," I said. "This was during last year's deer season?"

"Yep. What was Arnold doing by the water? He warn't huntin' no mergansers. You ever taste them? Fishy. Warn't fishing. Nothing but guppies and fingerlings in this pond. Hunting, he'd be in the trees. It's starting to drizzle again. If this had all been snow, we'd have three feet. You done here?"

I surveyed the area, tried to picture Arnold's death. The accident didn't make sense, but to outsiders how many of our actions do? Everyone knew Arnold poached, so if someone killed him, the list of suspects was endless.

Caws from a murder of crows cruising toward their evening roost brought me back to the present. Were they a sign? Only in a Bergman movie. I shook the rain off like a dog and got into Glen's truck. In the dusk, our headlights caught the scurry of hares at the side of the road and a coyote slipping into the brush.

"Slag heap's next," Glen said. After letting a gigantic truck pass, he turned onto the main drag. "A loaded dump truck developed an electrical problem with its lift mechanism at the top of the slag heap. Loaded, it was too heavy to tow, so Donny went up to work on it."

We turned onto a narrow road and serpentined up a hill. Eighteen-inch berms provided the only protection from dropping hundreds of feet into the mine pit. The outsized equipment below looked like matchbox toys. Butterflies tickled my stomach. I focused straight ahead, ignoring the increasing chasm out my window. We caught up to a three-story truck lumbering up the hill.

"Here's how it works," Glen said. "The engineers know the iron content of each face they're excavating, so if a truck's load contains enough iron, they cart it to the crusher. We'll visit that last. If the rock is overburden—not enough iron in it—the truck hauls it up here and adds it to the slag heap."

Partway up, Glen pulled so far to the right his tires rode slightly onto the berm. He yanked the emergency brake and hopped out. "Here we are."

I slithered onto the berm and inched around the front of the truck to join Glen. One slip and my next stop was a hundred feet lower. He pointed to the middle of the road. "Donny ended up here. Fell from up there." He waved vaguely toward the hill on our left. "Busted half the bones in his body. You be careful getting back into the truck now."

The top of the hill was flat, providing distant views of lights twinkling in the surrounding towns and, to the north, was the black void of Lake Superior.

"Can't build the slag heap no higher, otherwise we exceed the highest point in Michigan. Now *that* would cause a real stink."

The dump truck we followed proceeded to the far end of the plateau, deposited its load and a dozer pushed the slag over the far edge.

"If the trucks dump on the far side, why was Donny over here?"

"The accident inspectors found a cigarette butt nearby. Figure Donny took a break, slipped and met his maker."

"And you don't?"

"Probably happened that way. He liked the view from on top. Only other possibility is somebody took a chunk of ore and whapped him on the head, threw him over. Cops never found no motive."

I closed my eyes on the trip down and opened them once I felt the vehicle reach flat ground. Pale yellow light leaked from distant buildings, growing harsher the closer we came. Glen stopped at the far end of the building where they made iron pellets.

"Got your earplugs, right?" He turned off his truck and screwed plugs into his ears. "We'll need them once we're inside. You know how we make the pellets?"

"Not so much," I said, raising my voice to accommodate the earplugs.

"First we crush the rock. Watch this guy."

We hopped out. The dump truck, with tires taller than our vehicle, backed toward the side of the building, the beep-beep-beep loud enough to warn off folks a county or two away. The truck backed until a light on the building turned from green to red. I felt the rumble of the huge truck's diesel engine through the soles of my feet. Nothing happened until a second light changed from red to green. The dump truck raised its box and a load of iron ore rumbled into a circular hole in the ground with the sound of Niagara tumbling over its falls. Even before the truck's box returned to level, the dump truck had pulled out and a second truck maneuvered to back in.

"Not your mother's blender," Glen said. "Those big chunks of rock all end up as powder. Let's get in out of the rain."

We walked through a narrow door, down a corridor and into a control room where the operator monitored the crusher.

"See them gauges?" Glen pointed to a row of displays along one wall. "Show what's happening in the crusher. Only two things stop this operation. A rock jams up the works, and they gotta knock it loose. Or a gauge goes kerflooey. Then they call us."

The operator, half-listening to Glen's narration, shot me a "who-the-hell-are-you?" look.

Glen continued his narrative. "When a jam occurs, the sensors automatically trip a circuit breaker. The operator resets it once they clear the jam. It's different for electrical problems. The electrician cuts all the power to the crusher. See the red switch?" He pointed high on a wall in a dark corner. "Four hundred eighty volts. He turns off the power, tapes it down and signs his name. The operator's gotta leave the room. Only the signing electrician can remove the tape."

The operator was now paying more attention to Glen than to the gauges.

"Paul grabbed a live wire. Cops decided he didn't totally disconnect the power. Least it was quick."

The operator yelled to Glen. "More OSHA? Man, I'm glad it wasn't my shift. Stunk to high . . . never mind." He turned around and stared at the gauges.

We backed out of the room and Glen shut the door. "You want to see the exact location?"

I shook my head. "You think someone flipped the switch?"

"This is why Jon thinks if there's a killer, he's an electrician. You saw where the switch was located? Only people who know are electricians, a few managers and the operators in that booth. If he didn't screw up, it had to be one of us."

"Your tone of voice says you think he did screw up."

"That's what everyone except Margie believes."

I SPENT HOURS TALKING TO the electricians, alternately soaked in the rain outside the plant and steamed like a lobster inside. Nobody knew anything more than what Glen had told me.

Using my coat for a pillow, I fell asleep on a bench in the change room. Jon woke me in the morning. "Got the information." In his office he handed me a cup of steaming coffee. I don't drink the stuff, but it warmed my hands and maybe the caffeine reached me by osmosis.

Using the electrician seniority list, he marked those who had worked during each shift the "accidents" occurred. Only three guys were on the premises during all the events, and all three were currently on vacation.

"Guys choose vacation based on seniority?" I asked.

"We only let six guys off at a time. At the beginning of each year the first six put in for their vacation and then the next six and so on. First week of deer season . . . "

He nattered on, but I was in my own little world. The first six guys were out at deer camp, and numbers seven, eight and ten were buried six feet under. Glen was number nine. Maybe Margie wasn't so paranoid. Jon stopped talking and looked at me curiously.

"Sorry, wool gathering," I said. "How frequently do guys retire?"

"Depends. The top two announced awhile back that this was their last year. They'll both have thirty-five years in and get full retirement pay."

"So next year—" I forgot and took a sip of the coffee and had to stop myself from spitting it out. I tapped the list to buy time. "Glen and this guy, number eleven—Reginald Drum—will be eligible for vacation during the first week of deer season? How long will the next guys have to wait?"

He curled his bottom lip in concentration. "Hard to say…maybe four, five years."

"Wait a minute," I said. "We got one wrong. Arnold died while he was off-duty. How easily could someone sneak down to those holding ponds? Isn't it more likely someone off-duty killed him?"

He scratched the top of his head with both hands. "Could be. That would mean . . . " He trailed a pencil down the list. Now only one guy could have done it: Reginald Drum.

"Tell me about him," I said.

"Moose?" He slapped the metal desk. Made me jump. "You think he killed three people so he could go deer hunting on opening day? That's crazy." He paused, tilted his head and stared at the ceiling. "Of course killing three guys ain't exactly normal, is it?"

He turned to a file cabinet, ran his finger down the drawers, reading labels aloud. "Here we are," he said and opened a manila file. "Let's see what Moose was working on when Donny fell." He flipped through some pages. "According to this, both Moose and Donny were working truck maintenance. Donny went up. Moose stayed."

"But it's possible," I said, "that Drum also went to the top of the slag heap to help Donny?"

"Not according to this file, but..." Jon rooted through the cabinets again, pulled another folder. "At the time of the crusher accident everyone was on break. Before and after the break most of the guys were relocating sodium lamps over the separation room. Moose was by himself replacing three-way plugs about fifty feet from the crusher control booth. I can't believe . . . when the crusher ain't running, this place loses that low thrum you hear and feel. Everyone woulda known the crusher was down. If he used his break to see what was happening and found Paul working inside the crusher, he coulda tripped the breaker and no one knows the better."

I pictured all the guys I had met the evening before. Several were sized double or triple X. "Moose a volatile kind of guy?"

"When he gets a few under his belt." Jon scratched his head again. "You saw him at the meeting. Little guy—the one that stormed out after the meeting?"

"He's Moose?"

"It had something to do with Moosehead beer when he was a kid."

Only in the Northwoods. "We don't have near enough to go to the cops," I said, "but tell me what you think of this idea."

JON PARKED ME IN THE back stall of the men's room where I could overhear his prepared speech. He gathered the first shift at lunch break. "Sorry, guys, for another meeting. I got two quick announcements. Seamus McCree thinks Donny, Arnold and Paul were murdered. He's filling the manager in now and plans to head to Negaunee and talk with the State Troopers.

"I was gonna hold off the second thing until we're done with hunting season, but since I got you together now, I'll get it over with. Looks like next year management'll only let four of our guys off at a time—supposedly worried we'll be working twelves again and spread too thin during deer season. I checked: there's nothing in the contract says they can't do it. Questions?"

Guys grumbled and, Jon said, mostly stared at their shoes, except for Moose whose voice penetrated the bathroom wall.

"This sucks," he yelled. "If you think I'm waiting for two more guys to retire before I get that week—"

A slammed door cut off his tirade.

* * *

AFTER WAITING TEN MINUTES, I walked deliberately to my vehicle. I wanted to look over my shoulder and see who was watching. I wanted to shout, "I don't have any proof. I'm trying to smoke you out." My bright idea no longer seemed so bright. Leadenly, I placed one foot in front of the other until I got to my camp truck, an old Ford Ranger. Had Glen succeeded at the task Jon set him to before lunchtime? Would Moose take the bait? Had I surmised wrong and hooked someone else? I scanned the lot. Moose's black Tundra was missing.

I eased onto the mine's main road. At the four-way stop I looked right and left. No Moose. I surrendered my pass when I exited the mine property, a little surprised Moose hadn't taken a run at me while I was inside. Glen was supposed to remove the ammunition from Moose's rifle and follow him if he took his truck. I guessed I'd find out what happened from Glen when he was next at camp. At US-41 I turned away from the State Police in Negaunee, and headed home. At Michigamme, I entered the woods. The rain had stopped, but the roads were sloppy.

Halfway home, shortly before a one-lane bridge, a truck roared out of an abandoned two-track and slammed into the passenger side of my Ranger, toppling it into the creek. Water rushed into the upside down cab through the passenger door, which had sprung open from the impact. Elbowing aside the airbag, I released the seatbelt. Fighting the rush of water, I squeezed out the passenger door. The storm-swelled current swept me through the culvert, banged me on the rocky bottom, and spit me into an eddy on the other side of the road.

Shock from the collision and the near-freezing water kept me from making any noise. A heavy engine idled on the bridge, spewing out fumes. I peered through weeds and spotted a pair of legs on the other side of Moose's truck. Glen had screwed up.

Shivering so hard I had to keep my mouth wide open so my teeth didn't chatter, I crawled out of the water, staying below the truck's profile. While Moose continued to scan the Ranger's wreckage, I used an ancient trick and tossed pebbles onto the bank where I had exited the creek. The legs inched around the side of the truck and paused at the front. I held my breath for a millennium or two. Finally, he rushed to the far side of the road and pointed a rifle toward the creek. I followed and drove my shoulders into his legs, slamming him into the ground. My brain flashed that something was wrong. Momentum carried me up his body and my weight pounded his head into an underwater rock. It wasn't Moose; it was Glen.

The justice of letting him drown flashed through my thoughts. Instead, I dragged his limp body and the rifle to the road and checked the truck. Under a tarp I found Moose—dead from a crushed head. Glen was stirring and I couldn't find anything to bind him with. I covered him with the rifle.

When Glen came to, his justifications flowed like an artesian well from built up pressure. "If Arnold hadn't tripped and shot himself, none of this would have happened. What was I going to do? He knocked himself unconscious, and I was in trouble 'cause I'd boogied from work early. Then this thought came to me: Hell, if I can't get the first week of deer season off, at least I can take over Arnold's poaching. So he drowned, and you know… I was okay with that. Accidents happen.

"Those guys got ahead of me in seniority only 'cause I did my duty in Nam and they didn't. Now that's not fair, is it? The day Donny went to the slag heap to fix the truck, he and I came to work together. After the shift, I drove up to the top of the slag to pick him up. He razzed me about next opening day: him being in his blind with a 24-pack while I was stuck at work. Before I knew it, I whaled his head with a chunk of ore. Pitched him off the side and planted that cigarette butt."

"Why Paul?" I said. "He was behind you in the seniority."

"I never did like him and if anyone got suspicious, it might point the finger at someone else. Made you suspect Moose, eh? Everything was going fine until Margie got you involved. No one else tied it to deer season.

"When I got to Moose's truck, he was already there. I figured if you was both dead, they'd pin everything on him." He stood up. "Now Seamus, you got yourself a problem. Hypothermia will set in soon. I know you. You ain't gonna shoot me, gun's wet anyway. And you got no proof. I wore gloves, see?" He turned and took a step toward Moose's truck.

He was right, I wouldn't kill him.

I slammed the rifle butt into his knee. He crumpled to the ground wailing in agony. I thought about the victims and Margie's concern for his welfare and what this was going to do to her. I slammed the rifle into his other knee.

Accidents happen.

HOMEWORK

BRIAN COULDN'T WAIT FOR SCHOOL to end. Today was the last day of bird season in Michigan's Upper Peninsula. Tomorrow was a school holiday because it was opening day of deer season. Everything was setting up perfectly for three-days of hunting with his dad until his sixth-grade teacher, Mrs. Prichard, spoiled it ten minutes before school ended by handing out homework.

The closing bell rang, and in seconds the room emptied. Brian slung his book bag over his shoulder and stood before her desk. He didn't need to tell her his mother died six years ago and his father was retired; the whole town knew. Seemed like there weren't any secrets in Clear Falls. Instead he just stated the fact. "I can't do the second part of the homework."

Her mouth relaxed into a smile. "Your father always has interesting stories. Write about his last job," she looked up from packing her papers into a shopping bag. "Just make sure it's not one of his whoppers." She tousled Brian's hair. "Have a good weekend."

Brian raced out to his dad's woods truck, a mud-streaked F-150. The rusted door took two hands to open. He hopped into the cab, dropped his book bag by his feet and struggled into his orange hunting vest.

"Problem?" his father asked as they pulled out of the school lot.

"Nah. I had to ask Mrs. Prichard a question about the stupid homework assignment. Doesn't she know it's deer season?"

"Can you start it on the drive out and get 'er done while I make dinner so it's not hanging over your head?"

Brian pulled out the assignment and a blank piece of paper to outline his answers. He reread the first question: What has made this year special? (Minimum 100 words.)

Hunting birds, he decided. He'd learned to shoot when he was keyhole high, but his dad was strict about following the rules when it came to hunting. They had to wear orange and meet all Department of Natural Resources requirements, which meant no bird hunting until he turned twelve. His birthday had come the day before partridge season opened.

He jotted on his pad: "Birthday presents—bird gun and license from DNR." Brian turned in his seat to check the used sixteen-gauge, unzipped its carrying case and caught the faint whiff of gun oil he religiously applied after each outing.

Everyone in the U.P. called the birds "partridge," but Brian had learned from an old Peterson guide his father kept at deer camp that technically they were ruffed grouse. He flushed at the memory of trying out this knowledge at camp a few years back when all his Dad's friends were coming in from a day in the woods. He'd asked the first one through the door how many ruffed grouse he'd bagged. The guy looked at him as though he had two heads. "Well la-dee-da, ain't we just the scholar now?" As each man returned, the guy would drape an arm around the friend's shoulder and say loud enough for Brian to hear, "Brian wants to know how many *ruffed grouse* youse got today?"

That night his Dad did not sympathize at all and said the key to being smart was to use knowledge to help other people, not to show off. Brian closed his eyes to the memory and opened them to the nearly empty pad. Back to bird hunting. The night before his first hunt he'd hardly slept, and he had fidgeted through school the next day, impatient to get to the woods. The second hand crawled around the clock slower than a porcupine out for a Sunday stroll.

He missed two birds that day, but his father didn't get mad at him. Every afternoon it wasn't raining his father picked him up at school and drove fifteen miles north of town where they cut into the woods and cruised old logging roads looking for birds.

When startled, partridge exploded from the side of the road with a whirr of feathers. Always got Brian's heart pounding. His dad would ease the truck to a stop; they'd remove guns from their cases, jack in shells and head into the woods.

On their seventh day hunting, Brian got over his jitters and bagged his first bird. That night he cooked it over a campfire in their back yard. Beat chicken any day of the week once you added a little bacon, some salt and pepper and two shakes of paprika. Brian's mouth started watering. He rooted around in the cooler behind the seat and settled for an apple.

Brian jotted another note, "First bird – cook out and stories." That evening his dad had spun one whopper after another about the family and deer camps and big fish and even bigger ones that got away until it was way past Brian's bedtime.

"Can I drive today?" Brian asked a couple of miles before they would pull off the highway.

"Probably not. Too many guys'll be hauling last minute stuff up to their camps."

Brian wrote "Driving lessons" on his pad. He stared at the words before reluctantly crossing them out. Writing about illegal driving lessons might get his father in trouble, although everyone did it. Bird hunting and the cookout should be enough for 100 words.

They bounced off the highway onto the gravel road and a mile later veered left, taking a rutted dirt road. His father slowed to minimize the jostle and they both rolled down their windows. Brian inhaled the northwoods scent and couldn't help smiling. Wet maple leaves after last night's rain, cut balsam for deer blinds, a whiff of wood smoke from a distant camp.

To quote his dad, "It don't get much better than this."

They passed through a clear-cut planted five years ago with tamarack. The trees, yellow needles glowing in the late fall light, cast long shadows over the sandy soil.

"No driving today, Brian. Tracks all over the place."

Brian had already seen them and had his assignment sheet handy. "First question: Occupation? Mrs. Prichard told me to ask about your last job before you retired."

"What's this about?"

"Have to interview you and write it up. She called it..." He fumbled through the papers. "Creative non-fiction. You gotta pretend you're still working. How long have you done this job?"

Brian's father pulled to the side of the dirt road.

"Spot something?" Brian asked.

"Let me see what you got there." Brian handed over the photocopied assignment and watched his father's forehead change from smooth to ridged and back to smooth.

"What's funny about homework?" Brian asked, noticing his father's smile when he returned the sheet.

His dad engaged the gear and bumped into the middle of the dirt track. "Mrs. Prichard gave me the same blasted assignment when I had her. Mine didn't have any fancy stuff about 'creative nonfiction,' though. My father about bored me to death with his description of dairy farming in Wisconsin. I promise I won't do that to you."

"She make you write it the first weekend of deer season?"

"Probably. She never cottoned much to hunting."

"So, occupation?" Brian asked, pen at the ready.

"Let's say, 'exterminator.'"

"Exterminator? Aw, come on. That's as bad as Jimmy Swainhart having to spell 'statistician' on those forms we fill out at the beginning of each year. Spell it."

"Spell it what?"

"Please."

"Use 'pest control' instead."

Brian wrote it down and read the next question: "How did you become interested in your work?"

"Do you remember hearing about Uncle Donald?"

The name was familiar to Brian, but he couldn't put a face to it. His dad waited a beat and continued. "Great-uncle, actually. Your mother's father's brother. When your grandfather Maki died in the mine accident, Uncle Donald took your mother in. He didn't have any kids of his own. It wasn't one of my better decisions, but I hired on with him. Next question."

"Wait a sec, I got to make notes."

"I have to make notes."

"That's what I said."

"I have to. Not, I got to."

Brian rolled his eyes. "What did you want to be when you were my age?"

Brian's dad erupted in laughter. "An Alaska bush pilot. I was gonna fly into some remote lake before ice-up, trap all winter and fly out with my pelts the next spring."

"Cool. Why didn't you?"

"I met your ma. After that, being all alone in Alaska didn't seem so attractive."

"Last one. Most memorable incident from your job. Just tell me, 'cause I gotta—"

"I have."

Brian blew out a long sigh. "I <u>have</u> to write this in my own words."

"You're growing up fast. Time you heard this story. Not all decisions your old man made were good ones." He turned into a muddy two-track that curved through a young aspen grove. The rattle of the leaves in the light wind sounded like the rain stick Mrs. Prichard showed them earlier in the year. Brian looked for deer sign in the aspen grove as they crept through.

"It's a funny story, but sad too," Brian's dad said after twisting the Ford around a large boulder in the middle of the road. "About ten years ago – you were a toddler – I was mostly logging during the winter and working construction summers, and we hit a recession. No construction and no logging. Your ma had just gotten sick and had to quit her job. Tough times. Uncle Donald ran a distribution network in the U.P. – well, the western half anyway. Pharmaceuticals, but not the kind you'd get at a store. You get the drift?"

Brian got stuck on hearing about his mom. He still missed her, even after all these years. When his brain finally kicked in, he blurted, "Drugs?"

"Yep, big-time. You know how the Finns and the Swedes and the Italians are kind of clannish? Uncle Donald supplied the Finns and Swedes. The Italians had their own sources."

The brakes squealed as they stopped at the river where the bridge had washed out sometime before Brian was born. After turning off the ignition, Brian's dad pointed toward the river. "Look past the stump on the left. See it?"

Brian spotted the pine marten, nose to the ground, hunting in a zigzag path under the trees.

"Seems the Italians wanted to control the whole shebang. Guess they convinced the number two guy in Uncle Donald's organization to try to take over and then combine it with theirs. Uncle Donald heard about this and decided he needed some pest control."

Brian tried to figure out what to write on his pad. He started to doodle, listening to the engine tick as it cooled.

"Uncle Donald liked to keep everything in the family, and he knew I didn't have regular work. Your ma was laid up in bed, and we were hurting for money. He offered me ten grand to eliminate his pest."

"He have rats in a barn or something?"

"You're not listening, Son. The pest was his number two guy, who happened to be his cousin Larry. Larry was probably ten years younger than Donald. I don't know why he sold out to the Italians. Money maybe, or ambition or tired of being Donald's bagman."

Strange, Brian thought as he watched his dad. We're sitting here and he's not scanning the field for birds or looking for places where the bucks had rubbed antlers in preparation for the rut. It's like he's in a trance.

"I didn't want to shoot Larry."

"Why would you shoot him?" Brian asked, grinning because he'd finally figured it out. Mrs. Prichard warned Brian to avoid using any whoppers. He clicked the pen a few times and stuck it in a pocket. He wasn't going to be able to use this story for the homework, but he still wanted to hear it.

"Exactly. Too much forensic evidence, heh? One night, Uncle Donald threw a party at his house. I knew Larry would be there. I figured I'd wire his car. So I stole some TNT—mine security was pretty lax before the terrorist crap and there's still a lot of their missing inventory lying around here and there if you know where to look. I'd never used dynamite and I didn't exactly know how much to use. I started with several sticks, decided maybe I needed more and added a couple extra. Wrapped them together with electrical tape.

"In town, Larry drove a red 1963 Caddy—spit polish shine you could shave by, use those tail fins for the razor. What a beauty! His wife hated that car. Larry was supposed to redo their kitchen and instead he used the moolah to buy the Caddy. Anyway, while they partied, I wired the car. With all the other cars parked nearby, I didn't want it to explode as soon as he turned on the ignition, so I wired the ignition to a timer set for thirty seconds. Linked the timer to the coil. Figured after thirty seconds the coil would heat up and light the dynamite fuse. A real Rube Goldberg arrangement."

"A what?"

"Rube Goldberg." He winked at Brian. "Complicated beyond words."

"So what happened?"

"The party broke up around three in the morning and they were drunker than skunks. Nobody paid attention to DWI laws back then. Several cars took off before Larry. Uncle Donald stood on his porch watching everyone leave. He had no clue I had wired Larry's car. Did I tell you Uncle Donald owned that big house on the corner of Central and Maple? The painted lady?"

Out the window, Brian watched the undulating flight of a hairy woodpecker flitting from an ancient hemlock to a younger pine. His father always interrupted his stories. "Come on, Dad," Brian heard his voice whine in that way he hated 'cause it sounded like a little kid. "What happened?"

"You know there's no sense hurrying a story. Like a trout on a fly, you have to give it some line before you sink the hook and reel it in."

Brian tried to picture the house. "The law offices?"

"Yep. And where the car wash is now was his side lot where everybody parked."

"Got it."

"So Larry got into his car, started the engine and got out. Decided he had to take a leak."

"Right there?"

"He's drunk, heh? He's letting fly and the car explodes. Getting dark, think we should head back?"

"Daaad, finish the story."

His father tried to hide his grin with the back of his hand, then started laughing so hard it turned into a cough. "The ground shook, houses rattled, some old biddy called to report an earthquake. The engine block flew into the air, over the street and bounced twice. Ended up next to the Bethany Lutheran sign announcing the Sunday sermon. 'Nothing surprises God.' I'll tell you, He was the only one it didn't surprise, heh? The rest of the car blew the opposite direction into Pioneer Park."

Good story, Brian thought, but a little too dramatic. Playing along he said, "So what happened to this guy Larry?"

"Blast coldcocked him. God protects Irish and drunks, they say. Sure happened that night. No one was hurt except Uncle Donald. He had a heart attack and died on the spot."

"What?"

"Right on the porch. As it happened, Uncle Donald left all his money and the house to your mother. We sold the house and invested the money. That allowed me to stay home and take care of your ma while she was sick, and the money keeps growing so I can be home to take care of you. Turns out that was my last job." He turned the key in the ignition. "No birds, might as well head home."

"Okay," Brian said. "That's one of your best whoppers ever, but--"

"But, nothing." His dad's voice took on the don't-mess-with-me tone Brian had learned to respect. "That's God's honest truth."

Brian sat in stunned silence. Brian knew it <u>was</u> the truth. He couldn't use the story. They'd arrest his father for murder and then he'd be alone and…he didn't know what would happen. Tears leaked down his cheeks.

His dad reached over and brushed away a tear. "You worried I'm going to be in trouble over this?" He was back to smiling.

Brian nodded and choked back a sob.

"Larry refused to file a complaint about the Caddy and the statute of limitations is long past. They ruled Uncle Donald's death was from natural causes. His ticker was hollow as a Halloween gourd. Everyone in town knows the story; they're just not sure who planted the explosives. It's time they found out."

"Won't that Larry guy come after you?"

"That winter he plowed his snowmobile into a white spruce while chasing a coyote. Closed casket. God protects coyotes more than drunks. Anyway, you write this you'll get an A. Guaranteed."

"How do you figure?" Brian asked, wiping his cheek with the back of his hand.

"Larry's wife glommed onto the Caddy insurance money and got her new kitchen. She's been wondering who to thank for years."

"I don't get it."

"Larry's last name was Prichard."

"You mean Mrs. Prichard was—?"

"Larry's wife. Fine kitchen too."

James M. Jackson authors the Seamus McCree series.

Jim has also published an acclaimed book on contract bridge, *One Trick at a Time: How to start winning at bridge.*

He calls the deep woods of Michigan's Upper Peninsula home. You can find out more about Jim or sign up for his Readers Group newsletter at his website, https://jamesmjackson.com.